FOUR HOLIDAYS AND A WEDDING

MELANIE MORELAND

MORELAND
BOOKS INC.

DEDICATION

Christmas has always been my favorite time of year.
There is a magic that weaves itself into my heart,
filling it with the wonder of possibilities.
It is a time of love, dreams, and family,
and I wanted to write a book that contained them all.

This book is for you, my readers.
Thank you for your belief, your support, and your love.
I wish you a season filled with peace.

And to my Matthew—my greatest gift.
All my love.

MORELAND
BOOKS INC.

Edited by
Lisa Hollett—Silently Correcting Your Grammar
Sisters Get Lit.erary Proofreading
Cover Art: Abby O. Sweet of Bigfoot Creative

Readers with concerns about content or subjects depicted can check out the content advisory on my website:
https://melaniemoreland.com/extras/fan-suggestions/content-advisory/

CHRISTMAS SUGAR

CHAPTER 1

DYLAN

I lifted my mug, took a deep swallow of coffee, and grimaced. Slamming down the cup on my desk and ignoring the mess it made as the liquid splashed onto the dark wood, I hit the button on my phone.

"Amy! Get in here!"

My door opened, and she peeked around the corner.

"Yes, Mr. Maxwell?"

I drew in a calming breath, fighting to keep my voice neutral and even. "How long have you worked here?"

"Um, about two weeks."

I nodded. "How often have you brought me coffee?"

She stepped closer, no doubt encouraged by my mild tone.

"Every day, sir."

I narrowed my eyes at her. "Do you have a mental problem I'm unaware of?"

Her smile faltered. "Um, no, sir."

"Then why"—my voice began escalating—"is there fucking *sugar* in my coffee? I like a splash of cream—just cream. Is that such a difficult thing to remember?"

Her hand flew to her mouth. "I'm sorry! I must have mixed up the mugs!" She lunged forward, grabbing the mug and spilling more coffee over my desktop. "I'm sorry!" she repeated. "I'll clean that up." She turned, practically running out of my office. "I'll get you a fresh mug," she called over her shoulder, passing Mrs. Carson as she ran, babbling about different colored mugs.

I rolled my eyes and huffed at Arlene as she stood in front of my desk.

"I can't believe you're actually going to retire and leave me with the likes of her. She can't even get a fucking cup of coffee right."

Her brown eyes danced with mirth as she grinned at me. "I can't believe she's lasted two weeks. That has to be a record. I don't think either of the other two lasted a week. She's got some backbone."

I started to laugh. Nothing I ever said to Mrs. C fazed her. I leaned back in my chair. "Seriously, you're going to hate retirement. Rambling around in that big house of yours, playing bridge, and talking to your cats. You'll be a drunk in a month. Two, tops."

"Thanks for the vote of confidence, *Mr. Maxwell*. You have a better plan?"

"Stay here with me."

"And listen to your demands and bitching all the time? No thanks. I'll take my chances with the alcohol."

I smirked at her. "Simon is going to drive you nuts."

She shrugged. "Him or you. At least at home, I can wear my fuzzy slippers."

"I'll add that to your contract. Fuzzy slippers acceptable."

She shook her head, the white waves remaining firmly in place. Even her hair knew better than to disobey Mrs. C. "You'll be fine, Dylan. Just try to find a little patience. Stop yelling at everyone."

"I don't yell at everyone."

"Yes, you do."

"Okay, so I do. It's my thing. Keeps the staff on their toes."

"Your *thing* is going to lose you perfectly good staff."

I snorted. "I don't think you can consider Amy 'perfectly good staff.'"

"You'll never know unless you stop being such a hard-nosed ass. A little sugar isn't going to kill you—in fact, it might help sweeten you up a bit."

I waved my hand dismissively. "All right. Enough bad-mouthing the boss—I've changed my mind. You're fired."

"Good."

We grinned at each other, completely comfortable with our banter.

Arlene had been with me since I started my company, Maxwell Corp., and had watched it grow from a small, struggling business to the huge, multimillion-dollar land development conglomerate it was today. When my father had turned his back on me, telling me I would fail, she stood right by my side and supported me all the way. It was with her I celebrated my victories, and her I turned to for counsel. She was my right-hand, but the bottom line, it was still simply a job to her—part of her life, unlike me, who made it my entire life.

When her husband Simon retired earlier in the year, I knew it was merely a matter of time before she wanted to spend her days with him instead of me.

I was going to miss her like crazy.

And she knew it.

The door opened, and Amy walked in, a steaming cup in her shaking hand. I accepted it silently and watched as she mopped up the spill and stood back, waiting for approval. I sipped the brew and nodded at the lack of sugar. It was perfect. Mrs. C was glaring at me, and I set down the mug, knowing what they were waiting for.

"Excellent. Thank you, Amy."

A big smile broke out on her face. "You're welcome, Mr. Maxwell."

"Try to remember how I take it next time, all right? No sugar in my coffee or my food."

She nodded enthusiastically. "I put an X on the bottom of your cup. I won't mix them up again."

I stifled a groan, not wanting to hear if she planned to check she had the right mug before it was full. I was certain I didn't want to hear the answer. Even Mrs. C was smirking. Instead, I decided to check on the details of the next project I was working on.

"Do you have the travel arrangements I asked you to make?"

She nodded and thrust a file folder at me. "All done, sir. I'll be at my desk." She scampered off, shutting the door behind her. I arched an eyebrow at Mrs. C, who was watching me with an amused expression on her face. I flipped open the file and scanned the contents.

First-class flight to Halifax. A car would be waiting. A suite at the
. . .

I blinked. Then I read that line again.

An all-inclusive room at the . . . Sleepy Moose Inn?

What the fuck?

I slammed the file on my desk, roaring out in my anger.

"Amy!"

Mrs. C stood, shaking her head. "She's not at her desk."

"Why the fuck not? She needs to fix this, and then she's fired!"

"No, she's not. She simply did what I instructed her to do. The same way I told her to give you the file and go to lunch." She sighed. "I knew there'd be more yelling. You're always yelling, Dylan."

Ignoring her rebuke, I shook the file. "The Sleepy Moose Inn? What the fuck is that?"

"That"—she smirked—"is where you're staying."

"No, it's not."

"Yes, it is. It's part of the Ocean Bluff Resort you're planning to buy."

I vaguely recalled that detail. I remembered snickering over the name, thinking that would be the first thing I changed.

"Are you telling me there isn't a Ritz within driving distance? Or a fucking Hilton? I'll stay in Halifax if I have to!"

Mrs. Carson's voice was stern. "Dylan."

"What?" I muttered.

"You're flying to the East Coast to meet with Mr. Walsh."

"I know that."

She held up her hand. "He's agreeing to listen to your proposal on the condition you meet with him personally and spend some time there, at the resort."

I snorted. "He's not in any position to make demands. He's going to lose it all."

"Not quite yet, Dylan. He wants to meet you face-to-face, and you agreed to it."

"I did?"

"I did on your behalf."

I shot her a look that would have had Amy on the floor. Arlene barely blinked.

"Why, exactly?" I asked from between gritted teeth.

"I have a feeling."

"A feeling?"

"You have to go to the East Coast and meet with Mr. Walsh. Tell him your plans. He wants to know the *real* person he's selling his property to. Those are his demands. Otherwise, he'll sell to someone else." She studied me seriously. "You have to do this, Dylan."

I looked out the window at the gray, overcast sky. Winter was thick in the air, Christmas a mere few weeks away. The East Coast would be cold and snowy—far more than here. But I wouldn't be outside much. I had no reason not to go, other than not being comfortable with his demands. I was private and didn't understand his desire to know me before he sold the land. It was just land.

As much as I didn't want to go, I had no family to keep me here, no commitments, no big plans to prepare for—it wasn't as if Christmas was a big deal to me. Usually, I spent it wandering my condo, wishing the day were over so I could get back to work. Plus, thanks to Mrs. Carson's scheduling, I had the time. So, I had no excuse.

My head fell back against the plush leather of my chair. "I want that land. The plans I have for developing it will make me a very rich man."

"You're already a 'very rich man,' Dylan."

"Richer, then. I want this deal. I need this deal."

"Then I guess you're staying at the Sleepy Moose Inn and spending some of that time with Mr. Walsh."

Fuck.

"Make sure there's a bottle or two of Courvoisier in my room. The good stuff. I think I might need it."

She was laughing as she walked to the door. "Yeah, I'll get Amy on that right away." She paused, her hand on the handle. "Dylan . . ." she called.

I looked up, curious.

"There are many ways to be rich in this world. Not all of them involve money. Remember that." She smiled and walked out the door.

I stared after her retreating figure, wondering what crazy thoughts she was rambling on about.

CHAPTER 2

DYLAN

I glanced around, intrigued and amused. I'd never been to an airport as minute as the one I was standing in. The plane was much smaller than what I normally traveled on as well; even the first-class section didn't meet my standards. Wearily, I rubbed my hand over my face. It had been a long, trying day, one meeting after another, and a delayed flight to top it all off. Instead of arriving midafternoon, it was early evening and darkness had settled. I hadn't eaten on the plane, and I hoped the inn had a decent restaurant—or preferably, room service.

That bottle of Courvoisier had better be waiting. I needed it.

I walked over to the luggage carousel, irritated I had to carry my own bags, and went toward the front, expecting to find my limo driver waiting. Instead, I encountered an almost deserted terminal, with only a few people milling around. There was one young man sitting, texting furiously on his phone, glancing up on occasion. He was tall and thin with messy, light-brown hair and blue eyes. A heavy parka was tossed on the seat beside him. When he met my gaze, a wide grin split across his face, and he jumped to his feet, grabbed his parka, and hurried toward me.

"Mr. Maxwell?"

I nodded.

"I'm your ride," he exclaimed, wide grin still in place.

"P-Pardon?" I sputtered.

My ride?

"Yeah, I'm Seth. Alex sent me to pick you up. Flight delayed, eh?"

"Yes, there was a mechanical issue."

"Well, better you than me, man. Alex would tan my hide if I was the late one."

I arched my eyebrow at him. I had no idea who the "Alex" person was or exactly what "tan my hide," meant, although I had an inkling.

"Is the car out front?" I asked pointedly.

"Nah." He pointed his thumb over his shoulder. "I had to park it since you were late."

I sucked in a long, calming breath, reminding myself I wasn't in Toronto anymore. Obviously, they did things differently in Nova Scotia.

"Shall we go, then?"

He nodded. "Yeah, sure. Hope your coat's warm. It's colder than a witch's tit out there!"

I had no response to that cheerful announcement. He walked through the door, letting it shut in my face.

My coat billowed behind me, my eyes blinking instantly in rapid succession at the freezing temperature. I followed Seth's quick pace to the garage, almost groaning with relief when we walked into the cement structure. He looked at me askance.

"You should have done up your coat, man."

I glared at him, my patience thin. "You should have offered to take my bags, so I could button up my fucking coat. In fact, you should have had the car warm and waiting for me."

His cheerful expression fell. "Shit," he whispered. "Alex is gonna kill me." He lunged forward, almost ripping my case from my hand and dropping my garment bag. "Don't tell her, please? She trusted me to do this! I'll make it up to you!" He dropped my case as well, both of them sitting on the dirty, cold cement. He moved closer, trying to grab at my coat to fasten the buttons as he begged me.

Impatiently, I slapped his hands away. He looked so upset and young I didn't have the heart to keep yelling the way I usually would.

"Pick up my things, Seth."

Leaning down, he grabbed them.

"Can we go to the car? I'm damn well freezing," I grumbled.

"Right this way, Mr. Maxwell!"

I followed him, somehow not shocked when we stopped at a large minivan.

Why would I expect a limo or even a Town Car?

Seth threw my luggage in the back and grabbed my briefcase from my hands. He opened the passenger door, indicating I should get inside.

I resisted the urge to roll my eyes. It appeared I was riding up front.

He rounded the van quickly, started the engine, and grinned nervously when cold air blew out of the vents. "It'll take a minute to warm up, but the heater works pretty good," he assured me.

A long shiver racked my spine. "How long to the inn?"

"About forty-five minutes to Pinegrove." He regarded me anxiously. "Can I get you something?"

"I don't suppose you have any brandy?" I asked jokingly.

He shook his head. "I'm not old enough to drink."

"Are you old enough to drive?"

He chuckled. "Yeah. That I can do. How about some coffee? It'll warm you up."

"Sure."

Fifteen minutes later, we were speeding through the darkness, and I had a cup of coffee and a donut, courtesy of an insistent Seth. Tim Horton's was the one name I recognized as we drove into the town, and I was hungry enough to eat the donut, even though I rarely ate sweets. I was as rigid with my diet as I was with my business.

Snapping on the overhead light, I checked my phone, shaking my head at the number of emails and texts waiting. One was from Mrs. C inquiring if I had arrived safely. She always checked up on me—it was another thing I would miss about her. I answered her, adding in a humorous rendition of my arrival, including the "witch's tit" comment. I knew she'd like that one. A couple of minutes later, she texted me back.

Mrs. C
ROTFLMAO

I glared at the screen. I had no idea what that meant. I never used abbreviations in texts or email, and I hated it when others did. People butchered the English language enough without adding in silly expressions. I glanced over at Seth, remembering he had been texting when I arrived.

I cleared my throat. "Ah, do you by chance know what R-O-T-F-L-M-A-O means?"

His eyes flicked to me, then he returned his attention to the road. "Yes."

I tamped down my impatience. "Can you enlighten me, please?"

"*Rolling on the floor, laughing my ass off.* It means they found whatever you said funny."

I blinked at him, then returned my gaze to the screen.

> **Me**
>
> Obviously, your brain has already slipped into retirement mode. So glad I amused you. I hope you didn't break a hip when you fell, old woman.

Her reply was swift.

> **Mrs. C**
>
> If I had, it would have been worth it. I can imagine the look on your snooty face.

I had no clever comeback. I rarely used texting for personal reasons. I used the one word I knew drove her as crazy as abbreviations did me.

> **Me**
>
> My face is not snooty. But . . . whatever.

> **Mrs. C**
>
> Is so. And don't be rude.

I grinned at the screen. I was snooty; I knew that. It helped me keep people at arm's length.

> **Mrs. C**
>
> Be safe, dear boy.

I smirked a little as I typed her reply.

> **Me**
>
> Well, unless I get eaten by wildlife when I step out of the minivan, I think I will be fine.

> **Mrs. C**
>
> A minivan—I'd pay good money to see you in the back seat of one of those.

Me
I'll have you know I'm riding in the front seat. I am
nothing if not adaptable to my environment.

Mrs. C
Adaptable? Stop it, Dylan. I swear you're killing me. I
can't catch a breath from laughing.

Me
Fine. Good night, then.

Her reply made me frown with its strange message.

Mrs. C
This trip is going to be an eye-opener for you, Dylan.
Be sure not to miss anything.

Shutting off my phone, I stared out into the darkness, again
wondering what exactly she was talking about.

Seth pulled up to the front of the inn and I slid out of the van,
already shivering from the drastic change in temperature. "You go
inside and I'll park the van and bring your bags, Mr. Maxwell," he
instructed and pulled away, leaving me standing in the cold.

I looked around, not able to see much except the building in front
of me. The woods rose around the sides of the property, and I was
sure I could hear the crash of ocean waves slamming into rocks. It
was one of the key points of the property that made me want it.
That, plus the fact that I owned the land on either side of it and had
been waiting—not very patiently—for the piece to come up for sale.
The three areas formed a triangle—the one with the inn being the
uppermost point fully facing the water. When my contacts recently
told me it was the right time, I had gotten in touch with Mr. Walsh
before anyone else had a chance to find out it was going to be
available.

The inn itself showed me the age of the complex. A three-story
building that had been, I was sure, quite nice in its day. Now, even
in the dark, I could see it needed work. It wasn't overly large, but I
knew they also had cabins on the grounds, accounting for the
majority of their revenue. There weren't many cars in the parking

lot, which was hardly a surprise. All the information I had seen indicated they still did a decent business in the summer, mostly due to the location. However, once tourist season ended, they started bleeding red ink so fast it was as if a vampire had attacked its proverbial neck. Mr. Walsh needed the deal even more than I wanted it, no matter how hard to get he was playing. He was mortgaged to the hilt and teetering on the edge of financial disaster.

Still, there were lights strung around the building and the front decorated nicely with large pots of evergreens and bows. I hurried inside, grateful for the warmth that greeted me.

I glanced around at the old-fashioned lobby. A few well-worn sofas were in front of a roaring fireplace, which was double-sided and open to an older-style bar on the opposite wall. Tables and chairs were scattered around inside, a couple with people sitting at them. Business was about what I had expected: poor.

A throat clearing had me looking toward the sound, and for a moment, I froze in place. Behind the large desk was a girl. No, a woman—a petite one, but a woman, nonetheless. She had dark brown hair that glinted red under the lights. It tumbled past her shoulders and down her back in long waves. Her complexion was creamy, and her green eyes were wide and apprehensive as she regarded me. She was very pretty.

Then she smiled.

Warm, wide, and so sweet, her smile literally took my breath away.

No one had ever smiled at me like that. Ever. It was as if she was smiling for me. Just for me.

I'd never reacted in such a way to a smile before.

I smiled back.

Just as wide, and judging from the darkening of her cheeks, equally as warm.

For a brief moment, there was no one else, just that small woman and me in the room.

Smiling.

Until Seth hurried in, bringing with him a blast of arctic air. The sudden rush of cold burst the bubble that surrounded me and the beauty behind the desk. He stared between us, flummoxed. "Why are you just standing there?" Then he walked toward the desk, jerking his thumb in my direction.

"This is Mr. Maxwell, Alex."

For some reason, my smile grew wider. That was the infamous Alex who was going to *tan his hide*?

That little slip of a woman?

Seth kept talking. "He's tired, hungry, and thirsty." He leaned forward, dropping his voice, but not low enough I couldn't hear him. "And he's kinda grumpy."

My eyebrows shot up, my smile dropped, and I glared at him. I wasn't grumpy. I was doing my best to be polite.

The smile vanished off Alex's face, and her hand rose to her cheek in shock at his words. Her gaze flew to mine, knowing I had heard him. She reached over with her petite hand and pulled on his earlobe. "Seth! What did I tell you about learning to hold your tongue in front of guests?"

"Ow! I was only telling you so you were prepared. You like to be prepared."

She rolled her eyes. "Take Mr. Maxwell's luggage to his room, then go finish your chores. Now."

I stayed where I was and watched her, waiting for her to speak. The smile she offered me had turned distant, professional, and indifferent. I much preferred the one we'd shared moments ago. She held out her hand, her voice cool and low as she greeted me. "Welcome to Sleepy Moose Inn, Mr. Maxwell. I apologize for Seth. He's still learning his way around. I'm Alexis."

Ah. Alexis to customers, Alex to people she liked. There was no doubt what category I fell into for her.

I crossed the short lobby and wrapped my hand around hers, unsure why her composure had changed so drastically. It was as if the warmth I had felt disappeared as soon as she heard my name.

The desire to know why shocked me. The feel of her hand in mine was strangely . . . *right*. Looking down, I could see her tiny hand was completely hidden in mine—as if I were protecting it.

Shaking my head at my foolish thought, I broke our brief contact. Her green eyes regarded me coolly, and I felt my impatience reach its peak.

"Maybe you should consider hiring grown-ups instead of children."

She squared her shoulders. "Seth is seventeen, almost eighteen, and very capable."

"In your opinion."

"Is there something you'd like to tell me? Did Seth behave inappropriately?"

Opening my mouth, I was about to tell her exactly what he had done wrong in great detail. But I hesitated, remembering the way he'd begged me not to say anything. I shook my head and shut my mouth with a snap, unsure why I was keeping his poor behavior a secret.

"No, *Alexis*. It's fine. I'd like to go to my room now. It's been a long day."

"Of course." She handed me a key. "Room 240. Is there anything you require?"

"No, I'll order some room service to be sent up. There is wireless, yes?"

"Yes, we have wireless, but we don't offer room service."

I frowned. "Then I'll go to the restaurant."

"There, ah, is no restaurant."

My hand curled on the desk, a tight fist forming as I struggled to maintain my temper. "What do your guests eat, then?" I asked through gritted teeth.

"We have breakfast daily and coffee service all day. The bar offers some snacks. Typically, guests dine off-premises. We try to encourage them to support our local restaurants."

"Are they open this time of year?"

"Normally, yes, but not at this time of night."

"Well, I suppose I'll have to make do with *snacks*, then." I paused before continuing, gathering my rapidly thinning patience. "Should I order something to be sent to my room? Or is that not available either?"

"I'll have something brought up if you like," she stated.

I closed my hand around the key. "Thank you."

"George—Mr. Walsh—asked me to remind you he'll meet with you tomorrow morning. He apologizes for not being able to meet you himself tonight—he is indisposed. I'll show you to his office at ten tomorrow."

"Fine," I huffed, suddenly angry with the man who insisted I come to Pinegrove in the dead of winter and disrupt my busy life.

"Have a pleasant night, Mr. Maxwell."

I nodded, striding over to the elevators, not bothering to answer her.

I highly doubted it.

CHAPTER 3

DYLAN

My deluxe, all-inclusive room was exactly what I expected after the day I'd had: horrible.

I sat down heavily on the corner of the well-worn love seat and scanned the room—the dull beige walls, the queen-sized bed with a loud plaid bedspread and matching curtains. A tall armoire was in the corner, the doors open, showing the old TV on the top shelf and a minute refrigerator underneath. A coffeemaker was on the table, a short tower of foam cups ready to use beside it. The one other piece of furniture in the room was a chipped desk with a lamp on it and a lumpy-looking chair in front of it. A partially opened door offered me a view of a shower and dingy tiles in the bathroom.

I had to admit it was scrupulously clean, yet the entire thing was downright depressing—and the worst part . . .

No Courvoisier in sight.

I leaned over and grabbed the phone, almost laughing when I saw the push buttons and the old clunky square design—but the avocado green color was the topper.

I punched zero and waited.

"Front desk, Alex speaking, how may I help you?"

"Is it Alexis or Alex?" I barked out.

"Whichever you prefer, Mr. Maxwell."

"Fine, *Alex*," I snapped, knowing the familiarity would piss her off. "My Courvoisier."

"I'm sorry?"

"My assistant was supposed to have arranged a bottle of Courvoisier in my room. It's not here. Did you not get the message?"

"I'll have it sent up with your dinner."

I snorted. My snacks—right. It should be a great dinner.

"I'd like it now."

Alex's voice dropped, its tone icy-polite. "Right away, *sir*."

"Thank you." I hung up and sat back, wondering why it bothered me what her tone sounded like.

I returned some emails and a few texts, then stood to stretch, checking my watch. It had been twenty minutes. Apparently, *now* meant something different in Pinegrove from other parts of the country. Shaking my head, I grabbed my toiletry bag and went to have a shower.

At least the water was hot and the pressure in the shower strong. It felt good pounding on my back. I got out and dried off, throwing on a pair of sweats and a T-shirt. I realized I had only brought dress shoes with me, so I pulled on a pair of socks and decided to head downstairs to find out what the hell took so long to bring up a bottle of alcohol. Somehow, I doubted my lack of shoes would cause any great disturbance.

I yanked open my door, stepped into the hall, and froze. Sitting on the floor a little way down the hall, was a child, playing quietly with a doll. I looked up and down the empty corridor, then back at her. She gazed up at me curiously, her wide green eyes calm. Reddish colored hair, long and curly, tumbled past her shoulders, and she was dressed in fuzzy pajamas with slippers on her feet.

For a minute, I considered stepping back into my room and shutting the door. Children made me nervous. They were highly unpredictable—I never knew what they were going to do or say. Their hands were usually sticky, they often wanted hugs, or to feed you something they had already chewed. They darted places quickly and spoke in a language I often had trouble understanding, and the one down the hall didn't have a parent around to interpret.

As if she knew what I was thinking, she stood and smiled brightly at me.

"Hi!"

"Um, hello."

"I'm Nowowl. Wif two oowls."

What? She had owls?

I cleared my throat. "Pardon?"

She frowned and stepped closer. "N-o-e-owl-owl-e. Dat's how you spewl it." She looked proud when she finished her sentence. "My mommy taught me."

I mulled over her words in my head, then realized what she was saying.

"Noelle? That's your name?"

She clapped her hands, grinning widely. I noticed she was missing her two front teeth, which explained her odd speech pattern. "Yeth! What's yours?"

"I'm Dylan Maxwell."

She pursed her lips. "Dats a big name. And it has owls in it. I has twouba wif owls."

For some reason, I bit back a grin. Considering the large gap in her teeth, I'd say she had trouble with H, L, R, and undoubtedly, a few other consonants. Some of her S's were slurred, while others were clear. Strangely enough, I found it quite endearing rather than annoying. She didn't make me nervous at all. She was cute, actually.

"You can call me Dylan," I offered.

She held out her surprisingly clean hand. "Hewwo, Dywan."

Now, I was smiling. L's *were* a big issue, it seemed.

I folded my much larger hand over hers and shook it gently. "Hello, Noelle. That's a pretty name."

She nodded. "My birfday is on twitmath. Mommy thays I was the best gift eveh."

"I bet she does." I cleared my throat again. "Where, ah, is your mommy . . . and daddy?"

"I not have a daddy."

"Oh. Your mommy, then?"

"Mommy is wooking."

"Where does she work?"

"Heewer."

I frowned. Her mother worked here and left her alone while she did so? That was unacceptable. The child was no more than four—maybe younger. Even I knew that was too young to be alone. Anger started to burn.

"And you're all alone?"

"No. Sef is wooking afta me."

"Seth?"

She nodded, giggling as she looked down the hall. "He posda be. He fawed asweep."

She sat down again and picked up her doll. "Me and Ewwy came to pway out hewe so we not wake him up."

For some unknown reason, I sat down beside her. "I don't know if your mommy would like that."

She shook her head. "She not. I not tell her." Her eyes grew big. "Iz you gonna tell her? Mommy fink I'm bad! I not 'posed to be in da hawl."

"I won't tell her," I promised, even as I realized I was now keeping the actions of two strangers secret. Interesting Seth was involved in the current situation too. He certainly got around.

Maybe I should mention that to Alex when I went downstairs and retrieved my bottle of Courvoisier. Seth indicated she was in charge at the moment.

"Does your mommy work every night?"

She nodded. "She weads me a stowy when I go to bed. But not tonight."

"Why?"

She bit her lip, looking around. "I not fink I 'posed to say."

I leaned forward. "I can keep a secret."

"Mommy tell Sef she had to make suppa"—she paused, her quiet voice becoming a whisper—"for an ath-hole." Her eyes got bigger. "Dat's a bad word, ya know. I not 'posed to thay bad words."

I forced myself not to laugh. "Does your mommy say them a lot?"

She giggled, the sound adorable. "No. She wath mad."

"Ah. Well, I won't tell."

"I yike you, Dywan."

She grinned up at me. It was a big, toothy grin. Her little face beamed with the warmth of her infectious smile. It reminded me of another smile . . .

Just then, the elevator door opened and Alex stepped out. In her hands was a tray, and she stopped, staring at Noelle and me, surprise written all over her face.

Her weary face. How had I not noticed earlier how tired she looked?

For a moment, we regarded each other, then she moved forward.

"Noelle, what are you doing out of bed?"

Noelle shifted beside me. "Not sweepy, Mommy. I just pwaying."

"Where is Seth?"

I couldn't help snorting. "I think he was the sleepy one."

Alex's gaze was ferocious. "What are you doing out of your room, Mr. Maxwell?"

It was my turn to shift nervously—her look was enough to make anyone squirm. Breaking her gaze, I found my voice and my sarcasm. "I was coming to find my brandy. I didn't realize you had to brew it before the bottle came upstairs."

"Did Seth not bring it to you?"

"No."

She made a noise and thrust the tray toward me. "Take this."

Dumbfounded, I reached up and took the tray from her hands. I was sure she growled.

"Stay right here. Both of you."

Turning on her heel, she marched down the hall, disappearing into a room. Neither Noelle nor I moved. I knew she was obeying her mother, but I wasn't sure why I was following her orders.

"What's dat?"

I glanced down at the tray. "My supper, I think."

"Oh." Then Noelle gasped. "Dywan! Iz you da ath-hole?"

I blinked at her, then the tray.

I guessed I was.

Huh.

The door opened down the hall, and Seth stumbled out, followed by Alex. I pushed myself up to my feet as she pulled him along, stopping in front of me. One hand gripped his arm, the other around the bottle I'd been waiting for since I arrived.

"Apologize to Mr. Maxwell."

He looked at me. "I'm s-sorry—Alex sent me up as soon as she got back. I knocked, but there was no answer. I heard the shower running so I went to check on Noelle, and I guess I fell asleep while I was waiting."

"Got back from where?"

He stared at me as if I were crazy. "She had to go get your stuff, man. I'm not old enough to buy it."

I looked at Alex. "It wasn't here? You don't have it in the bar?"

Two bright spots of color appeared on her cheeks. "No, sir, we don't stock that. It's rather . . . expensive. Your assistant's request came in late this afternoon, and I hadn't had time to see to it. I had Susan watch the desk while I went to get it. Seth was to bring it to you, then relieve her while I did another task."

"Make da ath-hole his suppa," stated Noelle firmly. "Dat's Dywan."

Alex gasped, Seth started to laugh heartily, and before I could stop myself, so did I. In fact, I laughed so hard, I almost dropped the tray. Finally calming, I reached over and plucked the bottle from Alex's hand.

"Well, as interesting and eye-opening as this has been, this 'ath-hole' is hungry and needs to eat." I turned to Alex, who appeared mortified and maybe even on the verge of tears. I smirked at her. "I'm not as big an *asshole* when I'm not hungry—honest."

"Mr. Maxwell," she choked out, her voice panicked.

I lowered my voice, needing her to know I wasn't upset. I should be, but I was far from it. "I didn't realize you had to go and buy this special for me. I'll speak to my assistant about her lack of organization. Be sure to add it to my bill."

"Speak or yell?" She smiled hesitantly.

I winked at her, returning her smile. "Depends if I wait until after I eat."

Her smile came back again—the one that lit her face and made me want to say or do anything to keep her smiling at me like that. I was glad to see her shoulders relax a little.

I glanced over at Seth, who was still grinning. "If Alex trusts you enough to look after her daughter, you should take better care of her. I realize she is surely safe in the hotel, but she was still your responsibility."

His smile fell, and he looked at Alex. "Sorry. It was a long day."

She rubbed his arm. "I know."

I smiled down at Noelle. "Thank you for keeping me company. I enjoyed meeting you, Noelle."

"I see you in da morning, Dywan!"

"Be a good girl for your mommy. Go to bed," I admonished gently.

"Otay!"

I scanned the tray, with no clue as to what was under the lids, but it didn't matter. "Thank you for my dinner, Alex. I appreciate it a great deal."

"You're welcome," she whispered. "I hope you like it."

"I'm sure I will."

I pushed on my door and glanced over my shoulder at the unlikely welcoming committee I had been sent. A smart-mouthed teenager, a lisping little angel—who, for some reason, I seemed to adore instantly—and of course, Alex.

A mystery—one minute warm and smiling, the next cool and

frowning. Then, despite the fact that she found me an "ath-hole," made me dinner, after she went out to buy my requested brand of brandy instead of telling me to drink whatever shit excuse they had in the bar.

She certainly was an enigma.

And she smiled at me in a way that took my breath away.

Mrs. C was right—the trip was already full of surprises.

Astonishingly, I quite liked it.

CHAPTER 4

DYLAN

I woke gradually to strange and unfamiliar sounds. Sitting up, I
listened to the wind outside, the glass rattling in the windows from the
strength of it. For the first time that I could remember, I felt . . .
peaceful. Generally, when I woke, my mind was instantly crowded
with my hectic schedule: everything on the agenda for the day, what
was happening that evening, the next day, the next week—my brain
started firing as soon as my eyes opened.

But this morning, there was nothing. I had no idea what George
Walsh wanted to discuss, or why he wanted me to stay there for a few
days. Our lawyers could have handled it all, but he insisted.

It was an odd feeling not having to hurry and be somewhere.
Crossing the room, I pulled back the horrid plaid curtains and looked
outside. The sun was beginning to rise, and I could see all the
grounds around the inn. Towering, full pine trees encircled the
property. In front of me was a view of the ocean, the light dancing
across the surface as the sun rose. It was magnificent—a million-
dollar view.

Or, if I did my job well, maybe three-quarters of a million.

I glanced around the room, my gaze falling on the empty tray
from the previous night. The "snacks" Alex brought me turned out to
be a thick steak sandwich with a side salad. There had even been a
piece of apple pie on the tray. I'd resisted as long as I could before I
attacked it, literally scraping the plate, breaking my own rule of not
eating sugar. The entire meal had been as delicious as anything I'd

eaten in a five-star restaurant. Even if she had made it grudgingly for me. My lips twitched as I thought about what had occurred in the hall. Seth's non-filter, Noelle's adorable lisp and childlike honesty, Alex's embarrassment—and her smile.

Especially, her smile.

After another hot shower, and still not shaving, I went downstairs, not surprised to find the lobby empty. I could smell coffee and followed the aroma into the bar area. There was no one around, but I did see the large coffee urn, so I poured myself a cup and grabbed the local paper from the pile on the table, then sat at a table by the window.

As I scanned the headlines, a door opened and Alex emerged, carrying a large tray. She didn't see me, and I was able to watch her as she moved around, disappearing through the door and reemerging every few moments with another silver tray she placed on a long table. Her hair caught the morning sun, the red glints bright in the light. It hung in long waves down her back, almost to her waist. It wasn't styled or stiff with product, but natural and full. I thought it was incredibly sexy. She turned, stifling a gasp when she saw me sitting there watching her.

"Good morning."

She straightened her blouse and came closer. "Good morning, Mr. Maxwell."

"Dylan, please." I smirked. "After all, you allowed me to call you Alex."

She bit her lip, gnawing on the pink flesh. It made me wonder what she was thinking.

"Dylan. I hope you slept well."

"Surprisingly, I did."

"Surprisingly?"

"I don't sleep well in strange places, but I felt"—I paused, contemplating my words—"relaxed here."

That gorgeous smile broke out, and she nodded enthusiastically. "It's so lovely here. The wind, the water, and the trees—they surround you and help you forget the rest of the world exists. It's a small piece of heaven." Her face suddenly changed, and she looked sad. "I love it here," she whispered, almost more to herself than me.

I didn't like her sad. It made my chest feel strange. I rubbed my sternum, trying to rid myself of the ache. I wanted her to smile.

"I think another reason I slept so well is because of the dinner I ate last night. It was truly delicious." Reaching out, I took her hand

and squeezed it. "Thank you, Alex. I realize you went above and beyond for me." Then I winked at her, unable to resist teasing her a little. "Even if I am an *ath-hole.*"

She gasped and her cheeks blazed with color, then her lips twitched and the most adorable giggle escaped. She opened her mouth to say something, but a couple of other guests came in and she stepped back. "I have to get breakfast ready."

"Of course."

"Mommy!"

A little blur tore across the room as Noelle ran to her mother, flinging her arms around Alex's legs. Seth followed more sedately, sitting down at the table next to me, nodding his greeting.

Alex ran her fingers through her daughter's wild hair, smiling at her. "Are you ready for day care?"

Noelle nodded enthusiastically. "Iz pizza day!"

Alex laughed. "Your favorite." She looked at Seth. "Did you get all your homework done?"

"Yep. Even algebra."

"Okay. Your lunches and snacks are in the kitchen. Have some breakfast."

I cleared my throat. "While others are deciding, may I have an egg white omelet, vegetables only, and low-fat cheese? Whole wheat toast, no butter please."

Alex and Seth exchanged a glance. "Pardon?" she asked.

"I'm sorry. Is there someone else I should give my order to?"

She shook her head. "It's a breakfast buffet, Dylan."

It was my turn to be confused. "A buffet?"

"You serve yourself."

I blinked. "You expect me to make my own omelet?" I sputtered. "I don't know how to cook."

"There are no omelets." Alex's voice was patient and somewhat amused. "There are scrambled eggs and bacon. You can toast a bagel or grab a muffin. Make a waffle. There's yogurt and fresh fruit. Juice. Coffee. You help yourself to whatever you want."

Make a waffle? Toast a bagel?

I looked at the tables where Alex had carried the trays. Other guests were already helping themselves, seemingly comfortable at the way the inn did things.

Once again, I had to remind myself I wasn't in my world anymore.

I must have appeared shocked.

Noelle moved away from her mother and grabbed my hand. "I hep you, Dywan. I make da bethest waffas! Wight, Sef?"

"Right, kiddo. The best."

She tugged my hand. "Come on! I show you!"

Ten minutes later, I was staring at my plate filled with a waffle Noelle and I made together. When she said she "made" the best waffles, what she really meant was, she pointed to the foam cup full of goopy batter and instructed you precisely how to pour it into the pan. She was noticeably impatient at my lack of skill when it came to flipping the waffle pan. Seth had to help me the first time, but I was proud of myself when I flipped it back with precision, Noelle clapping her little hands in delight.

The waffles were covered with globs of butter and overflowing with syrup—both of which Noelle insisted I had to have. I did manage to convince her I didn't need the sprinkles she told me made it taste "even betta." There was definitely more sugar on my plate than I would eat in a year. There was another plate with bacon and eggs. Seth had assured me, as he filled his own plate, Alex made them, and they weren't the fake kind that came in a carton.

I had no idea you could get fake eggs in a carton.

"Twy it, Dywan!"

Gingerly, I picked up my utensils and cut into the thick, gooey mess. Noelle watched anxiously as I chewed and swallowed. It was sweet and dense, the butter and syrup melting in my mouth.

It was fucking awesome.

Seth started chuckling, and Noelle's eyes widened. "Dywan!" she whispered. "You thaided da baddest word of dem all!"

I stared at them both, realizing I'd uttered that thought out loud. Alex walked out of the kitchen, eyeing us all, and I knew she would not be pleased with me swearing in front of Noelle—especially, the *baddest* word of them all. Nerves I didn't even know I had anymore made my palms sweat. I leaned forward, lowering my voice. "Don't tell Alex," I pleaded. I looked at Seth. "You owe me."

"We won't say anything, right, Noelle?"

She grinned. "Secwet."

She and Seth shared a fist bump.

Somehow, I knew they now owned my ass and would use that information to their advantage at some point.

So, I kept eating my waffle.

It was fucking awesome, after all.

The view from the bar was not as scenic as the one from my room, but it was still pleasant. Huge, full pine trees surrounded the inn. I wanted to explore more of the grounds and see the ocean. I could imagine its beauty in the winter winds.

Seth and Noelle left for their day—a large yellow bus picked up Seth, and a few minutes later, I watched Alex bundle Noelle into the back seat of another minivan, waving at her as the van left. I noticed several more trucks, some SUVs, and vans in the parking lot, but no cars.

"Doesn't anyone drive cars here?" I muttered to myself. "Just regular, normal-sized cars?"

Behind me, Alex chuckled. "You need to get out more, Dylan."

I had to laugh. "I suppose."

"Do you want anything else? Can I get you something?"

I turned my back to the window. "No, thank you. I was thinking I'd go for a walk before meeting with Mr. Walsh, but since I doubt my shoes would provide much protection, I guess I'll go to my room and get ready."

"Wait here," she commanded, and for some reason, I did exactly what she said—again.

When she reemerged, she had a pair of boots in her hand. "A guest left these and never came back for them. Seth hasn't quite grown into them yet, so you can use them. They're fairly large so they should fit."

I couldn't contain my smirk. "Checking out the size of my feet, Alex?"

Her cheeks darkened and her green eyes flashed at me. They were an incredible color and reminded me of the pines that grew around the inn.

"I noticed them last night when you stomped your wet shoes on my freshly washed floor," she reprimanded me, pulling back the boots. "You were making a lot of noise . . . and mess!"

Instantly, my ire was piqued. There was something about the woman that drove me *crazy*. She could wind me up faster than even Amy—but in a very different way.

"My feet were frozen! They wouldn't have been so cold if the minivan you had that child pick me up in had a better heater."

"Seth is *not* a child. The minivan is perfectly acceptable."

"Maybe here on the East Coast."

"Well, a grown man such as you should know to bring boots when he travels to the East Coast in December! Or did your *assistant* neglect to mention the weather to you?"

My God, this woman was infuriating.

"She never mentioned it," I retaliated. "So, I forgot them."

"She doesn't pack for you?" She mocked me with her question and a raise of her eyebrows.

"No, I'm quite capable of packing myself," I informed her haughtily.

"Well, good for you, *Mr. Maxwell.*"

Was she questioning my masculinity?

"I'm perfectly able to take care of myself," I reiterated.

She snorted, not even bothering to cover up the sound.

"You think differently?" I growled, stepping closer.

"Why, no . . ." she drawled, sarcasm thick in her tone.

I scowled. "You don't exactly sound convinced."

"Well, why don't you check with your assistant about that? The one who booked your flight, ordered your liquor, and didn't think to inform you of the winter weather? I bet she heats your croissants for you as well, doesn't she? Brings you lunch daily?" She smirked knowingly. "After all, you don't even know how to make an omelet."

I stalked the rest of the way toward her until we were almost nose-to-nose. "That's what I pay her for."

"Money well spent, I'm sure."

"At least I don't have to worry about her being rude to guests at the hotel I own. Maybe I should mention that to Mr. Walsh when I speak to him."

"Go ahead," she challenged. "Tell him exactly what you think of me."

I would do precisely that if I knew what I thought of her. I wanted to pull out my hair in frustration.

"Are you of sound mind?" I snarled.

"*What?*"

"You blow hot and cold. One minute you smile at me with a warmth I've never experienced, and the next you're spitting fire at me with your words. Your mood swings are constant."

The anger melted away from her expression, making her appear vulnerable. Once again, I noticed how fatigued she looked. It caused an odd ache in my heart and made my own ire dissipate. Quiet yearning replaced the annoyance.

"I don't mean to," she whispered and looked away.

The air around us changed and became charged with a deep, tender energy I wasn't used to feeling.

I reached up and cupped her cheek, stroking the soft skin. "I like it better when you're smiling. Especially at me. You have a beautiful smile."

Her eyes widened and her breathing picked up. "Dylan, you can't . . . You shouldn't . . ."

I leaned down, my mouth hovering over hers, her sweet breath washing over my face. "I *want* to. Please."

Then I placed my mouth on hers. Her soft lips melded to mine. I wound my arm around her waist, dragging her to my chest as our mouths moved together as though they had done so for a lifetime—and lifetimes before that one. It felt as if I'd found something I didn't know I was missing. Heat settled in my chest, blooming like a slow, flickering flame, my entire being easing at her nearness. Groaning, I pulled her closer, the kiss morphing into carnal, blistering desire. Entwining my hands in her long, silky hair, I tugged and clutched it. Our bodies were meshed together, and I slipped my hand under the loose shirt she wore, pressing into the warmth of the soft skin of her back. Her hands fisted on my shirt, the most erotic, quivering whimpers low in her throat. I moved my lips to the smooth skin of her cheek, trailing light kisses over to her ear, pulling the lobe in my teeth.

"Alex . . ." I moaned.

She stiffened and stepped back, her face flushed, lips swollen. She was beautiful.

I tried to pull her back, but she pushed against my chest, stepping back farther. Her hand flew to her face, her eyes wide with fear. "I . . . I can't," she breathed out. "I'm sorry, I can't do this!"

She turned and fled from the room as if the hounds of hell were pursuing her.

I sat down heavily in the chair closest to me, my chest heaving.

What had I done? One moment, we were arguing, and the next . . .

Kissing!

I ran a hand through my hair. What the hell was I thinking, kissing a total stranger?

Except—she didn't feel like a stranger.

What was it about that woman? Why was I reacting to her that way?

She made me laugh, and smile, then angered me—all in the blink of an eye. She didn't take any shit from me, and I liked that. She was bossy and tough, but when I saw her with her daughter, her tenderness showed through. Add in the fact that she catered to my demanding ass, and I knew there was more to her than she let others see.

I ran my fingers over my mouth, still tasting her. I thought how it felt when I kissed her. The feelings she stirred in me.

God, she was sweet. Her mouth, the feel of her pressed close, wrecked me. I had no idea why I had kissed her, but once I started, I didn't want to stop.

Until, that was, she ran from me.

It took everything in me not to follow her. I wanted to drag her into my arms again and kiss her until she forgot about everything but me. Us.

I shook my head.

Us?

I had just met her yesterday and I was thinking *us?*

I groaned, dropping my head in my hands. It had to be the sugar. I never ate sugar. Between the pie last night and the waffle this morning, I was on overload.

That *had* to be the explanation. I never acted as impulsively as I had a moment ago with Alex.

The boots that had started the entire scene lay on the floor, forgotten.

Bending down, I picked them up. They were well-worn, although still in decent shape, and I remembered her words, *"Seth hadn't grown into them yet."*

Who was Seth to her? Why was she saving used boots for him?

I estimated she was about six years younger than I was, which would make her about twenty-eight. She was much too young to be Seth's mother.

Sister, maybe?

He'd been looking after her daughter last night.

While she worked.

I glanced around the room, my eyes narrowed. She'd been working last night. She was working again today. I knew she'd spoken with Amy yesterday afternoon.

Did she work all the time? Was that why she looked so exhausted?

Did she live in the hotel?

Where was Noelle's father?

I had so many questions—I wanted answers to them all.

I glanced at my watch. I had an hour before I was to meet with the mysterious Mr. Walsh.

Maybe he'd be able to give me the answers I was looking for.

I certainly planned to ask him.

CHAPTER 5

DYLAN

I approached the front desk warily, unsure of Alex's reaction. She glanced away from the woman she was speaking to, briefly meeting my eyes. Color stained her cheeks, but she didn't stop the conversation with her coworker. I waited patiently, even managing to keep my toe-tapping fairly quiet. My fingers drumming on the top of the scarred wood were a little more obvious, though.

Alex fixed me a look that would kill most men—and immediately, I stopped drumming my fingers.

The woman was confusing, and I was sure her bark was worse than her bite, but I wasn't stupid. I liked my fingers attached.

Finally, she finished and came around the front of the desk, indicating I should follow her. She was silent as she walked ahead of me down the hall. I admired the view, hoping she didn't realize I was checking her out. Her long hair swung as she walked, hitting the top of her ass. She had an amazing ass—high and round. I was glad she walked slowly.

When we stopped outside a door at the end of the hall, she smiled, looking businesslike and professional. I much preferred her breathless and dreamy, with her lips swollen from mine.

"Will you require anything this afternoon, Mr. Maxwell?"

I was back to being Mr. Maxwell? I didn't like that.

Fleetingly, I thought about telling her I required *her* for the afternoon, but I decided against it.

"Ah, is there a car service?"

"I'm sorry?"

"Can I hire a car and driver? I want to go into town."

"Do you drive at all? A car, I mean—I'm not referring to how you drive people crazy."

Once again, sarcasm laced her voice, and I knew she expected me to say no. Then she could ask me if my assistant did that for me too. As for the crazy remark, I chose to ignore it—she was one to talk.

"Yes, I drive very well."

"There's a car rental place in town, if you want a car for longer than a couple of hours. Otherwise, I can leave the keys for the minivan at the desk for you." She paused, her eyes lit with mischief she was trying to hide. "If you think you can handle it. It's *larger* than a 'normal' automobile."

I smirked at her. "Oh, I think I can handle it."

"I'll leave the keys, then."

"Dinner?" I asked before I could change my mind.

"I assume, Mr. Maxwell, you're asking if dinner will be available for you this evening? Or would you prefer me to recommend one of our local spots?"

"Actually, I'd like to take you to dinner, but if you have to be here, then I'd be happy to stay in. Whatever you could provide would be appreciated. Perhaps you can join me."

She blinked. "You-You're asking me . . . to dinner?" She breathed out the question.

I stepped closer, lowering my voice. "Would you say yes if I was, Alex?"

Her eyes grew large. "Uh, um, I have to work."

"Do you ever *not* work? Are you on the clock twenty-four seven?" I frowned at her. "Are you looking after yourself?"

She had a blank expression on her face, her voice returning to a businesslike tone. "I do what I have to do."

"I think too much is expected of you."

Her eyes flared. "It's not your concern. Now, about dinner, I'll have something sent to your room."

I tamped down the urge to tell her I was concerned and to make her talk to me.

Raising my hand, I ran down my finger her cheek, enjoying the feel of her skin and the way her eyes focused on my actions. "Will you bring it up to me?"

Her breath caught in her throat. "If I have time. Otherwise, I'll send it up with Seth."

I chuckled. "I'd prefer it was you. Then you could join me." I crouched down so my mouth was by her ear. "I might actually *get* my dinner, and I promise not to be an ath-hole."

Her slight laugh made me grin.

"You're never going to let me live that down, are you, Mr. Maxwell?"

I shook my head. "I need something to hold over you. And stop calling me Mr. Maxwell. It's Dylan. I like to hear you call me Dylan," I insisted, my finger drifting over to her mouth, remembering how her lips felt on mine. They were so soft under my callused fingertip. They felt so right under my mouth.

Our gazes locked, the warmth swirling around us again.

"Is there anything special you'd like for dinner?" she squeaked out.

"You," I murmured before I could stop myself.

She gasped and her cheeks flamed, making me chuckle. She reacted to me so easily.

"I meant . . . I meant for me to make you."

I sighed. "I figured as much, *dammit.*"

"Stop cursing," she admonished me.

"Have dinner with me, and I'll stop."

"I doubt that."

"So, that's a no?"

"Yes."

"Yes, you'll have dinner?" I grinned.

"Stop twisting my words! I have to work."

"Fine."

"Is there something in particular you would like me to make for your dinner?" she asked again, enunciating each word, making sure I understood her question.

"No. But I'd like some more pie," I requested, even though I'd sworn I wouldn't eat any more sugar.

One piece couldn't hurt.

"I'll see what I can do." She indicated the door. "George—Mr. Walsh—is waiting for you." She paused. "Enjoy your afternoon, Dylan."

She hurried away, her cheeks still flushed.

I chuckled and straightened my tie, lifting my hand to knock.

A deep voice stopped my movement.

"Come in, Mr. Maxwell."

George Walsh wasn't at all what I expected.

Of course, nothing was in Pinegrove.

He sat, tall and proud, in a wheelchair, everything about him screaming strength and dignity despite his useless legs.

His short, silver hair gleamed in the light. His handshake was firm, his blue gaze direct, and his approach honest.

I liked him.

We dispensed with the usual games straight away.

"Why do you want my property so much, Mr. Maxwell?"

"Dylan, please."

He dipped his head in acknowledgment. "George."

"Because I own the pieces on either side of you, George, and I have plans for it. For all of it."

"Which are?"

I indicated the chair beside him. "May I?"

"Please."

I sat down, crossing my legs. "I want to develop the property. Make it a high-end travel destination."

"You're going to tear down the inn and rebuild?"

"Yes."

"And destroy the forest?"

"No. I plan to use the land in a better fashion. Expand the entire operation."

"How?"

"In the summer, there'll be a new outdoor pool, tennis courts, and boats to use on the water with a huge pier overlooking the ocean. Hiking trails with guides. Ocean tours, whale watching—everything my R&D team can come up with to make this a destination people will flock to, all year-round. The hotel will be five-star—beautiful rooms and suites, as well as an indoor pool, spa area, and gourmet dining. The cottages will all be updated and made into luxurious getaways. In the winter, there'll be cross-country skiing, sleigh rides, snowshoeing, and other winter activities. It will draw a lot of people. It'll be good for the town and the local merchants. A win-win situation for everyone." Uncrossing my legs, I leaned forward, resting my elbows on my knees. "I plan to invest a great deal of money here."

"I'm not sure the town will be prepared for that."

I smiled knowingly. "George, I've been preparing for this for a long time. I've already purchased a number of the empty business fronts. There will be high-end shopping and local wares. I'll make sure the merchants are ready."

"You've planned this all out."

"I have. The final piece is your property."

He nodded, looking past me to the window.

"I always planned to live here until I die." He indicated his legs. "Until the accident happened."

"Is that why you're selling?"

He snorted. "We both know why I'm selling. If I don't soon enough, I'll lose the place."

He was right; we both did know that. But to my surprise, I wanted to know more. I wanted to understand.

"What happened?" I asked quietly.

"My son and I were on a trip down south. Foolishly, we didn't have travel insurance. We went down for a few days, and neither of us even thought about it. We were in a car accident." He blew out a long huff of air. "My son, Eric, was killed. I was left in this chair. Without insurance, the medical bills were horrendous."

"I'm sorry for your loss."

"That moment took away almost everything that mattered in my life. The only things I had left were this place and my daughter-in-law and granddaughter."

"Why have you decided to sell now?"

"Not long before the accident, Eric had convinced me to reinvest and do some upgrading. I took a huge mortgage on the place." His hands curled on the arms of his wheelchair, his anger showing.

"And?" I prompted.

"The contractor we hired screwed us over. He took the money, did next to nothing, and disappeared. Add in the accident and the bills I was left with, it's been a never-ending struggle."

I didn't say anything. His story helped explain how he ended up in such a mess. It was tragic and awful—and cost him everything he held dear.

"I held on to hope as long as I could, that one day I'd walk again, be able to find a way to make this all right. But instead, I'm getting older, and soon won't be able to care for myself at all. As it is, I need more help every week. I need to move to a place where I can get that care without feeling guilty for asking anything more from the one person who has given up her life for me. She deserves happiness—a home, and another chance at a real family."

"Your daughter-in-law?"

He looked me in the eye. "Yes. Alexis. Alex is my daughter-in-law."

ALEX

I hurried down the hall, my cheeks burning, my mind racing. I ducked into one of the doors marked *Staff Only* and leaned against the rough wood. My breathing was fast, my skin flushed all over, and my lips still felt him.

Dylan Maxwell.

When he had walked into the inn last night, my entire world fell off its axis. Standing in front of the fire, his fists clenched, he was out of place in my shabby lobby. Sharp cheekbones slashed across his stern face, and his deep brown hair shot with gray fell over his forehead in messy waves. His gaze was intense—light blue irises that stood out under heavy eyebrows. His overcoat stretched across his broad shoulders, suiting his tall frame. No doubt it cost more than I made in a month. Maybe two. He was frowning, looking around, seemingly almost . . . lost?

For one brief moment, I thought he was a stranger, someone needing a room, and I smiled at him warmly, wanting somehow to help him. His own smile changed his face. The detachment vanished, and his expression was open and inviting.

Seconds passed, and there was only us. Smiling at each other.

Until he spoke.

Until I knew for sure, he was the man who was going to buy the property and force me to move from the one place I had called home for so many years.

He was arrogant, demanding, and cold.

Infuriating.

I did my best to be polite and accommodating. I had to call a friend who owned a fancy restaurant down the road and beg her to sell me a bottle of Courvoisier since the liquor store was closed. She lived over the restaurant and met me partway to save me time when I explained about the error. Then I rushed back to the inn and made him dinner. I thought I'd finally done everything right for him, until I found him in the hall with Noelle.

And she repeated what I had muttered in a fit of anger.

Asshole.

To say his reaction stunned me would be an understatement. His laughter had been loud and rich. His forgiveness shocking. His acceptance of his dinner and his gratitude for it this morning, unexpected.

I couldn't keep my eyes off him as he ate breakfast with Noelle and Seth. His bewilderment was endearing. His patience with Noelle another surprise.

Until we were alone.

Until he spoke.

Until he kissed me.

The yearning that exploded when his mouth crashed on mine was overwhelming. He awoke feelings in me that had been dormant for years. The shock of the moment hit me, and I had run, unsure how to deal with him.

I couldn't believe he kissed me.

I couldn't believe how much I liked it.

When I took him to see George, his quiet words, innuendos, and teasing left me feeling off-kilter.

It had been so long since a man had made me feel that way.

I wanted him to kiss me again. I wanted to feel his hard body pressed to mine—to feel his strength and power as he held me. To feel his demanding mouth on mine again. To forget everything and everyone, and give in to the desire he stirred within me.

But I couldn't forget.

I was a mother, a caregiver, and I had a business to run with a lot of people depending on me. I came last, because that was how it had to be. I didn't have time for a fling. Because for a man like him, that was all it would be.

Dylan Maxwell was a guest.

A rich tycoon here to buy the property and nothing more.

He was sexy, handsome, and charming when he chose to be. Cold and blunt at other times.

And he would be gone in the next couple of days, returning to his life. I would remain in Pinegrove, trying to pick up the pieces, and find mine.

The strange attraction that sizzled between us would mean nothing. He wasn't the sort of man looking for a relationship. I wasn't the sort of woman that had flings.

No matter how attractive he was.

I pushed off the door, knowing I needed to stay busy.

At least here in the inn, that was never a problem.

I touched my lips, wishing they didn't still feel his touch.

I ignored the voice that whispered they wanted to feel it many times over.

CHAPTER 6

DYLAN

My mind was reeling as I went back to my room. I paced the small space, going over what George had told me.

Alex and Noelle were his family. The inn was their home.

Alex, he had explained, had always been an old soul and had few friends her own age. Her best friend, Tami, had been fifteen years her senior. When she died of breast cancer, Alex took in her son Seth, vowing to care for him as if he were her own. He became hers, and therefore, part of George's family as well.

After George's accident, and the death of her husband, Alex had cared for the children and him, plus ran the inn. She gave up the little house she and Eric lived in, and moved in to the hotel on the second floor. She renovated George's room on the main floor to accommodate his needs. Two years later, when Seth joined them, she made another room into his.

Between the medical bills and the constant need for repairs, as well as the dwindling guest bookings, George finally admitted they could no longer ignore the facts. He needed more care, and Alex needed to find her life. He had a place in Halifax that would meet his needs, but his greatest worry was Alex and her family.

He leaned forward, his tone earnest, honesty rolling off him in waves. "I need to look after my family, Dylan."

"Why are you telling me all this, George? How do you know I won't use it to lowball my offer?"

"I checked you out. You've always been honest in your business dealings. And . . ."

"And?" I prompted.

"I spoke several times with your Mrs. Carson. She, ah, has a very high opinion of you." He met my gaze. "I don't think you're going to try to screw me." He chuckled. "Besides that, Dylan, I'm infirm, not stupid. I know what the property is worth. I know you want it. If I don't like your offer, I'll accept another one and you can fight with them to buy it."

"What will Alex do? Will she move to the city?"

For the first time, he looked uncomfortable. "No. Alex went to the city once. The girl who left here and the one who came back were two completely different people. The big city and all the trappings there aren't for her. She likes, she needs, open spaces and friendly faces around her." He sighed. "My biggest regret is that the one thing she has always wanted, dreamed about, the one thing I struggled for so long to give her, will never happen."

"And what is that?" I asked, every nerve in my body on edge. I needed to know. I had no idea why, but I had to know what Alex's dream consisted of. It felt important to me.

"She wants to live on the bluff. In a house that lets her see the ocean everywhere she goes. The very tip of the property is her favorite place in the world."

My mind flipped through the scope of the property. "You can't sell it and leave that piece intact. There'd be no access without resurveying it. Changing the entire lay of the land, dividing it—and giving up the most valuable piece."

"I know. She knows it too. It can't be done and have the land hold the same value. She tells me it was simply a dream, and not one she ever expected to come true. She knows I have to sell. She's a smart woman and she's seen the numbers—but sometimes it doesn't make it any easier. I feel as if I've failed her, failed my son, by not being able to look after her."

"I'm sure she doesn't agree."

"She wouldn't say so if she did. Alex is, without a doubt, an angel. She never complains. She works too hard and takes on too much. Everything and everyone come first. She deserves so much more than a timeworn inn that is falling down around her, an old man who needs special care, and more stress than anyone should carry. She deserves love and laughter. She deserves to be looked after and to feel safe. And most of all, she deserves to be cherished."

He leaned back in his chair, fixing his all-knowing eyes on me.

"There's more to life than work and responsibility. More than money and success. Love is a rare gift not everyone is given, Dylan. If you find it, you should grab it and hold on to it. You never know when it might be taken away."

I stared at him, not knowing what to say.

What did love have to do with my buying his property?

"I'm headed into Halifax for some tests. I'll be back the day after tomorrow. You can present your offer to me then."

"I'm ready to present it now."

"I won't look at it until I come back. I want you to look around—really look around. Open your eyes and see what's here. Discover the hidden potential. Then we'll talk." He paused and sighed. "Alex will look after you while I'm gone."

I snorted. "Or kill me. I don't think she likes me at times."

His gaze was amused. "Alex is a strong woman, because she's had to be. Her bark is far worse than her bite."

I chuckled as he echoed my own thoughts from earlier.

"She doesn't deserve to be trifled with."

Realizing he'd probably heard our conversation in the hall, I felt a slight twinge of guilt. "I don't plan to do that." Thinking of her fiery temper, I smiled. "I think she is rather . . . amazing." I found myself confessing.

He nodded and returned my smile. "She's a complex woman—the perfect woman for a complex man who is ready to start really living life."

With those strange words, he had dismissed me.

I couldn't stay in my room any longer. I needed to move, to explore, and fill my head with thoughts other than Alex.

I stopped at the front desk and collected the keys for the dreaded minivan, approaching it cautiously in the parking lot. After adjusting the seats and mirrors, I drove into town, taking my time to enjoy the scenery. Both Mrs. C and George kept telling me to look around me; although, I wasn't sure what it was they wanted me to see.

In town, I walked around, checking on the various buildings I owned, some still with operational businesses, others closed. I could see a lot of potential everywhere I looked. Places for local artisans, a few higher-end stores, and fresh real estate ideas started forming in my head. Several of the buildings would make great condos on the upper floors, if remodeled and priced right. If the new resort brought the kind of traffic I projected it would draw, it could result in increased occupancies.

Once again, a win-win situation.

I enjoyed my walk. It was a nice town with lots of history and remarkable architecture. Nestled among the same sort of large pine trees that surrounded the inn, it was incredibly picturesque. The wharf was deserted this time of year, but I imagined in the summer it was a bustling place. If my plans came together, it would be that much busier in the years ahead.

Smiling, friendly faces greeted me everywhere I went. I rarely bought gifts, but I found a unique pewter sculpture I knew Arlene would love. Another store supplied me with the perfect handmade fishing lures for her husband. After I made the purchases, I had them shipped directly back home. They were the two people I always bought Christmas gifts for, along with their grandchildren. My staff received bonuses.

I wasn't sure what I'd do in regard to Amy. I wondered if there was a place I could send her to learn how to be a better PA, but then I realized Mrs. C would call me an ass for thinking that way. The problem was I'd had the best for so long, no one would ever be as good as Arlene Carson.

Especially not Amy.

I stopped in front of a window, examining the boots on display. I went inside and chose a pair I thought would be suitable for walking around the grounds of the inn. I wanted to see more of the property, but I couldn't do that in my dress shoes and I wasn't the type to wear someone else's discarded boots.

I had to tamp down my grin when I remembered my conversation with Alex over my shoes.

As I waited for the clerk to find my size, a pair of tiny red slippers caught my eye. Walking over, I picked them up, grinning at the foolishness of them. Boot-like, fuzzy, and graced with a red bow on the outside decorated with white polka dots, I knew instantly Noelle would love them. I could see her tripping up and down the hall in them, grinning as she held out her foot to show them off to me. *"Pwetty, wight, Mr. Dywan?"* I could hear her saying.

Except, I didn't know her size.

When the clerk reappeared, she smiled at me. "For your daughter?"

A strange thrill went through my chest at those words, but I shook my head. "A . . . friend's daughter. She's four, I think, but I don't know her size."

"Is she big for her age?"

"No, she's petite—like her mother."

"A small, then."

The words were out of my mouth before I even realized it. "I want a pair of boots for her son as well."

"Do you know his size?"

"Ah . . . no. Seth's seventeen, I think."

She looked surprised. "Alex's Seth? Alex is your friend? The boots are for him?"

"Yes." I replied, feeling as though I needed to justify my actions. "He's been a great help to me."

"He needs a twelve, and if the slippers are for Noelle, a small is perfect for her."

Remembering Mrs. C's words when it came to her grandchildren, I nodded. "I can't buy a gift for one without giving something to the other one."

"Of course not. That's very kind of you. They'll love it. And Alex . . . ?" Her voice trailed off.

"Alex?" I prompted.

Her eyes were sad as she spoke. "She's such a wonderful person and has given up so much for those kids. Everything she does is for them." Her fingers ran over the fuzzy red of the slippers. "Luxuries like these are rare for them."

I swallowed the sudden lump in my throat.

"Are there any, um, luxuries, Alex likes? Anything you could suggest?" I asked. "Something she would never treat herself to?"

She grinned as she handed me the boots I wanted to try on. "There's a chocolate shop on the corner. The dark chocolate-covered caramels are decadent. All made by hand. Alex is crazy for them."

"Thank you. I'll pick some up for her to say thank you for her hospitality."

She extended her hand. "I'm Jodi, by the way."

I accepted her handshake. "Dylan. Nice to meet you." I stood, testing the boots. "These fit well. I'll wear them, if you don't mind."

"Of course."

Twenty minutes later, I was on my way back to the inn. The passenger seat contained three parcels: a pair of winter boots Jodi assured me Seth would think were cool, a nonsensical pair of fuzzy red slippers Noelle would wear with delight, and the biggest box of dark chocolate-covered caramels I could buy at the chocolate shop.

Three simple gifts. None of them costing a lot of money—at least not for me—and yet, somehow, I knew they were the most important items I'd bought in a long time.

Gifts I was anxious to be well received.

I left the minivan in the parking lot and headed toward the bluff. The skies were getting darker, the temperature dropping. I knew a storm was coming, and I wanted to see the view before it hit. I followed a narrow path twisting between the trees, going uphill. I paused at the edge of the trees, my breath catching at the spectacular vista in front of me. The edge of the land was large and flat, bordered entirely by pine trees and rocks, leading to the edge of the bluff. You could see for miles in any direction, the vast scope overwhelming. It was as if you were on the edge of the world, with nothing around you. I could see why it was Alex's favorite spot.

I moved closer, mesmerized by the water, the blues and grays swirling, crashing against the icy rocks below. I could imagine how it looked in the summer, when the ocean was calm, the colors sparkling in the sun. Each season would bring its own beauty.

"Incredible, isn't it?"

Startled, I looked down. Alex was sitting on one of the lower rocks, her knees pulled to her chest. Her dark gray coat blended so well with the wet rocks, I hadn't even noticed her. Her hair was damp and plastered to her head, and I wondered how long she'd been sitting out in the frigid, wet air. Her voice sounded strange, and when I looked closer, I could see she'd been crying. My brow furrowed as I studied her—she looked so defeated.

I stepped forward, worried over two things: she'd been crying, and she was too damn close to the edge of the cliff. There was ice around, the frosty rocks glistening in the light. If she slipped, she could hurt herself or worse. I held out my hand. "Alex, come here."

She frowned up at me. "Why?"

I indicated the ocean that crashed against the rocks with a loud fury. "You're too close to the edge. It's making me nervous."

She craned her neck, looking over the cliff. She shrugged and hugged her knees closer. "I'm used to being close to the edge, Dylan. It's fine."

Her words made me shiver and my chest feel odd. I had a feeling she wasn't talking about the rocks.

"Please, Alex."

With a sigh, she took my hand, letting me pull her up. In my haste, I pulled her too fast, and she stumbled. My arms shot out, grabbing her, pulling her tight to my chest. I held her close, feeling her heart beating wildly against my skin. Mine was racing as well.

I stepped well back from the rocks, dragging her with me, not letting her go. I fisted my hands in her wet hair, tugging the strands so her head lifted. "Are you all right?"

She blinked. "I'm fine."

"Why are you sitting out here alone? Why are you crying?"

"I'm fine. It's the wind—my eyes were watering."

I didn't believe that for a second.

"I want to help."

"You can't."

"I want to make you smile."

To my horror, more tears filled her eyes, spilling over and down her cheeks.

"Tell me," I begged, a feeling of desperate helplessness running through my body. "Let me fix it."

"Fix it?"

"Yes." I wanted to tell her I'd fix anything that made her sad.

"But you're the cause, Dylan," she stated quietly.

"What?"

"You're buying the inn and the land. It's my home. The only one I know. The only one my children know. I don't know what's going to happen. I'm losing my home, George is leaving us, and I don't know what my future holds."

"Alex, I . . ."

She shook her head. "I know if it's not you, it will be someone else. I know George has to sell. My head knows this . . . But my heart"—she closed her eyes—"my heart hurts."

I touched my forehead to hers. "I'm sorry."

"Ignore me, Dylan. I simply needed to come here and think a little. I'll figure it out. I always do."

Her words sliced through my chest. Bending down, I cupped her cheek and pressed my mouth to her lips. Her hand grabbed my wrist, and I wound my other hand around her waist, tugging her close again. Time—the world—ceased to exist. All that was real, all that mattered, was how she felt, how she tasted. All that mattered was that moment.

Until she pulled away.

Tears clung to her lashes as she smiled bravely. "Take care of the land, Dylan. This is a special place."

I nodded, unsure what to say.

"I'll send your dinner up to your room about seven."

"That's fine."

"A storm is coming, so the inn will be pretty quiet. I need to go and make sure everything is done and secured, so I can send the staff home."

I reached out. "Alex . . ."

She stepped back, shaking her head. "I can't, Dylan. I've already lost enough. I can't afford to risk losing anything else."

I dropped my hand. Our eyes locked, her green gaze filled with so much pain it was blatant. I had nothing to offer her, nothing I could say that would make anything better. Her life was about to change again—and once more, not for the good.

The worst part? I was the reason for it.

CHAPTER 7

DYLAN

I paced around my room, running my hands through my hair in vexation. Over and again, Alex's words replayed in my mind.

I was taking away her home. No matter what else she said, or how accepting she was about it, it was still the honest truth. It didn't matter it was something that would happen even if I stepped back and didn't buy the property. George Walsh had to sell. The hotel had to go, and Alex and her family had to leave the place they all loved.

Common sense told me she would find a job in town—or another local area. Once George was settled and she had a new place, her life would become somewhat normal—maybe even better. Without the worry of looking after George or all the heavy responsibilities involved in running the inn, her life might get easier, in fact. She could devote all her time to caring for Noelle and Seth.

One thought kept nagging me, though. Who would care for Alex?

I slugged back another shot of brandy, unsure how many I'd consumed since getting back to my room. I squinted at my watch. It was almost seven, so Alex should be here soon with my dinner. Maybe I would talk to her some more.

When I heard the knock at the door, I lunged for it, throwing it open. Seth stepped back, startled. "Hey, Dylan."

"Oh." I peered around him into the empty hall. "Hey. Where's Alex?"

"She's, ah, busy. I brought your dinner." He grinned, thrusting the tray forward. "I didn't even forget this time—it's still hot!"

I took the tray, feeling disappointed.

"What is she busy doing?"

"She has some things to take care of. I'm looking after Noelle."

I sighed. "Yeah, fine. Thanks for dinner."

He looked at me strangely. "Dylan, you okay? You look weird."

"I'm fine. Hungry, I guess."

"You'll love your supper. Alex makes awesome Tater Tot Casserole. It's Noelle's favorite."

What the hell was a tater tot?

I had no idea, but it did smell delicious.

"Thanks."

"You can leave your tray outside, and I'll get it later."

"I can bring it down. I thought I might watch the hockey game in the bar later." I had noticed it had a decent-sized TV, unlike the small, out-of-date one in my room.

"Okay. You'll have the bar to yourself." He turned to go, then paused. "Alex asked if you need anything to knock on the door down the hall. Room 200. There isn't anyone at the front desk."

"Why?"

"You're the last guest. She's out right now. But I can get you anything you need."

"Oh. Okay, fine."

He left, and I sat down, lifting the lid, inhaling the fragrant meal in front of me. Beside the large portion of casserole still bubbling it its dish, there was a salad and some sort of cheesy bread, literally dripping with butter. A ramekin of salad dressing was on the side, which was thoughtful since I rarely used any—or had butter on my bread, never mind with the addition of more cheese.

I ate everything, including the salad dressing. I'd never tasted anything like it. I assumed the tater tots were the strange little puffy things on top of the casserole. I liked them—I liked them a lot.

I sat back, replete, but disappointed.

There was no pie.

I had really liked that pie.

I flung my napkin on the tray, wondering if maybe Alex would find me a piece when I went down to the bar. If I asked very politely, surely she wouldn't refuse.

Taking my tray, I went downstairs to the quiet main floor. It was strange not to see anyone anywhere, and I felt as if I was snooping as I pushed open the kitchen door and slid my tray onto the counter. It was small but clean and organized. I smirked. Of course, it was organized. Alex ran it.

I looked around, but I couldn't find any pie. There were lots of breakfast items and some containers I assumed held the "snacks" Alex had offered my first night. But no pie. Wandering back into the bar, I noticed something else.

There was no Alex. There was no one.

Grabbing the remote, I turned on the TV, finding the hockey game. I settled onto one of the sofas in the room, and after glancing around guiltily, lifted my feet to the coffee table and relaxed.

The hockey game was boring, and I started getting restless. I could hear the storm outside beginning to pick up, the wind getting stronger. Remembering that Seth said Alex was out, I began to worry. Why was she out on a night like that? She was the one who told me how bad the storms could get. Why would she leave the inn?

Maybe I had missed her. Maybe she came back while I was eating. Getting up, I tried the doors, but I found them locked. Obviously, no new guests were expected. I went back to the bar and checked the large coffee urn, but it was cold. I paced around the room, wondering about going upstairs and checking to make sure she hadn't come back while I was eating in my room. If she wasn't there, I was certain I could convince Seth to tell me where she was. I'd feel better knowing. But I hesitated. Alex might not want to see me, so I decided not to ask. I found a passable scotch behind the bar and poured a shot. Alex could add it to my bill. I sat back down and resumed watching the hockey game.

The elevator dinged, the doors opened, and I heard the sound of fast, tiny feet. I was already grinning when a tousled head of curls appeared around the corner and Noelle's mischievous smile beamed at me from across the room. Her green eyes, so like her mother's, were dancing as she peeked at me, not making a sound, waiting for me to encourage her to come closer.

Without a thought, I opened my arms. An affectionate nickname rolled off my tongue, surprising me, but it suited her.

"Hey, Little Owl."

She giggled, her little feet thumping against the hardwood floor as she rushed forward. Wearing a one-piece set of fuzzy pajamas with feet attached and clutching a container of something, she flung herself at me and I caught her, settling her on my knee.

"Are you supposed to be out of bed?"

"No."

"Where is Seth?"

"Sweeping."

"I see."

"He 'posed ta be doing homewok, but he fawed asweep," she explained. "I knocked on your doow, but you not dere. I come and find you," she added proudly.

"What do you have there?" I asked, indicating the container.

She grinned, showing off the empty space in her mouth. She was so adorable when she smiled. "Mommy and I made cookies. I share wif you."

I sat up straighter. *Cookies?* I couldn't remember the last time I had cookies.

"What kind?"

She lifted the lid. "Suga."

I groaned and looked in the container, my eyes widening. The cookies were all gone. I had eaten nine cookies. Nine sugar cookies. And, after raiding the refrigerator, downed two glasses of milk. Noelle had nibbled one cookie and sipped the glass of milk I poured her. She sat beside me on the sofa, her legs tucked under her, telling me all about her day in her lispy, breathless voice. I heard about pizza day, her best friend Lucy, how much she loved to "dwaw," and her "favowite teacha, Mrs. Webba."

I found it surprisingly easy to understand her, even with her strange speech patterns. Maybe it was because I wanted to hear what she had to say. I found her completely enchanting. She was beyond delighted when I told her how much I liked her favorite supper of Tater Tot Casserole, informing me she had "hepped Mommy make it."

"I puts on da tots, Dywan!"

I found a blanket on the back of a chair and draped it over her. She talked nonstop, pointing at the TV and asking questions about the hockey game, which I tried to explain to her. She yawned and stretched, clearly tired, and I smiled down at her.

"You should go to bed, Little Owl."

She shook her head no. "I wait hewe, wif you, fo Mommy."

"Seth might wake up and worry."

She giggled, shaking her head once more. "No. He sweeps yike da dead, Mommy thay."

I chuckled and leaned over, grabbing a pillow. I laid it on my lap and patted the fabric. "Lie down and watch the game with me, then."

She snuggled down, and I drew the blanket around her shoulders, not wanting her to get cold. I glanced at my watch and frowned. I couldn't believe Alex was still out. The wind was stronger, and snow had started falling.

"Do you know where Mommy went, Noelle?"

"Da pwane pwace," she mumbled sleepily.

I frowned. Plane place? My heart started to pound. She was at the airport? My gaze flew to the window where the snow swirled and the wind flung it against the glass. She was driving in that weather?

I glanced down, but Noelle was asleep. I started flipping channels, wanting to find the local news, fear filling my chest. Was she out on the highway? The news channel talked about the worsening conditions, the storm hitting harder and faster than expected.

Carefully, I slipped Noelle's head off my knee and stood, looking out the window. Thick, heavy snow was falling, the wind kicking it around. The tree branches were already laden with the weight. I peered toward the parking lot. I could barely make out the shape of the lone car sitting in the corner. I began to pace, tugging on my hair, unsure what to do. I couldn't go find her—I had no way of doing so. I didn't know whom to call. I couldn't even call Alex since I didn't know if she had a cell phone, or if she did, I had no idea of her number.

I glanced toward the elevator. If she had one, Seth would have the number. I had to try to find her. Make sure she was safe. I hurried forward, pressing the elevator button. As I stepped in, I heard the crunch of tires on snow and raced to the front, fumbling with the lock and flinging open the door.

Alex stepped from the van, looking exhausted, and somewhat alarmed. Her eyes widened as she took in my frantic appearance standing in the doorway. "Dylan?"

I was in front of her in three strides, ignoring the snow and the wet seeping into my shoes. I dragged her into my arms and lifted her up. "Thank God you're back safe."

"Dylan, it's snowing and you have no coat!"

Without releasing her, I pivoted and entered the inn, shutting the door firmly behind me. Setting her on her feet, I pushed the damp hair off her face. "Are you okay?"

"I'm fine. It took me longer to get back—the storm hit earlier than I anticipated."

"Why were you on the roads?"

She frowned. "Two guests had to get to the airport. They wanted to get away before the storm socked them in. I couldn't get a driver to take them, so I had to."

She shivered, and I unzipped her coat, pushing it off her shoulders. I pulled her toward the fireplace and pushed her into the chair beside it. I grabbed her hands, rubbing them briskly. "Where are your gloves?"

She looked down. "Oh. I lost them when I was checking the tire."

"Checking the tire?" I hissed.

"Something felt off with the van, so I pulled over to check I wasn't getting a flat." She shrugged. "It was just ice buildup. I guess after I cleaned the tires, my gloves must have dropped out of my pocket."

I stood and pulled at my hair.

"What's wrong?"

I turned sharply, leaning down, my hands on the arms of her chair, effectively pinning her in. "You risked your life to drive some people to the airport in a *snowstorm*, you left your kids here, and you didn't tell me you were going! No one knew where you were!"

She stared at me, blinking.

"You could have had an accident! Been hurt! All to please a couple of guests who wanted to leave, despite all the weather warnings? What were you thinking?"

She glared up at me, placing her hand on my chest, pushing me back—hard. She stood, her eyes narrowed. "First off, I've driven that route countless times, Dylan. I have all-wheel drive in the van and winter tires. Second, they weren't normal guests. They were some of our best customers who give us lots of business, and I knew they had somewhere to be tomorrow. If I'd had any other choice, I would have chosen it, but I didn't. As it was, they might not even get out since the storm hit sooner than we expected."

I started to speak, but she held up her hand. "Susan knew I was going to the airport, and if I had any problem, she would have been my contact. She would have come back to the inn to look after the kids if I needed her." She huffed. "I drove slow which is why I was gone so long, and I'm back safe and sound. I didn't say anything to you because, *you*, Mr. Maxwell, are a guest, and I would have no reason to inform you of my whereabouts since I wasn't aware you would care. Did you get your dinner?"

A guest? Didn't care?

She only thought of me as a guest?

That upset me, although I wasn't sure why.

"Yes," I said shortly. "Seth brought me my dinner."

"Are you down here because you've drunk all your own brandy?"

"I wanted to watch the hockey game. The TV in the bar is bigger."

Her gaze took in the TV, and she noticed her daughter curled up on the sofa. "Why is Noelle down here?"

I snorted. "Your babysitter failed again. He fell asleep."

"And?" she demanded.

"Your daughter was looking for company. She came to find me and found her way downstairs. Rather than send her upstairs alone again, I let her fall asleep here—with me." Still smarting from her remark about me only being a guest, I added, "It interrupted my evening, but I let her stay anyway."

"She was bothering you?"

"Seth isn't exactly the most reliable caregiver, it seems. And neither of your children know much about boundaries, do they? She just shows up and . . . injects herself," I muttered, instantly regretting my words when her face paled.

Brushing past me, she gathered up Noelle in her arms. "I apologize. Thank you for sitting with her and being so kind. I'll make sure she doesn't bother you again. Enjoy the rest of your evening, and I'll be down in a while to turn off the lights."

"Alex . . ."

Her voice was cool. "Is there anything you need, *Mr. Maxwell?* Something I can get you before you retire for the night?"

"No."

I watched her walk away, her head up, shoulders back. Leaning down, she punched the call button for the elevator. The doors slid open and she stepped inside. Our gazes met, and the sadness I saw in hers made my chest ache.

I put that sadness there.

The doors shut before I could apologize.

CHAPTER 8

DYLAN

I tossed and turned all night. The image of Alex's sad eyes kept running through my head. Twice, I had started down the hall to knock on her door before I retired for the night, but I thought better of it. I needed to talk to her in private and at length—not in the hall with her kids listening, and not when she was already tired and upset.

I got up later than normal and got ready for the day. The inn was quiet, the storm outside still going, but not as fierce as last evening. I knew I wasn't going anywhere today. I was determined to speak with Alex and apologize for my harsh words.

The front lobby was deserted, the fire burning low as I walked through, wondering where everyone was. I stopped and added a log, stifling a grin when I realized Seth had passed out on the sofa, softly snoring. He certainly loved to sleep. His hair was damp, as were the bottom of his pants. I guessed he'd been out shoveling snow. His boots were sitting on the mantel; I pushed them a little closer to the fire so they'd dry out—the way it was snowing out there, he'd be out a lot today. I lifted one up, noticing how worn-out it was. He really needed the new pair I'd bought him. With a frown, I placed it back beside its mate, wondering if Alex would let me give them to him. If she would accept any of the gifts I had bought.

I walked into the bar area, pleased when I saw the coffee was ready. Alex made great coffee. I grabbed a cup and strolled to the window, looking out at the storm. The trees were heavy with snow, even their strong limbs bending under the weight. The wind blew and gusted, the entire world white and blurry with the non-ending swirls.

I turned back, surprised to see the little figure in the corner. Noelle was busy coloring, her head down, shoulders hunched, her curls covering her face. I cleared my throat, waiting for her usual exuberant greeting, frowning when she glanced up, offering a trace of a smile, then lowering her head to her coloring again. I crossed the room and sat down beside her, setting down my coffee cup.

"Morning, Little Owl."

"Hi, Mista Dywan," she replied, her voice subdued. She went back to coloring, although her actions were less than enthusiastic.

"Are you feeling all right?"

"Yeth."

I leaned forward, not liking the sad version of my little girl. "Is something wrong?"

"No."

"Noelle, look at me, please."

She glanced up, her eyes unhappy and troubled.

I searched my mind, trying to figure out what was upsetting her.

"Are you angry with me? Did I do something wrong?"

She shook her head. "Not you, Dywan."

"What does that mean?"

"I-I not 'posed to bovver you."

"Bother me?"

"Mommy thaid I bovvered you. I 'posed to be a good gul today and pway by myself."

Immediately, I knew Alex had taken my words to heart. My rude, thoughtless words. They had hurt her, and she was trying to protect her daughter.

"Noelle, little one, you're not bothering me."

"I not?"

"No. I promise."

"But Mommy thaid . . ."

I smiled at her. "I'll talk to Mommy. You go back to being my Noelle, okay?"

The sadness vanished instantly, her delightful smile lighting her face. "You wanna cowwa wif me?"

I swallowed—I really had no idea how to color. Then I looked at the paper she was filling in and realized I could probably handle it. I was unsure what the image was she was creating, or if there was really an image there. It did kind of resemble something Christmassy with its holiday colors.

"Sure."

Then, to make sure she knew everything was okay, I leaned over and picked her up, settling her on my lap. She giggled and pulled her paper and crayons over, immediately lapsing into her usual chatter, her strange little lisp making me smile. I sipped my coffee, nodding and listening intently to her words, making out most of them. When she leaned back to my chest, tilting her head up as she grinned and laughed about her reindeer picture, I felt an intense wave of tenderness flow through me. The strange sensation of protectiveness I'd been feeling for Alex welled up for Noelle as well—I had even felt the tug of it as I watched Seth slumber. Feelings I had never felt for another person were strong for the entire family.

Alex came through the door, her arms filled with laundry. She stopped when she saw Noelle and me, a frown marring her face.

"Noelle," she began in a firm voice, "what did I tell you this morning?"

I held up my hand. "She's fine, Alex. *We're* fine."

Her shoulders were tense, and she looked exhausted. I lifted Noelle off my knee and placed her in my chair. I dropped a kiss to the top of her head. "You keep coloring, okay, Little Owl? I need to talk to Mommy."

"Otay."

I approached Alex, who was watching me warily.

"May I speak with you in private?"

She hesitated.

"Please, Alex."

She nodded. "I'm going to put this in the laundry and start your breakfast. We can talk in the kitchen."

"Thank you."

I entered the kitchen, waiting for her. She walked in, looking resigned and anxious. Before she could say a word, I reached out and dragged her into my arms. She stiffened in shock, trying to step back. Pressing my hand to the middle of her back, I held her tight.

"I'm sorry, Alex. I'm so sorry. I shouldn't have said that last night. I didn't mean it. Honestly. My Little Owl isn't a bother. Neither is Seth. None of you are."

"But you said it."

"I was so worried about you. I didn't know where you were or how to find you. The thought of you being hurt . . ." I swallowed hard. "I was an ass. Mrs. C would tell you, when I'm upset, I'm more of an ass than normal."

"That's a lot of ass," she mumbled.

A chuckle escaped my mouth. "It is. Even Noelle picked up on that."

She relaxed into my embrace, tilting up her head. Our eyes met and held.

"Why do you care so much?"

I slipped my hand up her neck, feeling the satin of her skin as I cupped her cheek. "I don't know. I just do."

"I can't . . ."

"Don't, Alex. Don't shut me out."

"Dylan," she whispered. "This can't work. I'm not a one-night-stand kind of woman, and you live hundreds of miles away. Live a different life from what I do. I have responsibilities, children . . . I can't just . . ." She shook her head. "I just can't."

"Alex, I feel something. I don't know what it is, but there's something. Please don't turn me away."

She didn't say anything, but she stared at me with those beautiful eyes, her exhaustion making them mossy and darker than usual. The air around us changed, becoming warm and charged. Slowly, I lowered my head, brushing my lips against hers. A quiet whimper escaped her mouth, and I tugged her to me, captured her mouth, and kissed her. All my worry, confusion, and the strange need I felt for her went into that kiss. Our tongues met, tangling and tasting, and I buried my hands in her long hair, tilting her face so I could get closer. Our mouths moved, the kiss deepened, and desire exploded.

In a second, I had shoved her against the wall, my body holding her captive as I explored her curves. It didn't matter her daughter was close by or Seth was sleeping across the room. I didn't care what happened in a few days, or even a few hours. All I cared about, all that mattered, was the way she felt in my arms. How perfectly she fit against me. The way she moaned low in her throat and how her fingers felt, tugging on the short strands of my hair, making me want her that much more. My cock lengthened, pressing against the seam of my trousers. I wanted her. Right there. Right now.

Until Seth's voice boomed through the thin walls and reality came crashing around us.

"Hey, kiddo! Where's Alex?"

Alex stiffened, and with regret, I pulled back, our eyes meeting. Her chest heaved, her cheeks were flushed, and her lips swollen. She looked stunning. I still had my hands tangled in her hair, and I bent down, kissing her softly. We'd have to continue it later.

Alex reached up, trying to calm the mess my hands had made of her waves. I tugged on her hand and kissed the knuckles.

"I'll go distract them. Give you a minute to, ah, calm down."

"I'll make you some breakfast."

"Sounds good." I ran a finger down her pink cheek. "We need to talk."

"Okay."

"And I want to kiss you more. Lots more."

"Oh," she breathed. Then she looked down at my crotch. "I don't know if you should go try to distract them looking like that."

I grinned at her. "It's all your fault. If you weren't so tempting, I wouldn't have this little problem." I adjusted myself.

"Not sure I'd call that little."

I chuckled and had to kiss her again, which didn't help with my raging hard-on.

I stepped back and grabbed the folded newspaper on the counter, holding it in front of me. I winked at her. "Don't want to scare anyone."

She covered her mouth, giggling. With a smirk, I dropped another kiss on her head before walking back to the dining room. Luckily, Seth was bent over, helping Noelle with her coloring. I took my time getting another cup of coffee, giving my erection a chance to soften. I stared out the window at the piles of drifting snow. It was as if the entire world was covered in a thick, white blanket.

Seth reached across the table, grabbing a mug. "Hey, Dylan. Morning."

"Morning."

"Sleep well?"

"Well enough. Unlike some people, *not* like the dead."

He laughed but looked bashful. "Alex told me Noelle escaped again last night. Sorry."

I sighed. "Seth, Alex trusts you. You need to make sure you live up to that trust. You can't keep falling asleep while you're looking after Noelle." I met his eyes. "You're old enough to be more responsible."

"I was tired."

I sighed, rubbing a hand across my face. "And you don't think Alex is tired? She runs this place, looks after the both of you and George, cooks, cleans, does laundry—" I paused, tired simply at the thought of everything she handled. "And God knows what else. She's run ragged, Seth. She needs help."

He glanced behind him at the kitchen door and exhaled. "She never says anything."

I put my hand on his shoulder, squeezing it lightly. "She never would. She's strong. But I'm telling you, she needs your help. Try staying awake on the nights she needs you."

"I will. I'll try to help more."

"Good." Unable to resist, I ruffled his hair. "You're a good kid, Seth."

His cheeks flushed, and he dropped his gaze in embarrassment. "Thanks."

Alex came through the kitchen, carrying a tray. "Dylan, I have your breakfast."

I sat down and, without hesitation, dug into the stack of pancakes. Noelle "hepped" me drown them in syrup, and she grinned when it dribbled down my chin. Alex sat down, sipping coffee, and Seth rambled on about snow days and no school. Noelle had lots to say on the subject of snow, and I ate my breakfast listening to them all talk. I didn't have much to add, but I talked about how I'd never seen that much snow. That led to many stories of the blizzards they'd been through over the years.

It was a strange sensation, sitting with them like that. It felt right. Listening to their stories, with Noelle back on my knee, coloring, and twisting around to make sure I was listening to her when she spoke. Often, she would tap at my cheek to get my attention, the gesture making me smile. Seth got up and filled all our coffee cups, and brought Noelle some more juice.

Alex frowned and looked out the window. "George won't get back for a couple of days, and I'm pretty sure you're stuck too, Dylan."

I wasn't surprised. Normally, I would be impatient, hating to have my schedule disrupted, but the news didn't bother me in the slightest. I shrugged. "Nothing to be done except weather the storm. What do you do when you're snowed in like this—besides trying to shovel your way out of it?"

Noelle clapped her hands. "Games!"

Seth grinned. "We have power, so we eat popcorn and watch movies."

Alex smiled. "We try to make it fun."

Fun. I couldn't remember the last time I had ever had *fun*.

I returned her smile, reaching for her hand under the table. "Can I join in?"

All three of them answered in unison. "Yes!"

That one word made my entire day.

CHAPTER 9

DYLAN

I sat back, chuckling as I watched Seth and Noelle battle it out to see who would win the highly competitive game of Snakes and Ladders that was happening. I had held my own pretty well, but they were too good for me.

Today had been one of the nicest days I could remember in a long time. After I ate my breakfast, I went upstairs to change when Alex informed me snow days meant casual. My dress shirt and pants were not going to cut it, she told me in no uncertain terms. When I confessed to not having any more casual-type clothing, she handed me a Sleepy Moose Inn T-shirt. I spent the day in my plaid sleep pants Arlene had given me as a joke for Christmas and the logo-emblazoned shirt. I wore my socks since my dress shoes looked stupid with pants. They were all dressed casually like me, and we spent hours in the lounge playing games. After lunch, I had offered my gifts hesitantly, not wanting Seth to use his worn boots when I heard him tell Alex he'd do more shoveling after we had eaten.

Noelle's exuberant shriek when she saw her slippers left me no doubt of her love for the fuzzy foot-warmers. Seth announced his boots were "sick," and judging from his delighted grin, I decided that was a good thing. Alex's eyes widened and that warm, appealing smile of hers lit her face when I handed her the box of chocolates. The girls gave me hugs and kisses, and I received a double fist pound from Seth, accompanied by repeated thanks. Alex's quiet protests, I stilled instantly with a hard kiss when the kids weren't looking. She stopped objecting once she had eaten a chocolate, and I heard no more "you shouldn't have" from her.

Noelle threw her hands up in victory. "I won! I won!"

Seth sat back with a grin. "You did, kiddo." He stood and stretched. "I'm going to clear a little more."

I started to stand. "I'll help."

He grinned. "Yeah?"

I nodded. "Let me get my boots and I'll shovel while you use the snow blower." I picked up my glass and followed Alex into the kitchen. "What about the rest of the grounds? The driveway and parking lot?"

She smiled at me, taking the glass from my hand. "As soon as the highway is clear, Mr. Johnson will be around to do those and make sure the front is good. It might not be for a couple of days, though. Since I pay him in trade, we aren't the first on his list, but he is usually pretty fast."

I frowned. "Trade?"

She smiled sadly. "Jeff knows money is tight, so we trade."

I stepped in front of her, resting my hands on the counter, effectively pinning her in. "And what, *exactly*, do you trade?"

Her brow furrowed. "Seriously, Dylan. His wife isn't a good cook. I make them some meals, he keeps the snow clear."

"Lucky man."

She narrowed her eyes at me. "What did you think I traded?"

I had the grace to look ashamed, and she frowned. "You live in a different world."

Dropping my head to her shoulder, I turned my face to her neck, pushing the edge of her shirt out of the way with my nose. I teased the delicate skin with my lips, swirling my tongue along the edge of her jaw. "Jealous," I whispered. "I can't stand the thought of someone else having your attention."

She moaned, a low noise in her chest, as I pulled her tight in my arms.

"I can't stand the thought of you kissing anyone else. Letting them hold you."

"No one has in a very long time."

I covered her mouth with mine. "Good."

Fiery heat ignited between us. Alex's fingers tugged on my neck, holding me close as I explored her mouth, groaning at her taste. The richness of the chocolates she'd been nibbling lingered, heightening the sweetness that was her—all Alex.

Seth's voice startled me. "Hey, Dylan! Are you coming?"

I groaned, pulling back. "I'd like to," I muttered. "But not much chance while you're awake."

Alex giggled, covering her mouth with her hand.

I grinned and kissed her forehead. "I have shoveling to do. Stop distracting me, woman."

"Dylan . . ."

I cupped her cheek, stroking it gently with my thumb. She looked nervous. "What is it?"

"I was wondering, instead of eating dinner in your room tonight" —she took in a big breath—"if you wanted to have dinner with us, in our room?"

"I'd like that very much."

"Me too. Six o'clock, in case I'm upstairs when you come back."

"I'll go work up an appetite." I kissed her again—long and hard. "Of a different sort."

She was giggling again as I left. The sound made my chest warm.

After I helped Seth for a while, I leaned against the handle of the shovel, watching as he finished cutting another wide pass through the thick snow. When the engine cut off, I walked over and clapped him on the shoulder. "Good job."

He grinned shyly.

I glanced at the still thick sky. "I'm not sure it's done yet."

He lifted his shoulders in agreement. "Probably not. But I like doing this. It's something that makes me feel like I'm helping."

I felt a slight pang of guilt for scolding him earlier. "I'm sure you do lots to help, Seth."

"I try. Alex and Noelle . . . they're my family. I hafta look out for them, you know?"

"I know."

He stepped forward. "Dylan, can I ask you something?"

His voice made me a little anxious. I swallowed, hoping he wasn't going to ask me anything about Alex.

"Sure."

"I, ah, I need some advice."

"Advice?"

"Yeah. There's, um . . . a girl."

My eyebrows shot up. "A girl?"

He nodded, moving closer. "I like her, Dylan. I really like her."

"And?"

His voice dropped. "I feel . . . *stuff* when she's around. We text every day, and I think about her . . . all the time."

I rubbed the back of my neck. "Shouldn't you, ah, talk to Alex about this?"

He frowned. "She's a girl. She doesn't understand about this stuff."

"This stuff?"

"Guy stuff. You know . . ."

My brow furrowed.

"I think about her *all the time*," he reiterated. "I *wake up* thinking about her . . . and, um, I have, ah, problems . . ."

Jesus. Now I understood.

He was talking about sex. Seth was looking for advice about sex. And morning wood.

I tried not to laugh. I could imagine how Alex would react to those conversations.

Then I realized he was serious. He needed to talk, and he wanted to talk to me. I draped my arm over his shoulder.

"Let's talk about respect, Seth." Then I grinned. "We'll move on to long morning showers and learning to do your own laundry after that."

I left a somewhat shell-shocked Seth outside and went to my room. After my shower, I flung myself on my bed and looked at my phone, surprised I had a signal. Weak, but it was still there. A message waited for me from Arlene.

> **Arlene**
> You snowed in, dear boy?

It had come in a few moments ago, so I answered her.

> **Me**
> Yes.

> **Arlene**
> Going crazy? Or is the Courvoisier keeping you sane?

I smirked.

Me
I've spent the day in my sleep pants and a T-shirt,
playing games, eating pancakes and chips, and having
a sex talk with a seventeen-year-old while we shoveled
snow. So far, it's been highly enjoyable.

> **Arlene**
> I'm sorry. I thought this was Dylan Maxwell.

Me
Of course, it's me.

> **Arlene**
> The Dylan Maxwell I know would never play games or
> eat chips. He dislikes pancakes, and he is far too
> snooty for lounge pants, T-shirts, or snow shoveling. I
> won't even address the sex talk.

I wondered what she would think if I told her about kissing Alex. And wanting to kiss her again.

Me
Guess you don't know me as well as you thought.

> **Arlene**
> Or perhaps . . . you didn't know yourself as well as
> YOU thought.

Me
Stop with the mumbo jumbo, woman. You told me to
try new things. I'm trying. And guess what?

> **Arlene**
> What?

Me
I love tater tots. Can you get me some for my condo?
I'm not sure where one purchases them. You have to
ask Alex how to make her casserole too. It's awesome.

> **Arlene**
> I think it's a good thing I'm retiring. I don't think I can
> take this change in you.

Me
Whatever.

> **Arlene**
> Well, it's definitely you, rude man. But I think I approve of these changes.

Me
Just going with the flow.

> **Arlene**
> Words I never thought I would hear from you. On that note, I'm going to get a drink. I think I need to lie down.

Me
I'm going to have a nap, then have dinner with Alex and the kids. I'm hoping for pie.

> **Arlene**
> Nap? Kids? Pie? When the real Dylan Maxwell shows up, ask him to get in touch.

I started to laugh.

Me
See you in a few days.

> **Arlene**
> Be safe, Dylan. Let me know if you need anything.

I stared at the screen. There was nothing I could think of that I needed or wanted. Right now, it was all right there. I signed off simply:

Me
Talk soon.

At six o'clock, I knocked on the door to Alex's . . . place. I wasn't sure what to call it. Apartment? Hotel room? Ten minutes after she opened the door and I was on her sofa, I knew exactly what to call it.
Her home.

She had taken two large rooms and made a modest quarter for her family. A tiny but functional kitchen held an old wooden table that was set for dinner. The rest of the space was filled with furniture and toys, books and games. Noelle dragged me into the next room and showed me her "princess place"—a bedroom full of frills and tulle, dolls, and pink things. There was the usual hotel functional bathroom and the smallest bedroom I'd ever seen, if you could even call it that. More like a closet. It held a single bed, a stand-up lamp, and a tiny dresser, and it was where Alex slept. I knew she hadn't meant for me to see it, but Noelle had been thorough in her tour. I nodded and smiled, even though I was horrified at the thought of Alex having so little space or comfort for herself. Seth, Alex told me when I returned to the living room and accepted a glass of wine from her, lived in the room across the hall, giving him the privacy he needed.

She leaned forward conspiratorially. "He's at *that* age. You know, Dylan."

I nodded, not wanting to tell her exactly how well I knew. I knew Seth wanted our little talk from earlier to be private, so I kept it to myself.

"What about you?" I asked, indicating the small room down the hall.

She shrugged. "I only sleep there. Once my day is over, I relax in here. It's not a big deal."

She got up and went to check on dinner. My gaze followed her every movement.

How much time did she ever really get to *relax*?

Regardless of what she said, it was a big deal. At least, to me. But I knew I had no right to say anything.

A fact that made me sadder than I realized.

Dinner was loud and entertaining. Unless it was business-related, or the occasional meal with Arlene and her husband, I was used to eating alone, and my meals were quick ones.

But not tonight. Alex's pot roast was, without a doubt, the best thing I'd ever eaten, and there was indeed pie for dessert. Seth and Noelle teased and joked, doing much more laughing than eating, although Seth did manage two helpings. When Alex rolled her eyes and pursed her lips, I pulled Noelle onto my knee and brought her plate close, handfeeding her mouthfuls while she chatted and giggled.

It didn't even bother me when she fed me off her plate—something I never would have imagined in my life. But it was Alex's pot roast, and I had already eaten three plates, so I felt asking for a fourth seemed rather greedy.

I helped clear the table and assisted Seth with dishes, while Alex bathed Noelle. When she returned, we had coffee on the sofa, and Noelle snuggled up next to me, tucked under my arm as though she belonged there. Alex put in a movie and we all watched, full from dinner and a long day of shoveling and games. Noelle grew heavier, leaning into my side until I shifted and carefully lowered her head onto my knee. Seth stood, yawning.

"I'm going to go catch up on homework. I might read after I'm done. I'm tired."

Alex smiled knowingly. "Sure, kiddo."

I glanced at my watch, seeing it was barely after nine. I hid my smirk, wondering if homework meant he'd be texting his dream girl for a while before "reading" in bed. From the smile on Alex's face, I was confident she knew exactly what would happen once he was alone.

Seth waved as he walked out the door, and Alex stood, reaching for Noelle.

"I'll get her," I whispered and slid out from beneath her sleeping form. I lifted her into my arms, liking how she curled into my chest, nuzzling the little old rag doll still clutched in her hands. I grinned at her bright nightgown and the red polka-dot slippers on her feet. Following Alex, I waited as she drew back the blankets, and I hesitated. "Should we take off her slippers?"

"No. Trust me. She'll want to sleep in them. She won't take them off until she absolutely has to."

Grinning, I slipped her under the warm covers and pulled them up around her shoulders, and without a thought, kissed her forehead, then ran my hand over her curls. "Night, Little Owl."

Turning, I saw the bemused expression on Alex's face before she bent, kissed Noelle, and turned off the light. She closed her door, then we went back and sat on the sofa.

"Her lisp," I began hesitantly. "How did she lose her teeth? I don't know much about kids, but don't they usually stay in longer?"

"Oh," Alex replied. "Yes, they do. She was on the swings at the playground and fell off. Face first into the ground and knocked out both her teeth. I rushed her to the dentist, but the cost of any type of repair was more than I had in the bank. He assured me she could do without them for a couple of years, and I really had no choice." She smiled sadly. "Her speech was quite good before, and once her teeth come back, it will be again, or at least I hope so."

I could tell how guilty she felt over the lack of funds. "I'm sure it will be. In the meantime, to be honest, I find it endearing. She is adorable."

"You're very good with her."

I shrugged, somewhat self-conscious. "I shouldn't be," I admitted. "I have no experience with children."

"You are with Seth as well. You talk to him like a man. He needs that influence." She sighed. "I can't give him that, and George is too tired most of the time."

"Your father?" I asked, leaving the words hanging in the air.

"My parents were killed when I was eighteen."

I felt my chest tighten. She'd suffered so much loss.

"I'm sorry."

Her voice was quiet. "It's difficult at times. George and Eric were my family. Eric died before Noelle was born, so she never knew him. George tells her stories about him, but it's more than she can really understand."

"Of course."

"I try to be enough for them both. Sometimes, I'm not sure I'm doing a very good job. Especially for Seth."

Reaching over, I clasped her hand. "Hey."

She looked up, her eyes sad in the dim light.

"You give him everything he needs. He is . . . *they are* both lucky to have you. I can see it clearly in them. You are more than enough."

"I try."

"You do it well." I caressed her hand I was still holding. "But who looks after you, Alex?"

It was her turn to shrug. "I'm fine."

I slid closer, draping my arm along the back of the sofa, running my fingers through her hair. "Of course you're fine. You're strong, independent, and amazing. But you still need to be looked after on occasion."

She shrugged. "There's no one to do that. I can't hope for it either. Who is going to want a single mother of two kids?" She paused, her lips trembling. "I'm not even sure where we'll be this time next year. I have nothing to offer anyone. Just my kids. So I can't rely on anyone else since they only have me to take care of them."

The urge to tell her she could rely on me was strong, but I held my tongue. Instead, I drew my finger down her cheek, the supple skin warm under my touch. "I think you have a lot to offer someone, Alex."

Our gazes locked, and like every other time we were alone, my body responded. The air around us bubbled with the heat I could feel, and before I knew what I was doing, she was in my arms. I pulled her onto my lap, and my mouth was on hers, kissing her deeply, losing myself in her softness. Threading my fingers into her thick hair, I tugged gently, exposing her neck. I trailed my tongue along the smooth skin, tugging on her earlobe. "God, baby, I want you."

She whimpered, and I covered her mouth again, kissing her with everything I had. I held her tight, sliding my hands under her loose sweatshirt, touching the supple, delicate skin of her back. I traced the ridges of her spine, groaning when I realized she wasn't wearing a bra. Reaching around, I cupped her breasts and stroked her tight nipples. The grip she had on me increased, and she made the most erotic sound I had ever heard, a breathless, moaning pant low in her throat. I pulled her down, letting her feel the effect she was having. My hard cock pushed against the material of my pants, feeling the heat of her so close.

We both wanted it.

A noise startled us, and Alex pulled away, panting. She scrambled off my lap, hurrying to Noelle's room. With a groan, I dropped my head into my hands. I was acting like an animal. If we hadn't been interrupted, I would have taken Alex right there on the sofa. The place she sat every night with her children.

I stood and paced. When Alex returned, I smiled at her, even as I saw the fact that her walls had gone back up. The interruption had broken the moment.

"I should go."

She bit her lip, appearing as though she was going to say something, but then she nodded. "I can't . . ." Her voice trailed off, her hand gesturing down the hall.

"I understand."

I walked to the door, turning with my hand on the knob. "Today was one of the best days I've had in a very long time. I loved spending it with you and the kids. Dinner was delicious." I paused, lowering my voice. "And although I didn't get to finish dessert, it was the highlight."

Her cheeks blazed with color, and with a chuckle, I ran my

knuckles over the hot flesh, still filled with desire for her. "Nothing on earth is as sweet as the taste of you, Alex. I'm afraid you've spoiled me for anything else."

She closed her eyes and sighed. "My children, Dylan, they have to come first. I'm their mother. The only one they have."

"And you're a woman. A beautiful, sexy woman who has been alone too long." I held up my hand as she started to protest. "I know we have two different lives, but right now we're together." I exhaled. "If you want to explore it further, you know where I am."

I dropped a gentle kiss to her head, then another to her sweet mouth.

Then I headed back to my room, feeling more alone than I had ever felt in my life.

CHAPTER 10

DYLAN

I tossed back a long swallow of the Courvoisier in my glass as I stood by the window, looking into the vast expanse in front of me. I had pushed the hideous drapes wide open and watched the snow as it swirled by, settling on the already laden branches of the massive trees that encircled the inn. Idly, I wondered how many we'd lose with construction. I'd have to make sure it was as few as possible. They were too beautiful to destroy.

Beautiful.

Like Alex.

I rubbed my bare chest, trying to push away the strange ache that had taken up residence there since I'd walked away from Alex earlier. All it took was the thought of her mouth moving with mine and how she felt melded into my chest to make my desire flare once more.

I wanted her.

I wanted her naked and writhing beneath me. I wanted to taste her everywhere, to feel her skin pressed tight to mine, to know how it felt to be held within her wet heat. I wanted to hear those low sounds she made, to watch as she shattered in my arms, and to know I brought her that much pleasure.

I wanted it all, and yet, I knew why I couldn't have it.

Alex didn't do casual. I didn't do relationships. She lived here; I lived in Toronto with a lifestyle she couldn't even comprehend. I glanced down at the Courvoisier I was drinking with a grimace. The most expensive cognac served in the cheapest tumbler made. It was our two lives captured in liquid and glass. One that was decadent and opulent, while the other so simple yet vital.

She hated the big city and never wanted to live there again, she had said. It was all I knew. It was all I would ever know since my business was there. My responsibilities were all there.

Alex took her responsibilities just as seriously. She would never jeopardize her life here in Pinegrove or her children's comfort for her own satisfaction. She would always put being a mother ahead of being a woman, or being simply *Alex*, first. Casual sex wasn't part of her plan.

It was all I knew.

I drained my glass and reached for the bottle, adding another generous amount. I stared out the window once more, for the first time realizing the profound silence that surrounded me. The wind continued to blow outside, but it was calmer. Inside the inn was still, only the occasional creak of wood or errant squeak could be heard. I shook my head in wonder. The city was so full of noise all the time, even at night; quiet was a rare gift.

An odd noise caught my ear and grew closer. It was the discreet pad of footsteps coming down the hall. Glancing at the clock, I saw it had been an hour since I left Alex's, and I couldn't help but wonder if Noelle was coming for a visit. She seemed to be a bit of a night owl.

Nothing shocked me more than when I heard the low click of the lock, and Alex stepped into the room. My startled gaze met her anxious glance in the dim light as she shut and locked the door behind her, stepping forward, stopping several feet from me. She placed a monitor on the table—I knew if Noelle stirred, Alex would be back down the hall before she was fully awake.

But for now, for as long as it could be, she was there. With me.

Dressed in a long, pale blue robe, with her hair tumbling over her shoulders, she was nervous—and beyond beautiful. Her fingers played with the sash on her robe as we stared at each other. Her gaze left mine, drifting over my torso, then lower. Her swift intake of air as she saw my physical reaction to her caused my lips to curl into a lazy smile. She liked what she saw.

So did I.

Wordlessly, I held out my glass, thinking she needed a little liquid courage. She took the glass, sipping at the brandy delicately, then handed it back. I held her gaze as I tossed back the remainder and set down the glass on the table. I cleared my throat.

"Are you certain?"

"I think so."

"You have to be certain, Alex. I want you. I want you so much I'm aching for you. But it's only now—not forever."

"I know," she whispered, breathless. "I want you too."

"Protection. I need . . ."

"I'm on the pill."

"And you trust me?"

She didn't hesitate. "Yes."

I maintained our gaze. "I'll ask you again. Are you certain?"

She didn't answer. Instead, with a quick tug, her robe opened, slipping off her shoulders, pooling at her feet in a puddle of silvery blue.

It was my turn to inhale sharply.

She was exquisite. Small but curvy, wide hips and supple breasts, all waiting for my attention. Her skin glowed in the moonlight, her hair like a dark cloud against the pale of her complexion. Smiling at her, I yanked on the cord of my sleep pants, pushing them off my hips so we were both naked.

Naked, panting with desire, and so close.

But not close enough.

In one step, she was crushed against me. My mouth was on hers, my tongue claiming and possessive, the same way I wanted my body to possess her. Bending, I scooped her into my arms, carrying her to the bed, covering her with my torso. The sounds I loved were already escaping her lips. Soft sighs, that low, breathless moan in her throat that turned me on as I explored her; all made me groan in return. Her touch, so caring and light as it drifted over my skin, moved up to tug on my hair, keeping me close as we discovered each other, and was unlike anything I'd ever experienced.

Everything about her was a mystery, a treasure I wanted more with each passing moment. Her silky skin, fragrant neck, sensitive lobes—I explored them all. I loved the way she reacted to my gentle bites to the juncture of her neck, my mouth on her nipples, my fingers stroking her where I wanted her the most. The pleasure of her exploration of me was intense. Her mouth, her seeking tongue, and nimble fingers caused long shivers to run down my spine and low curses to fall from my lips.

Hovering over her, I tenderly brushed the curls from her damp skin and met her lustful gaze. With my eyes, I asked her again, her barely there nod answering everything I needed to hear. Slipping my hands under her hips, I buried myself inside her, gasping her name as I stilled.

She wrapped her legs around me, drawing me in. "Dylan," she moaned, arching her back.

"Please."

I started to move, building our rhythm. Long, slow thrusts. Our mouths kissed, our hands stroked and caressed, and our bodies fused together as if they were meant to be joined. Two halves of a whole finding each other. Over and again, I thrust—I couldn't get deep enough. I couldn't taste enough of her—get my fill of her sweetness. I wanted her mouth melded to my lips, her tongue stroking mine, her body surrendering totally to me.

I wanted to claim her.

Alex's arms kept me close, her breath warm puffs of air across my skin and in my mouth. Her throaty sighs and soft mews spurred me on. I moved inside her powerfully, using my body to possess the one part of her I could have. How right we felt moving together wrecked me. When she pressed her head into the pillow, her neck straining as she succumbed, my name was a low, pleading gasp that fell from her sweet lips. I buried my head in her hair, breathing her in as my orgasm raced through me. Bright sparks of light exploded behind my eyes as I moaned her name, spilling into her, sated for the moment.

Keeping her close, I rolled, wrapping her up in my arms. The room was silent except for our breathing and the muted snuffling sounds I could hear from the monitor. Finally, I lifted up on one elbow, smiling down at Alex as I brushed the damp curls away from her face.

"Why?" I whispered, not wanting to disturb the stillness. "What made you change your mind?"

Lifting her hand, she idly traced my jaw. "I wanted . . ." She hesitated.

"Wanted what?" I asked. Whatever she wanted, I would give it to her.

"I wanted to be Alex again. Even if it was only for a night. Not Noelle's mother, Seth's guardian, or the woman behind the desk. You"—she paused, swallowing before she spoke again—"you make me feel things, Dylan. Desired, wanted . . . *needed*. Things I haven't felt for so very long. Years." Her eyes shut, and when she opened them again, they were damp. "Long before Noelle was born. I wanted to feel like a woman again."

"You are that. First and foremost. A beautiful, desirable woman."

She smiled dejectedly. "No, I'm a mom, a guardian, a coworker, and a daughter-in-law. You're the first person to see something else in a very long time. And as selfish as it is, I wanted to feel it again."

I shook my head. She had no concept of the word selfish.

"Were things . . . not good in your marriage?"

"Eric was a wonderful man. But we were better friends than husband and wife."

"Noelle?"

"She was a bit of a surprise to us. But a welcome one." She hastened to add. "We were trying to stay on track." She sighed heavily. "And then the accident happened."

"And you couldn't leave."

"George needed me too much. He'd already lost Eric. I couldn't leave him too."

"You put everyone first."

"I don't know how to do anything else."

I gathered her close. "I don't want you to lose yourself. You're . . . too special, Alex."

Her reply was so quiet I almost didn't hear her.

"I think I already did."

Alex drifted and I held her, liking how she felt nestled to my chest. She was obviously a light sleeper since every time Noelle shuffled or muttered in her sleep Alex sat up, ready to leave. Each time, I drew her back, until it was well past midnight.

"I should go."

"Stay," I urged, not wanting to lose her quite yet. "You sleep for a while, and I'll listen. If she wakes up, I'll get you."

She blinked up at me, suddenly shy. "If I stay, maybe I don't want to sleep."

Smirking, I crossed my arms behind my head. "However will we pass the time, then?"

My eyes widened as Alex flung her leg across my thighs, straddling me. Her fingers wandered down my chest, lazily swirling over my abs and back up, teasing my nipples.

"I'm sure, if we think *hard* enough, Dylan, we can come up with something," she murmured, shifting and sliding over my rapidly swelling cock.

I grabbed her waist, holding her in place. "You feel so good, baby." I arched my hips, hitting her right where she wanted me. "You like that? Huh? Is that what you want?"

"Yes," she moaned.

"Say it, Alex. Tell me what you want."

She leaned closer, her hands pressing on my sternum. Her hair fell forward, surrounding us with its silky texture, the ends tickling my skin. "You, Dylan. I want you to fuck me."

Then, without another word, she sank down, engulfing me in her heat. Cursing, I moved my hands to her hips, holding her tightly as I matched her rhythm.

"Feels like you're doing the fucking, Alex," I ground out between clenched teeth, wondering why hearing her say fuck turned me on so much.

"You like that? Huh?" she groaned, throwing my words back at me.

"Yes. *Fuck yes*, baby. Take me."

And she did. She flung back her head, gripping my wrists as she rolled her hips, moving like a wave over me. Her breasts jutted out, and her long tresses brushed against my legs as she moved, beautiful in her passion. We surged and ebbed until I felt the stirrings of my orgasm taking over.

"Come for me, baby." I strained up, needing to be as deep inside her as I could. "Come for me now."

She shattered, a long, low hiss escaping her lips as I shook and cursed, emptying myself inside her. She fell forward, collapsing onto my chest, panting. Tenderly, I moved her legs and pulled the blanket over her, holding her tight.

"Sleep for a while."

"Mmm-kay."

And she was out.

When I woke up, she was gone. The room was still dark, and it almost felt like a dream, except her fragrance lingered in the bed and my body could still feel hers. Groaning, I reached down, fisting my hardening cock. More than anything, I wanted her back beside me, to be in her warmth. Slowly, I stroked myself, then cursed. It wasn't my hand I wanted. It was her.

I rolled out of bed, squinting at the old alarm clock. It was only just past five. But I knew I wouldn't fall back asleep—I never did once

I was awake. I decided I'd get up and do some work. I knew Alex would rise early whether the inn was open or not. She'd have coffee on soon, and maybe I'd get the chance to make out with her in the kitchen before the kids were awake.

I stepped into the shower, the clouds of steam swirling around me. I leaned my arm on the tiles, resting my head against my forearm, still hard and throbbing with desire. Once again, I took my cock in my hand, stroking fast. I moaned her name, startling when arms came around my waist.

"Really, Dylan?" she murmured against my back. "I left you alone for fifteen minutes."

I turned and dragged her into my arms. "Fifteen minutes too fucking long," I hissed, capturing her lips. I kissed her passionately, my tongue possessing her mouth. Bending slightly, I grabbed behind her knees, lifting her up and spinning, pressing her against the shower enclosure. Her legs wrapped around my hips, my cock settling into her as if it belonged there. I dropped wet, openmouthed kisses to her throat, and pulled hard on her earlobe. "Now, Alex, it's my turn to fuck you."

She arched as I thrust, both of us groaning as I slid inside her. Bracing myself on the wall, I trapped her between the cold tile and my body, and I fucked her. My hips slammed into her hard and fast, and she met my movements, tilting her pelvis so I hit her exactly where she wanted. Her nails dug into my back, sinking farther the harder I took her. I covered her mouth, swallowing her cries, keeping them only for me. Her body tightened around me, milking my cock as she shattered. I dropped my head to her shoulder, drawing the skin between my teeth as I groaned out her name, my hand slapping the wall as my orgasm burned through me. I shuddered, my body melting into hers as the water poured over us.

"Fuck," she whimpered. "That was just . . . *fuck*."

I grinned against her skin, nipping it again, making her yelp. "Such a potty mouth you have for a lady, Alex."

"Only when I'm naked with you," she retorted.

I kissed my way to her mouth, hovering over her full lips. "Good," I breathed. "I like you dirty with me."

I moved back, helping her to her feet, and we let the warm water cascade over us. I shut off the water and stepped out, holding out a towel for her. "Best shower—ever."

She giggled, then looked down at the floor and grimaced. "Damn it, my robe is wet."

I chuckled and handed her my sweatshirt. "Wear this. It's long enough to be a robe." I picked up her wet robe with a teasing smile. "That's what happens when you're anxious to get in the shower with me."

She smirked. "Complaining?"

I shook my head. "Far from it. I like you like this. Teasing and frisky. I love hearing you curse. It's very sexy." I ran my fingers down her arm, suddenly serious. "You were . . . *we were* amazing."

She bit her lip, looking unsure.

"Hey," I called in a gentle voice. "Last night—this morning—it was indescribable. You were everything I imagined . . . and more."

She fingered the edge of her towel. "Eric didn't like that," she admitted. "He was very . . . reserved in the bedroom. He didn't like dirty talk, and he hated it when I cursed."

"I'm not Eric."

Her head snapped up. "I know that. I'm not comparing. But last night, I felt like I could be . . . *me*. You made me feel safe enough to just . . . feel and enjoy."

I pulled her close. "I like doing that for you." I stared down into her warm eyes. "I know this"—I motioned between us—"has to stay private and in this room, but in here, Alex, you're free to be you. My Alex." I kissed her sweetly. "My cursing, sexy Alex."

"I've never felt sexy."

"You are. You are incredibly sexy." I tugged her closer. "I can't stop wanting you."

Her eyes widened as she felt the evidence of my desire for her against her skin. Her shy gaze turned mischievous and bold.

"What . . . ?"

She tossed my sweatshirt behind me to the counter, dropped to her knees, and tugged on my towel. I stared down at her, my breath catching in my throat.

"Oh God, Alex, you don't have to."

"But I want to. And you said I could do whatever I wanted in this room, Dylan."

Then she wrapped her lips around my cock.

I couldn't argue with that rationale.

CHAPTER 11

DYLAN

It was another day of laziness and fun. We played games, watched more movies, and I made out with Alex every chance I got. While the popcorn popped and the kids were still engrossed in the movie in the other room. As I "helped" her make lunch. When the kids went outside for a snowball fight—Alex and I watched from the window, their antics making us laugh. They were so tired when they came inside, they fell asleep in front of the fire and didn't even finish the hot cocoa Alex made them. I tackled her to the sofa and kissed her until we were breathless. She fell asleep in my arms, and I watched them all before napping myself. Something that hadn't happened in years. Usually, I was too busy to take a nap. It was a great day.

After dinner was over and Seth had left for his room again, Noelle fell asleep between us, and once she was tucked into her bed, I had Alex alone. It was all I could do not to take her on the sofa in her small living room, but I left and waited for her to come to my room once she was sure both Seth and Noelle were settled for the night. Neither of us got much sleep, and when she slipped from my bed in the darkness, immediately I missed her beside me. I fell into a restless sleep and didn't wake until later the next morning, my chest feeling tight for some reason.

When the elevator doors opened, I heard the sound of a voice I didn't recognize. Walking into the bar, my heart sank. Through the window, I could see a large snow-clearing machine parked out front and massive piles of snow.

The cavalry had come.

The man I assumed was Mr. Johnson was standing and putting on his hat. "Thanks for the coffee and the meals, Alex. The missus will appreciate it. The roads are clearing up, and I know George is happy to be home."

She smiled at him, holding out a box that contained his food. "Thanks, Mr. Johnson, I appreciate it." She turned to me. "Good morning, Dylan."

Her words were friendly, but her voice was different. Distant, polite. I was back to being a guest, which I knew would happen, but a small part of me hadn't wanted it to materialize—especially so soon. And if George was back, that meant my time at the inn was almost done. I had to swallow a sudden lump in my throat before I returned her greeting.

"Morning, Alex."

"Coffee's on. I'll get you some breakfast."

"Just coffee is fine, thanks."

"Okay. George is free whenever you want to see him."

I nodded and turned away, busying myself getting coffee. The odd sensation in my chest tightened—the same ache I had felt the other night. I wondered if I was getting sick. Maybe I needed to see the doctor when I got home.

I stood in front of the window and sipped my coffee, staring blankly, unsure as to why I felt so strange.

Mr. Johnson left with a cheery wave, and Alex came and stood beside me, not touching, but close enough I could feel her presence.

"Where are the kids?"

"Susan came and took them sledding. She figured they'd be going crazy after being cooped up. School reopens tomorrow." She smiled sadly. "The airport reopened again a short while ago. Your assistant faxed your flight information for you—I left it on the front counter. You're booked out tomorrow at lunch."

Tomorrow. I was leaving tomorrow. The ache in my chest grew more pronounced, and my throat turned desert-dry.

"Fine," I managed to spit out.

My hand twitched, and my fingers brushed against hers. She slipped her hand into mine and squeezed, then pulled back. I flexed my fingers so our pinkies were still entwined, needing some connection with her—no matter how small.

"Alex," I breathed.

"Don't," she pleaded.

"I don't know what to do," I admitted. "Or what to say."

"There is nothing you *have* to do or say. We're both adults. You came here for a reason. Your reason will be done today, and it's time for you to go home."

"What will you do?" I asked. She knew what I was asking. I was buying her home. Where was she going to go?

She sighed, her pinkie slipping from mine, and crossed her arms. She took a step away, already beginning to separate from me. "I'll find a place and a job. It'll be a change for us all, but it was going to happen eventually. You don't have to worry about us, Dylan."

I turned to face her. "But I do. Let me help."

"How?"

"I'll buy you a place. Pick out a house, and it's yours. Anywhere you want. I'll open a bank account for you until you're on your feet. Whatever you need."

She stared at me, shock and hurt written across her face. "And what, Dylan? You'll drop by for some nocturnal visits when you're in town? A little somethin' somethin' on the side?" Her voice dropped. "Do you know how confusing that would be to my children? To me? Not to mention, how insulting?"

"No!" I gasped. "No strings, Alex. I want nothing from you. I expect nothing from you," I hastened to assure her. I was stunned she would think that way.

"Why, then?"

"Pardon?"

"Why would you want to do that? Because we fucked? You're feeling guilty?"

"No! Because . . ." I stumbled over my words. "Because I care." I stepped closer. "And don't call it that. It was more, and you know it."

"You set the ground rules, Dylan. Only here, remember? A limited time—no strings attached. Your offer feels as if you're paying me for what happened between us."

I ran a hand through my hair in vexation. "I'm not trying to do that." I searched for the right words. "I'm wealthy, Alex. Very wealthy. I can afford it, and I want to do it . . . I just—I want-I want to help," I sputtered uncharacteristically.

For a moment, she was silent. When she spoke, her voice was low and firm. "Thank you for your offer, but it's not needed. I will look after *my* family. That's *my* job, not yours."

"But—" I began.

She held up her hand. "The answer is no, Dylan. And the subject is closed."

I stepped back, defeated. I had royally fucked that up. Instead of making her see I cared, I made her feel like a whore. She had no idea how rare it was for me to care about someone. How special that made her to me. I had to figure out another way to help her. I lowered my voice.

"Will you come to me tonight?" I reached out and touched her hand tenderly. "Please."

"I don't know."

I opened my mouth to beg her, when I heard the slight squeak of wheels coming close. We weren't alone anymore. I had to remember that.

I turned back to the window, tumultuous emotions raging within me. I hadn't expected to feel like that—desolate and lost. I hadn't expected to feel anything at all. None of that was supposed to happen.

"Dylan," George greeted me. "Ready to discuss that offer now?"

Steeling myself, I turned to him and smiled, my emotions locked down tight and my business face on. Alex was right. I came here to do something specific, and it was time to finish it.

"Absolutely. I'll go get the paperwork."

I followed him out of the room, feeling Alex's gaze on me the whole time. It took everything in me not to look back at her.

"Your offer is very generous."

"I want the property, George. I don't want to risk someone else making you a better offer."

He looked past me to the window, surveying his land. "I'll be able to help Alex get settled as well," he stated, his eyes shifting back to the paperwork.

I shrugged, feigning indifference. That had been my plan when I changed the amount on the offer. I was determined to help Alex whether she knew it was me or not. "It's your money—you can do whatever you want with it. I'm glad if it helps your family. She and her children have made my stay very, ah, pleasant."

"Pleasant?"

I nodded. "It was a nice break, but I'm anxious to get back to my life," I explained, my voice flat.

Disappointment flashed across his face. "I see. I'm sure they enjoyed their time with you too."

I didn't say anything. My throat felt too dry.

"Do you mind if I have my lawyer look these over? He's coming by this afternoon. I'm sure they're fine, but I would feel better."

"Of course."

"I'll sign them as soon as he gives me the thumbs-up. You'll have them before you leave—tomorrow, I think?"

"Yes."

He stared at me intently. "You're welcome to stay longer."

"Thank you, but no. I have a lot waiting for me when I get back."

"Of course." He held out his hand. "It's been a pleasure, Dylan."

I gripped his hand firmly. "It has." I stood, walking to the door, pausing. "George . . ."

He looked up. "Yes?"

I sighed. "Never mind."

I stayed in my room all afternoon, keeping busy with emails and catching up on work. Seth had appeared at one point to deliver a sandwich and inform me dinner was in the bar at six and I was welcome to join them. I almost told him to have Alex send up a tray, but I couldn't bring myself to do it. I wanted one more night with all of them.

Everyone was quiet at dinner; even my Little Owl seemed subdued. George pulled me aside and told me the lawyer had checked everything and the papers would be in my hands before I left. I could merely nod; the usual spark of victory absent when I shook his hand.

After dinner, Noelle crawled onto my lap, demanding a story. I read her favorite book, enjoying her closeness. She had her little doll clutched tight in her arms as I read, and she helped me turn each page, making sure I didn't skip any.

"I haf a new book for 'morrow night, Dywan. It's cawwed *Thanta's Magic*."

I swallowed, looking at Alex, unsure what to do. George sighed quietly and wheeled out of the room. Seth didn't say a word, but he grabbed his books and stomped away. Alex leaned forward, stroking Noelle's arm. "Dylan won't be here tomorrow night, baby."

"Why?"

"He has to go home."

She looked up at me, bewildered. "Why?" she whispered. "You tay hewe."

"I have work to do. I have to go."

"Oh." She huffed. "Otay. You come back, den. We read *Thanta's Magic* afta."

I opened my mouth, but Alex mouthed "no." Instead, I dropped a kiss to Noelle's forehead. "You be good for Mommy, Noelle."

She nodded. "I will be."

Alex stood. "Bedtime, little girl."

Noelle looked at me, her eyes sad. "Come back fathst, Dywan. I miss you too much!" Then she pressed her lips to my cheek and hopped off my knee, taking Alex's hand.

I watched her walk away, that odd sensation in my chest swelling—again.

I seriously needed to see the doctor.

Alex came to me in the dark of the night, slipping into my bed, her warm body melting into mine. Neither of us spoke; instead, we let our hands and bodies do the talking. Buried inside her, I groaned at the rightness of being with her that way, suddenly hating the fact that we had to hide. Hating more that it would be the last time. I thrust into her, desperation growing, my thoughts wild and chaotic. I clutched her close, not wanting to let her go, but knowing I had to. Overwhelmed by the vortex of emotions swirling through my head, I took her hard and fast. She moved with me, holding me tight, but the teasing, cursing side of her was quiet. She was as conflicted as I was, and yet neither of us could express it.

Afterward, she nestled close, pressing her head to my chest, but still, she was silent. I could feel her walls coming back, feel her removing herself from me, even as she stayed physically close.

I wanted to beg her to let me buy that house. To let me see her again. But I knew she wouldn't allow it. She couldn't allow her children to be caught in a relationship where I constantly came and went from their lives. Plus, I couldn't hurt her that way. But the truth was, I wasn't capable of having the kind of relationship she deserved.

When she pulled away from me, I cupped her cheek, kissing her sweet mouth. "My Alex," I murmured. "My darling girl—thank you."

She held my hand to her face, a tear running down her soft skin and over mine. She bent down, and we shared one last kiss. "I would be, Dylan," she whispered. "I would be yours if I could be."

She turned and hurried across the room, shutting the door behind her. I pressed my lips to my wet knuckles, tasting her sadness, loathing the reality that I was the cause of it.

Still, there was nothing I could do to change things.

Nothing.

I was certain of that fact, yet sleep didn't find me the rest of the night.

Sunlight scattered across the white of the snow, its brilliance almost blinding, as I stood lost in thought and drank coffee, staring out my window. Draining my cup, I set it on the table beside me and ran a hand through my hair, tugging on the ends. My stomach ached. My chest felt tighter than ever, and the usual calm that prevailed over my body was missing.

I was tense, exhausted, upset, and I couldn't understand why.

I was leaving the inn—going back to Toronto—exactly as I had planned to do all along. A few days ago when I arrived, I could hardly wait to get out of here, but something changed.

That something was Alex.

Her, a gangly teenager, and a lisping little angel—who had broken my heart with her tears this morning. Seth was unusually surly, and for some reason, turned to Noelle while she nattered on at breakfast and informed her I wouldn't be returning—ever.

Alex gasped. "Seth!"

"It's true," he insisted. "He's leaving, and he isn't coming back!" He glared at me. "Are you?"

Before I could say anything, Noelle burst into sobs. Seth pushed away from the table, grabbed his books, and stormed out of the inn, muttering under his breath. I could still hear the anguished sobs as Alex gathered Noelle close, indicating I should leave. I stood, helpless, and watched her cry as my stomach churned, then silently, I returned to my room.

I groaned. That wasn't supposed to happen. They weren't supposed to affect my life. I couldn't allow it to happen. My life was somewhere else. Their life was at the inn. I had nothing else to give. Alex had firmly rejected my offer of a house and financial help, so we were at a stalemate.

The door opened behind me, and I turned to see Alex slip inside, holding a thick envelope.

"How is Noelle?" I asked, anxious.

"Fine. She left for day care a couple of minutes ago."

"I saw the van. I wasn't sure if she left or you kept her home."

Alex nodded. "There's only a few days of school left before the Christmas break. I don't want her to miss them." She grimaced. "It's best if she goes and gets back to her busy little schedule."

I swallowed the thick feeling in my throat. "She'll be all right?"

"She'll be fine. We all will be."

I was surprised at how those simple words stung.

"I didn't mean to upset her . . . to upset any of you."

"She gets attached. I had hoped to ease her into your leaving." She wrung her hands. "I'll be having a long talk with Seth tonight—this is odd behavior for him, but I suppose he got attached too."

I wasn't sure what to say.

"I'm sorry, Alex."

"It's not your problem. I should have known better."

I frowned, unsure what she meant. Before I could ask, though, she spoke again.

"Your car will be here at ten." She glanced over to the bed, a smile tugging at her lips. "I'm impressed, Dylan. You packed yourself."

I knew she was trying to lighten the atmosphere. I glared at her. "I am a grown man and quite capable of packing myself, Alex."

With a wry grin, she bent down and picked up the boots and my sleep pants from the floor. "Not very well. It all needs to go in the case."

We both chuckled.

I stepped forward. "Alex . . ."

She held up her hand. "Don't say anything, Dylan. We said it all. These past days have been wonderful, for both of us, but it's time to get back to reality."

She laid the envelope on the bed. "George asked me to give this to you. He signed your offer." Her voice dropped. "Congratulations —you got what you came for. You now own the Sleepy Moose Inn and the Ocean Bluff Resort."

I had no idea how to respond.

She changed her voice, forcing a lighter tone. "I bet you never thought you'd see those words in your portfolio."

I had to admit she was correct. But this inn had unexpectedly become my most prized piece of property. I had to ask her. "Do you hate me for that?"

She looked startled. "No. It had to be sold—I'm glad you bought it. You'll make it into a lovely place. I'm sure of it."

"I will. I'll protect the land. I promise."

"Then it's all good." She indicated the door. "I have to go and help Susan. We're going to shut down most of the rooms for the season." A sad smile flitted across her face. "For good, I suppose."

"Can I see you if I come back to town?"

"I'm not sure that's a good idea, Dylan. I expect we'll bump into each other, but we need to let personal things go."

Pain lanced through my body, and I steadied my suddenly shaky limbs by leaning on the table. I was being insane. It was every man's dream—snowed in with a sexy woman, amazing sex, and being able to walk away with no strings and return to his life with nothing but great memories.

A dream for most, yet for me, it felt like a nightmare.

"Will you come say goodbye?"

She shook her head, a small crack appearing in her carefully controlled façade. "No. We said our goodbyes already."

She held out her hand. "Thank you, Mr. Maxwell. I wish you much luck in the future."

I stared at her hand before wrapping mine around it, shaking it gently. It took everything in me not to pull her into my arms one last time, but I knew she didn't want that. Our time was done. "I hope the future is good to you, Alex."

She bit her lip, straightened her shoulders, and smiled. "Don't be late for your car. I went to a lot of trouble to get you something other than a minivan." Turning abruptly, she walked away from me.

The quiet click of the door shutting echoed in my head long after she left.

CHAPTER 12

DYLAN

A town car pulled up in front of the inn. The lobby was deserted. No guests were expected—Alex explained they shut down between now and the end of January. Usually, they took that time to make repairs and reorganize for the upcoming season. I wondered what she would be doing this year. Then, I realized she would be looking for a job and a new place to live. My stomach tightened, and my fists clenched at my sides at the thought of her having to do either.

I wanted her to be the last thing I saw before I left. I wanted to hold her, to taste her, to commit her to memory.

But that wasn't going to happen. I grabbed my luggage and walked out the door to the waiting car. I waved off the driver, tossing my bags in the back seat and climbing in.

He put the car in gear, the tires hesitating on the icy surface, then we began to move. A noise caught my ears and I turned, shocked to see Alex behind the car, waving frantically, crying out my name.

"Stop!" I yelled, already reaching for the door.

I was out of the car, running to her, gathering her up in my arms, holding her tight. I felt the tremble in her body, and I opened my coat, wrapping her up in the warmth.

For a moment, the ache left my chest and my tension eased.

She tilted up her head. "I had to say goodbye, Dylan. I had to thank you."

"For what?" I studied her face, even as the tension crept back. Her lovely, sweet face I never wanted to forget, because she was still saying goodbye.

"These past few days, you made me remember what it was like to be Alex—to feel something other than worry and duty. You gave me a great gift. I don't want you to think I regretted it. I don't—not a single second."

Leaning up, she offered her mouth, and I took it, kissing her with everything I had—claiming her mouth, claiming her. I poured every good feeling, smile, and touch we shared into that kiss. I kissed her until the brief honk of the car horn reminded me I had to get on the road or I would miss my plane. Reluctantly, I released her, setting her on her feet, dropping one last, lingering kiss to her mouth. I held her chin in my hand, looking into her eyes.

"You're the one who gave me the gift, Alex. And I'll never forget it, or you."

"Be happy, Dylan."

I squeezed her hand. "Be well, my darling girl."

I held her close one last time, then strode back to the car. Slamming the door behind me, in a gruff voice, I informed the driver we could go.

I didn't look back.

I didn't know how to cope with the feeling of emptiness and that I was leaving something important behind.

"Amy!" I hollered, slamming down my coffee mug.

My door opened and she crept in, already looking scared. She should be. I was gone days, not weeks, and she'd messed up my coffee every single time since I came back, as if she'd forgotten. How fucking difficult was it to make a cup of coffee?

I pushed my mug toward the edge of the desk. "Get me another one, and for God's sake, get it right or you're fired."

Arlene walked in, breezing past Amy, who was frozen, her mouth agape. Arlene came to my desk, lifted my mug, and took a sip. She turned to Amy. "It's fine. Go back to your desk."

Amy scurried out, shutting the door too loudly for my liking. I slammed down my hand on the wooden surface, glaring at Arlene. "Don't be overriding my authority with my staff. You don't even work here anymore!"

"Stop taking out your bad mood on the poor girl. And I do still work here until the end of the year."

I flicked my hand at the door. "Consider it an early Christmas gift. Go home. Send that useless girl away too."

Arlene laughed and sat down, swinging her leg. "And leave you alone without an assistant? I don't think so."

"I'm better off on my own than with the likes of her."

She huffed, not put out at all by my temper. "Shut up, Dylan, and drink your coffee."

"It's shit."

"It's exactly the way you like it."

I wanted to growl at her—it wasn't. Alex hadn't made it. She hadn't handed it to me with one of her warm smiles. It didn't have a sprinkling of sugar snuck into it. I knew Alex did that, and I liked how it tasted. But I couldn't get the amount right no matter how many times I tried with the sugar I had hidden in my top drawer— *that* was how I liked my coffee. I couldn't tell Arlene that, though. Instead, I glowered and sipped the brew.

"Have you slept at all since coming back?" she queried.

"I'm fine," I snapped.

"You keep telling yourself that."

"Drop it."

I had barely slept since returning to Toronto. Instead, I wandered my condo, finding the noise of the city too much to process and my bed too big and cold. My thoughts drifted to Alex constantly. I wondered what she was doing. If she was okay. I worried about Noelle and if she was still upset. If she still wore her slippers every day. If Seth still hated me for leaving. I worried about their future.

I missed them all, and I wondered if they missed me.

"Did you keep the appointment I made for you with the doctor?"

I snorted. "Fat lot of good it did me, but yes. I don't know why I'm paying so much for private care. I need to find a new one."

"Oh?"

"He did a bunch of tests and said I was fine." I rubbed my chest. "It's still aching."

She pursed her lips. "He had nothing to offer?"

I grunted. "A bunch of BS that sometimes physical symptoms have more to do with stress in our lives and emotions we're not dealing with, rather than being ill."

Sarcasm laced her voice. "You're right—a total quack. You need to find someone to perform unnecessary open-heart surgery instead of good, common sense."

I glowered at her.

"I can't find my gray sweatshirt—the one you gave me last year with those hideous sleep pants," I blurted out, wanting to change the subject.

She blinked at me. "I don't have it, Dylan. When was the last time you saw it?"

I couldn't remember, or figure out why it was so important. I had even torn apart my place last night looking for it. I shrugged.

"Did you take it to Nova Scotia with you?"

The sudden memory of tugging my shirt over Alex's head after our steamy shower hit me. She had my shirt.

My breath caught.

Had she tossed it? Was she wearing it? Did she think of me?

I had kept what happened between Alex and me to myself, so I couldn't tell Arlene any of that. But now I knew where my sweatshirt was.

"Maybe." I shrugged noncommittally. "Doesn't really matter."

I wondered if it was keeping her warm. I wanted it to keep her warm. I ignored the fact that what I *really* wanted was to be the one to keep her warm.

"We're going shopping," Arlene announced, startling me from my thoughts.

"No, we aren't."

"Yes, we are. You need to pick out your gifts for my grandkids. And something for Amy."

"Give them a gift card this year. They can pick out their own gift." I tilted my chin to the door. "*She's* getting a pink slip. I'll add a bow."

She stood and leaned over the desk, her face serious. "You are going to ditch the Grinch attitude, damn well plaster a smile on your face, and we are going shopping. Do you understand me, Dylan?"

I knew that look. If I pushed her any further, I was going to find myself at the receiving end of a lecture I would never forget.

"I have a meeting," I protested lamely.

"Which I switched until tomorrow. We're going shopping, and that is final."

I stood and grabbed my coat. "Fine. Maybe I can find a fucking Starbucks to make me a decent coffee."

She chuckled as she followed me. "I doubt that."

I hated shopping. I hated it during every other time of year. But at Christmas? God, I hated it even more. The stores were full of too many bodies, crying children, and stressed-out parents dragging them around. People frantically grabbing gifts they probably couldn't afford, desperate to complete their lists and get out of the box-like-hell they called the mall.

Dutifully, I followed Arlene around the toy store, while she showed me some options for her grandkids. I pointed to the items I preferred, and she set them in the cart. As we rounded the corner, I knocked an item off the shelf, grabbing it before it hit the floor. I stared down at the fluffy kitten that started meowing out some silly song. Instantly, my mind went to Noelle. She would love that. I could see her meowing along with the cat as she hugged it, running up and down the halls in her fuzzy slippers, smiling her wide, toothless grin.

"Dylan?" Arlene's voice was quiet, gentle. "Did you want to buy that?"

I glanced up and nodded. She took the box from my hands and set it in the cart. "Anything else?"

I looked around and allowed myself to think of Alex, Seth, and Noelle, my entire body aching with sadness as their faces filled my mind. Alex refused to let me help them, but she couldn't refuse Christmas gifts.

"Can we get a box of gifts to Nova Scotia before Christmas?"

"Yes, if I charter Roger and the private plane."

"Then, yes, Arlene, there're lots of things I want to buy."

She beamed at me. "I thought so."

Four hours later, the back of her car was full and so was the trunk. All the gifts were gift-wrapped with name tags and decked out with bows and ribbons. There were toys and clothes for Seth and Noelle, a warm, deep green coat Arlene helped me pick out for Alex, along with a pretty scarf and gloves in the softest leather I could find. I found some books and movies I knew she would enjoy. There was candy and chocolate, and I even remembered a box of cigars for George, like the ones I had noticed on his desk.

"My 'treat' on occasion," he had informed me. Then he had winked. *"When Alex allows it."* We had both laughed.

There was also a delicate gold necklace, adorned with a wide-eyed owl set with emeralds and tiny diamonds that I had seen in the jeweler's window as I went past. I kept going back, and finally, went in and bought it. I wrote a note to Alex and asked her to keep it for Noelle when she was older. She might not remember me, but I would remember my Little Owl for the rest of my life, and I wanted her to have it. It was her "birfday," after all.

I sat back, sipping a brandy, as Arlene groaned.

"For someone who didn't want to go shopping, you certainly changed your mind." She smirked, rubbing her calf.

I shrugged. "Alex and her family don't have much. If I can make their Christmas a good one, at least a little better than usual, I'll feel I've done something right for a change when it comes to them."

She leaned back, picking up her glass of wine. She took a sip, regarding me over the rim. "You feel guilty," she said.

"I'm taking their home."

"It was going to happen anyway."

I shrugged. "Regardless."

"Is it possible, Dylan, there's more to this than you're saying?"

"I have no idea what you're talking about."

"Do you know how often you've spoken of them since you came back?"

"I spent some time with them. It's fresh. That's all."

"Hmmm. Did you know the last deal you did, a dozen families lost their homes?"

"We compensated them."

"Generously. But it never bothered you. A dozen of them. One little family and you can't stop thinking about them." She set down her glass. "Do you know what I think?"

"I'm sure I'm about to," I stated wryly.

She ignored my sarcasm. "I think you became emotionally invested."

"I'm never emotionally invested in a deal."

"I'm not talking about the deal."

"Drop it."

"Hitting too close to home?"

I leaned forward, my voice low. "I'm not sure what you think you know, but there is no future. Alex has her life. I have mine. She won't leave the East Coast."

She snorted. "I know everything, because I know you, Dylan. And people can move."

"Did you not hear me? She won't leave."

"I wasn't talking about her, Dylan."

"Are we at that again?" I huffed. "I am not, repeat, *not* a family man. Alex and the kids need that sort of man. I don't know anything about being responsible for another person. I don't want to repeat the hell of my past. I don't want to look in the mirror and realize I've become my father."

"Like he did with you, you mean? Ignore the child desperate for your love and immerse yourself in strangers and business instead?"

"Yes." I shook my head. "I can't do that."

"Look again, Dylan," she said sadly. "It might be too late." She stood. "I'd like to go home now. I'll arrange for a car to pick you up."

I stared at her, unsure how to respond.

"For what it's worth, I think you're already feeling responsible, which is why you're so upset. I don't think you've given yourself enough credit. I don't think you're being honest with yourself about a lot of things." She hesitated, her hand gripping the back of the chair. "Sometimes what we want changes. How we do things has to be adjusted. Often, it's scary. But if you grab that chance, the end result is amazing, Dylan. Think about it."

She turned and left, her cryptic words resonating in my head.

I was tired and cranky the next morning—even crankier than I had been since arriving home.

As soon as Arlene appeared, I was at her, barely waiting for her to sit down before I asked. "Did you arrange for those packages to be delivered?"

"I handled everything, yes."

"I want them to have the gifts for Christmas."

"They will—one way or another."

"What does that mean?"

"Dylan." She sighed and shook her head. "It means the gifts will be delivered, even if you don't get your head out of your ass in time."

"If you have something to say, then spit it out, old woman. Stop with your innuendos and not-so-subtle attempts to get into my fucking head," I snapped.

She didn't react to my tone or my words. She never did. She regarded me calmly, her gaze drifting to the windows behind where I sat. She got out of her chair and walked over to the large panes of glass, standing in silence as she gazed out.

"It's a big city."

I rolled my eyes. "Yes."

"Lots happening—all the time."

"Uh-huh."

"Have you been to a play this year, Dylan?"

I frowned. "I took you to see *Les Misérables* for your birthday."

"That was two years ago, dear boy."

"Well, then, I guess not."

"Concerts?"

"No."

"Opera, symphony, a sporting event?"

I ran my hand over my face. "No. I'm busy, Arlene. I don't have time to do those things. Or much interest in them, to be honest."

She nodded, still looking out the window. "Nightclubbing?"

I snorted. "You know I don't go nightclubbing."

"Of course." She tapped her lip thoughtfully. "You took a couple of days off in the summer, correct?"

"Yes. What are you getting at?"

"Humor me, Dylan. What did you do while you were off? Explore the galleries and museums? Walk the waterfront?"

"No. I rented a small cabin up north and relaxed for a few days. I needed to get away from the city and the bustle."

"Right."

"I like it up there. It's peaceful."

"Yes, I could tell when you came back." She turned from the window and headed to the door. "I've decided to do dinner tomorrow, not Christmas Day. I'm planning on an early one. Be there for four."

I slammed my hand on my desk. "What the hell was all that about? All your hints and clues? Trying to point out the fact that I could give up my life and go east?" I stood up, waving my arm around. "What about my business? Have you thought of that?"

She paused, her hand on the doorknob. "A business can be run from anywhere, Dylan. Most of the business you do is via phone or computer. If needed, planes take you wherever you want to go."

"That's it!" I snarled in exasperation. "You think I should give up my life in Toronto and go to Alex. You think that's what I need to do?"

She tilted her head and studied me. "I would never dream of telling you what to do, Dylan." She pulled open the door and said, before walking out, "And you can't give up a life you aren't living."

Hours later, I paced the floor, my hands tugging on my hair in irritation, cursing Arlene Carson's name.

What the hell was she trying to do? Did she really think I could simply uproot my life? And do what? Become a family man and live in a small town? And live at the Sleepy Moose Inn?

I threw back a shot of scotch, the burn welcome as I moved restlessly around my condo.

What did she expect—I would go out east, marry Alex, and look after her and her children? Become a dad? I scoffed out loud. Marriage—children—neither was on my radar.

The image of Noelle's little face swam behind my eyes, and the sound of her sweet voice echoed in my head. Her adorable smile and the way she lisped all her words. I knew I would go to Pinegrove to check on the project once it was underway, and chances were, given how small the town was, I would see them, even if I didn't actively seek them out. Noelle's teeth would have grown in by then and that endearing part of her would have disappeared, but it would always be how I remembered her.

The next time I saw Seth, he would have grown up even more. He was already on that borderline between being a boy and a man. I knew, with Alex's influence, he would grow to be a fine one. I thought of our private conversation while I was there. He hadn't needed sex education—he knew all about sex, or at least, the mechanics of it. He needed someone to talk to about the emotion that came with sex— about how he was feeling for the girl he liked. A little part of me hoped my words would stay with him and help him be the man I knew he could become.

And Alex. My heart clenched as I thought about her. She'd been on my mind endlessly since I returned; no matter how hard I tried not to think about her—and what we shared. Somehow, she was always there, peeking around the corner, filling my mind with thoughts, images, and memories.

I shook my head. It was ridiculous. No matter what mumbo jumbo Arlene spouted about knowing me. I had known Alex a few days. Made love to her a handful of times. We had no history, no long-term plans. We had agreed on that. Other than the one call to let her know I was back safe in Toronto, I hadn't spoken to her. She had my number, but she hadn't reached out to me either.

Yet, I couldn't stop thinking about her. Worrying about her. Wondering what she was going to do when the inn was no longer her home. She'd refused every offer I'd made to help her; although, I knew George now had enough money to help her find a safe place to live.

Still, I worried about her. Was she managing? Would she be

angry over the gifts I sent? I wanted her and the children to have a good Christmas. To enjoy the day and let them all have a few Santa surprises.

To thank her in some small way for making me feel, even for a short time, as if I mattered. Not Dylan Maxwell the businessman— someone you wanted to have on your side and trade favors with for your own personal and financial gain. Just Dylan—the man. She had brought forth so much emotion—for her, Noelle, and Seth. She had shown me there was more to me than simply someone with a good head for business on his shoulders. She, and the kids, had liked Dylan.

I liked myself when I was with them.

I drained my glass with an angry curse. There was no point in thinking about it. Alex had her life there in Pinegrove, and I had mine here in Toronto. Regardless of what bullshit Arlene had been spewing earlier, I had a life and it was a good one. I had a fantastic condo, a business I ran well, and I stayed busy. I spent my evenings and weekends working out, at various functions, and I . . .

My thoughts trailed off.

I had dinner on occasion with Arlene and her husband. Even rarer, I had dinner with a friend who was in town or I'd bumped into. My last girlfriend had been two years ago, and she had walked out, saying I was emotionally unavailable and a grouch most of the time. I had to agree with her—she made me grouchy with her constant need to spend my money and her frivolous demands on my time.

Since then, though, there had been no one of significance.

Except Alex.

I slammed down my glass—bloody Arlene and her mutterings. I was fine.

I was fine before I met Alex, and I'd be fine once the stupid holidays were over.

I ignored the low jingle in my head that sounded like laughter.

The next day, I arrived at Arlene's promptly at four. She hated latecomers. I brought two bottles of her favorite wine, as well as had sent flowers earlier. I did it every year. Although, usually, dinner was on Christmas Day, but I assumed she was spending it with her grandkids.

I had spent the day in the office alone, after magnanimously giving Amy the day off. Before she left yesterday, I'd handed her a small bonus, which Arlene insisted she deserved, and a gift certificate for her favorite salon, which Arlene had picked up for me. I refrained from advising her to use it to color her roots and perhaps to embrace her natural hair color for a change. I knew that would be frowned upon, and Arlene would kick my ass, so I wished Amy happy holidays and got my own coffee for the day.

It still wasn't as good as Alex's was.

I got a lot done, including going over the plans for the Ocean Bluff Resort. I kept looking at the diagrams. At one point, I had sketched a different design over the top, moving the main entrance and adding a house on the bluff, before shaking my head in disgust. I rolled up the plans and shoved them back into their container.

I was being ridiculous.

Arlene and Simon welcomed me warmly, and we sat down to a pleasant meal, chatting about their plans for the holidays and after she retired. My appetite was off, and I pushed the food around on my plate, pretending to eat. They kept exchanging glances, which I ignored.

After dinner, we sat in their great room, admiring the gigantic Christmas tree in the corner filled with lights and packages spilling over in piles beneath it.

With a smile, I held out an envelope, containing the cruise voucher I was giving them, and the gifts I had purchased in Nova Scotia. After many hugs and handshakes, I opened my gifts: the special edition bottle of Courvoisier and a new pair of lounge pants —blue plaid this time. I arched my eyebrow at Arlene.

"Think you're funny?"

"You found a use for the last pair. I thought these would come in handy for the next time you tried to relax."

Again, I ignored her not-so-subtle hint.

She handed me another parcel. I frowned as I took it from her hands. Unlike the sleek, perfectly wrapped gifts that were under the tree, this one was awkward—the edges crinkled, the paper covered in reindeer and funny Santa faces, and it was cold to the touch.

"What's this?"

"Open it."

My hands trembled as I unwrapped the paper. Inside was a container with an envelope taped to the top. Opening it up, I stared at it as tears came to my eyes.

A hand-drawn picture—crude and childlike. There was no doubt

—Noelle. It was the couch in the lobby of the inn. All of us were on it. I held Noelle on my lap; Seth was on one side of me, and Alex on the other. She had even drawn my stick figure arm around Alex's shoulders. In scrawly, uneven print, the words, *Merry Christmas Dylan* were at the top.

Inside was Noelle's signature, about a thousand xxxx's and a short note from Alex.

Dylan,

Noelle couldn't bear the thought of her Dywan not having some of his favorite Sugar Sprinkle cookies for the holidays. However, I couldn't figure out how to send Tater Tot Casserole, so these will have to do. Mrs. Carson was kind enough to accept delivery and keep them fresh.

We hope you are well and your life is good.

Merry Christmas,

Alex

PS—She misses you.

We all miss you.

X

I blinked away the moisture and opened the lid. Inside the box, Noelle's "suga cookies" filled the space.

I offered the container to Arlene and Simon, and we each ate one silently.

My gaze kept falling on the words at the bottom: We all miss you.

I swallowed and lifted my eyes, meeting Arlene's knowing ones. She nodded, a small smile playing on her lips.

"They miss me," I choked out.

"Of course they do." She smiled tenderly. "You miss *them*."

The ache in my chest became a yawning chasm. I had to say the words before I fell.

"I think . . . I think I love her. I think I love all of them. How is that even possible? I only knew them a few days."

"It is possible. I loved you the moment I met you. That has never changed," she said. "Love has no schedule."

"They need me—they all need me."

"*You* need them, Dylan."

The lump in my throat grew.

She leaned forward, cupping my face. "Dear boy, I love you, and I'm proud of your success and everything else you've accomplished. But your life is empty, and you've been alone long enough. I heard more joy in your voice those few days than I have ever witnessed with you in all these years. It's time to start living. It's okay to need someone. To love someone." She paused, her voice fierce. "You are *not* your father, Dylan. You have so much love to give. Go and get it."

I wasn't my father—my cold, unbending father who never had time for me after my mother died. Those words resonated in my head. She was right. I wanted to spend time with Seth and Noelle. In fact, I wanted to spend lots of time with them. And I wanted Alex. I wanted to be with Alex every minute.

I was tired of denying it. I was tired of the empty, aching feeling in my chest.

"It's crazy."

She kissed my cheek. "Love is."

I grabbed her, hugging her hard. "I have to go. I have to figure out how to get to them."

She drew back, her eyes dancing. "Roger will be at the airport tonight at eleven. All your gifts are already on the plane I chartered. A rental car is waiting for you at the airport when you arrive. You'll be there when they wake up Christmas morning."

"How?"

"George left a key in the flowerpot. All you have to do is wait."

"George?"

She grinned, an infectious I-know-you-better-than-you-know-yourself grin. "Let's just say we covered all the bases . . . In case you finally took your snooty head out of your ass long enough to see what was right in front of you."

The fact that two people, one practically a stranger, had discussed and planned this should have upset me. But it didn't. Gratitude and love, the love I had for the woman who was so much like a mother to me, welled up, and I hugged her again. "Thank you, Arlene."

"I'll make certain the office is covered until you get back. I'll help you close this one down." She smirked. "I think you'll have lots of help setting up the new one. A certain, well-organized innkeeper comes to mind for that job."

I grinned back at her. "I think she's going to be the one issuing the orders."

She beamed at me. "That is exactly what you need." She pointed to the door. "Go and find your life, Dylan."

I kissed her cheek. "Merry Christmas."

"Merry Christmas, my dear boy."

CHAPTER 14

DYLAN

The roads were deserted as I drove toward the Sleepy Moose Inn. Boxes and bags filled the minivan, and every time I looked in the rearview mirror, I chuckled. I felt like Santa Claus. I had laughed when Roger walked me out to pick up my rental car and I saw it was one of the dreaded minivans. I had a feeling Arlene had done that on purpose. I didn't care. It held all my gifts, and it was getting me to where I belonged. On the front seat sat the almost empty container of "suga cookies." I couldn't stop eating them, and I really hoped Alex had more.

I pulled in the long, winding driveway, my heart rate picking up. I'd see Alex soon. Be able to feel her in my arms. Kiss Noelle's sweet little face. Tease Seth.

Feel complete in a way I hadn't since I'd left them behind.

The Christmas lights were on, glowing bright in the darkness. I parked the van in front of the door, surprised to see George in his wheelchair outside, puffing on one of his forbidden cigars, the smoke circling his head. A thick blanket draped over his legs, and he wore a heavy parka against the cold. I got out of the vehicle and walked toward him, extending my hand. He shook it, looking serious.

"Dylan."

"George." I smiled at him. "Are you enjoying a stolen cigar, or are you out here because you had another one of your feelings that I'd show up after your chat with Arlene?"

A huge grin broke out on his face, and his eyes crinkled, the wrinkles on his face prominent. "Wish I could say yes, but more like Mrs. Carson called me to tell me you were on your way."

"The two of you know way too much about my personal life."

He turned serious. "Before I let you in, I need to know what your intentions are, Dylan. I can't let them be hurt again."

"Again?"

"Alex may seem to be strong, but she hasn't been the same since you left. Neither has my Noelle. Even Seth has been quiet. You had quite the impact on them."

"As they did me. I haven't been the same either," I assured him.

"So, this is serious? Not just a visit?"

I slipped my hand into my pocket and withdrew the tiny box inside. I opened the case and held out the diamond ring I had brought with me. It had taken a lot of begging and favors to get my friend to meet me at his jewelry store on Christmas Eve so I could get it. As soon as I saw it in his backroom vault, I knew it was the one. Perfect for my Alex—simple, elegant, and symbolic. The three stones represented what they were to me—one for each of the people who had claimed my heart. I knew nothing about diamonds, but Garrett had assured me they were high quality and even sketched out a band that would go well with the setting. I liked how the light caught the jewels, reflecting their brilliance. He had larger, fancier ones, but I knew Alex wouldn't like them. But the one I chose . . . I knew she would love. If she forgave me and said yes.

"Is this serious enough for you, George? I'm here for them. All of them."

He studied the ring, then looked at me. "She doesn't want to leave here, but I think, for you, she will."

I shut the lid and slid the ring back into my pocket. "She won't have to. I'm going to come here. To her." I looked past him to the ocean. "I'm going to build her a house—on the bluff, or wherever she wants it. Create a home and a life with her."

He sighed, a long puff of white escaping his mouth. "Be the husband she deserves. The one my son couldn't be for her."

He shrugged at my raised eyebrows.

"I'm old, not blind. Alex and Eric were great friends, and that is how they should have remained. Alex has been a godsend to me, but she stopped living a long time ago. When Eric died, she mourned her friend and Noelle's father, but not her soul mate. She deserves that." He didn't say anything for a moment. "I saw how she looked at you. She found that with you. I think you found that with her." He hesitated and extended his hand. "You have my blessing, Dylan. I know you'll look after all of them."

I took his proffered hand. "With everything in me."

He smiled. "I know. Now, you'd better get that haul inside and set it up." He chuckled. "But I guarantee, nothing you've bought gift-wise will compare to the joy they'll have when they see you."

I smiled back at him. Being with them was going to be my greatest gift as well.

I paced the bar, nervous as I sipped on a brandy. George had offered me a room so I could get some sleep, but I knew it would be a waste. I wouldn't rest until I could be with Alex. He left me alone, saying he was sure Alex would be down soon anyway. I knew he was trying to give us our privacy for when she arrived.

Regardless of George's thoughts and his blessing, I had no idea how Alex would feel about seeing me. What her reaction to my proposal would be. I had spoken with her once—and it was brief—since the day I left. Daily, I fought against the need I felt, the yearning for her. And in doing so, I hurt not only myself, but also Alex and her children. I'd let my fears and doubt swamp me, and therefore, I denied us the one thing we all needed: to be together.

The elevator sounded, and I watched as Alex stepped out, carrying some brightly wrapped packages. I knew money was tight for her, and she made the day more about family and time together than about gifts. There had been some presents for each of the kids under the tree from her and George and some friends. George told me she always added the ones from Santa, sneaking back upstairs before Noelle got her up, anxious to go downstairs. I knew that was what she was carrying. Two gifts each and a fat stocking for them each to open.

She was wearing a pair of fuzzy pants and a long sweatshirt, which I realized was mine—the one I couldn't find when I went home. She still had it and was wearing it tonight—that made me happy. Her hair was hanging around her shoulders, a dark cloud of messy waves. She looked tired and sad . . . a fact I planned to change in the next couple of minutes. I wanted her smile—that wide, beautiful one she had especially for me. I hoped that it was still mine.

She stopped abruptly, shock evident on her face when she saw the piles of gifts now under the tree. Slowly, she came forward, setting down her gifts, hanging up the stockings by the fireplace. She lowered herself to her knees, looking at the surprise gifts, reading the tags. She sat stock-still for a moment, simply holding a box with Noelle's name on it. I was horrified to see tears running down her cheeks when she lifted her face.

"No, Dylan," she said and sobbed into the seemingly empty room. "We didn't want your gifts, we wanted *you.*"

Dropping the package, she buried her face in her hands, her shoulders shaking with the force of her tears.

They wanted me. Dylan. Not the business tycoon, not my money or the gifts it could buy. Me.

My sock-covered feet made no noise as I went to her. Kneeling and wrapping my arms around her, I drew her close. "You have me, my darling girl."

ALEX

I opened my eyes, the darkness of the night still around me. I pushed up off the mattress and pulled my legs up to my chest. I drew in a few deep breaths, hoping to dispel the constant heaviness in my chest.

I knew it was useless. I knew what it was.

I missed Dylan. Desperately.

From the moment his car had disappeared around the corner, I had missed him. It was crazy. I had known him mere days, yet his departure left such a hole in me, I found myself unable to cope. I spent hours thinking of him. Of the way his mouth felt on mine. How safe I felt when he was beside me. Of the way the haughty expression on his face morphed into something warmer, sweet, almost loving when he was in the room with us.

All of us.

His leaving had affected each of us in different ways. Seth was quieter, almost angry at times. Noelle bounced between her usual cheerful self and being withdrawn and misbehaving. She had begged me to send "Dywan" some cookies.

"He needs dem, Mommy. He be sad wifout dem."

I wondered if he had received them yet. What he would think.

I wondered if we ever crossed his mind at all or if he had returned to his life and ceased to think of us.

The thought of that happening increased the ache in my heart.

I slid from bed, knowing trying to sleep was useless. After checking on Noelle, I gathered the Santa gifts and stockings I had made and headed downstairs. Perhaps I would curl up on the sofa by the tree and wait for the kids to get up. I wanted to make the day a nice one for them.

The lobby was quiet, the tree lights glowing in the darkness. The one other light was the lamp in the corner. Something was different, but it wasn't until I got closer to the tree that I saw what it was.

Presents. Many of them, piled under the branches, the shiny paper catching the light. I stared, frozen at the mountain of Christmas gifts that had magically appeared since I went upstairs earlier.

Had George used some of the money from the sale and bought the kids more gifts than usual?

I crouched beside the tree and pulled one brightly wrapped package toward me, inspecting the tag. My hand shook as I read the words written in a bold, masculine script.

For Noelle:
Merry Christmas, Little Owl
Love, Dylan

Dylan. He had remembered us. Somehow, he had sent gifts. My gaze flew over the piles. So many gifts. I was sure all wonderful, thoughtful things. He didn't think he was good at relationships, or that he was a caring man, but he was. I had witnessed his caring. The things he had given my children. The way he spoke to them, the way he treated me. He simply couldn't see it. He could spot an incredible business deal instantly, but he had no idea of the value of his own worth.

Tears sprang to my eyes. "No, Dylan." I wept. "We didn't want your gifts, we wanted *you*."

Dropping the package, I buried my face in my hands, giving in to the despair I had been feeling. I would have given anything to find him there with me. *He* was all I wanted.

I started at the feel of arms wrapping around me.

Dylan's arms.

A warm, gentle voice in my ear.

Dylan's voice.

"You have me, my darling girl."

DYLAN

Gasping, she turned, flinging her arms around my neck. I pulled her close, breathing her in, holding her tight to my chest. I let her cry, enjoying the feel of holding her again and realizing the constant ache was gone. I felt complete and whole. That damn quack doctor had been right.

Finally, I dropped my lips to her ear. "Hush, now. Look at me, baby. Please."

She pulled back, cupping my face. "When . . . how . . ."

Leaning down, I wiped away her tears and kissed her—softly brushing her lips with mine. "A little while ago. George let me in."

Her eyes were wide—I could see the fear in them. "George did? He knows you're here? How long? Noelle . . . I can't let her . . ."

I kissed her soundly, silencing her words. "Forever, Alex. If you'll have me."

"I don't understand."

"Neither did I, until yesterday." I inhaled deeply. I hadn't planned to do it so soon, but the moment was right. "I love you, Alex. I want to build a life with you." Before she could protest, I held a finger to her lips. "Here with you. I'll build your house on the bluff. We'll make a life together. You, me, Seth, and my Little Owl. We'll be a family." I pressed the box into her hand. "Marry me, Alex. Make this the happiest Christmas I've ever known."

She looked down at the box, fresh tears streaming down her cheeks.

"Forgive me," I begged her. "Forgive me for letting my fears stop me from telling you how much you mean to me. I know I said it was only here, but I was wrong. You're everywhere, Alex. You're inside me. You changed me so completely; I'm lost without you. For the first time in my life, I need someone. I need *you*. I need to be with you. Please let me."

More tears ran down her face, and her bottom lip quivered.

"I don't know anything about love or caring for other people. But I want to learn. I want you to teach me," I pleaded. "I want to show you how much you—all of you—mean to me." I touched her cheek gently. "You said you would be mine if you could," I reminded her. "You can be. You simply have to say yes."

"This is crazy."

I grinned at her, using Arlene's words. "Love is."

"I . . . I have so many questions."

"And I'll answer all of them. Tell you anything you want to know. But let me do it with you as my fiancée. Please. Tell me you love me too."

Her voice quavered. "I do love you. I love you so much, and I've . . . *missed* you so much since you left."

"You don't have to miss me anymore. I'm here."

"You want to move here to be with me?"

"With all of you, yes. But especially you." I stroked her cheek. "I've missed you too," I added. "So much."

"You really love me?"

"I do."

"*And* my children?"

I gathered her close. "I love them now, and I will love them like my own for the rest of my life. And I want to make a bunch more Noelles with you. Maybe a Seth or two thrown in so we boys have some company."

"Yes," she whispered, smiling, pressing her mouth to my neck. "Yes."

My whole body froze. "Yes to marrying me, or yes to more babies?"

She tilted up her head, meeting my gaze. Love blazed from the depths of her eyes. Her all-encompassing love that warmed my soul and eased my entire being. "Yes to both."

I took the ring from the box and slid it onto her finger. It was as perfect as I knew it would be.

"Say it, Alex. I need to hear you say it."

She cupped my cheek, the ring glinting in the lights of the tree, as shiny and brilliant as the moment. "I love you, Dylan."

With a groan, I kissed her passionately. My memory of how she felt in my arms was nothing compared to the real thing. I was desperate to feel her against me, and I tugged her closer, trailing wet kisses down her neck. She gasped when I bit down on her skin, soothing it with my tongue. "I love you," I declared against her skin. "I don't ever want to be without you."

She whimpered as I slipped my hand under the loose shirt and my fingers traced over her nipples, teasing the tight peaks.

"*God*, I want you."

"You have too many clothes on, Dylan."

I groaned into her neck. "I can change that."

"We have to be fast."

"That's not going to be a problem, baby. I missed you . . . *a lot*."

Her fingers tugged at my waistband. "Good."

❄

We curled up on the couch, her back to my chest, the fireplace crackling, the tree casting its glow over the room. I had changed into my new sleep pants, since someone's anxious fingers had actually ripped my other ones. I had pulled on another sweatshirt, and when I sat down beside her again, I had to laugh. We both had on gray sweatshirts and plaid pants.

"We match." I grinned.

"I like it."

I kissed her nose affectionately. "Me too."

We didn't talk much, except the occasional murmur and "I love you" breaking the still of the room. We'd have lots of time to talk, clear the air, and make plans. Tomorrow, there'd be plenty of time for discussion. Right now, all we wanted, all we needed, was to be close. I pulled her snug to my body, dropping another kiss on her head. Contentment I never knew existed filled my heart, banishing the loneliness I'd known my entire life.

"I should make coffee," she said. "They'll be up soon, and Noelle is going to go crazy when she sees you." She looked up, beaming. "It's going to be quite the Christmas Day."

I chuckled. "I can't wait to see her and Seth. I would love some coffee. I haven't had a decent cup since I left here. Amy is incapable of it, apparently. How do you make it taste so perfect? I tried adding a little bit of sugar the way I saw you do it. It still wasn't right."

"I use natural sugar—it tastes better." She grinned impishly. "I noticed you seemed happier when you ate or drank something sweet, so I slipped it in."

I tweaked her nose. "You got me addicted."

She laughed, but she was serious when she spoke. "Have you been giving her a hard time—Amy, I mean?"

"At times."

She rolled her eyes and sat up. Turning around, she placed her hand on my chest. "Dylan," she admonished, "you have to be nice."

"I'll be *very* nice to my new assistant."

"You already know who that will be?"

With a wicked grin, I picked up her hand, kissing the ring she now wore. "I was hoping, since you won't have the inn to worry about, maybe you'd agree to keep me in line."

She pursed her lips, pausing to think. "Running the inn will seem like child's play compared to that," she countered.

I gasped in mock horror. "Don't think you can handle me, Alex?"

"You, Mr. Maxwell, are a demanding man."

"I am. But I promise there'll be lots of perks . . . bonuses . . ." I teased her. "Does that help?"

"Maybe."

"What if I promised to be good?"

"I'm not sure you can be."

"I will. I promise." I ran my finger down her cheek, tracing her full bottom lip. "I have a feeling you're exactly who I need by my side."

Her cheeks colored, and she tossed her hair. "Well, maybe we can do a three-month probationary period."

I smirked at her knowingly. "By then, we'll be married, so you can't dump me."

Her eyebrows rose. "We will?"

I became serious. "Alex, I finally found you. The key to something I never expected to have—happiness. I'm not taking the chance of losing you. I want to be with you. I assumed you would prefer to be married rather than living together."

"Things are moving so fast."

I kissed her. "We'll talk about it tomorrow. I'll refrain from booking a minister today."

Before she could answer me, the elevator pinged. Alex stood, smiling. "Brace yourself, Dylan. The squealing is going to commence."

I stood beside her. I could hardly wait.

The elevator door opened, and out stumbled the sweetest little girl in the world, wearing her fuzzy red slippers, her wild curls bouncing around her head. A sleepy Seth followed, rubbing his eyes. He spotted me immediately, halting in his tracks. Noelle was staring at the vast pile of gifts under the tree, her eyes huge, her mouth a wide O. Then she saw me, and, in a second, was tearing across the room, her arms outstretched.

"Dywan! Dywan!"

I fell to my knees, my own arms open as she barreled into me. She wrapped herself around me, all warm and soft, smelling of bubble bath and little girl. Tears sprang to my eyes at her greeting. She pulled back, dropping tiny butterfly kisses all over my face, turning my tears into laughter.

"I knew it, I knew it," she crowed. "I tolded Thanta I had a wifth I touldn't even tell him, and he thaid if I was vewy good and pwayed weally hawd, I would ged it!" She turned to Seth, who was watching us with narrowed eyes. "I toll you, Sef!" Her head swung back my way. "Iz you, Dywan? Iz you my wifth? I didn't ask for nuffin' else—not even fo my birfday!"

"You wanted me to come back, Little Owl?" I asked, smiling as she dropped more kisses on my chin, wrinkling her nose as the scruff tickled her face.

Seth snorted. "She wants way more than that." He huffed. "Asshole," he added so quietly, I almost missed it.

I had no doubt that, as happy as my girls were to see me, Seth had reservations.

Noelle gasped. "Dywan iz no an ath-hole! He iz onwy gwumpy when he no haf suppa!"

My lips quirked at her defensive words, but Alex stood, slamming her hands on her hips.

I stood alongside her, taking Noelle with me. Not that I had any choice, since she had her arms wrapped so tight around my neck I wasn't sure how much longer I could breathe. "Alex," I murmured. "Let me."

I held out my hand. "Seth."

"Dylan," he scoffed, ignoring my hand.

Behind me, Alex hissed, "Seth, your manners!"

I held up my hand. "It's fine, Alex. He's protecting you. Both of you."

"How long are you here for?" he asked with purpose. "You might as well tell her and break her heart now."

Noelle shook her head. "No, Sef! My wifth is Dywan would be a daddy for boffa us! And Mommy need a huband. He is bof! Dats why he's hewe!" She looked at me, the innocent belief of a child shining through. To her, it was so simple. If she was good enough, and wished hard enough, it would be true. Her smile was bright and filled with hope. "Wight, Dywan?"

I kissed her cheek and met Seth's stare. As strong as he was trying to appear, I could see the vulnerability he was attempting to cover up.

"I came back to ask all of you if it would be okay if I moved here, Seth," I explained. "If maybe you all liked me enough to let us try to be a family."

Noelle squealed, tightening her hands. I was certain I was about to start seeing black dots.

"I don't need a father," he muttered and began to turn away.

I stopped him. "How about a friend? I thought we got along pretty well. Maybe we could start there."

He hesitated. "You're really moving here?"

"I want to. I want to build a life here. I want to build you all a home and share it with you."

His gaze flew to Alex, who nodded. "All of us?" His tone was less combative and more like the happy teenager I had grown to love.

I extended my hand again and winked. "All of you," I stated firmly. "I think you need me to help even out the numbers. God knows I can't keep these two in line without you."

He grabbed my hand, shaking it hard. "Darn right, you can't."

All of a sudden, I was ensconced. I was holding Noelle and Seth, with Alex wrapped around all of us. The love I felt was astounding. I was exhausted and overwhelmed, in a good way, being cried upon, my hair tugged by happy little fists, choked to death with love, and I was pretty sure I was about to weep in front of all of them.

I had flown all night, driven a minivan, played Santa, proposed to a woman who could render me useless with one smile, and it wasn't even seven a.m.

It was the best Christmas ever.

CHAPTER 15

DYLAN

I had never known a Christmas like it. My childhood, especially after my mother passed, had been lonely. My father buried himself in work, and at times, he seemed to forget I existed. I had nannies, then tutors, to keep me company. Mrs. C had changed all that when she joined my father's household as his housekeeper. She became so much more to me: my friend, confidante, and staunchest supporter. When I opened my first office, she walked away from my father and stood beside me, even as he sneered at my business idea. Real estate was a foolish endeavor, and I was being irresponsible, he'd said. Once again, I disappointed him. Arlene's faith in me never wavered.

Nevertheless, Christmas had always been a day of sadness. Arlene spent it with her family, and that forced my father to spend the day with me. There was never a tree, and he simply handed me gifts, not wrapped or signed with: *Love, Dad* or even *From, Santa*. They were always useful items—my father didn't believe in frivolities or spoiling a child. I knew each year that I would receive three things: a gift certificate to a bookstore, some educational item, and an article of clothing. He didn't choose any of it—one of his assistants did, so none of them was special. I respectfully handed him a card and a small item I had picked out. Although, once I got older, I discovered he discarded it to charity the day after. Dinner was an early affair, usually late lunch, and afterward, he would stand, his duty done, and inform me he would be working the rest of the day. When I was able to get around on my own, I would go to Mrs. C's and enjoy the rest of the day. Her thoughtful gift was always treasured, but the company and love I found there more so.

Today was the Christmas that I always dreamed of as a child. It didn't matter it wasn't me getting the gifts—somehow, it meant more. Seeing the joy and surprise on their faces was gift enough. Boxes, wrapping paper, and squeals of delight abounded. Things I swore I would hate made me smile. Wet, excited kisses were rained on my face. Noelle's sticky fingers offered me chocolate and candies that I gladly accepted. Fist bumps and a few awkward hugs from Seth were shared.

I loved every minute of it.

Alex finally stopped shaking her head and muttering about me "going overboard" when she saw the happiness and glee on her children's faces. Her own quiet enjoyment at her gifts warmed my heart. Her effusive kisses of thanks warmed other parts of me. George was thrilled with his cigars, laughing at the way Alex rolled her eyes and scolded me.

As the frenzy wound down, Alex pulled out a gift from the back of the tree, handing it to me, her cheeks pink with shyness.

"What is this?"

She shrugged, not meeting my eyes. "Just in case."

I tore open the flat package, grinning broadly at the framed photo. It was from the bluff, the ocean wild with the wind kicking up the waves and the sun shining down, making the swirling colors vivid.

"I took the picture in the summer. I thought you could hang it in your office as a reminder."

Leaning over, I kissed her. "I love it." I kissed her again, lowering my voice. "I love you."

Noelle jumped up, clutching her singing cat, rushing to the elevator.

"Where is she going?"

Alex frowned. "I don't know."

She reappeared moments later, clutching a folded piece of cardboard. She stood in front of me, looking as serious as I'd ever seen my Little Owl.

"I made dis fo you."

I unfolded the cardboard and stared at the homemade gift. It was messy and chaotic—and the best present I'd ever received.

My Christmas Wish, it read across the top, obviously in her caregiver's hand. Underneath, my name, spelled out in pasta:

DYLAN and Noelle's crude, shaky rendition of my image, with curly macaroni for my hair, which made me grin. It suited me.

My tear-filled gaze flew to Alex's. She was watching me, her own eyes filled with tears. I could feel Seth's eyes on us, and I looked at Noelle.

"Thank you, Little Owl. It's perfect. I'll keep it forever."

Her eyes grew round. "Fuhevah? You lub it?"

I pulled her onto my knee and dropped a kiss on her messy curls. "I do love it. And I love you. Fuhevah."

She snuggled in with a happy sigh.

Mine echoed hers.

The mattress dipped beside me, and Alex's warm body curved to mine.

"Hey," she whispered.

I rolled over, pulling her to my chest. "What time is it?" I asked, still groggy.

"Almost two."

"You shouldn't have let me sleep so long."

She rubbed my arm. "Dylan, you had a three-hour nap. You were up all night."

I held her tighter. "I haven't slept well since I left you."

"Then I guess you have to stay."

"I guess so." I spoke quietly. "I'll have to go back and forth for a while . . ."

"I know."

I tilted up her face and kissed her. "But I'll hurry back. I promise."

"You better."

"Maybe you could come with me for a couple of days? We can take the kids with us over break or something?"

"Seth would like that."

"But not you?"

She hesitated, biting her lip. I could feel the tension in her body at the mere thought of coming with me.

I nuzzled her soft mouth. "Tell me, my darling girl."

"I was so lost when I was there, Dylan. I was scared all the time. I was broke, homesick, and I hated my job. I . . . I was attacked one night."

"Were you . . . did they hurt you?" I stumbled over the words, worried about her response.

"They didn't get that far—I fought them and managed to escape. But they got my purse, containing my ID and some money, and I knew they had my address. It scared me so much, I stayed with some friends. They packed up my things, and I came home. It took me a long time to feel safe again." She sighed. "I think maybe that was one of the reasons I married Eric. I felt safe."

I held her as I thought about her words. I hated hearing how scared she'd been and the fact that she was attacked. I didn't want to force her to do anything that made her uncomfortable.

"I know you had a bad experience, Alex, but it will be different this time. I won't let anyone near you."

"I know. You'll be there."

I kissed her forehead, my lips lingering. "I'll always be there for you now, Alex. I can't be without you."

"I'll come with you."

"Thank you. If you hate it, we can leave right away."

"It's only for a visit, right?"

The anxiety in her voice was evident, and I hastened to reassure her.

"Short visits. I'll bring you right back here where you belong. I promise."

She snuggled closer. "Okay."

I folded an arm under my head and glanced around. "I never thought I'd see this room again."

"I never thought you would either."

"Lots of good memories in here," I teased.

She pointed to the bathroom door. "In there too."

I groaned and rolled over, pinning her under me. "Alex, my darling girl, unless you tell me I have you alone for the next few hours, don't be reminding me of that shower . . . and how talented this wicked little mouth of yours is," I added, tracing her bottom lip with my finger.

She nipped at my finger. "I think we have about another five minutes before Noelle will burst in here. Plus, the fact that dinner is almost ready and there are a bunch of people downstairs wanting to meet and talk to my fiancé. But," she added with a wicked smile, "the kids were up very early, which means they'll both be flaked out by seven or so. And George goes back to Susan's every year to spend time with her and her family. He won't be home until tomorrow."

I lowered my mouth to hers, hovering over her lips. "So, after seven, you're all mine?"

"I'm already yours," she whispered. "But after seven, you can show me as often as you want."

I kissed her hard—a promise of what would be happening later. I planned to show her often.

The pounding of little feet heading our way made me pull back.

I kissed her once more, my mouth lingering on her smooth lips. "I can hardly wait until seven."

Her eyes were wide with desire. "Me too."

The bar area was full of holiday cheer. Alex had pushed all the tables together, making a large U shape, and had the room festively decorated and filled with her friends. Susan and her family, Jodi from the store in town and her husband Adam, and other people from the Pinegrove community. They all met and greeted me welcomingly, shaking my hand, kissing my cheek, congratulating both of us. No one seemed surprised by our news, but pleased for Alex. I couldn't keep my eyes off her, and Noelle hardly left my side, her little hand tucked into mine or perched on my hip as I walked around. Alex had let me give her the owl necklace for her birthday. Her face had been filled with wonder and her breathy little "so pwetty" made my heart warm. She promised countless times to take the "bethest care" of it, so Alex let her wear it. She showed it to everyone, which made me grin every time.

Seth spent a lot of time in the corner with his girl, Cindy. She was shy and sweet and gazed at him with adoration written across her face. Still, often, when I would glance over, he was looking in my direction, as if to make sure I was still there. I realized we would all be checking on each other for a while. It was going to take all of us some time to be sure and to trust fully. I was determined to do everything I could to set all their fears to rest.

After a huge meal, two slices of Alex's amazing pie, and more sugar cookies, I sat back, replete. I swore I had never tasted anything as good as Alex's cooking. She sat beside me, holding a sleepy Noelle, and chatted to Adam. She had her free hand tucked into mine, and I gazed at the two most important women in my life with a lazy smile. Unable to resist, I stroked Noelle's cheek and dropped a kiss onto Alex's.

Beside me, George chuckled. "You have it bad, son."

I tore my gaze away and turned to him. "I do."

"What are your plans?"

"Marry her as fast as possible and start our life," I stated with conviction.

He frowned.

I was confused. Surely, that was what he wanted?

"All well and good, Dylan. But where will you live? You'll tear this place down in the spring, and I'm assuming you don't want to stay in a guest room until that point."

My brow furrowed. I hadn't thought of that. All I had thought of was making Alex mine.

"Good point," I mused.

Jodi leaned across the table. "I heard the McAllister place is going up for sale."

George nodded. "So did I."

The name rang a bell. "McAllister?"

"The Gables. It's a family-run place about halfway between here and Halifax. Right on the ocean—great property."

I recalled looking at it once. The reason the name rang a bell was that it was on my list of properties I was watching earlier in the year.

"Really," I mused, my interest piqued.

"You know," he said and winked, looking amused, "Alex used to work there in the summers when she was young. Loved the place. Her second-favorite spot to here. It has a spectacular view—not as amazing as the bluff, but pretty damn close."

"Is that right?"

Jodi chuckled. "Fabulous house—they even recently did a bunch of upgrades. Huge family home and separate guest cottages. You could live in it and have a nice business at the same time on the side, if you wanted. For someone, you know, needing a place to live right away. I heard they wanted a fast sale—their daughter found out she is having triplets and needs them to be close."

I had to laugh at the pair of them. "I'm onto the two of you. You're about as subtle as a bat to the head."

George shrugged, his eyes dancing. "I was just telling you. I happen to be having lunch with Doug day after tomorrow. At his place. In case, you know, you were interested in coming along and checking out the view."

It wouldn't hurt. I could look into the place, get information before it went up for sale if I was interested, and it would solve a problem I hadn't thought of until now. A home for us while I had Alex's dream house built. The fact that Alex had a fondness for the property was also a deciding factor. I wanted to give her everything. Make every dream she'd ever had come true.

I started to chuckle. I had a feeling I'd be buying more property before the new year.

"What time is lunch, George?"

Alex sighed, a muted little breath that drifted over my skin. I pulled her closer. "Tell me what you're thinking."

"I'm not sure," she admitted. "Yesterday, I was trying to figure out how to get through the holidays, and today, you're here, we're engaged, and you told me you want to buy a place you've never seen for us to move to . . . and you want to get married right away."

"So, you're saying it's too much."

She tilted up her head, smiling at me. "It is a lot, Dylan."

I tucked a long strand of hair away from her face. "I know, but hear me out. I don't want to wait to marry you. You already said you don't want a big fuss, so we can do it here, some friends and us. I mean, why wait? We can start the new year as a family. As for the house, George is right—I can't stay in this room and have you running down the hall as if we're doing something wrong. I can't stay in your room." I snorted. "I don't think I could fit on your bed."

Alex laughed, and I kept talking.

"I'll go have lunch with George and Doug, and have a look at the place. If it's a good investment, and you love it, I'll buy it and sell it once our home is ready. But Jodi is right—if it works, you can run it as a business in the busy season, if that's what you want. If not, we can live in it."

She worried her lip. "You're buying it because you think I love it."

I shrugged. "That's part of it. But I checked it out. It's a good fit. Well-laid-out, in great condition, close enough it won't disrupt the kids' lives—they can go to the same school and daycare, keep their friends. You'll be happy." I sucked in a nervous breath. "And when I have to leave on my trips, I'll know you're somewhere you love and feel safe."

She didn't respond, so I continued.

"It's got a fabulous loft at the back. They added it a couple of years ago. I can use it as my office until I decide what to do—open a place in town or work from home," I added. "It ticks so many boxes."

"The money . . ."

Ah. And now we reach the real crux of the matter.

"Alex," I began gently, "look at me."

Her expressive eyes lifted to mine, the worry in them evident. "My darling girl, I'm rich. Very rich. You will never have to work yourself into exhaustion again. You never have to work if you don't want to. You will *never* want for anything. The kids will never want for anything again. I can afford to buy it—I can afford to give you anything you want. You don't have to worry about that." I brushed my knuckles down her cheek. "I'll take care of you all now."

"I don't love you for your money."

"That is what makes your love so sweet. I know you love me for me. And for the first time, I want to share my life and *everything* I have with someone. *With you*. That includes making all your dreams come true." I frowned when I saw her biting her lip. "Is that what you think? That I'm worried about why you love me? Or are you worried about what other people will think when they hear you got married. *Who* you married?"

"I don't know," she admitted honestly.

"I don't care what other people think or say. I know why you love me. Your friends and family know." I chuckled. "Hell, even Mrs. C knows, and she hasn't met you yet. We are meant for each other, Alex. Even if I didn't have a dime, you'd love me."

"Yes, I would." She nodded fervently.

"Relax about the money, please."

"How will I . . . contribute? I need to feel I'm bringing something to our relationship."

I gaped at her. "How will you . . ." My voice trailed off, and I yanked her to me tightly. "Alex, I was lost before you. As Arlene pointed out, all I did was go through the motions. You woke me up and showed me what living can be. Today was the happiest Christmas I've ever had—and the first day in my entire life I didn't feel truly alone. What you *bring* me is love. What you *give* me is you. What you *contribute* is your unconditional support of me and *us* becoming a family. That is worth more money or gifts than I could ever offer." I held her face between my hands and met her gaze. "It's me who needs to feel I'm offering enough, Alex. Not the other way around."

"I love you," she whispered, tears falling down her face.

"And I love you. Do you understand now? Your contribution is priceless. I need to know you understand that."

"Yes," she said, and I wiped away the tears.

"Good. So, New Year's Eve—we have a date? You'll marry me?"

"Definitely."

"Can I take you away on a honeymoon?"

She hesitated. I could see her struggling over what she wanted, and what she felt she had to do.

"We'll make sure the kids are looked after. We won't go for long, and we'll plan a family trip in the spring, okay?"

"Okay. Could we go somewhere warm? Do you . . ." She paused. "Do you think we could go somewhere warm with a beach? Like Florida?"

I frowned. "I think we could do better than Florida. Why don't we save that for a trip with the kids—we can take them to Disney World. I'll take you somewhere a little more exotic—and private. Maybe Fiji or the Bahamas."

Her eyes lit up.

"So, that's a definite yes to both?" I loved how happy such a little thing could make her. All she wanted was a warm place—I'd give her that—a private beach, a villa, and us naked. Naked a lot.

"Yes."

"Then we need to get the license when they open the day after tomorrow."

"Sounds perfect."

"We'll go there in the morning, then have lunch with George and Doug and see the house."

"You never do things half measured, do you?"

"Nope. I'm goal-oriented. And my current goals are simple. Marry you, move into a place where I can keep you beside me all night long, and start making more babies."

"I like these goals." She hummed. "But . . ."

"But what?" I asked, worried. Maybe she didn't want more children.

"Can we wait a bit on the babies? There's so much to grasp . . . and I don't want Seth and Noelle upset by so much change, and I just need . . ."

"A little time?" I finished.

She nodded. "I want more children, Dylan. I want them with you. But I want time for us first. Time for the kids to adapt and for this not to feel like a dream."

"So, it's not a no. It's a wait a little while?"

"Yes."

"I can handle that. It makes sense," I admitted. "I do like the idea of just us for a while."

"Thank you."

I grinned at her, then rolled, and in a second, I had her underneath me, my mouth hovering over hers. "I think we should practice, though."

Her hands tugged me closer, our bodies meshing perfectly. "Yes, yes, we should. Lots and lots of practice." She pulled me down to her mouth.

Once again, I was home.

CHAPTER 16

DYLAN

I walked around the main floor of the inn, the silence bliss to my ears. The tree lights were still on, some of the gifts under the tree, yet to be put away. It had been such an amazing day. Upstairs, Alex and the kids were asleep.

After we'd spent hours together, making love and talking, discussing plans and our future, Alex had fallen asleep. I carried her down the hall and tucked her into her little bed. A few more nights, we'd be married and I could keep her beside me, but for now, she needed to be close to Noelle. I couldn't sleep, though, and had come downstairs to get a brandy, hoping the liquor would help me relax. I glanced at my watch, to note it wasn't quite midnight yet, and suddenly, I knew why the day didn't feel *done*. Why it wasn't complete.

I reached into my pocket for my phone and dialed a number I knew by heart.

"Hello, dear boy." Arlene's warm voice came over the line. "I was wondering if you'd forgotten me today."

"Never."

"Was it a good day?"

"The best day of my life."

"Oh, Dylan."

"They were so happy to see me, Arlene. Me, not my gifts. Me."

"Of course they were. They love you."

"I asked her to marry me."

There was silence. "Well, my boy, you've surprised even me."

"I think I surprised everyone."

"And?"

"Are you busy New Year's Eve?"

"What?" She gasped.

"We're getting married here. I want you . . . I *need* you here. Please, Arlene . . . you're my family. I want you to be a part of the most important day of my life."

I was sure I heard a quiet sob before she replied, her voice thick with emotion. "There is no other place I'd rather be."

"Arrange with Roger to fly you and Simon out."

"I will."

"I need my blue suit."

She chuckled. "I already knew that would be the one you'd want. I'll pick it up and some more of your personal things."

I leaned my forehead against the window, taking in the vista that surrounded me. "How did you know?" I asked quietly.

"I didn't," she confessed. "But talking to George, and the way he spoke of her, I just . . ." She paused before continuing. " . . . I had a feeling you had to meet her. He was so worried about her future, I was worried about yours. She sounded perfect for you. It seemed . . . like fate."

"It was—and she is."

"I'm so pleased, Dylan. This is the best news you've ever shared with me."

"I can't wait for you to meet my girl."

"I can't wait to meet her either."

"So, I'll see you in a few days?"

She laughed. "You will."

"Thank you." I blew out a long breath. "I love you, Arlene. You're like a mother to me."

She didn't even try to disguise her sobs. "Thank you, dear boy. You're like my own. I'll see you soon."

"I can't wait," I replied and ended the call.

"Have you ever told her that?" Alex's voice startled me.

I turned, held out my hand for her, pulling her close, and placed a kiss on her head.

"No, I don't think I have. I think she knew how I felt, but I never said it." I sighed, looking down at Alex's sweet face. "I've only ever said it to two people. You were the first. You've opened up a side of me I didn't know existed, Alex."

She snuggled into my chest. "I like this side."

"Well, that's good to know. She's coming for the wedding. It wouldn't surprise me if she showed up tomorrow or the next day."

"I can hardly wait to meet her. I hope . . . I hope she likes us."

"Alex, she will love you—all of you. I have no doubt." I stroked her cheek with my finger. "I love all of you, so much—but especially you, Alex. You've become the most important thing in my world. I hope you know that."

"I think I do."

She shivered a little in my arms, and I pulled her closer. "You should be in bed."

"I was lonely without you. In fact," she admitted, "when I woke up in my own bed, I thought I had dreamed the whole thing. But your ring was there, so I knew it was real."

"I didn't want to confuse Noelle."

She tilted up her head. "Soon we won't have to pretend."

"Hmm, I like that."

She pressed against me. "I can still come to visit."

I grinned, lowering my face to hers. "We can use my room for alone time, and you sleep there?"

"It's only for a few nights."

Knowing she was right and soon we'd be together, I nodded. "I can work with that."

I was right. Arlene Carson breezed in the next night, bringing with her the two things I loved the most: her impeccable organizational skills and her need to make sure I was looked after.

An hour after she arrived, it was as if she'd known Alex and her family their entire life. Alex sat beside her on the sofa with Noelle perched on her knee. George listened with rapt attention to every word she spoke, and even Seth leaned in, anxious to hear what she had to say—which was a lot. Simon and I sat on another sofa sipping scotch, cast aside to the wonder that was Mrs. C.

"We might as well not be here," I mumbled, taking a generous sip.

"Get used to it," Simon snorted. "At least we have some good scotch."

"I heard you," Arlene sang, casting a frown in our direction. "Do not drink that scotch all night. We have a lot to do and only a few days to get it done. We have a wedding to organize, a house to buy, and then we need to get these two lovebirds off on a honeymoon."

I brightened a little at those words.

"Dylan," she ordered, "tomorrow you and Alex get the license. I'll arrange everything else. We'll go look at the house when you get back, and you can work on the honeymoon. You have to be back by the twentieth. I've changed our cruise date until then."

"Why?"

She looked at me as if I had six heads. "I'll be staying to look after Noelle and Seth while you're gone and also to help George with his move. I've already spoken with Jodi, who was very helpful, and she has recommended a contractor for anything that has to happen to the house before you get back."

Alex nodded. "Michael is great."

"Won't, ah, Doug be a little upset when you show up with a bunch of strangers, George?"

He grinned. "I spoke with him and he's fine. We'll visit after you leave. I'm certain you'll love the property, Dylan."

"Okay, then."

George was right. I did love it, and I could see Alex did too. It was called the Gables because of the many ornate gables adorning the house. An older, Victorian-style house, it had been well cared for and added to with the addition of a large loft and sunroom on the back that took full advantage of the view. There were six good-sized bedrooms, including a massive master with its own bathroom, a large kitchen, and a family room, with spectacular views from every window.

There was an expansive piece of property that contained five self-contained cottages, each a miniature version of the main house. It held immense potential for investment, but more importantly was the potential it held for being a home filled with happiness for my new family. By the end of the afternoon, I'd shaken hands on yet another large deal in the small province of Nova Scotia. They were thrilled with the offer, and the fact that we wanted in as swiftly as they wanted out. We could move in right after we came back from our honeymoon. They were taking all their furniture and personal items, but the cottages stayed intact. Arlene was already making notes with

Alex about buying beds and other pieces of furniture, so our plans were well underway.

It was all so fast, so unexpected, I knew I should be nervous, anxious, and feeling out of control. Instead, I felt as if things were falling into place in my life, and I was remarkably calm.

New Year's Eve dawned bright and filled with promises. When I went downstairs to find Alex, the lower level had been transformed. Flowers and tulle were draped everywhere, minute fairy lights scattered around. The mantel piled high with candles, flowers, and pinecones. As I stood gazing around, I felt my chest tighten in anticipation. Right there was where I would marry my Alex. In a couple of hours, she would be mine—forever.

A noise made me turn, and I saw her watching me. I held out my hand, smiling as she came closer. I tugged her into my arms, kissing her softly. "Are you ready for this?"

She nodded, eyes large in her face. "I have to keep pinching myself to know it's not a dream."

I chuckled. "I may be more of a nightmare at times."

She arched her eyebrow at me, a move I'd found very sexy since she had started doing it a few days ago. "As long as you're Dylan and not snobby Dylan we'll be fine."

I laughed and kissed her hard. "You've been spending too much time with Mrs. C—only she gets to call me snobby."

I became serious. "I can hardly wait to make you mine tonight."

She smiled up at me, a mischievous expression dancing across her face. "Here, or do you mean later at the hotel?"

I groaned, burying my face into her neck and dropping kisses onto her supple skin. Since Arlene and Simon had arrived, we hadn't been together. Their room was between Alex's and mine, and Arlene's hearing was too good. Given everything else going on, we agreed to hold off until the wedding and we were finally alone. At the time I agreed, I found it a rather romantic gesture, but that lasted a day or so. Every chance I got, I dragged Alex behind a closed door and kissed her until we were both panting with want. But no matter where I took her, someone always found us. However, tonight, I'd finally have her alone, and tomorrow we would leave on our honeymoon—two glorious weeks of simply us. I had the villa in the Bahamas booked. It was secluded and private, with its own beach and pool. Staff was on call for meals or anything we wanted, but other than that, she was all mine.

"I'm so ready to start our life," I murmured against her mouth, dragging my tongue over her plump bottom lip.

"Me too."

I tilted my head to kiss her as the elevator door opened and Arlene strolled out, a clipboard in hand. "Ah, there you are, Dylan. We have some things to go over, then I'm stealing Alex for the afternoon."

I leaned my forehead to Alex's, fighting a groan. It was as if Arlene knew I was about to kiss Alex and appeared. Every damn time.

Alex giggled, and I realized I'd spoken out loud. She leaned up and kissed me fast. "Tonight," she promised. "I'll make up for it tonight."

"You bet you will!" I growled as she walked away. I narrowed my eyes at Arlene, then burst out laughing when she grinned at me, not the least bit worried over my glare. She knew what she was doing.

"You'll pay, old woman!" I called after her, turning to get a cup of coffee.

"Whatever, dear boy," she replied, making me chuckle.

I glanced at my watch. In six hours, I'd be married, and Alex would be my wife.

Six hours until I could kiss her again.

It was dark by 4:00 p.m. The candles flickered, and the scent of the flowers wafted through the air as Alex and I exchanged vows in front of a small gathering of those we both loved the most. I had flown in a few friends, as well as Mrs. C's family, and the rest of the guests were Alex's crew. I never invited nor thought to let my father know what was happening. I knew he wouldn't care, and I had no desire to give him the chance to ruin the day for me.

Alex wore a gorgeous, knee-length, lacy dress and I wore my favorite dark blue suit Arlene had brought with her. My best man, Seth, stood beside me, anxious and proud, and behind him was Simon. Noelle was beside her mother, far more interested in the pretty flowers she was holding for Alex than the service going on in front of her. All she knew, all she cared about, was that, as of today, she could call me Daddy. When she had asked me, I was so overcome I could barely speak, and I'd had to look to Alex, unsure how she would feel about it.

She had smiled lovingly, running her hand over Noelle's wild curls. "I think Dylan would like that, but after we're married okay, sweetheart?"

"Otay," she said, her slipper-covered feet bouncing with happiness. "I can wait!"

Seth had snorted. "I ain't calling you Daddy."

I had to laugh, grateful for his humor restoring some lightness to the moment. "I think Dylan will do, Seth," I agreed.

"Yeah, well, for now," he stated, not looking my way.

My gaze met Alex's, and I knew there was another conversation we would have to have. I wasn't simply marrying her; I was marrying them as well. I would do whatever I needed to do to make sure they understood how important they were.

Alex squeezed my hand, bringing me back to the moment. Behind her, Arlene grinned at me, and I realized people were waiting for me to speak.

I said the words I never thought I would hear myself utter.

"I do."

Moments later, vows spoken, rings exchanged, Alex was mine. Forever.

Leaning down, I captured her lips, kissing her deeply. I held her close, not wanting the moment to end.

Then I felt it—the small tug on my trouser leg. I broke away from Alex and looked down into Noelle's sweet little face. She lifted her arms up, her smile wide.

"My turn, Daddy."

THE FUTURE

ALEX

"No. This isn't right." Dylan tugged on his hair, then waved his hand over the set of plans he was studying.

The architect sighed. "I've done everything you asked, Dylan. Can you explain what's wrong?"

Dylan huffed a sigh. "I don't know. I just don't know."

I shifted in my chair, my lower back feeling achy. I studied my husband and looked around the large office.

This was the Dylan I knew the least. The place I disliked the most. In the city, he became the Dylan I first met. Cool, removed—in control and exact with what he wanted, and how he wanted it.

No one but those closest to him saw the real Dylan. Warm, tender, loving, and patient to a fault. Nothing fazed him when it came to our family or our life. He was an amazing father, a good friend, and the sexiest, most loving husband a woman could hope for in her life. That man disappeared when he donned his expensive, well-tailored suit and stepped foot in his company's office. Businessman Dylan appeared, and he reminded me too much of the man Dylan had been when I had met him, the man hiding behind his pain. I knew it was his cover and the man I married was the real Dylan, but still, I didn't like coming to Toronto.

The day he exploded into my life was one I would never forget. He made me feel things I didn't think I would ever experience. Seth thought he was the coolest person ever, and Noelle . . . well, she adored him. She still did. He brought forth a passion I didn't even know existed within me, and I fell for him so hard and so fast, I didn't know which way was up. The day he left, it was as if the world had lost its light. He couldn't see his value—how special he was, or the non-material gifts he had to offer. He didn't see how he completed us or made us a family—all he saw, all he thought, was he had nothing to give.

When he showed up, bearing too many presents, a beautiful ring, and the perfect gift of his heart, was the best day of my life. I didn't care about his money, his company, or anything else. Only him. When he told me he loved me, my world was complete. That was the Dylan I knew—and loved.

I was looking forward to our flight home in the evening. I hadn't really wanted to come this time, but since finding out I was pregnant, Dylan was loath to leave me, no matter how short the trip. He also wanted me to see the plans for the new house. The same architect had done the design for the new Edgewater Resort. I had jokingly suggested Dylan keep the name Sleepy Moose Inn, but I had been outvoted quickly. Edgewater Resort did suit the property. Dylan had asked John to draw up plans for our house on the bluff. But nothing seemed to work.

I sat up and sighed quietly, rubbing my back. But it wasn't quiet enough. Dylan's head snapped up, and he saw what I was doing, immediately hurrying over. In the matter of several steps, he changed into my Dylan. His cool manner melted, his eyes warm and concerned as he dropped to his knees in front of me.

"Hey, darling girl." He reached around to rub my sore muscles. "Are you okay?"

"Just a little tired."

He leaned closer, laying his hand on my stomach and rubbing it in tender circles. "Are you being kicked everywhere?"

I chuckled. "They're both pretty active."

"We'll be home soon, and you'll rest better. I know you don't sleep well here." He stood and held out his hand. "Come look at these plans. Maybe you can tell me what's wrong."

He pulled me to my feet and dropped a heavy kiss on my head, leading me to the table. I looked over the plans, which confirmed what I already expected. I smiled at John, who was looking at me for any clue.

"Do you think you could leave us with these for a bit?"

"Of course. Take your time. Why don't you call me in a few days, Dylan?"

Dylan huffed out a sigh. "Fine."

John shook our hands and left.

Dylan stood beside me, frowning.

I traced the design. "I'm surprised you don't see it."

His voice wasn't impatient or upset but weary. "Don't see what, Alex?"

"Look again, Dylan. What are you trying to make here?"

He looked over the drawings. "Your dream house, Alex. A home for us."

I smiled up at him. "We already have that at the Gables. You're trying to recreate your favorite parts into another house."

He stared at me, then at the plans. "Oh my God, I am."

I leaned against the table. "Dylan, we all love it at the Gables. Why are you insisting we move?"

"Because the bluff was your dream, Alex. I want to give it to you."

"You already gave me my dream, Dylan. I have you."

"But the house . . . the bluff . . ."

"I have another bluff now. You built me a lovely place to sit and spend time. You know how much I love my sun-house."

"I wanted to give you this dream."

I shook my head. "I've been trying to tell you for months, Dylan. You already have. I wanted a home, love, and to feel safe. The bluff was my hideaway. It was where I went when I needed to feel centered. I have all that at the Gables. Our home—*you*—center me. The kids love it there. We have plenty of room, it's easy access to Edgewater or Halifax. You love your office, and I enjoy running the cottages . . . when they're not full of company, that is."

He chuckled. Most of the time, they were filled with personal guests. Arlene and Simon, their family, and George were constant visitors. We took guests on occasion, and even those were regulars.

He looked at the design. "So, you don't want to move?"

"One day, when we're older and the kids are gone and we want a smaller place. Change the design and build it as the honeymoon cottage, Dylan. Fill it with people in love. Let that soak into the walls for the next thirty years, and we'll move in and finish our lives there, together." I smiled up at him. "We can even rent it and have dirty weekends away when the kids drive us crazy." I nudged him in the ribs. "I know the owner, you know, I can get us a good rate."

He burst out laughing, wrapping his arms around me. "That would work. I can have John keep the private road, and the people renting the cottage have access. It gives them privacy. Then when we're ready—in *forty or fifty* years"—he cocked an eyebrow at me—"we can make it ours." He glanced back at the design. "A bungalow, two bedrooms, and the back wall all glass so we see the view from every room."

I leaned up on my tiptoes and kissed him. "Perfect."

He pulled me closer, bringing my mouth to his for another kiss. "Yes," he whispered. "You are."

I glanced over at my sleeping wife. She had been so exhausted when we arrived home last night, she hadn't even moved as I lifted her from the passenger seat and carried her inside. The one time she stirred was when I tugged her shirt over her head and tucked her into our big bed. She half smiled at me, attempting to pat my cheek and missing totally, falling right back to sleep.

I should have left her at home when I flew to Toronto. I knew she didn't like the big city—it frightened her still, even with me beside her, but since she had told me she was pregnant, my protectiveness had kicked into high gear. I hated not being close—she seemed to feel the same—and agreed to come with me since it was only for two days.

I rested my hand on her already rounded stomach. After we were married that New Year's Eve in front of the fireplace with friends, and had a perfect—but too short—honeymoon, we started our life together.

We went home, moved into the Gables, and became a family. After a long discussion, I adopted Noelle and Seth, who had surprised me when he told me he would like to be a Maxwell as well. Like Noelle, he had never known his father, and he felt his mother would be pleased he was part of a new family.

I still got a warm feeling in my chest when I heard my Little Owl call me Daddy. Seth waffled between calling me Dad and Dylan, depending on what he wanted at the time. On the rare occasion, he'd mutter "Asshole," but luckily they were few and far between—he was a great kid, and I was proud of him.

I was thrilled the day Alex threw out her birth control pills. It took us a few months before she was pregnant, but we did it thoroughly, and she was expecting twins. My masculine pride knew no bounds, which made Alex laugh.

I slid out of bed to leave her to sleep, dragged a T-shirt over my head, and headed down to the kitchen. I was still hopeless at making coffee or doing anything else in the kitchen, but Alex kept a Keurig on the counter for me. So, I made a cup of coffee and carried it over to table, sitting back and enjoying the view. George insisted the view on the bluff was the most scenic, but I actually preferred my current view. The vast expanse of openness from the bluff was wild and isolating. The view from the Gables was tranquil and welcoming. Farther inland, the water kissed the rocky shore in gentle swells, and at low tide, my Little Owl and I loved to walk together, searching for new treasures. The more protected cove made it a great place for swimming and boating.

I loved the house. The moment we'd stepped inside, I loved it, and I knew I'd buy it. It was everything we wanted and together, we had made it a home.

Alex was right—I didn't want to move. We were so happy at the Gables. Friends and family often occupied the five guest cottages, but in the busy summer months, Alex loved having new faces to introduce to her beloved province. It kept her busy, and with a slight smirk, I had to admit, it gave her a break from me. She was an excellent assistant, and she worked hard to keep me in line, never taking any of my shit. I loved working with her, and I'd be lying if I didn't confess I pouted a little on the days she had "other things" to do.

Edgewater was a booming success. After much thought, and many plans, I changed my mind on the scope of the project. It was still a high-end destination, but not as large as I had originally projected. I kept the main building smaller and added more cottages, catering to both families and couples looking to get away somewhere private. I used the land to scatter them around, and the place was booked year-round. And heading it up . . . was none other than Amy. She flew down with Arlene one trip, met one of the contractors, fell in love, and moved to Pinegrove. While she was there, she showed a remarkable aptitude for running the show. Whereas she failed at taking orders, she was amazing at issuing them, and she ran the guest services to perfection. She also ran Michael, but he seemed to enjoy it. She and Alex hit it off and had become fast friends. Amy and I had finally found a plateau on which we could both function, and to my surprise, we got along well too.

But knowing the magic of the place, nothing should surprise me anymore. It had certainly changed my life—for the better.

The sound of tiny feet heading my way made me smile. I turned in my chair, holding out my arms as the feet sped up.

"Daddy, you're home!"

Seconds later, I was holding my Little Owl, subjected to her usual greeting of wet little kisses all over my face. They were my favorite.

Her teeth were back, her lisp gone, and her vocabulary much larger. Silence was her enemy, but she was still my Noelle. She had remained tiny, her hair wild and curly, and my knee still her favorite place to sit.

"Hey, Little Owl. Miss me?"

She giggled. "Yes! Seth is too bossy."

I grinned. Seth had grown up. Now nineteen, his eyes were on the future. Unlike Alex, he loved going to Toronto with me, and I took him quite often. He had taken a year off after graduating, unsure what he wanted to do. Finally, he came to me for one of our talks, and he told me he wanted to go to the University of Toronto and get his business degree. Then, shyly, he informed me he would like the chance to work with me. The thought of him by my side, learning from me, had filled me with pride. With eyes for his Cindy alone, he was thrilled when she decided to follow him to Toronto to study nursing.

So, come the fall, he would be leaving us and starting a new life. Granted, he would have it far easier than most kids his age. I had never sold my condo, using in it when I was in town, so he and Cindy would be living there, and on occasion when I was in town, I would be their guest. I also insisted on paying for his tuition. He'd been through so much at a young age; I wanted to make it easy on him. Cindy's parents struggled financially, and I slyly found a way of paying her tuition as well without insulting them. Both Alex and I adored Cindy and were sure, when the time was right, she would be part of our family too.

We were also both certain, given the love Seth had for the hustle and bustle of the big city, that he would remain there. I already envisioned him taking over my company one day, and then passing it on to his son or daughter.

Noelle tugged on my arm, bringing me back to the present. "Can we go find some shells today?"

I nuzzled her head. "Sure."

"Will Mommy come with us?"

"Probably not. She's pretty tired."

"Maybe we can make her breakfast?"

I grinned. "Maybe lunch would be better." Sandwiches, I was good at. Plus, Alex always had soup in the freezer, and I could reheat things really well. "Maybe Seth will be awake by then."

She giggled, leaning back into my chest. "He likes to sleep."

"That he does."

Noelle tilted up her head. "Did you pick a house?" she asked, and for the first time, I noticed the lack of excitement in her voice. Alex was right about the whole thing. None of us wanted to move.

I brushed the wild hair back from her forehead and pressed a kiss to the soft skin. "Mommy and I decided we would rather stay here. Is that okay with you?"

Her face lit up, brighter than the sun bouncing off the waves out in the ocean. She bobbed her head, looking excited. "I love my room! And the beach is fun!"

"Good. Then this is where we'll stay."

"Can we make a nursery now?"

I thought of the room at the end of the hall Alex kept wandering into each day. She would lean against the wall and look around, but she had never said a word. She wanted that room as the nursery. She wanted our children in that bright room with the big windows. And I would make sure she had it.

I grinned down at my daughter. "Wanna go do some fun stuff with Daddy?"

She nodded.

"Okay. Go get dressed, and we'll go see Jodi."

She clapped her hands. She loved Jodi.

"Okay!"

Alex was at the table when we got back, her hair damp from her shower. A cup of weak tea was in front of her—it was all she could stomach lately. She smiled at us as we walked in, our hands filled with bags.

"I wondered where the two of you were. I was sure you'd be down on the beach, but I checked and you weren't there."

I dropped a warm kiss on her upturned mouth, then sat beside her, resting my hands on her rounded stomach. "My Little Owl and I had things to do."

She laughed. "I figured you'd be together. I just wasn't sure where."

"We had some things to pick up."

"I see."

"Is Seth in the land of the living yet?"

She nodded as she took a sip of her tea. "Cindy came and got him. They went into Halifax to look for some school stuff." She sighed, a sad smile on her face. "I'm going to miss him."

I lifted her chin, smiling into her teary eyes. "You have to let him live his life, my darling girl. And I'll keep an eye on them. He'll be back for Christmas."

"I know."

"I'm here, Mommy!" Noelle called out. "I'll help with the babies!"

I scooped her up, sitting her on my knee. "You're gonna be the best big sister ever," I teased her, loving how she spread her tiny fingers across Alex's stomach.

"Are they playing today, Mommy?"

"They were, but I think they are having a nap."

"Ooooh," Noelle whispered. "I'll be quiet."

I grinned against her head. She was still beyond adorable. "Don't you wanna show Mommy what we got?"

She clapped her hands. "Can I, Daddy?"

"Yep."

Alex smiled. "What have the two of you done now?"

"We went shopping!" Noelle crowed.

I met Alex's gaze over Noelle's head.

She smiled tenderly at me, shaking her head. "Dylan . . ."

I lifted one shoulder. "We enlisted Jodi's help."

"That's even worse."

I laughed and handed her a bag containing her favorite chocolates. She loved the new outfit Noelle had picked and chuckled over the multicolored sneakers that lit up when Noelle walked on them. Noelle's sweet laughter drifted down the hall as she ran to hang up her new dress and no doubt stand in front of the mirror, tapping her feet.

When I handed Alex the flat bag, she frowned in curiosity, then gasped in delight at the contents. Jodi had found websites with lots of baby furniture and designs and printed them out. She also typed up links for places that carried the hundreds of items it seemed babies needed. Part of taking Alex to Toronto with me had been to take her shopping there, but between my work and her exhaustion, it never happened. Thanks to the internet, though, I could bring the shopping to her. Jodi knew Alex's tastes, and she helped me choose some sites that carried the sort of items she knew Alex would like.

I leaned forward and kissed my wife. "We're staying here in our home, so decorate the room at the end of the hall for our children, Alex. Whatever you want for them is yours. Jodi will come to help you if you want, and Michael will make any changes you need made and paint it. Okay?"

She cupped my cheek and nodded, her eyes brimming with tears. "Thank you, Dylan."

"Thank you, my darling girl, for knowing what was right for our family. For knowing me." I turned my face to press a kiss to her palm. "You're my everything, Alex. I love you."

She smiled—the warm, wonderful smile I so loved to see. The one she had for me and me alone.

"I love you too."

Thick, white snow swirled outside our windows, the wind ferocious in its intensity. Wet, heavy clumps of drifts surrounded our home, the storm so intense, I couldn't see the ocean and beach that normally greeted me. I knew tomorrow I would be using the huge snow blower I purchased, and that once again, I would be grateful for investing in the massive SUV we owned. It was the closest I could get to a minivan without actually having to drive one. Alex still did, the one big difference being it was new, well-serviced, and very safe. It held the most precious cargo in the world—my family.

Inside our home, it was warm, safe, and dry. The storm that raged was muted by the heavy building protecting us. My Noelle slept soundly—completely unaware of the storm outside, her wild curls spread on her pillow, making her odd snuffling sounds. I grinned as I tucked her feet back under the covers, knowing ten minutes after I was gone, she would have kicked them off again. Leaning down, I brushed a kiss to her forehead and left her room, leaving her door ajar in case she did wake and was frightened.

I passed Seth's room and paused in the doorway. His bed was neatly made up, the room spotless—everything in its place, except for the boy. Happy and busy in Toronto, he loved his new world. Even though we spoke almost daily and Skyped all the time, I missed his cheerful disposition and our easy camaraderie. And I really missed having another male in the house—I was entirely outnumbered now.

I moved down the hall to my intended destination. In the nursery, I checked on my two tiniest daughters. They were both asleep, their little fists curled under their cheeks, the storm not bothering them in the least. I traced my finger over the downy cheek of our eldest twin, Joy. Born ten minutes ahead of her sister Hope, she weighed a whole pound more, and she was already the ruler of the nursery and the house. Her cry was distinctive and loud, and her temper rivalled mine. Her younger, tinier sister, rarely cried, seemingly content to let Joy take the lead and make sure someone looked after all their needs.

I couldn't stay away from either of them.

Hope's little arm shifted, her fist opening, and she bleated a tiny sound. Without a thought, I scooped her into my arms and sat in the rocking chair, holding her close. She nuzzled into my chest, her warmth seeping into my skin as we rocked. I knew she was fine, but I couldn't resist any opportunity to hold her or her sister. Alex often came in to find me dozing in the chair, both the girls nestled on my chest as I slumbered.

The tenderness I had for these tiny beings was overwhelming at times. I didn't think I could love anything or anybody more than I loved my wife, but their birth proved me wrong. It was as if my heart expanded—and the happiness and devotion they brought forth strengthened and grew the love I was capable of giving. The love Alex had helped me discover.

A quiet squeak of the floorboards had me looking up. Alex was leaning on the doorframe, a gentle smile on her face.

"I thought I'd find you in here."

"Just checking on the chicklets." I kissed Hope's head. "Noelle was obviously fighting dragons again, but I tucked her back in. Joy was good, but Hope was a little restless and fussing. I thought I could settle her down."

Alex crossed over, standing in front of us. Leaning down, she ran her finger over Hope's downy head. "Dylan," she murmured. "We have monitors you know. I heard her, ah, 'fussing.'"

I grinned, not at all upset she caught me.

She bent down, brushing her lips over mine. "You're such a good daddy. But you're going to spoil them."

"I want to spoil them, Alex. I never want them to doubt how much they are loved."

"They never will, Dylan. They will never experience the kind of neglect you did. You're too full of love for us to let that happen."

My emotions were dangerously close to the surface tonight. My eyes burned with unshed tears as I gazed at my wife—the woman who had changed my life, and shown me how to truly live.

Her eyes widened at the sight of my tears, and she slipped my daughter out of my embrace and nestled her back into her safe crib. I held out my arms, and Alex climbed on my lap, fitting her body to mine, drawing my head to her shoulder.

"What is it?" She ran her fingers through my hair.

"Do you know what today is, Alex?"

"Tuesday?"

I chuckled and kissed her soft skin. Glancing up, I met her concerned gaze. "Three years ago, I arrived in this province with one intention: meeting with George to buy his property." I smiled at her. "I walked into the Sleepy Moose Inn, and lost my heart instead."

"You got what you came for," she reminded me.

"I got a lot more than I expected. I fell in love with a bossy little slip of a woman who thought I was an *ath-hole*, but loved me anyway."

She giggled at the memory of that first night. "You were rather bossy yourself."

"I was lost. It was the only way I could deal with the world and nobody figured it out."

She cupped my cheek, wiping the lone tear that had trickled down my face.

"You gave me everything, Alex. You showed me what love was. With you, I got a new life, a family, and for the first time in my life—I wasn't alone." I touched her lips with mine. "You are my life. Our family is my life."

"I know."

"I love you."

She sighed and guided my head back to her shoulder. "I love you too, Dylan. We all love you."

I held her close.

"You want to go back to bed?" she whispered.

"No."

I felt her smile. "You want to go to the kitchen and have a snack?"

"Yes."

"Noelle and I made your favorites this afternoon."

I smiled at her. "Sugar cookies?"

She returned my smile. "You always feel better once you've had a little bit of Christmas sugar."

I captured her mouth with mine, kissing her deeply.

I could taste her sweetness.

Feel her love.

She was the very best kind of sugar.

AN UNEXPECTED GIFT

CHAPTER ONE

EVAN

The night was black around me. With no streetlights or other cars to be seen, the inkiness seemed deeper—the snow falling on the cold winter night bright in the headlights. It was accumulating fast, the road becoming icy and slippery. I had to concentrate on driving, and my hands were tired from gripping the wheel.

The car lurched, made a strange noise, then sputtered and huffed, slowly rolling to a stop on the side of the road. I roared out in frustration.

"Goddammit!"

I leaned my head back on the headrest, trying to rein in my anger.

I knew the unpredictability of the Canadian winter. When the weather report says "chances of snow," it was a pretty damn certain thing.

What the hell possessed me to leave the quiet safety of my house to drive across the country two days before Christmas, to go see my family? What stupid sense of duty prompted my action?

I barked out a laugh, the sound loud in the car. So much for a surprise for them. The joke was really on me. They didn't know I was coming, and now, I wasn't sure I'd get there. From the strange sound my car had made just before it died, I wasn't sure I'd get home either. I was screwed either way.

I tried the engine again, but it wouldn't turn over. I slammed my hand on the steering wheel in exasperation.

I peered into the darkness, taking in the bleak landscape. I searched the back seat for the GPS I had flung over my shoulder in anger when the damn thing kept telling me to turn hard right and I almost ended up in a snowbank.

It lit up and came to life, the annoying voice repeating the same word over and again.

Recalculating.

I tossed it aside again—what a piece of junk.

I had no idea where I was, except I knew I was about three hours away from a major city. Ottawa was far behind me. My parents' home, some four hours or more ahead. I shook my head in frustration. I should have been patient and not taken that detour, but the accident on the highway had snarled traffic for miles. Instead of waiting for it to clear, I had followed a line of cars headed off the highway, but they had all disappeared right about the time my GPS died, followed not long after by my cell phone. I always forgot to charge the damn thing.

A car flew by me, and I lifted my head, narrowing my eyes as I watched it travel down the road. I pursed my lips as I saw brake lights and then they disappeared around a corner farther up the road. It was a long way away, but I was sure I saw lights.

What was up there?

A house? A business?

I shrugged my shoulders, knowing I had little choice in the matter.

There was only one way to find out.

I leaned over and grabbed my toque and gloves, silently cursing the fact that my leather coat wasn't going to offer much protection from the cold. Neither were my sneakers. But it was either go try to find a phone or sit in the car and wait for someone to stop. Given how little traffic there was right now, that didn't seem to be a viable option. I liked to run and could cover great distances in a short period of time, so I was sure I could make it to the location where I saw the light up ahead in short order.

Except, when I got out of the car, I realized there was a third option.

Freeze.

Damn, it was cold outside.

And thanks to the fresh snow, far too slippery to run.

With a low groan, I trudged down the road, my head bent against the wind and hands buried in my pockets, concentrating on staying upright. By the time I got to the spot I thought the other car had turned, my teeth were chattering, and my body shook with cold chills. Luckily the snow had let up, so I didn't have that to contend with as well. I rounded the corner and heaved a sigh of relief. Up ahead was a small building, its lights a dim glow. My pace quickened, and I pushed forward, groaning with relief when I realized it was a quaint little diner and it was open. The parking lot had about a half-dozen cars in it, and I gratefully pushed open the thick, wooden door and stepped through it.

The warmth inside the diner hit me, and I stumbled to the closest table, sitting down heavily with a low gasp. The air around me felt almost too hot compared to my icy skin. I pulled the toque from my head and yanked off my gloves, bending and stretching my cold hands, trying to get the feeling back in them. My glasses were so cold there was ice on the lenses, so I tugged them off and tossed them onto the table. I should have left them in the car. Since my laser surgery, I only needed them for reading, but I had left them on out of habit. I shut my eyes and breathed in the warm air in long gulps.

"Here." A low voice startled me.

I opened my eyes, meeting a pair of the lightest soft-blue eyes I had ever seen. They were filled with worry as they met mine, the emotion in them so clear. I couldn't remember the last time I had known anyone to look at me with such concern. It was an unusual feeling.

Unable to break our gaze, I blinked, and a deep V appeared between the lovely eyes.

"Can you talk?"

I cleared my throat and sat straighter. "S-sorry. Yes." My voice sounded rough, as if I hadn't spoken for days rather than only hours. "C-cold, I'm so cold."

A cup appeared in front of me on the table, and gratefully I grabbed for it, only to have it slip from my frozen hands and rattle back into place on the saucer.

I cursed and looked back up into the warm gaze. The woman attached to the lovely eyes smiled in understanding and lifted the cup to my mouth, helping me drink the warm liquid. She sat down, cupping the back of my head, the heat of her touch hot against my icy skin as I gulped down the coffee greedily. She set down the cup, a satisfied expression on her face when she saw it was empty.

"Better?"

I nodded, feeling the warmth seep through my body. "Much. Thank you."

"Where did you come from?"

"My car—" I paused and swallowed. "My car broke down."

Her voice was horrified. "You walked here from the highway?"

"No. The highway was closed. I followed some cars trying to get around an accident, and I got lost. My car started making some weird noises, and then it simply died. I walked for about twenty minutes."

"That's still a long way in this cold north wind. No wonder you're freezing. You don't even have boots on!" She tsked loudly as she stood. "Take off your coat. It's holding in the cold. Stay here."

She walked away, and I grinned at her retreating figure, finding her authoritative tone amusing for some reason. She was awfully little to be so bossy. I glanced out the window with a grimace, thinking about her command.

"Stay here."

Where did she think I was gonna go? Back out in that cold? That wasn't happening anytime soon.

She reappeared with a steaming bowl of soup and set it in front of me. Then she draped a blanket around my shoulders.

"Eat that. I'll be back."

Her tone brooked no argument. I picked up the spoon and took a mouthful. It was delicious, thick with vegetables, the steam welcome on my face. I ate it slowly, grateful for its warmth.

As I ate, I watched her move around the diner, talking to the customers sitting at tables, obviously at home here. She was short, five foot nothing, I guessed. Her strawberry-blond hair was chin length, curly and wild around her face. She was cute. Impish. Adorable, actually. She had a Christmas ornament tucked behind one ear, the sparkle on it catching the light, and it jingled as she moved her head. She was curvy and lush, her uniform snug over her full breasts, and she moved with an easy grace as she flitted from one task to the next. I had the feeling she was the sort of person who liked to stay active.

She smiled and laughed, filled coffee cups, sliced pie, and wiped off the tables as she teased customers. Her laugh brought a smile to my face. It was high and feminine—an odd sound to my ears that were used to the quiet and solitude. More than once, her gaze met mine, our eyes locking for a brief moment, before she returned to her task. It was as if she were checking up on me. I liked the odd feeling of her concern.

Feeling warmer, I glanced around, taking in my surroundings. It was an old-fashioned kind of diner, with Formica countertops and mismatched tables and chairs scattered around. A pass-through showed one cook, busy preparing food. The place smelled of burgers and grease, and there was a lingering sweetness in the air, no doubt from the pies and cakes displayed in a case on the counter. The sign taped to the glass boasted all desserts were made in-house.

Christmas lights were strung around the windows, and beside me, a rather dilapidated tree was festooned with popcorn strings and ornaments fashioned from straws and bent utensils, giving it a whimsical air that made me smile. The entire atmosphere was one of a well-worn, long-standing local place to gather and meet. At this time of night, the diner wasn't full, but the sign outside said it was open twenty-four hours. I wondered idly what time my bossy waitress worked until.

She reappeared, smiling in satisfaction at the empty bowl in front of me. "Warmer now?"

"Yes. Thank you again." I glanced at my watch, seeing it was after ten. "I don't suppose there's a twenty-four-hour service station around here?"

She shook her head. "No, sorry."

"A hotel close by?"

She frowned. "There is in town. A motel anyway."

I grimaced. "How far away is that?"

"About a twenty-minute drive."

"Ah."

"More coffee?"

"Will you help me drink it?" I teased, surprised at my words. I felt very at ease with this woman, which wasn't a normal reaction for me.

Her wide smile was beautiful. It transformed her soft, adorable features into a stunning vision of loveliness. A dimple appeared in one of her cheeks. Her eyes danced with mischief. She was heart-stopping. My breath caught in my throat looking at her.

"The first one is on the house. I charge after that." She tilted her head and winked. Her hair ornament tinkled with the movement.

"Noted." My voice dropped. "Thank you for your help. That was beyond kind."

Her cheeks flooded with color, enhancing her subtle beauty, and her gaze dropped. "I'll get your coffee."

On impulse, I held out my hand. "I'm Evan. Evan Brooks."

Her hand was warm, clasped in mine. "Holly Cole."

I looked down at our hands and then back up at her.

"Hello, Holly. It's a real pleasure to meet you."

A fresh cup of coffee appeared in front of me. I took a sip of it and gasped. "Wow. That's hot."

She smiled as she nodded. "I added cold water to the first cup so you could drink it fast and start warming up. Speaking of which, you're still shivering. Here." In her outstretched hand was a bundled towel. Confused, I took it from her grip only to realize it was warm.

"Your hands are still cold, so your feet must be freezing. They're soaking wet," she explained calmly. "Take off your shoes and you can wrap your feet in the towel."

"Oh, um…here?"

She nodded. "Yes."

I hesitated.

"Your feet," she said pointedly. "Take off your shoes and socks. The wet socks aren't helping."

I looked around the diner. I didn't want to get her into trouble. She smiled at me. "It's fine, Evan."

I toed out of my wet sneakers and socks and wrapped the towel around my feet. She was right—they were freezing. "Thank you," I said again. A shudder ran through me as the heat hit my skin.

"I called a friend in town who owns a garage. He's coming out with one of his tow trucks to get your car. They'll look at it in the morning. He can drive you to the motel as well. It's going to take him a while to get here, though, so I'll throw your socks and sneakers into the dryer in the back."

Again, I was surprised by her kindness. "Holly—thank you."

"It isn't a problem."

I reached for her, wrapping my hand around hers once more. There was a strange warmth when our skin connected. "You are truly —" I hesitated "—an angel. Thank you."

"Drink your coffee, Evan," she admonished.

But she was smiling as she walked away.

"You're sure?" Tom asked me as he pulled back into the diner parking lot, my car on the winch behind his truck. He'd picked me up and drove us to my car, but instead of riding back into town with him as planned, I felt the intense need to go back to the diner.

Back to Holly.

She had looked as sad as I felt when Tom arrived to take me to my car, even though she smiled as she handed me my now dry sneakers and socks. She wished me well and a safe journey before she turned away, leaving me feeling strangely empty. From the moment I left, I wanted to go back.

She had chatted with me while I waited for Tom, and I enjoyed her low voice and sweet laughter. My usual shyness seemed to disappear around her. I couldn't keep my eyes off her, following her movements as she busied herself with a seemingly endless list of tasks. I drank an inordinate amount of coffee and ate two slices of pie, just to get her over to my table. She had a way of drawing me into her warmth, making me want more.

More of her time and beautiful smiles. More of her.

I realized Tom was staring at me, waiting for my answer. "Yes. I left my glasses."

"I can wait."

"I'm, ah, hungry. I'll eat and then grab a cab."

Tom chuckled. "This isn't the big city, Evan. A cab will be hard to come by out here."

"I'll grab a ride with someone."

He glanced toward the diner. "The food *is* good." Then he smirked. "So is the service—or should I say, the staff—one in particular."

I narrowed my eyes at him. He returned my gaze steadily. "Holly is a good friend of my wife, Leslie, and me. We're both fond of her. Tread carefully."

"I just want a cheeseburger, Tom."

He laughed. "We have a Wendy's if that's all you're after."

"Um…"

"Carefully, Evan. Just saying." He paused. "I'll call your cell when I know what the problem is with your car."

Clutching my duffle bag and cell phone, I nodded as I got out of the cab of his truck.

"Thanks. Goodnight."

I watched him drive away, wondering what the hell I was doing. Then I headed back into the diner.

CHAPTER TWO

EVAN

A sweet smell hit me as I entered the diner, rich with cinnamon and sugar—it was obvious pies were being made for the next day. The scent was tantalizing. The diner was emptier than it had been earlier. I made my way to a table and sat down, placing my small bag on the chair beside me. Holly came out from the kitchen, her face breaking into a smile when she saw me. Once again, I was struck by how lovely she was as she walked toward me. She held up my glasses. "I was going to drop these off at the garage for you in the morning." Then she frowned as she glanced toward the window. "Why is Tom leaving? What is he doing? I told him you needed a ride to the motel!" She began to hurry toward the door before I stopped her.

"It's fine. I sent him back to town."

"Why? I'll get him back. You came for your glasses, and now you have them!"

I shook my head and drew in a deep breath. "I didn't come back only for my glasses. I wanted to spend more time with you."

Her light-blue eyes widened. "Oh."

I hesitated, worried about her reaction. "Is that okay?"

Pink tinged her cheeks. "Yeah, it is."

"Good."

"Can I get you something?"

I smiled. I hadn't totally lied to Tom—I was hungry. "May I have a cheeseburger? With fries?"

She laughed. "Yes."

"Will you-will you sit with me?"

"Yes."

"Okay. Good."

She nodded, suddenly looking shy. "Yes," she murmured. "Yes, it is."

"Don't you need to call your family?"

I shook my head. I finished chewing my burger and swallowed. I sipped my coffee, trying to figure out the best response. "They, ah, didn't know I was on my way."

"Oh, you're surprising them? I'm sure Tom will get your car fixed and you'll make it. They'll be thrilled."

I snorted. "I doubt *thrilled* is the right word."

She wrapped her hands around her mug of coffee, studying me over the rim. I noticed how small and delicate her fingers were, barely reaching around the mug.

"What would the right word be?"

"Surprised. Maybe slightly displeased."

Holly frowned. "That would be a strange reaction to have when family comes to visit at Christmas."

"They aren't—" I drew in some much-needed oxygen "—like most families."

She tilted her head as she processed my words. "Why would you say that?"

I sighed. "I don't get on well with my family, Holly." I chuckled dryly at the understatement. "When my car broke down, I was wondering if it was a sign I was stupid for making this trip."

"Why did you make it, then?"

I shrugged. "I haven't had a Christmas with them in years. My sister had a baby a couple of months ago. I thought maybe I should try to reconnect. Enough time had gone by, I thought perhaps I needed to make the effort."

Her tone was gentle. "What happened, Evan? Can you tell me?"

Her eyes were tender and kind. There were no demands in them, only concern. For the first time ever, I *wanted* to tell someone. I wanted to share. Unconsciously, I reached out my hand, and she met it halfway, wrapping mine between both of hers. Again, I felt a surge of warmth flow through me at the contact. I noticed the contrast between our skin. The tan on mine was still visible from all the work I did outdoors. My skin was rough and callused. Holly's skin was pale, supple, and her hands looked small holding my larger one.

I glanced around. The diner was deserted except for a couple of truckers eating at the booth in the corner. They had already paid their bill and were finishing their coffee and pie. The cook was busy in the kitchen. No one was looking at us or paying attention to our discussion.

"I have two siblings. Both perfect in my parents' eyes. Popular in school, excellent at anything they put their mind to. Well-rounded students and now very successful adults. At least, their version of success. My sister is married, my brother an eternal bachelor. Both have great, high-profile careers." I smiled sadly, lifting one shoulder. "And then there's me. The baby of the family."

Holly smiled. "I thought the baby of the family was the most spoiled—the most loved."

I shook my head. "Not in my family. I've never quite measured up. I was always shy, quiet. I did well in school, but not like my siblings. I didn't participate in all the activities they did. My grades were good, and I liked to study and read. I liked to fix things and be on my own."

Memories pushed on the edges of my mind. My mother ordering me from the garage, telling me to stop working on a damaged table I had found and wanted to fix for my room.

"We do not have castoffs in this house." She grimaced in horror. "Throw it back in the garbage where it belongs."

She refused to listen to my pleas.

My father frowned at our exchange and muttered about my lack of ambition.

"Get your head out of your ass and concentrate, Evan. You'll never amount to anything at this rate. Brooks men don't use their hands like common laborers. We use our brains."

It never changed. I was constantly in trouble for wanting to fix and mend things I found and liked. Eventually, I stopped taking them home—instead using a friendly neighbor's garage, a man who liked to tinker and mend things as well. He taught me so many things I still used to this day. The day he died was one of the saddest days of my life. It felt as if I had lost my only friend, and I had no one to share my grief with. My family hadn't noticed how much time I spent with him. As long as I wasn't bothering them or doing anything to embarrass the Brooks name, they didn't really pay attention to me.

I shook my head to clear it, meeting Holly's eyes and returning to the present.

"I was never popular, good at sports, or outgoing the way they were. I was merely okay. Nothing exceptional like them. I was, as my father told me many times, an underachiever."

"Everyone is different. It's what makes us special."

I nodded because she was right. Except in my family—special wasn't allowed. It only made you different. Different wasn't good.

I studied our clasped hands, noting how well her fingers knit with mine. "My father is a lawyer. My brother, Calvin, is a partner in his firm. My sister, Kelsey, owns her own design company. My mother runs a high-end boutique. They all live in very large homes, drive expensive cars, and live extravagant lifestyles. They travel a lot, shop lavishly, and have lives I'm not comfortable with. I never was." I paused. "And then there's me. The odd man out." I barked out a low laugh. "The only thing I have in common with my siblings is our trust funds. And even those, we disagree on."

I stopped.

Why the hell had I mentioned my trust fund?

I never talked about it. Ever.

But Holly didn't comment on my trust fund. She didn't even look interested when I mentioned it.

"Tell me about Evan. Who is he?" she asked, squeezing my hand.

"I'm an antique restoration specialist. I live alone in a house on the edge of the water, in a little town on the East Coast. My world is a quiet one. My workshop is out back of my house, so I'm my own boss, and I don't socialize much. I live a simple, uncomplicated life. I don't live like my family. I like things… modest."

"Do you get lonely?"

I paused. I *had* been lonely until I took a job restoring an antique desk for Carol Whittaker. I hadn't realized how lonely I was until the Whittakers came into my life.

"Not the way I was when I was younger. I have a few good friends now who treat me like part of their family." I smiled as I thought about Dan and Carol. How they had practically adopted me, bringing me into their family, showing me what it was like to be *part* of one—accepted for who I was and not treated like an outsider. It took a lot of effort on their part to get me comfortable enough to accept their care and friendship since I wasn't used to being wanted. But they never gave up, and now I was no longer alone, although there were many times, I still felt lonely. Andrew, their son, and I were close friends, and I got along well with his wife, Tara, who treated me like the brother she'd never had, which meant she ordered me around a lot. Used to being ignored by my own siblings, I had to admit, I liked it.

"You repair broken pieces of history, Evan? Restore their beauty? Make them useful and vibrant again?"

I like how she phrased my work. "I suppose, in many cases, yes."

"I think that's wonderful. What else?" she prompted.

"I teach piano lessons in my spare time, and I like to carve things. I take a lot of pictures around the area I live in—it's beautiful there, no matter the season." I paused, searching my brain. "I like watching the history and nature channels. And I coach little kids' hockey in the winter."

She lifted our hands and studied mine. "You have long fingers—perfect for the piano."

I chuckled. "I never get them clean, though. No matter how I scrub them, there's always stain or paint under the nails from whatever project I'm working on."

She smiled and shook her head. "They're still beautiful hands, Evan. Capable, strong, talented hands."

I looked down at them in surprise. She thought they were beautiful? Capable and talented?

I was certain no one had ever used those words to describe any part of me.

I looked at her hands: small, tiny fingers that barely came to my knuckles as I held them against mine. I liked, however, how they felt nestled between my own fingers. They seemed to fit as if they belonged there.

"What about you?" I asked. "What do you like to do?"

"I rescue stranded men. Like a St. Bernard—except I have less fur. And no brandy."

I chuckled. "Happens a lot, does it? Strange men tripping in here half frozen, looking for warmth?"

She nodded. "A regular Wednesday night occurrence." She winked. "At least once a month."

I laughed at her drollness. "What do you do aside from imitating a big, furry dog?"

She paused, her hesitation making it seem as if she weren't sure how to answer. I wondered if perhaps no one ever asked her that question.

"I-I like to sketch. Paint with watercolors." She shrugged. "I'm not very good, but I like doing it."

"You're probably amazing."

"Why would you say that?"

It was my turn to shrug. "No idea—a feeling, I suppose. I think you'd be amazing at anything you did."

Her gaze skittered away and I knew I was right. No one asked, and she never talked about it. It was something private. But she had told me.

"What do you sketch?"

"I take walks and sketch animals in the woods. Sometimes the sunsets. I just enjoy it."

"You'd love it where I live. There is so much beauty, you'd be sketching all the time."

She offered me a small smile, her gaze unfocused as she looked past my shoulder into the night. I wasn't sure why I'd said that, but for some reason, I wanted her to know about the beauty of the place I called home.

"Do you have, um, a girlfriend?" she asked, looking at me bashfully from under her eyelashes. Then as if she realized what the answer to that question might be, she started to withdraw her hands from mine.

"No," I hastened to assure her, holding on to her fingers. "I'm, ah, not so good with…girls. Um, women. I mean, I've had them. Girlfriends, I mean. A few. But, yeah, um. No. No girlfriend." I huffed out a sigh. "The shyness I suffered from in my youth has never completely gone away. I have trouble talking at times."

God, I was lame.

"Seems to me you do okay. You're talking to me."

"You're different, somehow," I murmured. "You make it easy to talk to you."

The blush I found so charming appeared again. "Thank you."

I squeezed her hand.

"Tell me more about your home," she asked.

"I live in a log cabin. A family had bought it as a holiday place, then grew tired of it. I saw it one day when I was traveling and fell in love with it. I bought it and spent a year adding on to it, building my workshop and making it my own."

"You were traveling?"

I stared out the window, lost in thought. "I knew my life was never going to satisfy my parents. After I left school, I knew I didn't want a nine-to-five job. I had secretly been taking woodworking courses, and I knew that was what I wanted to do. I left home and traveled, learning more and more about antiques and restoration. I was in Nova Scotia when I saw the house." I shrugged. "Walking up the driveway felt like coming home to me, and I stayed."

"That's amazing."

"My favorite time of day is spent sitting on my porch watching the sun set over the water," I offered quietly. "It's so peaceful. I love living there."

"Sounds pretty good to me."

I snorted. "According to my father, it's a waste."

She lifted one shoulder dismissively. "It's not his life. He lives his life how he likes. You're entitled to live yours. You don't owe them anything. You only owe your life to yourself."

Her words hit me.

Unassuming. Direct.

My life.

Not his.

I stared at her in shock at the simple clarity of her statement.

"Still, they are your family, Evan. You should try to be part of their life. Family is important."

"Do you have family, Holly?"

Her glance was unfocused over my shoulder. The diner was now empty except for us, the only other sound in the place coming from the kitchen. It was well after two, and she had told me that she worked until three. I didn't want the time to be over.

I waited as she gathered her thoughts.

"I lost my parents a couple of years ago. They were away on one of their trips and died when the bus they were on crashed in the mountains of Brazil. I have no siblings. So, no family—I'm alone." She stopped as if searching for words.

"One of their trips?" I prompted.

"My parents were free spirits. We relocated a lot, never settling—always moving from some new adventure they wanted to have to another. They worked so many odd jobs, never saving for the future, and when they died, there was nothing left for me. I hadn't gone on that trip with them. I hadn't gone for a couple of years. I was tired of the travel, to be honest. After they were gone, I stayed here. I was tired of moving around, being dragged from place to place. I had a job and a few friends. I needed to stay in one place for a while and figure out what I wanted to accomplish in my life."

I frowned. It didn't sound like she'd had a very good childhood.

"Is that why you like to sketch?"

She nodded. "A pad of paper and a pencil were easy to carry

around. I could lose myself in the view—commit some place I liked to memory." She sighed. "We never stayed anywhere for very long, and I knew we'd probably never go back. My parents believed in experiencing something—someplace, once—and going forward." There was a beat of silence. "I often think I was one of those things."

"Sounds lonesome."

She met my gaze. "It was."

"How old are you, Holly?"

"Twenty-three."

"I'm thirty."

"It's just a number, Evan."

"True. Do you, ah, do you live alone?"

"With my cat, Chester. I have a roommate who is hardly ever there. Connie travels for a living and comes home every so often to swap her wardrobe, catch up, and she's gone. It's her place—I sort of take care of it while she's gone."

"You like it here?"

She shrugged. "I was so tired of never having anything to call my own—never feeling I truly had a *home*. I wanted someplace I felt I could belong."

"Did you find it?"

Her voice was so low, I almost didn't hear her. "Not yet."

The urge to lean forward and tell her I wanted to help her with that was strong. Instead, I squeezed her hands. "We all want that, Holly. We all need to belong—to someone and someplace."

She nodded.

"What do you want from your life?"

"I want to go back to school and get my degree. I want to work with kids. I love kids."

"You want to teach?"

"Teach or early childhood development. I'm still deciding."

"Is that—" I paused, unsure how to ask "—going to happen for you?"

"Soon." She nodded. "I work here and part time in town at the local grocery store. I'll have enough to go to school in the fall next year. I'll still have to work and find a place to live with roommates, but I'll be able to do it."

"That's great." I squeezed her hands in encouragement. I had a feeling she could do anything she put her mind to.

The door opened, and an older woman walked in. She stared briefly at Holly and me before nodding and heading into the back. It was then I realized how close we were. Our chairs were pulled together, shoulders touching. Our hands were entwined on the tabletop, and as we talked, our heads had drifted nearer together, almost touching. It was as if we were wrapped in a bubble of our own, sharing our lives with each other. I had never experienced this sense of intimacy with another person…or this sense of wanting to be even closer.

"My shift relief is here," she told me. "That's Barb."

"Does she work every night?" I couldn't imagine getting up in the middle of the night all the time.

Holly grinned mischievously and bent forward, her voice discreet. "Yes. Rumor has it she likes how Ronnie, um, *runs the kitchen*—" she winked "—if you know what I mean. Worth getting out of bed for, I hear." Then she giggled, and I chuckled with her.

"What about you, Holly? Do you like his kitchen *skills?*" I teased her, even though inside I was feeling a strange tightening of my stomach as I waited for her answer.

She relaxed back in her chair. "Nope. He's always too hot— working by the stove." She quirked her eyebrows, making her look adorable. "I prefer cold hands and feet. Gives me something to warm up while cuddling."

I laughed at her cheeky remarks. She *was* quite adorable.

She yawned—trying to cover the fact that she was doing so by turning her head.

My smile faded, because I knew what that meant. It was time to say goodbye to her. I stood.

"You must be tired, and it's time for you to go home. I need to find a ride into town."

She reached out her hand, grabbing mine, and pulling me back into my chair. "I'll take you."

"You don't have to—" I hesitated, but I really wanted a little more time with her.

"Don't be silly. I'm going into town anyway."

"Yeah?"

She nodded. "I, ah, just have to do a few things."

I released her hand regretfully. "Take your time." I grinned, pleased at the offer. "I'm not going anywhere."

She disappeared into the kitchen, my eyes following her movements, my head echoing with one small phrase I couldn't understand.

"Not without you."

"This is what you drive?" I gaped at the monster truck sitting in the last spot in the parking lot. "Can you see over the dashboard?"

Holly chuckled. "Yes. It was the one thing that came with us, everywhere we went. And one of the few things I have left of my parents. It's an old friend."

"Is it safe?" Old friend or not, it looked like it had seen better days.

She snorted. "Get in, fraidy cat."

I climbed in, and a few seconds later, Holly had the engine cranked up and the heater going. "It just takes a few minutes to warm up."

"Okay."

Our eyes met and held in the dim light coming from the dashboard. The cab got warm. Very warm. I swallowed nervously. Holly's bright eyes reflected the light as she stared at me, her gaze unsure. Slowly, I lifted my hand, grazing my fingers over her cheek. "You've been so kind to me all night, Holly. More than you know."

"I just helped you warm up," she whispered, searching my eyes with her own.

"Yes, you did that. But you talked to me and listened. You *cared* for me. That is so…*special*. I can't thank you enough."

"You're welcome."

Bravely, I slid closer, reaching over to stroke her round cheek again. "You truly are an angel to me."

"I've never been an angel to anyone."

I drew in a long breath, my fingers slipping into her hair. "Well, you're mine. My Angel."

Her eyes widened.

And then my mouth was on hers.

Warm, sweet, indulgent.

She wound her arms around my neck, clutching the back of my hair with tender fingers. When I slipped my tongue inside her mouth, the sound she made was erotic. I pulled her closer, my tongue stroking hers. I cupped the back of her head, holding her close. I never wanted to stop kissing her. It was only the bright lights of a car pulling in and reflecting in the rearview mirror that had us pulling apart, panting. My finger traced her bottom lip. "Should I apologize?"

"No."

"Can I do that again?"

"Yes," she breathed.

"Thank God," I whispered against her lips.

I had no idea how long I kissed her. I didn't know how I even got brave enough to kiss her in the first place, but now that I had, I didn't want to stop. Finally, though, she broke away, her breath warm on my cheek as she snuggled her head into my shoulder. I held her against me, enjoying the closeness.

"Evan?" Her voice was muffled against my chest.

I kissed her head. I liked how my name sounded on her lips. "Hmm?"

"Will you…will you come home with me?"

I tilted up her chin and studied her open gaze. No one had ever looked at me with so much emotion before. It was overwhelming. "*God*, Holly, I want to. I want to so much. Are you sure?"

"Yes."

I drew in a deep breath and kissed her again. "Take me there, then."

CHAPTER THREE

EVAN

The house she lived in was small. There was the glow of a tiny light coming from the inside. I could see the silhouette of Holly's cat in the window, no doubt waiting for her to come home. Holly shut off the engine, and for a moment the truck cab was silent.

I swallowed hard, thinking she had changed her mind. We had been quiet the whole drive, but our hands were entwined on the seat between us. I stroked her silky skin with my thumb, occasionally lifting her hand to brush my lips over it, when the urge to do so became too strong to resist. Now, I tightened my grip. "I can walk to the motel from here, Holly. It's okay."

Her gaze flew to mine. "No! I…I just need you to know I don't do this. I don't bring men home with me."

"I don't do this either," I admitted. "It's been a long time for me, and I don't have what you might call a great deal of experience with women."

This time, she squeezed my hand. "I don't have a great deal of experience either."

Her honest words made me ridiculously happy.

"I, ah, wasn't really planning on, um," I stammered. "I don't have —" My voice trailed off in embarrassment.

Holly chuckled. "Connie keeps a stock of condoms on hand. I'm sure she won't mind if we borrow a few…or, um, more if needed."

More?

My smile couldn't be contained. Holly's answering smile was shy but heartwarming.

"I feel something between us. Something I've never felt before with you. Can you feel it?" I asked.

"Yes."

"Are you sure about this, Holly?"

She drew in a deep breath and opened her door. "Yes."

❄

She led me into the dark house, flicking on another small lamp in the living room. I was surprised not to see any Christmas decorations or a tree. She was such a warm person—somehow, she seemed the type to surround herself with the season. Even I dragged home a small tree each year from the woods behind my house, and although my decorations left a lot to be desired, it was a nice thing to look at in the dark evenings when I was alone. I looked at her curiously. "No tree?"

She shrugged. "I work tomorrow, and then on Christmas Day, I'll have dinner with Leslie and Tom later in the day. I don't exchange gifts with anyone anymore." She laughed, the sound more sad than happy. "Not that I ever really did. My parents never made a big deal about Christmas. They felt it was too commercial, so they didn't do very much. Occasionally, there was a small gift by my plate in the morning."

"Occasionally?"

"Sometimes, there was nothing. It depended on if they were working, how long we'd been living in the place we were in, that sort of thing." She paused. "Maybe one day, it will be different. But for now, it seems silly to do anything only for me."

I swallowed around the painful lump in my throat. For the first time since I met her, she sounded despondent. Resigned. Whereas Christmas for me growing up had been excessive in the worst form, with too many gifts simply for the sake of giving gifts, hers had been the exact opposite. It also sounded to me as if she was as ignored as I had been as a child. I hated that she knew that feeling. I also hated the fact that she didn't feel she was worth the effort to add some holiday joy into her life.

What was it about this woman that made me want to give her every single desire she ever had missed out on? I wanted to fill her small house with lights and tinsel and put a tree in the corner that was loaded with gifts. I wanted to watch her open them and see the delight on her face. I wanted to be the one who made her smile. I wanted to share in her joy. I blinked at the peculiar feeling; it was another emotion I had never experienced before.

A strange noise had me looking down to see a pair of green eyes gazing up at me. Long dark fur stuck out everywhere and a patch of white was centered on his forehead. Bending down, I stroked the softness. "You must be Chester." I was rewarded with a deep purr as the cat wound itself around my legs, then stretched up, allowing me to pick him up. Holly giggled, the sound so much better than her earlier, sadder sound.

"He must like you. He never lets people pick him up."

"Have you had him long?"

"No. I found him last winter outside the diner. I think someone had abandoned him. I brought him home to keep him safe for the night, but I couldn't bear the thought of taking him to a shelter. So, he stayed."

I smiled at her. Of course, he did. Her rescuing me tonight wasn't a first for her. I wondered if maybe she would let me stay as well. The strange thought made me pause for a moment.

"He's so small."

She nodded, reaching over to scratch his head. "I think he had a hard life before I found him. He never grew very much." Then she giggled again. "He looks like you."

"What?" I chuckled.

"The green eyes and the white patch on his head. There is quite the resemblance."

I grinned. I had developed a white streak at the front of my hairline when I was young. My mother disliked it and had insisted on having it colored, but I stopped doing that as soon as I left home. "Your taste in strays is excellent."

"I only save the handsomest men."

I blinked at her. *Handsome?* She thought I was handsome?

"I'm a throwback," I blurted out.

"What?"

"I heard my mother tell someone once I was a throwback to my grandfather, whom my father didn't get on with. I looked exactly like him—right down to the white patch in my hair. I have his coloring and eyes too. She said it was probably why my father wasn't very fond of me."

Her eyes were wide. "Your mother said your own father wasn't *fond* of you?"

I shrugged. "It wasn't much of a secret."

"That is so…cold."

"I was never treated the same way as the other two." I paused. "I don't think any of them found me very handsome. I looked different, I wore glasses. The way I saw things, *did* things, was different." I laughed mirthlessly. "My entire family is opinionated, vocal. Far too much, in my opinion. I was always in the corner and quiet. I never fit in."

"You're a gentle soul."

"My father would say weak."

"Forgive me for saying this, Evan, but your father is an ass."

I couldn't help but laugh. She was so right about that.

Her voice became quiet. "They were wrong. About everything. You're wonderful—just the way you are."

"You think so? How can you be so sure?"

She shrugged. "I'm a good judge of character."

I set down the cat and stepped closer. "And you like my character, Holly? You think I'm handsome?"

She reached up and ran her fingers through my hair. "Yes. I like you. And yes, I think you're very handsome."

"All my family had light-colored hair and hazel eyes, like my parents. I have my grandfather's dark hair and green eyes, plus his white streak. Even physically, I was the odd one."

"You're not odd. You're Evan. You're perfect."

Her words were like a small shock running through my system.

Nobody had ever thought or told me I was perfect. I couldn't describe the feelings those words elicited.

I leaned into her touch as she continued to stroke my hair. The sensation was wonderful. No wonder the cat purred. If I could, I would as well.

"I'm not perfect. I'm far from it."

"Not as far as you've been led to believe. You look sad, the same way Chester did when I found him."

"I've been lost all my life," I whispered.

"So have I."

Her hand stilled. The air around us warmed again. Our eyes held, locked in a silent conversation.

Holly swallowed. "Do you want a drink, Evan?"

I shook my head.

"Something to eat?"

"No."

I pulled her closer.

"There is only one thing I want right now."
Her voice was hushed, almost shy. "What is it?"
"I want you, Angel."
And then her mouth was on mine.
I wasn't lost anymore.

There was no shyness between us. It felt as though I had known her forever. As though in some other life, we had experienced each other on this intimate level. It was as if I had found a missing part of me.

Holly's hands were so gentle; they touched me with such tenderness, I wanted to weep. The way she stroked my torso, played with my nipples, touched my face. Her mouth was talented and warm, her lips an artist's brush that painted my body like a canvas with bold strokes and delicate arches. I groaned and hissed my pleasure as she explored me.

Nothing was rushed or hurried. There was no screaming or wild thrashing. There was only a deep, abiding passion between us I had never experienced with anyone else.

Slowly, sensually, we shed our clothes, kissing and touching as each new piece of skin was uncovered. Our voices murmured and encouraged, whispering adoration and sweet promises. I caressed her curves, loving how she felt under my touch—supple and perfect. Her skin was warm, silky, and tasted sweet under my tongue. I discovered all her secrets, her ticklish right side I teased mercilessly, the small scar on her thigh I kissed tenderly. I learned the dip of her waist. The rightness of her rounded hips. The beautiful fullness of her breasts. I thrilled at how she whimpered as I kissed the juncture at the base of her neck, teasing it with my tongue. Moaned when I sucked on her nipples.

Our mouths locked together, our bodies in flawless sync. Being buried inside her was nothing short of perfection. Her warmth grounded me, her sighs filled my head, and feeling her coming around my cock, as I moved and rocked above her, was ecstasy in itself. She held me close as I stilled, a low, heavy groan escaping my throat, my own orgasm so powerful, there was only one word I was able to utter, the most important one in the world at the moment.

Angel.

Wrapped up in her arms afterward was like coming home. She was so right curled around me. I had never experienced contentment before or this odd feeling of happiness. Both were foreign and both were abundant, coursing through my body and leaving me filled with wonder at all the emotions she seemed to bring out in me.

I looked down at Holly, the source of those strange feelings. Her cheeks were flushed in the dim light, her eyelashes resting on them as she relaxed against me. I could feel her stuttering breaths against my neck as her body softened. I knew my breathing was still erratic. Slowly, we relaxed and calmed, still wrapped around each other. I nuzzled the top of her head, smiling as she tilted back her head, looking shy as she gazed up at me.

"Hi."

I kissed her full mouth. "Hi," I whispered against her lips.

"That was—" She bit her lip. "Wow." She grinned.

Now it was my turn to feel shy. I knew I wasn't the most experienced lover. It had certainly been the most intense experience I'd ever had. "Yeah? It was, ah, *good* for you?"

She pursed her lips. "Well, now that you mention it—"

"Um," I stammered.

She pressed closer, flinging her leg over my hip and cupping my ass. "Maybe we should try again, just to be sure?"

A slow grin broke out on my face. "To be sure of…?"

"That it was as beautiful as I think it was."

My heart soared. I rolled, hovering over her, already hardening and wanting her. "Yes. We need to make sure of that."

CHAPTER FOUR

EVAN

My cell phone rang from Holly's bedside table the next morning. She'd plugged it in for me the night before so Tom could reach me. I blinked in the bright morning light. We'd been up most of the brief night, only dozing, talking, and sharing long, lingering kisses. We'd made love again, and even now as I watched her lean over to grab the phone, I could feel myself stirring with desire for her. She handed me the phone, and I cupped her head, bringing her close for another kiss before answering it.

Tom's booming voice told me he found the problem and, luckily, was able to get the parts he needed. My car would be ready by noon. I thanked him and hung up, feeling an odd pull in my chest. I should be grateful I could get back on the road today, yet I felt only sadness that I would be able to leave in a few hours.

Holly kissed me, her voice quiet. "What time?"

"Noon."

"I can drop you there before I go to work."

"What time do you work until?"

"Only six today. The diner closes early since it's Christmas Eve."

"Holly—" I wanted to say something. What, I had no idea, but something.

She shook her head, her voice beseeching. "Don't."

My head fell back on the pillow, my eyes shutting against the burn I felt behind them. I pulled her close, breathing in the scent of her hair. She smelled like sun and flowers. Lovely. "I have so much to say."

"This was a stop in your life, Evan. A detour. Maybe one you needed, to be able to *find* your life. But you have to keep going. I don't expect anything." Her voice lowered. "Last night was so wonderful. I'll treasure it and the thought of you always. I'm glad you found my diner."

I swallowed. I was more than glad I'd found her diner. And her. She was an unexpected gift in my life. Perhaps the greatest I would ever receive.

"Tell me about your life, your friends," she whispered. "Don't tell me goodbye yet."

I tightened my hold and did what she asked. I told her about Dan and Carol. Andrew and Tara. How they had drawn me into their world, showing me what a real family was like. Loving. Caring. Supportive. Not judgmental and cold.

"I'm glad you found them."

I chuckled. "Carol found me, actually. And she refused to let me stay in my shell. It was as if she saw what I needed and was determined to give it to me, whether I knew I wanted it or not."

I described my house as best I could, telling her about the renovations I had made and the huge porch I had added on to the front.

"The sunsets, Holly. They're breathtaking and remind me every day how much I love living there. I make a point of sitting on the porch and watching them. I feel a sense of peace."

"It sounds beautiful. Maybe one day, I'll go there."

I had to bite my lip to stop myself from telling her I wanted her to come and be with me there—that I wanted her to see the sunsets with me every day. I knew it was only the emotion of this trip causing me to feel that way. Instead, I hummed. "You could sketch and paint something new every day."

I made her chuckle with some stories of restoration disasters— glued hair and throbbing thumbs from miscalculated blows of my tools. She told me funny stories of the diner and of growing up, as she put it, like a gypsy.

Throughout it all, we touched. She swept her fingers over my skin, warming it as they went. I kept her close, my hand often buried in her wild hair to tilt her head back for a kiss. Chester slumbered away at the bottom of the bed, frequently stretching, pushing on my feet as he made himself more comfortable.

The room became still. Finally, she asked, "How much longer to your parents' place?"

"About four hours."

"So you'll get there late afternoon."

"I have to stop somewhere and pick up some gifts. This was such a last-minute decision, I didn't bring anything with me." I shuddered, thinking about entering a mall on Christmas Eve. I wasn't big on crowds.

She sat up, tugging the blanket with her to cover her beautiful breasts. "Evan, there's a lovely gift shop here. Local artisans. Tom's wife, Leslie, runs it. She doesn't open until noon, but I know she would let me bring you in early, if you'd like. You could pick out some things, she would wrap them for you, and you could drive straight through." She paused. "Then I wouldn't worry."

"Worry?"

"It gets dark early. I'd like to know you got to your parents' before it got dark, especially today. I'll worry because of your car." She smiled even though I could see the deep sadness in her eyes. "I'm not sure there'll be another diner for you to find open tonight."

My breath caught. She was concerned about me again. She cared. I drew my fingers over her cheek and pulled her back down to me. She buried her face into my neck.

"There will never be another diner—or another you, Angel."

Her voice almost broke me. "Make love to me, one more time?"

How could I say no?

Hours later, I held out my credit card for the purchases. All picked out with the help of Holly, all tasteful, thoughtful gifts most people would be thrilled to receive. Handmade silk scarves for my mother and sister, carved business card holders for my brother and father, beautifully knitted items for my new niece, along with a handmade teddy bear with arms and legs that moved. There was even a hand-painted silk tie for my brother-in-law. I knew, though, my family would be unimpressed by the choices. No brand names, expensive trinkets, or extravagant gestures were in the gifts. None of them would be deemed acceptable. But I didn't say a word. I appreciated Holly's assistance and enthusiasm. I knew she thought the gifts would be accepted and enjoyed. I refused to tell her otherwise—she had been so delighted and wanted to help; I couldn't bear to disappoint her. The gifts would find homes elsewhere, but not with my family. Of that, I had no doubt.

The gifts Holly helped me pick for the Whittaker family would, I knew, be treasured and loved simply because they came from me. Those gifts, I found joy in purchasing. Holly had great taste, and surprisingly, the shop was filled with a vast assortment of beautiful and useful items. I saw the way Holly's eyes lit up at some of the items she looked at, and I had to resist the urge to buy them all for her. She would hate that. This was something she wanted to do for me, and she didn't want it to be about her at all.

I accepted the bags of wrapped gifts, Holly having asked Leslie to keep the two groups separate, and we walked to the truck, my heart growing heavier with each step.

We were silent on the drive back to her house, and I followed her inside, my stomach clenching and throat going dry at the thought of what would happen next.

She had to go to work, and I had to finish my drive and go see my family. Our time was done. The unexpected gift of her sweet, caring nature was about to end. After Tom had called, we'd made love, showered in her small bathroom, and shared some more time in her kitchen, sipping coffee, neither of us hungry for food. My car had been picked up and was now beside hers outside, ready to go.

For a moment, we stood in her tiny kitchen, staring at each other, and then she was in my arms. I lifted her up, holding her tight.

"My Angel," I whispered against her ear. "What you've given me these past hours—I can't even begin to say thank you."

Her arms tightened. "You are so much more than you give yourself credit for, Evan. You have such a beautiful soul. Don't let them take that away from you." Her lips touched mine in a gentle caress. "Live your life for you. Find what makes you happy and grab it. Act on that happiness."

She began to step back, but I held on. I couldn't let her go—not yet. The words were out of my mouth before I realized. "I need more time."

"What?"

"I need more time with you."

"But your family—"

"Will be there tomorrow. They don't even know I'm coming, so it doesn't matter if I show up today or tomorrow. You told me to act on what makes me happy. You make me happy."

"I have to go to work."

"That's fine. I'll be here when you get home. Spend the evening with me. Let me wake up with you tomorrow morning. *Christmas morning.* I want to wake up with someone who cares about me." I paused. "Whom I care about. I want to wake up with you."

She stared at me, her eyes wide with anxiety and longing. They reflected the same emotions I was feeling.

"Please give me this, Holly. A few more hours is all I'm asking."

"Yes," she murmured. "I want you to stay."

I pulled her close, feeling as if I could breathe again. I knew I was only delaying the inevitable, but for now, I could stay and be with her. Tomorrow was hours away.

Today, I had her.

CHAPTER FIVE

EVAN

"I'll drive you to work," I offered, my arms still looped around her waist. I felt as if a weight had been lifted from my shoulders. As if I had given myself a gift today—a gift of *her*.

"Oh, um, I have a couple errands to run. The diner won't be busy, so Judy and I cover for each other for an hour, then we can get things done—so I'll need my truck."

I glanced out the window at her mammoth vehicle in the driveway. In the light, I could see how old and decrepit it was. I had thought it a dull red in the dark last night, but today I could see the rust on the body was what was holding it together, covering the gray the truck used to be. But she insisted it was roadworthy, and I had no choice but to accept it.

"All right," I agreed. "But before you go, I need to know where a couple of places are in town."

Holly laughed, her eyes no longer sad. "What are you going to do while I'm gone?"

I grinned, feeling lighter than I had since I woke up. I had more time with her.

"I've got some stuff to do. Then Chester and I will hang out."

She narrowed her eyes, looking suspicious. "*Stuff?* What are you up to, Evan Brooks?"

I liked how my name sounded rolling off her tongue, the bossiness of her tone as she settled one hand on her hip and acted stern. She was too cute.

"I'm going to cook you dinner."

"You cook?"

I snorted. "I live by myself in a small town. There's no fast food close. It was either learn to cook or starve. I do pretty well." I winked at her. "You do like tacos, right?"

"Um, sure."

Laughing, I pulled her back into my arms. "I can do a little better than that. I'll follow you, and you can point out where the grocery store is."

"And you'll be here when I get back?"

I kissed her, liking the thought of being here, waiting for her. "Yes."

She sighed, the sound happy and content. She lifted up on her toes and kissed me in return. "Okay."

I followed Holly all the way to the diner, some odd sense of needing to make sure she was okay filling my head. She hopped out of her truck and approached my car, bending low into the window.

"Not necessary, Evan. The truck looks awful, but Tom keeps it running well."

"Maybe I just like following you. You have an awesome tailgate."

She blinked, then started to giggle. I grinned at her amusement, loving the fact that it was me who made her smile. She leaned in and kissed me, her tongue gliding along my bottom lip. I slid my hand up her neck and kissed her back, groaning low in my throat, desire for her building fast. She pulled back, her cheeks flushed.

"Wow, you can kiss."

I tugged on her neck. "Come back, and I'll show you some more."

She laughed and stepped away from the car. She touched her mouth, shaking her head. "Later, Evan."

I watched her walk away, leaning out my window, unable to help myself.

"Yep," I called. "*Awesome* tailgate."

Her laughter drifted across the parking lot. She paused at the door, peering over her shoulder. She blew me a kiss I pretended to catch, then she disappeared. I grinned all the way back into town.

I pulled back into the parking lot at Leslie's store, not surprised to find it busy. She looked at me oddly when I walked in, then approached me once she was finished with her customer.

"Changed your mind about one of your gifts, Evan?"

I ran my hand along the back of my neck. "Ah, no. Change of plans. I need a few more presents." I paused. "For Holly."

A smile lit her face. "That, I can help you with."

I returned her smile. "I was hoping you'd say that." I sucked in a deep breath. "I want to spoil her a little."

"Then let's go shopping."

Hours later, I looked around, making sure everything was in place. A small tree was set up in the corner, the white lights and pretty ornaments I had bought shining in the dark. Some bright parcels were nestled underneath. I had even remembered a small gift for Chester. Earlier, I had resisted the urge to buy everything I had seen Holly's eyes linger on when we'd been shopping together for my family's gifts, but I did get some things I knew she would like. Special ones, just like her. Leslie helped guide me to choose the perfect ones, although one I had chosen alone. But from the way Leslie's eyes had lit up, I knew I had chosen well. She had her assistant wrap them all, so they were festive and pretty under the tree.

I resisted adding any other decorations to Holly's place, but I did get some flowers for her and added some scented candles I had seen at Leslie's. As I was setting things up, I realized how sparse the house was of regular decor. Her roommate, Connie, kept the place only for a home base, but it made me unhappy to think that Holly was so used to having nothing static in her life, she simply didn't think to make where she was living into a home for herself. She had never known that, and she didn't think herself worthy of the effort.

While I was out, I had picked up a couple of Christmas movies to watch and some snacks when I was at the small grocery store. The thought of spending the evening on the sofa with Holly curled up beside me made me absurdly happy. I wanted the night to be a good one for both of us. Two lonely people enjoying spending some time together at a time of year when being alone seemed so much darker than usual. I ignored the small part of my brain telling me it wasn't going to be possible to be alone again after today. That I wasn't going to be able to walk away from Holly. I liked how I felt when I was with her; she banished the sadness that seemed to hover over everything I did.

I shook my head to stop those thoughts. I only had until tomorrow with her.

I checked the dinner in the oven and made sure the wine was getting cold. I hoped she would enjoy the meal I'd made for us. I wasn't a gourmet cook and the stuffing was from a package, but my roast chicken was usually pretty stellar. I did hope Holly could make gravy, though. Mine was always resembled dark water, usually with lumps.

Headlights shone in the window, and I hurried to the door. I had it open before she even reached the steps, and I stepped outside, pulling her into the warm house and my arms. We both sighed as our bodies met. I nuzzled the top of her head and then lifted her chin so I could kiss her.

It had been too long since her lips were against mine.

The bags she was holding fell to the floor, and she tugged herself against me. Groaning, I covered her lips with mine possessively. I cupped the back of her head, holding her close to my mouth, my tongue swirling and caressing, welcoming her home. She felt so right against me.

"Hi," I murmured against her lips. "How was your day?"

"It was fine," she responded breathlessly. "Although I'm hoping, not as good as my night."

I liked that.

I pulled her farther into the house, smiling at her reaction to the small tree I had bought.

"You can, ah, plant it later," I explained.

"Why are there gifts under the tree, Evan?"

"Oh, um…some fat guy in a red suit was here. I couldn't stop him."

She laughed as she bent down and added a couple of parcels to the small pile. "Funny. He dropped by the diner and left these."

"Wow, he gets around."

She stood, and I wrapped my arm around her waist. Christmas music played quietly in the background. The lights glowed in the dark—they reflected on the bows and shiny paper packages tucked beneath the tree. The candles flickered and danced, their shadows playing on the walls. It was peaceful and perfect.

Holly sighed, pressing herself back against me. "Thank you."

I kissed her head. "You're welcome."

❄

Holly sat back, smiling at me. The house she lived in had no dining room, so we ate side by side at the counter, our hands often touching, the occasional kiss shared as we ate our dinner together. Holly could, indeed, make gravy, and she patiently walked me through the steps as she mixed and seasoned, tasting until it was right. I doubted I would ever be as proficient as she was, but I let her think I had it down pat.

"That was amazing."

"Your gravy made it work. We're a good team."

She leaned forward, nuzzling my lips. "We are. It was a wonderful Christmas dinner. Thank you."

A realization hit me.

This time, this simple dinner, was how I would remember this Christmas. Not seeing my family. Not the disappointment I feared would happen with trying and failing to fit in with people who never seemed to want me.

No, I would remember Holly. Her warmth. Her acceptance.

Melancholy filled me, and I stood, needing to move. I grabbed our plates, walking over to the sink. A minute later, Holly joined me, wrapping her arms around me from behind. Her warmth soothed me, and I covered her hand that was resting on my chest. We were both silent for a moment, both of us feeling something in the air around us.

"Want to take a walk and see the lights before we have dessert and watch a movie?" she asked tenderly.

I turned and pulled her into my arms. "Yes."

Arm in arm, we strolled the streets, looking at the lights, stopping often to comment on a pretty house or chuckling over some badly done efforts. The night was dark, the moon full, and the stars in the clear sky bright and twinkling over us as we walked, often passing other couples and families out doing the same thing. The air was cold, but not as cold as it had been. Still, though, it was a good excuse to keep Holly close to my side.

At one point, we stopped at a house that was brightly lit, with a variety of decorations and displays out front. There was a large tree in the window, ablaze with colorful lights, and you could see the family inside—Mom, Dad, and two small children running around the room. We watched as, with help, they hung up their stockings before their parents lifted them, laughing, and carried them down the hall, no doubt to tuck them in for the night. I felt my throat tighten at the overwhelming feeling of sudden longing. Glancing down, I saw the expression on Holly's face. The vulnerable sadness I saw made me wince, and I knew she was feeling the same thing. Wanting something you thought you would never have.

"You want that, Holly? A house…kids?"

She sighed, a shaky, low sound of sadness. "I don't know how to be…*that*," she whispered, her hand indicating the now-empty window.

"Why?"

"I've never settled anywhere. My entire life has been one town after another. I only stayed here because I was so tired of moving. But even now, I know I'm not going to stay. I'll go to school and then somewhere else—" Her voice quavered. "I don't ever want to subject a child to that. Especially my own. It's just too hard. You never feel… safe."

I shook my head. She would be an amazing mother and partner. Her caring and warmth made her a natural. She couldn't see it, because she didn't see herself clearly.

I squeezed her against my side. "I think you're wrong. I think you're going to find your place. And you'll flourish. You have too much love in you not to."

She looked back at the window and sighed.

Pulling her close, I pressed a kiss to her crown. There was nothing else I could say.

CHAPTER SIX

EVAN

The movie was almost over. Holly was curled into me, the room dark except for the lights of our little tree and the dull glow from the TV. My arm was around her, my fingers caressing her shoulder as we chuckled over Chevy Chase's ridiculous antics. We had already watched *A Christmas Carol* and decided we needed something a little more upbeat for the second movie. She had been quiet for the last few moments and looking down, I saw her eyes were shut, her breathing deep and even. She was so tired. She didn't get much sleep last night because of me, and then she worked again today. Smiling, I shut off the TV and carefully lifted her into my arms, carrying her down the hall and laying her on the bed. She stirred, her eyes blinking open, and she gazed up at me sleepily. "Hi."

I nuzzled her head. "It's late. Go to sleep."

She held out her arms. "Stay."

I shut off the light and slipped in beside her after I pulled off my clothes. Wrapping my arms around her, I sighed. There was nowhere else I wanted to be.

Part of me, though, wished she were asking for forever.

The first thing I saw the next morning were Holly's blue eyes staring at me, wide and excited. Between us was a fuzzy stocking that she pushed toward me.

Grinning, I pulled myself upright. "For me?"

She nodded.

"I've never had a stocking before."

"Ever?"

I shook my head. "No. Lots of gifts, but never stockings." I looked at her sadly. "I didn't think to make you one."

She smiled. "I got one once. It was my favorite Christmas. I-I just wanted to make you one." She pushed it toward me. "Open it!"

It was full. Chocolate, socks, small puzzles, candy, and other items came out as I delved into it. Each one made me smile. Each item earned her a kiss. When it was empty, I pulled her onto my lap and showed her my own version of a full Christmas sock. I couldn't get enough of her mouth or her warmth. Joining with her was perfection. I groaned my orgasm into her neck, while she cried out her pleasure loudly.

Laughing and sated, we sipped coffee and ate toasted bagels sitting at the counter, then grabbed more coffee and entered the living room. Holly tried to hide her delight, but her eyes were dancing when we sat down by the tree. I loved seeing the expression of excitement on her face, knowing I had helped put it there. I handed her a gift, watching with barely suppressed enjoyment as she opened it. She took her time, relishing the process of unwrapping the gift slowly. Her smile of delight at the deep blue cashmere scarf and mittens was heartwarming. Her kiss warmed other parts of me.

She sighed in pleasure at the bath products Leslie helped me pick out, assuring me they were Holly's favorite scent. Holly immediately pulled out the hand lotion, insisting on testing it out not only on herself but me as well. I teased her, telling her it smelled far better on her.

I swallowed nervously handing her the last gift. The one I really wanted to give her and hoped she would accept.

She took it, eyeing the small, narrow box warily. She opened it with great care.

"Evan!" she gasped.

Smiling, I lifted the delicate handmade aquamarine necklace from the box. The color of the stone reminded me of her eyes, and I wanted to see her wear it. Surrounded by pearls, the gem was lovely and unique—just like she was. It looked perfect, nestled on her collarbone.

"It's so beautiful." Her kiss was warm and lingering. "I'll wear it every day." Another kiss followed. Her voice dropped, tinged with sadness. "I'll think of you when I wear it."

Before I could respond, she pushed a box into my hands. It was a large package, and I was filled with curiosity. I took my time opening the box and paused as I saw the contents. I ran my fingers over the smooth finish of the beautifully carved set of angel wings nestled in the tissue paper. I had seen and admired them in Leslie's store the day before. I had even chatted for a short time with the old man who had carved them, watching as he worked on another piece in the corner of the shop where he did his carving. I enjoyed wood carving, but my figures were nowhere near the delicate beauty of his. I had held these up and thought how great they would look over my fireplace, but then put them down, distracted by a question sent my way. Holly must have seen me look at them and gone back to get them for me. I remembered her casual remark of having errands to run in the afternoon. I could take them with me, and the memory of what they represented would stay with me always.

My Angel. Holly.

I smiled at her. "They're exquisite."

She returned my smile sweetly, but it didn't reach her eyes. "I saw you looking at them yesterday," she confirmed. "I thought maybe they would help you remember this Christmas."

My breath caught. I pulled her face close to mine. "I'll never forget this Christmas. I'll never forget you, Angel." My mouth covered hers, parting her lips and kissing her with all the emotion I was feeling. She returned my kiss with the same intense emotion. I pulled her closer so she was straddling my lap. She tugged on my hair as she whimpered softly. When we pulled back, I felt the loss of her warmth.

"There's one more," she whispered as she reached under the tree and handed me a long, heavier package. I leaned back, unwrapped the box and frowned. "Holly, it's too much."

"No," she insisted. "I heard you talking to Lionel about carving, and when I went back, he told me to tell you to get these chisels. He says they're the best. I asked him where to purchase them and he had an extra set, so I bought them off him."

"Holly—"

"Please accept them," she begged. "It means a lot to me. I could hear how much you enjoyed doing this while you spoke to Lionel, and I wanted to give you something useful for your hobby." Her smile was shaky. "Maybe you could make me something."

My gaze flew to hers.

"Mail it to me," she murmured.

I set aside the box. I had her in my arms again, lifting her, kissing her as I carried her down the hall, already feeling the pain of leaving her.

The morning was going too fast.

And there was nothing I could do to stop it.

She was so right in my arms. We fit together perfectly, and I wanted to lose myself in her forever. My mouth and hands memorized her taste, the feel of her silky skin. Her breathy, longing whisper of my name would forever be etched into my memory.

Being buried inside her heat was ecstasy. My mouth never left hers as I rocked, taking my time and loving her thoroughly. Her name fell like a prayer as I whispered it against her softness, my orgasm washing over me like a warm tidal wave, cresting and leaving me boneless.

I gathered her against me, holding her tight, fighting back unexpected tears. This was the last time I would make love to her.

My Angel.

How could I walk away from her?

It was time. I sat on the edge of the bed and tied my sneakers, my stomach knotted and my throat aching with suppressed emotion.

Holly was already in the living room, waiting for me. I knew she had put my gifts in the trunk of the car while I showered.

Our separation had already begun.

With a sigh, I pulled on my coat. I didn't want to leave, but I knew the longer I stayed and drew out our goodbye, the harder it would be for both of us.

I hadn't planned on this.

My trip to see my family had taken an unexpected detour, and now I wasn't sure I wanted to get back on the road I had started on only a few days earlier. It didn't feel right.

But Holly was correct. I had to go see my family, finish what I started. Once that was done, regardless of the results, I had a life waiting for me. She was still looking for hers. We had two separate paths.

It was time to leave.

I walked soundlessly into the living room. Holly was standing at the window, her back to me, her posture rigid.

"The weather forecast is good. No snow," she said, her voice sounding thick.

I stood behind her, my own throat aching. "Holly—"

"Don't. Thank you…for everything. You made this lonely time of year so unexpectedly wonderful for me."

I turned her around, slipping my fingers under her chin. "You did the same for me, Angel."

Our eyes locked. Her warmth and caring shone through the dampness I saw there. I pulled her into my arms, wanting her closeness. We stood silent and wrapped around each other. I didn't want to move.

I didn't want to leave.

"You have to go," she murmured.

I tightened my arms.

"Go see your family. Show them how wonderful you are."

I shook my head. "I doubt that is going to happen at this point. I'm hoping for a civil visit at best."

Her eyes were intense as she tilted up her head and met my gaze. "Try, Evan. You're so special. Show your family the person you are. Let them see how special. If they can't, it's their loss. But at least you tried. Then you can go back to your life and move on. But try."

"Holly, I—"

"May I ask a favor?" she interrupted me. I realized she wanted to send me off with a smile. I knew she didn't want me to say or do anything that would make my leaving more difficult on either of us. So, I smiled and nodded at her, masking my sadness.

"Anything."

"Will you call or text me—just let me know you got there?"

I pulled her closer. "Yes."

"Evan—"

I kissed her. Long, slow, deep. I wanted her taste in my mouth for the long miles ahead. I wanted to smell her lovely scent on my skin. I wanted to burn the memory of her eyes and the way they looked at me into my brain forever. Nobody ever looked at me the way Holly did. I doubted anyone ever would again.

When we broke apart, the air was heavy. Her eyes glistened under the lights, and I felt a tear run down my cheek.

How could I feel so deeply for someone I had only just met? Why was she so insistent that I had to leave? I could stay and forget about my family. We could talk about us instead, maybe figure out a way of seeing each other again. Thoughts and ideas swirled in my mind, but before I could say them out loud, Holly stepped back, breaking the silence.

"You have to go."

I reached out and dragged her back to me. I held her close, kissing the top of her head, unable to speak. Finally, she pulled back. "Text me," she ordered.

I smiled despite the sadness I was feeling. Ms. Bossy was back.

My voice trembled as I spoke. "Holly—"

She shook her head, her voice firm. "Be happy, Evan."

She wanted me to leave. I had no choice.

I touched her one last time. One last kiss. One last glance. "You as well, Angel."

I couldn't look back as I shut the door behind me.

CHAPTER SEVEN

EVAN

I pulled up in front of my parents' house. It was decorated with an understated elegance that spoke of money and class. And of being done by a company for hire. It was all about appearance, not for the love of the season. I couldn't even begin to imagine my father on a stepladder hanging lights, or my mother helping him.

When one was a Brooks, one simply didn't do manual labor. You hired that out.

No wonder they were disappointed in me.

I *was* the manual labor.

I shook my head, trying to clear the melancholy that had settled in my body since leaving Holly. She had been right—I needed to come and see my family and explore the chance of having a relationship with them—any of them. Given the fact that my sister now had a child, perhaps she would be more open to staying in touch. Maybe she would be happy to see me, and we could forge some sort of bond.

I ignored the small voice in my head that informed me perhaps pigs would fly tomorrow.

I stepped from my car, grabbed the bag of gifts from the trunk, straightened my shoulders, and approached the front door. I rang the bell and waited. I wasn't sure who was more shocked when the door opened—my mother seeing me standing on the doorstep, or me seeing her answer the door. She had people who did that for her.

Her greeting, however, didn't disappoint.

"Evan," she said with a frown. "What are you doing here? We weren't expecting you."

I forced a smile. "Merry Christmas, Mother. Surprise!"

Her eyebrows rose in annoyance. There was no smile, no return salutation, and no hug.

She stepped back. "Well, you may as well come in. I don't want to let too much cold air inside."

I tamped down my disappointment. The house might be warmer inside, but the atmosphere was as frosty as the winter weather I left behind as the door shut.

"What do you mean, you don't have a dinner jacket?" My mother's voice was shocked and appalled. I noticed her facial expression didn't change a lot, leading me to think some Botox was working overtime under her skin.

I shifted in my chair, uncomfortable and tense.

"As I said before, my lifestyle doesn't require a lot of dressing up, Mother."

"You don't own a *suit?*" Her voice rose at the end of the sentence as if not owning a suit should be a crime.

"Yes, I do. But as I said earlier, this was a last-minute decision, and I didn't think to pack it. I was simply trying to get here to spend the holidays with you. A suit never crossed my mind."

She sniffed. "Showing up on Christmas Day is leaving it rather late. You could have planned better, Evan. You always were bad at time management."

I counted to ten. "I told you I experienced car trouble."

Kelsey glanced toward the window. "What year is that Buick? Maybe you need a newer, better car." Her voice dripped with sarcasm. "Surely you can afford one."

I held back my sigh. My surprise appearance had been greeted with nothing but annoyance and barely concealed contempt. As I suspected, my gifts were opened then discarded. They had disappeared at some point, and I had no idea where they went. Although I'd expected it, I was stunned at the level of indifference to the items I had chosen for them. Holly, I knew, would be devastated if she saw how they had been received.

My hopes that my sister had tempered with motherhood dissolved quickly. My niece, Mia, was looked after by a nanny, and, after some staged photos of the family by the tree, had been whisked away to another part of the house. I was allowed to hold her, but only briefly. I sat with her cradled in my arms, admiring her sweetness, and talking softly to her before she was taken away. There was no doubt they didn't want her odd uncle to have much contact with her.

"My car is two years old, Kelsey. I don't need to replace it yet. I rarely drive it since I use my work SUV most days. I need a bigger vehicle for transporting furniture."

She and my mother made a face at my statement. I wasn't sure if it was the thought of me driving a work SUV or the work I did. Neither would meet their standards.

"You will have to wear one of your father's jackets for dinner," my mother announced and stood. "Now I have to go see about the seating arrangements. Your presence makes the table an odd number, Evan. It is most inconvenient."

She walked from the room, shaking her head and muttering under her breath. Kelsey met my gaze with a cool glance and followed.

I let my head fall forward.

An inconvenience. That was all I was to them. Other than his terse greeting, my father had ignored me except to remind me once more that my life was wasted. My brother sat in the corner, a drink in hand every moment, watching the entire debacle with a smirk on his face. I wondered if anyone else noticed the amount of alcohol he was imbibing. Surprisingly, my brother-in-law, Simon, seemed like a decent sort of guy, but Kelsey interrupted him every time we began to talk. He kept trying, but when she became irate, he gave up and, with a resigned look, left the room. I didn't see him again until dinner, and we sat at opposite ends of the table. I did wonder briefly what a nice guy like him was doing married to Kelsey, but it was a question I knew I would never have an answer for. He, at least, seemed to care for his daughter. Aside from me, he was the only one who held her and appeared upset when she was removed from the room. I had a feeling there was a story there.

My brother and father had disappeared into my father's study as soon as the gifts were done. I was not invited to join them. I had sat, as an observer only, watching them open their presents, noting with interest Simon didn't participate. There had been nothing for me, of course, since I wasn't expected, and I was ignored as they opened their over-the-top gifts, exclaiming over cruise tickets, custom-made suits, expensive liquor, and jewelry none of them needed, but wanted to have—simply for show. I tried not to feel slighted thinking of the fact that all I received at Christmas every year, this one included, was a card—not even personally signed.

I rubbed a hand over my weary eyes.

This had been a mistake of epic proportions.

I stood and climbed the steps to the guest room I had been given, albeit grudgingly. I needed a nap and a shower. In my room, I checked my phone. I had texted Holly and let her know I'd arrived, and I had hoped to hear from her. There was only one line waiting for me.

> **Holly**
> Glad you're safe. Remember what I said, Evan. Show them who you are.

I shook my head. They didn't want to know me, and they couldn't care less about the person I was. I would never fit into their world and mine made them uncomfortable.

I lay down, sadness engulfing me. The wish that I was beside Holly tugged at my chest. The thought of her filled me with a longing I had never experienced. I never should have left her.

Dinner was an awkward event as I sat in my borrowed jacket, listening to the talk that swirled around me in a roomful of strangers. I was rarely included in the conversation, so I spent the time instead thinking of the vast difference in the dinner with my family and their friends, compared to the one I'd shared with Holly the night before in her tiny kitchen. That small room had been filled with warmth and laughter. My parents' large, opulent room, lit with candles and heavy with the overpowering stench of hothouse flowers, was as cold and fake as the people in it. There I was, nothing more than the son who was constantly lacking, but whose presence had to be tolerated. Last night, I had been the center of Holly's small world.

I far preferred that role.

But I kept my promise to Holly and myself. I attempted to break through to them, but I failed. The following day was fraught with tension, and no matter how innocently a conversation started, it became hostile and turned into an argument. Finally, my father and I exchanged heated words over my choices in life, and for the first time ever, I stood up to him. I used Holly's words when I informed him it was my life—not his. I was happy, enjoyed my work, and my quiet life. He made sure I understood exactly how he felt and what an utter failure I was in his eyes.

After they had settled for the night, I grabbed my things and left, going through the kitchen to the back where they had asked me to park my car. Something bright caught my eye, and I was horrified to find the bag of gifts I had brought beside the garbage can. The symbolism wasn't lost on me. My gifts were worth nothing to them. Nor was I. I took them with me, knowing there were many people who would appreciate them back home.

Because Nova Scotia was my home now—not here. It never really had been.

I felt only relief as I left the house, and I knew they would feel the same way when they woke and found me gone. I no longer had to try or to spare them another thought. The only sadness I felt was at the fact that Mia would be brought up among such cold people. I feared she would become like them, and it bothered me, not that I could do anything to prevent it. I knew she wouldn't be allowed any contact with me. Silently, I wished her much luck, determined if she ever reached out, to be there for her.

I drove straight home without a break. It took everything in me not to pull off the highway as I passed the exit to the town where Holly lived. I had to wrap my hands tightly around the steering wheel and not look in the rearview mirror. I fought down the swell of desperate need to go to her.

Holly hadn't asked me to stay, so I didn't think she would want me showing back up a couple of days later on her doorstep, wanting to share my sad story. I didn't think I could handle more rejection— especially not from her. I needed to accept that she was right—my time with her had been a moment in my life. Not the future.

Somehow, that reality was far harder to handle than the disastrous finality with my family.

Holly was constantly on my mind, lingering on the edge of my thoughts. I compared everything that happened with my parents to her. Her warmth versus their coldness. Her giving, generous nature against their judgmental, rigid views. Her sweet acceptance. Their complete rejection.

With a weary sigh, I pulled into the driveway leading to my house. Lights beckoned to me, their warm glow a welcome sight after the long drive. Dan's car was parked in front of the house, and I knew he and Carol would be there waiting for me. I smiled sadly. Unlike my family, they would be happy to see me. I opened the car door, relieved to be home. Immediately, I was enveloped in Carol's embrace, a motherly action I needed more than I realized. Surrounded by her scent—vanilla and cookies—I hugged her back and let her lead me inside my house. Coffee, sandwiches, and a warm fire waited for me.

As did their patience and understanding.

"Evan, I'm so sorry. I had hoped things would go better for you." Carol's voice was hurt-filled. Hurt I knew she was feeling for me.

I leaned my head back on the sofa, enjoying the feeling of the simple comfort that being surrounded by my own things brought me.

"Pretty much a disaster from the get-go. Maybe my car breaking down was a sign. I guess I should have listened better to what the gods were saying." I smiled, trying to lighten the atmosphere, while my mind went over what I had just shared with Dan and Carol.

I told them everything about the time with my parents, holding nothing back about their displeasure or how I was done trying to be what they wanted. Moving forward, I was living life the way I wanted—with no apologies.

"Are you okay, Evan?" Carol's voice broke through my musings.

I nodded. "I'm just tired."

"You should have stopped. That is such a long drive."

I shook my head. If I had, I would have turned around and gone to find Holly. The urge had been strong. "I wanted to get home."

"We're glad you're back." Dan smiled at me. "Carol's got a big brunch planned for you. We'll give you tomorrow to rest up and come over the next day. It'll be our own little Christmas."

"I look forward to it."

Carol leaned forward, her hands resting on her knees. "Are you going to contact her? Holly?"

"Carol," Dan chided. "Not our business."

"Hush." She turned back to me. "Well?"

Carol had been full of questions about Holly. She was fascinated by the way we met and the time I'd spent with her. I had shown her the wings Holly gave me and the wood-carving tools. Talked about the time we spent together. It had been such a relief to be able to tell someone about her. I never brought up the subject at my parents', letting them think I had traveled even later than I actually had. It would have been blasphemy to have said Holly's name there. I could only imagine the biting comments that would have followed, and I didn't want to share that memory with them, only to have it tainted.

I shrugged. "And say what, Carol? 'Hey, thanks for the interlude. I'll look you up next time'? It was, as she said, a stop in my life. Something we both needed at the time."

Carol frowned. "Bullshit, Evan. That is *bullshit*."

I gaped at her. Carol never swore.

"She didn't ask me to stay," I insisted.

"And *you* didn't ask," she stated pointedly.

I stared at her, unsure what to say.

Dan let out a bark of laughter and stood. "I think we need to leave. Don't forget brunch. Come over whenever you want that morning." He pulled Carol off the chair. "We're going now. Get some sleep, Evan."

Carol paused beside my chair. "When you're ready to talk, I'm here."

Dan tugged on her arm. "Leave him alone, for heaven's sake."

She shook her head. "Stubborn fool."

I watched them walk out, not moving from the sofa.

Was she talking about Dan or me?

CHAPTER EIGHT

EVAN

My dreams were filled with soft blue eyes that were warm and kind. They looked at me with so much emotion, yet every time I reached for the person attached to them, they disappeared. I woke up in the late afternoon, unrefreshed and moody. I walked around the house, unable to settle.

The quiet and solitude I always enjoyed now seemed to be mocking me. The silence echoed in the house. Over and again, my eyes strayed to the wings on the mantle. Memories of my time with her played in my head.

Holly.

Her laugh.

The way she cared for me.

The sadness and fear she tried so hard to hide.

I thought of how I felt being with her.

The incredible sensation of making love to her.

How she made me feel about myself—not weak and lost. Unwanted.

Strong. Needed.

Loved?

I shook my head. I was being ridiculous. People didn't fall in love in a day.

Yet, I couldn't deny the longing I felt for her.

I glanced at my phone and picked it up. I hadn't texted her aside from the one I'd sent after arriving at my parents'. She hadn't texted me again—nor had I expected her to. But I wanted her to know I was home in case she worried.

> **Me**
> Holly, I am back home. Things went as badly as expected. Just thought you'd want to know.

A few moments later, my phone beeped.

> **Holly**
> I'm so sorry. You deserve so much better. You tried. I am proud of you—now make your own life and be happy for you.

Be happy.
I thought I was happy before I met her.
Now I wasn't sure.
I rubbed my eyes. I wasn't sure about anything anymore.

Watching my friends open the gifts I had chosen was a far different experience than I'd had at my parents'. Their expressions of delight were a direct contrast to the tight-lipped scorn the gifts I had given my family had drawn.

Carol's reaction to the lovely blown glass vase was effusive, and Tara squealed in delight over the earrings Holly had picked out after I tried to describe her "style" as best I could. Dan was thrilled with the prints I had selected for his office, and Andrew already had plans for a fishing trip for us to use the lures I had found.

I frowned in confusion when Carol handed me another small parcel. I had opened their thoughtful gifts already. "It has your name on it," she explained. "It was in the bag with the others."

I swallowed heavily.

Holly.

With shaky fingers, I opened the little package. Inside was a small Saint Christopher medallion. The patron saint of travelers. I unfolded the small note.

To help keep you safe. Always, H

My hand came up to rest on my chest, trying to quell the sudden ache. Holly worried about me. Even after I left, she was worried about me.

The memories hit me again. The feelings they evoked flooded my system. Holly's gaze. Her caring and warmth.

I needed that in my life.

I needed her.

As crazy as it sounded, I was in love with her.

For a moment, I was lost in my thoughts until the sound of a clearing throat made me look up. My gaze found Carol's right away. Her eyes were gentle, filled with understanding, and she nodded before I even got the words out.

"I have to go back."

She smiled. "Yes, you do."

Tara sprang to her feet. "Thank God. Let's figure this out."

"I'll leave tomorrow."

Dan shook his head. "There's a big snowstorm headed this way, Evan. It's heading across Quebec right now. You'll get trapped."

"You need to fly," Tara announced. "Tonight, before we get snowed in."

"I—"

"I'm on it," Andrew announced, heading over to the computer. He sat down, typing fast. He scanned the screen. "All the flights are booked except for the last flight out at eight. I take it all the time. There's a first-class seat left." He whistled. "It's gonna cost you."

I tossed him my credit card. "Book it. I need a car—make that an SUV—to pick up there as well. A nice one."

He chuckled. "You got it. Go home and pack. I'll get this done, and Tara and I will drive you to the airport. Then you can go get your girl."

I looked at Carol. "Brunch…" I started.

She waved me off with a wide smile and tugged me in for a hug. "Forget brunch. You can bring Holly for dinner when you get back."

"What if she says no?"

She shook her head and cupped my face. "Then you know you tried. But from what you've told me, she won't. I think she's missing you as much as you are missing her." She smiled. "*This* is your chance to find your life, Evan. Grab it. *Be happy.*"

"I will."

❆

The familiar scenery went by as I drove down the road. The diner was closed between Christmas and New Year's, the parking lot deserted and the sign dark. I hoped Holly would be home when I got there. If not, I would wait.

I was nervous, anxious, and tense. I knew Holly might say no. She might think I was crazy. But like Carol said, as with the situation with my family, I had to reach out and try. I only hoped this outcome would be better.

I had spent the afternoon wandering my house, imagining Holly there with me. I could see her sitting on the porch as the sun set, our hands entwined. Or curled up in the swing sketching. I could hear her laughter echo in the kitchen as we worked together making a meal. I wanted to see her warm gaze across the table from me. I wanted to feel her pressed up against me in my bed and wake up to her in the morning.

As crazy and fast as it sounded, I wanted to build a life with her.

She understood me, because she had lived through her own kind of neglected childhood. Her parents had dragged her around, only thinking of themselves, and never giving her the things she needed more than anything. Things she deserved.

A home.

To be safe and loved.

To belong.

She had helped me. Cared for me so lovingly—a complete stranger. She had not only opened her house to me; without realizing it, she had shown me her heart. She had shared her pain and let me share mine with her. She made me feel. The short time I spent with her had changed me now…for the better. And I didn't want to go back to being shut off anymore.

While Andrew and Tara were booking my flight, I talked to Carol. She made me understand why Holly didn't ask me to stay. It wasn't because she didn't feel the same way.

No. She felt something. I could see it in her eyes and feel the way she cared for me; I knew that.

Holly didn't think herself worthy of asking. She was sending me away to get on with my life, because she thought I had a good one. But she was wrong; something was missing. She was worried she didn't know how to settle in one place or be a partner to someone, because she'd never experienced that in her entire life. But she was wrong about that also. She needed someone to love her and to let her see how it felt to have someone put her needs and desires over their own. To show her she was worth that.

I knew what was missing for both of us.

Each other.

Now I had to convince her.

I pulled up outside her house. Her large, ugly truck was parked in the driveway. I could see the glow of a light in the window, and I sighed in relief, knowing she was in there. I sat in silence, gathering up my courage; I had no idea how she would react to seeing me.

There was only one way to find out.

HOLLY

I sat on the sofa, my legs curled under me, with Chester asleep beside me. A glass of wine sat on the table, untouched. I hadn't eaten dinner since my appetite was nonexistent.

It had been since Evan had cooked dinner for us. I had barely picked at the turkey dinner Leslie made for us on Christmas Day, and in the days that followed, I snacked on leftovers she'd sent, nibbling on a sandwich or some crackers and cheese. Nothing tempted me.

All I could think about was Evan. As soon as I received his text when he went home, I read his pain in the one line he sent me. His family had rejected him.

And he had left, not stopping to see me.

It had taken everything in me not to ask him why. I knew why.

I had been correct when I'd told him the time we had was only a moment in his life. He deserved someone who could be a partner to him. Who knew how to be part of a lasting relationship. I wasn't that person, and he knew it.

Still, I couldn't stop thinking about him.

His loving nature.

His kind personality.

His passion.

How desperately I missed him. I didn't understand it, but I did. I felt empty without him.

Chester stretched, lifting his head, and I tickled him under the chin. "Evan's little twin," I murmured, a smile pulling at my lips in memory. He did look like the feline version of Evan.

Evan was tall and lanky, but his shoulders were broad. His hair, long enough to touch his collar, was a midnight black with a white patch in the middle that gave him a rakish air. His green eyes were set under heavy brows, and when he slid on his glasses to read something, his sexiness level, which was already high, flew into the stratosphere. But he was unconscious of his appeal, which only made him more attractive. I was shocked when he first told me of his shyness and absence of a girlfriend. I was convinced the town he lived in must be lacking in women with good eyesight. How he hadn't been snatched up was insane.

The sound of a car, then hurried footsteps, made me frown. The sound of furious pounding on my door startled me. Connie wasn't due home for at least a month and I wasn't expecting anyone. Chester jumped from the sofa, running to the door. I followed, worried something had happened to Leslie and Tom needed my help. I flicked on the light and yanked open the heavy door.

To say I was shocked to find Evan standing in my doorway would be an understatement.

I met his gaze. He looked anxious and upset.

"Evan? What…what are you doing here?" I stepped forward, concerned. "Are you all right?"

He held out his hand beseechingly. "I-I have to talk to you," he begged.

I stepped back, grasping his hand and pulling him inside.

"You were home. You texted me and told me that." I stared at him in horror. "How did you get back here? You didn't drive again, did you?"

He shook my head. "I flew." He tightened his hand on mine. "I had to see you. I had to try. I have to talk to you, Holly."

I furrowed my brow in confusion but nodded. "Okay, Evan. Come in and talk."

EVAN

Once in her living room, I pulled off my coat. I stood looking at her, my eyes drinking her in. It felt like years, not days, since I had last seen her. She looked so good to me. Soft, pretty, warm. I wanted so badly to touch her, pull her into my arms and hold her, but I wasn't sure if I could.

"Holly, I—"

She moved closer, now clearly concerned. "Evan, sweetheart, what is it? Why are you here?"

Sweetheart. She called me sweetheart.

I wrapped my arms around her, thrilled when she leaned into my embrace, her face buried into my chest. I held her close, needing to feel her warmth and quiet strength.

Her voice was calm. "What did you mean you had to try? Try what? Why did you need to talk to me?"

There was a tone to her voice, one I prayed was hopeful.

"I made a mistake."

She leaned back, gazing up at me, but didn't leave my arms. "What? Going to see your family?"

"No. You were right—I had to. I'm glad I did that. It proved I was correct and I don't belong in their world. And I finally told my father off. I won't let his opinion of me rule my life anymore."

She smiled and cupped my cheek. "Good. I'm proud of you. But what mistake?"

I drew in a deep breath. "I should have come right back here."

"What do you mean?"

I released her, needing to move and let off some of my nerves. I started to pace. "I never should have left here, Holly. I never should have left you behind." I tugged on my hair. "When I left my parents', I should have come right back here and talked to you. But I didn't know how you would react. If you wanted me to come back." I clenched my hands. "You didn't ask me to stay. You let me walk away. Didn't you feel anything for me?"

Her voice quavered. "Yes, I did. I felt a lot of things."

"Then why?"

"I didn't want you to go," she admitted. "It took everything I had in me not to come after you when you left. I wanted to ask you…but I was afraid. I wasn't sure how I would handle it if you said no." Her voice became thick with emotion. "I didn't think I could be what you needed."

"You are. You are *exactly* what I need."

"Evan…"

I stopped in front of her, my entire body shaking. "I want you to come with me," I blurted out before I could change my mind.

"What?"

"Come with me, *please*."

Her brow furrowed. "Where are you going?"

"I want you to come home with me. To Nova Scotia."

She stared at me, speechless.

"Leaving you behind was one of the most painful things I've ever done, Holly. The entire drive, all I could think about was you. It's all I can think about now. How you made me feel. How empty I am without you. How empty my life will be without you in it."

Her eyes were wide with surprise. I kept talking.

"I thought I was happy before. I thought my life was settled. But it's not. *I'm not.* I've been waiting for something, and I didn't know what it was until I found you. I was meant to break down that night. I was meant to find you." I paused. "We need each other, Angel.

"You told me you wanted to find your place in this world. Stop looking." I wrapped my hands around hers. "Find your home with me." I stepped closer. "I've found mine with you." I kissed her hand softly. "You said you wanted to belong somewhere." I paused. "Belong to me."

"But…"

I shook my head. "No buts. This is real. It's right. I feel it. We'll figure out everything—together. What you want to do about school. Living together as a couple. We can do it all if we're together. I'll support whatever decisions you make about your life as long as I can share it with you."

She blinked.

"Our home can be your safe place, Holly. I can be your safe place. You can be mine."

One lone tear ran down her cheek.

I took in a deep breath. "I love you."

Her voice was incredulous. "You love me?"

I shrugged self-consciously. "I know I don't have a lot of experience with that emotion. But if loving you means wanting to be with you, to make you happy, then yes. I want to protect you, care for you, like you did for me. I want to watch you smile. Wipe your tears. Hold you at night. Wake up with you." I paused. "If wanting to do all those things and be that person for you for the rest of your life means that I love you, then yes, Holly Cole. I love you."

She stared at me, speechless. Her gaze moved between our hands and my eyes.

"A very smart person told me to be happy. You make me happy. Carol told me to hold on to whatever it was I found that made me feel this way. So, I am. It's you. It's *all* you.

"I love you, Holly. I know this with a certainty beyond

comprehension. Stop being alone and searching for your place in this world. It's with me. Let's live our lives together." I smiled at her, even as a tear ran down my cheek. "I want to give you what we saw the other night. A home. One filled with lights and love. A family we created together."

"You want children?"

"With you. Yes. I want everything with you." I tightened my hands around hers. "Please, Angel, rescue me one more time. For the rest of our lives."

Her eyes filled with tears. "Evan," she breathed.

"Don't say no, please. I couldn't bear it. I know it's fast, but please, give us a chance."

"I want to," she whispered.

I pulled her into my arms, relief and joy coursing through my body. In that one instant, everything in my life shifted and settled, becoming perfectly clear. If I had her, I could do anything. Be anything. As long as she was mine, I would be okay.

"What if I can't be what you need?" she asked, searching my eyes with hers.

"You already are."

"Say it again," she pleaded, her voice vulnerable.

I looked down at her sweet face. "I love you, Holly."

Her beautiful smile lit the room. "I want and feel all those things for you as well. I-I love you too, Evan."

The power of those small words hit me. She offered them without any conditions or reservations. Only truth.

I kissed her. "Those are my favorite words in the world. I will never tire of hearing you say them."

"Then I'll say them every day."

"You'll come with me?"

"Yes."

"Now?"

She frowned, confused. "Um, I need to pack up some things and let people know."

I nodded. "Of course. I'll help. What doesn't fit in the SUV, we'll ship."

"You don't want to drive my truck?" she teased gently.

"Ah, no. We'll ship it out if you insist."

"Maybe Tom could store it."

I winked. "Or junk it." I'd happily dip into my trust fund to purchase a nice car for her. But I'd pay to ship the thing if that was what she really wanted. Anything for her if it meant she came with me.

"Don't talk smack about my truck. It's been good to me." She slapped my chest, then frowned. "Chester?"

I grinned. "My cat twin is welcome. I hope he likes road trips."

"I like road trips."

"I like you."

She blushed sweetly. "What will your friends think when you come home with me?"

"They can hardly wait to meet you. I told them all about you, and they know how I feel." I drew my fingers down her cheek. "I've been searching for you. And now that I've found you, I'm not letting go." I kissed her warmly. "They are gonna love you. I have a feeling you and Tara are going to be best friends. And Carol will spoil you." I tightened my hand in reassurance. "Life will be good for us, Holly. I promise."

Her voice was quiet. "I know."

I pulled her into my arms, nuzzling the top of her head. We stayed locked together, enjoying the moment of unexpected happiness.

Holly tilted her head back. "What now?"

"I'll go find some boxes."

She chuckled. "Everything is closed. It's almost midnight. Tomorrow, I'll call Leslie and ask if she has empty ones from the store we can have."

"How do you think she and Tom will react?"

Holly smiled. "Leslie wanted to know why I let you leave. She said she knew we belonged together when she saw us together in her store." She sighed. "I'll miss them, but they knew I was leaving soon anyway. I think they might be surprised by the news, but they'll be happy for me. She and Tom will help if we need it." She looked around. "It won't take long. There isn't much. Most of this belongs to Connie. I'll have to call and tell her."

I lifted her chin. "They're just things. Take or leave whatever you want. We'll build a *life* together, Holly. One full of love. We'll fill walls with pictures and our hearts with memories. We'll do it together." I wiped away a glistening tear from the side of her eye. "You're never going to be alone again."

"Neither are you."

Our eyes met and held. My entire future was there inside the glimmering depths of soft blue. Gently, I traced her damp cheek.

"We'll start off the new year together, Angel."
"Together."
My mouth covered hers.
I was home.

Waking up to Holly the next morning was as amazing as I thought it would be. Nestled in my arms, her head on my shoulder, she slumbered with a smile on her face. I lay still, watching her for a moment, filled with wonder that I would no longer wake up alone. My days wouldn't be permeated by the sound of silence, and my nights an endless repeat of emptiness.

Holly would be there with me.

Unable to resist, I leaned down, slipping my fingers under her chin and nuzzling her full lips. She blinked awake, her smile growing against my mouth.

"Hi," she murmured, her voice thick with sleep.

"Sorry, I had to kiss you. You were making me happy."

"By sleeping?"

I chuckled. "By sleeping beside me. I realized I get to keep you." My voice caught. "I won't be alone anymore."

She snuggled closer, running her fingers through my hair. "Never again. Neither of us will be."

Our gaze met and held, our future bright and filled with love.

I slid my hand down her back, curving it over the swell of her ass, tugging her closer. "I think we should celebrate."

She whimpered at the feel of my hard cock pressing against her softness. She lifted her leg over my hip, arching her back so I settled into her heat. "Yes, Evan. We should."

I groaned at the feel of her. "You are so perfect," I whispered.

"We're perfect together."

I rolled her over, hovering above her. I gazed down at her sweet face. Her wild hair curled around her cheeks, and her lovely eyes were filled with love as she returned my stare. I slid inside her, dropping my head to her neck at the rightness of feeling her warmth wrapped around me. I began to move, my need for her overtaking everything else.

"Yes, we are."

CHAPTER NINE

EVAN

Over coffee, we planned our day and the trip ahead. I frowned as I studied the weather. "We need to leave today to beat the storm heading this way, Holly. Either that or wait a few days."

She wrapped her hand around her mug. "All I need is a couple of hours. I have to call John and resign from the diner. I already texted Connie, and she has another friend who is going to move in next week. Leslie and Tom will be here in an hour with some boxes and tape." She shrugged. "I don't have a lot to pack."

Her voice held a strange tone, and I realized she sounded almost embarrassed. "Hey," I called softly. "I told you we'll build our own memories."

She nodded. "There are a few boxes in the garage that were my parents'. I would like to take them if that's okay. And my sketchbooks."

"Holly," I started, waiting until she met my eyes before continuing. "You can bring anything you want. I'd rent a trailer if I had to, or ship everything if you wanted to bring this whole damn house."

A smile curled her lips, and the sadness faded from her eyes. "No shipping needed."

"Are you sure you're ready to do this?" I asked, my heart in my throat. "We can stay, or I can head back and you can follow when you're ready," I offered, hating the idea of leaving her at all. "This is sudden, and I don't want to rush you."

The frantic shaking of her head made me relax. She didn't want me to go without her. "No! I want to go with you. I'm just—won't your friends think it's odd when we arrive and I have, like, two suitcases, a cat, and a few boxes? Maybe they'll think I'm after your money."

I burst out laughing and leaned over to kiss her. Then I had to kiss her again. "Silly girl. When I arrived in Nova Scotia, I had a backpack. Your things don't make you the person you are. Your heart does. I already know you, Holly. I see your soul. It matches mine, and my money has nothing to do with it." I winked. "In fact, we can split the gas money."

"Good idea," she nodded sagely. "I don't think the bank is open today, but we can stop by the ATM and—"

Another round of laughter escaped my mouth, and I swept her into my arms and kissed her until she was breathless. "Not happening. I was teasing. I'm taking you home to Nova Scotia, I'm taking care of you, and you are going to let me. Understand?"

Her cheeks flooded with color. "Fine. No need to get all handsy and bossy, Evan."

I grinned. "Why don't I show you just how handsy and bossy I can get?"

Her eyes widened, and the grip she had on my arm tightened. I dropped my gaze to her mouth and I began to lower my head, when the doorbell sounded.

"Leslie and Tom," she murmured. "Bad timing."

"Nope," I said and kissed her fast. "Let's get you packed and get on the road. We'll revisit this later."

She giggled as she slipped by and patted my ass.

"So bossy."

I followed, feeling happier and lighter than I had in years.

She did that for me.

With a frown, I cast a last look at the boxes in the back of the SUV I had rented. There were six of them, plus two suitcases. That was the entire contents of Holly's life, sitting in the back of the vehicle. Three of the boxes held things from her parents—the rest were hers. I was determined her life would no longer be so empty.

I shut the liftgate and hurried back into the house. I stopped at the kennel waiting by the door and peered in at Chester. He hadn't been overly pleased at being placed inside the carrier, but he stared back at me, calm and resolved. I poked my finger inside and chuffed his chin. "You're gonna love it there, Chester," I promised. "Lots of rooms to wander around in and places to lie in the sun."

Then I went to find Holly. She had been quiet since Leslie and Tom had left, their goodbyes filled with promises of visits and keeping in touch. I liked them both and hoped they would follow through. I wanted Holly to stay close to people who cared about her.

I found her in her bedroom, opening drawers and cupboards, making sure she had everything. A small bag sat on the bed, the mittens I gave her resting beside the bag with her coat. She already had the soft hat on her head, pulled low on one side, giving her a rakish air. The blue looked pretty against her hair and skin. I leaned against the doorway, watching her. She was pale, her teeth caught in her bottom lip, and for a moment I felt a flash of guilt.

Was I pushing her too fast?

"Holly."

She looked up, a smile appearing. "Hey."

"You almost ready?"

"I was just checking I hadn't left anything." She sighed. "Not that I had a lot to bring."

I crossed the room and grasped her elbows. I bent and kissed her forehead, my lips lingering on her skin. "We discussed this. None of it matters, Holly. What you bring or don't bring. As long as you're with me, all of this is just stuff. We'll replace what you forget, and we'll build a whole bunch of new memories."

I felt her tension ease. "I know."

"Is it too much, Angel? Do I need to slow down?" My heartbeat raced as I waited for her answer.

"No. I do tend to overthink things." She laughed, not meeting my eyes. "Since my parents never really thought things out, I sort of took over that job."

I folded her into my arms, relieved. "You have me now. We'll worry about them together."

She leaned back, her smile genuine. "Together—I like that idea."

"Ready to start our adventure?"

She leaned up on her toes and kissed me. "Ready."

I slowed down as we passed the diner. It was still closed, but John had a private family party going on inside. "Did you want to stop?"

"No. John wished me well, and to be honest, I think it was the right time. His wife has been wanting to change the hours and close at eleven, instead of being open twenty-four hours. That would mean a lot of hours being cut back, and without me he can give the other girls my shifts. It used to be really busy all the time, but since they built the bypass he doesn't get as many truckers in at night. The regulars who have come for years, but not a lot of new people."

"Makes sense." I squeezed her hand, watching the way she peered over her shoulder at the building fading into the background. I knew, no matter how happy she was to be coming with me, she was going to be sentimental about leaving. "It's sort of our place, isn't it?"

"Yes, it is. But I'm so excited about where we are going, Evan."

I winked at her. "So am I."

She was quiet as she watched the scenery pass by. I hit the highway, pleased at how empty the roads were. I picked up speed, handed her my phone, and patted her leg. "Pick some music, Holly. And the route. If there is any place you want to stop, name it."

"Really?" she asked, taking my phone, her eyes excited. She had told me about the many trips she had taken with her parents. An added piece of luggage in the back seat, relegated to observer, not really part of the event or the planning. I didn't want this trip to be like that for her.

"The storm isn't going to hit for a few days. We have time to do some exploring if you want."

She leaned over and kissed my cheek, her lips warm on my skin. "Thank you."

She scrolled through my playlists, pursing her lips. "Well, thank goodness. No rap."

I felt a smile tug on my lips. "You don't like rap, Holly?"

She shook her head. "It makes me ragey. Probably not good for a car trip."

I laughed out loud, unable to imagine her "ragey." "Probably not," I agreed. "Best stick to a different genre."

"You know what goes well with road trips?" she asked, glancing at me.

"What?" I'd give her anything.

She pointed at the sign we were passing. "Coffee and donuts."

I hit the indicator and slowed down. "Your wish is my command."

She smiled—so wide and bright, it was a wonder to witness. "I'm going to like this road trip."

That was my plan.

HOLLY

Evan slowly drove up to the house, putting the SUV in park and turning to look at me. I stared at the place, awed and excited. The huge house sat on a plot of land that was astounding in its scope. Though it was snow-covered and icy, I could still see the beauty the winter hid. Mature trees and bushes surrounded a large log home. The ocean sparkled in the background. Two stories, with a huge wraparound porch and tons of windows, the house looked as if it belonged in that spot.

I turned to Evan, who was watching me with excited eyes. "Evan, it's beautiful!"

He smiled and lifted my hand to his mouth. "Yes, it is."

Except he wasn't looking at the house—he was looking at me. I felt my cheeks grow warm, and I wondered if I would ever get used to his affection.

The drive from Ontario had been so different from the ones I used to take with my parents. It was always their trip, their adventure, and I was simply present. This time, Evan made sure I saw anything I wanted. Teasingly, he told me I was in charge of the route and the radio. We strolled around little towns, spent the night in Montreal, planned another trip for when we had more time, to Quebec City. He kept his eye on the weather, but we were lucky and stayed ahead of any storm that might have stalled our journey, although he admitted, even though he was anxious to get me to Nova Scotia, he wouldn't have minded spending more time trapped in a hotel with me.

Chester proved to be a great traveler, sleeping in his kennel, sitting on my lap, watching the scenery go by, curious but calm.

Now he was sleeping in his kennel, not at all concerned the car had stopped—a seasoned traveler.

"I can't wait to see inside," I admitted. "I'm already in love with the place."

Evan grinned, kissing my hand again. "Okay."

I slid from the SUV, stretching to relieve my tight muscles. Evan opened the back door, lifting Chester out, and stood beside me. He wrapped his free arm around my waist and pressed a kiss to my head. He drew in a deep breath and smiled.

"Welcome home, Holly."

My heart stuttered with his words, but I felt only a sense of rightness. Being with Evan felt like home, and the house in front of us was going to be my sanctuary—the same way it was for him. There was no doubt about it. I returned his smile with one of my own.

"I love you."

He beamed, hugging me tight to his side as we walked toward the door.

"Those are my favorite words, ever," he murmured.

Two hours later, I was still wandering around in a daze. The house was massive. Four bedrooms, a big kitchen that took up half of the main floor, while the other half was a living-dining area. There were windows everywhere, with views of the ocean, the woods, and the lovely open areas around the house. Evan's workshop was tucked against the backdrop of massive fir trees, and as he showed me around, he explained how he loved to have the huge barn doors open so he could hear the sound of the waves and smell the fresh air as he worked. He pointed to the loft over his work area. "I'll turn that into a studio for you. You can paint and sketch to your heart's content."

I could only kiss him in thanks.

His shop was neat and orderly, as was his house. It was comfortable and furnished with pieces he had restored, along with newer sofas and chairs. The angel wings I had given him were the only decoration above the massive fireplace that heated the entire first floor.

As I stood, gazing around, Evan slid his arms around my waist, and he pulled me back against his chest. "The place needs a woman's touch," he murmured, his lips close to my ear. "*Your* touch."

"I've never had a home to add my touch to," I admitted.

He kissed my neck. "Now you do. I've always loved this house, but this is the first time it's felt like a home to me, Holly. Because you're in it. We'll make it ours."

Ours.

I liked the sound of that.

The sound of a car approaching made me lift my head to meet Evan's gaze. He grinned, the corners of his eyes crinkling. "Carol and Dan, no doubt. She insisted on 'dropping by' with dinner for us so we didn't have to worry about cooking." He chuckled. "The truth is, she's so anxious to meet you that I'm shocked she wasn't on the porch waiting when we got here."

I felt a wave of nerves hit me and Evan tightened his grip. "I'm right here, Holly. And I swear—they're gonna love you. And you will love them. I know it."

A knock sounded on the front door. He kissed my neck. "Ready?"

I huffed out a long breath. "Ready."

CHAPTER TEN

HOLLY

Carol and Dan were warmth personified. They arrived with dinner, groceries, and lots of hugs, and they stayed for coffee. By the time they left, I understood Evan's affection for them. I loved seeing her gently admonish him about making sure he kept the house warm enough for me and the way Dan teased him about how his firewood was stacked. It was impossible to feel nervous after a few moments. They seemed to accept me for simply being me and the fact that I was important to Evan.

Carol told me about all the charming spots in town, and we made arrangements to spend some time together.

"I'll show you all the best places to shop and introduce you around," she insisted.

"That would be lovely. I need to find a job as well. Is there a diner in town?"

"Yes, a few. They are quiet this time of year, but you never know. Once tourist season kicks in, they're always looking."

I nodded, already thinking ahead. I had enough money saved; I could be without a job for a while and still contribute. I had to discuss all that with Evan.

After Dan and Carol left, I poked around the kitchen, figuring out where things were and putting away the groceries they had so kindly brought with them.

Evan strolled in, leaning against the counter, watching me.

"Holly."

Something in his voice made me stop what I was doing and turn to him. "Evan?"

He inhaled deeply and crossed his arms over his chest. "I'm rich."

I stared at him with a frown. "Rich?"

"I have a trust fund, and my business does very well."

He had mentioned a trust fund before, but I hadn't paid much attention. Confused, I smiled. "Good."

He huffed out a breath and held out his hand, tugging me close when I slid my palm against his.

He looked down at me, pushing a curl behind my ear.

"Hear me out?" he asked, his voice serious.

I nodded.

"I told you my family lives a life I'm not comfortable with. Frivolous and greedy. I rarely touch my trust fund. In fact, it's larger now than when I got it. I've invested most of it, and I only use it for important things."

"Okay."

He tightened his arms. "*You're* important, Holly."

"I don't understand."

"I don't want you to work. I want to have you here with me. You can do whatever you like. Hang around the house with Chester. Sketch and paint. Take some online courses."

"But I have to contribute. I didn't come here to sponge off of you."

"You wouldn't be sponging." He regarded me intensely. "I want —*I need*—to look after you, Holly. *You* need that. No one has ever looked after you properly before. Put you first. *I will*. I will always put you first. Let me care for you. I want to see you sleep in, relax, putter around the house and make it ours. Read. Take baths. Make us sandwiches and have lunch with me. I want you around."

He paused. "I need it as much as you do. Settle in. Get to know Carol and Tara. Decide what you really want to do, because for the first time in your life, you can take the time to do so." He leaned down and kissed my nose. "I don't want you working and tired."

The thought of not being on my feet for hours at a time was tempting. Not smelling like grease and having to face endless strangers, smiling as I filled coffee cups and carried heavy trays. The idea of being here with Evan and making a home for both of us was a lovely thought. Exploring my options for school, not having to worry if not taking that extra shift meant dipping into my savings for the heating bill.

He met my gaze, his anxious for a different reason than mine. "Please," he whispered. "Let me."

"Only if I can help you with your business. I'm good with numbers."

His eyes crinkled in happiness. "Then you're hired. I hate doing the books."

"Okay, then."

He pressed his mouth to mine.

"Okay."

I relaxed against the porcelain tub, the steam rising from the water—a mist in the air. My gaze took in the room. Evan's en suite was larger than my whole bedroom had been in Connie's place. After an early dinner, he'd insisted I have a bath and relax.

"It's been a long trip, Angel. You must be tired."

"You're the one who did all the driving," I pointed out. As I discovered, Evan liked to be in control behind the wheel. He had looked affronted when I offered to drive, informing me that it was his job to do so and my job to enjoy the scenery. I had struggled not to laugh at his over-the-top reaction, realizing that it was his way of looking after me. And I was enjoying the sights. Having never been out East—even with the snow—the landscape was beautiful. He often pulled over so I could take a picture, and at one point, had stopped and bought me a new sketchbook and pencils in case I felt like drawing. He made the entire trip about me, and I loved every moment of being with him.

I sighed in contentment. I had never had a bath in such a large tub until now. I used some of the bath salts Evan had given me for Christmas and the room smelled of lilacs and roses.

The door opened, and Evan came in, carrying a glass of wine and a rolled towel. He set down the wine beside me and flipped his fingers. "Head up."

I lifted my head, and he slid the towel under my neck. The softness and warmth felt good, and I grinned at him. "You heated it up."

He returned my grin and dropped a kiss to my head. "I learned that from you. You heated up the towel and warmed my feet. Just repaying the favor. I ordered a bath pillow for you online, but this will do until it comes."

I gripped his hand. "Evan—you don't have to get me a pillow. Or anything else. I'm fine."

He stared down at me, his brow furrowed. "Yes, I do, Holly. It's my job now to look after you, and you need a pillow. I want you to use the tub, enjoy it. It's sat there for three years, ignored."

"You've never had a bath?"

"No, I'm a shower kind of guy. Apparently, the wife of the couple I bought the house from loved to soak in the tub and look at the stars." He indicated the skylight above me. "Never really got into that myself." He frowned. "You need candles too. Women like candles, right? We can get some in town tomorrow."

I had to stop my laugh. He was determined to make sure I had everything he thought I should have, whether it mattered or not. There was no point in fighting him. Instead, I held out my hand.

"You could join me."

He paused, his hand on the doorknob. "In the tub?"

I chuckled. "Yes, in the tub. Lots of room. I'd scrub your back if you wanted."

He stared at me for a moment, reached over his head and pulled off his shirt, then yanked down his pants. I watched his movements, admiring the way his muscles rippled.

"Maybe I need to give this tub thing a shot."

I held out my arms, welcoming him as he lowered himself into the steaming water. He leaned back into my chest with a sigh. I wrapped my arms and legs around him, then kissed the top of his head. He relaxed, his body loosening, and we lay together, staring up at the stars overhead.

"I see why she liked this," he murmured. "But I think having you with me makes it better."

I held him tighter.

"Are you nervous, Holly?" he asked, his voice low in the room. "About being here with me? Leaving your life behind?"

"No," I replied. "It wasn't much of a life, Evan. I was waiting— searching for something." A sigh flowed through my chest. "I think I was looking for you. For the first time in my life, I feel…content. As if I'm home."

He lifted my hand from his chest and kissed it. Tilting up his head, he smiled tenderly at me. "You are home, Holly. You never have to search or be alone again. I'm right here."

I lowered my face and our lips met. They moved and molded together, a perfect fit. Evan threaded his fingers into my hair, cupping my head while our kiss deepened. The water splashed as he rolled, his chest pressing me into the sloped porcelain. Our mouths never separated, if anything, our kisses becoming deeper. Our bodies sculpted to each other, the water warm around us, the air filled with his groans, my whimpers, and our heavy breathing.

Evan sat up, taking me with him. My legs straddled his thighs, his erection trapped between us. "Holly," he moaned. "I want you right here."

I nipped at his neck, running my hands over the taut muscles of his back. "Then take me."

"We're gonna get water everywhere."

I licked his ear, sucking his lobe. His shiver made me smile. His hard cock twitched, making me shiver in return.

"I hope you have a lot of towels, then."

He lifted me as if I weighed nothing, and I slowly slid down onto his length.

"I'll add those to the list. I have a feeling we're gonna be having a lot of baths," he mumbled. "Lots of baths."

I groaned at the sensation of him buried inside me, the water surrounding us, and the steam making the room a private sanctuary. I began to move, gripping the edge of the tub.

"Good."

CHAPTER ELEVEN

HOLLY

Springtime A Year Later

Sun scattered across the water, the late spring breeze warm on my face. I carried a tray to the porch and stood looking at the dance of the waves as they hit the shore. I loved it here. The sounds of the ocean, the smell of the fresh air, the warmth of the people— and the life I had built with Evan. I studied the waves, knowing I would probably end up back in my studio, trying to capture the endlessly changing colors of the ocean. The scope here was vast, and I never ran out of inspiration. Evan had his favorite paintings framed and hung around the house and his shop and had even given a couple to Carol and Dan. He was overly proud and boastful of my talent, but I loved him for it. I loved him for everything he was.

I couldn't help remember the day he had shown me the studio he had created for me.

"Evan!" I exclaimed, trying to take in everything in the room. I met his gaze, his green eyes dancing with excitement. He had refused to let me in his shop for over two weeks. He, Dan, and Andrew had been busy—the sounds of hammers, saws, and drills going on for days. Finally, I was allowed to see the space he created for me over his shop. A set of stairs ran up the side of the shop to a wide-open space above. The front was all windows, offering a great view of the ocean and the vista surrounding the house. Broad planks on the floor and reclaimed wood on the walls gave it a warm feeling. A huge set of shelves, an easel, and a vast selection of watercolor paints, paper, canvases, and pencils waited for me. There

was a loveseat facing the window, antique, recovered, the wood trim gleaming in the sun. I ran my hand over the arched back.

"You made this for me?"

"I did all this for you, Holly."

I flung myself in his arms and kissed him. I loved kissing Evan. He was passionate, warm, and giving. His mouth was magic against mine, and he held me as though I was the most precious thing on earth to him. He growled in pleasure, low in his throat, and sat down heavily on the loveseat, never releasing my mouth. We kissed until we were breathless, yet it wasn't enough. It was never enough with Evan. With a sigh, I rested my head in the crook of his neck.

"I'm so lucky," I murmured. "You are the greatest gift I ever got."

He chuckled, his breath stirring the curls around my forehead. "I'm the lucky one, Holly. I get you."

I tilted up my head, smiling. "We get each other."

His grip tightened. "Yeah. Perfect."

"You know what else is perfect?"

"What?"

"How we can see the world from this window and no one can see us. Very private."

He raised one eyebrow, his grin wide. "Private?"

I slid off his knee to the floor in front of him. I ran my hands up his thighs, feeling the sinewy muscles clench. "Very private."

He let his head drop to the back of the loveseat as I cupped his erection, then yanked down his pants.

"Good planning on my part," he groaned.

I lowered my head, my breath washing over his cock. "You can look at the scenery while I'm, ah, busy. It's pretty spectacular."

He grunted as my mouth closed around him. Our gazes locked, his dark and intense. "I'm already looking at the most spectacular, sexiest thing I've ever seen."

I winked, unable to speak.

It was rude to talk with your mouth full.

I grinned at the memories as I stared out over the vast horizon. I would never tire of this view.

There were times I still had to pinch myself that this was my life and Evan belonged to me. That I belonged to him. Evan Brooks was every fantasy I ever had…and every dream and wish I never spoke of.

The loneliness that had permeated my life had been banished. With Evan, I found a home and people to call my family. Light glinted off the rings on my finger, making me smile. We had been married for just over a year, exchanging our vows against the backdrop of the view I loved so much. Us, our adopted family, and the friends we had made here in this small town. I had a part-time job I loved, a husband I adored, and a life I never thought would be mine.

I touched my pocket with a smile. There was something else I never thought I would have. The sound of the shop door sliding shut made me look up, and my breath caught as I watched Evan stroll toward me.

He walked differently these days. Taller, his head held high, his broad shoulders straight. His dark hair gleamed in the sun, the white patch at the front bright. He had grown more confident—sure of himself and his place in the world. His place with me.

He climbed the steps and came directly to my side, sliding his arm around my waist. He lifted my chin with his slender fingers and kissed my mouth. Long, slow, sweet. It was his hello every single day. That, and his greeting.

He smiled against my mouth. "Hello, my beautiful wife. Miss me?"

I laughed as always. "Yes, the last hours without you have been terrible."

He kissed me again. "Cheeky. You've been with Carol all afternoon. I was lonely while the two of you were shopping up a storm."

I sat down, making sure to hide my grin. Shopping had been brief. I only bought one thing.

He sat down and picked up his glass of iced tea, sipping it and looking toward the water. "What a great day."

"In every sense."

He tilted his head, studying me. "Did you find some great bargain? A new piece of furniture you're trying to figure out where to put?" he teased.

Our home had changed a great deal since I'd arrived. Evan's once bare walls were now filled with artwork, photographs, and my paintings and sketches. There'd been many trips and memories—all captured on film, our favorites displayed on the walls. Pieces from local artists we'd picked out together. Our life's story told in frames and souvenirs that made us smile. Celebrations of moments of the love that we shared.

And I had the most special one to give him.

I slipped the small square from my pocket. "I bought you something."

He grinned eagerly, holding out his hand in anticipation. He loved presents, and I had a feeling this one might top them all. I handed him the package, smiling as he studied it.

"Too small for a sofa."

"Nope."

He pursed his lips. "Not a friend for Chester. Too square."

I laughed. "Open it."

He slid off the simple brown paper and rattan ribbon and lifted up the tiny square frame. It was simple, a creamy yellow with ducks on it. Evan frowned. "Ducks. How…whimsical. Ah, a new frame for our next adventure?"

I chuckled. "Actually, we've already had this adventure. Look closer, Evan. Look inside."

He stared at the black-and-white image which he had thought to be nothing. I knew the second he realized what he was looking at. His entire body froze, and he lifted his head, his expression one of such joy—filled with so much love and tenderness that it took my breath away.

"Holly?" he uttered. "Really? *A baby*?" He swallowed. "My baby? Our baby?"

I nodded, unable to speak.

In a moment, he was on his knees in front of me, and I was wrapped in his embrace. He pressed kisses to my cheeks, forehead, nose, and mouth, finally dropping his head to my lap. He looked up, his large hands spread wide across my stomach.

"Are you okay? Is everything all right?"

"Yes," I assured him. "Carol took me to see the doctor today, and he did the ultrasound. He said everything looked fine. Our baby is due at the start of January."

"I missed the ultrasound?"

"You can come to the next one."

"To all of them," he insisted. "I'll be there for everything."

"Okay."

"Say it, Holly. Tell me."

"You're going to be a daddy, Evan."

"I think I just found another set of favorite words."

I laughed. "I knew you'd like them."

His smile was wide. "*A baby*. Oh God, Holly, I love you."

I cupped his face. "I love you. We both love you."

His happiness couldn't be contained. He wrapped me in his arms, holding me safe and secure. "I love you, Holly. Thank you, my Angel."

CHAPTER TWELVE

EVAN

Christmas Eve Day

Holly was asleep on the sofa, curled up under the blanket I had draped over her. I loved watching her sleep. She always smiled and muttered, lost in a dream world I would never know about. Except the fact that she often said my name, which made me smile; I liked knowing I was in there somewhere.

Today, however, she grimaced more than smiled, and her feet moved restlessly. The storm was making her nervous and disturbing her sleep. I leaned up from my place on the floor, where I had been gazing at the lights on our Christmas tree, and rubbed her rounded tummy soothingly, murmuring nonsensical words to our daughter. That did the trick, as it always did. The rapid movements stopped for both of them, and my girls relaxed. Smiling, I left my hand on Holly's stomach as I watched her, thinking about the last two years.

The happiest two years of my life.

Holly was everything I had been looking for but never knew I needed. She filled a void in my life I hadn't even known existed. She showed me how to be happy being Evan, and I showed her how it felt to be someone's priority. Everything I did, every decision was made with her happiness in mind.

Together, we built a home and a life.

Together, we were strong.

As I expected, Carol, Dan, Tara, and Andrew loved her. Carol took her under her wing, and Holly blossomed. I stopped trying to gain the approval of my family and instead basked in the unconditional love of the Whittaker clan. They became the family both Holly and I never had.

Holly decided not to go to school and instead worked as an aide in the local kindergarten. She was loved by the kids and teachers alike, and she enjoyed the freedom of not having to worry about money anymore. My favorite days were when she hung out with me in my shop, handing me tools, singing along with the radio, as I'd discovered she loved to do on our winter drive here, or chatting about plans we had. Other times she painted or sketched in the studio above my shop, and I could hear her humming and moving around, content to have her nearby. We traveled and explored the Maritimes, falling more in love with the East Coast with every new discovery.

My Angel blossomed with the love that now surrounded her. I blossomed because of hers.

So many memories stirred as I watched my wife slumber.

The day I stumbled alone and frozen into Holly's life.

The day she said she loved me and I knew my heart would never again feel so cold.

Our quiet, beautiful wedding in our home, where we promised each other we'd never be alone again.

The poignant moment she told me I was going to be a father and the joy that I felt tear through my entire being.

All the laughter and tears we had shared. The deep peace and happiness she brought to my life.

One memory stirred, making my smile even wider.

I'd arranged an overnight trip for Holly, Carol, and Tara to a spa retreat I had heard a lot about. They had a special package that catered to mothers-to-be. Holly had been having difficulty sleeping—experiencing leg cramps, and struggling to get comfortable at times, so I sent all my girls off to be pampered, hoping some massages and relaxation would help.

As soon as the car was out of sight, Dan and Andrew showed up, and we got to work. We worked on the nursery, turning the room beside Holly's and mine into a woodland playroom for the baby. I had taken one of Holly's paintings of the woods around the house and had it turned into a mural for the wall. She had added some whimsical forest creatures into her painting, planning on hanging it in the nursery, and now the scene graced the wall behind the crib. A cute bunny, an inquisitive fawn, a pair of turtle doves perched on a branch, and even a sleepy owl could be found. We painted the walls a creamy yellow and moved in the furniture I had been working on secretly. A beautiful crib and dresser that had belonged to Carol and Dan now shone new and fresh under the lights. I had stripped and refinished them in natural tones, and Dan helped me build a changing table that matched. I added a thick rug, some stuffed animals, and a rocker Holly loved from my shop. Carol had been in on the project and had sewn the curtains and pretty bedding that went in the crib. All the room needed was our daughter.

From the day we found out it was a girl, I was beside myself in excitement. I vowed I would love and protect her with everything in me. She would never doubt how much she was loved, and she would always be safe and cared for in a stable, warm home. The loneliness Holly and I had each experienced in our childhoods would not be repeated. Not by my children.

Holly's reaction to the room was nothing short of effusive. She had stood in the middle of the room, slowly turning, taking it all in. Then she'd burst into tears and flung herself into my arms.

"Happy tears?" I asked. It was hard to tell these days. She cried about a lot of things, and I was never completely sure if I needed to kick someone's ass or simply hold her.

"It-it's beautiful! All we need is our girl."

I slid my hand over her rounded tummy. "Soon," I crooned. "A few more months."

In fact, the truth was that I was as impatient as Holly for our girl to arrive. I could hardly wait to meet her, hold her, and begin to show her the love I felt for her.

And soon, she would be here.

Suddenly, I needed to be closer to Holly. I needed to touch her. I moved up and tenderly traced her cheek with my mouth, her supple skin warm under my lips. Her eyes fluttered open, and she grinned at me. "Hey."

"Hi," I whispered.

"You okay, sweetheart?"

I nodded. "I just needed to kiss you."

"Well, then—" She smiled sleepily. "Kiss away."

I pressed my lips to hers happily, and we moved together effortlessly, our kiss indulgent and loving. I cupped her face, stroking her skin in gentle circles with my thumbs.

Holly abruptly stiffened and pulled away.

"What's wrong?"

Her eyes flew down to her stomach before meeting mine. "I think your daughter is ready to meet you. My-my water just broke."

I was on my feet in a second.

"*Now?* She's early and it's storming! Tell her to wait!"

Holly began to chuckle. "I don't think that's gonna work, Daddy." She held out her hand, and I helped her sit up. "Call Andrew. He has the truck ready in case." She grimaced. "That damn Tara is always right. She said it would be today."

I was already on the phone. After Andrew assured me he was on the way and Tara would call Carol and Dan, I hurried back to Holly. "He's on his way."

She smiled calmly. "My bag is by the door. I need to change. Can you help, please?"

I fumbled, trying to get her dressed in our bedroom, my hands shaking with nerves. "Evan," she soothed. "Relax. Everything is fine."

I nodded as I tugged on her boots, unable to speak and not sure how she could be so calm right now.

She tilted up my face. "Hey."

I looked up into her warm but worried eyes.

"Evan, I need you right now. You've been so strong my whole pregnancy. Don't lose it now."

I swallowed, unsure how to explain my sudden panic. "What if—"

"What if, what?"

"What if I'm an awful father? I didn't have a good example growing up." Another terrible thought occurred to me. "What if she doesn't like me?"

Holly cupped my face firmly. "You are *nothing* like your father. You are going to be an amazing daddy. You'll be funny, kind, loving, and affectionate. Your daughter is going to adore you. Just like I do."

I drew in a shaky breath. "Promise?"

"Promise."

"Okay."

"I love you."

The words never failed to make me smile. "I love you, Angel."

My daughter was perfect. Tiny and wiggly, her skin a mottled pink, and her fist jammed into her little rosebud mouth. I couldn't bear to put her down for a second. Angela Carol Brooks had already stolen my heart. I didn't know it was possible for one person to feel this much love.

Holly had worked so hard to bring her into this world. Her labor had been long, but finally, after seventeen hours, my daughter had screamed her way into our life, protesting loudly at being moved from her little nest.

I looked over at Holly, who was watching us wearily, a tired smile on her face. "You need to put her in her bassinet, Evan."

"Soon," I lied.

Carol and Dan had been there the whole time Holly was in labor, refusing to leave. Tara and Andrew came and went, bringing food, coffee, and support. Once Angela was born, they had all seen her and Holly, then finally left me alone with my family. I knew they'd be back in the morning, so I was determined to take advantage of the time I had with my girls.

A nurse walked in and checked on Holly. She smiled as she shook her head at me, knowing full well I had been holding Angela since the last time she'd checked on my wife. "What a good daddy," she crooned. "Get some sleep, Mrs. Brooks. You'll need it." She paused on her way out of the room. "Merry Christmas."

I smiled at her. "It certainly is."

I looked down at my slumbering daughter. "I met your mommy two years ago. She was like an angel to me." I chuckled as I stroked Angela's downy little cheek. "We shared our first Christmas together, and I fell in love with her on that special day as well. She was an unexpected gift to me then, and now I have another one." I stood up and placed her into Holly's outstretched arms. Leaning down, I kissed them both and smiled as I took in the sight of both of my girls. My family.

"Now I have two angels."

My wife smiled at me. "Merry Christmas, Evan."

I kissed her again.

My Holly. My life. I was so blessed.

"Merry Christmas, Angel."

EPILOGUE

A FEW YEARS LATER...

I stood back, eyeing the large sideboard critically. It was a find Holly and I discovered one weekend when we were traveling around the island. The piece was in disrepair, the doors stuck shut from being exposed to the elements in an unused corner of a shed on a farmer's property. It was still beautiful despite the dirt, wear, and cracked wood, and Holly fell in love with it, insisting it would look perfect in our dining room. I had to agree with her and after making a deal with the owner, made the trip back with Dan in my truck, pulling the heavy piece from the shed and bringing it to my shop. I spent hours filling, repairing, and sanding to get it to this point. The doors now swung freely, the cracks and damage restored. The wood was smooth, the details brought back to life, and it was ready to be cleaned, stained, then taken into the house.

Holly would be so excited.

I pulled off my mask. The atmosphere around me swam with dust motes, the smell of freshly sanded wood heavy in the air. A fine layer of sawdust covered my shop, but the end result was worth the days of effort, buckets of sweat, and hours of painstaking detail.

I pulled open the barn door, letting the fresh, cold air rush in. The sun that had shone brightly earlier, glittering off the water at the front of the house, was now dimmer, clouds gathering and casting shadows on the branches of the trees that were gradually coming to life. Spring was slow to arrive this year, the colder weather still keeping us in its grip. I didn't mind too much, whereas once I'd dreaded winter—the long nights, the days of endless hours on hand when projects were few. Now I loved them. It gave me more time with my family, and Holly and I passed the time with our girls playing games, reading, listening to their stories, watching them grow. And with the snow came our favorite time of year—Christmas. The once lonely holiday now held a vastly different place in my heart. It was a time of joy, celebration, and family. The family Holly and I shared, as well as Dan, Carol, Andrew, and Tara.

Still, I was ready for the spring to arrive and looked forward to the time I could spend in the shop. I still loved "repairing broken pieces of history," as Holly phrased it, and the hours I toiled in my shop were fruitful and satisfying. Because of Holly, I finally accepted the joy my work brought me and was proud of what I did. Together, we had a great life.

Turning, I once again studied the sideboard, running my hand over the smooth surface of the wood making sure it was finished. I heard the telltale squeak of the back-porch door and a smile broke out on my face, knowing it must be lunchtime. I walked back to the open door of my shop to watch my girls come to me.

Angela hurried down the path, her long, straight, dark hair blowing behind her. Tall for her age and slender, she resembled me, except for her eyes. They were the same soft blue as Holly's, and they danced with mischief and laughter all the time.

"Daddy!" she squealed, launching herself into my arms, acting as if it had been days not hours since she'd seen me at breakfast. She loved to be with me in the shop, but on days when I was sanding or using heavy machinery, I didn't allow her in, not wanting to expose her to the dust or danger. When she was older, I had a feeling it would be harder to keep her away—she loved "working" in my shop and "helping" me. She listened with fascination as I showed her simple things like how to sand a piece of wood or add glue to mend a broken board. Together we had built birdhouses and little projects I came up with, and I looked forward to when I could show her more. But for now, I practiced caution. At four, she was smart, stubborn, and sweet. I adored my little girl.

I set her on her feet, pressing a kiss to her forehead, brushing her hair behind her ear. "Hey, Angel-girl."

"We made a studio picnic!"

"Awesome." I grinned. Studio picnics were our favorite—all the fun of regular picnics, but in the warmth and comfort of Holly's studio, surrounded by blankets and soft cushions. My more "mature" bones thanked me at the end of the picnics, plus it was too cool to eat outside today. "Did you help Momma?"

She nodded furiously. "She said she couldn't do it without me."

"I bet she did."

I stood, my smile growing wider. Holly walked slowly, a huge basket in one hand, her other hand at her side. Our youngest daughter, Hannah, toddled beside her, her steps wonky and slow, but determined. Hannah was short, chubby, with a head of wild, curly red ringlets that bounced as she wobbled, clutching Holly's fingers to stay upright. When Hannah saw me, she stopped, letting go of Holly's hand, her eyes, the same green color as mine, lighting up. She began babbling in her high, animated voice, her hands flapping in excitement so fast she fell on her butt, still chirping in enthusiasm at seeing me. As usual, her exuberance made me laugh, and I hurried forward, lifting her from the cold ground and swinging her into the air.

"Hello, my little dumpling." I brought her close and blew a long raspberry on her cheek.

"Dadadada," she chortled, laughing and squirming, patting my face, reaching up with wet kisses and smiles.

My heart soared. Holly's love had brought such a sense of peace, acceptance, and light to my life, and my children's affection healed me totally. My past no longer mattered or held me in its dark grip. My girls' love was freely given, absolute, and complete. To them, I was the greatest man on earth and could do no wrong.

Unless I said no.

Luckily, that didn't happen very often.

I picked up Angela, holding both my daughters in my arms. I bent low and kissed my wife. "Hi."

She beamed up at me, laying her hand on my chest. "Hi, yourself. Hope you're hungry. Angela insisted you would be starving, so we had to make lots of sandwiches."

"Yep. Starving."

She winked. "Somehow I'm not surprised."

I laughed. I was always hungry these days. Holly was a great cook, and I had filled out over the years. My shoulders were wider, my chest broad, and my waist thick. Between my work, my girls, and life in general, my body had changed—growing sturdier the same way my determination and confidence had. I liked it. I felt strong and capable—a protector for my family.

Holly loved my muscles and showed her appreciation for them on a regular basis.

I liked that too.

A gust of wind blew through the trees, the branches swaying and bending deeply, dry leaves left over from fall dropping and swirling in the burst of air.

"Time to head in," I announced, looking at the deepening clouds. "We might be in the studio for a while."

"Can you light the fire, Daddy?" Angela asked. She loved the little potbelly stove I had in the corner of the studio. It threw a lot of warmth, making the room snug, even heating the shop below it. My girls loved to be warm.

"Yep."

Inside, I pulled the heavy door shut behind me after setting down Angela. She ran upstairs, Holly following her, and I carried Hannah up with me. She was nestled into my chest, her little fingers gripping my shirt the way she always did. She loved to be held and snuggled, and I knew if I let her, she would stay that way our entire lunch.

I had no problem with that. I never denied my children my affection. I knew what it was like to grow up with none—to yearn for hugs and love. Holly and I were very liberal with our love for our girls —and each other. After all these years, that hadn't changed.

Upstairs, I lit the fire, then shut the door once the flames licked at the kindling and paper, the heat beginning to build. Turning, I grinned at the sight in front of me. Hannah was waiting on the floor where I'd sat her, her chubby little legs kicking in impatience, her arms outstretched, anxious. I swooped her up with a flourish, delighting in her chuckles. She shoved a fist into her mouth, gnawing at her knuckles. She was a late starter when it came to teething, but she was making up for it fast.

Blankets were spread out in the middle of the room, Holly unpacked the lunch she brought, and Angela carried pillows from the pile in the corner, arranging them to her satisfaction. I sank to the floor beside Holly, nestling Hannah between my legs. She immediately pointed to the container of animal crackers, and I handed her one, amused by the way she grabbed it, chewing ravenously on it as if she hadn't been fed in weeks. Between teething and her appetite, she had something in her mouth constantly these days. I brushed my hand over her wild curls and pressed a kiss to her head. Her only response was a growly noise that made Holly and me chuckle. Hannah was serious when it came to meals, and she concentrated fully on the food in front of her.

"The sideboard looks beautiful," Holly commented, handing me another biscuit for Hannah.

"I'll stain it next week, then varnish it. It should be done by the end of the month." I glanced out the window as the glass rattled with the strong wind gusting outside. "Hopefully the sun will dry things out. It's gonna be heavy enough to carry without worrying about puddles."

Holly grinned, running her fingers along my bicep. "You'll manage."

Her touch made my body tighten. It always did. With a lewd wink, I leaned in and kissed her. Her full lips were soft underneath mine, and she tasted like coffee and something sweet and spicy—cinnamon.

"Did you bake today?" I asked eagerly.

Angela settled beside me, her cushions arranged to her liking. "We made pumpkin muffins, Daddy!"

"And raisin cookies," Holly added.

"My two favorites," I hummed. "Awesome."

Holly finished unpacking the food, and I held a plate as Angela picked out her choices. Hannah was easy when it came to meals—there wasn't a food we'd introduced she didn't love. Angela was far more selective. Some crackers, a piece of cheese, and a peanut butter sandwich. Meat was a no go for her, as were most vegetables, although she liked carrots. Luckily, she loved fruit and yogurt, and our pediatrician told us to relax when I expressed my worry over her limited diet.

"She's healthy and growing. She gets lots of protein with her choices. Let her find out what she likes and don't force her. Her likes will grow as she does." She patted my arm. *"You're doing good, Dad. Both of you are."*

I, like Hannah, loved everything, and I filled my plate with sandwiches, and all the extras Holly had made. I fed Hannah bits, listened to Angela's chatter, and sat next to my wife, brimming with contentment. I loved these times with my family.

The fire warmed the room. Holly's watercolors hung on the walls, and canvases were stacked neatly, ready to be used. I wasn't the only one who thought her talented, and in the busy tourist season, one local shop regularly sold out of her paintings. I was incredibly proud of her.

"Daddy, I'm going to school soon!" Angela announced.

I glanced at Holly, unsure how to respond.

School?

She smiled in understanding. "We saw Mrs. Anderson in town earlier," she explained. "Angela will be in prekindergarten in September."

I swallowed. *Prekindergarten?* Where the hell had the time gone? It was only yesterday Angela was a baby in my arms—and now school?

"Already?" I croaked.

Holly patted my arm. "Just part days, Daddy."

"We still get to keep Hannah," I insisted, tightening my arms around my baby girl.

Holly laughed, her head tilted back in amusement. "We get to *keep* them both. It's just a few hours during the day." She met my gaze, her eyes twinkling. "It's part of growing up, Evan."

Angela bounced from her spot on the blanket. "I'll get to spend time with my friends, Daddy. Carly is going too! I can teach you stuff when I get home!"

Carly was Angela's best friend, and I knew she was excited. Still, I had to force a smile. "That'll be awesome."

Angela jumped up. "Chutes and Ladders time!"

I pushed away my plate, my appetite suddenly gone. "Okay, Angel-girl. Get the board."

The wind rattled the glass again, and I looked up from where I was lying on the blanket. The sky was ominous and just as I was about to suggest we head to the house, the skies opened up and rain began to pour.

"Well, I guess we're stuck here," I mused.

"Not a bad place to be stuck," Holly responded. "Besides, the girls are down for the count."

I smirked. Hannah was a sleeping ball of warmth beside me, and Angela was sprawled across the blankets, having whooped my ass in three straight games. Hannah was too young to play, but she liked to move pieces around the board and, on occasion, attempt to eat them, so Holly had kept her busy, reading out loud to her while we played. Then both girls flaked out, full of lunch and happy.

"How is it possible to even think about school, Holly?" I asked. "Where the hell has the time gone?"

"This is really upsetting you," she murmured. "Why?"

"I'm not ready for them to grow up."

"But they are, Daddy," she protested. "School or not. Every day, they get bigger and more independent. And they are awesome little girls. Think how much more awesome they'll be once they get older."

I sighed. "As I get older, you mean."

"Well, there is that."

"They make me feel young *now*. As babies. I like how they need me," I admitted.

Holly offered me her hand, and I took it, tugging gently so she shifted closer. "They'll always need you, Evan." She smiled in understanding. "You're their nucleus, and they revolve around you. But they have to grow, and it's our job to help them." She cupped my cheek, her touch tender. "They love you more than anything or anyone in this world. They always will." She winked. "So will I."

I leaned forward and kissed her. "That goes both ways, Holly. They and I love you equally as much."

"I know. But you're *Daddy*. And they are *your* girls. That's special."

I ran my hand over Hannah's back. She huffed out a little sigh of contentment and snuggled closer. I smiled at her sweet little face.

"The house will seem empty," I mused. "Angela is always running around with Hannah trailing behind her. She's going to miss her big sister terribly." I sighed. "I'll miss her terribly."

"I'm sure there will be other, ah, *distractions* for both of you."

Something in her voice made me look up. She was smiling, biting her lip in one of her nervous tells.

"Distractions?"

She took my hand and placed it on her stomach. "Babies are *very* distracting."

My eyes widened. "Babies? Holly? Are you…?" My voice trailed off in excitement and disbelief. After Angela was born, we had a lot of trouble conceiving Hannah. Holly got pregnant after we stopped stressing about having another child. Hannah was another unexpected gift for both of us. After she was born, we didn't try not to get pregnant—but we didn't *not* try either.

Apparently, my old *bones* still worked. I felt my smile stretch across my face. Wide. Hard. Ecstatic.

"I am." She confirmed.

As carefully as I could, I shifted away from Hannah and knelt in front of Holly. "Angel—really?"

"Really."

I gathered her in my arms, holding her close. I dropped kisses to her forehead, cheeks, nose, then captured her mouth and kissed her deeply. Then a thought occurred to me. "How pregnant?"

She smiled against my mouth. "Another Christmas baby."

I laughed, dropping my head back on my shoulders in silent laughter. Angela was born on Christmas Day, Hannah on Boxing Day.

"What is it about spring with us?" I chuckled. "You're extra fertile."

"April Fools' every time."

I caressed her cheek. "So it seems." I ran my finger over her stomach, grinning when she giggled. She was always more sensitive when she was pregnant. "Are you feeling okay?"

"I'm fine. Tired, but fine."

"Have you seen the doctor?"

"Yes. Everything is good, and you'll be there for the ultrasound as usual."

"For everything."

She cupped my cheek. "I know." Her thumb brushed my skin. "Maybe we'll have a little Brooks boy this time. Would you like that?"

"I'd like him or her to be healthy and happy. Nothing else. I don't need to produce the next generation of Brooks men. My girls carry my name and my heart. That's all I need."

"I love you."

I cradled her face in my hands, her beautiful, sweet, wonderful face, and I kissed her. "Angel, love isn't a big enough word. It's not a big enough feeling for what happened to me when you came into my life. What you continue to do in my life. You make everything… *right*." I sighed. "You are the gift that just keeps giving, Holly. The best gift I ever got." I kissed her again. "Thank you for being you. My perfect Angel."

Her eyes were misty and her voice tender. "I'm hardly perfect, but I love being your Angel."

I slid beside her and wrapped her in my arms. She settled close, her head resting on my shoulder. I slid my hand to her stomach, spreading my fingers wide, knowing my child was resting under my touch. Holly laid hers over mine with a happy sigh.

I stretched out my legs, grinning when Angela grasped my foot in her sleep. Hannah slept to one side, and Holly was curled into my other side. I was touching every member of my family—safe and secure inside our little nest.

NEXT SUMMER

I lifted the baby swing and let it go carefully, the motion making my son laugh. I loved that sound. His sweet, high giggle that completed my world. I puckered my lips and crossed my eyes, making funny noises, and he squealed in glee. Laughing, I lifted him from the swing, holding him high. He kicked his feet and he gurgled in happiness as I slowly lowered, then lifted him back up a few times, and swooshed him around like a plane. My son loved that game.

I brought him to my chest and kissed his cheek, chuckling as he squeezed mine between his long fingers. For only seven months old, he was freakishly strong.

Brandon was another "throwback" to my grandfather. Hair so dark it was black clung to his head in wild curls, which he got from Holly. The rest was me. He was long, lean, with eyes of bright green, and Holly simply referred to him as my Mini-Me. He was the biggest baby I had ever seen, and Holly had a great deal of trouble birthing him. When they handed him to me, I was shocked by his size. Twenty-three inches and almost ten pounds in weight. I had no idea how she carried him to term. But she did, and on New Year's Eve, he was born—just like his sisters—in the middle of a storm. Holly joked it was tradition, and I supposed she was right.

We also decided three children were enough. I never wanted to watch Holly struggle that way again or feel the fear I did as we went through some tense moments. Holly was my world, and the thought of losing her was too much. Once she recovered and we talked, I had a vasectomy. We were so blessed, and I didn't want her taking birth control—the side effects she could experience frightened me as well.

Brandon gnawed at his hand, bringing me back to the present, and I dug a teething biscuit out of my pocket. Unlike Hannah, he was early for everything. His first tooth started coming in at five months, and he seemed to pop them nonstop.

"There you go, my boy. Let's go find Mommy and see what she's doing, okay?" He grasped the biscuit, gumming happily as I walked toward the house.

As I rounded the side, I spied Holly in the garden. Angela was at her best friend Carly's house but would be home by three. Hannah was on the porch, napping. My little dumpling loved her naps, but she never liked to be far away from Mommy, so I built a daybed and screened in the front porch so she could nap and be happy.

My footsteps carried me to Holly, who stood and brushed off her hands as we approached.

"There're my two favorite boys." She smiled and blew a raspberry on Brandon's cheek, then leaned up for a kiss. I happily obliged, capturing her face with my free hand and caressing her lips. She hadn't changed much, except to get prettier. Her hair was longer, still wild and curly, and she smiled all the time. As I suspected, she was a wonderful mother, a great partner, and loved by everyone who met her.

"Quite the harvest," I observed, indicating the basket beside her.

She nodded. "There is a pile of peppers, zucchini, and tomatoes. I thought maybe I'd jar up some of that homemade salsa you like so much. You can take some to Carol and Dan too."

"Awesome."

A car pulling into the driveway diverted my attention. It was an SUV, silver in color, with rental car plates. A man was behind the wheel, and as I watched, he shut off the engine, spoke to someone in the back, and opened his door.

I chuckled. "Another lost tourist, no doubt." It happened a lot in the summer.

Holly reached for Brandon and settled him on her hip. "Go give directions and get them unlost." She tickled Brandon's tummy. "We'll wait here."

I approached the SUV, prepared to give directions, my smile in place. But as I neared the vehicle, the man walked toward me, and something about him struck me as familiar. He was tall, with deep brown hair shot with silver. Sunglasses covered his eyes. He was dressed casually in jeans, a polo shirt, and a light jacket, but his posture was tense, his shoulders stiff. He had his hands buried in his pockets as I stopped a few feet away.

"Can I help you?"

He cleared his throat. "Hello, Evan."

I frowned at his deep baritone, its familiar tone striking a long-forgotten memory.

"I'm sorry, do I know you?"

He took off his glasses and stepped forward. Recognition hit me in the gut, and I stared at him. I had only seen him once, but I remembered him.

"It's me. Simon—Simon Fletcher."

Holy shit.

My brother-in-law.

It was my turn to clear my throat. "What are you doing here?" I asked, once I had made sure my sister wasn't in the passenger seat.

He scrubbed his face with his hand. "I realize seeing me must be a shock, but I needed to come and reach out."

"Why?"

He glanced over his shoulder. "My daughter—your niece—asked to see you."

For a moment, I was struck silent. Holly appeared at my side, Brandon still perched on her hip, chattering away in his baby voice, the sounds incoherent. She wrapped an arm around my waist in support. "Hello."

He smiled, the action causing his hazel eyes to crinkle at the corners. "Hello. You must be Holly."

"I am. And you are?"

"Kelsey's husband," I muttered.

He was fast to shake his head. "*Ex*-husband. We split up not long after I met you, Evan." He huffed out a long breath. "Look, maybe I should have called or written, but it felt to me like this was best done in person. It's a long story, but Mia wanted to meet you." He dug in his pocket and pulled out a well-loved worn little stuffed bear that I recognized. "She wanted to meet the man who gave her this."

I stared at the bear. I had never looked in the discarded bag, assuming all the gifts I had brought that Christmas were still in it. "I-I thought that had been thrown out with the rest of the gifts."

He shook his head. "I kept this and my tie."

"Your tie?" I repeated.

"It was a nice tie. I still wear it." He grinned, then became serious again. "Mia has carried that bear with her every day since. She loves every gift you have ever sent her."

Every gift? All these years?

It had been Holly's idea to try to keep some form of communication open with Mia. I thought it was a waste of time, but she had insisted, and every year, we sent Mia a gift and a card at Christmas. Simon owned his own investment company, so we sent the package to his office. He had been the only person even remotely kind to me that fateful Christmas, and I had thought he was the best chance of making sure the gifts were accepted. I had no idea until now if the gifts were received, but Holly wanted to keep sending them. Deep in my heart, I'd hoped Mia got them and knew that out there was someone who loved her, even if she couldn't know me.

I blinked. "I don't understand."

"I know. But I'd like the chance to explain. We've come a long way, and I'm hoping you'll be open to seeing her—to listening to my story."

I was on information overload. I had no idea my sister was divorced. The only information I had heard about my family was my brother had died in a drunk driving accident years ago and my father had retired not long after. Both pieces of news I had discovered via the internet. No one had reached out or let me know. I'd had no contact with anyone in my family since that disastrous trip home at Christmas years prior.

Holly squeezed my waist. "We'd love to meet her, wouldn't we, Evan?"

"Yes," I agreed, realizing how I must look. "I would love to meet her."

Simon smiled, his shoulders relaxing. He walked to the car and opened the back door, handing the bear to Mia inside. "Come on, sweet pea. Uncle Evan wants to meet you too."

Mia climbed out of the car. Small, with hair as dark as mine and eyes like her father's, she clung to his hand, looking nervous. "Hi."

Holly walked forward, smiling. She bent down and kissed Mia's cheek. "Hi, Mia. I'm Holly, Evan's wife. This is our son, Brandon."

Mia grinned, dimples appearing in both cheeks. "He's cute."

Holly winked. "We think so."

Mia looked past her toward me. My heart sped up at the look of vulnerability and uncertainty on her face.

My feet propelled me forward, and I stopped in front of her. "Last time I saw you, I held you on my knee. You were such a little thing. We shared a few moments together on Christmas."

She smiled. "My dad told me. We have a picture at our house."

"You do?" I glanced at Simon.

"I snapped it when no one was looking."

Huh. Another surprise.

"He said you came to see me that year."

"I did."

"I wanted to come and see you."

I held out my arms, smiling. "I'm glad you did."

She flung herself forward, and I caught her. She barely came past my waist and her arms didn't reach around me, but she held on tight.

I bent low and kissed her head. "Hello, Mia."

We went inside, chaos ensuing for the next while. Hannah woke from her nap, Angela came home, and there were a lot of questions and activity until things settled somewhat and we could talk.

Holly made coffee and brought out some of her homemade cookies. The kids were in front of us, talking, playing, and eating their snacks. Angela was fascinated with Mia, staring at her cousin with instant adoration. Hannah was a little shyer but stayed close, making sure she could see Holly from her place on the carpet. Brandon slept in his carrier, not interested in much expect his full tummy and the cookie he gummed, falling asleep with it half eaten and hanging from his mouth.

"She was so excited to meet you," Simon murmured.

"I don't understand," I repeated. "All these years. Why now?"

He ran a hand over his face and studied his daughter with an indulgent smile on his face. He obviously adored her, which made me happy. When he spoke, his voice was quiet.

"I met Kelsey at a low point in my life. She was beautiful and vibrant and seemed to be what I needed. We got married far too fast." He met my eyes. "Outward appearances are often deceiving, as I learned the hard way. We had a lot of problems, and just when I was ready to throw in the towel, she announced she was pregnant." He sipped his coffee. "I wanted to try for our child, but it was no use. Your sister is a viper, Evan, and drains people. I was shocked at her behavior—your family's behavior—when you visited, and things got worse between us." He looked sheepish. "To be honest, you were a surprise to me that day. Kelsey had never even mentioned you."

At one time, those words would have wounded me, but now, they meant nothing. They had no power over me. I shrugged. "Not really a surprise."

He sighed. "We argued bitterly that day and all the days that followed. It never stopped and, finally, I realized I was wasting my life being unhappy and hurting my daughter. We separated later that year, and the custody battle was long and ugly."

"I'm surprised she wanted custody, to be honest. She didn't strike me as maternal."

He snorted. "She isn't. What she wanted was to keep the marriage going. Her business had hit a rough patch. Mine had not," he stated, his meaning clear. "She wanted my money and used our child to try to get it."

"Ah."

"Finally, we settled. It took me a few years to come to terms with everything. Single fatherhood, recovering from a disastrous marriage. Kelsey cut off all ties to our daughter. Your parents never see her. I wanted nothing to do with anyone from your family. Even you. I convinced myself all Brooks were cut from the same cloth."

I lifted my eyebrows and swallowed a mouthful of coffee. "That's fair."

"No," he mused. "But it took me a while to figure it out. My one and only focus was Mia—making sure she was okay. Adjusted and doing well. She was, *is*, the one good thing I got from my marriage." He stared out the window at the water for a moment, then continued. "Every year at Christmas, without fail, a package would arrive for Mia. I was shocked by the first one—Kelsey and I had just separated so I didn't know what to do with it. To be honest, the first couple of years, I didn't even open them, then my counselor told me I should— not to be so fast to write you off since you were obviously trying. So I gave them to her. Every year she looked forward to them—a package from her distant uncle and aunt." He smiled at Holly. "I assume you had a lot to do with those packages."

I squeezed her hand, loving her soft blush. "She did."

"Anyway, it wasn't anything we ever talked about until this spring. You were just a name on a package. A face in a picture. Then her class did a genealogy project—a family tree sort of thing—at school, and Mia started asking me questions. In general at first, then more in depth. Mostly about you. Why she had never met you. What you did. Where you lived. Then one night, she told me she wanted to meet you. She's asked for months, and finally, I agreed."

"Why didn't you get in touch? Obviously, you had my address."

He stared at Mia, winking at her and blowing her a kiss. Then he turned to me. "She's a child, Evan. Her mother doesn't even remember her birthday. Her grandparents ignore her. I had no idea how you would react. You seemed decent. Kind, genuine. But I thought that of Kelsey once." He scrubbed his face. "I am very open with my daughter. I told Mia I was worried about your reaction. She's very smart. Intuitive. She reminded me that you sent her a gift every year and that you didn't have to. She told me she was sure you would want to see her, but that if you didn't, it was okay, because everyone had a choice. She said she realized, aside from me, you were her only family and she wanted to know you. I told her I would write you, but she wanted to come. She begged me, and she never begs for anything. So, I brought her. I arranged for a few weeks off to make a trip of it, and we came here. I prayed all the way here you wouldn't reject her—that my first impression of you had been the right one."

I sat back, stunned, then glanced over at my niece. She was staring, her eyes wide. I held out my hand, and she stood, coming to my side. I pulled her into a loose hug. "Thank you for being brave and coming to see me."

"I wanted you to know I got your gifts, and I love them." She smiled. "I love you."

My throat got thick, and I glanced at Holly. This happened because of her. Because she insisted on trying, *on hoping*, I was able to meet my niece. I got the chance to get to know her.

Holly watched us with watery eyes.

I tapped Mia's nose. "I love you too, kiddo."

I turned to Simon, who regarded us with an indulgent smile. His eyes were suspiciously glassy as well, and none of us tried to hide it.

"Where are you staying?"

"I booked a hotel—"

Holly interrupted him. "No, you're staying with us."

"We can't impose."

I spoke. "You're not imposing, Simon. You're family."

He looked startled, then grinned.

"Yeah?"

I nodded. "I want the chance to know Mia. And you. We have lots of room, and you're welcome to stay."

"Daddy, please?" Mia asked. "I want to stay with Uncle E."

I chuckled at her name for me. "Stay," I urged.

He nodded. "We'd love to."

A FEW WEEKS LATER

I groaned as we shifted the heavy desk I was working on into place. I stood back, rubbing the back of my neck.

"I'm getting too old for this shit," I muttered.

Simon laughed, dusting off his hands. "I hit forty-two this year. Talk to me about old."

I chuckled.

Over the past few weeks, Simon and I had grown close. He and Mia seemed to fit into our life effortlessly. Dan and Carol were crazy for Mia and liked Simon a lot. Andrew, Simon, and I went fishing. Tara spent time with Holly and Mia and our children. We had barbeques and lunches on the beach. Went out on the boat I had bought and explored the island. The kids all played together, Mia assuming the role of eldest sister and doting on the others. My children loved her.

Simon spent a lot of time with me in the shop, and Mia stayed close to Holly, enjoying her company. Mia and I took long walks, and we talked about a lot of things. Simon was right. She was smart, sweet, and sensitive, and I adored her. I was going to miss her like crazy—so was Holly.

We were all going to miss them.

Simon leaned back against my workbench. "So, Evan, I need to talk to you."

"What's up?" I asked, concerned at his serious tone.

"Mia doesn't want to go back to Ontario."

I sighed, wiping the sweat off my brow. "She told me that, but she'll adjust again. Holidays are always hard when they come to an end."

He rubbed the back of his neck. "What if it didn't? End, I mean?"

"What are you talking about?"

He sighed, looking over my shoulder. "I love it here, to be honest. The quiet. The people. Our family." He stood straighter. "I'm thinking of moving us here."

"Holy shit—that's a major decision. What about your business?"

He shrugged. "What I do, I can do anywhere. I can set up an office here easily. From home, even. Yesterday when you and Mia were hanging together, I did some checking. I saw a house I liked. There's a great school close by, Mia could transfer. Aside from me, you and Holly are all the family she has, and she adores you and her cousins. I've never seen her so happy or settled, and I want that to continue. I think it would be good for us—a fresh start. We haven't been happy for a while, and I think the change would do us a world of good."

I didn't hesitate. "Then do it."

"I have to go back and arrange things. I was wondering how you would feel about Mia staying here with you while I did? I'd be back in a couple weeks and have to go back and forth for a bit…"

"We'd love it." I didn't have to ask Holly—I already knew her answer. She had cried last night at the thought of them leaving. She'd be ecstatic. "Have you talked to Mia?"

He smirked. "It was her idea. She said she loved it here and wanted to stay." He grinned, unashamed. "The house I looked at is only ten minutes away."

"You already put in an offer, didn't you?"

"Yep."

I clapped him on the shoulder. "This is great news. Let's go tell Holly."

Later that night, Holly curled into me, her face excited. "I can't believe they're moving here! Angela, Hannah, and Brandon will have their cousin close by. We'll get to see her whenever we want."

I cupped her cheek, stroking her face. "I know. Mia is so excited."

"How about you?"

"I'm still processing the fact that I get to have my niece in our life. And that Simon is a great guy." I lowered my head to hers and kissed her. "All because of you, Holly. Your thoughtfulness and insistence have once again brought an unexpected gift into my life. More family. Every single good memory I have—every moment of joy in my life—is because of *you*. Every second contains *you*. Thank you, my Angel." I kissed her again. "Thank you."

She blinked away the tears that were forming and smiled. "I just want you to be happy. You deserve it."

Her love shone in her eyes, and her actions always spoke volumes. She did it all quietly, never asking for anything in return. All she wanted was to be loved, and I made sure she was surrounded by it every day. My love for her was, and always would be, paramount in my life.

"You make me happy. Every damn day."

She snuggled closer. "You do the same for me."

"Good."

Her fingers trailed along my skin. "Did you notice the way Simon watched Amy at the barbeque last week?" she asked.

"Amy? Really?"

"I thought I saw a spark there. They certainly talked a lot. I wondered if maybe that factored into his decision."

I mulled it over. Amy was a friend of Holly's who worked at the school. She ran the kindergarten class, and Holly still helped out on occasion. Amy had come to the barbeque last week and I had seen her and Simon talking. I hadn't thought anything of it, but now that Holly mentioned it, I remembered he had casually asked about her after, when we were cleaning up. Perhaps Holly was right, and his interest was more personal. Amy was a lovely woman—kind, sweet, and a good friend. She might be the right sort of person Simon needed to move on.

"I guess we'll see."

She laughed quietly. "I'm going to go have coffee with her and do a little digging."

I tucked her closer. "My little matchmaker."

We were quiet as thoughts drifted through my head. I could see the years ahead. Our families blending. Watching Mia and my children growing up together. Spending more time with Simon. He had already expressed an interest in helping coach hockey with me in the winter. We had sat down and figured out the next while as he went back and forth to settle things in Ontario and make the move here. Mia was excited about staying with us and seeing more of Carol and Dan, who had taken on the role of grandparents the same way they had with my kids.

I saw it all. Birthdays, celebrations, holidays—especially Christmas. From what Simon had said, they had never had one at home. He usually took them on a trip since he couldn't face the holiday on his own. When Holly talked about how we celebrated—especially with three birthdays at the same time—Mia's eyes grew huge in her face, excitement pouring off her. She'd never seen a real white Christmas, and we always had snow. We'd have to make this year's festivities especially good. And if Simon found someone to share his life with, all the better. After what he went through, he deserved it.

As if reading my mind, Holly hummed. "You're thinking about the holidays already, aren't you?"

I chuckled. "My favorite time of year for so many reasons. It was the start of us. Of this amazing life. Who knew a broken-down car would lead me to you?"

She cupped my face. "It was fate. And we have a whole lifetime together, Evan. We're still just beginning. Every day is a new adventure."

I kissed her full lips, grateful for her and all the blessings she had brought into my life. She was right. Each day was a new adventure, and with her by my side, life promised to be filled with them.

"I know, Angel. I know. I look forward to every single one."

She sighed in happiness. "I love you," she whispered.

I smiled, pressing my lips to her head.

Those were still my favorite words.

"Love you too, Angel. Always."

THE WISH LIST

CHAPTER ONE

ASHER

All around me were the sights and sounds of Christmas. Lights were strung everywhere. Trees, their branches so heavily decorated I was surprised they were standing, were placed in the most inconvenient places. Statues of Santa, reindeer, and elves peered at me from the shelves. Gift wrap, bows, ribbon, and tags were bright piles of glitter. A huge display of frolicking snowmen and the North Pole was set up in the middle of the department, and around it snaked a lineup of children and their parents, waiting to see Santa Claus.

They all looked miserable for different reasons.

The store was overly hot, overly bright, and overly crowded. The children wanted to see Santa—*now*—and the parents wanted to be anywhere but here. I had to agree with them.

Why the hell I did this to myself every year was a mystery.

But a few days before Christmas every year, I came to this store, walked to this department, found the one gift I required, and fled, grateful to be leaving the noise and confusion behind. Then I headed back to my quiet condo, where a good scotch and some soft classical music waited for me.

And silence.

I sat down, staring at the massive tree in the middle of the North Pole display, the fake mounds of snow and large bright-colored Christmas ornaments making my head ache. Despite my promise, I was seriously considering using my power and having the gift picked up by someone else and delivered to me. My sister, Suzy, wouldn't really know. I bought my niece's gifts that way, and she never complained. I picked the gifts; someone else had the hassle of picking them up. No complaints. Then again, Bonnie was five.

Except, I would know, and I hated lying to my sister. It was only for her that I would make this pilgrimage to this store and get her a gift she loved. One she expected each year from me.

"It wouldn't feel the same if someone else gave it to me," Suzy said once. *"It's our thing."*

And dammit, I loved my sister too much to let her down.

I glanced at the small bag in my hand. My job was done, and I could leave. Yet, I stayed sitting, staring at the chaos around me like a man unable to look away from a gruesome accident.

Suddenly, I heard my name being called. The voice was panicked, and for a moment, I was certain I was hearing things, until it rang out again.

"Asher!"

I rose to my feet as a woman rushed around the corner. Our eyes locked, and she hurried toward me. "Asher?"

I blinked at the stranger. Her bright-red hair glinted under the lights. It streamed down her back in a mass of waves. As she hurried closer, I stared at her creamy complexion that was covered in freckles. Thousands of them dotted the ivory skin, a large abundance of them on her cheeks and over the bridge of her nose. Her eyes were green —bright and clear like emeralds. She was small, dressed in a coat that looked too big for her, the hem almost to the floor. She carried a bag and another coat, this one smaller. And she looked upset. The need to help her hit me, and I moved toward her.

"Asher!" she called out again.

Did I know her? My name was unusual, so hearing her call it out confused me.

I stepped in front of her, halting her progress, our eyes once again meeting.

"I'm Asher. Can I help you?" I asked, laying my hand on her arm.

She blinked, her voice fraught with trepidation. She shook her head. "No. My son. I'm looking for my son. He-he disappeared."

I glanced over her shoulder, meeting the mischievous grin of a small boy I hadn't seen a moment ago. He was among the frolicking snowmen, hiding behind a mound of fake snow. I had no doubt it had to be the other Asher—her son. The red hair and freckles he obviously inherited from his mother gave him away instantly.

"Um, is he wearing a blue sweater with cars on it? And he has your freckles?"

"Yes," she gulped, gripping my arm. "Have you seen him?"

I tried not to notice how my body reacted to her touch. I could feel it—even through the layers of material separating us. I tilted my chin in the direction over her shoulder. "I think he's over there."

She spun, her entire body shuddering in gratitude as she found her son. "Asher, come here," she gasped, relief evident in her voice. "Now!"

The little boy I judged to be about five or six raced over, stopping beside his mother. "I was saying hi to the snowman, Momma."

She dropped to her knees, engulfing him in her arms. "You can't leave my side," she said, her voice thick with tears. "AJ, you scared me. I couldn't find you."

He patted her back, his small hand tapping on her coat in reassurance. He looked up at me, his eyes the same green as hers. They were sad-looking at the moment, the color dull. "I'm sorry, Momma. I could see *you*, so I thought it was okay. I won't do it again." He flung his little arms around her neck. "I'm sorry!"

She immediately began to comfort him, making soft sounds meant to soothe.

I sat back down, feeling guilty for witnessing the tender moment between them.

She stood, wiping at her cheeks. She turned to me, her beautiful green eyes watery. "Thank you."

I smiled. "Not every day I hear my name being called. Happy to have helped." I looked at her son. "Listen to your momma."

He grinned, his happy mood restored, and nodded. "I will. I'm a good boy."

Something about his grin was infectious, and I returned it. "I'm sure you are."

"Sit here while you wait for your husband," I offered, standing. The woman looked frazzled and exhausted.

"Oh no, we're good. No, ah, no husband to wait for," she rambled. "We're going to head home now."

She began to hand Asher his coat when she stumbled. Without thought, I was beside her in a second, wrapping my arm around her waist and supporting her.

"Are you all right?"

She blinked up at me, her face pale, her eyes unfocused for a moment. Then she shook her head. "Oh, I'm fine." She looked embarrassed. "It's hot in here."

"You're probably hungry, Momma. You didn't eat breakfast this morning."

A feeling passed over me as I looked down at her. A small unfurling in my chest. I held her close, liking how she felt against me. It was as if she belonged there for some odd reason. Concern hit me as her son's words sank in.

"No breakfast?" I asked. "You came into this store, this crowd, with no breakfast to sustain you?"

She shook her head, staring at me.

I tightened my arm. "Well, that won't do. Let's go."

"Go where?" she asked.

"Breakfast." I looked at her son. "You like pancakes, Asher?"

"Yes."

"Good man."

Ten minutes later, we were seated in one of the cafés in the expansive department store. I liked this one, and it was surprisingly empty, considering how busy the store was. I ordered coffee, eggs, toast, pancakes, and bacon, and chocolate milk for my little namesake. Then I turned to the pretty redhead who was still reeling in shock from her scare and my high-handedness. She regarded me cautiously.

"You know my name is Asher," I teased. "But I don't know yours."

"Rosie," she replied. "Rosie Duncan."

"Pretty name."

She lifted a lock of hair. "I came out with a full head of red hair. My dad thought it was appropriate."

"I like it."

"Your name is Asher?" her son asked. "Mine too! Did you know that, Momma?"

"Yes," she replied patiently.

He smiled. "Momma calls me AJ most of the time. So we won't get mixed up." He leaned forward, dropping his voice. "If she calls you by your whole name, look out. She is mad."

"I'll keep that in mind. Any advice?"

"Run," he said seriously.

I began to laugh, and he grinned. Rosie's lips twitched at the corner, but she still looked anxious.

I slid a full coffee cup her way after adding cream and sugar. "Drink up, Rosie."

Her brow furrowed. "How did you know how I like my coffee?"

I shook my head. "I didn't. But you need the sugar. You just had a scare."

"Momma, can I go look at the display?"

In the corner, not far from the table, was yet another Christmas wonderland. Asher seemed fascinated by it.

"Make sure your momma can see you," I admonished him gently as she nodded in permission.

"I will!"

He hurried away, standing and watching the animated scene in rapture.

"So, Asher," she said. "Do you have a last name?"

"Yes." I waited a beat.

She shook her head. "Care to share?"

I stuck out my hand. "Asher Hart. Asher William Hart, in case you need the whole name for when I'm in trouble."

She slipped her hand in mine. It was small and felt cool to my skin. The skin was pale, her fingers delicate. Her nails were short and natural, and she wore no jewelry. It was hard to release her from my grip. She blushed at my words, the pretty color suffusing her skin.

"I doubt I'll need it."

I winked. "I have it on good authority from my sister that I'm trouble."

She smiled and took a sip of her coffee. I found myself mesmerized by her actions. It was the oddest thing.

"Christmas shopping?" I asked, clearing my throat.

"Sort of. He loves coming here to Zoles," she murmured. "I did as a child too. I bring him every year."

"AJ?" I asked. "Short for…?"

"Asher Joseph."

"Ah. And how old is AJ?" I asked.

"He'll be five in January."

"You called out Asher when you were looking for him. Not AJ. Not his full name either."

"I panicked, and I wasn't thinking. It is rare I say his full name. He's a good boy."

"I can see that." I sipped my coffee. "So, you're *sort of* Christmas shopping?"

"Browsing, really. I have his gifts already." She smiled tightly. "I'm his only parent."

"His father is not in the picture?" I had assumed that somehow, but I needed to be sure.

She frowned. "No. He walked away when he found out I was pregnant. It's Asher and me."

"No family?"

She shook her head, color staining her cheeks again, this time darker. "No. They disowned me when they found out I was pregnant and not marrying the father."

I felt her hurt in the simple words and saw the flash of pain in her eyes. The high color in her cheeks was anger.

"My mother died last year. My father didn't even tell me. I heard he already remarried."

"So, you're alone."

She tilted her head, studying me. "And you?"

"I have a sister, as I mentioned. And a niece I adore. I tolerate her husband," I added with a wink. I actually liked him a great deal, and we got along well. "My business is my life, to be honest."

"Ah."

That was all she said. No inquiries about my job, my life, my financial status, nothing. She watched Asher carefully, tensing if he disappeared for a moment. I laid my hand on hers, squeezing her fingers. "He is perfectly safe in here, Rosie. I'm watching him as well."

"I was waiting to pay for his picture with Santa. I blinked, and he was gone." She shook her head. "He's never done that before. Disappeared on me. It-it was scary."

Flipping my palm, I slipped my hand under hers, unable to stop touching her. Our skin slid together, and I entwined our fingers. She stared at our hands, then lifted her eyes to mine. I wondered if she felt that odd connection I did. I hated seeing the worry in her expression. The exhaustion that showed under her eyes. Something inside me wanted, needed, to ease both negative inputs in her life. Anything that bothered her needed to be gone.

I was so shocked by my thoughts, I had to lower my head and clear my throat before I spoke.

"I'm sure it was frightening. It must be a difficult thing to be a single parent. But he's fine and safe. So try to relax."

She took in a deep breath, letting it out slowly.

"We come here every year," she said, sliding her hand away and wrapping it around her mug. I was surprised at the sensation of loss I experienced when we were no longer touching. I picked up my own mug and sipped as she kept talking. I liked the sound of her voice. Low, quiet, sweet.

"I did as a child as well," she continued. "My grandmother brought me until I was fifteen. She died then." She paused, swallowing. "Zoles always had the best Santa. They still do. And the displays are wonderful. I loved them."

"Well, obviously, AJ shares your feelings."

She smiled.

"So, you have his picture taken every year?"

She nodded, a small frown on her face. "The price skyrocketed this year. I wasn't sure I could swing it, but it's a tradition, so I scrimped and saved on some other things so we could do it. I knew AJ would be disappointed. And I couldn't bring him here to look at the displays and not see Santa," she explained. "You can't discuss finances with a small child."

I studied her. "Is that why you didn't eat breakfast this morning?" I asked.

She shook her head, looking embarrassed. "Oh, no. I was trying to get him ready, and we ran out of time."

She was a horrible liar. In my business life, I knew how to spot one, and she was one of the worst I had ever seen. But I let it go, understanding it was a point of pride for her.

But I didn't like it.

"Besides, it was on his wish list. I can't deny his wish list. He really asks for so little."

"I see." I crossed my legs. "Does his momma have a wish list?"

She laughed lightly, shaking her head. "No. Not one I would share anyway. I keep it pretty close to my chest."

I sipped my coffee, having a sinking feeling that her wish list contained far more sensible things than her son's did.

That bothered me as well, and I couldn't explain why.

Our breakfast arrived, and I filled a plate, sliding it in front of Rosie. I had ordered family style, so I knew there would be plenty. "Eat." I paused, using a word that rarely passed my lips. "Please."

AJ ran over, sliding onto a chair. He gazed at the table, his eyes wide. "Oh, Momma. This is a feast!"

I laughed and slid a pancake onto his plate and added some

bacon and scrambled eggs. Rosie cut up the pancake after adding some butter and syrup to it, and AJ dug in, chatting in excitement. He pointed out his favorite parts of the display, telling me about his school, his best friend, Charlie, and his second favorite friend, Ashley.

"Sometimes she says she's my girlfriend, and I just let her," he explained. "Momma says I'm too little to have a girlfriend, but I don't like to hurt her feelings." He grinned, showing me a mouthful of pancakes. "She's nice, though, and gives me her cookies at lunch sometimes, so it's okay if she wants to hold my hand in line."

I nodded sagely, finding him highly entertaining. He had good table manners, said please and thank you, and was intelligent. Rosie was obviously a good mother.

I watched her eat, noticing her seeming love of toast. She buttered each piece liberally, adding jam and enjoying the small triangles. Color returned to her cheeks as she ate some bacon and eggs, and I filled her coffee cup again, adding cream and sugar as if I had been doing it for years. It pleased me to know I was doing something to help her—even if it was in the smallest of ways.

It struck me how comfortable I was with the two of them. None of my usual impatience or terseness was present. I laughed and teased AJ, as well as his mother. I smiled in amusement at his ramblings. Watched his momma with concern and interest.

She fascinated me. From the way she ate her toast to her quiet observations. I thought she was lovely, her red hair and freckles enchanting. On AJ, they were adorable; on Rosie, they were sexy and playful. Yet, she seemed unaware of her prettiness. Our eyes met often, locking for brief moments and speaking volumes before she would drop her gaze to her plate or refocus on AJ. I wondered if she was feeling the same draw to me as I was to her.

We finished breakfast, and I paid the bill, silencing her protests with a dark look. When we were done, she was surprised but didn't object as I took her hand and led her and AJ out of the restaurant.

"I'll drive you home." She had mentioned the bus at one point, but I didn't want to say goodbye yet. Or have them wait in the cold for public transportation.

"Oh no—" she began, but I held up my hand, silencing her.

"I'll drive you home," I repeated.

She didn't reply or make a comment as we stepped outside and my vehicle was waiting by the door. She looked nervous, and it occurred to me I was a stranger and basically demanding she let me drive her home. I called the store doorman over.

"Mr. Hart?" he asked.

"This is Rosie Duncan. I am driving her and her son home."

He tipped his hat. "Yes, sir." He smiled at Rosie. "You're in good hands, miss. Mr. Hart will look after you."

She glanced at me with a smile. "Thank you."

"I want you to feel safe."

"I do."

"Good, then let's get you home."

I was grateful I had a car seat for my niece already and I knew how to use it. When she saw it, Rosie looked startled, but I explained. "My niece and I have a standing pizza night once a month. I drive." I winked. "She's a terror behind the wheel."

Her laughter made me grin. It was light and buoyant, the sound filling the air. I liked it. I wanted to hear more of it.

I buckled AJ into the back, made sure Rosie was safe in the front, and slid into the driver's seat.

"What?" I asked as I turned to look at her, seeing the look of confusion and wonder on her face.

"Where did you come from, Asher?" she asked.

I smiled as I touched her cheek. "Your secret wish list."

Her blush said it all.

CHAPTER TWO

ASHER

I didn't ask if I could come in when we reached her apartment. I simply got out of the vehicle and followed them inside. They lived in a small apartment block, the neighborhood decent for the area. Inside, her home was compact but spotless. A tiny living room and kitchen, a place for a table and chairs to one side. AJ took my hand and showed me his room, the boy theme making me smile. Cars and trucks were big for him, his toy chest overflowing with all sorts of little vehicles.

I left him in his room, returning to the kitchen. I spied a small artificial tree in the corner with a few gifts under it. I went closer, inspecting it. Handmade ornaments and some bright-colored lights decorated the well-used tree. It was very festive. On examination, I noticed all the gifts were to Asher and signed "Love, Momma."

I saw none for her. I wondered if that changed come Christmas morning.

Some other lights were strung up and decorations scattered around. The furniture was worn but comfortable-looking. Throw blankets and pillows made it a welcoming place.

I entered the kitchen, seeing Rosie sitting at the table, looking nervous. I sat beside her, reaching for her hand. "AJ obviously loves his room."

"He plays in there a lot."

I looked around, realizing, aside from the bathroom, the apartment had no other doors.

"Where is your room?" I asked.

"I sleep on the sofa."

"On the sofa?" I asked, shocked. She had no room? No privacy?

She nodded. "I haven't found a two-bedroom place I can afford. I like this neighborhood. It's close to AJ's school and easy transit. The sofa pulls out to a bed. I don't mind it. It's comfortable enough." She shrugged. "It will do until I can afford something better."

I had a feeling "until I can afford something better" was a mantra for her. I thought of her too-big coat, going without breakfast. Sleeping on the sofa. She went without so AJ didn't have to. I wondered how many other sacrifices she made without even thinking.

"What do you do for a living?" I asked.

"I'm an accountant. I put myself through school."

"While pregnant?"

"Partially." She smiled ruefully. "It wasn't as if I had a choice. I had to finish school to get a decent job. I had to work in order to go to school. Luckily, I qualified for some small scholarships, which helped."

"And his father never helped?"

She laughed and got up, pouring us the coffee she had made. "He ran as far away as possible. Last I heard, he was in the Northwest Territories as a guide or something. He always liked nature and hiking."

"Selfish bastard."

"It never would have worked out. We were too different. He was taking business courses so he could run his own company offering outdoor nature adventures. We met at a course we were taking together. He seemed nice. Sadly, nice and wanting the same things from life didn't mesh. He wanted adventures. To never settle down. I hated the sun and outside. I wanted to get my degree, settle down, and have a family. When I got pregnant, he walked fast."

"And you became a mother."

She smiled, her love for her son evident. "*Asher's* mother. Yes. He is worth everything."

"So, an accountant?"

"Yes. I finally got on with a good place. I'm still at the bottom, but it's steady and I plan to work my way up." She took a sip of coffee. "And you? What do you do when not finding lost boys or feeding strange women?"

I chuckled. "I only do that once a year. Otherwise, I'm a philanthropist."

"Oh." She frowned. "What is that exactly?"

"I own several companies, which are profitable. We turn the profits into investments. Those funds are there to help people. We do grants, support charities, fund causes. Scholarships. Foundations. We even give money to individuals."

"Wow. So you give away money for a living."

"I tried the usual route. I came from money and made more easily. But I was tired of corporate greed. The first time I gave away a large chunk of money was the first time I felt good about myself. I realized I could do both. Make it and give it away. Help others. So I restructured my life."

"That is amazing."

I opened my mouth to reply but my phone buzzed, and I frowned as I read the message. "I have to go," I said regretfully.

I was pleased to see she looked as disappointed as I felt. She stood, and I followed her to the door. "Thank you for your help today," she said. "And breakfast. It was delicious, and I enjoyed spending some time with you."

I stepped closer. "So did I." I paused. "I don't want to leave," I confessed.

"Oh," she breathed out.

"I want to see you again." I cupped her cheek, the skin beneath my fingers soft and smooth. I stroked it with my thumb, feeling the heat gather under my touch.

"Are you sure?" she whispered.

"Do you feel it?" I asked, keeping my voice low. "This…draw?"

She nodded, not speaking.

I dropped my head, brushing along her cheek with my lips. "I want to explore it. If you feel the same way," I added.

She gripped my jacket with her hand, fisting the material tightly. "I'm not alone."

"I know. I think you're a wonderful mother. I like your son. I like you." I took her hand in mine, lifting it to my lips. "Please," I asked again, the word coming easily when it came to her.

"I, ah, don't think I'm the kind of woman you're used to, Asher."

I liked the way she said my name. It was different from when she said it to her son. This was breathier, needier.

"I'm not used to any kind of woman, Rosie. I'm a bit of a loner. But I want to get to know you better—if you let me."

"I'm not in your league."

"I wasn't aware I had one. And if I do, I want you there with me. Let me see you again."

"Maybe you should think about it, and if you decide you want to, you know where I am."

I pressed my mouth to her cheek, my lips lingering. Her hair tickled my cheek, the scent of her, soft and feminine, swirling around me.

I didn't need to think.

I already knew.

I knocked on her door at nine o'clock that night. I heard light footsteps, and she opened the door, surprised. Her hair was up, and she was dressed in fuzzy pants and a long sweatshirt. Warm socks were on her feet. She looked adorable.

"Asher?" she asked, confused.

"I've been thinking," I said.

"I see." She chewed on her lip. "Did you want to come in and tell me your thoughts, or did you come to say goodbye?"

I stepped into the apartment. "I came to share."

"Okay."

She had the tree lights on, quiet music playing, and a book was open on the sofa. A mug of something warm steamed on the coffee table.

"AJ asleep?"

"He conked out about twenty minutes ago."

"Am I interrupting your quiet time?" I had a feeling she didn't get much of that.

"I don't mind," she replied. "I was going to read a bit and take some calls. I can put it off."

"Take some calls?"

"I work for a customer call center. I usually try to do a couple of hours in the evenings and the morning before AJ gets up."

"And you work all day?"

"Yeah." She shrugged as if it was nothing. "The more calls I log, the more I make. It helps me give AJ a few treats in the year and a nice Christmas."

I stared at her in wonder. Then suddenly, she was in my arms and my mouth covered hers. I pulled her tight to my chest. She flung her arms around my neck, returning my passion with her own. She tasted of the tea she had been sipping and something I couldn't identify. Something uniquely her. Despite the difference in our heights, she fit against me well, her curves molding to my hardness. She made a low noise in her throat as I deepened the kiss, exploring her, discovering all the sweetness of her sexy mouth. She gripped my hair, played with the ends, and ran her tongue along mine, making me shiver. I ended up on the sofa, her on my lap, as our kisses became frantic. She straddled me, impatiently pushing off my coat so I felt the heat of her skin through the thin layers that separated us. I lost myself to her. To everything about her. The weight of her on my lap, the press of her mouth on mine, the feel of her nipples grazing my chest. How my cock felt trapped between us. I knew we had to stop soon or we would cross a line neither of us was ready for. But I couldn't stop. I couldn't break away from the wonder of her mouth. The warmth of her embrace.

Until the plaintive sound of her son's voice cut through the fog that had surrounded us.

"Momma!"

She pushed off me, scrambling from my lap. I hated the cold feeling that flooded me without her warmth. Her eyes were wide and startled, her hair messy from my hands, and she was adorably rumpled.

Her gaze strayed to me then snapped back as a second summons was called. She hurried away, and I let my head fall to my chest with a low groan.

I hadn't planned on walking in here and mauling her like a college frat boy. I hadn't been able to stop thinking about her all day. The whole time I dealt with a client, I thought about her. Her smile. Her beautiful eyes. That wild hair. How it felt under my fingers. How soft her skin was. What a wonderful mother she was to her son. How awesome I thought AJ was. The fact that we shared the same name.

I thought about her until I had no choice but to come see her and ask her out again.

Until my body took over my mind and all that mattered was getting her close. I pushed off the sofa, rolling my shoulders and willing my body back under control.

I had only met her that morning, for Christ's sake. Why was I feeling so strongly about her? Why was she filling my every thought?

I blew out a long breath. I needed to get myself under control. Now.

ROSIE

I smoothed the blanket over AJ's shoulder, stroking the hair back from his forehead. He often called out to me not long after falling asleep. It had been that way since he was able to say "Momma." As if he needed to feel me close before drifting into his deep sleep.

I was normally prepared for it.

But not tonight.

Tonight, I had been locked in Asher's arms. Drowning in his taste. Reveling in his touch.

I caught a glimpse of myself in the mirror that hung on the wall across from AJ's bed. My lips were swollen and red. My hair was messy. My eyes were wide, and I looked as if I had been thoroughly kissed.

And I had.

My God, that man's mouth.

I had noticed him before AJ disappeared. He was sitting alone, staring at the crowds. There was something about his expression. A sorrow I felt deep in my bones as if it were my own. He was incredibly good-looking, even as serious and stern as he appeared to be. Everything about him was dark. He was dressed in jeans, a navy shirt, and a black leather jacket. He had black Doc Martens on his large feet. His rich brown hair was brushed off his forehead, and his eyes were so dark they were almost black. When he rose to his feet, reacting to my calling out what he thought was his name, I noticed how tall he was. When he stepped in to help, I couldn't help staring at his wide shoulders, slim waist, and long legs. I expected to see coldness when our eyes met, but instead, I saw only compassion and worry.

When he held my hand, I noticed how large it was compared to my own. When he closed his palm around mine, he engulfed me.

Much like when he held me close and kissed me.

Earlier, he'd been unexpectedly kind. He was obviously used to taking charge, the way he had taken us to breakfast, then driven us home. I had tried to tamp down my attraction to him, knowing it was a lost cause. When he confessed to feeling the same pull toward me, I was shocked. But after he left, I really didn't think I would see him again. I assumed he would come to his senses and realize he was simply reacting to helping a woman and had gotten carried away. I had googled him, and I knew he was wealthy. That he had been named Philanthropist of the Year three times in a row. I read a lot of articles about the good he did in the community. The pictures I found showed him at various functions. Always alone. He was dressed in a suit in every picture, looking polished and distant, always slightly to the side as if he didn't want to be there. I zoomed in, wondering if anyone ever noticed the sadness in his eyes. It was the same sadness I had glimpsed earlier. I was certain of it.

Then I shook my head, knowing he existed in a different world than I did, and I had no idea if he was sad or simply bored at one of the seemingly frequent events he attended.

I googled a little more, looking at the wealthy people he associated with. Faces I recognized from society columns. Newspaper articles. There were even a few pictures of him taken with the BAM group. They were huge in real estate, and their buildings were highly sought after. And although he was smiling in the pictures, I still saw the same distance in his expression. A man alone in a crowd.

I hadn't expected him to show up at my door tonight.

And I hadn't expected to feel this passion. Or long for his mouth on mine again.

I shut my eyes and scrubbed my face.

I needed to get a grip. Fast.

ASHER

She entered the room quietly, her posture saying it all. I stepped closer. "I apologize."

"You're sorry you kissed me?"

I ran a hand through my hair. "I should say yes. Assure you I got carried away and it won't happen again, but I'd be lying. I want to kiss you more, Rosie. Talk to you. Ask you a thousand questions and listen to your answers. Tell you anything you want to know about me."

She blinked, once again caught off guard.

"I don't understand."

I moved in front of her, capturing her hands in mine and lifting them to my mouth, kissing the knuckles. "You're so shocked someone would be interested in you."

"Well, that, and it's so…so—"

I cut her off. "Fast?"

She nodded.

"I know. But it feels right, doesn't it?"

"We're so different."

I frowned, not liking that statement. I knew what she meant. Our lives were polar opposites. Financially, we were yin and yang. Our worlds were two different places. Yet that didn't matter at all to me. I didn't want her thinking that way about us. I wanted her seeing the positives.

I wanted to make her laugh and smile, not look sad and pensive.

"You mean the penis thing? That I have one and you don't? The difference works well in this application, Rosie. Trust me on this."

Her eyes widened, and then it happened. She began to laugh—the same light, girly sound as earlier. Her frown faded, her tension disappeared, and she was gorgeous. She slapped my chest in pretend outrage.

"You're awful."

"Awful good," I assured her, lifting her hand to my mouth again and kissing it.

We shared some more amusement, and I pulled her into my arms, unable to resist touching her any longer.

"Opposites attract, Rosie. God knows I'm attracted to you."

"I, ah, looked you up on the internet."

I chuckled, not surprised. "The world I live in is different, but I'm just me, Rosie. I like that you see that. I get tired of being the center of attention because of my money. Of being sought after for what I could do for someone."

"I like the man I see, but I'm still worried…" She trailed off.

I shook my head and kissed her sweet mouth. "Baby, earlier you said you were out of my league. I have a feeling *you* are the one out of *my* league. But I want to explore this. Give me a chance. Please."

She bit her lip, staring at me. I pulled her teeth from the plump flesh.

"I won't hurt you. Or your son. Please."

"Yes."

That was all I needed to hear.

CHAPTER THREE

ASHER

She was shocked yet again when I appeared at her door the next morning, my hands filled with bags. We had talked, kissed more, and I had left, regretting the fact that I had to, but I knew she was tired. I had hoped once I was gone, she would go to bed, but I had a feeling she would log some hours on her second job. I had to push down my instinct to tell her to stop. I didn't have that right.

Yet.

During our talk last night, I was shocked when she admitted she had only been on two dates since Asher was born. When I expressed my disbelief, she only shrugged at my statement.

"Single mothers are a lot for most men to take on, Asher. We're too much work."

"I disagree. The best things in life are worth the effort."

"I think you're a different breed altogether."

I planned on showing her how different I was—in the best ways. She fascinated me, and I thought AJ was an incredible kid. I looked forward to getting to know both of them more.

I admitted to her I didn't date much. "My business has always come first," I explained. I met her worried gaze, running my knuckles over her soft cheek. "I think that might have changed."

I liked the fact that my words made her smile.

She opened the door looking so sexy and sweet, it took all I could not to drop the bag and pull her into my arms and kiss her until she was breathless. Her hair was everywhere. Lines from her pillowcase were etched into her cheek. Her beautiful green eyes were wide and blinking, hardly awake enough to comprehend my presence.

"Asher?" she asked. "How do you keep getting into the building?"

I grinned. "Magic." I lifted the bags in my hands. "I brought breakfast."

"Breakfast?" she repeated. "Or a whole grocery store?"

I breezed past her, stopping to drop a fast kiss to her mouth. "I didn't know what you had, so I brought everything to make my specialty."

AJ came running out of the bedroom, clutching a well-worn teddy. "Asher! Hi!"

"Hey, bud. I came to have breakfast with you and your mom. I'm going to make it."

"Can I help? Momma says I'm a great helper!"

"Great. I need an assistant."

"I'll go get ready!" he announced before running to his room.

I set down the bags, shrugged off my coat, and toed off my boots. Rosie stared dumbfounded at me.

"You're very, ah, goal-oriented, aren't you?" she asked.

I laughed and cupped her face, her skin warm under my cold hands. "If you mean making you smile is the goal, then yes." I kissed her again. "We'll make breakfast. You go have a nice leisurely shower. I don't imagine you get many of those."

"No," she admitted ruefully.

"Go," I encouraged.

"Why are you doing this?" she whispered.

I pulled her into my arms and kissed her deeply. Until she was whimpering and shaking in my arms. Then I pulled back, resting my forehead against hers.

"That's why."

"Okay, then. Just checking," she replied.

I turned her and swatted her ass. "Go before your son comes back and catches us."

I tried not to laugh as she walked into the sofa, then stumbled down the hall to the bathroom.

I picked up the bags, feeling somewhat light-headed myself.

Rosie shook her head as she finished the omelet and toast I had made. Once again, I noticed her love of the warm bread. I had bought extra butter, putting it in her refrigerator, assuming it was a treat she didn't get very often. I had, in fact, added a lot of things I had picked up "by accident" while getting the items I needed for breakfast.

"You like toast."

She blushed slightly, biting into another piece. "I love it. I always have. Just toast and butter. Nothing else. It's comfort food to me."

"You're in need of comforting right now?" I asked with a frown.

AJ laughed from the spot on the floor where he sat, cross-legged and enjoying cartoons. Rosie had told me she only allowed him an hour of screen time every day except the weekends. *"He loves cartoons, and my neighbor is kind enough to let me use her Disney+ sign-in. I let him watch some shows, and we often watch a movie together," she explained.*

"Comforting?" she replied. "No, but I'm wondering why a wealthy philanthropist is sitting at my old kitchen table after making me breakfast. It's a little disconcerting." She met my gaze. "I don't really understand this thing between us."

"I don't either," I confessed. "This isn't my usual MO."

She sat back, picking up her coffee cup. "What is?" she asked, her voice teasing. But I saw the flash of worry in her gaze and felt her tension. "Five-star restaurants, ballroom dancing, and quick trips to the islands with leggy blondes after a long week of making millions?"

I dropped my head in laughter at her words.

"First off, no to the ballroom dancing. Not a fan. Second, my days and evenings usually consist of me and my laptop, working, listening to my assistant call me a tyrant and a bore because I rarely leave the office." I shook my head. "My meals are normally what my housekeeper leaves me or takeout. As for the leggy blondes, those were around on occasion before, but lately, I much prefer the company of clever, sexy redheads who let me cook them breakfast."

"Why?" she whispered.

"Because I think she is fascinating. Strong. Beautiful. Inspiring."

She blinked.

"I assume you're not used to being thought of that way."

"Well, AJ thinks I'm awesome—most of the time. But other than that, no."

"Get used to it."

She worried at the plump flesh of her mouth with her teeth. I leaned forward, pulling her lip away from the self-inflicted torture. "I want to kiss that lip later," I murmured. "Stop hurting it."

Her eyes widened, and I tried not to groan as she kissed the end of my finger that rested lightly on her bottom lip.

"Why me?" she whispered.

"Why not you?"

"There is nothing special about me."

"I totally disagree on that. I think you're very special."

"I'm ordinary. There are lots of single mothers working as hard as I am to give their kids a good life."

I nodded. "I try to help them with my business and my money. I try to do good for a lot of people. That is important to me. As for being ordinary, I don't think you ever have or ever will be that."

"Why?" she asked again.

I didn't know how to explain this feeling. How intensely I felt this connection with her. Or even why I felt it. But it was there, a living, breathing thing between us. And I refused to push it away. I needed to find out how strong it was.

"Because I think it was meant to be."

She looked shocked at my words, unsure what to say. Right then, AJ chose to run over. "Momma, can we still go sledding?"

"Sure, baby."

"Can I watch one more cartoon?"

She sighed and stroked his wild curls away from his face. "Only one."

"Thank you!"

He turned to me. "You can come sledding if you want. We go to the hill by the park. It's fun."

"I think Asher has other—"

I cut her off. "I would love to, bud."

He raced off, happy, and she looked at me. "You don't have to do that."

"But I want to."

"You're not really dressed for sledding."

"I have some other clothes in the car. I often take Bonnie to the park, so I'm always prepared."

"Your niece?"

"Yes."

"I assume you'll be spending Christmas with them?"

"No, they go to his parents' place in Alberta. They've already gone, in fact. We'll spend the day together when they get back and have our own little Christmas."

"You don't go with them?"

"I went once. It was just…too much."

"Too much?"

"I felt like the odd man out, to be honest. All couples and families. And I don't like my sister worrying about me. So I stay here and do what I do best. Be alone. Find places to give money."

She frowned. "You can't be alone on Christmas." She looked around. "I mean, it's not much, but you're welcome here."

"Not much?" I repeated. "It's your home."

"I'm sure compared to where you live, it's, ah, lacking."

"You don't have other people joining you?"

"No. It's only AJ and me."

The thought of spending the day with them made me feel something I hadn't felt in years. An elusive fluttering of happiness filled my chest.

"I would be honored to come here for Christmas."

She beamed at me, her smile wide.

"Then consider yourself invited."

The snow began as we went sledding, the fluffy white flakes falling rapidly. The walk to the park was short, AJ chatting incessantly. There were two places to sled, one a small slope, the other much higher. Both were fairly busy with families and kids, the noise and excitement level high.

"There's a skating pond farther down the path," Rosie explained.

"I don't know how to skate," AJ said with a frown.

"I can teach you," I offered.

"I don't have any skates. Neither does Momma."

"I bet I have an older pair kicking around that would fit you," I said. "My sister left her skates last time. I bet they'd fit your momma."

"I'd like that!"

Rosie didn't look as enthused as her son did, which made me chuckle.

At the bottom of the hill was a food truck, and the scent of coffee, hot cocoa, and something sweet filled the air.

"That's where Momma sits while I sled sometimes." AJ pointed to the picnic tables set up. "She only goes a few times." He bent his finger for me to come closer. "She gets tired 'cause she is old."

I bit back my laughter. "I don't think your momma is old."

"She says so."

"Trust me, trudging up the hill, I feel old," Rosie said, sounding amused.

"Okay, well today, AJ and I will trudge." I pressed a bill into her hand. "You sit and enjoy the coffee. We'll have some cocoa when we've made a few trips."

She began to protest, and I leaned down and kissed her. "Please. I want to do this."

She smiled, and it felt as if the sun came out. "Okay."

"Let's go, bud."

We headed to the hill, and I paused. "Which one?"

He hesitated. "That one." He pointed to the smaller of the two.

"I don't mind walking up the bigger one," I offered. "It'll be fun."

He kicked the snow. "The little one is fine."

I got down on one knee. "What is it, Asher?"

He looked up, hearing his full name. "I went down the big one once, and I fell off the sled. I'm scared to try again."

I pursed my lips and nodded in understanding. "That would be scary. But this time, I'll be with you. We can go down together. I won't let you fall."

He looked over my shoulder at the higher hill. "You won't?"

"Nope. I'll sit behind you and make sure you're good." I winked. "If I hold you, I won't fall either."

He grinned. "Let's go!"

We headed up, pulling the wooden sled behind me. I noticed AJ's envious looks at some of the newer sleds on the hill, but he didn't say a word.

"You know," I confided. "I had a sled just like this when I was your age. Best kind around. The wood goes faster and straighter than some of the slippery ones."

"It's all right."

At the top, I put the sled into position and motioned for AJ to get on. He looked nervous, so I sat at the back, patting the space between my legs. "Sit here."

He did, and I grabbed the rope. "Hold tight to this. We're gonna go fast."

"We won't fall?"

"Nope."

I pushed off, guiding the sled down the slope. It was fast and fun, the wind in our faces, my arm around AJ, holding him tight. He whooped and laughed, raising one hand in the air as we hit the bottom, gliding to a stop. He jumped up, no longer afraid, his eyes gleaming with happiness.

"Can we go again?"

"Absolutely."

A few runs later, I joined Rosie on the picnic bench as AJ went to the smaller hill, confident on his own there.

I sat down heavily, accepting the cup of coffee she handed me. I took an appreciative sip.

"He was having such a good time," she observed.

"We both were. He wants to play with his friends for a bit, which is good." I leaned back with a grimace. "Apparently, I'm old too. My butt is killing me."

She laughed. "Nothing like an almost five-year-old to make you feel your age."

I chuckled.

"You're so good with him."

"I like kids."

"I can see that."

"Am I allowed to buy him a gift, Rosie?"

She frowned. "Allowed?"

"A Christmas gift. I don't want to overstep. Nothing extravagant."

"Like?"

"A new sled."

She smiled sadly. "The one he has is a used one. I'm sure he'd love a new one."

"I know the perfect one. It's not over the top or unsafe."

"If you want to, then yes."

"I want to."

"Okay, then."

I squeezed her hand. "Thanks."

"Uh-oh, he's headed back. Hope your butt is recovered."

I grinned. "If not, you can kiss it better for me later."

I left her laughing.

AJ's laughter rang out loudly as we went to the bigger hill again and again. We had a snowball fight, him and me against his momma.

She was far better at it, building up an arsenal and pelting us with them mercilessly. I loved seeing her happy and giggling. Her cheeks were flushed with the cold, her eyes dancing. She was beautiful, and I kissed her after tackling her in the snow. AJ jumped on top of us, and we rolled around, throwing handfuls of snow, chuckling and teasing.

We were all wet and cold when we got back to her little apartment. She made us hot chocolate and threw our wet clothes in the dryer at her neighbor's.

"She lets me use her machines," she explained. "She's away for Christmas right now."

We spent the rest of the afternoon watching a Christmas movie. Eating popcorn. I insisted on ordering in dinner, and we ate a feast of Chinese food, AJ exclaiming over every new dish he tried. It was simple, fun, and I couldn't recall ever feeling so content in my life.

After he went to bed, we ended up on the sofa, locked in each other's embrace, our mouths moving together with a hunger that couldn't be satisfied. She was beautiful in her desire. Achingly sweet in her pleas for more.

"I don't want to rush," I murmured, wondering who the hell was talking. I wanted her. I wanted her more than I could recall wanting another woman in my entire life.

"Please give me this," she whispered. "A memory I can think of and hold close."

I drew back, shocked. "No, baby," I whispered back. "No, that is not what this is. I'm not going to disappear. I won't fuck you and vanish. I'm not walking out of your life."

"I have nothing to hold you."

I rested my forehead on hers. "You have given me more happiness in a day than I have felt in years. You and AJ. That is priceless. What you give me is inestimable. Your heart is far more valuable than the millions I touch every day."

She clutched my wrists. "I want to believe that."

"Then do. I told you—I'm your wish list."

I hated to leave her. I had to force myself to walk out the door. I kissed her long and hard before leaving, promising to return the next day by lunchtime. It would be Christmas Eve, and I wanted as much time with them as possible.

In the condo, I prowled the vast space, noticing the emptiness of the rooms and the coldness of the décor. I had never given much thought to it before.

For all its shabbiness and cramped space, Rosie's place was a home. This was simply a place to live.

I thought of how, with one phone call, I could have the place decorated, a huge tree brought in. Presents delivered and enough food to feed an army by tomorrow. I could bring her and AJ here and give them a Christmas beyond their expectations.

Except, I knew she wouldn't like it. She would be overwhelmed and uncomfortable. Unlike women in my past, she wasn't interested in me for my money. I barked out a laugh in the silence of the room. She had no idea who I really was. What I did. How rich I actually was. She had admitted to googling me, but she hadn't dug very deep. It didn't matter to her.

But she mattered to me. How it happened so quickly, I had no idea, but it did. I cared about her. About her son. And I knew she felt it too.

And I wanted to make Christmas good for her—for both of them.

Without overwhelming her or scaring her off.

I picked up my phone and made a call. A shocked voice on the other end answered.

"Asher?"

"I need your help."

"With?"

"Pulling off a small miracle."

"Hit me."

CHAPTER FOUR

ASHER

I arrived just before lunch, knocking on Rosie's door. She opened it, and I grinned at the jaunty Santa hat perched on her head. I set down my bag and stepped forward, cupping her face and kissing her. "Santa has never looked so sexy," I murmured.

"It arrived this morning, along with a few other things," she said, shaking her head. "Asher—"

"My contribution to the day," I finished for her. "A few groceries and such."

"Your *such* is extravagant. Lewis refused to take any of it back."

"And she was pretty damn insistent." My assistant strode in from the kitchen, covered in glitter and tinsel. "AJ and I were making some ornaments while your woman was cussing me out and telling me off," he informed me with a twinkle in his eye. "You never said she was lippy. Just pretty."

I shook his hand, still amazed at how lucky I was. When he'd listened to my requests last night, he hadn't wasted time with questions or unwanted advice. He'd simply gotten to work and arranged some of the items I needed. The rest, I took care of myself this morning.

Some things a man needed to handle on his own. And as much as I appreciated Lewis's extra efforts, I wanted to do the more personal ones.

I walked into the kitchen, laughing at AJ. He wore even more glitter, but the smile on his face was even brighter.

"Asher!" he crowed. "We made things!" He held up a brightly colored ball, the glitter literally dripping from it. "I like Lewis!"

"Me too, bud. You had fun?"

"Yeah! And Momma said she'd never seen so much food in our kitchen."

I had made sure to add lots of extras to the list. I never wanted her to be without butter again for her toast. Or real cream.

I peered at her. "I assumed you wouldn't normally make a turkey for just the two of you. I got us one. I thought we could cook it together."

"And the rest of the stuff?" she asked quietly.

I shrugged. "Things I thought we might need. I had no idea what you had or didn't have."

She rose up on her toes and pressed a kiss to my cheek. "And you went overboard. But thank you."

I turned and captured her mouth, kissing her hard and fast. I was grateful and surprised at her acceptance.

I saw Lewis smirk as he reached for his coat. I walked him to the door. "I'll transfer everything to your trunk," he said quietly. "I got it all."

I shook his hand. "Thank you."

"I don't know what happened or how you met her, but she is amazing," he said. "I've never heard or seen you look like this."

"This, how?" I asked.

"Happy. Excited." He paused. "In love."

I blinked at his words.

Love?

I wasn't *in love*. I had only just met Rosie. That was impossible—

Or was it?

I grinned.

"Another Christmas miracle," I replied. "Your bonus is in your bank account."

"Boss man, what I did this morning was my gift to you. But I appreciate it, and I'll make sure Evan knows where the MacBook came from. He'll be thrilled. He's been wanting one of those in green for ages. Luckily, the Apple Store still had one in stock. I'm picking it up now."

I clapped him on the shoulder. "Merry Christmas."

He grinned. "Back at you."

He left, and I picked up the bouquet I had left in the hall. I walked into the kitchen, where Rosie was still unpacking bags and AJ was tidying up. I had a feeling I'd be sneezing glitter for the next few months, but somehow, the thought made me happy.

I helped her finish unloading the groceries. The flowers I gave her made her smile. They also got me a long kiss that only ended when AJ ran into the kitchen to tell us it was snowing again. He was excited.

"Momma, a white Christmas! We never get those!"

"I know, baby."

He stared up at me, his eyes round in his face. "Maybe we can go sledding again?"

I ruffled his hair. "I'd love to."

He paused. "Are you gonna keep kissing my momma?"

"Probably."

He crossed his arms. "She doesn't usually kiss anyone but me."

I matched his stance. "I see. Do we need to have a talk? Man-to-man?"

He pursed his lips. "Later. I don't wanna miss my show."

"Good choice. Later, when your momma is having a nap."

"A nap?" he questioned. "Momma never naps."

"It's Christmas. Naps are special."

"Doesn't sound like much fun, but okay."

He padded back to the living room. Rosie smiled at me.

"You're very good with him."

"He's the same age as my niece. I talk to her like an adult too—at least, most of the time. We're silly at times too. But kids are smarter than people give them credit for."

She was quiet for a moment, then stepped closer.

"I noticed your, ah, overnight bag you put in the closet."

"I was hoping you'd let me stay. Wake up with you two on Christmas morning." I swallowed nervously, surprised at how desperately I needed her to say yes. As someone used to getting anything he wanted whenever he wanted it, asking her came surprisingly easy. She controlled the situation—not me. It was an odd sensation, but not unwelcome. "If you'd let me."

"I sleep on the sofa. The mattress is sort of lumpy."

"I can handle it."

She tilted her head, and a smile tugged on her lips. "Not sure I can handle you, but I would like it if you stayed." She held up a finger before I could speak. "But if you decide a few hours from now it's all too much, I won't be upset if you head home to your own bed and some peace and quiet. You're still welcome for dinner."

I wasn't going to change my mind. I was tired of peace and quiet. Tired of being alone. I was right where I wanted to be—lumpy mattress, crowded apartment, overly excited child, and all.

Because everything was connected to her.

✳

"I am so full," she murmured, setting down her utensils. She sat back, picking up her wineglass. "Since when do wealthy single men cook for themselves?"

I laughed. "I can do breakfast, and I make this casserole. That is it. My housekeeper taught me this recipe in case she was gone for a while so I wouldn't starve." I winked at her. "You are totally in charge of dinner tomorrow."

"Speaking of that, a fifteen-pound turkey for three people?" she scoffed. "Plus all those vegetables for side dishes? And the desserts? We'll be eating like kings for weeks."

That had been my plan. Although, the more time I spent with her and AJ, the more I was convinced they would be in my life for a very long time. I would make sure the kitchen was well stocked. Preferably the one in my condo. I could already see Rosie in there making dinner, AJ playing on the floor in the living room, and me watching them both. Making sure they were warm, safe, and happy.

I kept my mouth shut, though. Rosie already thought I was too impulsive.

What she didn't realize was that it was only when it came to her. Everywhere else in my life, I was circumspect. Cautious. One encounter with her and that all went out the window.

"I like leftovers," I said simply.

She smiled, looking shy.

"What?" I asked, leaning over and stroking her soft cheek.

"I like knowing you want to be around for them."

"I do. More than you know."

Her brow furrowed, and I moved closer again. "I'm not going anywhere. I can't explain why or how I know, but I do know it. I trust my gut all the time. It has never let me down."

She became teasing. "And your gut likes me?"

I winked, leering at her. "Everything below my belt likes you, Rosie." When she began to laugh with me, I smiled. "Everything above the belt too."

"Okay, then."

"Finish your wine. I believe an excited little boy wants to go for a walk and watch a movie before he puts out his stocking. We have a busy night ahead of us."

She grinned. "Yes, we do."

AJ was out for the count. Between the walk, the movie, and the wrestling match we had, he was exhausted enough to fall asleep by nine. I helped her put out the few gifts for AJ from Santa and fill his stocking. "What about you?"

She smiled and added a couple of boxes under the tree. "I wrap up a few things from around the house so I have something to open."

I refrained from telling her this would be the last year that happened. In fact, it wouldn't be happening at all. Instead, I nodded. "Good thinking, Momma."

She went for a shower, and I called and left my sister a voice mail. I told her I wasn't alone and I would explain when she got back. We didn't make a big deal about Christmas apart. We celebrated when she returned, but I knew she would be pleased to know I was with someone.

Rosie returned, dressed in pajamas with Santas on them. They were fuzzy and warm-looking and made me smile. I grabbed a fast shower in her small space, missing my far more luxurious shower. I hoped one day soon to show it to her.

Back in the living room, she looked nervous. The pull-out bed was ready, and she was perched on the end. "Ah, do you have a favorite side?"

I bent and kissed her. "Whatever one you like is fine." I cupped her face. "Relax, my girl. I'll be a perfect gentleman."

She chewed her lips. "I hope I can return the favor."

I winked. "Just nudge me. I'll be ready."

We climbed into the bed, and I discovered quickly she was correct. The mattress was lumpy. But that ceased to matter when I pulled her close and she nestled into my chest as if she was meant to be there. I had to stifle a groan as she wiggled against me to get comfortable. My cock was fully ready for her. I tried to shift my hips back, but she obviously felt me against her.

"Oh, ah, sorry," she mumbled.

"Ignore it. It'll settle."

Maybe.

With a sigh, she relaxed and fell asleep quickly. I knew she was tired. She worked, looked after her son, and had the added stress of the holidays. And she did it all on her own.

I waited until I knew she was deeply asleep. I had never moved as carefully as I did for the next while. I slipped down to my car and pulled out the bags Lewis had left. I snuck back upstairs and added gifts to the ones currently under the tree, putting the reused gifts for her into the bag, which I tucked into the closet. I added a full stocking for Rosie. The sled I had purchased was too big to wrap, but I propped it against the wall, adding a festive bow. It was sleek and fast. AJ would love it. Then I crept back into bed, smiling as she snuggled against me again.

A while later, I woke alone, sitting up to see Rosie kneeling by the tree, staring at it and the pile of gifts. She was touching the ribbon on a package, shaking her head. I flung back the blanket, padded across the room, and sat behind her. "What are you doing, Rosie?"

"How did these get here?"

"Santa."

She turned, the soft glow of the tree casting her face in light. "I didn't expect…" She trailed off.

"I know. I wanted you to have a surprise too."

"You're incredible."

I touched her nose with mine, rubbing it affectionately.

"I think the same of you."

"Asher," she whispered. "What if there *was* something I wanted? Something only you could give me?"

"Ask me," I replied without hesitation. "Whatever you want, I'll get it for you."

She drew in a deep breath. "You. I want you."

I froze. "If we do this, Rosie, then you're mine. I don't play the field. I take sex seriously. I'll be all in. You understand that?"

She pulled her pajama top over her head, her breasts full and taut in the glow of the tree. "I'm all in too."

There was nothing else to say.

I yanked her into my arms.

CHAPTER FIVE

ASHER

She was liquid fire around me. Warm, soft, fluid. Her breasts were perfect in my hands, her nipples hard points under my tongue. She smelled like flowers and tasted like sugar. We kissed endlessly, never moving away from the tree. I laid her out on the floor, worshipping every inch of her body. She was ticklish on the right side. The sexy freckles I liked so much were scattered all over her body, and I enjoyed tracing them with my tongue. She whimpered when I sucked her nipples and moaned softly when I nibbled on the sensitive spot behind her ear. She was responsive and eager. As desperate for me as I was for her.

"Condom," I hissed.

"On the pill. I haven't had sex since AJ," she assured me.

"It's been a long time for me."

"Take me like this," she whispered. "I want you."

Her sharp gasp when I entered her was music to my ears.

"Oh, you feel so good," she groaned. "*So* good, Asher."

I reveled in the feel of her. Came alive under her touch. I shivered as she trailed her fingers down my spine, gripped my shoulders, and clutched at my back as I drove into her. With everything in my life, even lovers, I always held myself back, never giving everything. But there was no holding back with Rosie. I lost myself in her. Gave her everything I had. Took everything she offered and then some. I had never experienced such passion, such need, as I did with her.

And knowing this was only the first time?

It blew my mind.

She stiffened, her muscles fluttering around me. She whispered my name, tightening her arms around my neck and holding me close.

I buried my fingers into her hair, gripping it as my orgasm washed over me. It peaked and ebbed like a tidal wave, carrying me along its path and crashing me to the sand. Leaving me adrift and spent.

We lay wrapped around each other until I felt her shiver. I sat up, and we helped each other dress, sharing smiles, kisses, and whispered words of adoration. I wrapped myself around her in the bed, kissing her neck.

"Best Christmas gift ever," I murmured. "Thank you."

She giggled. "No returns."

"I don't want a return. I want to repurchase. Again and again."

"That was incredible."

"Yeah, it was."

I kissed her, pulling her tight to my chest. "Sleep, my Rosie. AJ will be up early, and he's going to have a banner day."

She peered up at me. "I just had a banner night."

I laughed and rubbed her nose. "Good."

I had never experienced a Christmas like it. It wasn't the gifts. It was the love that filled the room. AJ's excitement. Rosie's smile. The little surprises, like the stocking Rosie had filled for me with silly, fun things. How she had managed it, I had no idea. AJ adored the new sled I got him as well as the snowsuit so he could stay out longer and not be cold. Rosie exclaimed in delight over every gift, even the gloves and scarf I'd selected for her, the green reminding me of her eyes. I kept the gifts simple, not wanting to overwhelm her or the ones she had already purchased for her son.

There was a handsome muffler for me. A box of cookies she had baked. A coupon book filled with IOUs for dinner or a back rub. Thoughtful ideas I planned on cashing in. I made breakfast, we watched a movie, and then we went sledding, just AJ and me, leaving Rosie puttering in the apartment and cooking dinner. I knew she didn't get much time on her own, and I hoped she'd take advantage of it and curl up on the sofa and read or nap while we were gone.

The area wasn't as busy, but there were still a fair number of people around. One young boy ran up to AJ, looking excited.

"Cool sled!"

AJ grinned. "My friend Asher gave it to me."

"Maybe we can race later!"

"Sure."

At the top of the smaller hill, AJ looked up at me. "I was right before, wasn't I?"

I hunched down to his level. "About?"

"That you're my friend."

"Absolutely."

"Are you Momma's friend?"

I rubbed my chin. "That's a bit more complicated, AJ. Technically, yes. I'm your momma's friend. I like her a lot."

"I know." He wrinkled his nose. "You kiss her all the time."

I chuckled. "Noticed that, did you?"

"Yes. And you hold hands. Momma told me once that grown-ups do that when they like each other. She holds my hand because she loves me and doesn't want me to get lost."

"I don't want your momma to get lost either."

He suddenly looked older than his years. "She smiles more when you're here, Asher. She doesn't seem so sad."

"Your momma gets sad?"

He scuffed his boot in the snow. "She tries to hide it, but I see sometimes. She cries."

My heart hurt for them both. "Sometimes grown-ups cry," I agreed with him. "There's a lot of responsibility when you're big."

"Do you?"

"On occasion."

"I try to be good for her when she cries."

I ruffled his hair. "It's not you, bud. She loves you, and I think you're a good boy all the time. She just needs to cry. Mommas are like that sometimes."

"Will you make her cry?"

"I hope not."

"Will you go away and not come back like my dad?"

"No. I plan on staying." I drew in a deep breath. "Sometimes being a grown-up is a lot of work. I like your momma, and she likes me. We want to keep seeing each other. We'll need some time alone —and other times with you. Lots of it, really. If that's okay with you."

"I'd like that." He flung his arms around my neck. "I like you, Asher."

I hugged him back tightly. "I like you. Now, let's try out this new sled, okay?"

"Okay!"

We spent a couple of hours at the park, arriving back at the apartment cold and hungry. The scent of the turkey filled the small space, and the feeling of peace and belonging filled my soul as I stepped inside and saw Rosie's wide smile greeting us.

Midafternoon, I fell asleep on the sofa with AJ snuggled beside me, and when I woke up, Rosie was nestled into my other side.

And I was complete.

Dinner contained more laughter. More bonding. Afterward, cleaning up, I wrapped my arms around Rosie's waist, dropping my head to her shoulder.

"Did you have a good day?" she asked.

"The best. You?" I tightened my arms as I waited for her reply.

"Yes. You made all my dreams on my wish list come true."

I held back my smile. If only she knew I was just starting. I planned to give her every dream and wish she could think of.

"Can I stay?" I asked quietly. The thought of going back to my cold, empty condo felt wrong. I wanted to be right here. What happened after the next few days, we would deal with. But for now, this was where I wanted to be. For as long as she would let me stay.

"Yes."

I spun her in my arms and kissed her. "Thank you."

Our eyes met and held. "This is only the beginning. You know that, right?"

She nodded. "I do." She cupped my face. "Merry Christmas, Asher."

I kissed her again. "Merry Christmas, Rosie."

AJ bounded into the kitchen, wearing the new pj's Rosie had bought him. The Batman logo blazed on his chest, the little hoodie complete with the bat ears. He loved them, having vowed to never take them off. I had laughed, and Rosie had shaken her head. "He's serious."

"I know," I replied. "I gave Bonnie some *Frozen* pj's she was dying for, and she wore them constantly. Suzy had to strip her at night, wash them, and put them right back on, or the tantrums started."

Rosie chuckled, laying her head on my shoulder. "Sounds about right."

AJ was full of excitement over his day. "Momma, Christmas movies are on all night! Can I watch them?"

"May I," she corrected.

He grinned. "Yes, you may. So that means I can too!"

Laughing, he raced out of the kitchen. I had to join his amusement. "He's clever."

"Too clever for me some days." She smiled, but it was a sad one. "He's growing up so fast. Next fall, he'll be in school full time. I don't know where the time has gone."

I slipped an arm around her. "It goes fast," I agreed. "Where is his school?"

"Oh, the public elementary down the road. Bradshaw."

"Is he excited?"

"He's used to a schedule. He goes to day care and kindergarten. He is very advanced."

"What do you do in the summers?"

"Any free camps I can enroll him in, I do. I pay for a couple. Things he finds fun. Some day care. I take my holidays in August, so we have time together. My boss has always been very accommodating. I work extra in the winter and over tax time. And I work four days in the summer, so, financially, that helps. I take extra calls when I can." She paused. "But I have a new boss starting after the holidays, so I'm hoping she'll be as understanding." She lifted a shoulder in resignation. "I'll figure it all out."

I marveled at her. She wasn't complaining or whining. Simply stating the facts. Everything she did was for Asher. To make sure he was safe and happy. I pressed a kiss to her head, knowing that she had no idea how incredible she was.

From the living room, Asher shouted. "Momma! Asher! Grinch is on!"

"We mustn't keep him waiting," I chuckled. "Grinch is on."

I lay beside Rosie, her head on my chest, the room dark except the lights of the Christmas tree. We'd made love again, this time on the lumpy mattress. I needed to source a new one for her—it really was uncomfortable. I knew exactly where to get one. I would have to arrange it to be switched out while she wasn't at home so she couldn't say no.

I stroked my hand through her thick hair, the tresses soft against my fingers.

"I love your hair."

She hummed. "Really? It's annoying. The color, the curls."

"Those are two of the things I love most about it."

I felt her smile against my chest. "You're so sweet."

I laughed. "I'm hardly sweet. I made you blush not long ago." I lowered my voice. "And come a couple of times."

"Three," she responded.

"Oh." I grinned, feeling the male pride of making my woman orgasm. "I missed one. I'll have to pay better attention."

"You were kind of busy moaning yourself."

I hauled her up my chest, fisting her hair and kissing her. "When your mouth was around my cock, you mean? Baby, that was the hottest thing I've ever seen or felt."

I felt the warmth of her skin as she flushed. It amazed me that such a sweet woman could turn into a passionate lover one moment, then blush the next. It was intoxicating.

"Jesus, you turn me on," I groaned into her mouth. "I've never felt like this, Rosie. Ever."

"I want you," she breathed. "Again."

It was music to my ears. I kissed her until she was shaking with desire, then pulled her onto my thighs. "Ride me."

"I've never…"

If anything, those two words turned me on more. I loved knowing she was inexperienced. That I was the first man showing her all these things. She was a fast study.

I grasped my cock, sliding into her inch by inch until I was fully enveloped by her. Our bodies were so tightly connected it was incredible. I was deeper in her than I had ever been. I gripped her hips, encouraging her to move. She was slow at first, finding her rhythm, then she began to whimper, undulating her hips, moving easily, taking all of me.

"Grab the back of the sofa," I instructed, my voice rough. "Lean forward."

She did, and I sucked at her breasts, the new angle stimulating and different. I slipped a hand between us, stroking her hard clit, making her tremble. I thrust up, needing to be closer, wanting more. She rode me faster, her breathing picking up and the sounds she made becoming needier and louder.

I covered her mouth, and she licked at my palm before biting down, her teeth rubbing my flesh. She stiffened and came hard, strangling my cock, setting off my own orgasm. I shut my eyes, lost to the sensations. Her body, her sounds, the feel of her around me. The scent of her, me, us swirling in the air.

And then she collapsed on top of me. We were a mass of arms and legs, sweaty bodies, and stickiness. I held her close, chuckling when she lifted her head. "I need a shower."

"Go," I encouraged. "I'll follow."

"Okay." She pressed a kiss to my mouth, and I held her close, keeping her there until I was satisfied. At least as satisfied as I could feel right now.

I watched with a grin as she lifted off me and headed to the small bathroom.

I had a feeling I might never be satisfied when it came to Rosie.

CHAPTER SIX

ROSIE

The next two days were filled with a contentment and rhythm I had never experienced. The three of us were like a little family. The days were spent wandering around, eating in restaurants—not fancy places, but ones AJ and I enjoyed. The kinds of places I could afford once in a while as a treat if I put in extra calls or was given a gift card at work for a bonus. Asher never once pulled a face, made a disrespectful remark, or informed me he wanted to go elsewhere. We played in the snow, went to the park, watched movies on my little TV, snuggled while AJ played with his new toys, and took naps. Glorious, wonderful naps, wrapped in Asher's arms, his warm body close, his even breathing on my skin. Invariably, AJ would wake first, but he seemed happy to play or watch a cartoon while Asher and I looked over at him from the sofa.

The mornings were lazy, Asher cooking breakfast and the coffee ready when I woke. The nights were incredible. Once AJ was out, Asher had me in bed, doing all the things he whispered to me during the day he had planned that night. He was an incredible lover, giving and patient. Never angry if we heard AJ and I had to check on him. He was inventive and gentle. Passionate and intense. I never knew which Asher would greet me after I tucked AJ in, but I liked all of them.

I had no idea what was happening between us. What would happen once the holidays were over. But my entire life, I had done what was expected of me, played by the rules, and it got me nowhere. I was worried about AJ and how fond he was already of Asher, but there was little I could do about it. Asher asked me to trust him, and I did. I hoped, somehow, we would fit into Asher's life once reality set in.

If we didn't, I would care for my son and move on.

I tried to ignore the little voice in my head that asked who would look after me. Asher would be incredibly difficult to move past.

So even though the odds were against us, I refused to think about that.

I woke up in the morning, hearing Asher's low voice in the kitchen.

"I just didn't expect you back so soon, Suzy."

I sat up, pulling my legs to my chest. My heart sank. His sister was home, with his niece. He had told me he would be going to see them for a few days but didn't expect them back until the new year. We had plans for a fun evening on New Year's, but listening, I knew it wouldn't be happening now.

"Of course I'll come. I promised Bonnie I would, and I don't break my promises. But why the place in Quebec?"

There was silence, and I heard his sigh. "I see. Makes sense. I'll see you tomorrow, then."

Again, there was silence as he listened. "No," he said firmly. "I'll drive myself, and I'll see you tomorrow. I have something I have to take care of first."

I heard his phone hit the table, and I shut my eyes at the pain that swelled. He had to take care of us first. Would he be saying "see you soon," or would it be a "this was a fun break, take care of yourself," sort of farewell?

I pushed back the blanket, grabbing my robe. I shivered a little. The apartment was cold, and my robe had seen better days. I headed to the kitchen. Asher was at the table, his head in his hands, pulling on his hair. I walked up to him, tugging on his hands. "I like your hair where it is."

He wrapped his arms around me, pulling me close, his head resting on my stomach. "I didn't mean to wake you. Go back to bed, and I'll bring coffee."

I didn't think I could face this conversation on the sofa. Too many intimate moments had been shared on it. "I'm fine. I'll get us coffee."

I bent and kissed the top of his head, and he looked up, unhappy and worried. I pulled away and got the mugs, pouring the coffee and bringing it to the table.

"Your sister must have been up early."

He nodded. "They flew home ahead of schedule."

I injected a false note of cheer into my voice. "You must be excited to see Bonnie and have your Christmas with her. I'm sure she is thrilled, knowing she'll see you soon."

"They're headed up to their cabin in Quebec. They want me to come tomorrow. Well, today, actually. But I said tomorrow."

I stood and went to the counter, refusing to let him see how sad his words made me. I'd known this was coming. He wasn't going to stay in this ratty little apartment with us forever. He had another life —one filled with other people, very rich people, like him who had cabins and flew to and from places whenever they wanted. I cleared my voice before I spoke. "You must have a lot to do before you go. Do you have time for breakfast with us first? I know AJ would like to say goodbye."

He was behind me in an instant, spinning me in his arms. "I am not saying goodbye to either of you."

"Asher," I began. "I know you have another life—"

He cut me off, lifting my chin. "My other life was empty until I found you and AJ. Lonely. This is not goodbye, Rosie. I have to go see my sister and niece because I promised. I don't want to leave you."

"Oh."

He shook his head. "How could you think that after the past few days?"

"I-I don't know what to think. We never talked past the holidays…" I trailed off at his intense frown.

He pressed his forehead to mine. "I am not walking away. I thought they'd be at home and I'd drive up in the morning, spend the day, maybe one night like usual, and be back with you fast. But the cabin is a day's drive, and she wants me to spend a couple days with them, and I hate saying no…"

"I understand," I replied because I really did. That was his family.

"Come with me."

"What?"

He stood back. "You and AJ come with me."

I shook my head. "No, Asher. It's too soon. I-I wouldn't be comfortable. I wasn't invited."

He ran a hand through his hair. "You'd be welcome," he insisted. "I want you there."

I shook my head. "It's not a good idea."

"It is to me."

I pressed a hand to his cheek. "You go see your family. Spend some time with your niece. Asher and I will be here when you get back, if you still want to see us."

He held my hand to his skin, his voice incredulous. "What kind of statement is that?" he asked. "*If I want?* Of course I want to see you. I don't even want to go, Rosie."

His words eased my anxiety a little. "You have to go."

"We'd planned New Year's."

I had to laugh. "And we'll do that when you get back. AJ won't care if he eats Chinese food on the second or the thirty-first. All he'll care about is he eats it with you. So, we'll hold off until you get back."

He cupped my face, looking into my eyes. "I am coming back, Rosie. This is not over. Please come with me, though."

"Another time, Asher. I don't want the first time I meet your family to be, ah, now. And I am not intruding on your time with your niece. You need to go, and I need to stay here. We'll be waiting."

"You promise?" he asked.

"I promise." His plea made me feel better.

"Fine. You shower. I'll make breakfast."

"Okay."

He kissed me. Softly. "I will miss this. You. Me. AJ."

"It had to end sometime," I reminded him. "We couldn't stay here forever. Life has to go back to normal." I slipped from his arms, pausing at the doorway when he said my name.

"You have a new normal now. We both do. Do you understand me?" he asked.

"Yes."

"Good."

AJ hugged Asher. "See you soon!" he exclaimed.

Asher ruffled his hair. "Only a few days, bud. Then I'll be back, and we'll have supper, okay? We'll start your skating lessons."

AJ nodded. "Charlie's dad goes on business trips all the time. He always brings him something fun!" Then he covered his mouth. "Sorry. That was rude."

Asher laughed. "Nope. I agree. I'll bring something fun for you."

AJ clapped his hands in delight and sped off to his room. Asher had explained over breakfast he had to go away for a few days, and

AJ had immediately assumed it meant the same as when Charlie's dad was gone. It was easier than trying to explain everything else, so I had simply agreed with his thoughts. We watched a movie and had one last play in the snow before Asher left. I knew he had to get ready and that he planned on leaving early the next morning.

Asher turned to me. "Come here."

I slipped into his arms, and he held me close. "A few days," he said. "It's only a few days."

"Drive safely," I replied. "Let me know when you get there, please. I checked the weather report, and tomorrow looks okay for driving."

He smiled down at me. "Will you worry?"

"Yes."

"Then I'll call. And text."

"Use Bluetooth," I insisted.

He smiled. "I like having you worry about me. Few people do."

"I will. So, check in. And enjoy your visit."

"Are you sure you won't come?"

I leaned up and pressed a kiss to his jaw. "Yes."

He yanked me tight to his chest and covered my mouth with his, kissing me hard. Deep. Until I was shaking in his arms. "Asher," I whispered as he dragged his lips to my ear. "It's only a few days," I repeated.

"I'm going to miss your mouth."

"Is that all?" I teased.

"No. I'm going to miss everything, but especially this mouth. Your smile. Your voice."

"My mouth and my voice will be waiting for you when you get back."

"And you'll pick up the phone?"

"Yes."

"Not work every second I'm gone?"

"No."

"I'll call you later."

"Okay."

He kissed me again and opened the door, slinging his bag over his shoulder. "I left you something in the bathroom." He paused. "I'll see you soon, Rosie."

And he was gone.

CHAPTER SEVEN

ROSIE

It was confusing how I could miss Asher so much that quickly. He hadn't even left the building, and I wished he was back. I shook my head. I was being ridiculous. He'd only been in our life for a few days. He couldn't possibly have made that much of an impact on us.

Could he?

In the bathroom, he'd left a sweatshirt, which made me grin. I had told him I would miss his scent, so he'd left me this to borrow while he was gone. I slipped it over my head, inhaling deeply. It smelled like him. Rich, decadent, and intoxicating. I kept it on all day.

Around eleven, I closed my laptop and got ready for bed. AJ had fallen asleep around eight, so I signed on and logged some calls. It was a busy night, so I was pleased. I pulled out the sofa bed and sat on the mattress, running my hand over the blankets. I missed Asher waiting for me. His strong body, his warmth. He had called and texted, and I knew he was no doubt asleep since he planned to be on the road no later than six the next morning. I sighed as I picked up my book, deciding to read a little. My phone buzzed with a text from Asher.

Asher
You awake?

I smiled as I replied.

Me
Yes. You shouldn't be since you have to get up early.

His reply was swift.

Asher
Couldn't sleep. You weren't beside me, all sexy and sweet, drooling on my chest as you slept.

I laughed as I typed my response.

Me
I do not drool.

I loved his teasing.

Asher
You do. It's totally adorable.

I shook my head.

Me
Go to bed.

Asher
Baby, it's cold outside.

I laughed.

Me
It is winter.

Asher
It's lonely too. Your hallway is sort of dark.

I stared at the screen and flung the blanket off, rushing to the door. I opened it, meeting Asher's gaze.

"What…?" I asked, but before I could say anything else, he stepped inside, shutting the door behind him. He kissed me, hard, wet, and deep. His skin was cold, his mouth warm, and his embrace tight. He pulled back, leaning his forehead on mine. "Hi."

"You are supposed to be at home."

He tightened his arms. "I am now."

"Asher—"

He cut me off with his lips on mine again. "I was lying in my bed, wondering why I wasn't here. Even for a few hours. I've been pacing my empty condo all night, missing you and AJ. So, I came over. If you don't want me to stay, I'll start driving."

I slid my hands under his open coat, tugging on his T-shirt. "Get in bed with me."

He grinned against my mouth. "Your wish, my command."

I settled against his chest, his arms around me. "I didn't come here for a booty call," he murmured. "But, wow, lady. You missed me." He chuckled. "I think I might fear for my manhood when I get back. You'll drain me."

I laughed at his teasing. "I think you can keep up."

He slipped his finger under my chin, lifting my head. "I'll do everything I can to make sure you're satisfied."

I bent and kissed his finger. "You are the ultimate Snickers." At his low laughter, I smiled. "I had no idea…" I trailed off.

"No idea?" he prompted, tapping my chin.

"Um, sex before was okay. Not like with you."

"Obviously, aside from sperm donation, your ex wasn't much good at anything except running like a coward."

"I always thought it was me."

He kissed me soundly. "Trust me. It wasn't."

He pulled me back to his chest. "Sleep for a while, Rosie."

"What about you?"

"I can sleep now too."

He was gone when I woke up. For a moment, I thought I had imagined his late-night visit until I saw his note and another shirt.

In case my smell fades from the first one. I liked seeing you in my clothes. Back before you know it—Asher xx

He had loved the fact that I'd worn his shirt all day. He left me another one.

I planned on wearing it.

ASHER

"If you look at your phone one more time, I am going to pitch it in the snow. No business deal can be that important," my sister Suzy informed me dryly. "You've checked it a dozen times since you got here."

I slipped it into my pocket. "Just waiting on a reply."

I had texted Rosie three hours ago. She hadn't responded. My call went to voice mail.

Was she okay?

Was AJ sick?

Was she sick?

Had she already forgotten about me?

Internally, I shook my head. She was no doubt busy. Laundry. Playing with AJ. Out. Something.

But she hadn't answered, and I was worried. I almost started to laugh. I didn't worry about anyone. Aside from my sister and niece, and even they didn't get much of that worry. I knew James loved them fiercely and protected them both.

"A new project," she asked. "Or—" she grinned widely and took a sip of wine "—does this have something to do with your 'I'm not alone' comment over Christmas?"

I was surprised it had taken her so long to bring that up. Granted, since I'd arrived, I had been busy with Bonnie. Opening gifts, having tea, reading to her before she went with her dad to pick up pizza, leaving Suzy and me alone for the first time since I'd gotten here.

I was quiet for a moment. "I met someone. I was letting her know I arrived, and she hasn't responded. I'm a little surprised."

"And concerned," Suzy added, tilting her head. "She must be special to have your attention, big brother."

"She is."

"When did you meet her? How long have you been seeing her?"

"Just before the holidays."

"So, November?"

"More like a couple of days before Christmas."

Suzy's eyebrows flew up in shock. Before she could speak, my phone rang and I answered quickly, my voice filled with relief. "Rosie. Is everything okay? "

"I'm sorry!" she exclaimed. "It was so cold AJ couldn't play outside, and he was restless. The neighborhood theater had a cheap matinee and we went, and I guess I forgot my phone. We stopped for a burger, and we were gone longer than I expected and I missed your calls—"

"It's all right, baby. I'm glad you and AJ had a nice afternoon and you're both okay."

"I didn't mean to worry you. In your message, you sounded upset."

"I was concerned. But it's all good."

"Your drive was okay?"

"Boring and fast."

"Did you speed?" she tsked.

"A little."

"Asher," she scolded.

I glanced at my sister, who was watching me with narrowed eyes.

"We're about to have dinner. I'll call you later once the holy terror is in bed, all right?" I said, dropping my voice.

Rosie's lovely laughter drifted over the phone. "You adore that holy terror. I can see it every time you talk about her."

"I do. I adore you as well. I'll call you later. Give AJ a kiss for me."

"And me?"

"A hundred of them."

I hung up and caught sight of Suzy's shocked face. She leaned forward, her elbows on her knees, and met my eyes.

"Asher, you had better start talking. Really talking. And I mean now before Bonnie walks through that door and monopolizes you again. Spill it."

I told her everything. Mostly everything. Okay, the basics. Meeting Rosie and AJ. The connection. Spending Christmas with them. But I was honest about the draw I felt toward them. Especially Rosie.

She stared at me. "Who are you, and what have you done with my brother?"

I shrugged.

She narrowed her eyes. "Did you sleep with this woman, Asher?"

The front door opened, and Bonnie called my name, excited. "Uncle Ash, we got pizza!"

I stood. "I've been summoned."

Suzy said my name, and I paused at the doorway.

"We're not done."

I nodded. Knowing my sister, we were far from finished with this conversation.

I avoided her until almost nine. I read Bonnie a story, sitting with her until she fell asleep. She loved her gifts, told me all about Christmas Day with her Gram and Gramps and her cousins.

"Uncle Vince and Auntie Laura were there, but you weren't," she observed. "I missed you."

I chucked her under the chin. "We always have our own little Christmas, munchkin. You know that."

"Why?"

It was too difficult to explain to a child. "Uncle Ash likes having you to himself," I said instead. "I look forward to our time without everyone else."

She thought about it for a moment, her adorable little brow furrowed in thought. Then she smiled. "Me too. And Mommy says if you miss someone, it means you love them."

I thought about how much I was missing two people right now. All day and evening, they hadn't been far from my thoughts.

I bent and kissed her. "Your mommy is very smart. Now go to sleep."

I read a little more, and she drifted fast. I thought I was in the clear, but just as I headed to my room, Suzy appeared. "Not so fast, buster."

"Must it be tonight?"

"Yes. I have scotch."

"Well, at least that helps," I muttered. "A little."

In the living room, my brother-in-law handed me a generous glass of the amber liquid. "For the inquisition," he said with a droll wink. "Suzy filled me in, and I have to admit, I have questions."

I took the glass from his hand. "Thanks. I think I'm going to need it."

Suzy came in, carrying a glass of wine. She sat across from me,

James beside her, his hand on her knee. "Did you sleep with her?" she asked again.

I met her gaze. "Yes."

"Asher," she said, aghast. "There is a child."

"I am aware, Suzy. I was there."

"And you stayed there all this time?"

I laughed. "You make it sound as if I was there for a year. It was a few days."

"There is a child," she repeated. "An impressionable child."

I sat forward in understanding. "I am not playing around."

"What do you call it?"

I took a sip of scotch. "The start of something important and real in my life."

It was rare I saw my sister speechless. She gaped at me, looked at James, then took a sip of wine.

"You met her at Zoles?"

"Yes, I was getting your gift."

Suzy glanced over at the tree, her handmade crystal collector's ornament catching the light, along with the thirty-plus others she had. One for every Christmas she'd been alive. I had taken over the tradition of giving them to her when our mother died. Every year, there was talk of discontinuing the tradition, and every year, I vetoed the idea. Suzy loved the pieces—loved what they represented. It was different for me, but I carried on the tradition for her. They were a limited item, and each one had to be picked up in person and signed for.

"Is she pretty?" Suzy asked.

"Tiny, fierce, strong, and a great mother," I replied. "Her voice is soft, her heart is big, and she's simply the loveliest woman I have ever met."

Suzy blinked and looked at James again, taking another sip of wine.

"She has red hair, green eyes, and freckles that drive her crazy."

Me too, I added silently, but my kind of crazy was different. The kind I wouldn't discuss with my sister.

"Do you have a picture?"

I scrolled through my phone, picking one I had taken of her reading to AJ. With her head bent over his, it was hard to tell where her red hair ended and his began. He was staring up at her, and she was smiling at him, patiently explaining something he didn't understand in the story. It was one of my favorites. Suzy studied it, then scanned a few more. She stopped at one, lifting her eyebrow. I knew which one it was. Rosie staring at the camera, sexy, and freshly fucked. Her hair was a mess, her lips swollen and a shy smile pulling her lips.

"She is beautiful," was all she said, handing my phone back.

"Inside and out." I paused. "The moment I touched her, something flared between us. I couldn't deny it. I didn't want to. Then she almost fainted, and I took her to breakfast. That was all I meant to do, but…" I shrugged. "I couldn't stay away."

"Does she know who you are?"

"She knows I'm a philanthropist. That I'm single and I have a sister and a niece."

James cleared his throat.

"And a brother-in-law I get on well with," I added with a grin.

James inclined his head in thanks.

"Does she know *who* you are?" she asked again.

"No. I didn't share that information with her. It wasn't relevant at the time."

"You mean before you—"

I held up my hand. "Do not finish that sentence. I'll say something and we'll start fighting, and James will punch me in the mouth and I'll have to punch him back and this scotch will be everywhere but where it should be."

James grunted. "We could set the scotch in a safe place first."

"But it would take away the spontaneity," I pointed out.

"True."

"Can we get back to the subject at hand?" Suzy said crossly.

I sighed. "I don't know what you want from me. I met someone. Someone wonderful. We had this instant connection. She has a son from a previous relationship. His father has nothing to do with him— in fact, he has never seen him or even cared that he exists. She's a single mother—a wonderful one, I'll say again—and I'm interested in spending more time with her. Seeing where this goes. She likes me too. Just me. Asher. She has no idea of my past, how wealthy I am, or who my family is. That's all I can tell you." I drained my scotch. "The rest, frankly, is private." I set down my glass. "Except you should know, I wanted her to come with me. She felt it was too soon and said no. I wish she had come. You would love her."

"And if I don't?" Suzy challenged.

"I think you will. She's smart, strong, and witty. She cares for those around her. Very much like you. And if you don't, then I will see her without your approval. I'll see you and Bonnie other times."

"And me," James interjected. "I keep getting left out."

I laughed at his humor. "I add you silently, James. Always."

He tipped his glass. "Thank you very much."

Suzy gazed at me. "You have totally fallen for this girl."

I shifted in my seat. "I care about her a great deal, considering how short a time I have known her. I care about her son too. I think she is amazing."

"And you're sure she isn't, ah—"

I was already shaking my head. "She had no clue who I was. She was looking for her son. Not me."

"But she found you."

I sat back with a grin. "Well, I found her, actually. I went to her. I'm not even sure she had noticed me. She was too busy looking for AJ."

"Fate," she breathed out.

"Fate, kismet, or coincidence. I don't care. I met her."

"When can I meet her?"

"Soon."

"How soon?" she pressed.

"When I decide you won't frighten her away."

"Me?"

I laughed. "You, my sister. I am aware of your interrogation tactics."

"As we all are," James said dryly, pouring us each another finger of scotch. "Legendary."

Suzy laughed at him, and I joined in, then became serious. "Give me a little time. I'm not ready to share."

Suzy shook her head. "I can't believe it," she muttered. "You and a single mother."

I grinned.

Me and Rosie.

I liked the sound of it.

CHAPTER EIGHT

ROSIE

"Momma, that was so much fun!" AJ exclaimed. "Can we do it again tomorrow?"

I rubbed my shoulder. Sledding with AJ was fun, but we'd gone over a large bump and I'd fallen off the sled, hitting my shoulder hard on a patch of frozen snow.

"Sure, baby. If my arm hurts, I can watch."

He looked sorrowful. "Do you need an aspirin?"

I ruffled his hair. "I took a couple of Tylenol. I'll feel fine soon."

I opened the fridge, peering inside. It was still full of food. I had made soup with the turkey bones and frozen it, but Asher had bought so many other items, we were spoiled for choice.

"Want grilled cheese and tomato soup?" I asked, already knowing the answer. That was his favorite.

"Yeah!" he said, throwing up his arms.

I laughed and made our simple dinner. We ate it on the sofa, watching a movie. I relaxed my usual rules over the holidays and let him watch what he wanted. He still enjoyed playing and coloring, so it wasn't as if he was glued to the screen all day.

After we ate, he curled into me and fell asleep. I rubbed my shoulder at the dull ache. Maybe I was too old for sledding anymore.

When Asher had been here, the two of them had done most of the sledding, while I cheered on with a cup of coffee in my hand. I much preferred that.

I woke up AJ and ran him a bath. I washed his hair, and he talked nonstop the whole time about his day. He loved it when I wasn't working and we could spend time together. I had to admit, I loved it as well, but it only happened over the holidays and my once-a-year vacation, unless he got sick and I stayed home with him.

My phone rang, and I answered, happy to see Asher's number.

"Hey, you," I said, trying not to laugh at the soap monsters AJ was making in the tub.

"How are you, Rosie?"

"A little wet. AJ is having his bath."

"Hi, Asher!" AJ called out, excited.

"Put him on," Asher said good-naturedly.

I did as he asked and handed AJ the phone on speaker. "Don't drop it."

I headed to the kitchen and took a couple of Tylenol. My shoulder still hurt. I could hear AJ telling Asher how fast the hill was with his new sled and how many kids there were.

"My face got really cold," he said.

"You need an extra scarf. Tie it over your forehead and nose. You won't get so cold again."

"I'll tell Momma!"

"Good man. You taking care of your momma?"

"She fell off the sled and hurt her arm."

"What?" Asher said, his voice now worried. "She's hurt?"

I took the phone. "As we discussed before, I'm old, is what I am. And the frozen ground was hard. I'm a little sore. Nothing to worry about."

"Did you hit your head?"

"Barely. Just my arm and shoulder. I'll be fine."

"Barely?" he repeated. "Are you sure?"

"Positive."

"I can send my doctor to see you."

Those words stopped me. *He had a private doctor? That was a thing?*

I left AJ playing for a few moments and sat on a chair in the hall where I could keep an eye on him. "Asher, I smacked my arm on some hard ice. It'll be fine. No need to call a doctor."

He huffed. "All right."

"How is everything there?" I asked to change the subject.

"Great. Lonely without you."

I laughed. "I am sure your sister and niece are keeping you busy."

"Bonnie is. We had another tea party this afternoon. All the stuffed animals were invited, so I had a lot of voices to do. James and

I split them up and drank a lot of pretend tea. Luckily, the cookies were real. Suzy went and had a manicure."

"Nice."

"I am sending them out for New Year's, and Bonnie and I will do our own thing. They're going with friends for dinner at the club. I thought they'd enjoy a night out."

"I thought you were at a cabin."

He laughed. "I am. In a private resort surrounded by many other cabins and a huge clubhouse with lots of amenities. This is my sister's idea of roughing it."

I chuckled, not even able to imagine it.

"I have a cabin in the Niagara region," he murmured. "I bought it from a business tycoon. It's private and woodsy. No one else around. That's my idea of getting away." He paused. "It's a great spot. I'll take you there."

"Oh. That would be nice."

"What are you two doing tomorrow?"

"We're going to make homemade pizza and watch TV. He'll be out by nine, and I might work a little. Surprisingly, New Year's Eve is very busy on the customer service line. So, nothing exciting."

"I'd make it exciting for you if I were there."

Before I could respond, AJ called out.

"Momma!"

Asher chuckled. "Go see your boy. I'll call you later, Rosie." There was a moment of silence. "I miss you," he added before he disconnected the call.

I got AJ ready for bed and read to him for a while. He was chatty and happy, but he soon drifted off.

I settled on the sofa, putting an ice bag on my sore shoulder. My head was aching, and I was tired. It had been a long day. I chuckled thinking ice had caused the problem and was now the thing I needed to use for relief. My phone buzzed with a video call, and I answered with a smile at Asher's handsome face. "Hi."

"AJ asleep?"

"Yes."

"You're not working, are you?" Asher asked with a frown.

"No. Taking the night off."

"Good. You work too hard."

"I work because I have to, Asher. And I'm fine. You worry far too much." I winced a little as I moved.

"You need someone to worry about you."

His words made me warm, but he frowned. "You keep grimacing."

"My shoulder is sore. I'm icing it."

"Let me see."

"There is nothing to see."

"Rosie. Let me see."

With a sigh, I turned to the light, pulling my sweater off my shoulder, holding up the phone.

"Nice sofa," Asher said dryly. "Go to the mirror."

"My God, you are bossy," I muttered. Tamping down my impatience, I went to the bathroom and showed him my shoulder in the mirror. I was surprised how bruised it was, the dark stain coming out already on my skin.

"*Nothing* to see," he snorted.

I shook my head and headed back to the sofa. "Nothing I can't handle, anyway."

"And you're sure you didn't hit your head?"

I didn't understand his fascination with my head, but I assured him I had not hit it hard. "It sort of glanced off the snow, but my shoulder took the hit. I'll rub some Voltaren cream in before I go to bed, and I'll be fine tomorrow."

"I'd do that and kiss it better if I were there," he said, sounding frustrated. "And I wouldn't stop at your shoulder."

"When are you coming home?" I asked, ignoring the rush of desire I felt at his words.

"I'm leaving at lunch on New Year's Day. They're staying another week, but I'm done. Suzy and James enjoy the whole resort and the social aspect. Bonnie has friends she can play with. I've had a good visit, but I have something I need to get back to."

"Your business?" I teased.

"Yes. You and AJ are my business, and I miss you like crazy." He shook his head with a grin. "How, I don't understand, but I do."

"We miss you too."

"Soon, you won't have to."

"Okay."

"May I take you out when I get home?"

"Out, like a date?"

"Yes. A proper date. Dinner. Maybe dancing. Or my place. Just the two of us. Do you have someone who can watch AJ?"

"Yes."

"Arrange it."

I lifted an eyebrow, and he chuckled.

"Sorry. Please arrange it. Whatever night suits you best."

"I'll do that."

We talked a bit longer, about nothing important, just sharing bits of our time apart. He was reluctant to hang up. "This bed is empty and cold."

"So is mine."

"I'll be home soon."

"I'm looking forward to it."

"Call me in the morning and let me know how you are."

"Okay."

He disconnected the call after staring at me for a moment and touching his lips in a silent kiss.

I stared at the ceiling, wondering how this was going to work. We'd lived in a bubble for a few magical, wonderful days. But real life was about to happen. I'd go back to work and the daily grind of getting AJ out of the house and to day care, then coming home and making dinner, doing housework, dishes, and chores. Getting him to bed. Working some extra hours, catching sleep when I could. I wouldn't have long days of walks, snowball fights, stolen kisses, and afternoon naps. I had no doubt whatever he did kept Asher very busy. He'd mentioned dinners and events, lots of meetings and long hours.

Would we find time for us, or would we drift apart? I couldn't help but wonder if he had been reacting to the loneliness of the season and, now that it had passed and he went back to his real life, if what we shared would fade away. The idea of that happening made my chest ache with a sadness I couldn't comprehend.

I stood and got ready for bed, slipping on Asher's T-shirt. It still smelled like him, and I buried my nose in the neckline of it and drifted into an uneasy sleep, one thought on repeat.

That soon, his scent would only be a memory.

Like him.

Like us.

CHAPTER NINE

ROSIE

I was a little stiff in the morning and slow to get going. I'd fallen asleep after talking to Asher and my cell phone had died overnight, so I plugged it in. AJ and I went to breakfast as a treat. It was nice to have the meal out, and I could relax and enjoy my coffee as AJ colored the menu they'd given him. He loved the pancakes at the small diner, and he dug in as soon as they were in front of him, dousing them with syrup. I laughed and took away the bottle, enjoying my western sandwich. Food always tasted better when you didn't have to make it.

After, we walked to the store to pick up a few things for New Year's. I let him pick his favorite chips and one bag of candy. I bought the makings for homemade pizza. AJ was excited, and we headed home, walking slowly. I shifted the bags from arm to arm, my shoulder aching constantly. When we arrived at the apartment building, I was surprised to discover a man waiting for me by my door. He was middle-aged, with kind brown eyes, and he carried a black bag.

"Ms. Duncan?"

"Yes," I replied with a frown. "Can I help you?"

"I'm Dr. Sherman Hayes." He offered me a card.

I shifted the bags, taking the card. "Um, hello?"

"I was sent by Mr. Hart."

At my blank look, he smiled. "Asher. Asher sent me."

I was confused. "Why?"

"He was worried. He said you hit your head, and he hadn't heard from you as promised. He thought you might be in medical distress."

I gaped at him. "What? So he called you to come check on me?"

"Yes," he said calmly, as if that was normal.

I had no words. Asher had sent his doctor to check on me. I blinked, unsure how to handle the situation.

"Perhaps we could go inside," Dr. Hayes said quietly. "Have a cup of tea. Call Asher after I check you over and reassure him?"

I planned on reassuring him, all right. That he'd gone too far and was overreacting. But I wasn't going to take it out on the nice doctor in front of me.

"Yes, come in and have a cup of tea," I offered.

"That would be lovely," he replied.

"Not once I'm through," I muttered under my breath.

We entered the apartment, and AJ shrugged off his coat and headed to his room. I put down the bags and plugged in the kettle, looking at my phone. I had five missed calls from Asher and many more texts, each growing more frantic. I tamped down my frustration and typed a fast reply to them all.

I am fine. I will call you later.

I turned to the doctor, who was watching me with a calm expression.

"I'm afraid Mr. Hart has wasted your time."

He shook his head. "If it calms his fears, then my time is not wasted."

"I'm fine. It is a huge misunderstanding."

"You wince when you move. Asher said that you hit your head?"

"I hit my shoulder, and yes, my head fell back. But the headache is from the neck and shoulder stiffness. Not because of something else."

"May I look?"

I had a feeling this was not going to stop unless I agreed. I tugged off the sweatshirt I was wearing, leaving on the tank top underneath it. The doctor tsked as he saw the bruises and indicated for me to sit down. With a sigh, I did so, and he checked out my shoulder and arm, examining my head. He checked my eyes, had me do some reflex tests, and nodded. "You are badly bruised, but I agree, your head is fine."

The kettle whistled, and I stood, pouring the hot water over the tea bags in the pot. I carried the pot to the small table and poured us each a cup of the steaming, fragrant liquid.

"Asher overreacted. I'm sorry to have troubled you."

He wrote something on a pad of paper and handed it to me with a smile. "No trouble. Get this prescription filled and rub this cream into your neck and shoulder. It will help ease the ache. I am glad you didn't do more damage."

"Who knew sledding could be so dangerous?" I asked, trying to be light.

"You would be shocked at the number of serious injuries from sledding. Broken bones, head injuries, hidden sharp objects under the snow that cause stitches." He shook his head. "Asher was being cautious. I don't fault him for that." He took a sip of his tea. "I will let him know you are fine."

Before I could respond, I heard heavy, rushed footsteps coming down the hall. My door opened fast, so fast it almost slammed into the wall. Asher rushed in, meeting my eyes across the room. He visibly relaxed when he saw me standing. I stared at him, shocked.

"What are you doing here?"

He crossed the room, his eyes wild, tiredness etched beneath them. "You're okay?" His gaze swung to the doctor. "Is she okay?"

"*She* is fine," I said firmly.

Dr. Hayes stood. "She is bruised and sore, but otherwise fine." He turned to me. "You have my card should you feel unwell. Fill the prescription. It will help ease the aches." He leaned close. "Don't be too hard on him."

He shook Asher's hand and left. We stared at each other.

"You didn't call. You didn't answer my calls. Or my texts. I was so worried, I—"

I lifted my hand, cutting him off. "You overreacted. I told you I didn't hit my head directly. I hit my shoulder."

"You had a headache."

"From being jarred with the fall." I shook my head. "You overstepped, Asher."

AJ ran into the kitchen, a huge smile on his face. "Asher! You're back!" He flung himself at him, wrapping his arms around Asher's legs and hugging him. "We missed you!"

Asher kneeled in front of AJ. His smile was forced, but I doubted AJ realized it. "Missed you too, bud."

"Are you gonna have pizza and watch movies with us tonight?"

I interrupted before Asher could reply. "No. Asher has plans, baby. He just dropped by to say hello. Go to your room and play for a little, okay? Momma has to put away the groceries and start the pizza for later. I'll make you a snack."

AJ frowned but hugged Asher. "See you soon, right?"

Asher ruffled his hair, his eyes on me. "Hope so."

AJ padded down the hall to his room.

"I can stay."

"No. You are supposed to be at your sister's, looking after your niece."

"Suzy understood."

I frowned. "I don't. I told you I was fine. I am perfectly capable of looking after myself, Asher. If I thought there was a problem, I would have gone to the hospital. I don't need you to second-guess me. I certainly don't need you screwing up everyone's plans to rush here or send a doctor to check me over."

He began to argue. "You didn't answer your phone—"

"I fell asleep and forgot to charge it. I slept in a little and had to get to the store before they closed at noon. I wanted to take AJ for breakfast as a treat. My son and our plans were a priority. I had no idea you'd go off the deep end and jump in the car and rush here. Or send some strange man to my home."

"He is my personal, private physician. And I didn't drive. I chartered a helicopter. A service will pick up my car."

I could only blink before I shook my head at his words. A helicopter. A private physician who made house calls. Until he had told me that last night, I didn't know such a thing existed. It certainly didn't in my world.

Which was so different from his.

"Suzy is taking Bonnie to the care center, where lots of other kids will be tonight. So, their plans haven't changed. Bonnie will have a great time. I'll make it up to her and go visit in a couple of weeks. I was out of my mind with worry when I couldn't get a hold of you."

I rubbed my temple. "You overreacted."

"I beg to differ."

I shut my eyes, not wanting to go round and round on this. "You need to go home, Asher. Or better yet, go back to your sister's and keep your word. I'm fine."

"Are you?"

His insistence that I was not telling him the truth irked me. "I have an achy shoulder. I'm not going to drop dead of a head injury or whatever you're thinking. I'm a grown woman, perfectly capable of making decisions when it comes to my health and how it affects me and the welfare of my child. I have been doing it since I learned I was pregnant. You have no right to step in and make those decisions. Now I want you to leave."

There was a beat of silence. Our gazes locked, mine angry, his oddly vulnerable. Then a hood came down over his expression. He straightened his shoulders. "Are you sure?"

"Go."

He spun on his heel and walked out the door, closing it quietly behind him. I stared at it, hearing his footsteps fading away. I sat down, suddenly shaky. I had just ended it. I knew it. Asher Hart wasn't a man who begged. He was a man who took control, used to handling everything quickly in his life. He didn't ask for second chances.

Our bubble had burst quickly.

I rubbed my head, another headache coming on. This one wasn't from bumping it while sledding. It was from emotion. I had a feeling I was going to miss him more than I could express.

More than I anticipated.

And the thought of it made me sadder than I could fathom.

AJ picked at his snack. "Momma, why did Asher go?"

"He had plans tonight, baby. I told you that."

"Is he coming tomorrow?"

I forced a smile to my face. "No, he has to go away for a while on business again."

"When is he coming back?"

"I don't know."

"He's too busy for us now? I liked it when he was here."

"He is a businessman, and he has lots of demands on his time now that the holidays are over."

"You should call him and tell him I miss him. He'll come back," he said with the confidence of a child.

"I'll tell him that next time I talk to him."

"Good." He perked up and ate his cheese and crackers. Mine

tasted like ash and I was hardly able to swallow any of it, but I forced myself to so that AJ didn't question me.

We watched a Disney movie after we finished our late lunch. It kept him entertained, while I sat beside him, laughing when he did, pretending to eat the popcorn. All I could think of was Asher. The look on his face when he left. The genuine worry in his expression when he showed up. His over-the-top reaction and sending his personal physician to see me.

I wasn't sure anyone had ever cared enough to go to such lengths over me.

I remembered Dr. Hayes's whispered plea not to be too hard on him.

Had I been too hasty?

I sighed as I rubbed my eyes. It was too late now. Asher was gone, and my phone was silent. I had a feeling it would remain so.

Outside, the snow fell softly, and AJ looked out. "Momma, can we go for a walk? Maybe sled again?"

It would do both of us good to go out and get some fresh air before darkness fell. "Sure. I'll just watch this time."

"Okay!"

We went out in the cold, heading to the park. He went down the hill a few times with some friends he met up with. I stood with some other moms, laughing at the antics of our kids. One of the dads took turns going down with his daughter and AJ, so he was happy. It felt normal, although I had to admit it wasn't as fun as when Asher was with us. I had no warm kisses to look forward to, and I couldn't be bothered to get a coffee from the food truck. Asher had insisted on it the other day. And he had stolen sips from my cup when he would come to check on me while AJ took a turn down the hill on his own since he was feeling braver. I had no interest in drinking it alone.

Today, I tried not to notice how that happened to other families at the hill. Watching them pulled at something in my chest. Something that hurt.

But I kept a smile firmly in place. I was determined to make this a nice evening for AJ the way I had planned.

Back at home, I made hot chocolate, and AJ had a bath to warm up. He watched a cartoon while I showered fast and got into a pair of fuzzy pants and a warm sweatshirt. Together, we made homemade pizza, laughing at our oddly shaped pies and putting on our favorite toppings. I turned on the tree lights, and he chose a movie and helped me carry our plates and drinks to the sofa. We snuggled under the blankets and watched his chosen show while we ate the pizza and sipped ginger ale from the two champagne flutes I'd bought at a garage sale years before. I rarely let him have pop, but tonight was a treat, and he loved the fancy glasses.

He made it through to the end, and I brought out a plate of cookies left from the bounty Asher had brought on Christmas. AJ ate a cookie, snuggled into my side. He talked about going back to school, seeing his friends, only mentioning Asher once. I turned on a New Year's Eve show, but he was bored with it, so I told him to pick another movie and we'd watch it after I tidied up the kitchen. But when I got back, he was sound asleep on the sofa, wrapped in a blanket, little cookie crumbs on his chin. I lifted and carried him to his room, placing him on the bed. It was only seven, and I knew he'd be up early the next day, but he was tired so I decided to let him sleep.

Back in the living room, I logged on and clocked a couple of hours, finding the time went by fast as the customer service line was steady. I stopped around ten and poured myself a glass of wine, putting the TV back on but not paying much attention to it, the background noise helping dispel the quiet of the apartment.

I wondered where Asher was now. Had he driven back to his sister's? Was he at home? I swallowed down the lump in my throat as I wondered if he'd decided to go out with someone else for the night. If he would be kissing another woman at midnight.

I was shocked at the tears that welled in my eyes at the thought of it.

I wiped at my eyes and took a sip of wine, reaching for my book and opening it, determined to put all other thoughts out of my head.

A short while later, there was a soft knock on my door. I assumed it was a neighbor coming to wish me a Happy New Year or the super's wife had come to check on us. She did that on occasion, which was kind.

I was shocked when I opened the door to find Asher there. He filled the doorframe, his broad shoulders straight. His overcoat had a dusting of snow on it, and a few flakes glistened on his head.

"Asher."

He nodded, looking determined. "Rosie."

"I assumed you went back to Suzy's."

"No. I stayed here. I know you told me to leave, but I was hoping you would allow me to come in."

"Why?" I asked.

"To talk."
I paused, his next words surprising me.
"Please, Rosie. Let me in. Give me a chance and hear me out."
I couldn't ignore the plea in his voice.
I stepped back. "Come in."

CHAPTER TEN

ROSIE

He stepped in and shed his coat, hanging it in the closet. He toed off his boots and stopped, looking uncertain.

"Do you want some coffee? Or a drink?"

He glanced at the sofa, seeing the champagne glasses. He looked at me, puzzled.

"Ginger ale New Year's celebration with AJ. He had too much sledding again today and passed out a couple of hours ago."

His eyebrows drew down, and worry crossed his face. "You didn't—"

I stopped his question. "I watched today."

He nodded, looking relieved. "A drink would be welcome."

I waved at the kitchen. "You know where your scotch is."

He had brought a bottle with him, plus an expensive liqueur for me to drink, before Christmas. Some of each was left in the bottles.

"I'm going to check on AJ."

In his room, I looked down at my son. He was sleeping, having kicked off the blanket he'd been wrapped in, and was now on the bottom of his bed. I carefully moved him and tucked him back in, knowing I'd do this again later. I brushed back the hair on his forehead, smiling as it flopped back into place. He needed a haircut. I'd give him a trim tomorrow. I bent and kissed his forehead, inhaling. He smelled of bubble bath and shampoo. I straightened, thinking how fast he was growing. Soon, he wouldn't fit in this single bed. Or this room. I shook my head to clear my thoughts. Hopefully by then I would be in a better place financially. I would have a better-paying job and find a larger place for us to live. One step at a time, I reminded myself, the way I had since finding out I was pregnant.

In the living room, Asher waited, a scotch in his hand. He had poured me a liqueur, and I sat beside him. For a moment, there was silence, then he spoke.

"I owe you an apology and an explanation." He took another sip. "I had no intention of making you feel as if I questioned your ability to make sound decisions for yourself or your son. I think you're an amazing mother, and I'm sorry if I made you doubt my feelings on that subject."

"Why did you call the doctor, Asher? Why did you race here? And hire a helicopter, of all things?" I questioned.

He turned and met my eyes. "I was frantic."

"Explain why to me. Please."

He hesitated, then reached for my hand. I let him clasp our fingers together, and he stared down at them, lifting our joined hands and kissing my knuckles.

"I was seven, Suzy was five and a half. My father was away on one of his constant business trips. It was Suzy, Mom, and me as usual. She hadn't been feeling well all day—Mom, that is. Tired. Out of sorts, she would call it. I had heard her ask my father not to go away that morning—to stay home and help look after us because she wasn't feeling herself. He told her that was what nannies were for and to hire one, and he left. Mom was quiet all day, and she didn't eat much supper. She kept rubbing her temples, but she would smile and say she was fine when I asked. After dinner, she said she was tired and going to have a nap and asked me to watch over Suzy. We played for a while, but Mom was still asleep." He paused, his voice getting thicker. I could hear his barely contained emotions, and I braced myself for what he was going to say. I already knew how this ended, and I was horrified.

"I helped Suzy get ready for bed, and I brushed my teeth and got in my pajamas. I thought Mom would be so proud of me. I went to tell her and let her know I was going to bed, but—" he swallowed convulsively then took a sip of his scotch "—I couldn't wake her."

"Asher," I breathed.

"She had an aneurysm. She'd fallen a couple of days before and knocked her head on the edge of the counter. She'd gotten up and laughed, saying how clumsy she was, and did nothing about it. It caused a blood clot. If my father hadn't been so wrapped up in business, he could have stayed home. Made the connection between her fall and how she was acting. Taken her to the hospital and maybe saved her life."

I moved closer, and he tightened his grip on my hand. He hadn't looked at me once as he spoke, as if too wary to make eye contact. "I was seven. Alone with my baby sister and my dead mother. We lived in a large house, and the staff wasn't there. We had a housekeeper, but she only came three times a week. Mom refused to have anyone help her 'raise her babies,' as she used to say, so no one was around. Not even a close neighbor, as we lived on a large estate."

"What did you do?" I whispered.

"I was panicked. Scared. Emotional. But I remembered what Mom taught me. Called 9-1-1. The police and ambulance came. They took her away. Put Suzy and me in a foster home for the night. Tracked down my father." He wiped a hand over his face. "My entire life changed that night, Rosie."

"I'm sorry."

He nodded and turned his head, finally looking at me. "When you said you had a headache, it all came rushing back. Finding my mom. Being alone with her. Scared and not knowing what to do. When you didn't answer your phone, I became irrational. All I could think about was getting to you. To little Asher. Suzy told me I was overreacting. She warned me. But I had to come. I had to call Sherman and get him to come see you. I prayed so hard that I would find you okay. That there was a simple explanation for your not returning my calls." He swallowed before speaking.

"That you weren't lying dead on the sofa and AJ finding you. That through some sick twist of fate, I'd lost another woman the same way I'd lost my mom."

His voice cracked, and I couldn't stop myself. I climbed into his lap, wrapping my arms around him and holding him tight.

"I'm here, Asher. Right here."

He gripped me tightly. "Thank God."

ASHER

I had taken a chance, coming back to Rosie's place. One I knew could blow up in my face. I had crossed a line that morning. Suzy had tried to warn me, begged me to be patient, but I hadn't listened. I couldn't listen. The images from my childhood hit me hard, wrapping around my brain until that was all I could see. Feel. Think about. I had to make sure Rosie was okay. And on the off chance she wasn't—I wanted AJ to have someone there to care for him. I never wanted a child to feel the swamping panic and grief I'd felt at a situation they couldn't control.

But she had let me in and listened. Now I had her in my arms again, a warm, soft weight on my lap. I inhaled her feminine scent, feeling the calm she brought with her. It settled into my chest and thawed me. Eased away the tension I had been carrying around all day. First the fear of something happening to her, then her anger when I stuck my foot in my mouth.

I had wandered my condo all day, unsure what to do with myself. How to put aside the feeling I had somehow lost something intrinsically precious to me with no idea how to get it back.

She eased back, cupping my face. Her lovely eyes were damp.

"I'm sorry," I said, sliding my hand around to the nape of her neck, the skin silky under my touch. "Please tell me you forgive me and we can go forward."

"Is that what you want?" she asked quietly. "To go forward?"

"Yes," I insisted. "Aside from this morning, has anything indicated I don't?"

"Our lives are so different. You need to get somewhere fast, you take a helicopter. I take the bus. You can buy anything you want. I save for the smallest of treats. I don't think I can compete, and I wonder how long it will be until those differences become too much."

I shook my head, the panic returning. "I don't want you to compete. Yes, I can buy anything I want. For me. You. AJ. Anyone. Those are material things. I can't buy the feeling I get when I'm close to you. When AJ makes me laugh. How much of a man I feel like when I do something and you smile at me. Kiss me. Those things are far more precious and rarer."

She frowned, and I pulled her close, kissing her again. "The time I spent with you and AJ made me feel alive. Happy. I have missed you so much and was so anxious to get back here. The only other person I have ever missed is my mother."

"What about your dad?"

I sighed, hating this subject. "My dad wasn't a bad person. He didn't beat us or hurt us in any way, except to avoid us. Mom was the main parent. He was driven to succeed. Work was his top priority all the time. The only disagreements they ever had were about his being gone so much. I remember her telling him that his presence was more valuable than more money in the bank. But he was obsessed with wealth. He'd grown up dirt poor and made himself into the business tycoon he became. He always said he'd stop when he had enough money to relax." I barked out a low chuckle. "He was never satisfied. After Mom died, we had housekeepers, babysitters, tutors. He buried his feelings and his mind in accumulating more wealth. Power. Status."

"He never remarried?"

"No."

"He must have loved your mother very much."

"She was easy to love." I ran a finger down her cheek. "She would have liked you."

Rosie smiled, a gentle expression on her face. I loved her softness, the way emotions played out on her face.

"Suzy and I were close. Dad was just a figure who passed through the house at times. He wasn't mean or nasty—simply withdrawn. There was no lack of money. Anything we wanted, we got. We could have ended up spoiled and entitled, but somehow, I inherited my father's work ethic and my mom's love of family. Suzy got my mom's heart—she loves as fiercely as my mom did. I made sure to keep my feet on the ground. When Dad died, all the money was split. I inherited most of the businesses. Dad was old-fashioned and always thought men should run things. I sold some of the companies and gave Suzy half, but I kept many of them. They're profitable and let me keep giving money away. I have the right people in place running them. I oversee most of the time."

"You must be a busy man," she murmured. "No time for anything but work."

"I thought so."

Our eyes met and locked. "I can find the time for something better, Rosie. For you and AJ. I want that. I don't want to be my father."

"Your world is—"

I cut her off. "Lonely. Empty. It'll be lonelier if you don't forgive me."

"I do forgive you."

The weight pressing on my chest vanished. "You do?"

"We need to talk about boundaries. You have to understand something, Asher. AJ comes first. You might call or text, but if I am busy with him, he is my priority. If he were sick, I would cancel plans with you. If he needed me, I would stay with him."

I nodded in agreement. "I do understand, and it's one of the things I adore about you. You put your child first. Your love for him is fierce. I get that and respect it. I wish my father had been the same way."

"How did he react when your mother died? Did he comfort you? Stay with you?"

"No. He sent people to pick us up from the foster home. He greeted us when we arrived home but was reserved. I went to their room the next day and barely recognized it. The furniture was different, all traces of her gone. I asked him, and he ignored me. I never saw him shed a tear or break down. He was never warm and loving like Mom, but he was Dad, you know? After she died, he became a polite stranger."

"What kind of business did he run?"

"He was into real estate, shopping stores, hotel chains, so many things. He loved getting in on the ground floor and making money. He was brilliant. He could spot a solid investment, and he was never wrong." I took a deep breath. "His very first venture, one only he owned, is still one of the most profitable and privately owned stores here. Zoles."

She blinked. "Zoles."

"Yes."

"Where I met you?"

"Yes."

"You own Zoles."

"Yes."

"Why were you there? You said you hated it."

"I did. I do. It took so much of my father's time. I used to hate what it represented. It robbed me of him. If he had to choose between it and me, it won every time. I still resent it, but I own it." I tucked a lock of hair behind her ear. "I can't sell it because my mother loved it. Everything about it. He named it after them. Zoe and Les. *Zoles*. Selling it feels wrong because of the love my mother had for it. When I grew up, I realized maybe my father spent so much of his energy on it because of what it meant to her. That maybe he was as lost as we were, but unable to admit it. That helped me forgive him. So, I keep it. In her memory."

"Asher," she whispered.

"I was there because every year, Zoles comes out with a limited crystal Christmas ornament. It was my mother's idea, and it was and is huge. She gave Suzy one every year until she died. I carried on the tradition. The first Christmas after she was gone, I figured out my father wouldn't think to buy her one, and I made my way to his office, which was on the top floor of the store in those days. I spoke to his secretary, and she took me downstairs and helped me buy the ornament."

"At seven years old," she said. "You went all by yourself?"

"Yes. I had the driver take me to the store, and I used the money my father gave us every week as an allowance. Mrs. Fairmount made sure my name was on the list so I could buy one every year for Suzy. I have never missed one. She insists I buy it for her."

"And your driver still takes you to pick it up?" she teased gently.

I laughed, grateful she was trying to lighten the atmosphere. "I usually drive myself."

She nodded. "Your story would have been more dramatic if you'd had to take the bus instead of being chauffeured. Sort of takes away from the whole image. The big allowance thing was sort of a letdown too. Most seven-year-olds can't afford crystal. You should have had to save for months by collecting bottles and stuff. You should rethink it the next time you tell it."

I pulled her into my arms, chuckling. "I have only ever told you, but I'll keep that in mind."

She held me tight. "I'm sorry for what you went through, Asher. I hate thinking of you alone, even if it was in a limo."

I pressed a kiss to her head. "I'm not alone now."

She looked up, cupping my face. She pressed her mouth to mine. "No, you're not."

CHAPTER ELEVEN

ROSIE

I held Asher close, his embrace tight. We sat for a while, not speaking, not moving, simply locked together.

He was a proud, strong man, and he had just allowed me to see his vulnerable side—one I was certain few ever saw. Instinctually, I knew he needed my embrace. To be held and comforted by my touch. I felt safe in his arms, and it made me feel incredible to know he felt the same way about my hold.

As a mother, I was horrified that he had found her dead at his young age. Left alone to figure out what to do. The thought of that happening to AJ was overwhelming. I understood Asher's panic now and could allow for his feelings. He still had gone overboard, but given his history, I wasn't angry anymore.

Asher shifted, and I eased back, cupping his face. His eyes were still dark with emotion, but some of the tension had fallen away.

"Thank you," he said simply.

I leaned forward and kissed him affectionately. "Thank you for telling me."

"Am I forgiven?" He sighed, his hands gripping my hips. "I'll try to do better, Rosie. Sometimes it hits me, and I react—"

I pressed a finger to his mouth. "Forgiven. I understand."

"I do, as well. AJ comes first. I'll try to hold back on my impulsive panic."

"I'll try to remember to look at my phone more often. I'm not used to anyone calling or checking in on me. If AJ is with me, I tend to forget."

He smiled, tracing a finger down my cheek. "We both have things to learn. Me, some patience, and you, that you have someone who deeply cares."

"We'll figure it out."

He lifted my hand to his lips and pressed a kiss to the knuckles. "I like the sound of that."

"Me too."

His stomach grumbled, and I frowned. "Are you hungry?"

"I didn't eat. I was upset."

"I'll make you something."

"I don't want you to work. I'll order something."

I laughed. "Asher, it's late on New Year's Eve. Do you know how busy every place is? You won't get delivery for hours."

He looked mischievous, reaching for his phone. I rolled my eyes.

"Not even you," I challenged.

He grinned. "Oh baby, now I have something to prove."

Forty-five minutes later, I was nibbling on an egg roll as Asher dug into a container of noodles. He fed me a mouthful and opened some orange chicken, muttering about how delicious it was. He offered me a piece with his chopsticks, and I took it, agreeing how tasty the morsel was.

"How?" I asked.

He smiled. "I went to school with the owner. We're still close. I bankrolled the restaurant. He always comes through."

"Even on New Year's Eve," I hummed, impressed.

Asher chuckled, licking at some sauce on his mouth. "I actually rarely ask. He knew it had to be important." He dug in the bag and handed me a set of chopsticks. "Eat with me. I saw the leftover pizza in the fridge, so I know you didn't eat much either."

"I was upset," I admitted.

He paused, leaned forward, and stroked my cheek. "I'm sorry."

"I know. I'm better now."

"Me too."

We ate, the TV on low in the background, music playing, mostly by groups I had never heard of, but it was white noise. Asher appeared famished, polishing off every dish he had ordered. I picked at the food, nowhere near as hungry as he was.

"Did you not eat today at all?" I asked.

"No." He peered into the bag, handing me a fortune cookie. "No leftovers. I should have ordered more. I'll get more in for dinner tomorrow. AJ loves Chinese." He stopped, meeting my gaze. "If that's all right with you."

"You'll spoil us."

He placed the bag on the coffee table and opened his fortune cookie, breaking it in half. He placed a piece on my bottom lip, and I let him feed me the sweet-tasting cookie. He popped the rest into his mouth and chewed slowly. "I need to make this clear, Rosie. I want to spoil you. Both of you. I have money. Lots of money. What seems extravagant to you probably doesn't to me." He held up his hand before I could say anything. "I'm aware of how that sounds. I'll try to watch myself and not go overboard. But you should know part of my 'love language,' if you want to call it that, is buying gifts. I do for my sister and my niece. I'm generous with employees. It's part of my nature."

"Love language?" I repeated, a smile pulling on my lips.

He chuckled. "That's what Suzy calls it."

"I know you're generous. More than most people," I replied. "Christmas is a good example."

"I held myself back," he argued.

I sighed. "I can't reciprocate, Asher."

"Yes, you can," he said, sounding eager. "You can cook me the food I bring. Let me enjoy a meal with you and AJ instead of eating alone. Wear the scarf, which will make me happy knowing you love it. Relax in the tub using the bath bombs I picked out because they smelled great and I wanted to inhale that fragrance on your skin. Being here with you makes me happy. That is far more valuable than the cash I spend. Happiness is much rarer."

"Says someone who has lots of it."

He shifted closer. "I can make you happy too, Rosie. Give me a chance. Let me into your life and trust me. Let me spoil you the way I can. You spoil me the way you can. It all equals out."

"Hardly," I said with a grimace.

"You're right," he agreed. "I'll never be equal to what you give me."

"Asher," I protested.

"You are priceless to me." He took my hands and cupped them with his, kissing my palms. "You mean so much already, and we've only started. I cannot fathom what you'll mean over the next while."

My breath caught at his words. "You mean a lot as well."

"Then we'll start the next year off together, yes?"

Behind him, the TV show began the countdown. His gaze slid to mine, waiting, hopeful, and filled with adoration. "Say yes, please, Rosie."

I smiled because there was no way I could refuse this man. "Yes."

He slipped his hand to the nape of my neck, pulling me close.

"Happy New Year, Rosie," he whispered against my lips.

"Happy New Year, Asher."

With his mouth on mine and his promise ringing in my ears, I looked forward to what the year held in store.

I woke up to low voices coming from the kitchen. Asher had stayed, but we hadn't done anything other than hold each other. He needed the closeness, and I loved his warmth. He had held me tightly, and we had slept after the midnight celebration.

I sat up, running a hand through my hair. I was bundled up, but the air in the apartment felt cool. I shivered a little and wrapped the blanket around me. I checked the thermostat, wondering if the heating was on the fritz again. It occurred a lot here. I turned it up but nothing happened, and I groaned low in my throat in frustration. It always got fixed, but it often took a few days. AJ and I would have to bundle up to stay warm. I had one small heater I would set up in the living room then move to AJ's room at night to keep the apartment from getting too cold. I could only hope they would fix it soon.

I washed my face and brushed my teeth, then I headed to the kitchen, leaning on the doorframe, observing AJ and Asher in silence. They were eating breakfast and playing checkers—a game Asher had bought AJ for Christmas. They were concentrating, leaning on their elbows, studying the board. AJ had a piece of toast with peanut butter in his hand, Asher was holding a half-eaten granola bar. Their serious expressions made me smile.

"I feel the tension in here," I drawled.

They looked up, grinning when they saw me.

"Momma—I beat Asher once, and he beat me. This is the tie breaker!"

I stepped closer, ruffling his hair and kissing his cheek. "I see."

Asher smiled at me, his eyes dancing. "Do I get a kiss too?"

I bent to brush my lips over his cheek, but he pulled me close, capturing my mouth. "Morning," he breathed.

"Morning."

"I made coffee."

"Okay."

I poured a cup and topped his up, then sat down and watched them finish the game. AJ won, and he lifted his arms in celebration. Asher fist-bumped him. "You've caught on well, bud. We'll move on to chess next."

AJ laughed in delight at the thought of spending more time with Asher. I smiled at him. "Go get dressed, baby. Wear something warm. It's cold in here."

He ran off, and Asher studied me. "I noticed the temperature drop. Why is it cold?"

"We often lose heat in the winter. They fix it as fast as they can."

"What if they can't?"

"So far, they have."

"I don't like the idea of you two being cold."

"We'll survive."

"Come to my place."

I shook my head. "AJ goes back to school the day after tomorrow. I return to work. We'll add layers, and if it gets really bad, they'll do something. The system is old, but they do the repairs when needed." I shrugged. "A little chill is better than when we lost electricity for four days. No heat, lights, hot water, any way to cook anything. AJ was only two. It was awful."

"I hate thinking of you in any discomfort."

"I'm tougher than I look."

He smiled. "I know you are. You're exceedingly strong."

"Not always."

"I think you're incredible."

I waved off his compliment. "You're biased." I stood, stopping to drop a kiss to his mouth. "It's the sex. It's clouded your mind."

He tugged me to his lap, wrapping his arm around me, pressing a kiss to my forehead. "It's you, Rosie. I'm in constant awe of you."

I snuggled close, loving his scent, his warmth, and the way he saw me. "Thank you."

He tipped up my chin and kissed me again. "You're welcome." Then he grinned. "But if you want to remind me about the sex thing, I'm all for it."

I laughed. "With AJ awake? Good luck."

He returned my amusement. "We'll have to wait until he's asleep, then."

"Good plan."

The apartment was chilly by the time the heat was fixed. Asher was anxious and upset as we waited. AJ and I were used to it and added blankets. I had to admit, as the temperature dropped, the invitation to go to Asher's condo looked better than ever. When the pipes clanked and hissed, indicating the heat had returned, I blew out a relieved breath. We were snuggled on the sofa watching a movie when it happened, and Asher frowned.

"Took them long enough."

"Sometimes it gets cold out here," AJ informed him. "But Momma puts a heater in my room so I'm okay." He bounded away to get a drink, and Asher studied me.

"So, you make sure he's warm, and you suffer?"

"I sleep on the floor of his room. In the daytime, I bring the heater out here so we are warmer. It's rare when it's off longer." I lifted one shoulder. "I can't afford to go to a hotel, so we do the best we can."

He shook his head but didn't respond. I knew he couldn't imagine living the way we did, but AJ and I were fine. We did the best we could with what we had, and we were happy. One day, we'd have more. I was working toward it. I headed to the kitchen and put on a pot of coffee to brew. Asher followed, sitting at the table.

AJ came into the kitchen, and I smiled at him. "Time to cut your hair."

He rolled his eyes, always hating to have his unruly locks trimmed, but I had an ace up my sleeve. "I'll cut Asher's first if you want."

They both stared at me. "Um," Asher said, for the first time sounding hesitant. "Cut my hair?"

"It's beginning to hang in your eyes."

"I can see my barber in a couple of days."

I held up my scissors. "But I have time now." I pulled a chair in front of me and patted the seat. "It'll only take a minute."

He sat down, and I unfurled the cape, draping it around his shoulders. I spritzed the water on his hair and combed it. Standing in front of him, I pursed my lips. He looked decidedly nervous, which I found amusing. Asher was never nervous.

"Have you cut any hair aside from AJ's?" he asked.

I tilted my head. "I watched lots of YouTube."

He swallowed, and I had to laugh. "I took a course. You'll be fine."

I was done in five minutes, tidying up the ends and trimming the front. As a joke, I pretended to make a mistake, widening my eyes and looking at my closed hand. "Well, thank goodness it grows back," I muttered, my voice horrified.

"Oh God, how bad?" Asher groaned.

I began to laugh as I uncurled my fingers and showed him there was nothing there. "Gotcha."

AJ began to chuckle, and Asher narrowed his eyes. "You'll pay for that."

"Promises, promises."

I handed him the mirror. "See for yourself."

He glanced at his reflection, brushing at his temples. "Once again, I'm impressed, Rosie."

I could only smirk.

AJ sat down once Asher stood, and his took a little longer. But it looked much better, and it didn't take me too long. Afterward, they insisted popcorn had to be their reward. We ate it as we played a game of Trouble, AJ winning the game soundly.

Asher and AJ picked the dinner menu, and more Chinese food arrived. Way more than we could eat, but I knew Asher did that deliberately, wanting my fridge full. We ate in the living room, the food spread out on the coffee table. Watching Asher try to teach AJ how to use chopsticks was funny.

He leaned over AJ, showing him with his fingers how to hold them. "Like this, bud. Put your fingers like this. Yes. Now, the other chopstick here. Great. You got it. Pick up a piece of chicken," he encouraged.

The chicken got away, and Asher laughed. "Again."

They practiced as I ate, happy just to see them together. Asher was endlessly patient with AJ, and in the end, he was able to pick up a piece of the teriyaki chicken and eat it. Rice was a grain at a time, and the noodles ended up being wound around the chopsticks like spaghetti, but they had fun. AJ's face and fingers were a mess, so when he finished his meal, I sent him to wash up.

Asher filled his plate again, relaxing against the sofa. "Thank you," I said quietly.

"For?" he asked, popping a piece of chicken into his mouth and chewing.

"For your patience with him."

Asher shook his head. "He's easy to be patient with. He makes me smile." He paused, chewing a mouthful of noodles. "I think he and Bonnie would get along well. I'm sure Suzy will be demanding an intro soon enough."

I smiled, knowing he was probably correct. If she was like her brother, patience wouldn't be a strong suit.

We ate in silence for a few moments, and he set down his plate. "I don't want to leave you tomorrow."

"We have to go back to normal life," I replied. "The holidays are over. AJ goes back to school, I go back to work, you go back to giving away money."

He nodded. "But I can see you, right? Besides a date?"

"If you want to," I said cautiously. "I know the holidays are lonely and people do odd things, so if you go back—"

He cut me off with one word. "No." He shook his head, his gaze fierce, his voice firm. "This was not just me being lonely. We are not ending, Rosie. This is simply the start. We'll adjust and figure things out. But you and AJ are part of me now. Don't think for one moment you were nothing but a temporary panacea. You are so much more. Tell me you know that."

"I'm trying."

"You are."

"Okay," I whispered, wanting with everything in me to believe him. To know this wonderful man would be around once the holiday decorations were gone and real life stepped in.

"I'll prove it to you."

"I look forward to it."

CHAPTER TWELVE

ASHER

My condo felt empty when I returned to it. Vast, filled with furniture, the air warm, and completely lacking any life. I wandered around, looking at the rooms. Four bedrooms, plus my large primary suite. The others rarely used unless Bonnie spent the night or Suzy and she stayed a few days. The kitchen was great for heating up takeout and the furniture rarely sat on. My office was the most lived-in. I spent a lot of time there, even sleeping on the sofa on occasion, watching a movie on the big screen. The rest of the rooms were just…space.

Rosie's tiny apartment was crammed. The furniture didn't match, the heat was iffy at times, yet I sensed the love that saturated the rooms. Felt the lives they lived in that tiny space.

I longed to be back on that lumpy sofa with her wrapped in blankets to ward off the chill rather than here in my perfectly temperature-controlled condo with nothing out of place. It was devoid of warmth. Rather like me before Rosie and AJ came into my life.

I loved my sister and my niece. But even with them, I tempered my feelings. I got on well with my brother-in-law. I had a few friends I cared about. But with all of them, I drew an invisible line in the sand. I cared only so much.

That line was erased when it came to Rosie and AJ. I had no control over my emotions. My actions. Normally, I was rock solid. I made rational decisions, and I stuck to them. There was nothing rational about how I acted with Rosie. It was as if she had woken up something inside me that had been locked away.

Last night after AJ had fallen asleep on the sofa, I'd carried him to his bed and stood back as Rosie tucked him in. Seeing the sweetness of her mothering him, pressing kisses to his forehead, brushing his unruly hair off his face, made my chest ache with the tenderness of the moment. Something she was used to, no doubt, but being denied that so much of my life brought out a sensation I wasn't used to feeling. I wanted to be part of that nighttime routine. To give and get sloppy goodnight kisses. To know the satisfaction of having my children warm and safe, tucked up for the night.

She had impressed me with the haircuts she gave the two of us. Mine looked neater, and AJ's was far shorter and he had stopped pushing it off his face every few moments. She was a woman of many talents, even though I realized some of them, like cutting her son's hair, were more of a necessity than a pleasure.

Rosie had bent and bestowed one last kiss to AJ's nose and tucked the blanket around him. She snapped off the light, leaving the small one in the corner lit. She had told me he didn't like total darkness, so it was on for him every night.

We had walked to the living room, coming together without words. Our clothing was discarded, and I sank onto the sofa, pulling her to my lap. We kissed endlessly, whispered words of desire, emotion, and shared quiet secrets. I slid inside her, the feeling of rightness at being surrounded by her settling over me. We moved and rocked on that old sofa, our pleasure blanketed by lips and tongues, our bodies releasing the tension we'd been carrying since being apart. Afterward, we dressed, and I held her close, wishing this was how I could end every day. Wondering, hoping, that one day it would be the normal.

I stared around my condo, thinking of that wish. I could see Rosie in the kitchen here. AJ and possible siblings playing on the floor. Studying and doing their homework. Having dinner as a family. Tucking them in and finding Rosie in our bed, waiting for me. Losing myself in her for a while and drifting off to sleep with her beside me.

At the moment, I loathed the fact that I was here in a warm, empty condo and she was across town, prepared to face the cold if need be. Alone. She handled everything alone.

I couldn't allow that. I couldn't stomach the idea of it happening.

I shook my head and strode into my office.

I had arrangements to make.

❄

I didn't sleep well and was up early, heading into the office. I knew it would be busy after the holiday break, and I wasn't wrong. The building buzzed around me all day. I had investment people who made sure the money source would never end. Another group that scouted for opportunities. Staff who went through applications, sorting out the bad from the good. Lawyers and accountants.

My office was at the end of the hall, the windows overlooking the small park behind us, a rare treat in downtown Toronto. I owned the building, refusing to pay rent to someone else. I used the top two floors, and the bottom two were rented from me. That money got reinvested and used to help make others' lives easier. My world was a constant circle of money in and money out. The bottom line was that no matter how much I gave away, it would always be replenished. My father, although lacking in emotional support, had built a strong portfolio of investments, real estate, businesses, and land. Once I was no longer an angry man, I focused on the good the money could do and stopped selling off businesses and giving away money like an idiot, and I made a career of it. I had quadrupled his portfolio, making it mine.

The sunlight bounced off the snow, reflecting on the window behind me as I studied the picture on my phone. I had snapped it yesterday while Rosie was busy. It was the January calendar for her and AJ. Her work, his school and activities, the online second job hours she had penciled in as much as she could. She was a single mother who struggled every day to be both parents to her son, while working two jobs and still making sure AJ was looked after, had outside activities, and was happy.

As I told her, she amazed me.

The one thing this schedule confirmed was that Rosie had zero time for herself. If she wasn't working, she was shuttling AJ around, taking care of him, and once he was in bed, taking care of the apartment and her second job. She had mentioned wanting to continue her accounting education as well.

"When I can afford it," she had added. *"Maybe a couple of years away, but I'll get it done."*

Everything she did focused on AJ. He had good, warm boots. Hers had seen better days. His winter coat was newer. Hers was well-worn and ragged along the hem. They took the bus or walked everywhere. Yet she never complained.

And now, I wanted some of her time. Which she had precious

little of to spare. I wanted to figure out a way to help her, which, in turn, helped me. It was selfish, but I didn't care.

I made a call to a friend who owned a nanny service. After describing what I wanted, Maureen was quiet for a moment. "I don't really offer babysitting services, Asher."

"I'll pay double. Surely some of your nannies want extra money."

"This is highly unusual."

"I just need a couple of nights a week. Please."

"I'll see what I can do."

I hung up, hopeful that she would figure something out. She always did. Her business had a stellar reputation. If I could prove to Rosie that AJ would be well looked after, maybe she would go out with me. I knew she didn't want to take advantage of her neighbor all the time. And I wanted to see her more than occasionally.

I had an email with some photos attached, and I grinned as I chose the options I liked best from the selection my designer had provided. Part two of my plan was moving ahead swiftly. It helped when you owned the business you wanted a quick turnaround from.

Then, satisfied there was nothing more I could do at the moment, I turned my attention back to business. I had back-to-back meetings the rest of the day. It was always busy after returning from the holidays, and this year was no different.

Except I was different.

In ways I had never expected.

And I rather liked it.

Six o'clock appeared in the blink of an eye. I had been busy all day, yet Rosie invaded my thoughts often. I wondered how her day was going. If AJ had enjoyed being back at day care. If she had eaten lunch. I knew she had a new boss starting today, and I hoped the transition had gone well.

Selfishly, I hoped she'd had time to ask her neighbor if she would watch over AJ one night so I could take her out.

I picked up my phone, dialing her, suddenly wanting to hear her voice.

She answered, her tone cautious. "Hello."

"Hey, sweetheart. How was your day?"

"Asher?" she questioned.

I laughed, even as a ripple of possessiveness ran through my chest. "Do you have a lot of men calling you up and addressing you as sweetheart?"

She hummed in amusement. "I didn't recognize your number."

"Oh. I called you from my other cell phone. I only use it for business, and I was on it most of the day," I explained. "I picked it up out of habit."

"I'm in your business contacts?"

"You're in both business and personal. Now you have this number, and you can reach me anytime. But use the personal one first. I always answer that, no matter what."

"More than business?"

"Yes," I replied firmly. "Family first."

"Ah."

"How was your day?"

"Chaotic." There was a noise behind her. "Still is. AJ is starving."

I felt a flash of disappointment I tamped down. She had priorities that were far more important than chatting with me.

"Go feed him, and call me when you can."

"How was your day?" she asked.

"I missed you."

There was a beat of silence. "Oh."

"You were on my mind a lot, Rosie."

"I asked Mrs. Watson if she could look after AJ one night. She said Wednesday worked for her. She has bingo tomorrow."

"Wednesday seems so far away."

She laughed. "The way my week is shaping up, it'll be here fast."

There was a note to her voice. Was it tension? Worry? I couldn't tell. She sounded tired, but it was the first day back from the holidays, so no doubt it would take her a bit to settle back into her routine. One that I hoped included me now.

"I will look forward to it. What time can I pick you up?"

"I can be ready for six thirty."

"Perfect."

"Momma!" AJ's voice called.

"I have to go."

"Call me later."

"I will." She paused. "Asher?"

"Yes, Rosie?"

"I missed you too."

She hung up, but her admission made me smile.

I sent her flowers the next day. I had casually confirmed the name of the company she worked for when we spoke later that night. I wanted to send her something that reminded her of me and let her know I was thinking of her. She texted me in the afternoon, thanking me and telling me she was looking forward to seeing me the next day.

It does seem forever away.

Your flowers are beautiful.

I replied swiftly, ignoring the people sitting in front of me.

Not possibly as beautiful as you.

The little heart emoji she sent back made me grin. The proposal we were going over was granted more money than I had planned to give. It seemed right somehow, given they were working on helping single mothers.

My staff left the room wondering if I had taken leave of my senses. It was rare I doubled the suggested contribution.

But my respect for single mothers had changed drastically. I'd admired them before Rosie. Now I thought they should be revered.

I had a feeling she would be pleased with my decision.

And even though I was going to see her the next day, I showed up at her door at nine that night, knocking quietly in case AJ was in bed.

She opened the door, looking surprised and, to my delight, happy to see me. She was in a long nightgown sort of thing. Shapeless, huge on her, and, no doubt, fuzzy and warm. She looked sexy and sweet all at once.

"Asher? What are you doing here?"

"I missed you," I replied.

She pulled me in, throwing her arms around my neck. I held her tight, enjoying the feeling of having her close, then slipped my fingers under her chin and kissed her. Our mouths moved together, lips and tongues touching, tasting, exploring. She was sweet tea and mint. Warm hellos and soft whimpers. I drew back, gazing down at her. "Hi."

"Hi," she replied.

"Can I come in just for a few moments?"

"Yes."

I toed off my shoes and laid my coat over the sofa arm. "AJ out?"

"Yes. You missed him by about fifteen minutes. I was just having supper."

"You didn't eat with him?"

"I had a really late lunch. I sat with him while he ate his dinner so I could hear all about his day."

She tugged me into the kitchen, and I shook my head. "Toast and tea? That's your dinner?"

"I love toast."

"I know, Rosie, but you have to eat more than that."

"It's all I wanted. Do you want some?"

I wasn't going to argue with her. "Yes."

She put some bread into the toaster and poured me a cup of tea. She handed me the peanut butter with my toast, but hers only had butter. I made a mental note to check her butter supply. I would make sure she had bread as well. If all she was going to eat was toast, I needed to know she had the supplies for it. We carried our "dinner" to the sofa and sat down.

"Why such a late lunch?"

She sighed quietly, and I noticed she looked tired.

"My new boss is rather, ah, demanding."

"Oh?"

"She has different ways of doing things. She's very brusque. To the point. And likes things her way. She's almost rude, if I'm being honest. I get the feeling she wants to make an impression."

"Sounds like she has. A negative one."

"I was lucky with Albert. He was a family man. He understood that with my being a single parent, sometimes I had to leave early, or if AJ was sick, I would work from home. He knew I always got the job done. Ms. Wells, as she prefers to be addressed, informed me she won't *cut me any slack* for my situation."

"What 'situation' exactly?"

"Being a single mother."

Anger flashed through me. "How is she possibly judging you on her first couple of days?"

"She wasn't happy that I left on time yesterday. Or that I was fifteen minutes late this morning after dropping AJ off. The sidewalks were slippery, and I slipped on the ice. I missed the bus."

"Are you hurt?" I asked, getting to my feet.

She shook her head. "Relax. Sit down. Other than my pride and a sore butt, I'm fine. I didn't hit my head or any other vital part."

I sat down, shaking my head. "Your ass is pretty vital. At least to me."

She began to laugh, and I had to join her. "Thank you," she said, wiping her eyes. "I needed that."

"Did you explain?"

Rosie nodded, stood, and placed her hand on her hip. She pretended to stare down at me. "Life is filled with mishaps, Ms. Duncan. How we overcome them shows our inner strength," she intoned in a nasal, holier-than-thou voice.

I blinked, amusement making my lips curl. "Your new boss, I presume?"

She flopped on the sofa next to me with a sigh. "She wasn't pleased when I informed her my inner strength needed some ice and a Tylenol. She told me to settle myself and get to work."

"Sounds lovely."

"She loves to bark orders all day. Not only at me, but she does love to stick her head in my door and tell me what she wants done. Frequently. My old boss sent out texts and emails, the occasional call. He was polite and knew the word please. And he knew exactly what was happening in the department at any given moment. He never barked. She wants daily update reports sent before we leave for the day. And God help me if it is a minute before four. She informed me she wasn't happy with my special hours."

"Track it all," I encouraged her. "You might need it for HR. It sounds rather bullying to me. And you can't discriminate against a single mother." I shook my head. "Better yet, quit and come work for me."

She blinked at me and laughed. "Yeah, so not a good idea. I am not coming to work for you. I will not be that woman sleeping with the boss."

I already knew she'd reject that idea. I pulled her to my lap and slid my hand up her leg. "There'd be perks, Rosie." I covered the nape of her neck, drawing her close and skimming my mouth along her skin. "So. Many. Perks."

My mouth hovered over hers, grinning as she whimpered. I kissed her. Deeply. Passionately. Without intent, but wishing there were. Except she surprised me, tugging off my tie and unbuttoning my shirt, slipping her hand inside and trailing it over my chest in light touches.

"Rosie, I didn't come here for this," I groaned, dropping my hands and palming her ass. God, I loved her ass. It fit perfectly in my hands.

She pressed wet, openmouthed kisses up my neck, pulling my lobe between her lips and sucking. I shuddered as the heat rolled through me. "Did you want to, though?" she whispered. "Come, I mean?"

"God, yes. I suppose I should do a thorough inspection of your injured butt. For purely medical reasons."

"Are you playing doctor now?" she purred in my ear, dropping her hand and cupping my erection through my pants.

"Yes. You have a fever, Ms. Duncan. There's only one cure. A special injection just for you."

"Give it to me," she whispered against my mouth. "Please."

I was only too happy to do exactly as she requested.

CHAPTER THIRTEEN

ASHER

The next day felt endless, which was unusual for me. I had left Rosie sleeping on her sofa, hating to depart, but not wanting to risk being found by AJ. I didn't want him thinking I snuck in at night after he went to bed. After our frantic coupling on the sofa, we had held each other, talking about everything and nothing. It was something I enjoyed about Rosie. She found the world around her interesting. At times frightening, but still intriguing. She talked about people at work, those she saw on the bus. She told me about the homeless man she saw every day. She often brought him a sandwich and made sure he had blankets. *"He tries so hard to be dignified,"* she said quietly. *"I worry every time there's a storm and I hope he's found shelter."*

I adored her tender heart and her way of looking at things.

She was on my mind all day. It was odd for me to think of anything but business. Even after hours, I was usually handling emails and messages. Once I sat at my desk, the rest of the world faded away, and I concentrated on the task at hand. But since the holidays, Rosie and AJ slipped into my thoughts all the time. Especially today. I swore I could still taste her, smell her skin. When I tugged on my overcoat to head to a meeting, I realized her fragrance clung to the material. I had wrapped it around her last night, after noticing her shiver. The apartment was chilly, given its age and the poor insulation and drafty windows. *"Even with the heat working, it never is very warm,"* *Rosie admitted.*

Except, I couldn't help but notice when I went in to peek at AJ, his room was toasty, with the little heater pumping away in the corner. I hated and loved the fact that she made sure he was fine, while she did without. She was a selfless mother, but she needed someone to look out for her as well.

I wanted that someone to be me.

Six o'clock couldn't come fast enough, and I was out of the office before the chimes on the large wall clock I had in the waiting room had finished their song. I made record time getting to Rosie's and was knocking at her door at six fifteen. She opened the door, smiling.

"This is becoming a habit."

I grinned, stepping inside and handing her the small bouquet I had picked up earlier. I cupped her face, her skin soft under my cool palms, and kissed her. "One you can't break, I hope," I murmured against her lips before kissing her. "You look beautiful."

AJ rushed over, so I kept my caress PG. I hunched down, exchanging fist bumps. Rosie went to the kitchen to put the flowers in water, and I listened to AJ tell me all his news. Like his mother, he was observant and loved to watch people. His world contained more crayons, nap times, and cookies, but I still enjoyed hearing him talk.

"You and Momma going for supper?" he asked.

"Yes."

He twisted his lips. "Not me."

I ruffled his hair. "Not tonight. This weekend, we all will. Okay?"

His sunshine smile broke out. "Okay!"

I grinned. He was easy to please.

Rosie returned, her pretty green dress swirling around her legs. She had her hair up, showing off her neck, tendrils dancing around her face. The dress had long sleeves and a bow on the hip. The color set off her eyes and ivory skin. I found myself wondering if the bow was for show or actually worked.

I hoped to find out later.

I met Rosie's neighbor when she came over. Mrs. Watson set down a large bag containing wool and knitting needles. She looked me up and down, pushing her glasses higher on her nose as she did so. Rosie introduced us, and I shook her hand. She grinned at me. "You're a fine specimen, aren't you?"

I had to laugh. "I clean up well."

She stepped closer. "She's a good girl. A good mother. You gonna treat her right?"

"Absolutely."

She nodded, watching as I helped Rosie on with her coat. It was different from the coat I'd seen her wear the first day. Shorter. Newer and fancier, but thinner. I frowned at the feel of it, but I didn't say anything, not wanting to embarrass her. Mrs. Watson beamed at her. "That looks lovely, dear."

"Thank you for the loan," Rosie replied.

"You have a good time. Don't rush to come back. I have my knitting, and I can sleep on the sofa. You enjoy yourselves." She winked at me.

"Thank you."

AJ got lots of hugs and kisses from his momma. He held up his arms, and I picked him up, getting a hard hug and a kiss on the cheek. His show of affection warmed my heart, and I felt that tug toward him, the same way I felt toward Rosie.

I turned up the heater in the car and put on the seat warmers. Rosie thanked me. "She insisted I borrow her coat. Mine is old, and I didn't want…" She trailed off. "This one looked nicer." She glanced down. "My dress isn't new either, but—"

I leaned across the console and cupped her face, kissing her until I felt her relax. "You look beautiful. I don't care if the dress is new, if the coat is borrowed. I want to spend the evening with you. That's all that matters."

"I don't want to embarrass you."

"You could never embarrass me," I replied firmly. "Ever. I'm proud to have you on my arm. Please forget about the dress, the coat, everything—just for a little while. Please?"

"Okay."

I winked at her. "Good. Because if you don't, I'll open up Zoles only for you and make you pick out a new coat and dress. Boots too."

"You wouldn't," she gasped. "You can't do that!"

I laughed as I guided the car into traffic. "I can, Rosie. The store belongs to me. I can do whatever I want, so…" I trailed off, glancing her way.

"I wouldn't allow it," she said primly.

I chuckled and took her hand. Little did she know I had plans to shower her with gifts, both the useful and frivolous varieties. And I was going to enjoy it. I had no doubt she was going to fight me on it, but I was looking forward to the scuffles as well.

I was looking forward to anything that had to do with her.

The restaurant was small, quaint, and homey. We walked in, and the owner stepped forward. "Asher!" he said, shaking my hand. "And who is this lovely lady?"

"Rosie, meet Franco. Best Italian food in the city."

He beamed, lifting her hand and kissing it. She smiled, and he looked at me. "What a beauty. Come. I have the best table, and I will cook for you myself."

We slipped into a circular booth, and without asking, a bottle of my favorite red appeared with two glasses. A plate of warm focaccia and a bowl of the most beautiful olive oil was added for dipping. The bread was studded with sun-dried tomatoes, rosemary, and pink salt. A bowl of mixed olives and thinly shaved slices of parmesan accompanied it.

Rosie looked around in curiosity. The wood walls and beams gave the place an exceptional ambiance. Candles and low lighting made it feel warm. The seats were comfortable and the place not overly crowded. Our spot in the corner was intimate, the small booth set back, giving us privacy.

"I love this place," Rosie said quietly.

"It was my mother's favorite spot. We came often. It's been family-run since the day it opened."

"And it's still here," she marveled.

"Great food. An amazing wine cellar." I picked up a piece of focaccia and dipped it in the olive oil, the subtle flavor of the oil bursting on my tongue. I pressed another piece to Rosie's lips. "You have to try this."

She took a bite and chewed, closing her eyes and humming at the taste. "That's incredible."

"I know."

She picked up her own piece, dipping it as I had, then added a sliver of the cheese. "Oh my God," she hummed.

She was sexy as she shut her eyes, chewing slowly, savoring the flavor. She smiled as she swallowed. "I'm going to move in to the kitchen."

I chuckled. "Franco would probably let you."

"So your mom brought you here?"

"We used to come as a family. After she died, we stopped, but I would beg the nanny of the month to bring me here. Suzy and I loved the place. When they fell on hard times, I bought it, gifted it back to them, and I make sure they will never have to sell. My mother loved it. I refuse to let it go."

"Like Zoles."

"Yes, but this place is personal. It has nothing but positive memories. I won't let that fade away."

She leaned over and kissed me, her lips soft and warm on mine. "I love your sentimental heart, Asher."

"My father felt it was a weakness."

"No, it's your greatest strength."

I kissed her back, needing her touch. "Thank you."

She beamed. "Anytime."

Rosie oohed and aahed over every dish. Protested she was full, yet her eyes lit up when the next round would appear. I had told Franco to go all out and I wanted leftovers. It would ensure Rosie and AJ ate well for the next couple of days. I noted the stuffed shells and chicken piccata were her favorites. The risotto was a huge hit, but we ate all of it, Rosie cleaning her plate with more focaccia. Finally, she sat back. "No more. I will burst out of this dress."

"No objections here." I waggled my eyebrows at her, and she laughed.

"One-track mind."

"When it comes to you, yes."

Franco presented some Italian cookies and espresso, along with small glasses of amaretto. We relaxed and enjoyed the ambiance and the quiet. I liked that I didn't have to fill in the silence with chatter. The quiet between us was comfortable.

"Do you have plans this weekend?" I asked.

She shook her head, swallowing her mouthful of cookie. "Working a little on the help desk. Probably sledding. Some errands."

I took in a deep breath. "Would you consider taking the weekend off and you and AJ come to the condo for the weekend? There's a great park not far from me. We can sled there. Skating too." I paused. "The three of us spending some time. I'll take you back on Sunday."

She placed her cup in the saucer carefully. "Where will AJ sleep?"

"In the guest room."

"And me?"

"With me in my room. His room would be right down the hall."

"That's a big step, Asher."

I tilted my head, studying her. "Every step we take is big, Rosie. We don't seem to have a small one in our roster."

"Does that worry you?"

"Not a bit."

"Okay."

"Great. I'll pick you up Friday after work."

"I thought you said the weekend. As in Saturday and Sunday."

"The weekend includes Friday night, Rosie. I'm sure most of the world would agree with me."

"So, two nights, then?"

"Yes."

"I assume you expect to get lucky?"

I chuckled. "I am lucky if you agree to this."

"You know what I mean."

I slid closer to her in the round booth. Glided my hand up her arm, over her shoulder, and wrapped my fingers around the nape of her neck. She shivered at my touch. I pulled her close and kissed her. "You, me, in my bed, so when you leave, the sheets smell like you? Like us? Yes, I want to get lucky. I want to hold you all night and wake up with you beside me. I want to make love to you in a big, comfortable bed. I want you to like it so much that you come back. A lot."

Her eyes were wide and shocked in her face. "I see."

"So, is that a yes?"

Her breath was warm on my skin as I pressed closer.

"Yes."

I kissed her. "Good answer."

CHAPTER FOURTEEN

ROSIE

I checked on AJ when I got home, still high on my evening with Asher. It had been so long since I had been on a real date. I had been nervous about my dress, my borrowed coat, but Asher made me feel beautiful. He refused to let me worry, smoothing all my rough edges with his sweet words and gestures.

I was touched that he'd taken me to a place that meant so much to him, that held such personal memories. I loved the restaurant. The casual way he told me of saving it and giving it back to the family showed me his real heart. I had seen so many glimpses of it since we met, but that showed me his honor.

We'd had dinner, sitting for hours simply talking. I loved hearing his stories. He was an excellent listener, asking questions and showing me that he was actually paying attention to me when I spoke. So many men tended to check out, barely paying attention. Asher truly listened.

I had been equal parts sad and happy when he'd brought me home, walking me to my door, kissing me goodnight, and leaving me.

"You're not coming in?" I asked.

He drifted his knuckles down my cheek. "No, Rosie. Tonight was to spend time with you. You're not just a booty call. You're so much more than that."

"Coffee?" I asked.

He bent and kissed me again. "We both know I won't be able to resist, and coffee will become more," he murmured. "I want tonight to be the first of many wonderful nights."

"All right," I agreed.

That didn't stop him from kissing me until I was a shaking mass of want in his arms. He felt the same way, judging from the erection pressed between us as he held me tight. But he left, trailing his finger over my lips, shaking his head, and muttering about "red-headed sirens."

I curled up on the sofa, my makeup scrubbed off, dressed in my warm pajamas. I pulled a blanket over me, once again feeling the coolness of the apartment after being warm and cozy beside Asher all evening. I hoped the heating wasn't failing again. The building was so old, it seemed to happen more and more often.

I was looking forward to the weekend with him at his place. I could only imagine what his condo was like. I asked him if I could cook for him, and he had been enthusiastic, telling me to send him a list of what I needed and he would ensure it was there for me. AJ would love it. He adored Asher, and part of me worried about that, while another part of me knew Asher didn't take that lightly. He assured me he had no plans on going anywhere.

I sighed as I rubbed my temples. I was falling for him. Fast. Hard.

I let out a small laugh.

Who was I kidding? I had already fallen. I'd fallen for him before Christmas was over. Maybe even the first day. I tried to recall how I lived before him, but everything seemed so black and white. I existed. Since he'd come into our lives, everything felt full of color. Of hope.

I curled up, pulling my blanket around my shoulders. My phone pinged, and I looked at my screen.

> You were so beautiful tonight. It hurt to leave you.
> Looking forward to the weekend.

> Good night, Rosie, my love. Asher

Rosie, my love.

He'd never called me that before.

I smiled as I replied.

> Looking forward to it.

> PS – I hated seeing you walk away, but the weekend is soon!

> Sleep well. Yours, Rosie XX

His reply was fast.

Mine. Yes. I like that.

Asher xx

I fell asleep dreaming of Asher, AJ, and a bright future.

Ms. Wells was on a tear the next couple of days, killing the high I had been feeling since my date with Asher. She loved to control everything and everyone around her. It wasn't only me, but I had the feeling she watched me extra closely. I kept track of all our emails and interactions, as per Asher's suggestion. She did like to refer to my "single mother status" far too often. It had rarely ever come up with my old boss or any of my coworkers, but she seemed to focus on that fact. I was on time every day, ate lunch at my desk as usual, and didn't leave before four p.m. Still, I had a feeling she found me lacking. I wasn't sure why she disliked me, but that feeling lingered.

Friday afternoon, I left work with an extra bounce in my step. I picked up AJ, and when we got home, I helped him pack his knapsack for the weekend.

"What toys should I bring, Momma?"

"Oh, ah…" I grimaced, unsure. Would Asher want toys strewn around his place?

A knock on the door interrupted my thoughts. I glanced at the watch on my wrist. It was barely five. Asher wouldn't be here for another hour, but when I opened the door, there he was. Tall, handsome, and sexy in his suit and overcoat. He held a large laundry basket in his hands, and he was smiling, looking sheepish.

"Rosie." He bent and kissed me. "I'm early. I couldn't wait."

I stepped back, unable to stop returning his smile. "I don't mind."

He came in, shutting the door, and placing the basket on the floor.

"Is that invisible laundry?" I asked. "Does your fancy apartment not have a washing machine?"

He chuckled as he took off his overcoat. AJ came running out. "Asher!"

Asher bent, lifting AJ over his head. "Hey, bud."

I had to turn my head at the sight of the joy on my son's face. He flung his little arms around Asher's neck. "I missed you, and I'm so excited!"

"Me too." Asher stared at me, his gaze heated. "What about Momma? Is she excited too?"

"Yes," I managed to get out, my breathing suddenly picking up.

"Good. Then we're all excited."

"Asher, what toys should I bring?"

Before I could speak, Asher set AJ down and lifted the basket. "Bring whatever ones you want that can fit in here."

"You have to be tidy at Asher's home," I reminded AJ. "Just like in your room."

"I know, Momma. I'll clean up my toys before bed." He picked up the basket, the size almost dwarfing him. "I gotta pick the best ones." He glanced at Asher, a furrow between his brows. "I don't know if I have this many."

Asher laughed. "Just pick your favorites. There are a few waiting for you at my place as well. I'll carry the basket when you're done."

AJ hurried away, the idea of other toys exciting him.

"You're spoiling him," I admonished gently. He stepped forward, wrapping one arm around my waist and drawing me close, while he cupped my face with his other hand. "I want to spoil him. And you. AJ is easy. You are far more challenging, Ms. Duncan. I have a feeling you'll fight me at every turn."

"Not every turn. I accept coffee."

He pressed his mouth to mine, our lips moving in perfect synchronicity. "How about the best coffee you ever tasted?" he murmured, dragging his mouth along my cheek. "A big sofa in front of a warm fire, curled up under the softest blanket I could find in this city?"

"And you beside me?"

"Oh, baby. You know it," he whispered, his voice husky. "I plan on staying close all weekend."

"Then go ahead and spoil me."

He grinned, dropping a kiss to my nose.

"I plan to."

I was nervous on the drive to Asher's place. He pulled into a private parking lot, using a pass that got him through an extra garage door. The level was bright and quiet, not very full, with six cars and a large, square truck-like vehicle parked in a row. All were gleaming under the lights. He parked beside the large vehicle and got out.

AJ stared at the truck. "That's a Hummer. It's so cool."

Asher grinned, handing me AJ's knapsack and my small bag. "It is."

"Does it belong to a neighbor?" I asked, trying not to laugh. AJ was staring at it like it was the holy grail. He stepped closer as if to touch it, but I patted his arm. "No, AJ. It isn't yours."

"He can touch it," Asher objected. "I don't mind."

"Is it yours?" AJ asked, sounding awed.

"Yes." He glanced around. "All of these are. This is my private parking area."

I tried not to gape. All of these cars were his? I didn't know much about cars, but I knew all of them were expensive.

Asher ruffled AJ's hair. "If your mom is okay with it, I'll take you for a drive in the Hummer this weekend."

AJ's eyes lit up, and I tried not to groan. "You have to behave," I said.

"I will!"

We stopped at an elevator, and Asher pressed his thumb to a panel. The doors opened, and we stepped in. "Yours, too?" I asked.

"Yes. I have a private entrance."

Of course he did.

Nothing prepared me for the condo we walked into. Soaring ceilings, an open floor plan, a massive fireplace, and a view to die for. I wasn't sure where to look first. The kitchen was gorgeous, with rich wood cabinets and stainless-steel appliances. The fridge would hold enough food to feed AJ and me for a month. The freezer beside it would keep us stocked for a year. Corridors led to the left and right of the great room we were in.

"Guest bedrooms and gym that way," Asher said with a tilt of his head. "My office and my room that way." He indicated the other hall.

I could only stare, trying to take it all in. My entire apartment would fit in his kitchen with room to spare. The thought of him even being at my shabby little place made me blush. Never mind all the time he spent there with us. The awful little sofa he slept on with me.

I was embarrassed. Horribly so.

But I forced a smile to my face. "Asher, it's incredible."

He gave me a strange look but took my hand. "Come on, I'll show you the rest."

My head swiveled constantly as we toured the condo. Asher

showed me the room he had for AJ. It was the first one off the hallway, with a spectacular view of the city. It was painted a cheerful blue, and it held a double bed and dresser. Some Lego and a couple of other toys waited for AJ, who was far more interested in those than the room, the en suite, or the rest of the place. He sat down, eagerly reaching for the Lego, waving us off when Asher asked him if he wanted to come with us.

The other two rooms were more neutral than the room AJ was going to sleep in, and I had a strange suspicion that it had been painted recently. Asher assured me that we would be able to hear AJ if he needed us in the night. "I bought a monitor," he said proudly.

After showing me the gym, he tugged me through the living room and past his office, leading me to his bedroom. Once again, I was speechless. I was certain I had never seen a bed so big. It dwarfed the room, the beautiful black-and-white comforter setting off the iron bedframe. Aside from the nightstands and a chair in the corner, it was the only piece of furniture. The dark colors with splashes of blue and gray were masculine and suited him.

He had a large walk-in closet and an amazing bathroom. I counted seven shower heads and an overhead rainfall shower in the glassed-in enclosure. A large slipper tub was in the corner, a set of long narrow windows at the perfect height to see the view as you relaxed in the tub. The entire condo bespoke wealth. It was rather overwhelming. I was at a loss for words.

Asher wrapped his arms around me, drawing me back to his chest. "Breathe, Rosie. Just breathe," he soothed, as if sensing my inner turmoil.

"It's so…incredible."

"It's where I live. That's all."

"I'm embarrassed about you being at mine," I admitted.

He spun me around. "What?"

ASHER

I was horrified by her words. "What?" I asked, meeting her eyes, aghast to see how pale she'd become. The moment we'd stepped into the condo, I'd felt her withdrawal. She became tense. Her smile brittle.

If I'd had any idea seeing this place would do that to her, I never would have brought her here.

"My place—" she began.

I cut her off. "Is your home. You welcomed me there. I loved every single second I spent with you there." I looked around. "Bigger isn't better, Rosie. A fancy tub doesn't make it a home. *You* make it a home. I felt that every moment I spent in your place." I stepped back, running a hand through my hair. "I wanted to bring you here so you could get comfortable in my space too. So we could go to either spot and feel relaxed. I didn't do it to upset you or make you feel embarrassed. *God,* that is the last thing I wanted."

"I'm sorry, it's just so…vast."

"And empty." I cupped her face. "Every moment since I came back to this condo, I felt its emptiness. I couldn't wait to get you and AJ here to bring some life to it. To make it feel like home, not just a place I sleep."

Her entire body relaxed. "Really?"

I kissed her. "Yes. I want to see you everywhere. Curled up on the sofa. Sitting by the fire. I want to watch you cook in the kitchen. I'm looking forward to building Lego with AJ and being able to see you as you move around. I'm going to fill that tub and watch you lie in it and relax. I want to be in there with you. Then I'm going to take you to bed and make love to you all night. I want to be able to see you everywhere, so when you're not here, I have something to hold on to until you are back again."

"Asher," she whispered, her eyes bright.

I leaned my forehead on hers. "You mean so much, Rosie. So much. I would never do anything to hurt or embarrass you. I'm sorry. I didn't think how this place would make you feel."

"I'm overreacting," she admitted. "It's so incredible. Really incredible. It just…"

"What?" I asked tenderly. "Finish it. Tell me."

"You have a private parking lot. I have a bus pass. You have a condo that I think my entire apartment block would fit into. I have a space that is hardly warm enough to live in at times. You buy restaurants to help people. If I can scrape enough together for takeout, it's a bonus. We live such different lives. How can I satisfy you?"

"By being you. My wealth doesn't talk to me and make me laugh or feel good about myself. My huge condo doesn't welcome me with a brilliant smile and warm green eyes. My cars are only good if they take me to you. My money only means something if it is making your life better. You, Rosie, have become the pinnacle I set everything else up against."

"Just like that?"

"Just like that."

I swept her into my embrace and kissed her. She held me tight, letting me command her mouth, hold her close and ravish her. I wanted to carry her to my bed and bury myself in her for hours. Until she believed the words I was speaking.

But the sound of running feet broke us apart. Rosie was breathing fast, her cheeks flushed.

"Do you understand what you mean to me?" I asked. I knew my wealth overwhelmed her. That the life I led was different from hers. Different, but not better. I had to be patient and let her figure it out. I wasn't worried that it was insurmountable. She needed some time to get used to all of it.

"I'm beginning to."

I held out my hand. "Then come with me. I need dinner, and you promised me shepherd's pie. After AJ goes to bed, I'll finish showing you." I paused. "If it takes all night, you'll understand, Rosie. I promise you that."

She relaxed as she puttered around the kitchen, exactly the way I knew she would. She grew more comfortable, the glass of wine I poured her helping, as much as the fact that she was in her element. She loved to cook, and I had been told the kitchen was a chef's dream.

I used it to heat up leftovers and make the occasional easy meal.

But Rosie was cooking. I heard her humming as she chopped and stirred. I surreptitiously watched her as she opened cupboards, investigating and finding what she needed. I'd had the kitchen department at Zoles fill it with everything. Pots, pans, baking implements. All sorts of gadgets and things I would never use, but I knew Rosie would. I heard her soft exclamations of delight as she discovered something she was looking for. Her pleasure at the self-lifting mixer in one of the bottom cupboards made me chuckle. It also inspired her to "whip up a batch of cookies" while the shepherd's pie cooked. My condo had never smelled so appetizing.

She watched us as well. Commented on the Lego creation we

were making. Chuckled at some of AJ's random thoughts. I heard all about the kids at school. The new girl missing her two front teeth that made her lisp when she spoke.

"The other kids laughed, but I got mad," AJ told me. "She fell off a swing in the summer, and they came out."

"What did you do?" I asked.

"I told them to stop being mean. I held her hand and told her she was pretty and I liked her even if she talked a little funny. I thought it was cute. I think she could be my friend. Now that Ashley moved, it would be nice."

I nodded in understanding. He had told me about Ashley moving on the phone, and he was sad. From what Rosie had said, I gathered it was sudden, and he didn't get to say goodbye. I was pleased he had a new friend to play with. And I was proud of his actions.

"Good man. You should always stick up for people."

He nodded. "I sat with her at lunch, and she gave me a cookie. I wanted to give her a bite of my apple, but she said it was too hard since her teeth were gone. I am gonna ask Momma to give me a knife so I can cut it up next week and share."

"Maybe take a banana," I advised. "Or some grapes. I don't think your momma will give you a knife."

His eyes lit up. "Good idea, Asher! They would be easy for her to eat."

I ruffled his hair. This kid slayed me with his good heart.

We ate dinner, AJ not overly impressed with the shepherd's pie, but I was. I ate two large helpings, plus salad and bread. Then I ate four cookies, still warm from the oven, and drank a large cup of coffee.

"You won't be able to sleep tonight," Rosie admonished me.

I grinned and winked. "That was my plan."

I loved her blush. And the way she rolled her eyes as she picked up the plates. Pretending to be affronted but smiling at the same time.

We watched a movie, AJ marveling at the size of the screen. He was crazy for the big chair he sat in that had a cupholder and a wide arm to put the bowl of popcorn I'd made in the microwave. I was certain I had impressed Rosie with my skills when I made it for us, adding the butter with a flourish as I informed her I was a microwave genius. Her laughter was music to my ears.

I sat beside her on the sofa, a blanket over our knees. I turned on the fireplace, the flames dancing in the low light, the heat making the room cozy. She sighed in contentment, nestled against me, a bowl of popcorn on my lap, her head on my shoulder. At one point, I glanced down at her. She was asleep, her eyelashes resting on her cheeks as she slumbered. I looked over at AJ, amused to see he, too, had fallen asleep, one hand still in the popcorn bowl. I felt a rush of tenderness for them, plus the internal pride that they were comfortable and safe because they were here with me. The condo was warm, they were content, and somehow that was all that mattered. I let the movie end, then shut it off, easing from Rosie. I picked her up and carried her down the hall, frowning as she stirred when I laid her on the bed. "Go back to sleep," I whispered.

"AJ," she protested sleepily.

"I'll put him to bed."

She mumbled something incoherent, falling back asleep. I stood over her, brushing her pretty hair off her forehead, pleased that she trusted me enough to let me handle the task.

Then I returned to the living room and repeated the same thing with AJ, wiping his buttery fingers with a damp cloth, grateful Rosie had put on his pajamas before we started watching the movie. I turned on a night-light and switched on the monitor in case he woke up. I left another light on in the living room and headed to my room, stopping at the little voice I heard call my name.

"Ash-er."

I hurried back to AJ's bed. He was asleep, burrowed deep in his covers already. I brushed his hair back and bent to kiss his head. He muttered in his sleep, and I remembered his teddy bear, tucking it close to him. He let out a long sigh and made a contented sound in the back of his throat. I gazed down on him fondly. He had called me tonight, not Rosie.

I wanted to be there for him every night. To make sure he was safe and warm. That they both were.

I slipped out of his room and stopped in the doorway of mine, grinning. Rosie was a curled-up bundle under the blankets, reminding me of AJ. She was tiny and perfect on the large mattress. I got ready, slipping in beside her. I reached for her, and she came easily, resting her head on my chest, her arm snaked around me. I held her close, pressing a kiss to her head. I had longed for her to be here with me in this bed. To feel her pressed against me.

It wasn't how I had planned for the evening to end, yet strangely enough, it was even better. The little family I thought of as mine were with me. Sheltered, content, and happy.

It was all I needed.

CHAPTER FIFTEEN

ROSIE

I woke in the early morning, confused. The last thing I remembered was watching a movie with Asher and AJ. I vaguely recalled being carried and put to bed, Asher's lips on my forehead telling me to sleep and he would look after AJ.

Currently, I was draped across Asher's chest, the steady beat of his heart under my ear. He had one arm around me, holding me tight to him. I lifted my head, studying him in the low light. He had his other arm tucked behind his head, his face turned slightly. A low sound escaped his mouth every few seconds, his breathing deep and even. His hair was tousled, and his face was relaxed, his mouth pursing and releasing with his breaths. I carefully eased away, slipping from him, and I used the bathroom, then checked on AJ, who was sleeping hard, curled up in the middle of the bed, his blankets pulled tight around him and his favorite teddy in the crook of his arm.

Then I headed back to Asher. He had frowned in his sleep when I moved away, but he was flat on his back, still slumbering.

Well, most of him was. The comforter was tented, and I bit my lip, holding in my grin. Someone was up and ready to say good morning.

I carefully climbed in beside him, settling close. This bed was heaven, plush yet firm, and I had slept better than I had in months. That deserved a reward.

I slid my hand under the covers, then the waistband of Asher's lounge pants. He was hard and hot in my hand. Heavy.

He groaned in his sleep, his back arching at my touch, but he didn't wake up. I stroked him a few times, loving the quiet moan from the back of his throat.

Carefully, I pulled back the comforter and slid under the sheet. It was easy to move his pants down since they had loosened in his sleep and were already low on his hips. His cock sprang free, already glistening at the head. I engulfed him in my mouth, taking in as much as I could, slowly sucking. I felt it the moment he came awake, his gasp of air and the way he immediately threaded his fingers through my hair.

"Jesus, Rosie, what…"

The rest of his words were garbled and lost in his groan of pleasure. I flicked my tongue along his shaft, and he shuddered.

"Baby, what if AJ…"

Once again, his words were cut off with another groan. I sucked him deep, humming around him, and he thrust into my mouth, going deeper. I swallowed around him, and he began to pant and mutter, begging for more, pleading for me to stop, threatening me if I did. Whispering dirty words. Praising me. Pulling at my legs to bring me closer. He slid his fingers into my leggings, finding me slick and ready.

"Sucking my dick makes you wet, doesn't it, Rosie? You like my cock down your throat," he hissed. "Such a good girl, taking my cock."

I whimpered as he played with my clit. Softly at first, then in tighter circles that made me moan around him. He slipped a finger inside me, then two, using his thumb to keep a steady pressure and rhythm on my clit. I began to shake, the pleasure hitting me in waves.

"Come on my hand, Rosie," he commanded. "I'm going to come down your throat. Oh God, now, baby, *come now*. I can't—*fuck*!"

He filled my mouth, and I swallowed, my body locking down as a hot, intense orgasm burst through me. I was lost in a sea of sensation. His talented fingers, his hot release, his noises, my moans, the lewd act itself. Something I had never enjoyed as much as I was right now.

He stopped moving, his breathing harsh. I shuddered as the last of the pleasure dwindled, leaving me feeling listless and relaxed. I released him, laying my head on his stomach. He lifted the sheet, gazing down at me with a grin. "You must need some air, baby. Come up here."

He tugged me up, and I rested my head on his chest, his heartbeat still rapid and his breathing ragged.

"One hell of a wake-up call," he said.

"I agree."

He pressed a kiss to my head. "Morning, my love."

I looked up, feeling shy suddenly. He smiled, running a finger down my cheek. "God, I love that."

"What?"

"That after waking me up with my cock in your mouth and riding my hand, you can still blush. You are such a contradiction, Rosie Duncan." His gaze was tender. "And I wouldn't want you any other way."

We heard the sound of AJ jumping from the bed and rushing down the hall at the same time. Asher grinned. "Good timing." He pressed a kiss to my head. "Thank you."

I grinned back. "Same to you."

The morning passed in waves of happiness. Pancakes and coffee. Secretive looks and smiles being shared between Asher and myself. Stolen kisses as AJ got dressed. Whispered promises, dirty and sweet in my ear as Asher cupped me from behind while AJ worked on his Lego treasure, his voice low in my ear.

"I'm going to ravish you tonight, Rosie. You, me, that big bed. My cock inside you until you scream." He nipped at my lobe. "I won't even stop then. I'm going to make you come so often, you'll lose count."

AJ called me over, and I sat with him, piecing together a couple of bricks. Asher joined us, sitting behind me. *"You are such a good mother," he praised. "I love watching you with him." He rested his chin on my shoulder, observing AJ with me. "Would you want another one?" he asked, his voice soft.*

"With you?" I replied.

He drew in a fast breath. "Yes. With me."

I could see him with a baby. His care and patience while I was pregnant. The way he would love us.

"Yes."

"I already see it. You, me, AJ, and a little one. Maybe two." He kissed my neck. "Maybe three."

I had no words to reply.

We went for a walk, AJ between us, holding our hands. We swung him a few times, and he was excited when we reached the skating pond. Asher had gifted him a pair of skates, and he was anxious to get on the ice.

I sat on the bench as Asher laced up the skates for both of them, explaining patiently to AJ how he was going to teach him. I watched as they hit the ice, marveling how quickly AJ caught on. Even Asher was impressed. AJ managed to stand more than he fell, and he held on to Asher's hands, learning to find his balance and move his feet. I loved observing them while I sipped the coffee Asher had gotten for me. He wanted me to try, but I was leery and passed this time. My butt was sore enough from the slip on the ice the other day.

After skating, we went back to the condo and ate grilled cheese sandwiches and tomato soup. I loved how Asher appreciated everything I cooked, even something as simple as an easy lunch. He ate two sandwiches, a huge bowl of soup, and a handful of the cookies I had made last night.

He had wanted to order in lunch, but I said no. I knew he could easily afford to order in every day, but it seemed extravagant to do so when the fridge and pantry were filled with food.

"I'm in charge of dinner, then," he said. "No arguments."

I saw how AJ's eyes lit up, and I knew Chinese would be on the menu. But I didn't argue.

After lunch, Asher and I sat on the sofa as AJ built more Lego. He glanced out the window. "Can we go skate more?"

Asher laughed. "Sure, bud." He turned to me. "You stay here and relax. Read. Nap. Have a bath. Just enjoy a little me time. AJ and I will skate."

Before I could protest, he lowered his head to my ear, whispering, "It'll tire him out. Then we get tonight. *I* get tonight. I get *you*." He pressed a kiss behind my ear.

"O-okay," I stammered.

He stood with a grin, AJ jumping up in excitement. There was a flurry of activity, and then I was alone. The condo suddenly seemed vast. I filled the bathtub, not surprised to find that Asher had thought of bath products. I sniffed a few bottles, settling on a light citrus scent. Soon, the bathroom was filled with the fragrance, the steam gently wafting upward, beckoning. I slipped into the warm water, groaning as the heat surrounded me. I relaxed against the built-in pillow, sighing in pleasure. I couldn't recall the last bath I'd had where I could just relax. The one in the apartment was shallow and not comfortable like this, plus, with AJ, it was hard to find time for a leisurely soak. This was a treat.

One I intended to enjoy fully.

※

An hour later, I was back on the sofa, book in hand. Asher's office had a lot of books on the shelves, and he had a suspense one I had wanted to read. I made a cup of tea, and it sat beside me, the scent drifting to my nose. I was wearing one of Asher's sweatshirts and a pair of my leggings. His socks covered my feet. I was content, cozy, and sleepy. More content than I could recall being in years. The sun was still out, and a few flakes flew around outside. AJ was with Asher and no doubt enjoying himself thoroughly. I looked around, wondering what it would be like to live like this. A warm home, a fully stocked kitchen. A car to drive. A comfortable bed.

No bus. No budgeting every penny to make sure there was enough food. Saying goodbye to piles of thin, well-worn blankets when the temperatures dropped and the heating didn't work so well.

I shook my head to clear it. That sort of thinking was dangerous. I was grateful for what AJ and I had. I couldn't be envious of the things we didn't.

Clearing my thoughts, I rested my head against the soft fabric of the sofa, drifting. The sound of the elevator opening woke me, and I blinked, unsure of what I was seeing. I met a pair of familiar dark-brown eyes across the length of the condo, but it wasn't Asher and AJ. Instead, it was a woman, holding the hand of a little girl. They both looked at me quizzically, then the woman smiled. Widely.

"You *must* be Rosie."

Ten minutes later, I sat across from Asher's sister, Suzy. She had his eyes and smile, but her features were more delicate. She was tall like him, forward, and blunt. I liked her.

Bonnie, his niece, was sweet. She didn't have a shy bone in her body. She declared the cookies I set out delicious and informed her mother they had to get some. Then she spied the Lego being built and sat down in front of it, studying it closely.

"Does she like Lego?" I asked.

"Not as much as dolls, but she'll give it a go. Do you want me to tell her no?"

I shook my head. "AJ and Asher won't mind."

Suzy sat back, picking up her tea and taking a sip. She studied me over the rim. "You have my brother tied up in knots. Acting like a crazy man."

Before I could say anything, she grinned. "I like it. I have never seen him act like this. Out of control. Out of his depth. I can understand why. You're very pretty."

"Um, thank you?"

She grinned. "He is besotted." She tilted her head. "In love, actually, I'd say."

"Oh, no…ah…" I stumbled over my words.

She shook her head. "I know my brother. And it's in our nature. I fell for my husband in ten minutes. I knew I was going to marry him. Asher recalls my mom saying she fell in love with my dad from across the room. It only makes sense when Asher finally fell it would be hard and fast." She paused. "It's kinda fun to watch from afar."

I had no idea how to respond. She picked up a cookie. "Want some stories about when he was younger?"

That, I could get on board with. "Yes."

Twenty minutes later, the elevator doors opened and Asher and AJ walked out. Asher stopped when he saw me and Suzy. Bonnie streaked across the room, her arms outstretched. "Uncle Ash!"

He bent, swinging her into his arms and pressing a kiss to her cheek.

"Oh, you're cold!" she squealed. Laughing, he set her down, and AJ smiled at her.

"Hi. I'm AJ."

"I'm Bonnie. I like your Legos."

A commotion ensued as coats were discarded, boots kicked off, and the kids ran to the Legos. Asher came over, bending to kiss his sister.

"I wasn't expecting you," he said dryly.

"Obviously."

He stood beside me, placing his hand on my shoulder. He squeezed it gently. "I promised AJ hot cocoa when we got home."

"I'll make it."

"Great."

I stood, and he stopped me moving, his hand still on my arm. He captured my mouth, kissing me hard. "Want me to throw her out? I will," he said quietly. Suzy heard him, laughing behind her hand, knowing he was full of it.

"How rude," I said. "I like her. And Bonnie."

"We can keep Bonnie," he insisted. "She and AJ can hang. But this one is gonna be full of questions and not so subtle suggestions."

I patted his cheek. "We'll be fine."

He sighed. "Good thing her husband isn't around. He encourages her."

"James will be here in an hour. He wasn't going to come up, but when I told him your woman was here, he was all for it. Then Rosie invited us to stay for dinner. She said Chinese was on the menu."

"Dammit," Asher muttered, hanging his head.

I tried not to grin. "It'll all be fine, Captain Highliner."

His eyes went wide, and he spun toward Suzy. "You told her that?"

She waggled her eyebrows.

"I was seven!" he exclaimed. "I thought he was a real fisherman with his own boat, and I wanted to be like him!"

I chuckled. "So sweet."

He glared at Suzy. "No more stories."

We laughed, and I headed to the kitchen. "Too late, Asher. She's been here a while, and I got lots of dirt."

He sat down, glowering. "Not fair. I need extra marshmallows now." He sat up straighter. "And I have stuff I can tell about her too."

They started to squabble, and I laughed as I filled the pot with milk for hot cocoa. I had a feeling I was going to be laughing a lot this afternoon.

Suzy hugged me. "You have my number. Call me, and we'll get together." She glanced over my shoulder with a wicked smile. "I have lots more stories about my brother."

Asher stepped close, pulling me away from her. "She's busy that day," he said emphatically.

"We didn't choose a date."

"She's busy every day," he replied.

Suzy laughed, and James shook his head. "Give it up, Asher. They'll get together one way or another."

I hugged Bonnie goodbye. James was holding her, but she reached out and I couldn't resist. She was a delightful child, and AJ liked her. They played well together and after dinner watched a movie as we sat around talking. It was obvious she adored Asher, and he felt the same about her. He and James had sat on the floor cross-legged with them and worked on the Lego blocks, acting like kids themselves. Asher was a natural with children, and the thought of seeing him with a baby did something to my ovaries. I kept thinking about his words from the morning.

"Maybe three."

I had to avert my eyes when he glanced up, but his grin told me he knew exactly what I was thinking. He was thinking the same thing.

The elevator doors closed, and I looked down at AJ. "Time to get ready for bed."

"Okay." He scampered off, stopping at the edge of the living room. "I like it here, Momma. It's warm and has lots of room. I like the people. Especially you, Asher." Then he hurried away.

Asher wound his arm around my waist. "Do you like it here, Rosie?"

"It is lovely."

"Can you see yourself living here?"

His words made me tremble. He spun me in his arms, looking down at me, his gaze gentle.

"What?" he asked tenderly. "It surprises you that I would ask?"

"It's a big question."

"Would you think about it?"

"Asher, we're so new."

"We're *so right*. You fit me perfectly, Rosie. You and AJ. Look how easily you meshed with my sister and her family. How well suited we are. Eventually, we're going to move forward." He tilted his head. "My bed won't fit in your place, so this is far more logical." He lifted one eyebrow so I knew he was teasing.

"One step at a time," I whispered. "I have to think of AJ. I can't cause him upheaval twice."

He frowned. "Twice?"

I drew in a deep breath. "In case it didn't work out."

He frowned. "I have every belief it will."

"I need…" I swallowed, feeling overwhelmed.

He kissed my nose. "A little time. I understand. I'll show you how serious I am, Rosie."

"I know that. I… AJ…"

"I know. I know. But I'll prove it."

AJ came running out of his room, grinning. "I brushed my teeth, Momma!"

Asher swung him up in his arms. "What a clever boy. Isn't he clever, Momma?"

I ruffled AJ's hair. "He is."

"Asher is clever too. Right, Momma?"

I smiled looking at them. They both looked at me with so much love in their eyes. As if I was the center of their world. I had to blink away the emotion I felt building.

"Yes," I agreed. "Both my boys are clever."

They high-fived each other, and AJ looked at Asher. "Will you and Momma read to me again tonight?"

Asher set him on his feet. "Go pick a book, and we'll be right in."

AJ rushed off, and Asher looped his arm around my waist. "One book, then you're mine the rest of the night, Rosie. All mine."

I followed him into the bedroom, hoping the book AJ chose was short.

Really short.

CHAPTER SIXTEEN

ROSIE

The next few weeks, life was different. The office wasn't as great a place to be anymore, at least not for me. Ms. Wells loved to micromanage and everyone in my department felt the effects of her daily reports, but she was especially hard on me. She noted my comings and goings meticulously. I made sure to arrive as early as I could, and I never left a minute before four. I wondered bitterly if she ever accounted for the fact that I rarely took a break and ate my lunch at my desk. I kept my phone on silent and replied to Asher's texts while in the bathroom or when I ate my sandwich at my desk. He checked in on me every day without fail, his sweet words the only thing making me smile.

But as draining as the days were, the evenings made up for it. I never knew when Asher would appear. Sometimes, he was waiting when we got home; other times, he would show up after dinner or while we were eating. A couple of times, he was waiting outside, driving me to pick up AJ and taking us out to supper. The nights he had meetings, he always called to talk. He told me about his day, a new venture, or a large donation that pleased him. I missed him when he wasn't there. His comforting presence, his warmth and laughter—I felt their absence. He rarely stayed the night, but he took AJ and me to his condo on the weekends. It was like a mini vacation from reality.

One I was finding hard to return to.

I hated Sunday nights. So did AJ. Last night after we got home, he threw a tantrum. The first I had ever witnessed.

"I want to go back to Asher's," he insisted. "It's nice and warm. I have a big bed, and you smile when we're there. Call him and tell him to come get us!"

The temptation to do exactly that was strong.

Asher was careful not to overstep or go too far. But the difference in our worlds was so clear every time I stepped back into my small apartment after leaving his more luxurious space. It surprised me how comfortable I was there. How much it felt like home. *He* felt like home. How tempting it was to ask him to let us stay. Because I knew if I did, he would arrange it in a heartbeat. He had already added to AJ's room. A race car bed frame now stretched along one wall. New toys and toy box. Racing stripes on the walls, a soft rug on the floor for when AJ was playing. A big chair in the corner all three of us sat in to read a book at night.

Items for me appeared as well. A thick, soft robe and warm slippers. Luxurious bath and beauty products. Another big chair to curl up in and look out the window of the bedroom. Every type of cooking implement and ingredient I could think of to use in the kitchen. Blankets and pillows in the living room. Some new comfortable shirts and leggings appeared in the closet. A pretty, warm jacket I had yet to wear.

All added for our comfort, slowly turning the condo into a haven of warmth for us all.

But I had only known him a short time, and I still worried. It frightened me how much I was beginning to rely on him. How much I needed him.

My phone rang, bringing me out of my musings, and I frowned when I saw the day care number.

"Hello?"

"Rosie, it's Gwen from Happy Faces Day Care."

"Is AJ all right?"

"He's fine. But we're closing early due to the storm."

"Storm?" I repeated, standing up and peering out my door. My little office had no windows. I was surprised to see the heavy snow swirling around outside from the window across the office.

"Wow. They forecast a few flakes," I said, shocked.

"They updated it an hour ago, and now they're calling it the storm of the season. We're asking all the parents to pick up their kids. They're advising people to head home and get off the roads."

"I'll get there as soon as I can."

I headed to Ms. Wells's office, knocking on her door. I noticed a lot of desks were empty as I went past the other offices.

She glanced up, the perpetual frown on her face evident. "Yes."

"I have to leave."

"I beg your pardon?"

"The storm outside. I have to get my son."

She glanced at the clock. "You have two more hours until you can leave."

I shook my head. "I have to leave now. I have no choice."

"I said no."

Anger grabbed hold of me. "I haven't taken a lunch in weeks. Or a break. I'm not asking permission. Half the staff has already left. I have to get my son."

"I'll dock your pay a full day unless you work it."

"I'll report you to HR."

She shrugged as if she couldn't care less. "I have lots to share with them about your attitude."

I was done. "I have no idea why you dislike me so much, but do whatever the hell you want. I'm going to pick up my son now."

"You're fired."

I blinked. "What?"

"You leave, and I'm letting you go. Take your personal things, and don't come back."

I pulled off my pass and flung it on the floor. I rushed to my little office, grabbing the few things I had. A picture of AJ. A pencil holder he'd made me for Christmas. A couple of small items. I didn't have much. Ms. Wells stood in my door, watching me, her gaze cold and unfeeling. I ignored her, adding my shoes to the bag and pulling on my boots and coat. I felt ill and wanted to cry, but I refused to let her see.

I didn't touch the work on my desk or the computer. I pushed past her, and she followed me to the door. I blinked away the moisture building, grateful not many people were around to see this, and I walked out the front door, the icy cold temperature and the snow hitting me in the face.

I couldn't think of what had just happened. I had to get my son and make it home. That was my priority. I would call the owner of the company and try to tell my side of the story later. I would let my old boss know what had happened. Maybe he could help find me another job. I knew I could never work for that woman again.

Then I put aside all other thoughts and headed to the day care.

AJ and I stumbled into the apartment, cold and shivering. The temperature had dropped, the buses were crammed full, and we'd had no choice but to walk after two buses passed by us so full, people were jammed against the door. Normally, it was about twenty minutes, but with the snow and wind, plus the ice everywhere, it took longer. The apartment felt warmer than the outside but not by much. I hung our wet coats in the bathroom, and we changed into dry clothes. I found a note under my door from Mrs. Watson saying her son had come and gotten her and she would be staying with him. "Use anything you need," her note read.

Her dryer would come in handy, but first, we needed to warm up.

AJ huddled on the sofa, his eyes big as the heavy snow hit our window. I made a cup of coffee and sat beside him, needing a moment to gather my thoughts. I turned on the TV, the local news broadcasting the weather warnings and the city asking people to stay off the streets. Buses were no longer running, malls were closing, shelters were already full, and only essential services would be available.

I had tried to call Asher, but the call went straight to voice mail. He was in Kingston at an all-day meeting, and I wasn't sure he would make it back to town, given the weather. AJ and I were on our own.

I heard the sudden loud clunk that indicated the heating had gone out, and I shut my eyes. My head was spinning. I had lost my job, we had no heat, Asher wasn't around, and it was only AJ and me. It couldn't get much worse. I struggled to stay calm, deciding to push aside the job crisis until this one was over.

I plugged in the heater in the living room, deciding AJ would sleep with me out here so we could both stay warm. I heated some soup and made sandwiches, the routine helping to soothe me. We had gone through winter storms before and been fine. We would be again.

After we ate, I handed AJ a cup of cocoa and a plate of cookies I had made last week and sat beside him. The lights in the apartment flickered, the TV died, and suddenly we were thrust into darkness.

"Momma?" AJ asked, sounding scared.

"It's okay, baby. We lost power for a few minutes. It'll be back on soon," I assured him. "I'll light a couple of candles."

Once they were lit, I set them on the coffee table and added another blanket over us. I checked my cell, not surprised to find I had no service. I had a cheap pay-as-you-go, and at times, it was unreliable. This was such an instance. I pulled AJ close and kissed his head.

"We'll just wait for the power to come back on, baby."

"Okay."

As time passed, I longed for Asher. If he were here, I would feel so much better, but I couldn't get hold of him. This storm had caught us all by surprise. I imagined him in a small motel in Kingston, pissed off he couldn't reach me, upset that he wasn't with us. He would know what to do.

I wondered if the whole city was without power, and I stood and peered out the window. I could see lights in the distance, so I knew it was probably the street or maybe only this building.

The power would be back soon, I told myself, cuddling beside AJ again. Using the candlelight, I picked up a book, and read to him, not surprised when he fell asleep, a heavy weight pressed against me.

Alone, the worries filled my head. No heat. No power. Nowhere to go. I had little cash on me, and I had no idea if ATMs were working or how badly the storm was affecting the city. I carefully eased away from AJ and searched the cupboard, finding the small, battery-operated radio I had. The temperature in the apartment was dropping quickly, and I fretted, wondering how long we could stay here, but unsure where to go.

I wondered if I took AJ and went to Asher's building if the doorman would let me in. We always entered with him through his private entrance, although the doorman had seen us leave together to go to the park. I thought of calling Asher's sister to see if she could help me by contacting the manager there, then I recalled my phone wasn't working.

I was stuck.

I rubbed my head, willing myself to stay calm. I had to make it through the night and hope by morning things were better. The news on the radio was bleak, the announcer saying more snow and ice were expected. Temperatures were still dropping. They advised people to stay off the roads, stating traffic lights were down all over town and electrical outages were affecting some areas.

I shut my eyes, my fear taking hold.

Then I heard it. Heavy footsteps coming down the hall. A knock at my door and a voice I was desperate to hear calling my name.

"Rosie! Open the door—it's Asher."

I raced to the door, stumbling around furniture, flinging it open.

Asher filled the doorway. "How…?" I gasped.

"Thank God you're safe," he said, pulling me into his arms.

I didn't care that his overcoat was cold. All I felt was the safety of his embrace. His scent surrounded me, calming me.

"How are you even here?" I asked.

He shook his head. "I'll tell you later. I'm overstepping right now, and you're going to let me. Do you understand?"

"Yes."

"Then get our boy and your things." He shook me slightly. "I'm taking you home."

ASHER

I cursed as I stumbled up the stairs to Rosie's apartment. When I pulled onto the street, I wasn't shocked to see her building in darkness. A lot of streets were that way, the storm affecting the power. Knowing she and AJ were upstairs sitting in the cold and dark, alone and no doubt worried, was what kept my eyes on the road and my speed even as I drove back from Kingston, ignoring the warnings not to be on the road. The Hummer Suzy had teased me mercilessly for buying was perfect for this weather. The heavy body and the wide tires ate through the snow. My attempts to reach Rosie on the phone failed, and I knew the cell systems were faltering as well as power in many places. I couldn't get through to Suzy either, so I concentrated on my driving, my only goal getting to Rosie and AJ.

The streets were deserted, abandoned cars littering the roads. I parked in front of her building, leaving the vehicle locked and running. The door lock to her building wasn't engaged, and I was grateful the stairwells weren't secured since the elevator wasn't working. When she opened the door, the look on her face told me I'd made the right call in getting here. I could feel the cool air of her apartment and felt the tension in her body as I held her.

"Pack what you need for AJ," I said to her. "I'll grab some things for you." I glanced to the sofa. "He can sleep through anything, can't he?"

"Yes."

"Don't wake him up. I'll carry him down in blankets. We'll take his coat."

"Asher," she said, pausing.

I cupped her cheek, feeling the coolness of her skin. "What, my love?"

"Thank you."

I bent and kissed her. "I'll always come for you, Rosie. Now get your stuff so I can get you warm."

Twenty minutes later, I had them in the Hummer. Rosie was in my overcoat, her wet outer garment still hanging in her bathroom. I made her leave it, planning on getting her a new one. Overstepping and I were about to become best friends.

I wasn't going to let her and AJ do without any longer. I had been patient enough.

The car seat I owned was in one of my other vehicles, so I laid AJ on the back seat, managing to get a seat belt around him. He barely stirred. The two small bags Rosie brought were tossed on the floor. I lifted Rosie into the passenger seat, fighting against the wind that threatened to slam the door on me, then hurried to the driver's side and slid in. I cranked up the heat for all of us, grateful the vehicle was already warm. Rosie held her shaking hands over the vents. I peeled off my gloves, doing the same thing. Even outside for only a moment, I was chilled.

"Can we get to your place?" she asked, nervous.

"Without a doubt."

I eased back onto the road, driving slowly. We barely spoke on the trip, and I sighed in relief as we got to my building, the garage door closing behind us and the lights on the parking level still glowing.

"You have power," she said.

"And heat. How long was yours out?"

"About three hours. Maybe more. The heat before that. My cell didn't work either."

I gathered AJ in my arms, and she grabbed the bags. Upstairs, she followed me into AJ's room, and we tucked him in. He stirred, his eyes opening. "Asher," he muttered sleepily.

"I'm here. You and your momma are safe. You're back in your big bed, bud. You sleep well, okay?"

He made a little noise of contentment, already slipping back into sleep. I made sure his teddy bear was tucked close.

I took Rosie's arm, heading to the primary bedroom. Turning on the shower, I stripped off her clothes, then did the same, pushing her into the warmth. I followed her, wrapping her in my arms and holding her until the shaking stopped and her body warmed. I needed to hold her as much as she needed to be held. I had been so worried I wouldn't be able to get to her. That she would be on a bus that broke down or unable to get home. I feared the power outage the radio talked about, certain it would affect her older building. All sorts of terrible scenarios had played through my head on the drive.

That she was safe and here helped me relax.

Until I realized she was crying. Rosie never cried.

"It's okay, my love. I have you. AJ is safe. Everything is fine."

"I got fired today," she wept. "Because I left to get AJ."

Fury tore through me. "Wells?" I asked.

"Yes."

"We'll figure it out." I tilted up her chin, meeting her tear-filled gaze. I hated to see her green eyes clouded over with fear and worry. "You will be fine. You have me, and I won't let anything happen to you or AJ. I'll take care of you. I promise."

I could see her struggle. "I know you're independent, Rosie. I love that. But it's okay to accept help from someone who loves you and only wants the best for you," I said, holding her gaze. Letting her see the adoration in my eyes.

She blinked. "You love me?"

"Yes."

"You. Love. Me."

"And AJ."

She flung her arms around my neck, sobbing hard again. I held her and let her cry. She needed the release. She'd had to be strong for so long, and today was the proverbial last straw. I rocked her, letting the heat and my closeness soothe her. When her tears stopped, she rubbed at her eyes, staring up at me.

"I love you too," she whispered. "So much, Asher. You're incredible, and I feel so much, I can't even express it."

I bent and kissed her. "Good. Then together, we'll figure everything out. You're not alone anymore, Rosie. Never again."

She nestled into me, and I smiled, finally relaxing.

They were here. They were safe.

And she loved me.

CHAPTER SEVENTEEN

ROSIE

I woke up feeling hot. Bundled in so many blankets I felt like a burrito. Asher was gone, his side of the bed cool, so I knew he'd been up for a while. He obviously wanted to make sure I was warm without him. I preferred his hot skin next to mine, but it was still nice to wake up and have my first thought not of being chilled.

I sat up, looking around. A glance at the clock told me it was past ten. I never slept this late.

Then again, I was rarely home on a Tuesday.

The other thought absent was the dread of going in and facing Ms. Wells. Untangling myself from the blankets, I padded over to the window, opening the blinds. It was still snowing, the world outside covered in white, the tree branches laden with snow and ice, bending under the weight they carried.

I got ready, dressing in leggings and a cozy sweatshirt. Asher hadn't packed a lot, but I could make do. It was only for a few days.

The thought of that made me sad, but I tamped down the feelings. I was here now.

I found Asher and AJ stretched out on the rug in front of the fireplace, the flames dancing behind the glass. Between them was the checkerboard, and they looked thoughtful as I crouched between them.

"Good morning."

I received two enthusiastic responses. AJ was thrilled to be back at the condo and with Asher. He talked and grinned for five minutes.

Asher waited his turn, then drew me close and kissed me. "Hello, my love. You look better."

"I feel better. Lazy."

"No. Long overdue. I made coffee."

I stood and stretched. I saw how Asher's gaze followed the hem of the sweatshirt lifting and exposing my skin. His eyes gleamed, and I shook my head. "Behave."

I got a cup of coffee as AJ jumped to his feet. "I won! I beat Asher! Momma, I hardly ever beat him!"

Asher stood, laughing, and shook his hand. "Good game."

AJ nodded. "You too."

Asher ruffled his hair. "Go get dressed. I'm gonna talk your momma into making pancakes."

AJ scampered away, and Asher came into the kitchen. I poured him a cup of coffee, and he sat at the counter.

"Pancakes?" I asked with a smile.

"And sausage," he said with a decisive nod. "I took it out of the freezer for you."

"How helpful."

"I know." He studied me. "You slept well. I'm pleased."

"You rather wore me out."

He'd made love to me twice before I fell asleep, once hard and fast in the shower and once in the bed, slowly, sweetly, making me come twice.

He grinned. "My favorite job."

My smile faded at the word, but he shook his head. "I spoke with my lawyer. Wells had no grounds to fire you. It's being handled."

"Handled?"

"Sam is friends with the owner of your company. He called him this morning. You are free to return to work. Ms. Wells will not be there." He took a sip of coffee. "If you want to go back. If not, there is a nice severance package for you."

"I have to work."

He lifted his eyebrows but said nothing.

"I do," I insisted. "Rent, food, clothes. They all cost."

He nodded.

"What about her?"

"Yours wasn't the only complaint. It was by far the most serious. Turns out she is the daughter of a friend who called in a favor. Her résumé looks awesome, but it's all a pack of lies. She's great at manipulation. He is 'moving her along.'"

"Oh. Good. I don't know why she disliked me so much."

"Because you were up for her position, and she knew it. She wanted you out of there so you couldn't show her up."

I gaped at him. "I had no idea. I'm not qualified…" I trailed off.

"Your old boss thought you were. He thought you were the perfect person to take his place. He recommended you." He smiled. "She disliked what you represented. A threat."

Her dislike made sense now. I didn't like it, but now I understood it.

"The office is closed for the rest of the week. You can work from here if you want, or you can take the rest of the week off—your choice."

"Wow."

"I have connections, and I will use them to make your life easier." He looked fierce. "I will do anything to make your life easier."

I blinked and set down my coffee. "I think I have pancakes to make."

He slid off the stool and rounded the counter. "Too much?"

"I'm not used to it, I suppose. Being cared for. That's my job with AJ."

"I can help with that, but you are mine to care for." He kissed me, holding me tight and commanding my mouth until I was lost to everything but him. "Mine," he repeated. "Got it?"

"Loud and clear."

"Good." He dropped another kiss on my nose, rubbing it affectionately with his. "Now, make me pancakes, woman. I'm depleted."

I grabbed a bowl, smiling.

I was rather depleted as well.

The snow finished falling late that night. The next evening, I watched the plows still hard at work with the long task of clearing the roads from the floor-to-ceiling windows of Asher's condo. The wind had died, but it remained cold. All day, the sun had glinted off the snow, looking pretty but dangerous. It was treacherous with the hidden ice and the below-normal temperatures. They were still asking people to stay home and off the streets.

I had managed to get through to the super in my building, but he told me that the heat was still out. The electricity had come back about an hour before I called. *"It's cold, Rosie,"* he said. *"If you have a warm place, stay there. I'll let you know when it comes back. And I'm worried the electrics will shut down again. Stay safe."*

I hung up, knowing I had to move. Joe and his wife did their best, but if the owner of the building wasn't willing to fix the main issues, what they could do was patchwork. I couldn't keep living with a small space heater and a prayer.

I sighed as I looked out at the snow-covered city. I feared for those homeless. I was grateful not to be one of them. Yet I worried.

Asher came behind me, his reflection a tall shadow that hovered over me. "You look very serious, Rosie."

I shook my head. "Just looking at all the snow. Where will they put it all?"

"They have dumping places, plus a couple of the stations use melting machines. Some goes down the sewers, and the rest is piled at corners and on boulevards."

"I don't remember ever seeing this much snow before."

He hummed in agreement, pulling me back to his chest and wrapping his arms around me.

"There is a huge amount."

"Did you get hold of Suzy?"

"Yes. They're all fine. Hunkered down and safe. She was relieved to find out you were here with me. She was worried."

I patted his hand. "I'm relieved too."

He held me tighter. "Not as much as me. I can't stand the thought of you cold, scared, and on your own."

"I've done it for a long time."

"Not anymore."

I stared out at the white-covered city. But I would have to. I had to go back to the apartment and figure out my life.

"What?" he asked, spinning me around. "What do you mean, go back?"

I sighed, realizing I had muttered my thoughts out loud.

"It's where we live, Asher. Today was lovely. I'll stay tomorrow too if that is okay, then we have to go home. I have to figure out what is going on with my job, make sure everything is okay at the apartment, and keep going with life."

I had been thoroughly spoiled the past couple of days. Napping, eating, watching movies. Reading. Comfortable and safe. It had been wonderful. Amazing. But it was time to get back to reality.

"You can't."

"Pardon me?" I asked, confused. Why was he so upset?

He paced in front of me, back and forth, his steps fast, his face like thunder. He stopped mid-pace and met my eyes. He was determined. Serious. I suddenly realized the businessman had appeared.

"Do not ask me to take you back there."

"All right," I said quietly. "I'll take the bus."

He gripped my arms. "You cannot go back and live there."

"Asher, I have no choice. It is what I can afford."

"You do have a choice."

"Asher, if this is about—"

He cut me off with his mouth on mine. He kissed me senseless. Until I was clutching his shoulders, kissing him back with the same intensity he was devouring me with.

He pulled back. "*That* is what this is about. You aren't going back there because you and AJ are staying here with me." He shook me gently. "Don't you see, Rosie? This is where you belong. With me. Where I can see you. Feel you. Where I know you're safe. I can't begin to think of you back there in that cold little apartment, wondering and worrying if your lights will go on. If you have heat."

"We've made do before."

Again, he shook me. "You don't have to 'make do' anymore. Ever."

"Asher, it's so fast. You can't possibly think this is a good idea."

He leaned close. "It's the best idea I have ever had."

"You're overstepping."

"I'm aware. But I'm not stopping."

"Your sister—"

"Agrees. She can't believe I haven't moved you in already."

"AJ—"

"Can be taken to day care every day and picked up. By me. You. Someone I hire. He loves it here, so you can't use him as an excuse."

"I'm not trying to find excuses. I'm trying to point out…" I waved my hand, trailing off. I wasn't sure what I was trying to point out. Then I remembered my argument.

"We've only known each other a short time. What if we're not compatible?"

He hauled me back to his chest and kissed me again, his tongue doing things to my mouth that should be illegal.

"Stop it." I slapped his chest. "You're clouding my head."

He pressed his forehead to mine. "We are compatible. We were meant for each other. That is why I went to the store. That is why you named your son Asher. He hid that day because that was what was supposed to happen. I was meant to find you. You were meant to be mine."

I searched his gaze, seeing only truth and longing in it.

"Asher," I whispered, frightened. Scared he was right, terrified he was wrong.

"Describe your life to me in two words," he said, his gaze intense.

I frowned at the abrupt shift in conversation. "Hard. Rewarding."

"Because of AJ?"

"Yes. He is worth all the struggles."

He nodded. "Ask me."

"Okay, describe your life in two words."

"Desolate. Solitary."

I felt my eyes widen. "What?"

"I've always held back from everyone. Even Suzy and Bonnie. I kept a little piece of myself locked away. But I can't do that anymore. Not with you. And I realized every time you walk out that damn door, I hate it. I loathe it. I had no idea how lonely I was until you came into my life. How empty my world was. I had everything money could buy and nothing my heart needed to live." He paused, swallowing. "Don't leave, Rosie. Stay with me. Make this your home. Our home. When you and AJ are here, that is exactly what this place is. Home."

"Asher," I began, my voice thick.

"I love you. I love you both. I don't want to be without you. I want you here when I come home. I want to know you're safe. I want to be the one to take AJ to school and pick him up. I want us to be a family. I want to build a family with you. Stay here with me and make it happen, Rosie."

My head was swimming with his sweet words. He slipped an arm around my waist, tugging me close. He pressed his lips to my forehead. "I want to look after you. Both of you. Nothing would make me happier."

"I have to work, to pull my weight," I protested.

"Let me carry it for a while, Rosie. Lean on me, and let me show you how good life can be. Let me spoil you," he murmured against my skin. "Marry me and make me the happiest man on earth. Stay." His sigh was a warm breath across my forehead. "Please."

I tilted up my head. "*Marry you?*"

"I want it all with you. Marriage, babies, love. I want you forever."

"I love you."

He smiled. "Is that a yes?"

I stared at him.

He ran a finger down my cheek. "I told you that I was your unspoken Christmas wish, Rosie. But you know what? You are my *life* wish. Everything I wanted, everything I needed but had no idea how to ask for. Please—" he bent, his mouth brushing mine "—make my wish come true."

I flung my arms around his neck.

"Yes."

EPILOGUE

FOUR MONTHS LATER

ASHER

I glanced at my watch, seeing it was almost three in the afternoon. I had a meeting with my personal accountant. She was a new hire, extremely efficient, and very tough on my expenditures. She also looked after my company expense reports and seemed to take great delight in questioning my submissions. I enjoyed our biweekly sparring.

As soon as the meeting was over, it would be time to pick up AJ. He was a highlight in my days now. Always happy to see me, full of stories and laughter. Then tonight, I was taking my wife out on a date. I kept Maureen's nannies busy with overtime, using them at least twice a week for date nights. AJ loved it—especially one of them. George was his favorite, the two of them bonding over dinosaurs and Legos.

A knock on my door brought me out of my musings. "Come in," I called.

She walked in, bringing with her a thick file, a calculator, and a stern expression. She sat across from me, crossing her legs, setting her files on the edge of my desk. "Mr. Hart," she greeted me.

I couldn't help but stare at her. Dressed in a pale green silk blouse and black pencil skirt, she was extremely sexy. Her hair was up, wispy tendrils around her ears and neck. Emerald earrings glittered in her lobes. Her wedding rings sparkled in the sunlight, the diamonds catching the light.

I should never have hired her—she was far too much of a distraction to me.

But one I loved having around.

"Mrs. Hart," I replied in a low voice.

She pursed her lips, making me smile.

"May I remind you we are at the office?" she said tartly. "That is not an office voice."

Rosie insisted on proper behavior during business hours. I liked to throw the rules out the window on a regular basis.

I stood, rounding the desk. I bent over her chair, resting my hands on the arms of it and trapping her there. I stared down at her. "I'm aware," I murmured. "But you are too sexy today, Rosie, my love."

"Behave," she said, but her voice was breathless.

I bent and captured her mouth, kissing her deeply. She whimpered, wrapping a hand around my neck and holding me tight. I enjoyed the closeness, the way her soft scent wrapped around me. The feel of her mouth under mine. The taste of her.

I drew back and dropped a kiss to her nose, then sat in the chair across from her. "How was your day?"

She blinked, patting her hair. "Good. It was good."

"Ready to go get our boy?"

"We're not done yet. We haven't even started."

From the look of the sticky tabs on my expense report, I had a feeling I was in for a good tongue-lashing. I settled in to enjoy it. I did love it when she chewed me out.

"Let's begin, then. I want to finish, go home, get AJ to bed, and finish something else."

I smirked as she opened the file, her cheeks flushing with color. I loved the fact that I could still make her blush.

"Business first. You cannot claim the car you bought me as a business expense."

"Why? It's for you to use for business."

"Because you insist on a driver or driving me yourself, Asher. You can't write both off."

I waved off her concern. "Then strike it."

"It was an unnecessary expense personally as well. You should return it."

"It's not a scarf, Rosie. It was a gift. You're keeping it. You won't drive any of my cars, so I got you one you are comfortable with."

She snorted. "I'd be comfortable with a Mazda or Hyundai. I don't need a Mercedes SUV."

"I thought you did. Case closed. Next."

"The business trip last month was anything but business."

"I met with some people."

"Accidently. For drinks." She eyed me over the file. "Not a scheduled meeting. And you talked zero business. I was there."

"I meant to," I protested. "But you looked so fucking sexy in that little sundress. It was hard to discuss business while trying to make sure my dick didn't explode out of my shorts trying to get to you."

It had been a fabulous break. Rosie, me, a private villa. Sun, sand, and time together. We hadn't had a vacation since we got married. Our honeymoon was wonderful but brief. Then Suzy and her family flew down with AJ, and we met them in Florida and did Disney World and a cruise. It was a belated birthday gift for AJ as well as a family trip. It had been one of the happiest times of my life. When we came home, I started the adoption process to make AJ mine officially. He already was in every other sense.

I still loved it when I heard him call me Dad.

But last month, I had needed my wife alone, so I'd chartered a plane and flew us to the Bahamas. I shook hands with a few people. It was sort of business.

She blinked. "You can't—"

"Take it out, then," I chuckled. It was all my money, so I didn't really care. "Next."

"The chair in my office."

"Office furnishings."

"Only because you broke it while having sex with me in it."

I waved my hand. "No one knows that. It stays."

She huffed. "I'm unsure on the flowers you send me weekly."

"I put some in the reception area as well. That is a real expense."

"Fine."

"Do whatever you want, Rosie. Leave them, include them. It's all the same to me."

She closed one file and opened another. "Now, your personal expenses."

"Are fine."

"You're spending more than you have in the past on a consistent level."

I began to laugh. "Rosie. Of course I am. I'm finally living. I'm spending it on you. AJ. *My family.*"

"You're spoiling us."

"Then my plan is working," I replied. "Spoiling you makes me happy."

"You should stay on a budget," she argued. "Plan for the future. For unexpected expenses."

"I'm certain I can cover any 'unexpected expenses.'" I leaned close. "I make more in an hour than I spend in a week, Rosie. You know that." I ran a finger down her cheek. "I know money still makes you nervous, but baby, we have a lot of it. More than we'll ever spend, even if I bought you a car every week. If I never brought in another dollar, you will never have to worry about money again."

"Still, I drew up a budget." She handed me a file, the look on her face nervous.

I sat back, opening the folder, running my finger down the columns. All well-thought-out, all generous, although I noticed she had put a restriction on takeout meals, which made me grin. I liked to order in dinner and save her the work. She had done this before and I always refused, but I did like to humor her. She had added a "spur of the moment gifts" column with such a low number I blinked. I wouldn't be paying attention to either of her "suggestions."

I tried not to laugh at her new additions and notes, frowning in confusion at one set of notes.

Reasons for budget planning:

Loss of wages.

Unexpected additional household expenses, such as: baby clothes, diapers, more childcare.

I was about to ask her why she had noted those items, when it hit my befuddled brain.

I froze, my gaze flying to meet hers. She held a small white tube in her hands that she passed to me. Two lines and the word "Pregnant" were in the small window.

Pregnant.

Rosie was pregnant.

Instantly, I was out of my chair and on my knees in front of her. "Really, my love?"

She nodded. "Really."

"Say it, Rosie. Tell me."

"I'm pregnant." She drew in a deep breath. "You're going to be a daddy again."

I wrapped her in my arms, holding her. Dropping hundreds of small kisses on her face. Pressing my mouth to hers, my tears mixing with hers. AJ was my son in every way that mattered, and now we were having a baby together.

"I'm about to overstep," I warned, pulling back, cupping her face. "And you're going to let me."

"Okay."

"No more working. You're staying home with this baby. With all our babies. I'm going to be around more. I can work from the condo. And we need to buy a house. With a yard. James and I can build a swing set. Can it be a girl, Rosie? I'd like a little girl."

She sniffled a little. "I can't do much about that, but we'll find out soon enough." She swallowed. "I don't want to work after the baby is born," she confessed. "I had to with AJ because I had no choice, but this time—"

I cut her off. "You never have to work again. I'll look after all of you. I'm going to be overstepping all the time now."

"I know you will."

"And you'll let me."

"Yes."

I wrapped her in my arms. A baby. We were going to have a baby.

This was the best meeting of my life.

CHRISTMAS THE FOLLOWING YEAR

I held my son, cradling him in my arms. Only eight months old, Brandon was remarkably advanced. At least, I thought so. He was crawling, trying to walk. Jabbering nonstop at times. I pretended to understand everything he said. I thought he was pretty much perfect, aside from the crying and the pooping. He did more of the latter, it seemed. Rosie handled it far better than I did. On the nights he fussed, I sat with him nestled on my knee in a huge chair I had bought Rosie that she loved to read in. As I discovered one night, it was extremely comfortable, and I used it whenever I could. We talked for hours, me imparting wisdom, him grunting and gnawing on his fist as he absorbed everything I told him. AJ often joined us, and Rosie would find the three of us asleep, a blanket over us, one boy on each side of me in the large chair.

From the moment we had dragged in the tree, Brandon had been fascinated. The lights mesmerized him, and Rosie had started laying him down for his nap by the tree. He would stare at it, slowly falling asleep with the glow of the lights. Rosie played music all the time, and the sounds soothed him as well.

Rosie came in, carrying his bottle. She handed it to me with a smile. "How is he?" she asked, bending down and brushing a dark curl off his head.

"Good." I patted the spot beside me, and she snuggled in with a sigh. "Tired?"

She rubbed her stomach, looking thoughtful. "This one is even more active than Brandon. I didn't think that was possible."

"You didn't think it was possible to get pregnant again so quickly either."

She sniffed. "You and your overactive libido. And determined sperm."

I chuckled. "Fertile Myrtle, I think the doctor said."

"Whatever it is, we are a dangerous combination. No sex for a year after this one."

"Shit," I muttered. "Don't even joke about that."

She laughed, pressing a kiss to my jaw. I captured her mouth and kissed her. "I can't keep my hands off you for that long, Rosie. Ever."

She settled her head against my shoulder.

"So, another boy," I mused. We had decided to find out this time. Rosie chuckled. "Yep. Your sister has girls. You have boys."

"Maybe the next one."

She tilted up her head. "Um…"

I grinned. "I bought us a big house, Rosie. We need to fill it."

"It might be easier to move."

I laughed, laying my hand on her stomach. "Whatever you want, baby. If you're happy, I am."

"I love you."

I pressed a kiss to her head. "I love you."

Christmas four years down the road

I woke up, my hand reaching out for my wife, already sensing she wasn't there. I sat up, glancing at my phone. It was four a.m. We had gone to bed past midnight, getting everything ready for Christmas Day. Why was she already up?

I threw off the blankets, pulling on my robe, and went in search of her. I peeked into AJ's room, the boy who was trapped between being a child and growing into a kid, but his room was empty except for him. I stopped to pull up his blanket, unable to stop smiling when I noticed his favorite teddy from years ago tucked by his pillow.

I checked on Brandon, but he was sleeping, curled up under the blankets of the race car bed AJ had let him have once he decided he was "too old" for it. No kicking off the blankets for our son. He liked being warm too much.

Next door, Carter slumbered in his bed, a thumb in his mouth, a stuffie clutched in his other hand. I stopped for a moment, gazing down at him. Brandon had my dark hair and his mother's green eyes. Carter was the opposite. Rosie's hair color was evident in the curls, although it was a darker hue than hers. His eyes were my dark brown, and according to my wife, so was his impatient temperament. Our child liked to overstep on a daily basis. I could only imagine him as a teenager. I had a feeling gray hair was in my future far sooner than I ever expected.

I shut his door, listening. The house was silent, but downstairs, I saw the flicker of the fire reflecting on the walls, and I headed that way, thinking Rosie had come down to add something to the tree or maybe her back was hurting and she was resting on the sofa. She liked to lie there.

I found her in front of the tree, staring up at it. Her long hair hung down her back, the flames highlighting the red curls. She was in a fuzzy robe, a pillow under her butt. How she got down, I had no idea. She mostly waddled and perched places these days. I wondered if she was stuck.

I crouched behind her, wrapping my arms around her, settling my hands on her tummy.

"Rosie, baby, it's the middle of the night. Why are you down here?"

"I couldn't sleep."

"Are you okay?" I rubbed her swollen belly. "Is our girl keeping you up?"

We were having a girl this time. I tried not to gloat about it, but it made me incredibly happy thinking about it. After Carter was born, we decided three was enough. Pregnancy was hard on Rosie, and I hated seeing her struggle. But as we discovered, one way or another, no matter what we did, we ended up pregnant—although this time, it took a few months longer than with the boys. When I found out it was a girl, I was ecstatic. I loved my boys, but I had always wanted a little girl who looked like Rosie whom I could spoil.

Rosie leaned back into me. "No, she is quiet tonight."

"Getting ready for her grand entrance in a couple of weeks."

"I suppose."

Her voice was different. Thick.

"Rosie, my love, what is it?"

"It's snowing outside."

I glanced out the window. "Yes, it is." I looked over her shoulder, seeing something clutched in her hands. "What is that?"

She held it up. "The scarf you gave me that first Christmas."

"You still have that?"

"Yes. You gave it to me because you were worried about me being cold." Her voice caught. "You were the first person who cared about me in so long."

I held her a little closer. "Feeling sentimental?" I asked, pressing a kiss to her head. I loved her tender heart.

"I guess. Remembering how alone I always was all the time. How frightened that I would do something and not be a good parent to AJ or lose my job and mess us up. Not be able to provide for him. I was always scared."

"You never showed it. You always were so brave."

"I felt it. And then you came into our lives, and suddenly I wasn't scared anymore. I had you. You and your generous heart and incredible love. You were larger-than-life. I kept thinking you'd disappear, but you kept getting better. Your love was—is—so wonderful."

"Rosie," I murmured, overcome by her words.

"For the first time that I could recall, I wasn't afraid. Because of you. This scarf represented so much to me. I could never get rid of it. Every time I see it, I think of meeting you. How my life changed." She leaned back and looked up into my eyes. "And the life I have now is so wonderful, so full. All because of you. You're a wonderful husband and a fabulous father. I love you, Asher Hart. With everything in me. You are my world."

I shook my head in wonder at her words. "You brought such joy to my life, Rosie. You have given me so much I didn't know I was missing. Your love and goodness. Your sweetness. I fell in love with you because of *how* you loved. Completely. Without reservation. I love you right back." I bent and kissed her.

She nestled back into me, and we sat looking at the lights on the tree. She stiffened then melted back into me with a small sigh and a low laugh.

"I have a last-minute Christmas gift for you."

I chuckled. "I don't need anything."

"You're gonna want this." She looked up. "My water just broke. I think your daughter decided it was time to meet you." Her eyes went wide as a contraction hit her. "Now."

"Holy shit."

Two hours later, I held my daughter. Tiny fuzzy red curls were all over her head. I swore I already saw freckles on her skin. She'd entered the world screaming loudly, demanding attention, and angry at leaving the warm nest she'd been encased in for so long. She didn't stop crying until they placed her in my arms.

I fell as hard and as fast for her as I did her mother. All our children inspired a protectiveness that I never knew I had in me. But what I felt for our daughter was ten times that fierceness. I glanced over at my wife, who was watching us with sleepy eyes. We'd barely made it to the hospital this time. I had hardly gotten a gown and cap on and she was crowning. Moments later, Daphne appeared, and I hadn't stopped smiling.

I stood, sliding her into her mother's waiting arms. "Wait until the boys wake up and find out they have a sister for Christmas." I tucked a curl behind Rosie's ear. "Are you certain you want to go home later today?"

She smiled. "There is nothing they can do for me here, and I hate hospitals. Besides, I don't want to miss dinner."

I chuckled. "We could do it tomorrow."

"No. Today is Christmas. I want to be with my family."

"Highly unusual, the doc says."

"I don't care. Even he agreed I'd be fine at home. So, I'm going."

"I'm going to overstep and spoil you. Make you stay in bed and be catered to."

"Whatever. Just take me home."

I bent and kissed her. "Okay, my love. I'll take you home this afternoon. As long as you sleep now. Suzy has the boys, and James will bring the girls over once they wake up."

I took Daphne from her and sat down. "We'll be right here."

"Are you going to let anyone else hold her?"

"Of course," I scoffed. "In a month or so."

Rosie smiled. "I love you."

I stood and kissed her again. "Thank you for my daughter, Rosie Hart. Merry Christmas, baby."

"Merry Christmas, Asher."

She fell asleep, and I stared down in fascination at my little girl.

Our daughter.

I had Rosie. A great, full life. Three sons. The girl I'd longed for. My little alphabet, as Rosie called our kids. I now had ABC and D. I was good with that.

"Merry Christmas, little one. Welcome to the world. I've been waiting for you, and I can't wait to show you everything."

A tear splashed on my hand, and I realized I was crying.

My final wish had come true.

And life was perfect.

WRAPPED IN LOVE

CHAPTER ONE

CALLIE

With a weary sigh, I flipped the sign to *Closed*, turned off the outside light, and pulled down the blind. I looked around the store, shaking my head at the chaos left behind by the last-minute shoppers. They didn't buy very much, but they certainly made a mess. I would have plenty to do to keep myself busy over the next couple of days until I reopened after Christmas.

I stepped away from the door and was almost to the counter when the sound of furious knocking on the glass startled me. I turned to see the silhouette of a man in the glass, his hand never ceasing in its rapping.

"Callie James? Mrs. James, are you there? Please be there!" a deep, low, husky voice pleaded.

"Hello?" I called, not recognizing the voice.

"Oh, thank God. Please, Mrs. James, I need you."

I approached the door with trepidation. "How can I help?"

"My parcels, all my parcels were lost. Please!" He knocked again. "Mrs. Cooper sent me!"

Mrs. Cooper?

Frowning, I flicked on the light, pulled up the blind, and stifled a gasp at the tall man in the window. Wild, thick hair glinted chestnut in the illumination from above. Broad shoulders and a face that made my heart beat faster were framed in the glass. The man staring at me was ruggedly handsome. A sharp jaw was set off with scruff. Full lips smiled, dimples on both sides giving him a mischievous look. But it was his eyes that captivated me. Under thick brows, they glowed green. As green as the evergreens that wound around the wrought-iron railing of the store. They were tired, pleading, but gazed at me with such warmth, it flooded my entire body. Before I realized what I was doing, I had slipped the lock and pulled open the door.

"Your parcels?" I asked, confused. Had he ordered something from me?

He stepped in, bringing the cold with him. Snow dusted the shoulders of his heavy wool overcoat, but his hand was warm as he captured mine within his grasp.

"Thank you for opening the door. I beg of you for help."

I moved back, allowing him into the store. Never letting go of my hand, he shut the door behind him and introduced himself.

"My name is Shane Foster. I'm traveling to see my family over in Brighton. Do you know it?"

Brighton was a lovely town about two hours away. "Yes."

"It's been a day. My five-hour trip has been almost thirteen, and it's not over. There's a huge storm by my sister's, so I had to stop here for the night. When I was talking to her, she told me my Christmas parcels never arrived. All my gifts for the family!"

I stared at him, mesmerized. His face was so expressive when he spoke.

"The closest mall is an hour in the other direction from my family, and they'll be closed by the time I get there. I asked at the inn, and Mrs. Cooper said there was a chance you'd still be open. She said if anyone could help me, it would be her *'Callie-dear.'*"

I had to smile at his imitation of Sheila. It was perfect.

"Your light clicked off just as I was parking my SUV. I took the chance you might take pity on me, extend the Christmas spirit, and allow me to borrow a few minutes of your time to shop for my family." He paused, taking a breath. "Please?"

I couldn't resist his open, honest plea. It wasn't as if I had anywhere to be, and if I could help him, then it was a good thing.

His hand tightened. "Please."

I didn't know why I was hesitating. He already had me. "Of course. Please look around."

He lifted my hand to his mouth, his breath floating over my skin and making me shiver. His eyes met mine, warm, melting pools of green. "Thank you."

When his lips touched my skin, I swore I felt an electric shock jolt through my body. His grip on my hand tightened, then he stepped back, releasing me. Oddly, I missed his touch right away.

He shrugged off his coat, laid it carefully over the banister by the door, then turned the lock, and drew the blind at my request. One late-night shopper was enough. Looking around, he ran his fingers through his hair, causing the already unruly strands to lift and ruffle. He offered me a wide smile. "Can you please give me some advice?"

"How many people are you looking for?"

"Six children, six adults, and a cat." His voice turned teasing. "Any of those you can help me with would be much appreciated."

I arched my eyebrow. "I think you're going to need more than a few moments."

He instantly looked chagrined. "Am I keeping you from your family and friends?" He shook his head. "What a stupid question. It's Christmas Eve—of course I am. If I could grab a few books, I'll be on my way. The adults can wait until the parcels arrive."

I reached out, placing my hand on his arm. "I was teasing, Shane. I have nowhere to be, and I'm happy to help you pick some things for your family."

"Your, ah, husband won't be upset?"

"I'm not married. It's Miss James, actually. But you can call me Callie."

"Oh. Boyfriend?"

"No."

"Um, girlfriend?"

I shook my head, trying not to laugh at how adorable he was.

"Well, it's 2024. I felt I had to ask."

"All that is waiting is a casserole in the oven, a bottle of wine, and an old cat named Jake, who does nothing but sleep, fart, and lick his, ah, long-lost mistletoe." I winked.

A wide smile made his eyes crinkle. "Well then, Miss James, I'm at your mercy. Lead the way."

As we walked around the store, I pointed out the various sections. "That area is books, both adult and children's. This section is local artists—I have some lovely leather goods, stained glass, and scarves. My own line of handmade soaps and bath essentials is over there, and at the back are toys and games for all ages. Even pets. Handmade chocolates and goodies are in the far corner. I have a line of custom-made jewelry by the cash register if you're interested."

"I'm interested in it all. May I browse for a little bit?"

"Of course. I was going to get a cup of coffee while I do some closing-up items. Can I get you one?"

"That would be most welcome." He captured my hand again, squeezing it. "Thank you, Callie."

My cheeks flushed under his intense gaze. "You're welcome."

I brought him a coffee, adding the cream he said he liked. I placed a few cookies I'd had out for sampling on a napkin, handed them to him, and then left him to browse. I did a quick tally for the day, trying not to stare at him as he roamed around the store. He was intent, tilting his head, studying things as he sipped his coffee and gobbled down the cookies. He held up the last one.

"Do these come by the dozen?"

I peeked over at the basket. "Yes, there are some left."

"I'll take them all."

I chuckled as I grabbed the last three packages and put them on the counter. Good thing I had set a few cookies aside for myself already. He drained his mug, setting it down on the counter beside mine.

"Who made the stained-glass pieces?"

"I did."

"As well as the bath, ah, things?"

"Yes."

"I'm impressed. Did you bake the cookies too?" he teased.

I felt myself blush again. What was it about this man that made that happen?

"Yes."

He lifted a finger, tracing it over my cheek. "How unexpected," he murmured.

He moved past me to the books, leaving me to wonder if he meant the cookies, the stained glass…or me.

Shane Foster had to be the most generous man ever to enter my shop. After perusing the books, he returned with a dozen children's books, then went back, adding three huge tomes to the pile. "This is amazing," he stated. "You have books my brothers and father will love. Well, one brother and one brother-in-law. And I prefer giving the kids some books. I love reading. What about you?"

"It's one of my favorite pastimes."

His gaze was intense. "Excellent to know." He reached behind me, snagging another cookie. "Now, I need a toy for each of them— and a few games for the family."

I helped him pick something, listening as he talked about his nieces and nephews. Love dripped from his voice as he described them. Elly and John's identical twin girls. Alan and Tracey's three sons and one daughter—who, Shane laughed, "might as well be another boy—she can take them all." He also added candy for each of them, insisting all gifts from Uncle Shane had to be equal.

"What about the parcels that will come? Shouldn't you just buy something small for them to open tomorrow?"

"No—I like these better. I bought what their parents had sent me from a list. They can have those as extras later." He clapped his hands. "Now, the ladies. There, I need the most help. And I think I've decided on some of those gloves for the guys along with their books."

At his request, I made up a basket for each woman of my various soaps, lotions, and bath bombs. He chose a piece of stained glass for his mother, saying how much she would like it in her sunroom, then picked a set of earrings for both his sister-in-law, Tracey, and his sister, Elly. He took his time, choosing carefully with every item. Never once did he look at or ask a price. I kept a mental tally in my head, knowing he would purchase more with this transaction than I had made all month. It was mind-boggling.

Finally, he smiled. "I think I'm done."

I moved a box out of the way. "All right."

He looked down, stopping. "Wait." He tapped the glass. "What is that?"

I pulled the item his long finger pointed at out of the case with a sad smile. "This is my favorite piece in the shop."

He lifted the bracelet, the petite emeralds and diamonds catching the light. It was delicate, the loops all hand-cut and scattered with the tiny jewels. "It's absolutely beautiful."

"The woman who made all the jewelry did that as an experiment. She used gold and the very best gems she could, wanting to see if there was a market for it here."

"It didn't sell?"

"No. I've had it for over a year. She was retiring, so I bought out everything she had. She only sends me a few pieces now and then that she does as a pastime."

"Emeralds are my mother's favorite gem."

"Because of your eyes?" I asked before I could stop myself.

He grinned, those mesmerizing eyes dancing. "I have my father's eyes, so probably, yes. She says they're what made her fall in love with him."

"Oh," I breathed out. "I could see that."

"I, myself, prefer dark eyes. Deep, chocolate eyes you can lose yourself in."

Cue my blush.

Shane chuckled and laid the bracelet on the glass. "I'll take this as well, please."

"Would you like me to put the stained glass back?"

"No."

"Shane, this bracelet is $1700."

"That's fine." His lips twitched. "Does it come with a box?"

"Yes. A very pretty one."

"Sold. Now, once we finish here, do you suppose there is a store around still open that has gift wrap and tape?"

I glanced at the clock, shocked to see he'd been in the store for well over an hour. "No. Everything will be closed."

"I thought so. I'll have to try to get it all done at Elly's."

I pointed at the sign behind me. "I gift wrap."

"All of this?"

"It's part of the service."

"Callie, it's way past seven now. I can't ask you to give up more of your Christmas Eve wrapping my gifts."

Just then, his stomach growled, and he laughed, embarrassed. "Sorry. I haven't eaten since breakfast, and the cookies barely took the edge off. Ring me up, and I'll let you get on with your evening. Hopefully, I'll find a diner still open and get something to eat. Maybe Mrs. Cooper has some paper stashed somewhere at the inn. I'm sure I can charm her."

He smiled as he said it, yet it felt to me like, for the first time, his smile was forced. For some reason, I didn't want him to leave, and I had the feeling perhaps he felt the same way. I drew in a deep breath and gathered my courage.

"You're not asking, I'm offering. And, I have an idea."

"Oh?"

"You aren't going to find anything open around here tonight. If you don't mind a simple meal, I have one ready in my oven—I live behind the shop. We could eat, then I can help you wrap your gifts. It sounds as if you've had a long day, and maybe a little downtime would do you some good. And I would enjoy the company." I paused and smiled. "If you're okay with that."

"Are you serious?"

"Um, yes?"

"You're offering me a meal, more of your lovely company, to help wrap my purchases, and you're wondering if I'd be okay with that?"

"You'd have to help with the wrapping."

He flexed his fingers. "I'm great with corners. And a whiz with tape."

I laughed at his humor.

"I would love that, Callie James." He held out his credit card with a wink. "Ring it up so you know I'm good for it, then please feed me." He licked his lips, his eyes locking with mine. "I'm starving."

I had to turn away. The low timbre of his voice and the way he looked at me made me think he meant for more than food.

CHAPTER TWO

SHANE

I'd had a shit-tastic day. I grabbed the early flight, got rerouted, only to be stuck on my second connection when a storm blew in. I cursed at the hordes of people milling around the Ottawa airport. My first Christmas off in three years, the first Christmas my whole family would be together in five years, and I got stuck in an airport?

Fuck that. I needed to get back to the Toronto area.

I headed to the row of car rentals and yelled out, "Who has a four-wheel drive SUV for rent? I don't care about the cost!"

Four hands went up. I went with the one who added a wave for good measure, and within thirty minutes, I was on the road. I was going slowly in the poor conditions, but I was moving. Using the Bluetooth device, I spoke to Elly periodically, assuring her I would arrive later that night. All was going okay until she called to say another storm system was crashing down on them, and they were all worried about me driving in it. She suggested I get as close as I could, then hole up in a hotel for the night and come later the next day when the roads were cleared, even though it would be Christmas Day.

"We'll put everything off a few hours, Shane. We want you to be safe. We have the whole week."

It made sense, but it still pissed me off. I got even angrier when she told me the parcels I had sent never arrived.

"They were supposed to be there three days ago," I insisted.

"I think they're backed up. There have been so many storms. It's fine," she soothed. "We get you—the gifts will come later."

I drove another hour until I knew from the weather reports I was getting I couldn't go any farther. I pulled into the small town of Simcoe and was lucky enough to find an inn. It was older but still well-kept and, most importantly, had a vacancy sign. The elderly woman was chatty, and when I asked, she gave me the information about the only place I might be able to find some presents at the late hour.

"Callie is usually open until six." She scribbled down directions to Toys and Treasures. "If you hurry, you should make it."

I got turned around but finally located the quaint store, parking with minutes left to spare, only to see the light switch off. Desperate, I knocked, calling her name.

"Callie James? Mrs. James, are you there? Please be there!"

I was expecting a woman around Mrs. Cooper's age. That wasn't what I got.

A woman, my age or younger, peered at me from behind the glass. The lights caught the red of her mahogany hair that tumbled over her shoulders, and her deep, soulful brown eyes were nervous as she regarded me. She was short, with a lacy white blouse that fluttered as she moved. Her skirt was a festive red, scattered with glitter. Even her hair sparkled. She looked like an angel.

Which was exactly what she turned out to be when she let me inside. My own personal angel. She allowed me to browse; she fed me cookies and made me coffee. She listened to me chat about my family. The truth was, I knew almost instantly what I was going to buy. The store was well laid out and the items were all unique, but I found I wanted more time with her, and after her soft confession that she had nowhere else to be, I took full advantage of it. I was thrilled to learn she was indeed a Miss, not a Mrs. I was intrigued by this woman and her sad, expressive eyes. They called to me, igniting a feeling I had never experienced before today. I was desperate to know why she had nowhere to go and nobody to be with on this holiday.

I followed her to the back of the store, where she unlocked a heavy-looking door and let us into her home. It was a large, cheerful room with a couch and an overstuffed chair in front of a small fake fireplace where a lazy cat slumbered. He opened one eye, looked at me, then stretched, farted, and went back to sleep. I chuckled at Callie's admonished, "*Jake!*"

The kitchen was along the back wall, and the room smelled delicious.

"The bathroom is through my room over there, if you want to freshen up," she offered.

"Thanks."

Her room held a queen-sized sleigh bed and a simple dresser. The bed was a jewel of colors—reds, greens, golds, plaids, stripes—a symphony for the eyes. It was like Christmas in linen. I used the bathroom, sniffing at the soap. I recognized it as one of the ones I had chosen as a gift.

I hurried back, finding Callie already placing a heavy pan on the small round table. A bottle of wine was open, and she had set two places.

"Help yourself. I'll be right back." She brushed past me, and I couldn't stop myself from reaching out to halt her. It was as if as soon as she was close, I wanted her closer. Her eyes widened as I leaned down and brushed a kiss to her cheek. "Thank you."

I felt the warmth of her skin heat up as she bit her lip and whispered, "You're welcome," then hurried from the room.

I sat down, looking around. It was a comfortable room, filled with pictures and pieces of Callie. Stained glass hung in the windows, reflecting the lights from outside and the snow still falling. A tiny tree was by the fireplace, the twinkling lights soft in the room. I frowned at the mere two small parcels under the tree. She deserved more than that. Maybe she would go somewhere tomorrow to celebrate. I certainly hoped so. For some reason, the thought of her alone made my chest ache.

She returned, with her lacy blouse and festive skirt gone. In their place was a pair of fuzzy pants and a sweater. I chuckled at her slippers decorated with snowmen.

"You didn't start," she scolded gently.

"I was waiting for you."

My voice sounded odd, almost as if I had just issued a proclamation. She bit her lip and lifted my plate, placing a large square on it.

The aroma hit me full force, and I had to hold myself back from grabbing the plate and devouring whatever it was. I waited until she had served herself before I picked up my fork and cut into the dense offering. I chewed and swallowed, my eyes drifting shut in appreciation.

"What *is* this?"

"Mexican chicken lasagna. It has tortillas instead of noodles."

"I think it's the most delicious thing I've ever tasted."

She laughed softly. "Or you're starving."

"Both, I think."

She lifted the wine. "Would you like any?"

"One glass."

She poured, and I lifted my glass to hers. "To the greatest treasure I found tonight."

She looked at the table, flustered, the color in her cheeks deepening again. I wasn't sure the last time I had seen a woman blush. Where I lived, and in my line of work, it was pretty rare. I found it highly attractive—at least on her.

I smiled and returned my attention to the food on my plate.

CALLIE

He wasn't lying when he said he loved the casserole. He ate three huge pieces, then devoured a half dozen more cookies with a cup of coffee.

We never stopped talking during dinner. He asked question after question, finally laughing when I told him it was my turn.

"What do you do for a living, Shane?"

"I'm a doctor. A pediatric specialist."

"Really?"

"I love kids. I work in Calgary, and I've drawn the short straw the last three years and haven't been with my family during the holidays. With other people's commitments, it's been five years since we were all together."

"That's why the gifts were so important."

"My mom always made Christmas so special, and I know how sad she's been every year when one or more of us isn't there. I wanted this year to be great for her." He traced the edge of the table with his thumb, looking sad. "We had a scare with her this year and almost lost her." He looked up, his eyes serious. "But she's okay, and I did everything I could to get here this Christmas. We all did."

I covered his hand with mine. "You'll get there. I heard the storm is going to lessen overnight, and it's only a short drive. You'll make it."

He flipped his hand, encasing mine. Once again, I felt that strange surge of warmth. "Thank you, Callie. For the meal, your company, your help—everything."

The air around us grew heavier. Warmer. His eyes darkened, and my breathing picked up. He leaned forward slightly, and I stood quickly. "We should get those gifts wrapped. We can bring them back here where there is more room."

He blinked and cleared his throat. "Right. Good idea."

I hurried down the hall, Shane behind me. At the counter, I grabbed his bill to hand to him, then widened my eyes. "Um, Shane?"

"Yes?" He glanced at me from the pile of boxes he had in his hands.

"Your credit card was declined."

His face blanched. "*What?*"

I bit my lip and giggled. "Ho-ho-ho."

"Not nice, Callie. I think that just put you on the naughty list."

He was laughing as he went down the hall again, and my goal was accomplished. We were back on easy terms.

As for the naughty list? I was sure I was already on it as I watched his ass move in those tight jeans.

He was good with corners. Meticulous, even. It was strange how easy it was to be with him. He teased and tossed ribbons at me. Critiqued my corners compared to his. Tsked over my lack of proper usage of enough tape. In turn, I called him anal, which made him laugh, informed him the amount of tape he used made the gifts Fort Knox-worthy, and told him his ribbon-curling skills sucked. He picked up gifts, comparing them, then agreed and announced that, between us, we were awesome partners. Slowly, the pile of presents disappeared as the time passed, and I sorted them into bags, adding in the baskets, cookies, and candy. I made sure the earrings for the women, plus the bracelet he purchased were in a separate bag and slipped it inside one of the larger ones, showing Shane where they were.

I glanced at the clock, shocked to see it was eleven. My usual lonely evening had not only flown by, it had been the nicest one I'd had in a long time.

"How long have you been here?"

"Most of my life."

"You lived here? At the store?"

"Not this store. Another one."

Shane stood and stretched. "What's upstairs?"

"My studio."

He held out his hand. "Will you show me?"

I led him upstairs, and he walked around, looking at the different areas. He hummed over some stained-glass pieces I was working on, sniffed some new bath lotions I was mixing up, then paused at my newest workstation. "You make jewelry?"

"I'm learning."

He held up a leather cuff I had embellished with silver. "This is awesome. Wow."

"It's a work in progress." I moved closer and snapped it on his wrist. "It has a flaw. See?" I pointed. "Right here. I have to learn the technique better."

"Sometimes, the flaws are what makes something perfect, Callie," he whispered.

"Maybe."

He went to unsnap the cuff, and I reached out, halting him. "No. I-I'd like you to have it."

"Really?"

"Yes. Thank you for sharing Christmas Eve with me, Shane."

His eyes darkened again, and before I could stop him, he reached out and pulled me into his arms. His scent washed over me, filling my head. I fit under his chin, and his arms enveloped me totally. "Thank you, Callie. For everything."

He stepped back but kept his arms around me. "Why are you alone? Why aren't you surrounded by family and friends on Christmas?"

I smiled sadly. "My parents split when I was young. My mother walked away from us when I was nine. She got tired of small-town life and being the wife of a shopkeeper, as she called him. He ran the general store in town—his parents had run it before him. He liked living in a smaller town where he knew everyone and everyone knew him."

He nodded, encouraging me to continue.

"My dad was pretty helpless, so I learned to cook, do housework, and look after him. I helped out in the store after school and on weekends."

"He never remarried?"

"No. I don't think he ever got over my mom. We never heard from her again, but I think he always hoped she would reappear."

"It sounds like you had to grow up overnight."

"I suppose. Anyway, I went to school and graduated, then went to college. I wanted to be a teacher. I loved kids. I loved teaching."

"I know how that feels." He grinned.

"I got a call one day. There had been a fire, and my dad was hurt. I came home right away. Dad was in the hospital. The strain of the fire was too much, and he had a heart attack." I paused, tamping down the sadness. "He never really recovered. I looked after him for the next few years until he died."

Reaching out, he grasped my hand. "Callie, I'm so sorry."

I was quiet, lost to the memories in my head. "The store burned to the ground. There was literally nothing left but ashes. The insurance paid for the building, and I kept the property but used the money to look after him." I sighed. "When he died, I sold the land. There was no need for a general store anymore. People drive to bigger towns for what they want at a better price. Dad had barely been scraping by, and it made the most sense."

"And this place?"

"While he was ill, I needed to stay busy. I started making my soaps and stained glass, and I sold them at little fairs and markets. I really enjoyed doing it."

"You're very good at it."

"I had allowed a building company to put up this model home here on the edge of the cleared property of the general store. They did well for a bit, but then interest fell off. When I sold the land, I had been able to have it divided, and I kept this piece and bought the model home from them. They finished it off inside so I could have my little store and live here. Things had started to pick up in Simcoe, and I thought a place like this would do well. We were getting lots of tourists, and the townsfolk needed a place where they could pick up gifts that were unique."

"And?" he prompted.

"I did well the first year. Not so well the second, and this year has been bad." I smiled slightly. "Your shopping spree was more than I made all month, Shane. Thanks to your lost parcels, I can stay afloat for a few more months."

He frowned. "And then?"

I sighed. "Then I start again. It's the same every year. But I suppose that's life, right?"

CHAPTER THREE

SHANE

Instantly, I wished I had spent more. I wanted to do something, *anything*, for this selfless, wonderful woman.

"Start again?" I asked, wanting to know more about her.

She smiled and shook her head as if she knew what I was thinking. "I close in January and February. I learned that lesson. I'll make more inventory, replenish stock, and get ready for the next season. Unfortunately, I can't afford more than one part-time person in the summer when I'm busier, so it's me all the time."

"What about school?"

"I would have to start over. I simply didn't have the heart for it anymore." She sighed. "I guess I gave up. I'll be just like my dad and live my life here in Simcoe."

I hated her words, and it bothered me to hear them. "But you're alone."

"Christmas is a time for family, Shane. I have a few close friends. Tomorrow, I'll volunteer at a shelter a few towns over. Mrs. Cooper and a couple of other widows come with me. We spend the day being busy, and on Boxing Day, we cook a big dinner at the community center. Everyone brings potluck, and we have a great meal."

The words were out before I could stop them. "You deserve more than that for Christmas. You deserve to be spoiled and loved."

"I am loved, just in a different way. You have your family—what a gift that is. Treasure them. Spend as much time with them as you can. Visit more often." Tears glimmered in her eyes. "One day, you won't have them, and you can never go back."

"I do treasure them. I love spending time with them…"

"Why do I sense a but?"

I sighed, perched my hip on the table beside me, and scrubbed my face roughly. "I love my family. I really do. But I get tired of being the odd man out. Always the fifth wheel. My parents have each other, Elly and John are incredibly close, Alan worships Tracey. Don't get me wrong, I'm thrilled they're all happy. It's just, at times, it's hard to take being surrounded by so much love and not have the same thing."

"You don't have anyone in your life?"

"No. I've spent so much time on my career that everything else just fell by the wayside. Now that I finally have a life outside of work, I haven't met anyone significant." I lifted my shoulder. "I've dated, but I've never found that person who makes me want to change my life for them, you know?"

She nodded. "Yes. I know what you mean."

"I have no idea why I told you all that. I've never said it out loud to another living person." Leaning forward, I tucked a strand of hair behind Callie's ear. I met her gaze—her warm, understanding gaze. "Somehow, you make it okay for me to be honest."

"We all feel like that at times. There were times I resented my dad —hated him, even, for being sick and making me change my life plans. But the feelings were just the result of being sad or lonely. They always passed, and I loved him. Just the same as you love your family."

"Yes," I breathed out, amazed at her wisdom. "I'm surrounded by people, yet I feel so…lonely. I smile and laugh and do everything I can so no one knows, yet inside I'm…"

"Sad?"

"Yes." I clasped her hand. "You too?"

"Yes."

Her eyes captivated me. They were so beautiful. Once again, I had to reach out and touch her. "Why do I hate the thought of you being lonely or sad?"

"I don't like the thought of you being that way either."

I pulled her in, and she slipped between my legs, her hands clutching my shoulders. "Can I say thank you properly, Callie?"

"Yes," she whispered in a shaky voice. A shiver ran down her spine as I slipped my hands up her neck, cupping the soft skin of her cheeks.

Slowly, I leaned in, pressing my mouth to hers.

Our lips touched.

Time stood still.

I yanked her close, sliding my tongue into her mouth, and groaned as she sighed, her breath filling my lungs. Our tongues danced, tasted, and teased. I stroked her cheeks with my thumbs, tilted her head, and deepened the kiss. She fit perfectly against me, her softness molding to my harder form, as if she was made to be in my arms. She moved her hands restlessly along my upper arms, clutched my shoulders, then moved them down and wrapped them around my waist. She burrowed her fingers under my shirt, touching the warm skin of my back. I grunted into her mouth in approval. I wanted to feel her hands everywhere. I slid my hands down her hips and gripped her ass, pulling her closer, feeling the heat of her through the fuzzy pants she wore. I glided my hand down her thigh and, with a tug, hitched her leg high, bringing us even closer.

She whimpered into my mouth, pressing her fingers into my skin, sliding them under my waistband. Her touch left a trail of fire on my skin. "Callie," I groaned.

"Shane," she responded on a soft breath.

"I want you," I stated honestly. "I want you on that pretty bed downstairs surrounded by the colors of Christmas. I want you surrounded by me. And it's been a long time since I wanted that."

Our gazes locked and held. We both knew what I was asking. One night. I would be gone tomorrow and heading back to my life in · Calgary once the holidays were over. But I wanted this night with her more than anything I could remember wanting. There was something about this girl—a draw I couldn't fight. One I didn't want to fight.

"Please," I breathed out. "Don't send me away. Let me stay with you. Just this one night, let me be a part of something good in your life."

"Yes," was her quiet reply.

I held out my hand, and she led me to her room.

Dim light cast shadows on the walls. Her bed shimmered in the glow. Callie's eyes were wide and dark, but for the first time since I had met her, they weren't sad. Desire and lust filled her gaze, matching the beat of need I was feeling for her. We came together, our mouths fused, our bodies pressed together. Clothing fell away, my eager fingers finding purchase on her silky skin. Under me, she was pale and soft against the vivid holiday colors of her bedding. Her hair was spread out—a shimmering wave of chestnut against the pillows.

I discovered all the sweet secrets of her little body. The indent of her waist, the subtle flare of her hips. The lushness of her breasts.

The way she tasted under my tongue. Felt under my touch. Sounded as she lost herself to pleasure. Her touch made me shiver, the way she stroked and caressed me. Gripped at my waist as we moved. Wrapped her legs around my hips, our bodies aligned perfectly. Kissed me as if she couldn't get enough of me.

I couldn't get enough of her.

I groaned my orgasm into her neck. She cried out my name in the quiet of the room. We rested together, wrapped up in the ecstasy of the moment. Callie lay on my chest with her head nestled under my chin. I ran my hand up and down her back, gently tracing the bumps and ridges of her spine.

"Not how I expected my Christmas Eve to end," I teased, pressing a kiss to her head. "I thought I'd be alone in my room or stuck in a snowstorm somewhere."

"I'm glad you're here."

"Me too." Then I chuckled. "I'm glad you remembered the Christmas condoms you had in stock."

Callie giggled, and I felt the heat of her blush as she pressed her face to my chest. It had been almost comical when we'd realized neither of us was prepared. I hadn't bothered since I was going to see my family, and Callie had confessed she hadn't been with anyone for a long time, so she didn't keep any on hand. Then her eyes had grown round, and she'd dashed from the room, returning with a handful of Christmas condoms.

"I ordered these on a whim!" she exclaimed with a silly grin. "I got them as joke gifts for some of my quirkier customers. Some of them are even glow-in-the-dark!"

I grabbed one. "Joke's on them," I growled and ripped it open. The bright red and green colors made me laugh, but they worked. God, did they work.

And I planned to use as many of them as I could.

She peeked up at me, her expression mischievous. "We should try a glow-in-the-dark one to see if it works."

"Why, Miss James." I grinned and rolled over, taking her with me, pinning her under my chest. "You little hussy. Are you propositioning me?"

"It's strictly for quality assurance purposes," she insisted, her eyes dancing. "I take my job as a shop owner very seriously."

I threw back my head in laughter. "Insatiable," I muttered as she tilted up her hips, her warmth brushing against my growing erection.

She hummed in agreement, flinging a leg over my hips, making me hiss in pleasure at the feel of her.

I had a feeling we were both insatiable.

And we only had one night to quench that thirst.

Hours later, I finished brushing the snow off my rented SUV. I was exhausted—even more so than I had been the night before. I hadn't been able to keep my hands off Callie all night. It seemed she felt the same way. One of us would begin to drift, and the other would start with the touching, and then another condom got used.

Five in total. I was quite proud of that number. I'd take the exhaustion—my body had never felt as alive as it had the past hours spent with Callie.

It came to a screeching halt when my cell phone chirped a message from my sister telling me the weather had cleared enough that the roads were open, but another storm was coming so I needed to leave as soon as possible. Callie smiled sadly when I showed her the message, slipping from her bed to get ready to leave.

"We need to get you organized."

I grabbed a shower, dressed, and met her in the shop. My gifts were ready, Callie bundled up in a parka. She followed me out, handing me a thermal mug emblazoned with *Toys and Treasures* on the side, filled with coffee.

"To keep you awake."

"Thank you."

"You have to get your things at the inn?"

"No, I never even went to my room. Mrs. Cooper will think I met with some sort of accident."

Callie shook her head. "I'll tell her you were here and decided to try the drive. I'll say you forgot your gloves and sent me a message via the store site, saying you had arrived and would arrange for your gloves to be picked up. Leave me your key, and I'll see she gets it."

"Another thing I owe you for," I murmured, handing her the key.

"You don't owe me for anything, Shane. You paid for your gifts, we had a wonderful night together, and handing a key to Mrs. Cooper isn't a favor. But I do have one to ask of you."

"Name it."

"Please text me when you arrive so I know you got there safe." She handed me a business card with a cell phone number on the back.

"I can do that."

We stared at each other under the lone light of the parking lot. The wind scattered snowflakes around Callie's face, resting on her messy hair and flushed cheeks. Her lips were swollen, her eyes tired, but she was unbelievably beautiful. I felt a strange ache in my chest at the thought of leaving her. An unexpected thought occurred to me, and I spoke it before I could stop myself.

"Come with me."

She blinked. "What?"

"Come to my sister's with me. Have Christmas with my family. With me." I indicated her store. "I don't want you to be alone here. Not today."

Not any day, the voice in my head added.

"I can't do that."

"Why?"

"What on earth would you say—this is Callie? We fucked last night, and I brought her with me for some more holiday fun?"

I slammed the door of the SUV and gripped her arms.

"I didn't *fuck* you last night. Don't you dare call it that." I shook her slightly. "It was more than that. You know it. I know it. I'm asking you to come with me and let me spend more time with you." I lowered my voice. "As for my family, I'll tell them I met a wonderful woman and asked her to spend the holidays with me. The simple truth."

"To what end?" she asked, tears filling her eyes, her false bravado disappearing. She hated this as much as I did. "You want to get to know me more so you can fly back to Calgary and out of my life? It already hurts to say goodbye to you, Shane. If I have more time with you, I'm not sure I could."

"I don't know," I admitted. "All I know is I don't want to say goodbye yet. My family would make you welcome, Callie. In fact, they'd love you." I yanked her close. "A few days with me is all I'm asking. A chance to explore whatever it is I feel between us. We'll figure out the after later. Please."

"You're crazy," she whispered, touching my cheek.

I kissed the end of her nose. "About you, yes. I've never felt this draw to someone. Ever. Come with me."

"I'm not packed. Or showered. I have no gifts—I can't go to someone's house without gifts!"

Hope soared in my chest. "You have a whole store behind you. Pick something for the kids if you want, but I have all the stuff I bought. You can grab a shower and throw a few things in a bag. I'll wait. Whatever you forget, we can get or you can borrow from Elly. She has an entire store in her closet. Trust me. While you're getting ready, I'll call her."

She hesitated.

"Don't ask me to leave you by yourself today, Callie." The thought of her lonely on Christmas hurt me. "If you say no, I'm staying here."

"You can't do that."

"Then I guess you have no choice."

She sighed, and I knew I had won.

"I'll be ready in twenty minutes."

I kissed her hard. "You have thirty. Merry Christmas."

She smiled up at me, her lovely eyes sparkling in the overhead light. "Merry Christmas."

Then she hurried away.

But knowing she'd return made me look up at the wintery sky and smile.

I called Elly as I walked toward Callie's store.

"Are you on your way?" she asked by way of a greeting.

"In thirty minutes. I hope you have room for one more."

"You brought someone with you from Calgary? You never said—"

I interrupted her. "No. I met her yesterday."

"*Her?*" Elly's voice was shocked. I had never brought a girl home —not once in my life. Especially one I had just met. "Shane, what's going on?"

I walked up the steps, watching Callie race through her store. From the pile on the counter, it wasn't only the kids getting a gift. She was being overly generous, yet I knew that was her nature, so I wouldn't stop her.

"I don't know," I admitted. "But I'm bringing someone home. Her name is Callie. And Elly?" I said with a pause. "She's important."

"How important?"

I drew in a long breath, finally saying out loud what I had been feeling since the moment I'd seen Callie. "Life-changing important."

"Then we can't wait to meet her."

"See you soon."

I hung up and went inside to find Callie.

CHAPTER FOUR

SHANE

Callie's fingers worried the sleeve of her red jacket. Then the hem. They moved on to her jeans, tugging at the seam as she stared out the window into the early dawn. Reaching over, I covered her restless hand with mine, pulling it across to rest it on my thigh.

"Your clothing is suffering with your unnecessary worry."

She met my sidelong glance with anxious eyes.

"This is crazy. You should pull over and I'll walk home."

I burst out laughing at her absurd remark. "We're an hour away from the shop, Callie. I am not 'pulling over' and dropping you off. You're coming with me and spending Christmas with my family. We're going to get to know each other more."

"And then?" she asked quietly.

"Then we'll figure out the next step." I lifted her hand and kissed the knuckles. "I have never felt this connection to another person before, Callie. Ever. I am not going to waste this chance to explore something I feel is going to be significant."

"But—"

I shook my head. "No. Don't overthink this. We both feel it. You told me so. Whatever this is, we'll figure it out. I have no permanent ties in Calgary. You have no permanent ties here. If we have a future, we'll figure out the wheres, whys, and whens later. But for today, we're together, it's Christmas, and I want you with me. Can that be enough? For now?"

She sighed. "Yes."

"My family are awesome. Honestly. They're going to love you."

"They are going to wonder what kind of weird woman shows up with their relative on Christmas Day, having only met him the night before."

"They're going to wonder where you have been all my life."

Her quick intake of breath made me smile.

"Relax, love. Enjoy the day. I promise it'll be a good one."

She regarded me with wide eyes. "*Love?*" she repeated.

I smiled. "Since you personify it, yeah. It just came out. You okay with that?"

She glanced out the window, remaining silent. Then she nodded. "Yeah, I'm okay with that."

I picked up her hand and kissed it. "Good."

I withheld the information that my phone had been blowing up in my pocket. It had started about ten minutes after my conversation with Elly. My family was equally as curious as they were shocked. My mother was demanding to know all about Callie, wanting as much information as I could give, while my father's texts were slightly more cautious. Alan sent me a thumbs-up and some rather rude emojis, and Elly's messages were constant. I ignored them all after sending one group text.

> **Me**
> You'll meet her soon. Be nice. She is going to be around the rest of my life.

That caused another frenzy of texts to which I didn't respond. I was driving, and Callie was with me. They could sate their curiosity soon enough.

And they would love her—of that, I had no doubt. She was sweet, warm, and genuine. My mother would react to the quiet need in Callie's eyes. My father would feel a protective instinct. Alan would tease her simply to see the rush of color on her cheeks. Elly was going to want to be her best friend. John would be John—sit back and observe, all the time forming his own opinion. Tracey would recognize how alone Callie was and respond positively. She was as tenderhearted as Callie. And my nieces and nephews were going to go mad at having another aunt to love.

And I was going to enjoy watching them all fall under Callie's spell the same way I had.

We pulled into the driveway as the first of the heavy flakes began to fall. I eyed the sky with worry. "It is looking bad again. You might be stuck here with me for the entire week." I had hoped she'd stay the whole time, but I was prepared to drive her home sooner if she insisted.

Callie blushed. "I asked Mrs. Cooper to post a sign on the shop door when she goes to check on Jake. So, I'm not seeing a problem with that unless you change your mind. Or your family dislikes me."

"Neither is going to happen." I glanced toward the porch with a grin. "In fact, I have a feeling I'm going to lose you as soon as we walk up those steps." I indicated my sister and mother waiting by the door with a tilt of my head. I leaned across the console and captured Callie's mouth with mine, kissing her fast and deep.

"What was that for?"

"It's gonna be a while until I can do that again." I kissed her again, this time my lips lingering on hers. "Stocking up." I winked. "Get it? *Stocking up?*"

She slid her hand around my neck and kissed me in return. Regretfully, I pulled back and groaned. "I should have thought about that a mile back. I could kiss you for hours."

Her cheeks flooded with color. I found it sexy, especially knowing I had put that color there.

I chuckled. "Let's go, love. We'll meet them head on and endure it together."

She peeked at the crowd gathering on the porch and sucked in a long breath. "Okay."

I sipped a cup of coffee, watching with amusement and delight as my family fell under Callie's spell as quickly as I had. She was shy and sweet. Caring and inquisitive. Gentle and kind. She listened as people spoke. She paid attention to my nieces and nephews, giving them her full concentration when they wanted to monopolize her time. She asked questions of my father, praised my sister's home, pleaded with my mother to allow her to help cook the Christmas dinner, and blushed every time she met my eyes.

Which was often because I couldn't tear my gaze away from her. Callie was artlessly beautiful, her mahogany hair tumbling over her shoulders and her beautiful eyes lit from within. She sat cross-legged on the floor, surrounded by my family, looking as if she was exactly where she belonged.

I had a sneaking suspicion it was.

Elly stood and clapped her hands. "Okay! We've been waiting for Uncle Shane, and now he's here so you can open presents!"

For the next while, gifts were handed out, paper torn, and delighted shouts filled the air. How they did it, I had no idea, but my family had a few parcels for Callie waiting under the tree. Her shock and delight were evident and her thanks heartfelt and enthusiastic. The gifts I had bought from her store were met with great enthusiasm, and I was touched by the ones she had picked this morning. She had even taken the time to put each in a gift bag, adding candies and bows to make them look even prettier. She had done it in the car as we drove, staying busy the first while, her nervousness coming in handy as her fingers put together the packages.

We took a break—the adults needing more coffee, and the kids already knee-deep in gifts and wanting to explore what they had received. My mom stood.

"I need to get the turkey in." She smiled at Callie. "We eat early, so we can snack later."

"Please let me help."

Mom held out her hand. "Of course, dear girl. I would love it."

I smiled, watching them walk out of the room, Tracey and Elly trailing behind. Tracey handled dessert, and Elly always set the table. The men were in charge of the cleanup. It was tradition.

I had a feeling both Callie and I would be grilled while we were on our own.

Dad chuckled. "Relax, Shane. She's perfectly safe with your mother."

"I'm aware," I muttered. "I just don't want them badgering her."

He laughed. "You bring home a woman—the first one ever, I might add—out of the blue, and you expect them to hold back?" He shook his head. "Especially given the fact that you met her last night. And the way you look at her."

I had to admit he was right.

"You care deeply about her," John stated.

I smiled as I nodded. John was always able to see things clearly. He had a gift for sensing people and their emotions. "I care a great deal. Far more than I realized until I tried to walk away from her this morning." I sighed. "There's something special about her. Something…"

"Warm," he finished for me. "She's filled with warmth and love."

"She is," I agreed. "And the thought of her being alone did

something terrible to my chest. The pain was almost physical. I couldn't leave her." My gaze drifted down the hall, where I could hear the sounds of feminine laughter. I was surprised how easily I could pick out Callie's sweet laugh.

"What is going to happen in a few days?" Alan asked with a frown. "You live and work hundreds of miles from here."

His words were like a bucket of ice water running down my back.

"I know," I murmured. "I haven't figured out that part yet."

My dad spoke up. "Don't jump ahead. Live for today, Shane. Each day is a gift."

We all nodded in silent agreement at his words. He had started pulling back when Mom became ill. My workaholic father began cutting hours at the hospital. Saying no to lectures and business dinners. Spending more time with my mother. Telling us all to live for today. Grab each minute and live it.

"Don't put off happiness," he would say, shaking his head. "Stop waiting for it. Find it yourself."

Even after Mom recovered, he hadn't gone back to his old ways. They were closer than ever with a new zest for life and each other. I had a feeling it was one of the reasons they were so open to Callie being here.

"I think Callie might be the best gift ever, Dad," I mused.

He winked. "I think you might be right."

I wandered into the kitchen, inhaling the scent of the turkey roasting.

"God, it smells good in here."

Callie looked up from the pot of potatoes she was mashing with a smile. "It does."

I looked to the dining room, where Elly was busy setting the table, making sure everything was perfect. I held in my laughter. It was the same all the time. She spent hours making it look like a magazine spread, and five minutes after we sat down to eat, her perfection was destroyed. Still, she loved it, so I never bothered to ask her why.

Tracey glanced up from the pastry she was rolling. "The kids behaving?"

I chuckled as I went over to Callie and pressed a kiss to her head, quietly asking if she was okay.

She nodded and focused on her task at hand.

"Alan and John are taking them out sledding."

"Good plan." She smirked. "Wear them out. Once they eat, they'll fall asleep for a while." She lifted her pies from the counter and slid them into the second oven. "You must be tired, Shane. All the travel, the worry, and the driving?" she asked.

I nodded. "I am a bit."

My mom clucked her tongue and took the masher from Callie's hand. "Of course you are. You both must be. I can finish these. Take Callie and go have a nap. Dinner is in about three hours. It'll do you a world of good."

"I'm fine," Callie protested, even as a yawn escaped her lips.

Laughing, I pulled her toward me. "Come on, Callie. We'll have a little rest so we can visit with everyone tonight."

"But…"

"No arguing," Mom insisted. "We're way ahead, thanks to all your help. Go." She shooed us out of the kitchen, and I climbed the stairs, Callie following me, her hand still cradled within mine.

I opened the door to the room I always used, not surprised to see my cases and Callie's bag sitting at the foot of the bed. I sat down and pulled Callie between my legs. "My family didn't ask, but if you want your own room…" I let the words trail off, my grin wide as Callie shook her head.

"No. I want to be here with you."

I slipped my hand up her neck, pulling her down to my mouth and kissing her. She tasted sweet, her breath warm in my mouth, and I groaned as she kissed me back. Together, we fell back on the mattress. In seconds, she was under me, our kisses morphing into more. Deeper. Harder. Lips pressing, tongues stroking, hands sliding under clothes, seeking the warmth of bare skin. She made the most erotic noises low in her throat. She drove me crazy with desire, all else fading from my mind. I was no longer tired, no longer worried about tomorrow or next week. All that mattered was getting as close to her right now as I possibly could.

"I hope you brought more of those condoms with you," I moaned against her neck.

"All of them. Including the glow-in-the-dark ones."

"Excellent."

I planned on using every single one of them.

Callie curled up against me, her head on my shoulder. We could hear the kids outside, their laughter echoing. I stroked my fingers up and down Callie's arm in gentle passes, enjoying her closeness.

"Maybe we can go out with them tomorrow," she murmured.

"They'd like that."

"It's been a wonderful day, Shane."

I pressed my lips to her forehead, lingering against the soft skin. "Yeah, it has."

"Oh." She sat up, her long hair tumbling over her shoulders as she clutched the blanket against her chest. Her cheeks were flushed, her skin still damp from our lovemaking. Her hair was a mess from my hands, and she had a small bite mark over her left breast.

My mark.

She was so beautiful, my chest ached just looking at her.

"What is it?"

"I didn't give you your gift." She scrambled from the bed, bending over and digging in her case. The view of her ass was spectacular, and I needed her back in my bed right away so I could show her just how spectacular it—and she—was.

She placed a small box on the bed beside me and sat down, her hands twisting with nerves.

"Callie, I didn't expect you to give me something. Having you here with me is all I wanted."

"I wanted you to have this." She pushed the box toward me, and I sat up, accepting the gift. I opened the box and took out what looked like a small alarm clock. I glanced at her, my brow furrowed in confusion.

"It emits a soft blue light and various sounds—like waves on the ocean or the wind in the trees," she explained. "You told me you had trouble sleeping at times—that you couldn't turn your mind off after a long shift. This will help you to relax."

I was touched by her thoughtful gift, and I wrapped my hand around her neck and pulled her in for a kiss. "Thank you, love. It's perfect."

"You can use it and think of me at times," she whispered.

I wasn't sure how to tell her I would think of her more than only the times I couldn't sleep. I had a feeling she would be on my mind a lot. Rather than make both of us sad, I kissed her again.

"Your turn."

She frowned as I slipped a familiar box into her hands. Before she could protest, I opened the lid and took out the bracelet I had bought from her shop.

"You said it was your favorite piece," I said as I clasped it around her wrist. "I want you to wear it and think of me."

"But your mom…"

I shook my head. "It was never for my mom. I only bought it because you looked sad when you said it was your favorite, and I just didn't want someone buying it and taking it away." I kissed her wrist. "It was meant for you."

We locked eyes, and the words were out before I could stop them. "Just like *I* was meant for you, Callie."

And my mouth was on hers again, not letting her speak.

I couldn't bear it if she said no.

The days passed too quickly. For the first time in years, I wasn't ready to leave. Somehow, with Callie there, everything had more meaning. Laughing and playing with the kids. Late-night conversations with my father. Spending time with my mom in the kitchen. The silly card and board games we all played once the kids went to bed. Making love to Callie every chance I got. Food tasted better. Wine sweeter. Laughter came easier.

And hours flew by.

My time was over, and I had to return to Calgary. Luckily, the weather cooperated so I could fly back from Toronto where I should have landed originally.

My family hugged us both, Elly promising to stay in touch with Callie.

"We're only a few hours away," she insisted, her eyes bright with tears. "I can come visit, and you're welcome here anytime!"

Callie smiled and nodded. Her eyes welled up as my mom hugged her, adding to Elly's statement. "We'll see you soon, dear. I promise."

We were quiet on the drive back to Callie's. There was so much to be said, yet I couldn't find the words. I held her hand, running my thumb in restless circles over the skin. When we pulled up to her shop, I put the SUV in park and shut off the engine. Callie smiled at me as she unclipped her seat belt and opened the door. I grabbed her bags from the back and followed her up the steps, waiting as she unlocked the door and disarmed the security system. Silently, I carried her bags to her apartment, watching her pat Jake's head as he looked up with a yawn, another one of his horrific farts, and then curled back up to sleep.

"Hard life," I said with a smile.

She shook her head. "He was my dad's cat. He's old and grumpy, but still a little company at times." She chucked him under the chin. "I hope you didn't give Mrs. Cooper a hard time."

I laughed dryly. "Other than farting on her and sleeping, I doubt it."

We both chuckled, then silence descended.

"Callie," I began.

She held up her hand. "I know, Shane. It's been wonderful. The whole week. Meeting you and your family. Spending the holidays with them. With you. I loved every moment of it. But it's time to head back to reality. I understand."

I gaped at her. Her voice was quiet but certain. She was putting up a brave front, but I had gotten to know Callie well the past week. I knew her tells. The slight twitch to her eye. The tremor in her shoulders. The way her hands clenched in tight fists. How she blinked rapidly to hold back the tears. She was trying to let me go—thinking that what we had was a pleasant interlude and nothing more. That I would return to my life in Calgary and recall our time together as a nice memory. She felt that was all she was worth—the sum total of her value.

She was so wrong.

"You understand nothing, then, Callie."

"I'm sorry?"

I stepped forward, wrapping my hands around her biceps, feeling the tremble of her body under my touch. "You should be. Don't *ever* discount yourself like that again. This past week is the beginning. Today is not the end. Not by a long shot."

She shook her head. "How? How do you think this is going to work? You live hundreds of miles away."

I pulled her close, wrapping her in my embrace. "I have no idea, but the thought of walking away from you is killing me. Simply the idea of never seeing you again is tormenting me. We can figure this out, Callie. I can come visit. You can come to Calgary. We'll work at it—together. But don't put an end to something so special."

She leaned back, meeting my eyes. "The chances of this working are slim. The obstacles—"

I cut her off. "We'll take it a step at a time. Tell me you don't want that. That you don't want me, and I'll walk away."

"I can't do that," she confessed, a tear trickling down her cheek.

"Then try with me. I'll check my schedule when I get back and fly you out. I'll come back too. We can meet partway. Plus, we can call, text, FaceTime…*please*, love. Don't send me away without knowing you want to try." I took in a long breath. "I'm falling in love with you, Callie. I know it's fast and I know it sounds crazy, and who knows, maybe it was a Christmas miracle"—I smiled—"but it's the truth."

"Me too," she whispered.

Hope soared. "Then you'll try? With me?"

"Yes."

I pulled her to my mouth, kissing her deeply. "My plane isn't until tonight," I mumbled against her lips. "Late tonight."

"I thought it was dinnertime. That's what you told your family."

"I changed it. I wanted some time alone with you."

Her eyes lit up. "I think you need a nap, then."

I grinned down at her. We'd had an afternoon "nap" every day during the holidays. Not much sleep had happened.

I scooped her up in my arms, carrying her to her room.

Not much sleep was going to happen this time either.

CHAPTER FIVE

SHANE

A MONTH LATER

"Love, I'm sorry."

Callie's tear-filled voice broke me. "I know he was old and did nothing but sleep, but he was my last tie to my dad." She sniffled.

Jake had died—curled up on his chair, one last fart lingering in the air. Callie discovered him when she went to get a cup of coffee and stopped to stroke his fur. It happened yesterday, but it was the first chance I'd had to talk with her.

Long-distance relationships sucked.

Callie had flown here once in the weeks since Christmas. The first few days were great, but then all hell had broken loose at the hospital with an outbreak of flu, and I was constantly called in. I barely saw her the rest of the week, and since then, we hadn't been able to connect. I missed her terribly—especially once she'd been here. Once I'd had her in my space, in my bed. I wanted her back here, but I knew she wasn't interested in living in a big city.

Lately, I hadn't been either. After the quiet time with my family, Calgary seemed too loud, too chaotic—too lonely.

"I understand," I soothed. "It's okay to be sad, love."

"I wish you were here," she confessed.

Pain lanced through my chest at her words. That was the problem. I wasn't there for her. Despite my words of assurance, FaceTime, texts, and phone calls were cold comfort, compared to what I wanted. What she needed.

Her beside me. I needed her touch. I longed to feel her close.

"I know," was all I could offer.

"We'll see each other soon, though," she said with hope in her voice.

"Ah…" I swallowed.

"You didn't get the time off?"

"I did, but not the weekend we talked about. It's two weeks later," I confessed, hating the fact that I was disappointing her again.

"So, March."

"Yes." Not Valentine's, like I'd promised. "I'm sorry."

"I understand," she whispered. "Shane, I—"

My pager buzzing and my name over the loudspeaker interrupted us.

"Damn," I groaned. "Finish what you were going to say."

"No, it's fine. We'll talk later."

"Callie, I'm sorry about Jake."

"I know."

"And the weekend."

"Okay." She sighed. "I'll talk to you soon."

"I love you," I told her. I had expressed the words to her when she was here. I had no doubt in my mind. Her sweet response left me no doubt as to her own feelings, and it was the one thing that kept up my spirits.

But today, she didn't echo my sentiments.

"I know, Shane," she whispered.

Then she hung up.

I hated the sound of the dead line.

FOUR DAYS LATER

"Shane," a voice called.

I turned, meeting the eyes of my boss, Thomas Grant. "Hey, what's up?" I asked. I was anxious to get home. I had put in another long day, caught up on all my charting, and wanted to try to call Callie. It felt like days since we had spoken. She was still sad about Jake, and our situation wasn't helping. We were both hurting. I was worried about her and, if I was honest, about us. I let Elly know what had happened, and she was great, but Callie needed *me*.

And frankly, I needed her.

"Can we talk for a moment?" Thomas inquired.

I hid my impatience and followed him to his office. I slid my messenger bag from my shoulder and sat down.

"How are you?" he asked.

I frowned. "Good, Thomas."

"I was talking to your dad last night."

I nodded. Thomas and my dad had gone through med school together and were still close. I had been thrilled to discover I would be working with him here, and we got along well.

"He told me something interesting."

"What's that?"

"He said you'd fallen in love with a pretty shopkeeper over the holidays and are pining over her. He said how much you hate it here."

I felt the heat creep up my neck. I had spoken with my dad last week and confessed how frustrated I was lately with my life. How I didn't want to be in Calgary anymore. How much I missed Callie. How fed up I was with the nonstop workload here.

I didn't think he'd tell my boss.

"Ah…" I scrubbed my neck. "*Hate* is a strong word."

He threw back his head in laughter. "I'm kidding. He said you were frustrated. I've sensed that lately, Shane. Longer than the last few weeks. More like the last few months."

"Sorry, I didn't realize—"

"I know," he interrupted me. "That's the thing. You're an excellent doctor, Shane. One of the best. In fact, I had planned on nominating you to take my place when I retire in a few years."

My eyes flew open wide, and I felt panic swell. I didn't want his position. In that split second, I realized I didn't want to be here anymore.

Thomas held up his hand. "Except I've seen the signs. You give everything to your patients, Shane. You give until there isn't anything left, and for the first time ever, you need something left over. There is someone outside this place more important now, isn't there?"

I nodded and cleared my throat. "There is, but we seem to be at an impasse. She isn't a big-city girl, and I'm stuck here. Sorry," I added hastily. "I meant my job is here."

He regarded me quietly for a moment. "What if I told you that you weren't stuck? That I had an idea that might help you."

I leaned forward. "I'd like you to tell me more."

CALLIE

I sighed as I read the proposal in front of me. I was torn as I read the words, wondering if I would have been at all hesitant if I had received this offer in January.

In January, my life looked as if it was going to be different. Still in the thrall of Shane and his determination we were meant to be together, I had flown to Calgary to see him. It was perfect—until his overwhelming duties got in the way. Still, I loved being close to him. After I left, the calls and texts continued. We FaceTimed. Planned another weekend that he had to postpone. We replanned another weekend, only for it to happen again when his responsibilities interfered.

And the past two weeks, I had barely heard from him at all. His calls were sporadic and brief, and he was distracted when he did call.

Part of me wasn't shocked. I feared once the emotion of the holidays was over and he got back to his life, this might happen. I simply didn't think it would happen so soon. Shane seemed so adamant. Certain we had a future together. He told me over and over there had been a reason his flights were delayed. He swore he was meant to find my shop—to find me.

When Jake died, Shane sent flowers. Had Elly come see me. She insisted I go stay the weekend, and being at her house, while lovely, made me miss Shane more. He was everywhere—I even stayed in his room, and it smelled like him.

His parents—especially his mom—kept in touch. His family was wonderful.

It hurt knowing, when I lost Shane, I would lose them too. And it felt as if I was losing him.

It all seemed inevitable. We had burned hot and fast. It was unexpected, wonderful, and far too quick to be lasting.

Yet my heart ached as if I had lost the most precious thing in my life.

I looked around my shop and the unpacked boxes. Normally, by now, I was organized and getting ready to reopen in a few weeks. These days, I was distracted and sad. I was tired all the time, yet it felt as if I slept more than normal. My appetite was off and my energy level at an all-time low. I had barely put away the Christmas items, never mind gotten prepared to open up again.

I looked down at the papers in front of me. Maybe, despite things not working with Shane, it was time. The offer to purchase the building and the land was unexpected, but it was a good one. I could move and buy a place somewhere. Finish my education. Open another shop. For the first time, I would have the choice. As I pondered, one thought drifted through my head.

I wish I could talk to Shane about it.

Furious banging on my door startled me. I slid off the stool, heading toward the door. No doubt another delivery of inventory I would need to sort through.

Opening the door, I was shocked to discover who was on the other side. He had his hands locked on the doorframe, his hair wild and disheveled, looking intense, determined, and so handsome that my breath caught in my throat.

Shane.

SHANE

Callie was surprised to see me. She gripped the edge of the door, her brow furrowed, her voice shocked.

"Shane?"

God, she was beautiful. But thin and drawn. I prayed it was because she was missing me as much as I was missing her.

I stepped closer. "Miss James, once again, I must beg you for help."

She blinked. "Help?"

"Yes. I have misplaced something of great value, and I think perhaps you might have it in your possession."

I saw her eyes drift to the bracelet I had given her. She thought that was the thing of great value. "Not the bracelet, love," I prompted.

She met my eyes, the pain in hers evident, her confusion clear.

"My heart," I stated. "I left my heart with you. I've come to get it." I paused. "And you."

Tears filled those dark eyes of hers. "Me?"

"Yes," I responded, moving closer so I could wipe away her tears. "I'm empty without you. Nothing is right without you beside me. You have my heart, Callie. Will you take the rest of me?" I paused. "Forever?"

"Forever?" she repeated.

"Yes."

She was in my arms in an instant. I held her close, feeling complete for the first time since leaving her weeks prior.

I was never letting her go again.

Callie was curled up beside me on her small sofa. "Here? You're going to be a doctor here?"

"Well, in Grimsby. Only three hours from here. And I'm going to be part of a team there. My hours will be more stable." I gathered her hands in mine. "I'll get a place as close to here as I can. We can see each other more. I'll drive here every chance I get. Evenings, weekends…"

Callie shook her head. "Shane—I've had an offer on this place." She jumped up and hurried away, returning with a thick stack of papers. She thrust them at me, and I glanced at the number.

"This is generous." I looked up. "What about your store?"

"I can reopen someday if I want, or I was thinking of going back to school." She looked at me, suddenly shy. "Maybe I could do that in Grimsby."

I cupped her face and kissed her. "Yes. *God*, yes. Live with me, Callie. Be with me every day. *Please*."

Her breath caught. "I thought you were breaking up with me," she whispered, holding my wrists. "I've hardly heard from you."

"I know. I'm sorry. I was so blown over when Thomas told me about this position. I flew here and interviewed, and they offered me the job right away. I had to go back and settle things in Calgary." I paused and sighed. "Part of me was afraid to tell you in case you said no. The other part was so excited, I wanted to make it a surprise." I smiled. "I only told my family last night. And I decided if you said no, I was going to woo you until you changed your mind and decided to love me again."

"I never stopped."

I pulled her into my arms. "Good."

"I've missed you so much, Shane."

"Me too, love." I kissed her tenderly. "You're never going to be alone again. Neither of us will be."

"I like the sound of that."

"So, you'll live with me? We'll get a place together?" I asked, anxious.

"Yes," she said simply.

"Thank you, love. I don't ever want to be without you again." I held her tighter. "God, Callie, when Thomas told me about this job, my first thought was of you. Of us. Of being close to you—being able to see you."

I recalled my reaction and the way Thomas had laughed at my words. I had basically said the same thing to him, then realized what I had blurted out to my boss.

He waved away my apologies.

"Don't be sorry, Shane. There is more to life than being a doctor. Find that balance. Be with the woman you love. If you're happy at home, it will carry to your career. And the same goes the other way. You've been adrift for a while, without even knowing it. And since the holidays, you've looked downright lost. When David told me about your girl, I knew it was you who was meant for that position."

He stood and shook my hand. "I'll arrange the intro and start looking for a new body."

"Perhaps it won't work out."

He shook his head. "You're too good, and they need you. At least I have Nelson to torture." He winked and sent me on my way.

"I've been working on getting to you ever since."

She sighed, and I kissed her, studying her face. She looked exhausted.

"I think I got here at the right time. You need looking after, Miss James. And you're lucky. I have a degree that certifies there is no one better than me."

"You're a pediatrician, Shane," she pointed out with a grin, but she didn't object as I carried her to her room and laid her on the bed.

"Hush. I am a Callie expert caregiver. It's nap time, then I'm making you dinner and we're having a bath."

"What about you?"

"I'm locking up, then getting in there with you. Tomorrow, we'll talk about everything and make plans."

"Doctor's orders?"

I bent down and kissed her. "Doctor's orders."

THE NEXT CHRISTMAS

I pulled into the garage and killed the engine. I stretched and yawned, then quietly made my way inside the house. The colorful lights from the tree in the living room cast a dim glow into the hall, and after kicking off my shoes, I walked into the room, stopping at the pretty tableau I found.

Callie sound asleep in the big corner chair she loved so much, and our daughter slumbering on her chest. They were covered by a light blanket, a discarded bottle on the floor. I watched my girls, the intense feeling of happiness flooding my chest as I looked at them.

Our Madeline—or Maddy, as we called her—had been a surprise to us both. It turned out those glow-in-the-dark condoms weren't totally effective, and the tiredness and despondent mood Callie had been experiencing had been more than simply missing me. Her body was raging with pregnancy hormones. The biggest joke of all was neither of us realized it. I was so busy with the move and looking for a place to live, and Callie was going crazy with packing up her shop after accepting the offer on her place that we missed it. She was used to irregular cycles and thought nothing of it. I was so distracted, I was blind. It wasn't until I was there one day with Elly, helping Callie pack up the shop. Callie became dizzy, and something clicked as I caught her. Her emotions, the constant tiredness, the occasional nausea. I had missed the obvious signs completely. Elly procured a pregnancy test, and later that day, I learned I was going to be a dad.

Joy wasn't a big enough word to describe my feelings.

Life ramped into high gear. Within a month, we bought a house, moved Callie, I started with my new position, and we settled into a life together. It was as effortless as breathing with her. My family loved her, both my parents and Elly visiting often. As I expected, Callie and Elly were incredibly close.

I surprised Callie one summer day, getting down on one knee in the garden.

"Callie James, will you do me the extraordinary honor of marrying me?"

Her beautiful eyes filled with tears. "Yes."

I slipped a ring on her finger and kissed her hand. I held her palm to my cheek. "Soon?"

"Name the day," she replied.

A month later, we were husband and wife.

When Maddy arrived in September, our family was there, helping Callie, making sure I didn't drop my infant daughter, and stocking the house with food and every other essential we could need. When they left, the quiet was welcome and the terror real. But like the team Callie and I had become, we worked through it together.

I crossed the room and kneeled before my girls. I laid a hand on Callie's arm and the other on Maddy's back, rubbing it lightly. Callie's eyes flickered open, and a smile curved her mouth. "Hi."

I bent closer and kissed her. "Hi, Mommy. How are my girls?"

"Good. We fell asleep waiting for you." She paused. "How is Josh?"

One of my patients had had surgery then spiked a fever. I'd stayed late to make sure he pulled through. "Good. Fever broke, and he is responding well to pain meds."

"Good."

"May I have her?"

Callie smiled and slipped Maddy into my arms, knowing how much I needed her close. The feel of my little girl snuggled against my chest relaxed me. Her dark hair was curly and wild. She looked like Callie, right down to her mouth, except she had my green eyes. I looked up with a smile, and the light glinted off the pretty emerald necklace hanging around Callie's neck. I had given it to her when Maddy was born, and she never took it off. Callie smiled at me in return and stroked Maddy's head—the action making the matching bracelet twinkle in the light.

I loved holding my daughter. The way she looked—content and warm. Her baby smell. How her eyes followed my movements and she seemed to track my voice when I was in the room. Her sunny smile made me feel ten feet tall.

"Your parents arrive tomorrow," Callie reminded me.

"Are you sure, Callie? We can always tell them we changed our mind, and we can go there. You just gave birth. Hosting Christmas seems too much."

She chuckled and sat up. "I gave birth almost three months ago. Mom and I will do some baking while Maddy hangs with Grandpa. Everyone else is coming on Christmas Eve, and they're all staying at a hotel. It'll be fine."

I sighed, lifting Maddy to my shoulder and rubbing her back in long passes. I was almost grateful our house was small and couldn't hold them all. It would have been wild. Then I grinned.

"Christmas Eve. I can't believe, a year ago, I was hammering on your shop door, hoping the nice old lady who owned the store would let me in to pick out some gifts."

Callie laughed quietly. "Not so old, I guess."

I leaned forward and kissed her. "But *very* nice."

She traced my jaw with her fingertip. "I thought you were the most handsome man I had ever seen." She quirked her eyebrow. "And generous."

I laughed. "I have never been as grateful for lost parcels as I was that night. I didn't care how much it cost me if it meant spending a few more moments with you."

Callie frowned. "Did they ever get them? The lost parcels, I mean?"

I lifted one shoulder. "I have no idea. I totally forgot to ask. I assume they showed up at some point." I bent close, teasing. "And this year, I didn't have to worry. I have a wife now who does all that stuff."

She laughed with me, and I kissed her. We had shopped together, decorated the house, and I found joy in small things I had never noticed until now. The season had taken on a whole new meaning, thanks to the birth of my little girl and the gift of my wife.

"Last year was all about the lost parcels. This year, it's all about the very best thing. My own family. I never could have imagined how my life would change when you opened the door. How blessed I would be." I held her gaze. "Thank you, my beautiful wife."

"I love you," she whispered.

I cupped her cheek. "I love you, my Callie. Merry Christmas."

Her smile was bright. "Merry Christmas."

A MERRY VESTED WEDDING

PART I

PRESENT DAY

CHAPTER 1

BRAYDEN

The morning of December 22, I stood in the kitchen, staring out the window as the sun began to rise. Slowly, its rays lightened the sky, scattering over the beach, glinting on the frost-covered rocks.

Winter in Port Albany was magical. The water in the inlet usually froze, while the open waters farther beyond our tiny cove remained alive and frothy. The sand mingled with snow and ice, creating sculptures and divots everywhere. The trees hung lower with ice, and the ground was often covered with snow.

I loved it here. It was my favorite place on earth. A smile stretched across my face. My favorite place on earth, my favorite time of year, combining into my favorite day of my life.

My wedding day.

Today, I would marry my Addison. My little elf. Here in this place created by my uncle Bentley—soon to be my father-in-law.

His vision of a special place, a place where family could gather and be together—to de-stress and find your center—had grown and changed over the years. As a child, I could recall the six houses, all clustered—a small community, as it were. All of us kids running around, parents always close. Sandy and Jordan were never far. Adopted uncles, aunts, cousins—there was always someone to play with, hang around with, enjoy life.

The property hummed, especially on weekends. When they added the building we named the Hub, it became the focal point for all our celebrations.

Then our families grew. And my father and his partners knew exactly how to accommodate. They bought as much land as they could surrounding the original six houses. Created an entire village. "The BAM Compound," Uncle Aiden referred to it as.

Twenty houses dotted the area. Some small weekend cottages, some larger live-in-all-the-time dwellings. You never knew who would be there, but there was always an abundance of people.

I lived here year-round. I had loved this place as a child when we would come out on weekends. Unlike my urban-dwelling parents, I yearned for the wide-open spaces of Port Albany. The sound of the waves, the endless scope of the water stretching out in front of me. Often, I begged my parents to let me stay when it was time to head back to the city. Uncle Aiden understood my love of the place and would urge my dad to let me remain behind. I could run and move here. The city always felt more constrictive.

And besides, often when I stayed behind, my best friend was here. My Addison. There was no one I liked to spend time with more than her.

She had always been in my life. I couldn't recall a single memory from my childhood without her in it. Every happy moment, she was there. We attended the same schools, went to the same dances, hung out with the same friends. We celebrated the good moments and bolstered each other during the sad ones. We were always friends.

Until, one day, it changed.

I was sixteen, and it was the start of summer vacation, which meant I would spend most of the summer on the beach, walking the various trails, with Jordan on the boat or Uncle Aiden and my dad doing reps in the pool. Long, carefree days spent in Port Albany. Next summer, I planned on working at BAM, so I was going to make the most of my final season.

Sitting on the beach, I saw Addi come out of her house and head my way. I waved at her as she approached. Her hair was down, rippling like gold in the sun, and she wore a pair of shorts and a T-shirt. As she grew closer, I couldn't help but notice how her T-shirt clung to her curves. I wasn't sure when she got those curves or how I'd missed noticing them. The way she walked made her hips sway—she looked sexy. My board shorts grew uncomfortably tight the closer she came, and I had to sit up, drawing my knees to my chest to hide my erection. I was confused and annoyed. It was Addi—my best friend. Why the hell was I reacting as if she was a girl?

She sat down, looking dejected. "Hey, Bray."

Reaching over, I ruffled her hair, noticing for the first time how silky the strands were against my fingers.

Was she using a different shampoo?

"Hey, little elf."

She huffed in annoyance. "Stop calling me that. I was six when I dressed up as an elf for Christmas."

I chuckled. "Addi, you still wear elf pajamas every year."

"Whatever." She tossed her head, clearly dismissing me, but her shoulders remained drooped, and she looked sad.

"What's wrong?"

"Todd broke up with me."

I felt two things at once. Relief and jealousy. I didn't like Todd. I used to until he'd asked Addi out, and after that, every time his name was mentioned, I found myself wanting to snarl and spit like some sort of demented dog.

"Good. He didn't deserve you."

She sighed, mimicking my pose and resting her chin on her hands. "He said I was too much work."

I snorted. "What a dick."

"Derek said the same thing—a couple weeks of dating me, and they were done." She looked at me, her wide blue eyes confused and upset. "What's wrong with me, Bray?"

I forgot everything in a second. My erection was gone, my confusion dissipated, and all that mattered was she was hurting and I had to help her. I scooted closer and wrapped my arm around her shoulders.

"Nothing is wrong with you, Addi. The problem is them. All they see is the outer package—how pretty you are. They aren't prepared for how incredibly clever your mind is. How you can talk circles around them. They have no idea how advanced you are." I snorted. "The reason they say you're too much work is they think with their dicks, not their minds." I shrugged when she gaped at me. "They aren't looking for a relationship, just to get laid." I held up my hands. "Only telling you the truth."

She gazed at me, and for a second, I saw Uncle Bent. Serious, determined, and older than her years. Then she began to giggle.

"You're awful."

"It's true, though."

She sighed and leaned into me. "I guess I'm just going to die alone, then."

It was my turn to laugh. "You're a little young for that, Addi. Give it some time. You need to find the right guy." I turned my head and kissed the top of her head. "You're too amazing to be alone forever."

❄

A week later, I was in turmoil. Addi was suddenly everywhere. Everything about her was different. She was prettier, smarter, sexier. Her smiles taunted me. Her body tempted me. Her laughter was low and sultry.

I spent so much time in the cold water of the lake, even my father was beginning to notice. Every time I would see Addi, my dick would spring up, and I had no choice but to escape to the water to settle him down. I started avoiding her, unsure what to do about my feelings and how they had changed toward her.

Unable to sleep one night, I padded down to the beach, listening to the sound of the water. The breeze was light and felt good on my bare chest, the sand cool under my toes as I walked. I leaned against a pile of rocks, admiring the moon hanging high in the sky. I startled when a soft voice broke through my thoughts.

"Couldn't sleep either?"

I turned and met Addi's eyes. She was sitting five feet from me, cross-legged on a large, flat rock. I had been so deep in thought, I hadn't even noticed her.

I noticed her now. Her hair was up, loose curls hanging around her face and shoulders. Her skin gleamed in the moonlight. She was wearing a baggy shirt and leggings, one shoulder bare. She was sexy and beautiful, and in that single moment, everything became clear. I was totally in love with her. I always had been. It was all I could do not to groan out loud.

"Uncle Bent know you're out here? Alone?" I asked, my voice low and gravelly, even to my own ears.

She shook her head. "He had to go back to the city. Mom is asleep. Everyone is. But I was restless." She shrugged. "I'm perfectly safe here, Brayden. Even Uncle Aiden admits that."

The grounds were protected with a private fence and gate. There was a security system in place. I knew all that, and still, I didn't like it.

"No swimming alone," I snapped.

She huffed and scampered off the rocks, crossing her arms. "I'm not stupid, Bray. I know that." She shook her head. "I don't know what your problem is or why you're mad at me, but when you stop being a jerk, let me know."

She turned to leave, and I grabbed her arm, spinning her back to face me. I was shocked to see the tears in her eyes. "What? Why are you crying?"

"Why do you suddenly dislike me too? You've been avoiding me all week!"

"I don't dislike you," I replied. "That's the problem!"

"What?"

I didn't think; I only reacted. I yanked her into my arms and covered her mouth with mine and kissed her. She flung her arms around my neck and kissed me back. I slid my hands to cradle the back of her head, and deepened the kiss, groaning when her tongue touched mine. I lifted her to the rock, stepping between her legs, and for endless minutes, we explored each other. Learning and tasting. Our tongues stroked together, our breath mingling. I was aware of everything. How she fit against me. The subtle shiver that ran through her body as I touched her. The air surrounding us, the sound of the waves. How her nipples brushed against my chest. She fit against me seamlessly, melding against my chest. She tasted of chocolate and moonlight and all things Addi. It was a life-changing kiss for us both.

Breathing hard, I broke away. Our eyes met and held, hers wide and shocked, mine pleading and determined.

"I don't want you dating Todd or Derek or anybody else."

"Oh," she breathed out.

"You're mine, Addi. You have been your whole life. No one knows you the way I do. No one will ever understand you like me."

"But you've never…" She trailed off.

"I didn't know. Until this week. But it hit me. That's why I've hated every guy who looked at you twice. Why I go crazy thinking about someone else kissing you. Holding you. Because you're mine. You belong to me."

She swallowed, the tears spilling over her cheeks.

"What?" I asked again, wiping away the wetness. "Tell me."

She gripped my wrists, a shaky smile ghosting her lips.

"I thought you'd never figure it out."

Laughing, I kissed her again.

The next week was filled with ups and downs. I was on a high the next morning until I saw Addi on the beach. She looked pensive and upset.

"What's wrong?"

"We can't do this, Bray."

"Do what? We're not doing anything wrong," I insisted, yanking a hand through my hair.

"We're practically family. And I'm older than you."

I rolled my eyes with a snort. "By a little over a year. We grew up together, but we're not family in that sense, Addi. We're not related in any way." I grabbed her hands. "Don't overthink this. We're perfect for each other."

She shook her head. "I need time to think."

That was never a good thing. Addi would think and analyze to the point we would never have a chance. She would talk herself out of this. Out of me.

In desperation, I went to Sandy—the adoptive grandmother of all of us. She had been the assistant to our fathers, her role growing and adapting as the years went by. She became their nucleus and had been part of our world our entire lives.

I confessed everything to her. My feelings. Addi's sudden hesitance and worry.

"Am I wrong, Nan? Am I wrong to have these feelings for her?"

She studied me. "Wrong? No. But have you thought of all the implications if this doesn't work out?"

"It will," I insisted. "Addi is mine. She always has been."

She smiled. "You sound just like your father."

"I know I'm young, but I see my whole life with her. As soon as I kissed her, I knew." I lifted my shoulder. "Maybe even before."

"What do you need, Brayden?"

"You know how she gets. Stubborn. She'll overthink and decide the risks are too great. She'll push me away."

"You want me to talk to her?"

"She'll listen to you, Nan. She always does."

I waited for two days. I was sitting on the rocks, watching the sun sparkle on the water. Addi lowered herself beside me.

"Hey."

I peered at her warily. "Hi."

"Nan called me over. We talked for a long time."

"And?"

She slipped her hand into mine. "Forgive me. I panicked."

Relief tore through me. "So, we're good?"

"She said a year was nothing, and I was being foolish."

"She's right."

"She told me she isn't shocked by this 'development'—" Addi used her fingers to make the quotations "—and that we're both more mature than most kids our age. She told me sometimes we're lucky and find our soul mates early. That what was important was how we felt, not what others would think."

"Ah," I murmured, hope beckoning.

"She told me to look in my heart." Addi squeezed my fingers. "She said that was where my future was, not in my head."

"Nan is a wise woman."

"I want to try."

"Then let's do it."

After talking to Addi and letting it settle for a few days, I spoke to my parents. It was a surprisingly short conversation. They weren't shocked, telling me they had seen it long before I did.

"We were waiting for you to make up your mind," my mother told me, cupping my face. "Your head had to catch up to your heart."

My dad had asked some good questions but informed me he wasn't really surprised about my feelings for Addi.

"You two have always had a bond." He paused. "But you need to come clean with Bent," he stated.

"I am. Tomorrow."

The next day, I paid a visit to Uncle Bentley and Auntie Emmy. My dad came with me for moral support.

Addi was sitting with her parents on their deck, drinking coffee, when my dad and I approached. I sat beside her, my hand finding hers under the table and squeezing her fingers. I swallowed nervously then met Uncle Bent's eyes. His expression was stern, his brow furrowed as he looked between us. Then he spoke.

"You are aware the table is glass and I can see that," he said, indicating our clasped hands.

I glanced down then began to laugh. I had forgotten that fact. Addi joined in my laughter, and I relaxed when the adults did as well.

"So, you're together now?" Emmy asked, smiling at us.

"Yes."

"Have you thought this out? What will happen if this doesn't work?" Bentley asked. "How it will affect everyone around you?"

My dad and Nan had asked the same question, so I wasn't surprised to hear him ask it as well. I drew in a deep breath before I responded.

"I'm young, Uncle Bent, not stupid. We talked about that. But it's not going to happen." I met his serious gaze. "Addi is it for me."

"You're sixteen. She's a year ahead of you. What happens when she goes to university and you're still in high school?"

I shook my head. "I'm in advanced classes, Uncle Bent. I'll be going with her. And if we choose different schools, we'll figure it out." I didn't bother to tell him we already knew we would be going together.

Addi leaned forward. "You tell me all the time I'm like mom—young in years with an old soul."

Uncle Bentley's gaze grew warm, softening his stern look. "You are," he admitted.

"So is Brayden," my dad pointed out. "Come on, Bent, we always said this was going to happen. They've always been entwined. You can't possibly be surprised. It was inevitable."

He sighed and rubbed his eyes, then held up his hand. "Ground rules."

I bit back my grin. Uncle Bent always had ground rules.

He pointed at me. "You be careful. She's still young."

I felt myself flush, knowing exactly what he was saying.

"We're both too young," I mumbled. I knew we were both still virgins. For me, sex and love went hand in hand, and Addi was the same way. Although we had dated a few people, it had never gone that far for either of us.

"Good. Keep it that way until you're thirty—or even better, when I'm dead."

Auntie Emmy burst out laughing. "Stop it, Rigid. You're overreacting as usual. They're both good kids and plan to take this slow." She looked at us, one eyebrow lifted. "Right?"

We were both quick to agree.

"Same curfew and rules apply, Addi. I don't care whose son he is." He looked at me. "You pick her up and have her home at the set times. We prefer group outings. And no sneaking off while we're here.

"Same rules apply when we go back to Toronto. And when you start driving, you keep both hands on the wheel."

"Done." I had my learner's permit and planned on taking my test as soon as possible.

"You both will be respectful to us. Both your sets of parents. If we think things are getting too serious or you aren't following the rules, we're addressing it."

I agreed, nothing he said surprising me. I was actually shocked he didn't have more to say, but I had a feeling he would come to me later and talk to me privately. I also knew it was going to be far more personal and I wasn't going to enjoy it. But I would take it because it was for Addi.

"We're just starting, Uncle Bent. We wanted to be upfront with you. I don't want to hide anything or be deceitful." My parents were big on the truth and had drummed that into my head my whole life.

He smiled, some of the tension easing from his shoulders. "I appreciate that, Brayden." He met my gaze. "You take care of my little girl, and we won't have a problem. Otherwise…" He let the words trail off, then grinned. "I'll set Aiden on you."

"I will," I promised after the laughter had died down. I hunched closer, everyone else disappearing as I spoke directly to him. "I care about her a lot, Uncle Bent. I won't hurt her. But seeing her with anyone else hurt me, so I had to speak up."

He clasped my shoulder with a firm nod. "I trust you, Brayden. If I didn't, you'd be in the lake by now." He winked. "We'll save that for another day." He squeezed hard in warning. "I'll be watching."

I sat back, relieved. Addi watched her father with amused adoration. He shook his finger at her. "You behave. You're too much like your mother."

She laughed. "Everyone says I'm like you."

"Then you'd be hitting the books, not mooning over Brayden."

She smirked and grinned. "I'm a woman. We can multitask."

He groaned. "Don't remind me."

I smiled at the memories. The years that followed. School, work, growing, and learning. Together. We were always together, and neither of us wanted it any other way. Ours wasn't a typical relationship. It never had been. Growing up together. Falling in love so young. We'd never been in a hurry to get married, because we knew how solid we were. We went to school, although Addi followed in Bentley's footsteps and left before she got her degree, with the same bug he possessed in that she was bored and was eager to enter the business world. I pushed and worked hard, and at twenty-five, I held my CPA degree. Addi was a young president at the age of twenty-six, but she had earned the title. Bentley was too smart a businessman to entrust the role to anyone who wasn't qualified—daughter or not.

And today was the day I'd been waiting for since I first kissed her. Our lives had settled enough that we could move on to the next step in our journey—husband and wife. We were ready.

Here in this place I loved. We had all our firsts here. First kiss. First declaration of our feelings. The first time we made love. The day I asked her to marry me. Our entire world was linked to this spot.

And it would continue. Our parents had gifted us a house here. BAM had slowly bought up every piece of land around the area. There was a bustling resort a couple of miles down the road run by a new division in the company. A successful winery run by another department   and where I would marry Addi today. The rest of the land was personal holdings of the company and its directors.

Our house was set away, still overlooking the water, close enough to the main area we were still part of the group, but with a little more privacy. A bluff was a natural wall with an easy access path toward the other grouping of houses. There was room by our place for three other houses—and more space behind us if needed. For some members of BAM, this was a fun place to escape, a weekend getaway, or a place to vacation. For others, it was our home.

I had lived here for a few months, while Addi divided her time between her parents' place in Toronto and here. Addi amused me with her objections to our living together before we got married, even when I reminded her both her parents and mine had done so.

"We're not them, Brayden," she replied, lifting her eyebrows.

"So old-fashioned, Addi," I teased back. "Let me get this straight. You'll stay with me in a house our parents gave us on weekends, but you won't live here until we're married."

She had tossed her hair. "The occasional weeknight as well."

I laughed. "Right. You realize that makes no sense, right?"

"It does to me."

I leaned close and kissed her. "Whatever makes you happy."

She cupped my cheek. "You do."

When she looked at me like that, and kissed me the way she did, I'd give her anything.

I always would.

CHAPTER 2

ADDISON

I woke up, throwing back the blankets and getting out of bed, regardless of the fact that the sun wasn't up yet. I threw on my favorite robe, added a wrap to my shoulders and stuffed my feet into a pair of warm socks. I always felt the cold—not the way my mom did, but more than most people. Layers were my friend. And strangely enough, my favorite season was winter. I had learned to dress properly and not let it stop me.

I headed downstairs, not bothering with lights. My feet knew the way, the incline of the stairs, the layout of the rooms I walked through. I pushed open the kitchen door, not at all surprised to find my dad sitting at the table, a pot of coffee at his elbow. His ever-present laptop was open, but he wasn't busy typing or reading emails. Instead, he sat at the table, staring out the window. The overhead light glinted on his dark hair, highlighting the shots of gray that were scattered throughout it. He was a handsome, distinguished man, his posture straight, his shoulders still broad. He worked out with my uncle Aiden daily and could easily run circles around my brother or cousins. Something he liked to do on the basketball court weekly.

I smiled at him, crossing the room. "Hi, Dad."

His return smile was tight. "Addi."

I grabbed a cup and held it out. He filled it for me, indicating a plate. "Your mom made you some cinnamon raisin scones last night. I knew you'd want them this morning."

I loved my mom's scones—especially the cinnamon raisin ones. I bent and kissed his cheek, sliding my arms around his neck for a hug. "Thanks."

He wrapped me in a fast embrace. "No problem."

I sat beside him, picking up a scone.

"You're up even earlier than I thought you'd be," he observed, taking a sip of coffee.

I peeked at the clock—it was barely after five.

"Big day."

He huffed into his cup. I studied him in the low light. He looked weary this morning. Still calm and unruffled—stoic and stern, but weary.

Bentley Ridge was a legend. He was known as a hard-nosed, brilliant businessman. Unflappable. Detached. His company, BAM, was synonymous with quality. What started out as a dream for him in college had grown beyond even his expectations. Together with my "uncles" Aiden Callaghan and Maddox Riley, they had built an empire. Land development, construction, office buildings, housing, house flips, and everything in between, they were known for their excellence. And now, the next generation, including Brayden and me, ran ABC, focused on the outskirts of Toronto and finding new income streams, concentrating on the commercial aspects. A successful resort, a winery I had rescued from ruin, and a small private grouping of retirement cottages were some of our most profitable triumphs so far.

I was often compared to my father. I had inherited his business acumen and his stern resting face. While other little girls were playing with dolls, I sat on my dad's knee, listening and learning. I was known as severe and humorless. Emotionless. I had been referred to often as "a chip off the old block." Strangely enough, that comparison didn't bother me at all. I considered it a compliment. Like my father, I didn't much care what the business world thought of me personally. I let my record speak for itself.

But the faces we showed the world and those we showed the people we loved were vastly different. My dad was one of the kindest, generous, and most loving men in the world. Behind closed doors, with his family and those he treasured, he smiled and laughed. Teased and cajoled. Thought nothing of getting on the floor and wrestling my siblings or giving me a piggyback ride when we were younger. Sitting beside us, explaining homework and helping us understand. His patience with us always amazed me, given his cut-and-dried persona with business. With his extended family, he showed the same love and caring. He was loyal and protective. Always ready to help out or offer encouragement.

His adoration for my mother hadn't diminished over the years. Their love was a constant, steady light—a beacon for me and an example I wanted to live by. They still looked at each other with love and lit up when the other would enter a room. My father fussed over my mom, constantly bringing her gifts of soft shawls or fuzzy socks to keep her warm. Every floor in the house had been redone with radiant heating—he couldn't bear to see her cold. She watched over him zealously, accepting his need to care for her easily, knowing how much it meant to him. She made him smile, even on the darkest days, and reminded him, more than once, life and family came first.

The same lesson she drummed into our heads.

I touched his hand. "You okay, Dad?"

He smiled. "Of course."

"You look tired. I'm getting married today. You should be happy." He'd seemed fine when I went up to bed last night. "You're finally getting rid of me. All that is left is Chloe and you'll have the place to yourself again."

He sighed and flipped his hand over, encasing mine. "Forgive my moroseness, my girl. It hit me after you went to bed, it would be the last night I had you under my roof. Still mine to look after. As of today, Brayden will be the one who cares for you." I was shocked to see the glimmer of tears in his eyes. "Your home will be with him."

"Daddy," I whispered, the childish word slipping out.

"I walked the house all night, thinking—remembering. The day you were born and we brought you home. I was terrified. You were so small and helpless, and you needed me so much. I was so sure I would mess it up. But your mother told me I was being ridiculous, and as usual, she was right. I learned all of it. The diapers, the feedings, the tricks of surviving on no sleep and endless parades up and down the halls when you wouldn't settle." He paused. "I used to snuggle you right here—" he patted his shoulder "—in the crook on my neck and hum and walk. Sometimes it was the only thing that soothed you."

I squeezed his fingers.

"I watched you grow from a baby into this incredible young woman sitting in front of me, Addi. I cheered every accomplishment and success, even though I knew each one was a step that took you further away from me." He shook his head. "I am so incredibly proud of you—of the person you are, the businesswoman you've become." His voice caught. "I'll miss having you here."

"You didn't get this emotional when Thomas moved out." My brother had gone to university in BC, studying to become a marine biologist. He was still in school, working on his master's and had plans to pursue his PhD. He came home on occasion, hardly looking like the baby brother who had left when he was eighteen. My parents flew out regularly to see him, and we kept in contact via text and phone.

He smiled, lifting a shoulder. "That was different. You're my baby girl. My firstborn."

"And Chloe is still here," I reminded him. My younger sister eschewed anything to do with the business world. Her love was animals, and she was in school to become a veterinarian assistant. She lived at home; although her hours were so crazy, I rarely saw her anymore.

He smiled. "Not for much longer, I think. She graduates soon and has her eye on a clinic in Burlington. She's getting ready to fly on her own, as she should be. I'll suffer then too." He paused. "All my children—gone from my house. It's too fast."

I was out of my chair in a second. My dad caught me and pulled me into his lap, hugging me. It was rare for him to be this emotional. I snuggled my head onto his shoulder, feeling the strength of his embrace and the warmth of his love surround me.

"It's been a long time since you sat on my lap," he chuckled.

"I think I used to fit better."

He held me closer. "You fit perfectly." He kissed my head. "I want you to be happy, Addi. It's all I ever wanted for you."

"Brayden makes me happy, Dad. He loves me so much." I plucked at the sleeve of his heavy sweatshirt. "I love him. He gets me."

"I know," he sighed, resting his chin on my head. "That is the only reason I can do this. You two were always meant for each other." I felt the press of his lips on my forehead. "Forgive your old dad, Addi. Today is a happy day, and I'm thrilled. Brayden is going to take good care of my little girl, and you're going to have a wonderful life together." He hugged me again and released me. I slid to my chair, wiping my eyes.

"Promise me you'll save me a dance or two."

"Always."

"Be happy, Addi. And if you ever need me—I'm right here."

"I'll always need you."

"Brayden is going to step into my shoes. In many ways, he already has. He'll watch over you and be your protector." He smiled ruefully. "Just like you will be for him. But I'll be watching, and I'll be right here. Always. You always have a place here." He squeezed my hand. "Not that I expect you ever to need it. Your mother and I love him like one of our own, and despite my silly emotions of the moment, I am overjoyed for you."

"I kinda like your silly emotions."

"Your mother will kick my ass and withhold scones if she thinks I've upset you on your wedding day."

I grinned. My father fell in love with my mother and her scones simultaneously. She was tiny but fierce, and most people would be shocked to know who the real boss was in the household. My father deferred to her in most things, always saying she was smarter than he was by far.

"You haven't upset me, Dad. I like knowing how much you love me."

"I do."

I winked. "That's my line today."

He laughed. "So it is." He slid a box my way. "For you, my girl."

I opened the slim box, unable to hide my tears. A delicate bracelet lay on the satin, the white gold shimmering in the low light. A small heart embraced a pearl, creamy pink and pale. The tiniest of diamonds highlighted the curve of the heart. I knew that pearl. It was one that belonged to my grandmother—one of the few precious items my dad had of hers. Its mates were worn around my mother's neck—she rarely took off the necklace. As a child, I was fascinated with them. The smooth texture, the pretty color, the way they glimmered in the light. My mother let me touch them, quietly telling me how precious they were and that I had to be careful. I would trace them with the greatest of reverence. When I was older and knew the story behind them, my love for them, and my father, only grew.

"Dad," I breathed.

"Your mom thought you should have one of the pearls. We redesigned her necklace and had this made. We know you prefer bracelets to necklaces." He leaned over and helped me put it on.

"I'll never take it off."

He smiled. "It's your something old for today, Addi. Besides me walking you down the aisle."

I laughed as I wiped away my tears.

"Thank you."

He leaned close and pressed his lips to my cheek.

"Love you, baby girl."

My breath caught. "I love you, Daddy."

He winked. "I know."

The sounds of laughter and gaiety filled the room. I looked in the mirror at the cluster of women around me, smiling as I took a sip of champagne. I met my sister's eyes in the reflection, and she winked, knowing what I was thinking.

How incredibly lucky we were to be surrounded by these amazing women.

The winery had been designed to accommodate weddings and other events. I discovered it one day while out with Gracie. The wine was superb, but the land underutilized, the main building crumbling, and the business dying. ABC purchased it, kept the people who knew about wine, and demolished and rebuilt the rest. When I saw the designs, I knew it was where I wanted to get married, and we had, in fact, deferred our wedding until it was ready. The room I was in was on the top floor, facing the water, the wide sweep of windows showing the waves as they danced in the afternoon sun, the scattering of snowflakes delicate and beautiful amid the wildness of the water.

My mom sat on the sofa, a glass of wine in her hand, her golden hair catching the light. She was laughing at something Cami said, her head thrown back in amusement. She was a tiny dynamo, the center of my father's world, the rock for my siblings and me. She was always there, a constant in my life, my father by her side. Every school event, outside activity, achievement, victory, punishment—they handled together—for my siblings and me. They were hands-on, dedicated, loving parents. I knew we were wealthy, but we weren't spoiled. We earned our allowance, followed the rules, and acted like kids. My mother often joined in on the antics and dragged my father with her.

There was no doubt who the free spirit in the relationship was.

She was sitting with Cami and Dee, Becca, Liv, Fee, Katy, and of course, my Nan, Sandy. A close-knit group of women, strong, fierce, and the role models I tried to live up to. All were special, all a significant part of my life. Aunts in name only, they were as close to me as if joined by blood. So were their offspring.

Flitting around the room were my attendants. Shelby, Brayden's sister; Ava, Aiden's daughter; and Heather, Richard's younger daughter, were checking on gowns, chatting, helping one another with their hair. We didn't want stylists or makeup artists with us today. It was all about family, so we were spending the hours before my wedding together. The only one missing was Grace, Richard's eldest daughter and my best friend.

I frowned at my sister. "Chloe, where is Gracie? She should be here by now."

Chloe shrugged, glancing over her shoulder. "Hey, Hedda," she called, using an old nickname, "Where is your sister?"

Heather picked up her phone. "She's en route."

Katy VanRyan, her mom, frowned. "She's cutting it close. That's not like Gracie."

Heather poured some more champagne. "I think this case has her distracted. Something has."

She stood and came over to the small area we had called the salon. She bent to pour some more champagne in my glass, keeping her voice low. "Her text says she's bringing a plus-one and she hopes that's okay." She snorted delicately. "She says you don't have to feed him. Stick a chair outside for him, I think was her quote."

I lifted my eyebrows. "*Him?* Gracie is bringing a date?" I whispered. Gracie never had time to date. She was too busy with her career.

Heather looked perturbed. "She hasn't said anything to me until now. I'm as shocked as you."

"We'll have to grill her," Chloe muttered.

I laughed. "That'll produce nothing. You know how intensely private she is. We'll have to sic Nan on her."

If anyone could get Gracie to talk, it would be Sandy.

Cami stood, cinching the belt on her robe. Her dark hair was swept into an elegant chignon, and her face was youthful, the small lines around her eyes only evident when she smiled. She clapped her hands. "Girls, you need to get dressed." She met my eyes. "And we need to get you into your gown."

I looked at the elegant, gossamer dress hanging in the window, designed and made by Cami. She had done the girls' dresses as well. The bodice of my dress was tight-fitting, heavily beaded with shimmering pearls and crystals. Strapless, it clung to me like a second skin. The bottom was layers of ivory tulle that burst forth from my waist like a cloud of air. Delicate flowers were embroidered on the skirt. Brayden was going to love it. I could already picture his smile as I walked toward him. The way he would bend low and whisper how beautiful I was. The way his eyes would glow. How his voice would deepen as he told me he looked forward to getting me out of my dress later.

I felt my cheeks flush simply at the thought.

Hanging beside my dress was a thick, knitted ivory sweater with matching mitts and a pair of ivory, faux fur-lined ankle boots. A matching sweater hung in Brayden's closet.

Because ours was not a traditional wedding. No church, no long ceremony or wait time between the wedding and reception. No gifts —we'd asked our guests to donate to a local animal shelter instead.

We were getting married downstairs in a room filled with garlands, trees, lights, music, and flowers. Surrounded by our family and closest friends. Then, thanks to the staff and the muscle of all the boys, Brayden and I would don our heavy sweaters and boots and would have our pictures taken outside surrounded by the woods and snow. They had cleared a couple of areas so the pictures would be lovely.

Brayden and I loved everything about this place and this season. Skiing, skating, walking in the snow. Snowball fights and cold noses. We wanted the winter backdrop, and it was the winery's manager who suggested the two areas for pictures of the two of us. The rest, including family pictures, would be inside, although my mother insisted she wanted a couple done outdoors.

My father had looked askance at the idea, reminding her of how easily she got cold. In reply, she shook her head, laughing. "Relax, Rigid. I often sit by the fire pit in the winter. And we go for walks."

"Not in a dress," he argued.

"It's for a couple of pictures. I think they'll be charming." She leaned close to him, brushing her lips on his cheek. "If I get cold, you can warm me up."

He turned his head, kissing her hard. "I will." He looked at me. "You get a few pictures fast, and then she goes back inside."

"Done." I chuckled over their exchange. I was used to their displays of affection and my father's overprotectiveness with her.

Chloe interrupted my musings, setting down a box beside me. "Jen brought the flowers. Here's your headpiece."

"Where is he?" I asked, anxious to see him. The eccentric wedding planner would make sure everything was in place for me.

"Downstairs, checking on everything. He's in his element down there." She grinned. "Dressed to the nines as usual, bossing them all around. He says he will be up shortly."

I laughed. Jen had come into my parents' lives when they were getting married and had become a member of the family. Outrageous with his own style, he was elegant and perfect with details for events. It was he who suggested the color of the dresses for the girls, insisting the red and green would be so "cliché." He had been right, and the color scheme of ivory and gold, with punches of red and green, was beautiful. Each girl had a dress designed especially for her, and Cami had done an exquisite job. The boys would all be in simple black tuxes, their ties and cummerbunds a striped combination of the ivory and gold. I loved all of it.

I opened the box with eager fingers, and Chloe settled the circlet around my head. It matched the bouquets and decorations everywhere. Holly, ivy, sprigs of balsam and cedar, entwined with red roses, tiny pinecones, and white freesias. My headpiece had a few crystals to match my dress woven into the greens. Chloe skillfully pinned the headpiece and stood back, nodding happily.

"There. You're ready."

My hair, the same golden wheat color as my mother's, hung in loose curls over my shoulders. Chloe had woven some pearls and sparkles into the front, and the headpiece looked pretty. I smiled at my sister as she bent down, laying her head alongside mine. Our facial features were similar, but other than that, I had my mother's coloring with my dad's blue eyes. Chloe had my dad's hair and my mom's wide, dark eyes. We were both small like my mom. Our brother, Thomas, had my dad's height, coloring, and his eyes.

"If you decide the vet helper thing isn't your calling, you could always fall back on hairdressing," I teased.

She winked. "I'll keep that in mind."

The door opened, and Gracie stumbled in, dragging a suitcase. Her dark hair was a mess, her usually calm blue eyes filled with panic. Her coat was half buttoned, and her cheeks were flushed.

"Oh my god! I made it." She dropped her bag, shrugging off her coat, hugging and kissing everyone. "I'm so sorry!" She made a beeline for me, and I stood and hugged my best friend. Though she was older than me by a couple of years, Gracie and I had always been close.

"Thank god." I held her fiercely. "The day wouldn't have been right without you."

"Not happening. A bad engine, a delayed takeoff, a snowstorm—nothing was keeping me from being here."

I studied her closely. "Are you okay, Grace? You look frazzled."

Grace never looked frazzled. She always had everything under control.

She waved me off. "I've been running since yesterday, trying to get here." She accepted a glass of champagne from Heather, downing it in one long tip of her head. "I need another one of those."

I met Heather's shocked gaze. I had never seen Grace drink like that. Small, measured sips were all she ever took. I noticed a couple other things. A patch or two of pink on her neck as if she'd rubbed against something rough. A tiny bruise not quite hidden by the collar of her blouse. The brightness of her eyes. I held back a gasp when I noticed her finger. There was a thin pink line on her left ring finger. Her wedding ring finger. It looked as if a band had been there, then removed recently.

"Grace," I whispered. "What's going on?"

She ignored my words. "I'm here to see my best friend get married."

"We're going to talk about this," I hissed.

"Not today," she said, keeping her smile wide and her words low. "Today is about you."

"Just tell me you're okay."

She pressed a kiss to my cheek. "I promise."

I had to take her word for it since we had no time to delve deeper. But I had to ask.

"Who is the plus-one?"

She rolled her eyes. "A necessary pain in my ass. But I owe him for getting me here, and he wanted to come to the wedding. I hope it's okay." Her words were simple, but I noticed her cheeks flushed as she spoke.

"It's fine. You know we're casual."

"Thanks."

Our conversation was interrupted when Cami clapped her hands together again. "Girls, it's time."

"I need a fast shower," Grace insisted, wrinkling her nose. "I smell like I've been travelling for days."

Her mother stood. "Come, and I'll show you where."

I watched her walk away, trying to tamp down my curiosity. She hadn't smelled like she'd been travelling to me. She smelled like a man had been all over her. The scent was deep—citrusy and musky. Gracie's fragrance was very light and floral.

My curiosity grew, and I was suddenly anxious to meet her plus-one.

CHAPTER 3

BRAYDEN

My dad showed up a short time later in the morning, along with
Aiden and Bentley. Although in my mind they were still my uncles, I
had begun using their first names once I started working at BAM.
When Addi and I got engaged, we had talked to Bentley about the
whole Mom and Dad thing, and we agreed to stick to names. Since
our parents spent so much time together, it would have become
confusing. Bentley knew what he meant to me. So did Aiden. They
were as close to me as I was to my own dad, and I was grateful to
have three such strong men as role models. We walked over to the
Hub, the morning air crisp and cold. It was a massive building we all
used for various things. It had a full gym, a basketball court, a games
area, as well as three bowling lanes in the large, high-ceilinged
basement. Upstairs was a wide-open space with an attached fully
outfitted kitchen that we used for our gatherings. A glassed-in
swimming pool for the winter that overlooked the lake and a huge
movie room were on the main floor. It had been well-planned and
thought-out. There was a little library at the back next to the pool,
filled with books and comfortable chairs. My mom often sat there
reading, with Emmy or Cami for company.

We hadn't even poured coffee yet when Richard VanRyan, Van,
Halton, and Reid showed up. A few moments later, Jordan, or Pops
as we called him, strolled in, dragging the Callaghan boys, Theo,
Thomas, and Reed.

My tribe was all here. We had way more adopted "cousins" than
we could fit into a wedding party, but they would all be in attendance

and all had a job. We needed ushers, drivers for guests, various errands run for the wedding party—and the group all happily volunteered, and we considered them as much a part of our day as the ones standing beside us at the altar.

We hadn't wanted stag or doe parties, so the younger members of the group hosted a party for us here last night. We laughed, drank, ate, and danced, no parents or grandparents allowed. We sent them all out to dinner at their favorite place in Toronto, and they hosted some of the out-of-town guests. They enjoyed themselves, we cut loose, and everyone was happy. Hardly traditional, but Addi and I were anything but.

A wedding days before Christmas, pictures outside, a two-night honeymoon in our own home, followed by a full-blown BAM Christmas? Most women would have refused, but the entire thing was my Addi's idea.

Which was why she was perfect for me.

A hand on my shoulder broke my thoughts. My dad's warm blue gaze met mine. "Quit daydreaming, son. You'll be at the altar soon enough. We've got breakfast, some basketball, and a bunch of work to do."

I grinned. "I'm looking forward to the altar the most."

He chuckled. "I know. I felt the same way the day I married your mother."

"We all felt that way," Bentley said, adding a couple of scones to his plate. Everything else had been catered, but the scones came from Emmy. He wouldn't eat any others.

Bentley clapped my arm as he went by. "Knowing my Addi, she's as anxious as you. Emmy said she was enjoying her girl time, so you need to enjoy us."

I snorted. "They sit around, have their nails done, drink, and discuss us." I grinned widely. "They conspire together on how to keep us in line. All we do is work and let you old-timers beat us at basketball on occasion."

"Hey, who you calling old?" Aiden protested, flexing his muscles. "I can beat you—all of you—with one hand tied behind my back."

I smirked. Aiden was still huge. Tall, his posture ramrod straight. He worked out daily and could tire me out most of the time. His hair was completely gray now, with silver woven into the strands, and his scruff matched. But he was strong and agile, and he made sure we all were as well.

Like a single unit, Ronan, Paul, and Jeremy all stopped shoveling food into their mouths and looked up. Aiden's triplets weren't identical, but they were similar, all taking after Aiden in their size and looks. Dark-haired with green eyes, they were large and liked to work out and do most things together.

"You're on, old man," Ronan teased, always the spokesman for the group. The boys all high-fived one another, tilting their chins toward their father in a threatening way that made me laugh. Aiden narrowed his eyes.

"You're going down, son."

"Which one?" They spoke in unison.

"All of you." He jerked his head toward Bentley and Maddox. "I got my boys."

"Hey," Richard interjected. "I'll get in on that."

Ronan chuckled. "The three of us will take on all of you—except Pops. He's ours."

Everyone laughed as Jordan rolled his shoulders. "You heard them, gents. I'm the ace in the hole."

"That you are, Pops," hooted Reed.

The rest of the meal was filled with taunts and general ribbing. The breakfast disappeared as if none of them had seen food in months, leaving Bentley shaking his head. "I ordered double what I thought we needed." But he didn't look surprised.

After breakfast, we divided into teams and hit the court in the basement. There was a lot of trash-talking, unnecessary roughhousing, and taunts. Aiden took on his triplets, his eldest son, Liam, adding himself to his dad's team, and they held their own, although they had to admit defeat. The triplets were like a well-oiled machine, knowing one another's moves before they happened. You could never win if they weren't on your team. Still, it was fun to watch.

My dad got my attention. "We need to get you ready. Our tuxes are at your place. Everyone will get ready at their own homes and meet back here. The cars will drive us over."

"Jen with the girls?"

He smirked. "His favorite place to be. I think he arrived with the flowers and was making sure everything was perfect. We'll have to pass his inspection before he lets us in the building."

I laughed. The quirky male wedding coordinator was part of every celebration we ever had, as well as many family functions. He was outrageous, droll, and his eccentricity had only become more so as he aged. He walked with a cane now and only worked on select, personal weddings. He had been a huge help for ours.

I glanced at my watch, knowing in three hours I would be meeting Addi at the altar. I could hardly wait.

"Let's do this."

I came out of my room, pulling on my bow tie. "Dad, I need help."

He laughed, standing up and approaching me. His once silver hair was now pure white, and his laugh lines were deep around his eyes and mouth. But his back was straight, his shoulders broad, and he was strong. We had a close relationship. My mother said I was him made over except for my eyes, which were like hers. I did bear a strong resemblance to him, although I liked to tease him and say I was better-looking.

He was a great father, always there for Shelby and me. He was endlessly patient, never raised his voice, and was fiercely protective. He had been thrilled when I developed my love of numbers, encouraging me and helping me every step of the way. He'd been so proud when I graduated early and continued on to become a certified accountant like him. Shelby was the exact opposite—a dreamer and artistic to the core. She painted and drew, her fingers constantly covered in paint and ink. Her room was too until Dad had Van build her a little studio in the BAM building, where she happily spent most of her time after she left school. She worked at a local gallery, surrounded by art, and dedicated the rest of her time to creating.

He straightened the ends of the fabric with a shake of his head. "You have never got the hang of this."

"Didn't need to," I quipped. "I had you."

His hands stilled, and he met my eyes. His light blue shimmered, and he blinked. "You always will, Brayden."

I was shocked at the emotion on his face and in his voice. My dad gave us lots of hugs and always told us how much he loved us, how proud he was, but other than rare occasions, he kept his emotions hidden. I knew he shared them openly with my mother, but it was uncommon to see a crack in his façade.

I laid a hand on his shoulder. "I know, Dad. You have always been there for me."

He nodded, looking over my shoulder. "I never had that growing

up, and I wanted to make sure you knew how important you were—
you are—to me."

I knew about his childhood. When I was old enough, he had told
me. He was worried he wasn't a good enough dad, but I hadn't lied
when I told him I couldn't have a better one. Maddox Riley was
everything I wanted to be for my own kids. Strong, loving, and
generous. I wanted to be the kind of husband he was to my mother. I
wanted Addi to look at me years down the road and know she was as
important to me then as she was when we began. More so, even. My
parents' relationship, although not perfect, was strong and
unbreakable. They laughed and loved, fought and cried. Made up
and carried on. Devoted themselves to each other and to us.

"I do know, Dad. You've always told me how much you
loved me."

He cleared his throat, but the words were still choked.

"I know wedding days are mostly about the bride. Bentley is
having an inner meltdown over Addi getting married today." He tried
to smile, but his lips trembled. "But I am as well. You're my boy,
Brayden. Something I did right from the moment you were born."

He didn't let me say anything. "I wanted to give you something
today. Impart wisdom and sage advice, but to be honest, you don't
need it. You're amazing, son. You're loving and giving. Your mother
and I are incredibly proud of the man you've become."

I felt tears gather at his words.

"Bentley gave Addi something today for her old. Something that
meant a great deal to him. Again, I know it's the bride's tradition, but
I wanted to give you something as well. Something as precious to me
as you are." He sucked in a deep breath. "Something for your future
I hope you'll use."

I couldn't speak. My throat was too thick, so I nodded.

He tilted his chin, and I turned, noticing something I hadn't
until now.

A small lamp I recalled from my childhood was sitting on the
counter. I'd learned the history of it as I got older, finally
understanding the reason it was so special to my father. A broken
piece of his childhood my mother had restored. It sat in the nursery
when I was a child, and I often touched the paint, gazing at the truck
and the streetlight that stood over it, almost protecting it.

My dad would use it every night as he read to me. Turned it on
when I was scared, to comfort me. Take off the shade and make

hand puppets in the light thrown against the wall. It was always there when I was growing up.

The same way he was.

I met his gaze, not bothering to wipe the tears off my cheek.

"For your son," he said. "Or daughter."

Shelby never liked it. She preferred girlie things. Once I grew older, the lamp disappeared from the nursery and sat high on a shelf in his office. Protected.

And now, he was giving it to me. A symbol of his past so dear to him, I knew right then how deeply he loved me. More than I had ever imagined him doing. That was the real gift.

I embraced him, suddenly six years old again. Seeking his strength and warmth, which he gave freely. We stood for long moments, the love in the room tangible and rich. Then he stepped back and clapped his hands on my shoulders, letting me see his emotions.

"Be happy, Bray," he murmured.

"I will. I love her, Dad."

"I know. You'll be a great partner for Addi. You were meant to be together."

I nodded. He was right. She was my soul mate.

I indicated the lamp. "I'll take good care of it."

He smiled. "I know. I look forward to reading to my grandson with it."

"I'll get right on that."

He threw back his head, the moment lighter.

"I'll keep that to myself."

For a moment, our eyes locked, and I knew I would never forget this moment with my dad.

He squeezed my shoulders. "Let's go get you married."

"Sounds good."

CHAPTER 4

ADDISON

My stomach fluttered with nerves as I stepped into the cloud of tulle and lace. Cami slipped the dress up, making quick work of the hidden zipper and covered buttons that graced the back of the gown. I drew in a deep breath as the boning cinched in, and I ran my finger over the scalloped edge of the beading that hugged my breasts.

"This isn't going anywhere."

Cami met my eyes in the mirror, winking. "I'm sure Brayden will consider it a challenge later. Tell him to be gentle. I worked hard on this one."

My breath caught as I looked in the mirror. "You've outdone yourself," I whispered in awe. "It's beautiful."

"*You're* beautiful," Cami replied.

I felt like a princess or a fairy queen. The skirt billowed out around me, the sparkles catching the light. I never considered myself particularly beautiful. Brayden insisted I was, and the way he looked at me made me feel special and beautiful in his eyes, and that was enough. My dad called me lovely all the time and my mom insisted I was as well, but I always thought it was because they, like Brayden, looked at me with love. I was just me. Nothing special.

But today, in this dress, I felt beautiful.

My mom stepped behind the divider, her hand flying to her mouth. Tears filled her eyes. "Addi," she breathed out. "Oh, your father is going to lose it when he sees you."

"You as well, Mom. You look gorgeous."

She smiled and stepped close, laying her head along mine. Her golden hair was interwoven with silver, highlighting the color. She refused to have it dyed, and my father loved it. It was gathered in an elegant braid that hung down her back, laced with sparkles and ribbon. Her dress, a rich green, suited her coloring. It was long-sleeved, cinched tight at the waist, the sweetheart neckline showing off her throat and the redesigned necklace she wore. She was elegant and beautiful.

She kissed my cheek. "We'll both wow him."

Chloe slipped in, grinning. Her dress shimmered in the lights, the soft gold creation perfect on her. "Dad is going to blubber like a baby when he sees us. He's already emotional."

My mom smiled. "Your dad is having a hard time that his baby is getting married and her sister probably not far behind."

Chloe rolled her eyes. "I'm too busy for a man. I plan on staying at home until I'm fifty. Rent is cheap. My laundry is done, and the food is good." She winked. "And dad has a driver for me, and he lets me shop. Why do I need another man?"

We all laughed. Chloe loved all the benefits of living at home, including the car and driver Dad had at her disposal. He always worried with the hours she kept that she would fall asleep at the wheel, or worse yet, get mugged on a subway or bus. She had resisted at first, then decided she liked it. As for the rest—I couldn't argue. She did, on occasion, do her own laundry, and I knew my dad gave her a budget for her "shopping," although I was certain it was generous. Otherwise, she had it nailed. Our parents had been the same with all of us, including paying for our education. They insisted they wanted us to concentrate on studying, not having to juggle jobs and school. My mother had done it on her own, and my father didn't want us having to go through what she had, struggling to keep up.

"Not my children," he vowed. "I worked hard to make your life easier, so indulge me."

And we did.

I was grateful—we all were—we knew how lucky we were to have Bentley Ridge as our father.

Mom smiled. "He will be very proud."

She hugged us, and we stepped out from behind the screen. I gasped in delight at the girls. All in varying tones from cream and ivory to soft gold and their dresses styled to suit them, they were beautiful. The bouquets matched my headpiece, and each had a little piece of festiveness in her hair—a spray of holly, some ivy, the glitter of sparkles—some tiny sprig of the theme. They brought tears to my eyes.

They all loved my dress, oohing and aahing at Cami's creation. Jen came forward, clucking as he fixed the hem, fussed with my headpiece, and tamed a stray lock of hair back into place.

"A masterpiece of loveliness." He glanced over my shoulder. "Cami, you have done yourself proud. The entire wedding party is perfect."

She hummed her thanks, smiling widely.

I leaned close. "Is he here? Has Brayden arrived?"

Jen smiled, his eyes soft. "Your groom is waiting anxiously downstairs for you." He looked at Chloe. "You have the ring?"

She nodded, sliding her fingers into the hidden pocket added just for that reason. "Yep."

He turned to the group. "Remember. Slow and graceful. I don't want anyone charging down the aisle." He threw me a wink. "Even you. Once you get an eyeful of your man, you might want to, but don't. Enjoy the walk. Take in the splendor the room has become. The ambiance is—" he paused and brought his fingers to his lips in a kiss "—pure romance."

I nodded, my nerves easing a bit now I knew Brayden was here. Not that there had been any doubts, but somehow, I relaxed more knowing he was in the building. I fiddled with my bracelet, sliding my finger over the smooth surface of the pearl. My mom noticed and smiled. Then she slipped a small box into my hand.

"Your groom asked me to give this to you."

I held my breath as I opened the box. A set of earrings, pearls so similar to the one my dad gave me this morning, were nestled in dark velvet. They were surrounded by tiny diamonds that twinkled in the light. Delicate and elegant, they could be worn any time, but for today, they would be special. Brayden knew me so well. There was a small note, and I plucked it from the top.

Wear for me. I love you. B

I stifled a sob, and Mom helped me put them in. She nodded. "Perfect. He chose well."

"I think he had help."

She smiled. "He and your father may have had a talk. But the idea was his."

"Did he get his cuff links?"

"Yes. He loved them."

I drew in a deep breath and glanced at the clock.

"Oh god, ten minutes," I whispered.

My mom slipped her fingers under my chin. "Are you ready?"

"Yes."

Jen lifted his arms. "Then, ladies, in your positions. We're heading down to the back room now." He looked at me. "I'll send your father up in five. I'll get the girls in order. You'll be at the back. I'll send them down at the right moment."

"My sweater…" I asked, suddenly anxious.

"I will have it for afterward. Everything is handled." His smile was wide. "All you have to do is be the bride. We've got the rest covered." He handed me my bouquet. "All right?"

"Yes."

I waited, listening for my father's footsteps. When he appeared, he was silent, staring at me for a moment. His eyes misted over, and he wiped at his face, not at all embarrassed by his emotions. He leaned down and kissed my cheek, his voice thick. "The last time I saw a bride this beautiful, it was your mother."

"Thanks, Dad."

"Brayden is going out of his skin, waiting for you." He smiled, although his eyes were watery. "It's time to take you to him."

"Please."

He tucked my arm into his. "You sure you don't want to duck and run? We could go get ice cream." He winked, letting me know he was joking.

"Maybe after."

"Anytime, Addi. Anything, anytime."

I squeezed his arm. "I know."

He sighed. "Then let's get you married."

I peeked through the door before the girls started their walk. The room was resplendent. The glow of candles, the scent of pine and roses, the garlands and trees twinkling with lights. I spied the groomsmen, dashing in their tuxes, waiting patiently. Ronan, Paul, and Jeremy all stood out, their broad shoulders towering over everyone. Thomas was smiling at something Liam said as they sat down, their usher duties done. Beside Brayden was Reed, standing proud, his hand on Brayden's shoulder.

My breath caught at the sight of him. Tall, his shoulders straight, his hands crossed in front of him, looking anxious, was my Brayden. The light glinted off his light-brown hair, carefully brushed and gleaming. His chiseled jaw was smooth, and his tux fit him perfectly. He was built lean like his father, but his clothes hid the perfection of his taut torso, muscular biceps, and toned body. I knew those muscles all too well. How they felt under my fingers, the way they rippled as we made love.

His verdant green eyes were fixed on the aisle. Waiting for me. As anxious as I was to become united as one.

The music swelled, and Jen spread his arms.

"Ladies, it's time."

BRAYDEN

I tugged on my sleeves, the new cuff links that had been waiting for me when I got here making me smile. Like my father, I enjoyed dressing up, and cuff links were something I liked to collect. These were amazing, inlaid with mother-of-pearl and a small sapphire the color of Addi's eyes in the center. They were now my favorite pair, and I would think of this day every time I wore them.

I tried to concentrate on the girls as they drifted by, each one lovely, their gowns no doubt perfect. But I only had eyes for one woman today. And when she appeared, she took my breath away.

Far too slowly, she came down the aisle, her arm tucked into Bentley's, his hand covering hers. It took all I had to stay in place, not to meet her partway down the flower-strewn carpet and pull her from her father and into my arms.

Had she ever been more beautiful?

Her hair tumbled over her bare shoulders, the pretty circlet on her head making me smile. Her breasts were high, set off with the ivory material. Her skin shimmered in the muted lighting. She didn't walk; she glided. Glints of beads and crystals reflected around her. Her full skirt seemed to float, diaphanous and delicate. She was a vision.

And her eyes. Her beautiful eyes were focused on me as intensely as mine were on her. The blue glimmered and shone, her love clearly written in her expression. My heartbeat picked up, and I had to remind myself this wasn't a dream. This woman would be mine now. Mine to love, to care for, and to hold. Forever.

I stepped forward as they reached the evergreen-covered arbor and held out my hand, shaking Bentley's and waiting as he kissed Addi's cheek, then transferred her hand to mine. I felt his reluctance. I saw how his hand shook, and I knew how deeply emotional this moment was for him. How much she meant to him.

"I will guard her with my life," I murmured for his ears only. "You never have to worry about her happiness."

He met my gaze and squeezed my shoulder. "I know."

He moved to sit by Emmy, who reached for his hand. He covered hers with both of his and leaned forward, brushing his mouth over hers. It was a moment of love between them, and I wondered how I would feel years ahead when it was my turn.

I gazed down at Addi. I couldn't move until I told her. "You are exquisite," I whispered to her.

"You're not so bad yourself."

"Ready to do this, little elf?"

"You lead, I'll follow," she replied quietly.

"How about we do it together?"

"Even better."

The ceremony was simple and uncomplicated. Short. Neither of us wanted a long, drawn-out affair. We stated the vows we had written for each other, exchanged rings, the traditional I do's, and we were married.

I flexed my hand, the thick platinum band heavy and warm on my skin. It looked so right there. It was simple, with a row of diamonds in the center and squared-off edges—modern-looking and sleek. Addi's engagement ring glinted in the light as she signed the paperwork, the diamond now joined by a matching band, marking her as taken. As mine.

The minister finished signing and handed me the paperwork, which I tucked into my pocket.

"It's official, Addi." I winked. "You can't get away now."

"Don't think I can run in these heels anyway."

I bent low and kissed her. "Good thing. I'd catch you anyway."

She drifted her fingers down my cheek. "Maybe we can play that game later."

A throat clearing beside me reminded me we weren't alone. I kissed her again. "You're on."

We followed the minister to the center of the arbor. My smile couldn't be contained as he lifted his voice.

"Ladies and gentlemen, I present to you, Mr. and Mrs. Brayden and Addison Riley."

The catcalls and clapping were loud as we made our way down the aisle.

We had done it. Addi was mine forever.

The weather cooperated, and outside was cold but not frigid. I had removed my tux jacket and donned my heavy cable-knit sweater and tugged my pea coat over it. I switched out my dress shoes for some warm boots. I made sure Lucy, the photographer, had extra blankets on hand, and I knew one of the photo sites had a fire pit going.

I watched Addi walk toward me, still beautiful, but also adorable at the same time. Her sweater was buttoned up, and she had a pair of matching mitts on her hands. A warm scarf topped her sweater, and when she held up her skirt, I grinned at the cute ankle boots trimmed in faux fur on her feet.

I greeted her with a kiss, keeping her cool lips underneath mine until they warmed up. Then the fun began. Lucy was all business, and for the next while, we posed with the backdrop of the snow and trees around us. Addi was a trooper, even sitting in the snow for a few shots while I stood over her, resting against a fallen log. Even with the benefit of the blanket under her, I felt her shiver and called for a moment. I took her to the fire, standing behind her and tucking her into my coat. She nestled against me, and I bent low, kissing her ear.

"Almost done. Then a couple of family shots, and we go inside."

She peeked up at me, her cheeks and the end of her nose pink from the cold. "I'm fine. This is fun!"

I had no choice but to kiss her again.

One of the assistants came over with steaming mugs of hot chocolate and some cupcakes. Addi grinned in delight, and I laughed as she bit into one, icing smearing on her nose. I kissed it off and let her feed me a bite, knowing the entire exchange was being captured on film. I had a feeling it would be one of my favorite pictures.

I took the wrapper from her, tossing it into the bin, just as a snowball hit me square in the back. I turned around, lifting one eyebrow.

"Really, Mrs. Riley?"

She grinned, her expression teasing and joyful. She tossed another snowball up in the air, catching it in her mitt.

"You dare me, Mr. Riley?"

It was on. Regardless of the fact that she was in a wedding dress and I was wearing a tux. We frolicked and threw snowballs, laughing and trash-talking. I made sure the only one that hit her landed on her arm, but my Addi was competitive and got me a few times in the chest. Then in a move I didn't expect, she lowered her shoulders, gathered her skirt, and tackled me. I fell back, luckily more on the blanket than the snow, and rolled her under me, kissing her with abandon. I loved seeing the free spirit come out in her. Sharing her joy of the day. Few saw this side of Addi, and it was one of my favorites.

We kissed, the world around us melting away. Her lips were cold, but her mouth warm as my tongue stole inside, licking and tasting her. Sweet icing, a hint of mint and chocolate, and all Addi. Groaning, I kissed her harder until a throat cleared.

"We should really wrap this up."

I gazed down at my bride. Her blue eyes were filled with mirth, dancing in the waning light.

"Look what you've done, Addi," I whispered, flexing my hips subtly. "A hard-on outside, with a photographer watching."

She grinned, wicked and happy. "I will remember this moment the rest of my life. Every time I see these pictures, I'll know."

I kissed her one more time. Hard and fast. "Little minx."

I stood, pulling her to her feet and brushing the snow off her dress. "You'll be cold and shivering the rest of the day." I fussed over her, the worry helping soften my erection.

"You'll keep me warm."

"Addi," I warned.

She shook her head. "The tulle will dry fast. And I'm wearing thermal leggings under here that I'll take off. We're all good."

"Time for the family shots," Lucy called. "They'll be here in a moment."

I was grateful as her assistant ran over, straightening the headpiece and fluffing Addi's hair. Luckily, her lipstick was kiss-proof, although I could see her lips were swollen from mine. I patted my hair into place and brushed off my pants. God forbid Bentley see us and figure out we were up to more than just some staged photos. I hadn't been his son-in-law long enough for him to be quite that forgiving that I was ravishing his daughter outside in the snow on our wedding day.

I'd save that for New Year's.

Hearing the sound of voices and laughter, I turned to greet our family.

While we were gone and our guests sipped various wines and champagnes offered here at the winery and indulged in decadent hors d'oeuvres, the hall was rearranged into a dining area with a huge dance floor. Candles flickered everywhere. The tables were covered in gold and ivory, with evergreens piled in the center and hurricane lamps glowing. Darkness was falling outside, and the trees and garland twinkled with white lights.

"It's so magical," Addi breathed beside me, her hand tightening on my arm.

"Is it what you wanted, Addi?"

She rose up on her toes and kissed my cheek. "The whole day has been perfect. More than I ever dreamed of." She pressed another kiss close to my lips. "Especially my groom."

"Then let's join our guests. We need to be sociable for the next few hours, then the fun really begins." I winked.

"Oh, you have a new board game you want to play?" she asked, blinking her eyes innocently. We loved playing board games—it helped us both to relax—and I liked finding older ones and learning to play them.

I grinned. "Oh, I'm going to play something, little elf. I plan on playing it all night long."

Her breath caught, and that delicious pink color surged under her skin, highlighting her cheeks.

"Well then, Mr. Riley, we'd best get at it."

"Excellent answer, Mrs. Riley."

ADDISON

I loved hearing Brayden call me Mrs. Riley. We had agreed, for business purposes, I would remain Addison Ridge, but in my personal life, I would be Addison Riley.

I had been half in love with him my entire life. He was always there, a constant friend and supporter. I tried to date, feeling as if I shouldn't have the feelings I had for Brayden since we were almost family. But the few boys I had dated never measured up. I didn't feel the same way when they held my hand as I did when Brayden would. They looked bored when I would talk, as if they really didn't care what I had to say. Brayden always listened. Asked questions. Argued with me on subjects we didn't agree on. He challenged me. The bottom line was, he completed me. We fit as if made for each other. Once I got over my worry about our family ties, I accepted that—and him—entirely, and I had never looked back. Neither had he. Our course in life was tied with the other, and we were both happy to go with it.

I couldn't help my smile as they announced us, and we walked into the reception amid the loud applause. It wasn't a huge wedding by society standards. My dad and his partners kept their business and private life separate, so there were few unknown faces—mostly the plus-ones. Our social circle, and that of our parents, was tight-knit, so the numbers weren't large—our family made up most of the crowd.

Brayden swept me into his arms, and we danced our first dance as a couple, alone on the floor. He was an excellent dancer, and we moved well together. He held me tight in his arms, resting his head along mine and humming with the music, occasionally making quiet remarks.

"Our first dance of forever."

"You look beautiful in the candlelight, Addi."

"I love how you feel in my arms."

"Have I mentioned how much I love this dress?" He slid his hand up my *spine, his long fingers splayed wide. "I'm looking forward to seeing how it looks on the floor of our bedroom later."*

He pressed a kiss to my head. "And seeing what surprises you have on underneath it."

He dropped his head to my shoulder, running his mouth over my bare skin with light brushes of his lips. "Making love to my wife. Fucking her until she screams my name," he whispered darkly into my ear.

I felt flushed and breathless by the time we took our seats for dinner.

Brayden seemed calm, smiling and laughing, but I saw the desire in his eyes. Felt it in the grip he had on my hand. The way he kept me close, finding excuses to touch me. Throwing himself enthusiastically into the crowd's demands for kisses during dinner. The glasses would barely start clinking and he would be on his feet, dragging me into his arms, his mouth hard and possessive on mine.

Brayden had been my first and only lover. I was his. When we started dating, we had a frank discussion, and I told him I had always envisioned waiting for my wedding night. My virginity meant something to me, and unlike many girls at school, it wasn't something I was anxious to get rid of or give away.

The shocked look on his face would have made me laugh except for the seriousness of our talk. He was quiet for a moment, then took my hand.

"If that's what you want, Addi, I'll wait. We have the rest of our lives."

The next five years were filled with temptations. We kissed and touched, explored, learned the pleasure we could give each other, the pleasure we could take, without ever having actual intercourse. Orgasms were plentiful and enjoyable. I knew his body as well as he knew mine. We learned it all together, and although I knew there were times that Brayden wanted more, that his frustration levels had reached a maximum, he never lost his temper or pushed. He respected my decision, and although sometimes I was strongly tempted, I remained steadfast in my decision.

Until the night of Brayden's twenty-first birthday.

All he wanted was dinner with some friends, then to head to Port Albany. It was his favorite place on earth. We were surprised to find ourselves alone. Aiden was away with my dad and Maddox, looking at a piece of land up north. My mom was in Toronto, and although Cami had waved as we drove in, she didn't come to the house. We wandered to the beach, the night warm, the breeze light. We sat on a blanket, my back to Brayden's chest, looking at the stars as the night deepened and the silence surrounded us. I fingered the watch I had given him, the heavy silver links cool under my touch.

He pressed a kiss to my head. "I love it, Addi." He paused. "I love you."

I lifted my head, offering him my mouth. "I love you."

Our kiss started the way it always did. Soft and gentle. Then it changed, becoming deeper, longer. Taking and giving to each other, our tongues sliding and exploring. With a low groan, Brayden gathered me close, and seconds later, I was under him on the blanket. I loved how he felt on top of me. Solid, warm, and present. How his hands felt as they slid under my skirt, pushing up the fabric and teasing my skin. I whimpered as he ran his fingers over my center, the ache between my legs deeper and heavier than ever. All night, I had been watching him. He seemed different. Taller, his shoulders broad in the close-fitting shirt he wore, his muscular arms evident in the tight sleeves. We'd been so busy with school, work, and life, we hadn't been alone for a few weeks, and I had missed him. The desire I felt for him was overwhelming, and suddenly I knew.

"Make me yours," I whispered.

He drew back, surprise on his handsome face. "But Addi, you wanted to wait for your wedding night."

"I changed my mind." I slid my hand through his hair, cupping the back of his neck. "It's going to be you either tonight or then, right?"

"Absolutely."

I already wore a promise ring on my hand, and I knew he planned on changing it to an engagement ring soon.

"I don't want to wait anymore, Brayden. I want to be yours—in every way."

His green gaze was intense. I knew he was having an inner argument— wanting to give me what I said I wanted, yet worried I would regret it.

Except I wouldn't. This was us—and we were forever.

"Make love to me."

"Here?"

I smiled. "This is our place. We're alone. I want you. Yes, here."

He crashed his mouth to mine and kissed me. Lifted me into his arms and carried me to his room. The house was silent as he set me on my feet.

"Are you sure?" he asked one last time.

I answered by tugging on the bows that held up my sundress. I rolled my shoulders, letting it fall to the floor, and I stood in front of him, my breathing hard. "Yes."

I smiled as I thought about our first time.

It wasn't perfect by any means. Our hands shook and searched, there were times our mouths were overeager, and our teeth clashed. He fell off the bed reaching into his nightstand for a condom. "Thank God Aiden gave me these as a joke last year," he mumbled. "I never thought I would need them, but I tossed them in here."

I giggled too hard when he struggled to rip it open, mumbling how much easier it looked in movies. We rolled and fumbled. Laughed, groaned, and apologized.

"I don't want to hurt you," he confessed. "I know the first time will."

"I'll be fine. I have you," I assured him. When he was finally seated inside me, he gazed down, his eyes burning in passion.

"Nothing prepared me for this," he hissed. "Jesus, Addi—" He hung his head. "I'm not gonna last. You feel too good."

I was reeling from the way he felt. Filled by him and needing something. Something only he could give me. "Move, Brayden. Please move."

It was fast, intense, messy, and perfect. It was us.

And Brayden, it turned out, was a quick learner. He grew to be an amazing lover and, to this day, could turn me on with a look or a smile.

I expected very little sleep over the next couple of days.

And I was fine with that.

Another round of clapping brought me out of my memory-gathering. Brayden was standing, his hand held out, waiting for another kiss.

I was happy to accommodate. He grinned as he pulled me close. "What were you thinking about?" he asked quietly, gazing down at me. "Your cheeks are flushed again."

"Our first time," I whispered. "How amazing you felt inside me."

With a low growl, he kissed me. "Jesus, *wife*, you are killing me." He pulled me in tight, letting me feel his growing erection. "You keep doing this."

I grinned at the word "*wife*." I liked it. "I'll take care of that later, I promise."

Those words got me another deep kiss.

"I promise to take really good care of *you* tonight." He kissed me quickly. "Tomorrow." Another longer kiss followed. He bent me low, making me gasp and grip his shoulders. "The rest of our lives." Then he kissed me so long and hard, I forgot where I was.

It was perfect.

We had agreed to keep speeches short. Our parents kept theirs brief, my father far too emotional to say much, letting my mother speak. As the best man, Reed stood, approaching the microphone. Knowing his distaste for anything to do with public speaking, I knew it would be fast.

Except, he grinned into the microphone and looked over at us. "Sorry, friends. He's bigger and stronger. And he gave me a hundred bucks."

I watched as Aiden stood and approached the mic, pulling it from the stand. Both my father and Maddox dropped their heads, already grumbling, and Reid started laughing before Aiden began to speak.

Brayden groaned. "It's a wedding, Aiden. Not a roast."

"Have some faith, kid."

He turned to the mic. "For those of you who don't know me, I'm Aiden Callaghan. Adopted uncle, best friend, and all-around favorite boss of tonight's couple."

There was much laughter and taunts, which made Aiden smile.

"I've known these two kids since they were born. Before that, even. Twinkles in their fathers' eyes. The reason business suffered so greatly for a time because they were too busy with their own erections than the ones that the company was trying to build."

Everyone groaned. My dad dropped his head to the table in mock disgust. Maddox laughed, slapping him on the back. "Reed, Bent will give you five hundred to take back over," he called out.

Aiden pointed his finger at Reed. "Keep your ass in that chair, young man. I'll give you a grand to stay there."

Reed held up his hands. "I like where this is going."

I heard my dad groan. "I don't."

I chuckled. This was all too funny.

Aiden held his hand over his heart. "Imagine. My two best friends' kids getting married. Who would have dreamed that, all those years ago when we were poor university boys just trying to get by? Living hand to mouth, or in Bentley's case, million to million. Poor guy. We felt sorry for him, which is why we took him in. He was floundering, dripping money out of his pockets with nowhere to go."

That made my dad laugh.

"We're here today to celebrate something truly magical. Something so rare and fortuitous, it *has* to be celebrated. I am, of course, talking about the open bar. Holy shit, Bent. Did you know how much these people would drink? Good thing the groom's dad has access to the accounts—you're going to need it."

There was more laughter.

Aiden made some other jokes about us as kids but stuck to his word about keeping it brief and not going overboard.

Until the end.

"Marriage between the right two people is an amazing thing. It completes you in a way nothing else can." He looked over at us. "I wish you as much sex as I have had in my own marriage." He paused, scratching his head. "Wait. I mean success. I wish you a successful marriage."

He snorted with laughter at his own joke, while shaking his head at the whooping from the tables. "You guys are sick. I meant success."

"Sure, Dad!" one of the boys hollered.

Aiden winked. "I just want to add—may your ups and downs only be in the bedroom."

After the groans settled down, he became serious. "Stand with me and join in a toast. To two young people meant to be together. Their love is strong and beautiful. I'm proud to be their uncle, and I can hardly wait to see what the future brings for them. Or see Bentley bounce their child on his knee and be able to call him Gramps and get away with it." He lifted his glass. "To Brayden and Addi—the couple of the day."

He engulfed us both in his massive arms, lifting me right off the ground. "I did good, right?"

I chuckled. "Sure, Aiden." I pressed a kiss to his cheek. "You did real good."

Hours later, I smiled, remembering how proud he was of himself, as I sat down in a dark corner, the unexpected moment of quiet welcome. I had danced with my husband, my father, my new father-in-law, my brother, and Aiden. One turn with Aiden and I wasn't sure my body would recover. His strength and size didn't make for a good partner. And during the faster numbers, we all knew to give him a wide berth. His enthusiasm knew no bounds and made up for his lack of coordination. Cami usually just "held on for dear life," she told me once.

Pops, Reid, Van, Halton, Richard. My "cousins" insisted on their turns, and Ronan, Paul, Jeremy, Liam, Reed, Gavin, Theo, Matthew, and all the rest had claimed a dance. I bent low, rubbing my aching feet. I was grateful for the reprieve, although I didn't expect it to last long. Brayden would find me once he finished dancing with his mom and would want to dance some more. He loved to dance with me. In fact, he loved to dance period and moved with an easy grace. I was grateful for that.

Brayden's mom, Dee, looked lovely today, her mossy green dress complementing her soft red hair nicely. She smiled up at Brayden, their conversation constant since they'd started to dance. He was smiling indulgently down at her, towering over her as he did me. She had a couple of inches on me, but Brayden was six three, so he dwarfed both of us. He adored his mom, and she him. I was thrilled to have her as a mother-in-law. Like my own mom, she had been supportive of us from the beginning, saying it was destined to be.

It had been a great night, but I was grateful it was starting to wind down. Some guests had departed, and the ones who remained were mostly family. I liked it best that way. Brayden and I were in no hurry to leave since it was our wedding and party, and we were enjoying ourselves. But I knew soon he would come take my hand, and we would leave the last of the partiers to shut the place down.

I had a feeling the night would end with my father, Aiden, Maddox, Reid, Van, Halton, and Richard sitting at the last table, feet kicked up, a bottle of whiskey between them, lamenting how their kids had grown up too fast. They'd trade stories and heartbreaks, trying to outdo one another. For such stern businessmen, they were a bunch of softies when it came to their families. I loved them all for it.

I leaned back my head, the sound of a hushed conversation behind me making me perk up my ears. I recognized Gracie's voice. Her plus-one had been unexpected and mysterious. She had introduced me to him as he came through the receiving line. Her lips had been tight as she spoke.

"Brayden, Addi, this is Jaxson Richards, my, ah, coworker. He helped get me here."

Jaxson's eyebrows lifted at the introduction, but he didn't say anything. We thanked him, and he shook Brayden's hand, congratulating us on our nuptials, then lifted my hand and kissed it. "A pleasure."

I noticed a few things about him immediately. He was drop-dead gorgeous. His hair was so dark, it was almost black. He was tall, broad, and his suit was custom tailored. His jaw was chiseled, with a deep cleft in the middle. He carried himself easily, his confidence evident. He looked stern and haughty—serious, without humor. His eyes were a startling blue, piercing and shrewd.

And they were focused intently on my best friend, whereas she was trying to look everywhere but at him. Her over-the-top casualness made it obvious that whoever he was, whatever he was to her, it was not casual.

And the third thing was the fact that around his ring finger was the same pinched pink line I'd noticed on Gracie's hand earlier.

I could tell I was the only one who noticed. Brayden was already greeting the next guest, and everyone else was too busy enjoying themselves.

Jaxson lingered in front of Gracie, speaking in a low tone, then moved on, heading to the bar. He took a glass of champagne and headed toward the table where Katy was sitting. Beside me, Gracie tensed.

"Did you put him with my parents?" she asked, horrified.

"I don't honestly know. Jen arranged a spot for him. Is that a problem?" I asked.

"Um, no, of course not. It's just he and Dad will probably talk business all night."

I lifted my eyebrows so she knew I knew how full of BS she was. Then I turned to greet the next guest. We would continue this conversation later.

Even though Jaxson had only spoken a few words to me earlier, I recognized his deep tenor.

"Why should I leave, Gracie? I'm enjoying myself."

"Stop calling me that. It's Grace."

"All your family calls you Gracie."

"You aren't my family."

"Hmm. I beg to differ."

I sat up straighter. *What?*

"You shouldn't be here," Gracie insisted.

"You're here. I belong at your side."

"No, you don't," she hissed.

"I imagine the law would agree with me."

"Fuck the law," she almost growled, shocking me. Grace rarely swore. She rarely got upset. It was one of the reasons she was going to be such a good lawyer.

The next words I heard shocked me even more.

"I would rather fuck *you* again, darling. Far more enjoyable."

There was an odd choking noise, and then I heard the sound of footsteps hurrying away. High-heeled ones. Then a low chuckle and that deep voice murmuring a quiet promise.

"Run, Gracie, my darling. I'll catch you, regardless."

Jaxson Richards stepped out from behind the corner. He noticed me and lifted his eyebrows with a smirk. He bent close. "Your boss is funny."

"He's not just my boss."

He smiled suddenly, changing his face. It went from haughty to open. His dimple deepened as he grinned, and his eyes danced. He was devastatingly handsome. He tilted his chin toward the direction he and Gracie had been standing. "I'm not just her boss either."

Then he headed toward the table he'd been sitting at, leaving me gaping at his retreating back. He didn't appear upset or worried. If anything, his confidence was higher.

I slipped around the corner and into the ladies' room that was at the end of the hall. It was deserted except for Grace. She stood, gripping the counter, her head down, and her shoulders taut.

I stepped behind her.

"Gracie."

She whirled around, her eyes wide and startled.

"What is going on?" I asked quietly. "Don't tell me nothing because we both know that's a lie."

She sighed. "Remember me telling you about the pompous jackass I work for?"

I nodded. "It's Jaxson?" I guessed. "He's not just a coworker, but your boss. Your *direct* boss."

"Yes. He specializes in corporate law. I'm his intern. The firm sent us both to Vegas to work on this copyright mess we've been dealing with."

"Is he any good?"

"He's brilliant," she admitted. "When we're in the zone, we work really well together. The problem is we strike sparks the rest of the time. We're constantly battling with each other."

I waited. There was more to the story, but she wasn't telling me everything.

"When I missed my plane, and the snowstorm hit, he helped me get here. I never would have made it if it weren't for him. Part of the deal was he got to come to the wedding."

"Okay?"

She waved her hand. "I told him it was enough. To go home. He's been here far too long already. He refuses to leave."

"Why?"

She pressed her lips together. "Can we drop it?"

"No. Why is he refusing to leave, Gracie? Why were you so upset that he was sitting at your parents' table?"

"I don't want him getting comfortable with them."

"Why? If he's your boss and he helped you, what's the big deal?"

She began to turn away, but I refused to allow it. I grabbed her arm. "What happened in Vegas, Gracie?"

She met my eyes. "I married him."

CHAPTER 5

ADDISON

Before I could recover from the bombshell Gracie had just dropped, the washroom door opened, and Heather, Gracie's sister, came in.

"There you are. Nan and Pops are leaving, Bray is looking for you, Addi, and Gracie, that sexy coworker of yours is prowling around like a dementor. Does he suck the happiness out of every room he enters?"

She finished off her rapid announcement with a hand on her hip, looking exasperated. "He's a bossy SOB, isn't he?"

Gracie blinked, then let out an uncharacteristic giggle. My lips quirked at Heather's tone. The two sisters physically looked alike. Both small with dark hair and delicate features like their mom, Katy, but while Gracie had blue eyes like their mom, Heather had Richard's hazel eyes that seemed to see everything. That was where the resemblance ended. Gracie was calm, quiet, and unflappable, while Heather was exuberant, creative, and loud. She spoke her mind and used her hands to make a point, as if she were painting a picture for you. Despite their differences, they had always been close, but Gracie had obviously not shared her news with her sister.

"He is a bit over the top," Gracie stated, smoothing her hands down the front of her dress. "I imagine he's leaving and wanted to say his farewells."

Heather shook her head. "I don't think so. He told Mom he's alone at Christmas since he has no family, and she invited him to stay. She offered him the spare room."

Gracie paled. "What? He doesn't need the spare room. He has his own home in Toronto."

Heather glanced in the mirror, tucking a loose tendril behind her ear. "He told her that."

Gracie blew out a relieved breath. "Oh. Okay."

Heather grinned. "He said he'd love to come back, though, so he'll be here Christmas morning." She grabbed the door handle. "I guess Christmas just took on a different feel. I hope he learns to smile by then. Come say goodbye to Nan and Pops."

She left in traditional Heather style, a whirlwind of fabric and her signature lilac scent.

Gracie and I exchanged glances. "Well." I smirked. "This is gonna be interesting."

She grabbed my hand. "You can't say anything, Addi. It was a mistake, and it will be corrected. It's private." Her eyes widened. "My dad cannot find out. He'll go berserk."

"I won't say anything, but I want the whole story."

"I'll tell you," she promised. "Just let me get through this mess first. I need to go and uninvite Mr. Richards."

I couldn't help it. "Gracie?"

"What?"

"If you stayed married to him and hyphenated your name, maybe you could use Grace Richards-VanRyan. Sort of a twist, you know? Your dad might actually like that." I tried to hold in my laughter, but a chuckle escaped my lips.

For a moment, her lips quirked, then she frowned. "Addi, that was uncalled-for. I think you're channeling your inner Aiden." She yanked open the door. "And this marriage is history. It never happened," she hissed quietly.

Still chuckling, I followed her slowly, thinking about Jaxson's remark and the determined look on his face.

I had a feeling Mr. Richards might not agree.

BRAYDEN

Gracie rushed past me, heading toward the table where her mother sat with the guy she'd brought as her plus-one. Jason? Justin? I couldn't remember. He seemed pretty intense, but I had other things on my mind right now.

Specifically, finding my bride.

She appeared ahead of me, and I strode toward her. "I've been looking for you, Mrs. Riley."

She grinned. "Are you ever going to get tired of calling me that?"

I bent and kissed her. "I have waited a long time to be able to call you that, so nope. I will never tire of it. Pops and Nan are leaving, and I think I've partied enough."

She grimaced. "I won't argue there. My feet are aching from all the dancing. And I'm hungry."

"If you'd eat something, you wouldn't be so hungry. You've only picked all night."

"I can barely breathe in this corset thing, let alone eat," she admitted. "I want out of it."

"That's a plan I can get behind. Go say good night to Pops and Nan. I'll get you a snack."

She rose up and kissed me, her lips warm and soft. "Thank you."

"Anytime."

She floated away, her skirts billowing around her. I headed to the kitchen and ten minutes later found her still talking to Nan. Pops stood to the side, Nan's coat draped over his arm as he listened to their conversation, a bemused smile on his face.

Sandy looked incredible. Her pure-white hair was swept up and away from her face, the vivid blue of her dress lovely with her coloring. She had lots of laugh lines around her eyes and mouth but refused to worry about them. *"I've earned them," she liked to say.*

Still, her eyes were bright and her smile wide. She walked with a slight limp since her hip replacement, but she was active and energetic. Aiden made sure of that. Jordan was tall and strong, always close in case she needed him. They were a great couple and the best grandparents around. We were all lucky to have them as part of our lives.

Nan saw me approach and beamed. "There he is. You ready to take your bride away from all this?"

I kissed her cheek. "Her feet hurt and she's hungry." I indicated the basket I was holding. "I had the kitchen pack up some tidbits for us."

"Already a good husband." She patted my cheek. "Just like your father."

My dad doted on my mother. She was devoted to him as well. It was a good example to try to follow.

I glanced around, noting Gracie in a serious conversation with her plus-one. He was listening to her, leaning on a pillar, sipping a brandy with a small smirk on his face. She looked pretty hot and bothered, but he seemed at ease and not at all put out by her gestures or the words she was flinging at him. Cami, Emmy, Mom, Katy, Liv, Fee, and Becca were at a table together, watching them. Heather was dancing with Reed, the two of them wrapped around each other as per usual.

"Where are the guys?"

Jordan snorted as he slipped Sandy's coat over her shoulders. "On the balcony with a bottle of scotch. I think Bentley is wallowing, and his boys are with him for moral support."

Addi's gaze drifted to the glass doors. "Daddy," she murmured, looking sad.

Sandy chuckled. "He's fine. Let him have his pout with his band of misfits. It'll be their turn soon enough." She indicated Grace and Heather. "I think Richard needs to prepare himself."

"I think he's accepted Reed. He likes him."

"It took a while, though."

"True." Richard had thought Reed and Heather were only friends. Until the time he flew in unexpectedly and caught them kissing in the office. That had been an interesting day.

Reed and Heather were still a fairly new item. When she arrived in Toronto, he had been friendly and offered to show her around. None of us thought anything about it, until they started arriving at the office together, holding hands. I knew Bentley had spoken to them, reminding them of the policies in the office.

"You break up? You keep it between you. I have zero problem getting rid of trouble. You understand?"

They only seemed to grow closer. They kept their PDA behind closed doors for the most part. Although their teasing and quips often made me chuckle during meetings.

I was talking to my dad in the hall when a familiar voice rang out.

"Mad Dog!"

We turned to see Richard striding down the hall.

He and my dad shook hands and gave each other a one-armed hug. "What are you doing here?"

"Heather sounded strange on the phone. I was a bit worried, so I decided to come see for myself what was going on."

My dad and I exchanged a glance. I hadn't noticed anything off with Heather. "She seems fine to me," I offered. "But I'm sure she'll be thrilled to see you. She's in her office," I added.

"I'll go surprise her."

He disappeared around the corner, and I heard a knock, then silence, followed by another knock. Heather only ever closed her door if she needed privacy.

I frowned and looked at my dad, panicked. "If Heather's door is closed…" I let my voice trail off. "Does he know about Reed?"

"What the hell?" Richard bellowed.

"I think he does now." My dad smirked.

We raced around the corner. Richard was standing in front of Heather's desk. Reed and Heather were behind it, both looking rumpled. Heather's mouth was swollen, and Reed's hair was messy, as if someone's fingers had been in it. Namely, Heather's.

"You had better tell me that Heather was choking and you were providing assistance," Richard snarled.

"Daddy," Heather protested. "Don't be ridiculous."

"Don't you 'Daddy' me," Richard demanded. "What is going on?"

Reed straightened his shoulders. "I was kissing Heather." He put his hand on her shoulder. "My girlfriend."

Richard inhaled sharply. "Your girlfriend?"

Heather slid her hand over Reed's. "His girlfriend," she repeated.

Richard looked at my dad. "Did you know?"

"Recently, yes. I thought she had told you." My dad pulled on my arm. "We'll leave you to, ah, talk." He paused. "And Richard?"

"What?"

"No blood. We don't allow blood during business hours."

"I can't promise anything."

"Dad! Stop overreacting!"

"I'll decide when I'm overreacting, young lady."

She rolled her eyes. "Give me strength. I'm calling Mom."

"She'll be on my side on this one."

Heather picked up the phone. "We'll see."

My dad and I backed out of the office, pulling the door shut.

"Is that a good idea?"

He grinned. "If you survived Bentley, Reed can handle Richard. He's been working out with Aiden and Van. He can take him."

"You're really not worried?"

"I have no doubt Heather will calm him down. Especially if Katy is involved." He clapped my shoulder. "I am getting too old for this shit."

Richard had calmed down eventually. He had always liked Reed, so that helped. His trips to visit happened more frequently for a while, though.

Nan's throat-clearing brought me back to the present. "And Jaxson?" she asked, her eyebrow raised.

"Ah, that's just Gracie's boss," Addi replied, looking uncomfortable. "He helped her get here today."

Sandy leaned forward and kissed her. "And Richard was Katy's boss. History has a way of repeating itself."

They left, and I slid my arm around Addi. "Ready?"

"I think so."

Bentley suddenly appeared in front of us. He smelled of cigar smoke and scotch, and his normally shrewd gaze was cloudy. He cupped Addi's cheek. "Be happy, baby girl. Don't forget me."

She struggled to hold back her grin. "I'll see you in two days, Dad."

"I know. Cut me a little slack, okay? I love you."

"I love you too. Now go back to the balcony and finish your cigar. No more scotch."

He chuckled and reached out for my hand, shaking it wildly. "Welcome to the family, Brayden. I'm happy you're my son-in-law."

"Thanks, Bent."

"Hurt her, and I will dissect you into such small pieces, they'll never find you."

I blinked. "Good to know."

Then he grinned. "Nah. Kidding."

He walked away, calling over his shoulder. "Aiden will, though."

He stopped by the table and bent to kiss Emmy. She said something to him, and he waved his hand. He headed back to the balcony, and all the women at the table burst into laughter.

I chuckled. "I think your dad is a bit drunk. I've never seen him drunk."

"It's been a hard day for him."

I bent close and kissed her. "You okay?"

She sighed and leaned her head on my shoulder. "Yeah, but I can't take much more emotion tonight. Can we slip out, or is that rude?"

I looked over to the mothers' table and indicated the door with my chin. Emmy and my mom nodded and waved, both still looking amused.

I kissed Addi's head. "We're covered. The car is out front. Let's go."

She picked up her purse and the cardigan. "I'm with you."

❄

"I can walk!" Addi protested as I slipped her from the car and into my arms.

"Nope. I'm carrying you over the threshold. It's tradition."

"Oh." She relaxed in my arms. "Okay, then."

I chuckled, dropping a kiss to her head. "Besides, you fell asleep before we even left the parking lot. You're exhausted, my little elf."

Inside, I set her on the sofa. "Stay." I waggled my finger.

She rolled her eyes dramatically. "So it begins."

Laughing, I returned to the car and grabbed the basket, returning to the warmth of the house. I set down the basket and held out my hand. "Let's get you out of that dress so you can eat."

She sighed. "I imagined you peeling it off me in the bedroom and ravishing me right after."

"How about I peel it off you, kiss every inch I uncover, then we can eat and relax." I smiled at her indulgently. "We have the rest of the night for me to ravish you." I chuckled at her trying to cover up her yawn, and I held out my hand. "Come with me."

In our bedroom, she gasped. I'd had it filled with flowers and candles while we were gone, wanting it romantic for her. There was a bottle of champagne chilling and a single rose on her pillow.

"Bray." She turned to me, her hands clasped. "It's so beautiful."

I bent and kissed her, pulling her close. Our lips moved effortlessly, soft and sweet. I pulled back, spinning her, and got to work on the buttons that had mocked me all day. One by one, I slid them open, tracing her spine with my lips. The small zipper at the bottom slid down easily, and in an instant, the dress was a pile of froth and glitter on the floor. I traced the indents of the stays that remained on her sides, hating the fact that they had marred her skin and amazed she had walked around all day smiling while they had pinched at her flesh.

She turned with a smile. "They don't hurt." I held out my hand, and she stepped from the material. I bent down, unbuckling the strappy shoes and sliding them off her feet. I kissed each instep, rubbing them. I looked up at her.

"You were so beautiful today for me, Addi. Breathtaking."

Color flushed her cheeks. I slid my hands up her calves, the silky skin smooth under my fingers. I stood slowly, letting my fingers trail over her body as I drew to my full height. "But I think you are the most beautiful when you're just Addi. Alone with me, without the corset or the makeup. I see the real you. The most beautiful woman in the world because you are that way inside and out."

Tears filled her eyes. I cupped her cheeks. "I'm the luckiest man in the world because I have you. Now I want you to wash your face, put on one of my shirts, and come to the living room. I want to sit by the fire and feed you. Hold you. That's all I want right now. Let me do that."

She covered my wrists with her fingers, squeezing them. "How did I get so lucky?"

I nudged her nose with mine. "I guess we both did."

Then I winked at her. "Now go, before my dick overrides my head and I ravish you first. My god, you are sexy." I traced the wisp of lace at her hips. "Keep these on. I want to take them off—with my teeth."

She sashayed away, winking at me over her shoulder.

"Whatever you want, Mr. Riley. I'm all yours."

It was all I could do not to follow her.

"Married?" I gasped. "Gracie is *married?* To that guy? Jerome?"

She giggled around a mouthful of a sandwich. The kitchen had packed up a veritable feast. We had sandwiches, cheeses, assorted pickles, and condiments from the midnight buffet. Plus cake and cookies. I had refused their offer of the filet of beef and other items, asking them to donate it all to a shelter as we had requested. What they gave us barely made a dent in the leftover food, and I was happy to know the rest would help feed those in need. I had filled a plate for us to share, and we had both tucked in.

"Jaxson," she corrected.

"Whatever. Gracie is *married?* Holy shit, Richard is going to blow a gasket."

"She doesn't want him to know. She says it was a mistake and it will be handled."

I snorted as I reached for another sandwich. I had hardly eaten earlier either, and now I was starving. "Katy invited him for Christmas. You know it's going to come out."

"I'm the only one who knows. Well, and you now. You can't say anything."

I shook my head in disbelief. "I can't believe, of all of us, Gracie would be the one to get drunk and marry someone in Vegas. Her intense, I-could-kill-you-with-my-bare-hands-looking boss, of all people. And she expects it to remain a secret. The way he was looking at her? Good luck with that."

"I think she was going to tell him he couldn't come."

I sat back and pursed my lips. "I don't think he is gonna listen. This is going to be one for the records."

Addi worried her lip. "This is so unlike her."

"No shit. It's something one of the triplets would do. Maybe even Shelby. But Gracie?" I let my head fall back. "Do you think she's in love with him?"

"All she has ever said was he was hard to work for. I never even knew his name until today." Addi shrugged. "He is handsome, though. Sexy with that smolder."

I narrowed my eyes. "I beg your pardon? He's *what*?"

She laughed. "Not as handsome as you, of course. He's way too dark and broody for me. For Gracie too, I would have thought. But who knows?"

I huffed.

Addi picked up a slice of cake and nibbled it. She licked her lips, staring into the fire. I loved the way she looked right now. Dressed in one of my hoodies, her legs bare. Her face scrubbed clean of makeup and her hair down around her shoulders. I had changed as well, wearing only a pair of sweatpants and a loose Henley. Comfort was the key. Sitting across from each other on the blanket I had spread out, eating an indoor picnic, sipping champagne, and talking was exactly what we needed to do. Reliving the day and, of course, the bombshell Addi had dropped. It made no sense to me. Gracie— married. She was the most sensible of us all. Level-headed. She thought everything through. An impulsive marriage to a brooding, older man? Her boss, no less? I really wanted to hear that story.

But as I studied my wife, I wanted something else more.

Reaching across the blanket, I tugged her over, settling her between my legs. She leaned back into my chest with a soft sigh, drawing her legs up to her chest. I wrapped my arms around her, content to feel her close for the time being.

"For the next two days, you're mine, Addi. I'm locking the cell phones and laptops away. No one is coming near the house. I'm not sharing you until Christmas Day."

"I like the sound of that."

"I got a little tree we can put up tomorrow if you want. I even bought some decorations."

"I love that!"

"I figured there was no point in a big one since the Hub has the family tree. But I wanted you to have a little one this year. We'll pick a bigger one next year and put it up earlier."

Addi loved Christmas. We all did. The tradition had been the same since I was a small child. Each family had their own Christmas morning, then at lunch, we gathered together at the Hub. We exchanged gifts, went sledding or ice-skating, played outside. Ate cookies and drank hot cocoa. Everyone, right down to the youngest, pitched in for dinner. The women mostly handled the cooking, and the men the cleanup, although I recalled my dad often in the kitchen.

I remembered folding napkins, setting the table, crumbling bread for the stuffing. Years of memories were in that building. The hot cocoa became cider, the cups of milk at dinner replaced by wine, the board games after dinner replaced by movies. But it was the gathering of our families that remained constant.

There was always one gift under our tree at home from Santa and a stocking filled with goodies and little trinkets. My parents had explained that Santa could only leave one gift as he was too busy to do all the shopping, and they helped him with the rest. Family gifts were opened at home, and at the Hub were the ones from Pops and Nan, and the rest of the crew. Names were drawn months in advance. Otherwise, with the number of us, it would have gotten out of hand. But Nan and Pops insisted on buying everyone something.

When we were all really little, Santa came to see us on Christmas Day. His sack would be filled with candy, and we all got to sit on his knee. We never knew when he would show up, but he always did. His laughter was loud and familiar, and it was a long time before we caught on to the fact that it was Aiden under the beard and false belly. I think Gracie took it the hardest when Santa stopped visiting—even if she was older and knew the truth long before the rest of us did.

It was always a day filled with love and laughter, and more times than not, we drifted off, exhausted from the long day. We would fall asleep in the Hub and wake in our own beds the next morning. Even now, once dishes were done, lots of naps happened, especially by the men, sitting on the sofas, replete and tired from the constant craziness of the days leading up to Christmas, not to mention the day itself.

"Our first Christmas as husband and wife," Addi mused. "I feel as if we should have our own tradition."

I kissed the crown of her head. "How about each year, Christmas Eve is just us? Here in the house alone."

"I like that."

"Okay. This year will be the first."

We were silent for a moment, watching the fire, listening to the wind outside, wrapped in the warmth of each other.

"Are you sorry we didn't wait, Addi?" I asked quietly. We hadn't made love since December 1. In a stupid moment of remembrance, I had suggested it would build anticipation for tonight. I had regretted that impulsive idea until this very moment. The longing I felt for her couldn't be any deeper. My desire was so intense I could taste it in the air. Feel it pulsating under my skin.

Still, I wondered if she had any regrets.

She tilted her head back, meeting my eyes. "To make love?"

"Yes. I know you had wanted to wait for your first time to be your wedding night."

She smiled, stroking my jaw softly with her fingers. "It will be, Brayden. It will be our first time as husband and wife. It's still special, because it's us. It will only ever be us."

Her words filled my heart, and I lowered my head, kissing her. As soon as my mouth touched hers, heat filled me. I gathered her close, sliding my tongue into her mouth and kissing her with all the love and passion I felt for her.

Addi whimpered, wrapping her arms around my neck and pulling me in deeper. Endlessly we kissed. Long, hot kisses of passion. Soft, loving presses of our lips. Gentle nips and deep passes of our tongues as we explored. I ran my hands over her, groaning as I delved under the long hoodie to her bare skin. I fingered the lace on her hips, recalling the small band of silk between her legs. I kissed up and down her neck, laving my tongue on her skin, nibbling her ear, my breathing picking up, my cock hardening.

She gripped my hair, tugging on the short strands. Slid her hands up my back, tracing along my spine. Ran her nails along my skin, making me shudder. Straddled me, pressing her heat down onto my erection.

In one fluid movement, I stood, taking her with me, grateful for the lunges Aiden made me do. In our room, I set her on the bed, tugging the hoodie over her head. She leaned back on her arms, looking small and sexy against the deep gray of the comforter. In seconds, I was naked, and she shifted back into the middle of the bed. I leaned over her, hooking my fingers around the lace and silk that hid her from me. I was too impatient to use my teeth. I would save that for the next time.

"These have to go. *Now.*"

They joined the pile of clothes on the floor, and I stared down at my wife. She was perfect. Tiny enough to fit under my arm but formed for me and me alone. Her high breasts with their rosy nipples that I loved to kiss and suck. Wide hips and a sweet indentation at her waist that I could span with my hands. Small feet with even smaller toes and nails that she kept covered in polish—changing the color constantly so I never knew what it would be. Surprisingly long legs for someone so short, and at the apex—the sweetest, tightest pussy in the world that was all mine. I loved being inside her. The clutch and pull of her muscles, the heat that encased me when we were joined so closely you couldn't see where I ended and she began.

"Brayden," she murmured, breaking me from my thoughts.

I crawled up the mattress, kissing her. Settling between her thighs, stroking her skin. Passion flared, and we moved together as the heat kicked in. We kissed and caressed. Tasted and licked. I nipped at her breasts, teasing the tight peaks. She rolled us over and did the same to me, kissing her way down my abdomen and taking me in her mouth. I arched off the bed as she sucked me, rolling my balls in her hand and taking me deep. I could only take it for a short time before I rolled us again and lapped at her. She cried out as I sucked her hard nub into my mouth and slid two fingers into her, pumping slowly, drawing out her pleasure. We feasted on each other until we were breathless, sweaty, and aching. Frantic. I flung her legs over my shoulders and slid into her. I shut my eyes at the feeling of her surrounding me. It felt like the first time, all over again.

"Welcome home, Mr. Riley," she murmured, cupping my face.

"God, I love you, Addison Riley," I replied, aching with the emotion of the moment. Aching for her.

"Please, Brayden," she begged, drawing me down to her mouth. "Please."

I kissed her, the taste of us on her lips. I began to move, holding her leg high, hitting her where she liked me the most. As deep as I could get inside her. She whimpered my name, clutching at my damp skin, moving with me. Like the waves outside, we flowed and ebbed. Rose and fell. Cresting together until she shook, her eyes going wide as her orgasm rushed through her and my name fell from her lips. I thrust once, twice more and succumbed to the mind-numbing pleasure I had only felt with her—would only ever feel with her— racing through me. I groaned her name, gathering her close, riding out the ecstasy.

Then slowly, carefully, I eased her back to the bed and slipped from her. I lay beside her, tucking her close.

She pressed a kiss to my damp skin. "I love you."

I held her tight. The love of my life. My precious wife.

"Always, Addi. Always and forever."

PART II

CHRISTMAS

CHAPTER 6

BRAYDEN

I woke up, my hand reaching for Addi and only finding an empty bed. It was still new and wonderful to wake up beside her, knowing it would happen for the rest of our life together. The weekends and occasional night she would stay here were never enough.

We had barely left the bedroom since we got married. Except when we grabbed something to eat or a shower, and even then, something would happen. Addi would wink or look at me *that* way, and instantly my dick was hard, and we'd end up on the floor, on top of the counter, by the fire, or against the cold tiles in the shower. We'd christened a lot of spots in the house, but luckily, we had many left to try.

I should be exhausted, but I'd never felt more alive.

Except my wife was missing. I peered at the clock—it was barely six. She should be asleep beside me, tucked into a ball the way she always slept. Nestled close for warmth, hogging all the covers, her head on my pillow, and her warm breath on my skin.

Our bathroom door was open, but the door to the hall was pulled closed, and I knew I would find her by the tree, dressed in her elf pajamas, as excited as a five-year-old, and waiting for me. She always liked to get up early and sit in the darkness with only the lights of the tree in the room. She told me once she loved greeting Christmas morning that way. When we were dating, I would sneak over to her house and scale the balcony to sit with her, enjoying the peacefulness of the early morning with her before the frenzy began. When Bentley found me with her one Christmas morning, there was hell to pay, and from then on, I used the front door.

It was still dark when I snuck out of the house, pulling the door shut quietly behind me. I hiked across the snow-covered beach, the route familiar although more treacherous this time of the year. I scaled the balcony of Addi's family home and peeked in the window. My little elf was beside the huge tree, wrapped in a blanket, the glow of the lights reflecting on her face. I tapped lightly, and she looked up, waving me in. The door slid open without a squeak, and I left my shoes on the deck. I flung my coat over the sofa and headed toward her. She opened the blanket, and I slid in behind her, wrapping my arms around her and pulling her back to me. I dropped my face to her neck, kissing the skin. "You're so warm."

She shivered. "And you're freezing. I told you not to come, Brayden—it's too dangerous."

"It's fine. I want a little time with you today alone."

Although we'd been together for over two years, Bentley still preferred when we hung out as a group. We would be surrounded the rest of the day, with maybe a chance or two to sneak off for some stolen alone time, but it never lasted long. Someone, usually Bentley or Aiden, always found us. Ronan was good at it too, although he at least dragged his feet while searching. I never got to kiss her as much as I wanted on Christmas. I looked forward to the day I could.

I slipped a small box into her hand. "For you."

She lifted her head and offered me her mouth. "Thank you."

I kissed her softly, knowing we couldn't get carried away. She opened the box, gasping in delight at the promise ring inside. Delicate like her, it was a simple band of gold with tiny emeralds in it. She loved my eyes, and I wanted the ring to remind her of me.

"Wear it until the day I replace it with a diamond," I whispered, sliding it on her finger.

"I love it."

She took my wrist, snapping on an intricately woven leather and silver band. The medallion in the middle had our initials engraved, the A and B entwined. It was heavy and masculine.

I kissed her again. "It's perfect. You're perfect. I love you, Addi."

"I love you."

A light snapped on, startling us. "And I'd love to know what the hell you're doing in my house at five thirty in the morning, Brayden Riley. How the hell did you get in here?" Bentley's voice was dark and angry.

Both Addi and I scrambled to our feet, the blanket falling away.

"We aren't doing anything," I protested. "I just wanted to give Addi her gift."

"And that couldn't wait until the sun came up?" He narrowed his eyes.

"Where the hell is your coat?" He stepped forward, anger turning to fury. "Have you been here all night?"

I held up my hands. "No! No, Uncle Bentley! I just got here, like, ten minutes ago. I just wanted a little time alone with her today. You know how much she loves Christmas. I got her something special, and I wanted to give it to her. I swear!" I knew I was rambling, but the look on his face was scary.

"How did you get in?"

"Over the balcony."

He looked over my shoulder. "You climbed over the balcony? Something wrong with the front door?"

"I knew Addi was in here, so it made more sense," I replied, my answer sounding more like a question.

"You knew she was in here," he repeated slowly. "You've done this before, I take it."

Shit. I shouldn't have said that.

Emmy appeared. "What is going on?"

"Young Brayden here decided to pay our daughter a little Christmas morning visit."

"How sweet." She smiled at me.

"It's not sweet," he snarled. "It's practically the middle of the night."

"You're overreacting, Rigid."

"Overreacting? He came over the balcony, Emmy. He's done it before."

"Oh." She looked at me with a slight frown, although her eyes were dancing. "Maybe you should use the front door next time."

Bentley dug his phone from his robe pocket, hitting a button. He waited a moment, then spoke.

"Mad Dog? Your son is in my house, having a little morning visit with my daughter. He came in via the balcony. I just thought you should know he's going out the same way. And he's heading home fast because I'm not giving him his shoes. Maybe he'll remember that next time."

He hung up, heading my direction. I had no choice. I grabbed Addi, kissing her. "Merry Christmas, little elf!"

I took off running, not bothering to try for my coat or shoes. I headed toward the steps, swinging myself over the railing when I got close enough to the bottom. I gasped at the cold of the icy ground, but I didn't stop. Behind me, Addi was yelling at her dad, and Emmy was giving him shit. I sprinted over the beach and used the shortcut to head to my parents' place. My nipples felt like shards of glass, and my dick was so cold, I swore it was trying to crawl up inside my body. My feet were numb, but I kept going. My dad was waiting for me, shaking his head as he opened the door.

"Brayden—"

I held up my hand. "I know. I'll apologize."

"You'll have to."

"We weren't doing anything—just exchanging gifts," I defended myself.

He chuckled. "He's gonna be hell on wheels for the next while, you know that."

"The way Addi and Emmy were yelling at him, he might not be as bad as you think." I shivered.

He pushed me toward the fire. "Warm yourself, and I'll make coffee. I don't think I'll be going back to sleep now."

I headed to the fire, the heat feeling good on my feet. The rest of my anatomy began to warm up as well. My phone buzzed in my pocket, and a message from Addi appeared.

> **Addi**
> I'm sorry.

I replied.

> **Brayden**
> So worth it. I love you.

Her response warmed my heart.

> **Addi**
> I love you too. Heather is going to cover this afternoon.
> I'll thank you properly in the library at two. Be there.

I grinned as I felt the feeling come back to my feet.

> **Brayden**
> Wouldn't miss it for the world.

I chuckled remembering that day and Bentley's cool attitude that lasted about three hours. I apologized and promised only to use the front door and not show up before dawn. He brought my coat back but informed me since he couldn't toss me in the lake, he'd sacrificed my shoes instead.

"Consider yourself lucky," he informed me.

I took him at his word.

But it reminded me of needing to find my wife.

I sat up, and a Santa hat fell from my chest to my lap, the bright red and white vivid on the dark comforter. Laughing, I pulled it on my head and went to find my wife.

She was by the tree as I expected, the fireplace going, the lights bright in the early morning dimness. I slid behind her, pulling her back to my chest and wrapping my arms around her.

"Merry Christmas, Mrs. Riley."

She tilted up her head. "Merry Christmas, Mr. Riley."

Our lips met, moving gently. I pulled back, and she leaned into me. "I love this time of the day."

"I know."

"Our tree is so cute."

I chuckled. The little pine tree I had bought was only about two feet tall. We were barely able to get one small strand of lights and about half a dozen little ornaments on it before it looked as if it would collapse.

"We'll have a bigger one next year," I promised. "I thought we'd plant this one by the deck."

"I love that idea."

"Did you want to open your gifts?" I asked. We'd agreed to keep things simple this year, but we had each bought the other a few gifts, and they looked pretty with the bright wrapping under the tree. Addi's looked far nicer with her neat corners and perfectly centered bows, but I thought my slightly askew wrapping job was at least decent. She'd like what was inside for sure.

"Later."

She picked up a cup of coffee and sipped it, then offered it to me. I hummed in appreciation at the intense flavor. We both liked it strong and black, and this cup tasted even better knowing Addi's lips had been where mine were.

We were quiet, enjoying the stillness around us. Filtered light came in the French doors, gray and dense.

"Foggy today." I noticed.

"A storm is coming. The weather report said it was going to be a bad one."

"I hope everyone is able to make it home in time for the day before it does."

She lifted her head again, and I was surprised to see tears in her eyes. Worried, I cupped her cheek. "Addi, baby, what's wrong?"

She covered my hand with hers. "Nothing. I'm just so happy. I'm here. With you. Our family is all around us. We're all safe." She sniffled. "You married me."

I had to smile as I bent and kissed her. It was rare she showed such a sensitive, vulnerable side of herself. Very few people ever saw it, but I knew the tender heart her outside shell hid. It was one of the many things I adored about her.

"We'll think good thoughts for everyone so they get home with their loved ones too."

"Okay," she replied, laying her head on my shoulder. Tenderly, I wiped away the wetness under her eyes. "No more crying, little elf. It's Christmas."

She reached up and tugged the jaunty pom-pom on my hat. "I like this."

"I found it on my chest. I assumed you wanted me to wear it." I tweaked her nose. "I confess I'm disappointed not to see you in your elf pajamas, Addi. I thought we'd both be festive this morning."

"Oh." She slipped out from between my legs and took a few steps back toward the fire. "You don't like my robe?"

It was a deep shade of forest green, long and thick, no doubt keeping her warm. "It's pretty."

"I have slippers."

I began to laugh as I noticed them for the first time. They were bright red, with bells on the curved toes. She wiggled her foot so the bell tinkled.

"Very cute."

"I got new pajamas," she murmured as she undid the belt of her robe and shrugged her shoulders. "What do you think?"

I swallowed at the sight of her in a red camisole, delicate and frothy, tied with a bow and trimmed in white fluffy stuff. It ended at her hips. The tiniest scrap of lace nestled between her legs. She held herself straight, her breasts high, the hard nipples visible through the thin material. Her hair hung past her shoulders in golden waves, and her eyes were sparkling with mischievousness. The firelight danced behind her, casting shadows and glimmers on her skin.

My cock hardened at the erotic tableau in front of me.

Rising up on my knees, I crooked my finger. "I think you need to come closer."

When she was in front of me, I slid my hands up her legs, pressing my face into her soft skin. I wrapped my fingers around the thin straps at her hips. "I think you're going to need a new set once I'm finished with you."

Then I tore the lace away from her body and took her to the

floor. She wrapped her legs around my waist, the sound of the tinkling bells loud in the room. She grinned up at me. "You know they say every time a bell rings, an angel gets their wings."

I rocked against her. "Well, I have something for you, baby, but it ain't no wings. It's gonna make you fly, though." I slid through her heat, hitting her clit.

She whimpered.

"Santa's got a big package—just for you."

"Let's go then, Santa," she moaned. "I want my present."

I tugged open the bow between her breasts with my teeth, groaning at the sight of her nipples. "Trust me, little elf, I want to give it to you." I wrapped my lips around a plump nipple and sucked.

"Oh," she whispered. "Merry Christmas to me."

I grinned against her skin. I planned on making it very merry.

At least twice.

With the bad weather approaching, I insisted on driving the ATV we owned. We had gifts to take, making going by foot awkward, and if the storm was as bad as they were predicting, walking home might prove to be treacherous—even with a short distance. As we pulled up to the Hub, I noted many others had thought the same way we had. There were a few vehicles parked there, as well as Aiden's 4x4. With its heavy tires and chains, he would make sure everyone got home safely.

We smiled in delight as we took in the building. Lights were strung around the windows, framing the wreaths hanging in each one. There was a tree outside decorated with red bows and suet balls for the birds. Santa and his reindeer were set up on the big deck—something I recalled from when I was a small child.

When we got inside, Addi gasped. Our family had been busy and decorated the entire place the last two days we'd been locked inside our home and lost in each other. Garland was strung, glowing with lights. Candles were plentiful, the scent of pine, holly berry, and cinnamon heavy in the air. Everywhere you looked, there was something Christmassy. The railings were wrapped in greenery and more lights, the mantel on the fireplace piled high with evergreens and pinecones. Bows adorned picture frames. Vases were filled with more pinecones and red balls. It was beautiful every year, and every time it felt as if we'd never seen it before. Something new had always been added, and it was fun to see familiar things as well as the unique additions.

The gift-laden tree was ablaze with color, the ornaments reflecting off the thousands of twinkle lights on the branches and the bows on the presents underneath. Every year, Bentley, Aiden, and my dad went out and chopped down a tree tall enough to fill the enormous space. The ceiling soared to twenty feet in the center, and the lowest point was still over twelve feet tall. Every year, they argued and measured and always brought home a tree Aiden was certain would fit. Every year, some had to be cut off the bottom and the branches trimmed. Every year, they quarreled like schoolboys. It was odd as a child, but as an adult, it was amusing. I realized it was simply their thing. One year, Van went with them and brought home a perfect-fitting tree. He gloated over the magnificence. The other three men sulked for days. He never went with them again.

The air was filled with delicious aromas. Turkey, ham, spices. The sweet fragrance of pies mixed with the scents of the candles. Christmas music was playing, and I heard the sounds of our family laughing and talking. I added our gifts to the pile, and we headed toward the kitchen and were greeted by our mothers and aunts. Hugs and kisses were plentiful.

Nan stood back, cupped my face, then Addi's, and kissed us. "No need to ask how you are." She winked. "You both look very happy."

"I'm sure Aiden will still ask," Cami chuckled. "Rudely, of course."

"And Bentley will smack him," Emmy added.

"So will Maddox," Mom smirked.

And they were right.

Bentley shook my hand, my dad enveloped me in a hug, and Aiden smacked my back. "How's married life?"

"Aiden," Bentley warned. "That's my daughter."

"And my son," Maddox added.

Aiden held up his hands. "Just asking." He grinned my way. "She calling *you* daddy now?"

I tried to hold in my laughter, but I couldn't. The remark was so Aiden. My dad tried to hide his smile and failed. Van and Halton both smirked, and Bentley choked on the cup of coffee he was drinking.

Luckily, the rest of the crew came up from downstairs and

interrupted the moment. There was more laughter and teasing, although most of it didn't reach Bentley's ears. I knew Addi was getting some teasing as well from the flush across her cheekbones, but it was all in good fun.

Drink in hand, I followed the crew into the games room and admired the new air hockey table "Santa" had brought. Along with the foosball and pool tables already in place, it was a great addition.

"I wanted to add an ax-throwing area, but I was voted down," Aiden pouted.

"A little dangerous inside," Pops pointed out. "Fun, but dangerous."

Van perched on the edge of the pool table. "You know, the small area by the woodpile would be a great place. We could build an enclosure there. Safe. All cement walls lined in wood. A wood burner to keep it warm in the winter."

Aiden brightened. "Love it."

"Great sport," Bentley mused. "It could be fun. As long as it's not inside here."

"I'll draw up some plans."

Aiden high-fived him. "Awesome. I'll take on the boys."

"And we'll beat you," they said in unison.

"Whatever."

I headed toward Addi. I hadn't touched her in fifteen minutes—far too long. She was talking to Gracie, who smiled as I approached.

"Missing your bride?" she asked as I kissed Addi, then leaned over and brushed a kiss to her cheek.

"Yep." I looked around, lowering my voice. "Where's your, ah, *boss*?"

"You told him?" Gracie hissed in a low voice.

"Of course I did. It's Brayden."

"I'm not going to say anything. I won't give away your secret, Gracie." I shook my head. "But you really don't think it's going to come out?"

"No, it isn't," she snarled. "I'm not going to say anything, and neither are you."

"What about Jaxson?" I had a feeling he wasn't as anxious to hide this marriage as Gracie was.

"He isn't here and he's not coming, so there isn't going to be a problem. We'll get a fast, quiet divorce, and that will be the end of it."

"Wouldn't an annulment be faster?" Addi asked.

Gracie's face flushed, and I met Addi's startled gaze.

"Gracie," she whispered. "You didn't tell me that!"

"It doesn't matter. It happened. It's water under the bridge, and I'll deal with it."

"Does Jaxson have a say?" I asked.

"No. He knows it was a mistake. He's fine with it."

"Are you sure about that?" I asked, glancing over her shoulder out the window.

"Yes. No one will even remember meeting him in a couple of weeks."

"And you're sure he's not coming?" I asked again.

She glared at me. "First off, I uninvited him. And second, there's a huge storm coming, Brayden. Only an idiot would head out to Port Albany with the weather about to change."

I leaned close. "Then I guess your husband doesn't listen so well. And apparently, he *is* an idiot."

"What are you talking about?" she asked.

"Hey, look!" Ronan yelled at the same time. "Santa is outside!" Heads turned, and a ripple of laughter followed.

Gracie spun around and gasped.

Outside, Jaxson was on his way to the front door.

He was dressed as Santa, minus the beard, his dark hair unmistakable. He carried a large sack of what I assumed were gifts over his shoulder.

Addi looked at Gracie. "What is he doing?"

"He's playing Santa," she hissed.

"Why would he do that?" Addi queried, sharing a confused glance with me.

Gracie covered her face with her hands, her voice muffled. "Because apparently I talk too much when I'm drunk."

Addi began to laugh, covering her mouth with her hand to stifle it. "Oh dear."

I had to bite back my smile.

By now, Jaxson was almost at the door. Aiden was heading toward it, looking far too excited for a man his age.

Gracie grabbed my arm, her eyes wild with panic. "You need to stop him, Brayden!"

"Too late, I'm afraid." I murmured. "Even Aiden's into it."

"Oh god," she mumbled.

I couldn't help my smirk. "Good luck with that secret, Gracie. And by the way? We're *all* gonna remember this."

I was pretty sure she told me to go fuck myself as she brushed past me.

I had to be mistaken, though. Gracie didn't swear. But the Gracie I knew wouldn't have gotten drunk and married in Vegas either.

I guessed I had heard right.

Huh.

CHAPTER 7

ADDISON

I moved closer to Brayden, watching as Gracie hurried toward the door, determined to beat Aiden there. Her short legs had no chance of catching up to his long strides, especially when he was hurrying. He beat her, throwing open the door.

Jaxson filled the frame. He looked ridiculous and yet totally perfect. He wore a heavy red Santa jacket, complete with a belt cinched over an obviously padded stomach. His hat was perched on his head, slightly askew, the white pom-pom bouncing in the wind. The red was vivid against his almost black hair. His chiseled jaw bore a trace of scruff on it, highlighting the rugged handsomeness of his face.

Brayden leaned down. "Stop staring, little elf. Or I'll get jealous."

I rolled my eyes. "I'm married, not dead. Santa didn't look like that when we were kids."

He chuckled.

Aiden greeted him, his booming voice filling the room. "Santa! Come on in!"

Jaxson stepped in, lowering his bag to the floor. His gaze found Gracie quickly, and I saw the way his eyes lit up when he saw her. She was glaring at him, her hands tightened into fists at her sides. He winked at her, not at all perturbed by her lack of warmth or greeting.

He cleared his throat and put his hands on his hips. "Ho ho ho."

I tried not to laugh but failed. He wasn't exactly jolly. He tried again, lifting his arms. "Merry Christmas!"

He looked shocked at the chorus of Merry Christmases he got in return. But he smiled, and the gesture transformed his face from handsome to sinfully sexy.

"What's in the bag, Santa?" Ronan yelled.

"I hope it's booze!" Thomas added.

Jaxson blinked and looked at the bag by his feet. "Some of it," he said, sounding doubtful.

Aiden laughed and clapped him on the shoulder. "Some is good. Let's get this party started."

I sat beside Gracie, watching as Jaxson slowly walked around the room. I was fascinated observing him. He spoke to every person, called them by name, reached into his bag and handed them a present. They were simple things, but thoughtful. Chocolates or bath bombs for all the girls, cigars or small totes of alcohol for the men, each one tailored to the individual's taste. Every single one had a festive ribbon attached.

"He must have spent hours buying everything," I mused. "Never mind getting a suit and braving the weather to come here."

Gracie made a low noise in her throat. I glanced at her. She was focused on him intently, her hands clenched into fists on her lap.

"How on earth did he remember everyone's name?" I wondered out loud. "He hasn't made a single mistake."

"He does that," she murmured. "He remembers faces and names. Facts. The smallest details others forget."

"Amazing."

"It makes him a good lawyer," she admitted.

I grabbed her hand and squeezed it. "It makes him a good person too. He's extremely generous. And thoughtful."

"I told him not to come," she muttered almost to herself. "Why did he come?"

"Apparently, he wanted to," Brayden interjected cheekily. "Maybe it was his Christmas wish."

"Shut it," Gracie snarled.

Brayden smirked, clearly enjoying himself. I had to admit it was amusing to see Gracie acting so un-Gracie-like. Normally unflappable and still, she was a bundle of nerves. Her color was heightened, and her foot swung in agitation. Her little huffs of annoyance were adorable.

She tensed further as he approached the parents. He'd handed out something to all the "juniors," as Aiden called our generation, except for the three of us. I had a feeling he was saving that for last.

He shook all the dads' hands and kissed the mothers on the cheek. He thanked them profusely for including him today and handed them each a present. They were gracious and warm in return. Gracie was so anxious when he stood in front of Richard, I was sure she had stopped breathing. She almost growled when her dad clapped him on the shoulder, thanking him for the scotch. Her mom, Katy, spoke to him at length, listening to his low-voiced replies. At one point, her hand lifted to rest on his bicep as if in comfort.

"What is he *doing*?" Gracie whispered. "Why is he still up there? Why is he acting so…*nice*?"

"Is he not usually nice?" I asked.

"He's known as 'the dick' around the office," she replied. "He yells a lot."

"Just like your dad in his younger years—on both counts." Brayden rubbed his hands together in glee. "Oh, the apple doesn't fall far from the tree, does it, Gracie?"

"You want to wear that coffee, Bray? Keep it up," Gracie snarled. "*Why* is he still talking to my parents?"

Brayden chuckled. "Chatting to his new in-laws. I think your dad likes him. Your mom does, for sure. He'll fit in nicely once they get over the shock."

"Shut it, asshole," she growled.

I lifted my eyebrows at her vehemence.

"Just answering your question." Brayden defended himself. He grinned widely. "Maybe you should join him. Get them used to you as a couple."

"I'm going to slash your tires, and you'll have to walk home. I hope you freeze."

"What about my wife? Your best friend?" he asked, not at all concerned.

"She can stay with me."

"Hmm," he mused. "Three's a crowd. If the storm is bad, Jaxson is gonna have to stay over. I bet he chooses your bed to rest his weary bones." He winked lewdly at her. "His *rights* and all as your hubs."

She glared, her gaze colder than the wind blowing outside. "Get stuffed, Bray."

"I think that's his job."

"Stop it, both of you," I interrupted. As amusing as their banter was, I didn't want to miss a second of the action happening around me. Jaxson didn't strike me as only acting nice. He seemed intense but not mean or nasty. I wondered if perhaps people found his forceful nature off-putting. Maybe it was an act. People found me cold. Those who knew me best knew I was anything but. It was the persona I used to protect myself from the outside world. I peeked over at Gracie. Had she ever considered that? Had she really never seen this side of Jaxson?

Jaxson handed both Nan and Pops their gifts and received another kiss from Nan and a handshake from Pops. Again, he stood and spoke to them, seemingly at ease. Then he turned and headed our way.

Gracie pushed herself farther into the corner of the sofa.

He sat across from us, pulling off his hat and running his hand through his hair. He offered us a rueful smile. "This being Santa is tiring stuff. No wonder it only happens once a year."

Gracie shook her head. "There was no need for all the gifts, Jaxson. Or to risk your life to drive here. You should probably head back before the storm gets worse."

I gaped at her rudeness, but he only smiled. "Your mother and aunts were kind enough to invite me here today so I wouldn't be alone on Christmas. I still have the four-wheel drive, so I was perfectly fine on the roads, although I appreciate your concern. And to show up empty-handed would have been rude."

"A bottle of wine would have sufficed. This—" she waved her hand "—is a little overboard."

"There, I beg to differ. I recall being told that Santa's visit made the entire day magical. How can one ignore a chance to do that?" He paused, his voice lowering as he stared at her. "Especially for you, Gracie."

I tried not to giggle.

She sniffed, turning her head as if she could ignore his presence. Brayden and I exchanged a glance. The sexual tension between them was palpable. His gaze locked on her no matter where he was in the room, and whether Gracie admitted it or not, hers did as well. His words said so much. Why wasn't Gracie listening?

With them sitting that close to each other, you could feel something between them. How on earth they thought no one would catch on today was laughable. I had a feeling today was simply a ticking time bomb, and I wondered who would be caught in the explosion.

Jaxson handed me a lovely box of chocolates and Brayden a small bottle of his favorite whiskey. As with his dad, it was his preferred alcohol, although he didn't enjoy sampling as much as Maddox did. Brayden had a brand, and he stuck to it.

Ignoring the look Gracie threw me, I stood and kissed Jaxson's cheek. "Thank you. How on earth did you know these are my favorites?"

He smiled. "I listen." He glanced at Gracie. "I'm always listening." He reached into the bag and withdrew a box of chocolate caramels—Gracie's favorite. The box was larger than the others had been and decorated beautifully. "For my favorite intern."

"I'm your only intern."

"Yes, you are. You are both."

She took the box, touching the lovely bow. I noticed the way her fingers trembled. "Thank you."

Jaxson folded the bag beside him. "I guess my work is done." He stood and pulled off his heavy Santa coat and removed the padded stomach. His actions revealed a white dress shirt, covered in a deep navy cable-knit cardigan. He looked casual but dressy at the same time. I noticed the way Gracie's gaze flickered up and down, then she looked away. He was incredibly well built and sexy. A cross between Aiden and Brayden. Tall and strong. Broad yet slim. I could only imagine the muscles his clothes hid. I had to avert my eyes.

He reached into a pocket of his coat beside him and handed me an envelope. I frowned.

"What is this?"

"For you and your husband."

Confused, I opened it, finding a wedding card with a donation receipt to the local no-kill shelter we supported. It was generous and kind. Thoughtful.

"You didn't have to do this."

He shook his head. "I enjoyed being at your wedding. Meeting your family. Being welcomed so warmly—" his gaze drifted to Gracie, then back to me "—by your family. I wanted to contribute to a cause so dear to your heart."

It was a thoughtful gesture. I met his gaze, seeing the flare of pain in his eyes as he spoke. He was intense and deep. Serious. But I had a feeling underneath was a man with many complex layers. And whether or not Gracie wanted to admit it, he was trying to open himself up to show her.

I stood and hugged him. "Thank you. I'm glad you're here today, Jaxson."

I ignored Gracie's muffled gasp of outrage. Brayden stood and shook his hand. "Up to a game of air hockey?"

"Sounds like fun."

"I'm going to help with dinner preparations. You coming with me, Gracie?" I asked.

She pursed her lips. "I would like a moment with Jaxson first."

Brayden grabbed my hand. "Okay. See you downstairs shortly."

I tried not to grin as I heard Jaxson's mutter. "If I survive."

BRAYDEN

Christmas was always fun. I knew this Christmas would be even more so, having just gotten married. Add in the unexpected behavior and the secret Gracie was hiding?

It was awesome.

When Jaxson joined us, he was cool and calm. He admitted he had never played air hockey but caught on quickly. It was a top-of-the-line machine, complete with all the bells and whistles. Sounds that echoed when you scored. Buzzers. Crowd noises. The kids inside us loved it.

Jaxson was competitive and smart—a great opponent—and the room was loud with smack talk and laughter. I didn't push or try to get information. I liked to tease Gracie, but I wasn't an asshole. It was her secret to share, and I wouldn't break her confidence. It wasn't hard to notice the way he kept looking for her, though. Every time someone would walk into the room, his gaze would snap to the door. When the sound of a feminine voice would come closer, he would lift his head, and I knew he was hoping it was Gracie. He seemed genuinely infatuated with her, and I was dying to hear the story. His version. I had a feeling it was way different from hers.

We played, taking turns until Addi appeared downstairs. Her face was flushed, and she was wiping her hands on a dish towel. "Snacks are ready, and Aiden wants to get to the presents."

Everyone laughed. Aiden was always big on the presents. Funnily enough, his favorite part was watching people open the gifts and seeing their enjoyment. The big man was really just a giant teddy bear.

For the first time since arriving, Jaxson looked uncomfortable. He set down his pusher as the room emptied, the offer of food and gifts too tempting to resist.

"I believe I'll find a quiet corner and perhaps read for a while."

Addi shook her head, walking over and wrapping her arm through his. "No, you have to come join us."

"This is for family. Your gift time. I'm quite fine on my own."

She leaned close, smiling at him. "It's Christmas, Jaxson. Santa visits everyone here." She tugged on his arm. "*Everyone.*"

A delighted smile tugged on his mouth. "I don't wish to intrude. It wasn't my intention."

"You aren't intruding. And you have to come."

Watching how he responded to Addi, the way his tension melted under her gentle urgings, I understood. She was hard to resist. They walked past me, Addi holding on to his arm, making sure he wasn't left alone.

I followed behind, smiling.

And I fell in love with her all over again.

There were platters of sandwiches, bowls of chips and snacks, and trays of cookies. The spicy scent of hot cider laced the air. We all helped ourselves and headed toward the tree. Outside, the sky was heavy and the snow falling thick and fast.

"Thank god we're all here and safe," Nan breathed. "No one is leaving this compound until it's over."

We all laughed since none of us planned on doing so. Jaxson looked pleased at the thought, and I noticed the glance he and Gracie shared.

We ate, enjoying the food and one another's company. It was the same way all the time when we were all together. We seemed to drift into our own little pods. The triplets sat close together as usual, their dark heads bent over their plates. Liam sat next to them, and beside him, Aiden. All were quiet as they consumed their lunch. In the Callaghan family, eating was serious business. Cami and Ava were the softness in the family, yet I wouldn't want to cross either of them. Both were fierce and strong—in many ways, stronger than the boys. They were adored by all the males in the family.

Shelby was perched on the stairs, eating as she drew. She always had a sketchbook close at hand, and I knew she would be busy all day. My mom and dad were together on a sofa close to her, my mom making sure my sister ate since she tended to get lost in her art. My mom fussed over them, chiding my dad about how many stuffed pepper poppers he took and teasing him about heartburn. He responded by kissing her nose and telling her he was fine.

Bentley sat in a chair, Emmy perched on his lap. They always stayed close. He would often tuck a blanket over her knees and tug her shawl over her shoulder if it slipped off. She fed him tidbits, their intimate gestures never changing over the years. Thomas sat in a chair close to Bentley, the two of them talking quietly as they ate. I heard him telling his parents about some changes to the marine biology program and being excited by the new direction. They listened intently, obviously pleased to have their son close for a short time. Chloe sat nearby, her knees tucked to her chest, nibbling away, lost in thought.

Richard and Katy were nestled in the corner, Gracie perched close by and the twins, Gavin and Penny, talking up a storm as usual, often finishing each other's sentences. Their youngest, Matthew, was the quiet one of the group. He sat on the ottoman, listening and observing as always. Addi and I were beside them, and Jaxson had eased his big body to the floor, angled so he faced Gracie directly. She had relaxed somewhat and was cordial, although I had a feeling it was more to show her parents that all was well rather than how she really felt.

Not far away, Reed sat on the floor in front of Heather, his head leaning against her lap. They always sat between their two families, equal and happy.

Van and his girls sat together, Liv watching Reed with a smile. They loved Heather, and I knew they were hoping Reed made it official soon.

Reid and Becca and their crew were close to the tree. That was their spot and always had been. Reid was a big kid himself and loved the holidays. Halton and his gang rounded out our group. They took up a whole section of the room, and the laughter was constant with them.

Nan and Pops never sat anywhere for long. They perched and visited each group, checking everyone was good and that we were all happy. I knew Nan was disappointed that her grandson Colin and his family weren't here this year. It was his wife's turn to have Christmas with her family, but they would be here before New Year's. Jordan's kids stayed home this year since his eldest granddaughter was pregnant and too far along to travel. He and

Nan were headed to BC in a few days and would have their holiday time with them then.

It occurred to me that one day, hopefully not too far in the future, Addi and I would have our own little pod. That our parents would be fussing over our child, and we would claim our own space in the room. The thought did something to my chest, warming it and making me smile.

Addi leaned close, whispering. "What are you thinking about, Brayden? You're smiling like you just won the lottery."

I bent low and kissed her. I could do that now without worry. She was my wife, and Bentley could no longer clear his throat if he thought I was getting too close or lingering on her lips too long. I could kiss her anytime I wanted to. But I kept it respectful. For today.

"I did win the lottery. I got you." I kissed her again, making her smile. "I was thinking about the future, Addi. Adding our kids to this crazy mix. Watching them grow up the way we did, surrounded by this outrageous family."

Her eyes widened. "Can you imagine?" she whispered back.

"Yeah, I can. It's gonna be awesome."

"But we're going to wait a while."

I brushed my mouth to hers again. "Yes. I need you to myself for a while. Just you and me." I touched her cheek, drifting my fingers down her skin. "I'm not ready to share just yet." I moved in for another kiss when the familiar sound of a throat clearing caught my attention. I looked up and met Bentley's eyes. He waved his fingers between us, indicating he was still watching me, but he did so with a wink and a grin. I couldn't resist kissing Addi one last time.

He and I both chuckled.

After eating, we turned to the tree and the mountain of gifts it contained. Our tradition was that each person got a gift to open, and we all admired them. Nothing was hurried or rushed. When we were kids, it was different, but over the years, we had learned how to enjoy it. Savor the time. Admire the wrapping and the gift that lay under the festive bows.

Jaxson looked startled when he was handed his first gift. It was a handsome scarf, one I had, in fact, been admiring, and from the fast, apologetic look my mother cast me, I knew it was, indeed, the same one. But I was fine with it, especially seeing his delight. There was a nice bottle of scotch from Nan and Pops, and a few other gifts that he opened. Each one, he exclaimed over—even the socks we all got every year—and with each gift, I saw him relax and enjoy himself. I always knew the women in my family were special, but seeing how they had strived to make sure this man was included made me proud to be part of this family.

There were the usual gag gifts. Silk underwear for Aiden he was all too happy to model. A book, *101 Ways to Relax,* for Bentley. A pocket calculator for my dad. A tiny hammer for Van. Small things that made everyone laugh.

Addi got the raciest set of lingerie I had ever seen. Her cheeks were bright red as she held up the scraps of black lace, and I felt my ears get warm as I pictured her in it. The catcalls and whoops made me chuckle. The way the triplets high-fived one another left me no doubt who the culprits were.

The Costco-sized box of condoms I got made me laugh out loud.

After the gifts were done, we cleaned up the paper and lunch remnants. Some people drifted back to the basement. The women checked on dinner and then decided quiet relaxation with some wine was called for in the library. The snow had stopped, at least for now, so some donned their skates and headed outside.

I wanted a little time alone with Addi. We bundled up and went for a walk down by the water. The beach was covered in snow, piles beginning to accumulate by the rocks. The inner bay was frozen, and the laughter from the skaters floated over the air. We walked into the woods, finding a quiet spot. I pulled her into my arms and kissed her. She wrapped her hands around my neck, returning my caresses with enthusiasm. Moments passed as we lost ourselves to the other. The cold ceased to exist, the raging fire of desire racing through me. I gathered her close and pulled her to my lap as I sat down heavily on a broken tree behind a clump of bushes. We were hidden and private. We kissed, our tongues stroking together, at times deeply, other times teasing and light. I nibbled on her bottom lip, and she licked along my teeth and teased the roof of my mouth. I slid my fingers over her neck, holding her close. She whimpered as I thrust against the heat of her, wrapping her legs tight around my waist.

I broke away, burying my face into her neck. "If we don't stop, I am taking you right here," I warned.

"What's stopping you?"

"Explaining to your father how you got frostbite on your ass."

She began to giggle. Light, airy sounds that made me chuckle. I pulled her closer, letting her nestle into my chest. "Ah, Addi. I love you."

"I love you."

We sat in the silence, wrapped around each other.

The sounds of footsteps approaching startled us, and we looked at each other. Addi raised her finger to her lips, telling me to stay silent. Hopefully whoever it was wouldn't notice us sitting off the path and keep moving. I knew Aiden was planning on a marshmallow roast, and it was probably him looking for branches to whittle for it later.

But it wasn't Aiden.

"Okay, Jaxson, we've gone far enough. You wanted privacy, you got it. Now say whatever it is you want to say."

Addi's panicked gaze met mine, and I shrugged.

"Is it wrong for a man to want a few moments alone with his wife on Christmas Day?"

"I'm not your wife."

"I have a certificate that says otherwise."

"Stop it, Jaxson. It was a mistake."

"I disagree."

She huffed a sigh, the sound so Gracie-like, I had to bite back my laughter.

There was movement, and Gracie spoke.

"What is that?" she said, sounding horrified.

"A Christmas gift for you."

"I don't want a gift."

"Too bad, my darling. Take it."

There was a beat of silence, and he spoke again. "Take it now, or I'll hand it to you in front of your family."

The sound of paper being torn met my ears, and I shared an amused glance with Addi. Jaxson was a determined man.

"*What* have you done? This is not necessary, Jaxson."

"Our rings didn't fit. I wanted you to have a real one. One as beautiful as you."

"I am not your wife!"

"Yes, you are."

"We both know I married you drunk and out of my mind. We're getting a divorce."

His reply cut through the air, the lone word potent. "No."

"Give me one good reason why not."

There was the sound of rustling and a muffled gasp, followed by silence, then a low, almost painful sound.

Curious, Addi and I leaned over, tugging aside the branches that concealed us.

Gracie was locked in Jaxson's arms, and he was kissing her. The interesting part, considering how much she protested, was that she was kissing him back. He had her hair fisted in his hands, holding her tight to his mouth. She gripped his neck, her fingers moving restlessly on his skin. The low moans they both made were erotic.

I sat back, letting the branches fall into place. I gazed at Addi, her eyes wide with shock. I knew she wanted to stand up—let them know we were here, but it was too late. We had to hope they moved on.

I only prayed they didn't get carried away and stumble in our direction, looking for a place to continue their amorous clutch.

That was going to be awkward.

Suddenly, there was movement, and Gracie gasped. "Stop doing that!"

"Why? Give in, Gracie. Admit you feel something, and let's work on it. Tell your family. I'll stand by you."

"I am not staying married to you."

"Yes, you are."

Something shiny and bright sailed over our heads. It landed beside Addi, and she picked it up, staring at it. A thick band set with diamonds glittering in the overcast, muted light. It was beautiful and elegant. Much like Gracie.

When she wasn't furious and spitting like a crazy person. I wasn't sure I could get used to this side of her.

"That's what I think of your gift and this marriage. It's not happening, Jaxson. Keep your gifts and your lips to yourself!"

"Gracie," he admonished gently.

"I mean it, Jaxson. I will be polite because my mother and aunts invited you. You leave as soon as dinner is over, and I don't want to see you until I return to the office. And the first thing we're going to do is file for divorce."

She stomped away. I waited for an outburst from Jaxson. Expletives. But he was silent. Then he spoke up.

"Please tell me you found the ring."

We shared a startled glance, and he appeared around the bushes we were behind. Addi held up the ring. "We did."

"You knew we were here?" I asked.

He shrugged. "If Grace hadn't been so irritated, she would have noticed the footprints as well. She was determined not to go farther, so I just let her speak."

"She's not usually so…" Addi trailed off.

"Angry? Hurtful?"

"Yes."

He held out his hand, and she dropped the ring into his palm. He studied it for a moment, then slid it into his pocket.

"I hurt her first. I need to make it up to her." He paused. "I was correct then when I had assumed she confided in you, Addi? She told me how close you are."

"She did," Addi confirmed, her voice low. "She's determined to end this marriage. She insists it was a mistake."

He frowned, looking sad and forlorn for a moment. Then he shook his head. "It was not. And I am as determined to keep her as she is determined to be rid of me."

"Why?" I asked before I could stop myself.

He looked at me as if I were crazy.

"Because she is the only warmth in my life. Without her, the cold will destroy me."

His words hung heavy in the air. I had no idea how to reply to a statement that profound.

He cocked his head to the side, studying us. "Thank you for keeping our secret. One day, you will no longer have that burden."

He turned and left, his footsteps heavy and measured.

Addi looked at me. "What the hell was that?"

His footsteps faded, and I whistled. "I hope Gracie is prepared. That was a man determined to win." I looked down at her. "And I don't think he'll fight fairly."

"Oh boy."

ADDISON

Taking advantage of the break in the storm, Brayden and I walked a bit more, watched the skaters, and even had a snowball fight. We sat by the fire Aiden had started, warming up and enjoying the quiet. Brayden whittled some sticks for marshmallows later. Aiden joined us, and between them, they got a large pile done. Aiden was quiet at first, his knife moving over the ends fast.

"Great wedding," he suddenly said.

Brayden snickered. "Yeah, it was."

"You're not mad at me, are you? I really wanted to give the toast."

I flung myself into his massive arms, hugging him tight. "We would have been disappointed if you hadn't," I assured him. "You were very funny."

"Bentley smacked me later and refused to give me a cigar. Mad Dog snuck me one, though, so I figured if he was okay with it, you would be."

"We were more than okay."

He relaxed and started telling us some funny stories, sounding more like Aiden. It hadn't even occurred to me he'd be worried. It was strange how weddings and holidays seemed to make people more emotional. I was glad he said something so we could reassure him. He hugged me again before we left to head inside, holding me tight.

"Love you, Addi-girl," he whispered, using his old nickname for me.

"Love you back, Uncle A."

He stood with a grin. "I'm still your favorite, right?"

"Always."

We left him smiling and happy.

I was beginning to feel tired, and I wondered how early we could head home. Between the wedding and Christmas and all the hidden drama, I felt drained.

Brayden kissed my head. "I'll whisk you away after supper. We can have a bath and some sleep, okay, little elf?"

"You know me too well."

He stroked under my eye, his touch gentle. "I know this little bruise forming means you've had enough. No one will think twice about us cutting out a little early. Technically, we're on our honeymoon."

I was grateful for that excuse.

I wasn't sure what to expect when we got back to the Hub, but luckily, everything seemed fine. Jaxson was in the library reading, and Gracie was in the kitchen. Brayden kissed me, then went to find his dad, hoping for a game of chess. They started one each Christmas day, and it usually lasted until the New Year. They would take long breaks, sometimes a day between moves, trying to outdo each other. Maddox often won, although Brayden had beaten him two years in a row.

Gracie smiled as I walked into the kitchen. Her cheeks were flushed and her eyes bright. I spied a bottle of wine on the counter—

her favorite kind—and it was half empty. It was unusual for her to drink so much, but I supposed given the stress she was feeling, it was understandable. I poured myself a glass of red and asked what I could do to help.

My mom smiled at me. "You can make the gravy in a bit. The boys set the tables, the turkeys will be out soon, and dinner is in about an hour. Did you and Brayden have a nice walk in the woods?"

Gracie's gaze snapped to mine, and I smiled innocently. "We walked on the beach and watched them skate. We mostly sat by the fire and whittled sticks with Aiden."

I saw Gracie visibly relax.

"Why don't you take your wine and sit by the tree? You've been going all day. I'll call when it's gravy time."

I took her up on her offer and curled up by the tree. Shelby was busy sketching on the other end of the sofa. Ronan was asleep on another. Thomas was busy on his laptop, listening to someone in his earbuds, but he offered me a smile and a wink as I sat down.

Outside, the snow was getting heavier and harder. The wind was picking up as the sun went down, and I had a feeling Jaxson wouldn't be going anywhere. I thought about what he'd said about hurting Gracie. I wondered if she would ever tell me the whole story.

How had I missed the fact that something huge was happening in her life, and I didn't know about it? I had been so caught up in the opening of the winery, the wedding, and everything else, I had missed the signs. She had been quieter than normal, and we hadn't seen much of each other outside of work. I vowed to do better once the holidays were over.

She walked into the room just as Jaxson appeared across the way. They stood looking at each other. His pain was evident in his gaze. Her anger colored her vision, and she glared at him and turned on her heel and walked away.

He watched her leave with a slight shake of his head, and he headed downstairs, disappearing from view.

For the first time ever, I wanted Christmas done. We really needed to talk.

BRAYDEN

Dinner was its usual loud, boisterous affair. There was so much food. Platters of turkey and ham. My mom's garlic mashed potatoes plus a huge dish of roasted ones. Liv's curried cheese vegetables—the yams, carrots, and cauliflower tasty with a bite of curry and the rich sauce. Massive containers of stuffing. Platters of warm buns. Vast boats of gravy my wife had made.

Dishes of homemade cranberry sauce, festive in color. An area filled with nothing but cookies and tarts, pies, and sweets. A feast made with love by all the women in our lives, including my wife. I grinned, thinking about how much I loved calling Addi *my wife*.

Tables were set up like a U, and there was a lot of shouting and passing of platters. It always shocked me that no matter how much food was prepared, it disappeared. The Callaghan boys, their father included, were frightening when it came to meals. I noticed Jaxson was fascinated, watching them devour plate after plate of food. He informed the mothers he had never seen a feast such as this or tasted food so delicious. There was no doubt all the women found him charming, Addi included, except for the one he wanted to charm the most.

The food vanished, the wine flowed freely, lulling us all into a sated, quiet mood. The dishes were loaded into the two dishwashers, and everyone drifted to their favorite spot for some downtime. A lot of bodies were napping. Some reading. Some simply relaxing. Richard sat across from Gracie, scrolling through his phone, showing her amusing pictures at times. She had finally relaxed, the wine she had been sipping catching up to her. I felt relief at the fact that the day was almost over and Gracie's bombshell remained a secret. She could figure it out with Jaxson and move on. I knew she would tell her parents once it was done, although I was sure some of the details would be glossed over. She would make it sound like an amusing incident, and she would close this chapter.

I was an idiot to think so.

It happened so innocently. So quickly. Jaxson stood, announcing that he was going to leave. There was a chorus of objections he waved aside, insisting he would drive slowly and the vehicle he had rented had four-wheel drive and snow tires. He assured everyone he had only drunk one glass of wine and was fine. He stated he had work to do and had to return home. He kissed all the mothers and

Nan, shook the hands of the dads and Pops, his gratitude sincere and honest.

He headed in our direction, obviously planning on saying goodnight to Richard and the rest of us. Gracie set aside her wineglass, watching him come closer with mounting anxiety. Richard glanced her way with a frown, as if noticing her reaction to Jaxson. He narrowed his eyes, suddenly watchful.

One moment, Jaxson was striding toward us, and the next moment, he stumbled over the edge of a throw rug. He righted himself quickly, but his cardigan caught on the edge of a table, pulling at his pocket. The ring he had slid inside earlier flew out, soaring through the air and hitting the floor with a metallic thud that seemed to echo. It rolled on the wood floor, landing in front of none other than Gracie. The heavy platinum band spun like a top, the diamonds catching the light, the last few circles reminding me of a lazy drunk wobbling side to side, before it stopped. Jaxson hurried forward, but Richard bent, picking up the ring and studying it.

"Pretty ring." He narrowed his eyes. "Why is it in your pocket?"

"I forgot it was there." Jaxson held out his hand. "If I may have it back, please."

Richard held out the ring, then pulled back, squinting as he read something inside the ring. Jaxson went pale, and I shut my eyes, knowing whatever was inside the ring had just brought the secret out.

"My Saving Grace?" Richard snarled. "Why does this say 'My Saving Grace'? Are you…" His eyes widened. "Are you having an *affair* with my daughter?" His voice rose. My dad jumped to his feet, heading in our direction, Aiden following. Addi and I stood, knowing what was about to happen would not be pleasant.

Richard's gaze swung to Gracie. "What is going on?"

"This is why I don't drink," Gracie said, then, once again, burst into tears.

"Are you screwing with my daughter?" Richard bellowed. "You're her *boss*!"

He stepped toward Jaxson, who shook his head. "No. Absolutely not."

Richard shook his hand, the diamonds catching the light. "Explain this!"

Jaxson sighed and dropped his hand. There was nowhere to hide anymore. "We're not having an affair, Richard. We're married."

For a moment, only the sound of Gracie's sobs filled the air.

From behind us, one of the Callaghan boys muttered, "Well, holy…*night*. I wasn't expecting that."

Then it happened. Richard's fist shot out so fast, none of us had time to react. I heard the sound of bone meeting bone, and Jaxson stumbled backward, the ring once again hitting the floor. It rolled under the sofa.

My dad sprinted over, wrapping his arms around Richard to hold him back. He was yelling and cursing, trying to get to Jaxson. Oddly enough, Gracie stood, blocking his way as Jaxson straightened up, holding his jaw. Katy stood mute and confused across the room, watching the scene unfold in front of her. My mom stood beside her, wrapping her arm around her shoulders in comfort as Katy covered her mouth.

"Talk about decking the halls," another voice spoke up.

"I told you this wouldn't stay secret," I stated to Addi.

Richard's wild gaze turned on me. "You knew?" he yelled. "You knew about this?" He struggled harder against my dad's grip. Dad looked startled then lifted his eyebrows, indicating the door, telling me silently to get out. Others began to file from the room. It was like the proverbial sinking ship. The rats were getting out.

Holy shit.

Another Christmas I was going to have to run for it. At least this time I had my shoes. I grabbed Addi's hand. "Time to go."

I tugged her unwillingly behind me. I heard my dad tell Jaxson to get out, and he followed close behind me. We headed to his rental, and I took the keys from his hands. He looked as if he was in shock, and I wasn't sure he should be driving.

I headed to our house in his SUV, the normally short drive seemingly taking forever. The windows were so covered in snow and ice, visibility was almost nonexistent, and I didn't stop to scrape them. I pulled up and turned off the engine, grateful to have arrived.

"I should just go," he muttered.

"You can't drive in this, Jaxson. It would be suicide."

We led him inside, and he sat down heavily on the sofa. Addi went and got the ice pack, pressing it to his rapidly swelling cheek.

"Gracie," he breathed. "I need to go back."

"No," I insisted. "You need to stay right here and let Gracie figure this out with her family. You'll be involved soon enough."

"What just happened?" he asked in a daze.

I clapped him on the shoulder. "Welcome to the family, Jaxson. Brace yourself. It's gonna be a bumpy ride."

I sat down, pulling Addi to my lap. "Enjoying your honeymoon?" I quipped, trying to lighten the air. "What's a family holiday without a secret being leaked and fistfights happening? I mean, usually, it's the triplets and eggnog is involved, but at least this one was different."

"This is awful," she whispered.

"Christmas took an unexpected detour," I agreed. I hugged her close. "It's going to be okay, Addi. Somehow, it will be."

"What are we going to do?"

I looked over at Jaxson. I thought about Gracie's tears. Richard's fury. The chaos that had no doubt continued after we'd made our escape. I indicated Jaxson, sitting with his shoulders hunched over on our sofa. I kept my voice low.

"They need to figure it out, Addi. It's their story to tell. Their future to decide."

She rested her head on my shoulder. "Will we ever know what happened?"

I had to admit, I hoped so.

It was a tale I wanted to hear.

THE FATHER CIRCLE OF TRUTH

BENTLEY

I stared inside the large, elegant room, watching Addi move around, her dress floating like a cloud around her tiny frame. She looked so much like Emmy did when I married her. Young, beautiful—with her whole life ahead of her.

Where the hell did the time go?

It seemed like only yesterday I was holding her in my arms, cradling her safely. Protecting her from the world. I was the one to slay the monsters under her bed. I held her when she had a nightmare. Kissed away the tears when she scraped her knee. She always looked at me as if I were a hero who could do no wrong. As if I were the center of her universe.

And now, I had been replaced.

I took a long draw on the scotch in my glass, ignoring the cold that surrounded me.

I should have worn a coat.

I should have brought the bottle of scotch outside instead of just asking for a triple shot.

I should have pitched Brayden over the balcony when I had a chance.

I drained the glass, holding it against my chest.

Addi looked to Brayden now for comforting. It was his arms she sought for protection. His counsel she listened to. The little bastard had usurped me.

"Bent, you're growling."

I startled at the sight of Aiden and Maddox standing beside me. I hadn't even heard them come outside. Aiden handed me my coat.

"Emmy said you needed this."

I shrugged it on, not letting go of my glass.

Maddox chuckled and held up a bottle of scotch. "I thought maybe you needed this as well."

"You're going to have to share." Richard VanRyan appeared beside Maddox.

"I brought glasses," Reid offered.

Hal Smithers chuckled darkly. "I brought a second bottle."

Van's deep laughter echoed in the dark. "You guys are a sorry lot."

I glared at him. "Wait until Sammy's getting married. When some little shit steals your baby girl."

"Hey, that little shit is my son," Maddox protested.

I waved my hand. "I was talking in general terms."

He laughed. "You were talking in scotch-soaked terms. You know they were meant to be together, Bent."

He was right. Brayden was perfect for Addi. He respected her. Encouraged her. Let her fly. No one could be as proud of her as he was, aside from me. She was smart. Brilliant at running ABC. Another man might have felt diminished by her, but not Brayden. He was comfortable enough in his own skin to know how special she was. He knew the real Addi. The sweet, loving woman behind the stern mask she wore as a businesswoman. She was lucky to have him.

Maddox added some more scotch to my glass and filled up the other ones. We toasted in silence and sipped the liquor.

Jen appeared, a hand on his hip. "A BAM convention on the balcony. Six sorrowful-looking men, drowning themselves in scotch." He shook his head sadly, although his eyes danced with glee. "Six hot-looking men, I might add. I had hoped you would bypass the sob fest, but I came prepared." He walked over and lit the propane heater, the warmth almost instant. He indicated the cleaned-off table and the closed box on the surface. "You can sit and drink. I don't want any of you pitching over the edge into the water. And there are some cigars. At least be civil, sit, wallow, and have your smoke. Your wives will drag your sorry asses home when you're done."

"Our asses aren't sorry," Aiden chuckled. "We're here to support Bent."

Jen pursed his lips, ignoring Aiden. "And soon you'll all be crying about whose turn it is next. Wailing about the lost years." He sighed. "I've seen it before." He focused his gaze on me.

"Brayden and Addi are perfect for each other. You should be thrilled your daughter fell in love with such an upstanding young man. Have your little sulk and be done with it." He grabbed the second bottle of scotch. "One is enough. My god, for such brilliant businessmen, you're all such idiots at times. We'd be pouring you all into the limos."

He left, and we all stared at his retreating back.

"That was uncalled-for. We can handle our liquor." Aiden frowned.

"Some of us better than others." Maddox smirked.

"Shut up all of you," I grumbled, leaning forward and snagging a cigar. "It's not your daughter who got married." I cut off the end and lit it, letting the smoke escape. I rarely indulged, but I decided today I deserved it. "And I *am* happy. Brayden is an amazing partner for Addi. I just don't have to like it. Not right this minute. Right this minute, I get my goddamn wallow. My baby girl is all grown up, and I feel old."

Maddox blew out a perfect smoke ring. "So do I. Wasn't it just yesterday they were babies and Reid here still dressed like a homeless bum?"

Aiden chuckled. "Remember the day he sat in his office with no pants on because he needed to do laundry?"

Reid laughed. "That was a long time ago. Before Becca."

"Thank god for Sandy," we all said in unison.

"Remember Friday afternoon meetings?" I mused. "Us and the babies."

"I loved those," Maddox mused.

"The baby circle of truth," Reid sighed.

Richard laughed. "You guys *are* a sorry lot. We have awesome kids. They have to grow up—it's part of life."

"I'll remind you of that when Gracie drags some schmuck home to meet you."

He chuckled. "I didn't kill Reed."

Van laughed. "He said you tried."

Richard sniffed. "If I had really tried, I would have succeeded."

We all laughed, knowing he was full of it. Richard got along well with Reed and had been surprisingly relaxed over their relationship.

"I found it hard when Heather first moved here," Richard

admitted. "I worried constantly. Was she safe? Lonely? Was she eating? Would she tell me if she wanted to come home? Knowing she had Reed and the way he cared for her was, and is, actually very comforting."

That made sense in an odd sort of way.

"Gracie will be different," I warned. "The firstborn thing." I eyed Richard through a haze of smoke. "What's with her boss? He's pretty intense."

Hal snorted. "Pot meet kettle."

I flipped him the bird, ignoring the laughter from the rest of them.

Richard shrugged. "He helped her get here. Apparently with all the problems with weather and broken-down planes, they got as far as Calgary, and it looked like they were stuck. He rented a four-wheel-drive SUV and drove like a madman to get her to the wedding. I had a good conversation with him. He's a little uptight, but decent. He thinks Gracie is a brilliant intern and will be a great lawyer. I know she says he is hard to work for, but they must get along all right. She said he asked to come today. I think he wanted to see the winery."

"Is that all?" Reid asked dryly.

"What else could there be?" Richard asked. "He's her boss and mentor. He's older than her. I think he was just curious."

I met Maddox's gaze, and he lifted an eyebrow. I was sure I had noticed a few glances between the two of them that were not boss/intern-like. I was certain Richard was in denial, but I wasn't about to argue with him. I could be wrong—my head was a little mixed up today, and it seemed to be getting worse.

The table was silent for a moment, the music from inside muted. I looked at the bottom of my glass, wondering who drank my scotch. The glass was full only a minute ago.

Wasn't it?

"She's leaving," I groaned, peering through the patio glass. "She isn't coming to say goodbye."

Everyone laughed. "Because she'll be five minutes away and you'll see her in two days, Bent," Aiden pointed out. "Two days."

"Still." I stood and headed to the doors. Someone yelled about a cigar, but I kept going until I found Addi.

I made sure she knew I was happy for her and I would see her in a couple of days. I didn't want her to think I was too busy checking that all her uncles were okay not to say goodbye. She would be upset, and I couldn't have my baby girl upset on her wedding day. I welcomed Brayden to the family. It was the least I could do. Emmy pulled me in for a kiss as I went by, and I was pretty certain she propositioned me, but for some reason, none of the conversations were sticking in my head. Words floated by, but they were hard to grasp.

I returned to the table and picked up my glass.

"She's gone," I said morosely.

Someone clapped me on the back, and I shut my eyes.

Suddenly, Emmy was in front of me, shaking my shoulder, her beautiful dark eyes staring into mine. "Come on, Rigid. It's time to go home."

I looked around, noticing the balcony was empty except for Aiden. He winked at me, sipping his scotch. Someone had drunk all of mine.

Bastard.

"Is the wedding done?"

She smiled. She was so beautiful. Even more beautiful than the girl I married. I loved her more now than ever.

Her smile became wider. "I know."

"Am I drunk?" I whispered.

"Ah, a little. You knocked them back pretty fast." She tugged on my hands. "You need to go home to bed and sleep. You'll feel better in the morning."

"Weren't you going to have your wicked way with me?"

She laughed, wrapping her arm around my waist. "That was your line, and maybe we'll save that until the morning."

"Oh." I glanced over my shoulder. "Is Aiden coming with us?"

He stood, laughing. "Right behind you, Bent. Always am."

I had to smile.

He was. My best friend and business partner was always there. So were Maddox and my whole extended family. And I had my Emmy.

I was a lucky man.

Emmy squeezed my waist. "Yes, you are."

"Aiden?"

"Yeah?"

"I survived my baby girl getting married."

"You did good, Bent."

The balcony tilted a little. I leaned into Emmy but spoke over my shoulder to Aiden.

"Gonna pass out now."

"I was expecting that."
"Okay. Thanks."
And I was gone.

Unscripted With Mila (Vested Interest: ABC Corp #6)

Men of Hidden Justice

Vigilante Justice - Different Couples

The Boss

Second-In-Command

The Commander

The Watcher

The Specialist

Men of the Falls

Canadian mafia duet - Different Couples

Aldo

Roman

The Irishmen

Canadian syndicate duet - Different Couples

Finn

Niall

My Favorite

Romantic Comedy standalone

My Favorite Kidnapper

My Favorite Boss

My Favorite Hero

Reynolds Restorations -

Blue Collar heroes in Small Town - Different Couples

Revved to the Maxx

Breaking The Speed Limit

Shifting Gears

Under The Radar

Full Throttle

Standalones

Tropes from high angst to romcom

Into the Storm

Beneath the Scars

Over the Fence

The Image of You

Changing Roles

The Summer of Us

Happily Ever After Collection

Heart Strings

A Simple Life

Unexpected Complication

Titles published with Scarlett Scott

Historical Romance standalone

Maid for the Marquess

Titles published under M. Moreland

Insta-Spark Collection

Low Angst and all standalone

It Started with a Kiss

Christmas Sugar

An Instant Connection

An Unexpected Gift

Harvest of Love

An Unexpected Chance

Following Maggie

The Wish List

Wrapped In Love

ABOUT THE AUTHOR

NYT/WSJ/USAT international bestselling author Melanie Moreland, lives a happy and content life in a quiet area of Ontario with her beloved husband of thirty-plus years and their rescue cat, Amber. Nothing means more to her than her friends and family, and she cherishes every moment spent with them.

While seriously addicted to coffee, and highly challenged with all things computer-related and technical, she relishes baking, cooking, and trying new recipes for people to sample. She loves to throw dinner parties, and enjoys traveling, here and abroad, but finds coming home is always the best part of any trip.

Melanie loves stories, especially paired with a good wine, and enjoys skydiving (free falling over a fleck of dust) extreme snowboarding (falling down stairs) and piloting her own helicopter (tripping over her own feet.) She's learned happily ever afters, even bumpy ones, are all in how you tell the story.

Melanie is represented by Flavia Viotti at Bookcase Literary Agency. For any questions regarding subsidiary or translation rights please contact her at flavia@bookcaseagency.com

facebook.com/authormoreland

instagram.com/morelandmelanie

bookbub.com/authors/melanie-moreland

amazon.com/Melanie-Moreland/author/B00GV6LB00

goodreads.com/Melanie_Moreland

tiktok.com/@melaniemoreland

threads.com/@morelandmelanie